BLOODMARKED

Also by Tracy Deonn

Legendborn

BLOODMARKED

BOOK TWO IN **THE LEGENDBORN CYCLE**

TRACY DEONN

SIMON & SCHUSTER BFYR

New York   London   Toronto   Sydney   New Delhi

SIMON & SCHUSTER BFYR

An imprint of Simon & Schuster Children's Publishing Division
1230 Avenue of the Americas, New York, New York 10020

For information about special discounts for bulk purchases, please contact Simon & Schuster Special Sales at 1-866-506-1949 or business@simonandschuster.com.
The Simon & Schuster Speakers Bureau can bring authors to your live event. For more information or to book an event, contact the Simon & Schuster Speakers Bureau at 1-866-248-3049 or visit our website at www.simonspeakers.com.
Interior design by Laura Eckes
The text for this book was set in Perpetua Std.
Manufactured in the United States of America
First Edition
10 9 8 7 6 5 4 3 2 1
Library of Congress Cataloging-in-Publication Data
Names: Deonn, Tracy, author.
Title: Bloodmarked / Tracy Deonn.
Description: First edition. | New York : Simon & Schuster Books for Young Readers, [2022] | Series: Legendborn cycle ; 2 | Summary: "When the leaders of the Order reveal that they will do everything in their power to keep the approaching demon war a secret, Bree and her friends go on the run so she can learn how to control her devastating new powers"— Provided by publisher.
Identifiers: LCCN 2021056035 |
ISBN 9781534441637 (hardcover) | ISBN 9781534441651 (ebook)
Subjects: CYAC: Secret societies—Fiction. | Magic—Fiction. | Fantasy. | BISAC: YOUNG ADULT FICTION / Fantasy / Contemporary | YOUNG ADULT FICTION / Mysteries & Detective Stories | LCGFT: Fantasy fiction.
Classification: LCC PZ7.1.D46837 Bl 2022 | DDC [Fic]—dc23
LC record available at https://lccn.loc.gov/2021056035

For every Black girl who was "the first"

THE ORDER OF THE ROUND TABLE

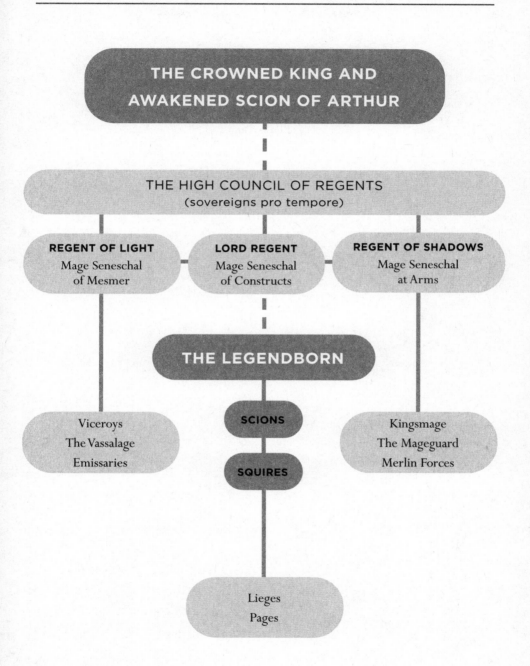

THE CROWNED KING AND
AWAKENED SCION OF ARTHUR

THE HIGH COUNCIL OF REGENTS
(sovereigns pro tempore)

REGENT OF LIGHT
Mage Seneschal
of Mesmer

LORD REGENT
Mage Seneschal
of Constructs

REGENT OF SHADOWS
Mage Seneschal
at Arms

THE LEGENDBORN

Viceroys
The Vassalage
Emissaries

SCIONS

SQUIRES

Kingsmage
The Mageguard
Merlin Forces

Lieges
Pages

BLOODMARKED

PROLOGUE

MY VEINS BURN with the spirits of my ancestors.

Twenty-four hours ago, I pulled Excalibur from its stone. Now, I am paying the price.

The ancient blade shattered me. Who I was. Who I could be. Who I'd never be again.

I became shards of myself.

The Briana Matthews who held Excalibur had been broken apart—and forged into something new.

Something new. Something powerful. That's how William described me.

Last night, as I'd raised Excalibur high, two spirits were *pounding* inside me like dual drums: Vera, my ancestral foremother, and Arthur Pendragon himself. Even though they'd lived centuries apart, they'd each used magic to lock power to their bloodlines, and to me. Vera, with a plea to her ancestors. Arthur, with a spell for his knights. When the battle was done and I'd finally fallen into bed I thought they'd both faded. Gone wherever spirits go when they are done possessing their Medium descendants.

Arthur fell silent. Vera seemed to say goodbye: *'There is a cost to being a legend, daughter. But fear not, you will not bear it alone.'*

But her words were not a personal farewell; they were an ancestral welcome.

Now, in the wee hours, I lie in bed at the Lodge, the historic home of the Legendborn. But I am not resting. I am painfully awake. Covers shoved off the bed, skin and spirit stretched tight. My curls lay damp against my neck.

I twist to my side, gasping, and squeeze both eyes shut. Crawl to the ground. Feel and hear my nails scrape the floor, a desperate sound in the night.

When my eyes open, the room around me is gone, and I am no longer Bree. Instead . . .

I am Selah: Vera's daughter, now grown and pregnant with her own child.

It is night. Long ago. I am being ushered into a home by a Black woman with sharp brown eyes that dart over my head the way I have come. Her warm, strong fingers grip my shoulder. "Hurry, girl. Hurry!" she whispers. I do not know this woman, but "girl" is uttered with urgency and sisterhood both.

She leads me to a door set into the floor at the back of the house. Lifts it to reveal a hidden cubby of earth and rotting wood.

I will pause here for a moment, but tomorrow I will run again.

I blink—and the Lodge bedroom returns. Dark and familiar. Shiny, wide planks of oak stretch out beneath me.

Inhale. Exhale.

Close my eyes. Open them.

I am in a diner. My name is Jessie. I am twenty years old.

My hands hold a stack of menus. Fifties music plays from a jukebox.

"Hey, you! Girl!" A rough, rude voice yelling my way. "Girl" is uttered with such clear derision that it barely cloaks the word he really means. That slur is written all over his face. I find the white man in the booth near the entrance, wearing the smug grin of someone who knows he will not be stopped. "Service, please?" he sneers, voice sarcastic. A jeer and a lure. Daring me to talk back.

A flare of anger, the furnace of root in my chest lit and growing—but a smile on my face as I walk toward him through the restaurant.

I'd like to ignore him, or shout, but I can't.

Not here, not today. But somewhere, someday.

As I pass by another booth, a white woman in a black-and-silver dress whips around. Her hand shoots out, fingers gripping my elbow. Her deep amber eyes narrow, and sparks of suspicion dance across my face. A tendril of spiced smoke hits my nose, like a match just lit, ready to grow.

All at once, I know who she is. She is one of them. The Order magicians my mother warned me about as a child. "Don't let those Order Merlins catch you. Don't let one get you alone. If you see their blue flames, run."

Heart racing, I swallow the furnace. Douse it. Hide it away.

"Ma'am?" My voice is clear and steady.

The Merlin woman looks me over. Doubt flickers across her face. A beat passes. Can she hear my heart? My fear?

Finally, she says, "Never mind. My apologies." Her fingers loosen, then drop, and she turns back to her meal. The scent of her magic fades—a weapon, sheathed.

I sigh with the escape. The close call.

It's not just the man who deserves my rage. One day, I hope to face the Merlins, too.

Not here, not today. But somewhere, someday.

When I return to the room in the Lodge this time, Bree once more, my sweaty palms have stained the hardwood floors.

Inhale. Exhale.

Eyes close. Eyes open.

My name is Leanne. I am fifteen. I am walking past a park at sunset with a friend. We are giggling. Silly.

In the darkness, faint and yards away, a creature. A near-translucent glowing hound in the park—and a figure surrounding it casting weapons made of light. The figure moves faster than they should be able to. Ozone fills my nose. The smell of honey, burning.

I freeze. Draw a silent breath. Become as stone, just like my mother taught me.

My friend stops, her brown eyes confused and laughing. "Leanne, what—"

I don't hear her speak. All I hear is the mantra I inherited from my mother. Her voice is hushed and furious in my ears: "Never let a Merlin find you. If you see one, run. You hear me? Run."

I slip off my shoes, down to my stockings. Quieter that way. Mumble an excuse to my friend. And I run.

I am flung back and forward, writhing between time and space.

Selah. Mary. Regina. Corinne. Emmeline. Jessie. Leanne. I even see a glimpse of my mother, Faye.

Eight visions. Eight sets of memories that aren't mine. Eight bodies that I inhabit, sucked down into lives I've never lived. All running.

Every daughter of the Line of Vera in the last two hundred years has run from the Order. Every mother has passed on the warning. And here I am inside its home.

Eventually, I slide into a shadowed space with no walls. In front of me, a pair of naked brown feet surrounded by flames.

"Daughter of daughters."

I push to standing to see Vera. She is much as she'd been before: a woman in an empty, dark world. Blood and flame swirl around her deep brown arms, hair stretching up and wide like it is reaching for the universe.

"Where——?"

"This is the plane between life and death."

The plane between . . . I look around at the darkness and feel the *waiting* of it, and the completion, too. Like smoke, ready to become matter or dissipate. Sound, ready to be heard or silenced. This is an *almost* and *already* place.

"You . . . you brought me here before," I pant. "When I pulled the sword."

She nods once.

I speak around the tears, through the memories that ache in my chest. "All of those lives . . . all of the *running*——"

"You had to see, because you need to understand who you are."

"'Who I am' . . . ?"

"You are the point of our arrow." Her voice grows louder with every word. "The tip of our spear. The bow of our ship. The flare of our long-simmering heat. You are the living embodiment of our resistance. The revelation after centuries of hiding. The pain-welded blade. Wound turned weapon."

"I know . . . ," I say. "I know . . ."

"No. You do not."

The flames on Vera's skin glow brighter. "From the first daughter to the last, our furnace has grown. Each life burns hotter than the life before. You are my lineage, at its sharpest and strongest. With all that flows through you, you have the power to protect what evil would destroy. You can face what must be faced."

Her words flow directly into my chest, searing me from every direction.

"We ran for many reasons. We ran to protect ourselves. We ran so we would not die, so that our daughters could *live*." Vera steps forward, and her voice is slow, rich lava against my skin. "But one purpose, one dream reigns above all others. Do you know what that is, Bree?"

I shake my head, gasping. "No."

The flames on her skin grow higher, her hair extending out and up so that I cannot see where it ends. I blink again . . . and I am a shivering, sweat-soaked teenage girl on the floor of a historic home. I am sucking air into burning lungs. I am shedding tears that are mine and not mine.

If Vera's voice was once volcanic flow, it is now cool obsidian. Razor-sharp.

"We ran . . . so you would not have to."

PART ONE

STRENGTH

THIS IS THE part where I hesitate.

Logically, I know I'll be fine. I've escaped half a dozen times, no problem. Wards are barrier magic, but the one outside my bedroom window was cast to keep intruders *out*, not to lock occupants in.

Still . . . it feels like a smart idea to test the silent, shimmering curtain of light that surrounds the Lodge before I fling my whole body through it. Just in case.

I raise a hand to the open window and *press* until my palm hits aether. The silver-blue ward flares at my touch, but doesn't put up a fight. Instead, it ripples in a sluggish wave over my knuckles and wrist. Prickly and warm, but harmless. My fingertips ease through the iridescent layer to meet crisp night air on the other side. When I withdraw my hand, the magic calms again.

Excellent.

The wind picks up, blowing a wave of harsh scents in my face: Bright, spicy cinnamon. Warm whiskey. Smoke from long-burning logs.

Sel usually recasts his wards in the early evening before Shadowborn activity rises, so his aether signature is still fresh. He can only place barriers around specific and immobile locations. Buildings, circles of land, a room. I was moved into the Lodge—against my wishes—precisely *because* it sits behind a fortress of protective wards. This one in particular wraps the brick and stone and is stronger than the ones he used to cast, making it impossible for someone to enter the home without the assistance of a Legendborn or Merlin.

I've only been the Scion of Arthur for a month and already I know a little of what Nick must have felt his whole life. Stifled. Trapped. Powerful and powerless, all at the same time. *Restless.*

"Phew." Another gust hits my sensitive nose. I wince and turn. Glance at the bedside alarm clock. Ten thirty.

Almost time.

I fall back on the bed with a huff. Sel and the Legendborn are probably just now reaching the first stop on their patrol route, the small tract of woods down near the south end of campus. No matter how hard I try to relax, my entire body is a coiled spring. Even my jaw is clenched tight while I wait.

A biting breeze blows through the open window, this time tickling my cheeks with the chill of early fall. A reminder that winter is on the way, and that time is passing us by.

I shouldn't be here.

The same phrase runs through my mind every day. No matter where I am or what I'm doing, those words will bubble up from somewhere deep in my gut, flow up the back of my throat, and sort of . . . crash around in my brain.

I shouldn't be sitting in this English classroom, listening to a lecture. I shouldn't be eating a four-course meal in the Lodge dining room. I shouldn't be sleeping on a soft bed, safe behind the Lodge's walls.

I'm certain my friends have guessed what I'm feeling by now. How could they not? Greer sits beside me in that classroom, so they see my bouncing knee. They can probably tell that I'm ready to launch out of my chair at any moment. I sit down for the four-course meal, but Pete is right there at my elbow when I poke at the food on the plate and forget to eat it. When the Legendborn return at two a.m. from their late-night patrols, I am always awake, waiting at the door to greet them.

The Legendborn are in a holding pattern. *I* am in a holding pattern. We have been, ever since the events of the ogof y ddraig, the cave of the dragon. Ever since I—*we*—faced murder and betrayal and ever since bitter truths were revealed.

Ever since Nick was taken from my side as I slept, abducted by Isaac

Sorenson, the powerful Kingsmage bound to Nick's own father. No one has heard from or seen the three of them since.

Frustration lives in my stomach like a piece of coal these days—and just *thinking* about Nick's capture stokes it into a painful flame, bright and familiar.

A month ago, deep under Carolina's campus, the spirit of King Arthur Pendragon Awakened into the world—and within *me,* his true descendant. His Awakening signaled that Camlann, the ancient war between the Legendborn and Shadowborn forces, was coming once again. And the very next day the Regents, the current leadership of the Order of the Round Table, instructed us to do . . . nothing. We are to attend classes, take tests, even go to parties if we're invited. We can't afford to draw attention to the chapter—or to me— while the Regents' intelligence agents gather intel about our enemies and about Nick's capture by a well-known loyal servant. Until further notice, the Legendborn have been ordered to sit tight and stay here.

For us, *here* is *weeks* of holding our collective breath while on the brink of war. But for me, *here* is sitting alone inside my room in the Lodge while the Legendborn are out hunting our enemies.

My father already knew the Order as an old academic student group. Knew Nick had invited me to join. But after he found out about my sudden move to their off-campus housing, he'd demanded an explanation. It took the dean of students, my best friend Alice, *and* my former therapist, Patricia, to convince him the Lodge was legitimate and safe. I couldn't tell him the whole truth, but I told him there was nowhere more secure. That's not a lie, it's just that . . .

I shouldn't be here. I don't *want* to be here.

So recently . . . I have decided I *won't* be here.

At least for a few hours at a time.

Another glance at the clock. Ten forty-five now. That should do it.

As I climb up on the sill, I have to chuckle. Even with Arthur's strength, I *never* would have considered jumping out of a two-story window if I hadn't experienced Sel do it from three—with me on his back.

"Thank you for the inspiration, Kingsmage," I murmur with a grin as I balance on the narrow strip of wood.

The difference between a jump and a fall? A decisive, hard push off the Lodge's stone exterior.

"One." I inhale. "Two." I grit my teeth. "Three!" I jump.

When I land, I hear my trainer Gillian's voice telling me to take the impact *intentionally*, bending my knees rather than locking them. Back when Gill was first training me, before I inherited Arthur's preternatural strength, my legs couldn't have absorbed even a half-story of shock. A jump like this would have sent all that force from the ground straight up my ankles into my knees and hips.

Now, Arthur's strength keeps me from breaking something, but it does nothing for my balance. When I stand, I wobble a bit but manage to remain upright. Progress. I'm only one step away from the building before a voice stops me.

"He's going to catch you one of these nights, you know."

I twist back to see a figure emerge from the shadows. William, in a green denim jacket and blue jeans, wearing a wry smile.

"And do what?" I cross my arms. "Yell at me again?"

William's mouth twitches. "Yes. Loudly." He tilts his head up to my darkened window. "Not a bad jump. Or landing, for that matter. You're acclimating to Arthur's strength."

"Yeah, well"—I shake my head—"strength is not enough."

"It never is." William would know what strength is and what it's not. For two hours a day, he is the strongest of us all. Stronger than me. Stronger than Sel. Stronger even than Felicity, the Scion of Lamorak.

Silence. I bite my lip. "You here to stop me?" He could, if he wanted to. He probably *should*, but . . .

William sighs and slips his hands into his back pockets. "No. If I stop you, you'll just keep sneaking out. In increasingly creative ways, I imagine."

The first time William met me, I'd been injured by a hellhound. He healed me while I was barely conscious, without knowing my name or even asking for it. Not long after—when he knew enough to suspect that I wasn't being fully honest about why I was joining the Order—he healed my injuries again. William understands the value of secrets and doesn't judge others for keeping them. A blessing, really. Especially tonight.

In lieu of judging, he watches me with a mild expression, waiting for me to own up to my crimes. I sigh. "How long?"

"Have I known you've been sneaking out?" He nods toward my right arm. "Since Monday morning when I spotted the poorly wrapped burn on your wrist at breakfast."

That was four days ago; the burn is mostly healed now. I tuck my arm behind me. "Thought I hid that under my sleeve."

"You did. From everyone other than me."

I am grateful for how much William just . . . *knows* . . . without saying anything. But I don't want to discuss the burns I'm not yet skilled enough to prevent.

"Sel would have spotted it, too, if he'd seen you that day."

"Well, he didn't see me that day," I mumble.

William doesn't comment.

"I thought you'd be out patrolling with the others." I gesture between us. "Or is this another one of y'all's bodyguard shifts?"

"Bree." William regards me for a long moment, letting the gentle admonishment settle like a soft weight around my shoulders. "You can't blame us, can you?"

"No." I look away, and repeat the lore no one will let me forget since that night in the cave. "'If a fully Awakened Arthur is struck down by Shadowborn blood, the Legendborn Lines will be broken forever.' I get it."

I didn't plan to sneak out, not at first. But then one day last week Greer confessed that Sel had ordered the Legendborn Scions and Squires to escort me from building to building on campus. *Quietly*, so I wouldn't notice that the others were protecting me from potential attacks. *Secretly*, so I wouldn't get offended by their hovering.

I got offended anyway.

Hot frustration wells up even now, and I clench my fist——until my nails break the skin. I hiss and unclench immediately. Arthur's strength is more annoying than useful when I'm not allowed to use it. I release a sigh and turn back to find William eyeing my hand. God, he notices *everything*.

William raises a brow. "If you get it, then why are you angry?"

"I should be able to defend myself just fine. I should fight in this war just like everyone else."

"You will. Just not yet." He gazes past me, along my intended path into the woods. "Heading to the arena?"

No use in hiding it. I nod.

His expression turns doubtful. Sneaking out is one secret; going to the arena alone is another. "It's already late, and the memorial is in the morning. . . ."

"I know." I chew on my lip. I hadn't forgotten the memorial. How could I? The Order's formal ceremony for Russ, Whitty, Fitz, and Evan will be the first funeral I've attended since my mother's. "I won't be out long. Promise."

"Bree . . ."

I pout harder. "Please."

With a sigh and an amused eye roll, he relents. "Okay." Then, to my surprise, he steps to my side. "But if you're going, I'll join you."

I blink. "You will?"

He shrugs. "Lead the way."

We both know the path through the woods well enough that we can walk it even without my flashlight. If Sel were here, he could light the walk with a palm full of aether.

But if Sel were here, he'd be dragging me back into the house, even though his wards form a triple-layered perimeter around the Lodge now. The one at the window was just the first.

When we press through the second ward, William notices my reaction to it. My wrinkled nose and watering eyes. "That Bloodcraft ability of yours is fascinating."

"Smelling aether?" The only Bloodcraft power readily available to me all the time is the passive ability to sense magic: Sight that allows me to see aether, touch that allows me to feel it. A nose that tells me that someone has used it in a casting.

"Not just scenting aether. The Legendborn can tell when there's aether around and if it's been weaponized, but *you* can discern between individual casters, their moods. . . ." He shakes his head in wonder.

Vera's Bloodcraft spell was designed, first and foremost, to help her descendants sense nearby aether users who might hunt us—Merlins, in particular.

"I'm curious." He points back at the ward we passed. "What did you pick up just then?"

I take another breath. "It burns a bit, so Sel was angry when he cast it."

He chuckles. Pauses. Turns my response over in his analytical, medical mind. "You sound congested. Are you allergic?"

I consider it. "No. More like . . . when someone walks by with *really* strong cologne."

William ducks beneath a branch. "Sel *does* leave an impression."

I groan. "Even when he's not around! The wards, the Legendborn bodyguards, the demands. It's *suffocating*."

William laughs then, gray eyes sparkling.

"What?" I ask.

He smiles softly. "You sound like Nicholas."

For the second time tonight, pain strikes me from within. Worse now, because I'd shoved it away earlier. The deep ache of losing Nick is not the obliterative wave of grief I still feel when I think of my mother, but something sharper. This grief slips between my ribs like a scalpel. A thing I gasp against but can't prevent. The trees blur. My eyes sting. I stop walking.

Nick was *right* beside me when he was taken. He'd just lost his title and been betrayed by his father, and yet he chose to stay with me while I recovered in his bed. Sometimes, I think I remember the heat of his breath against my collarbone, the reassuring weight of his arm across my middle. Words, whispered into my shoulder: *"You and me, B."*

"Bree." William steps in my line of sight. His voice is low, to soothe. "We don't have any reason to believe his father would harm him."

I blink away the prick of tears. "Harm will *find* him. At this rate, well before we do."

William chooses his words carefully. "It's been two hundred and forty-five years since a Scion of Arthur was last Called. No one alive has ever witnessed the moment in which we are living. Everything I know of the High Council of

Regents would support their being . . . measured. Careful in how they proceed when war is on the horizon and Onceborn lives are at stake—"

"Onceborn lives aren't the only lives at stake," I insist. "Nick was abducted by a murderer. His life is at stake too!"

William presses his lips into a patient line. "As is yours."

I don't usually argue with William, not really. But on this topic, we *have* gotten into a regular dance of point, counterpoint.

"Except that anyone who knows about the Order still believes that Nick is the Scion of Arthur." I take a deep breath. "And his father and Isaac have him out there on the run with some unknown number of Shadowborn still hellbent on killing him. Which means his life is currently in far more danger than mine is."

There is no arguing with this, and William doesn't try to. Keeping my identity secret for my own safety was the very first order that the Regents handed down. Up until Arthur Called me in the ogof y ddraig, Nicholas Davis was the Scion of Arthur. To the Legendborn world, Nicholas Davis is *still* the Scion of Arthur. But in reality, he's not. I am. Nick is not on a leave of absence from school to prepare to ascend the throne; he's been kidnapped, and *I* am the one preparing. Right now, there are fewer than twenty people in the world who know that—and my life depends on that circle of trust remaining as small as possible.

As the Awakened Scion of Arthur and anchor of the Spell of Eternity, I am the living, breathing embodiment of Legendborn power. Like an engine, my blood and my life fuel the magic that binds the spirits and enhanced abilities of the original thirteen knights to their Scion descendants. If I die by the hand of a Shadowborn demon, the spell will die too, and fifteen centuries of Legendborn power will end. No Scion will ever be Called again, and humanity will fall to Shadowborn rule. Demons will be free to feed on human emotions, stoke chaos and conflict, and attack indiscriminately and without recourse. So, you know, no pressure or anything.

William sighs. "You will have more say—in everything—after the Rite."

I roll my eyes. "The Rite where I pull the sword from the stone again. This time for an audience?"

William frowns. "Pulling the sword in battle was spontaneous and necessary—"

It also wasn't just me, I think. *It was Vera, Arthur, me. All together. Not one hand, but three.*

"You must formally *and intentionally* claim your title before the Regents to initiate the transfer of power, make it official. Especially in wartime."

I snort. "The only time that Arthur Calls his Scion *is* wartime, William."

"War against *known* enemies, perhaps. If that goruchel mimic, if Rha—" William's sentence ends abruptly. He inhales before trying again, as if he has to *force* his mouth around the name of the demon who murdered and mimicked Evan Cooper so perfectly that he fooled the entire chapter. "If *Rhaz* was telling the truth, there could be other impostors on this very campus. Even if Rhaz was lying, we still can't risk drawing undue attention to you or to Nick's absence. Not with Gates opening every night and Camlann on the horizon. Our forces are incomplete."

It's true. A completed Round Table is made up of twenty-six Legendborn members: thirteen Scion descendants, each with a bonded Squire to fight alongside them. The Table gained me when Arthur Called, but Rhaz murdered four: *Fitz. Evan. Russ. Whitty.* Their names are written in William's eyes. Lost Table members, lost warriors, lost friends.

When Fitz died, his younger brother was Called by Sir Bors to replace him immediately. But Evan, Russ, and Whitty were chosen Squires, and the Scions have been slow to select replacements. Not that they have many options. After word got out that Whitty was killed by a demon in battle mere *hours* after becoming William's Squire, most of the Pages who competed to become Squires in this year's tournament withdrew their names from consideration.

And then there's Nick and me. Nick may not be the Scion of Arthur any longer, but he is the Scion of Lancelot. As Scions, Order law dictates that we will need to choose our own Squires.

Merlin bespelled the original Round Table for twenty-six; our peak power *requires* twenty-six—and we are five members short.

War is coming, and we aren't ready.

"The Regents will hand you a kingdom in grave circumstances, Bree. But they will not deliver you an inner circle that you cannot trust. I, for one, am glad of this." William's brow pinches in a rare show of pain. "We have had too many losses to not proceed with caution and with Oathed allies at our side."

My hand finds his forearm in the dark and squeezes it before we keep walking.

I gnaw at my lip. "Speaking of Oaths . . . Sel . . . ?"

"Would have alerted us if his Oath indicated that Nick was in danger," William says evenly. "Nick is a valuable chip. Lord Davis will want to make the right play."

"Still can't believe Merlin didn't design that Oath with some sort of tracking spell or *something*. What's the use of a bodyguard knowing their charge is in danger if they don't know where they are?"

"In the old days, Kingsmages never left their charges' sides." William raises a brow. "Modern times have made that . . . challenging."

The empty arena is near silent when we arrive; the night air too cold for wildlife and insects. Our footsteps echo as we descend the stairs carved into the cliffside. The cloying, sour-sweet smell of dying leaves and damp wood beckons from below.

The night of the first trial, I'd walked down these same steps with my eyes cloaked by Sel's mesmer and Nick guiding me. As I walk down now, I can almost feel his hands, large and warm on my shoulders. Almost hear his voice—a low, amused laugh from a forgotten memory.

"Steady, B, steady. See, the problem *is that if you fall, the code of chivalry says I have no choice but to dive after you."*

"You still wear his necklace?" William's voice jolts me from the memory.

We've reached the bottom of the stairs and he's behind me, peering down at where my thumb is rubbing the Pendragon coin hanging from the chain at my chest.

My ears heat. "Yeah."

The coin may have been a gift from Nick, but it feels like something we share now. The sigil of the Line of Arthur, the dragon rampant, the mark of the king, on one side, and the Legendborn symbol—a four-pointed diamond overlaying a circle—on the other. I remember how indignant I'd felt when Nick first gave it to me, that he'd claimed me as "his" in a way that wasn't right. Later, I let myself think that maybe I *could* be his in a way that *did* feel right. And then I was.

I shake my head to clear it and lead us onto the grassy arena floor. When we reach the center, William stops mid-step. "Sel's last ward—"

"Follows the tree line. I've checked." I jerk my chin to the other side of the open field. Sel's third and outermost ward starts a few feet from the ditch where I'd once hidden with Sydney, a Page, during the tournament. From there, it stretches in a wide curve to make a massive circle of Battle Park with the Lodge at the center.

William nods, satisfied. "All right. Show me what you've got, newbie."

I know what he's doing. Teasingly reminding me that even though I—not Arthur—succeeded in the combat trial using my own hard-earned skills, the other Scions are still *years* ahead of me when it comes to knowing how to fight with aether. They'd started preparing for the possibility of inheriting their knights' aether abilities when they were six years old. Began training with rubber and wooden practice versions of their knights' preferred weapons at seven. I'm sixteen—ten years behind everyone else and just getting started.

William is reminding me, I think, to be kind to myself. To remember that even as adept as he is, he is human, like me. And humans must learn to wield aether, one step at a time.

Mediums can't control the dead. Even if I could contact Arthur at will, I can't—and won't—rely on possession to wield his power. If I am to lead, I have to be able to access and control aether on my own, like the others do.

My own breath is loud and raspy in my ears. My heart kicks at my rib once, twice. I close my eyes. Try to slow it down. Take another breath. Open my palms to the sky.

"Aether is all around you." William's voice is soft in my ears. "Already at your fingertips."

Aether is all around me. It's already here.

"A whisper. That's all you need."

I grin. "Sel doesn't whisper for power, he *pulls*."

William snorts. "A model you don't have to follow, not here."

I breathe deep and reach without reaching until warm air—aether—begins to dance along my skin. Then, I open my eyes—and *call* for that aether. Invite it to transform from its invisible gaseous state to the energy I can see and manipulate—and blue fire ignites around my hands and arms.

"Good," William murmurs, "Calling aether to mage flame is the first hurdle. Now, forge it. . . ."

The mage flame grows hotter. I hiss but hold steady and imagine the whirling wisps falling into the solid mass of Excalibur. I craft Arthur's hilt in my mind and *push* the flames into my image. I visualize a swirling storm of aether collapsing into the length of Arthur's blade, then layering over and over itself until thin sheets of magic become a sharp-edged weapon.

But my will isn't enough to cool the mage flame into a solid. My images don't work.

There is only burning.

Instead of concentrating into solid mass, my flames roar *higher*. The fine hair on my forearms singes; there's a charred smell in my nose. "Come on . . . ," I mutter.

William steps forward. "Bree, stop. We'll try again."

"No." I need to try again *now*. While the flames are here. *The blade is a . . . a longsword. Thick and silver, a blood groove down the middle . . .*

"Bree—"

"I can do it." I grit my teeth. *Pommel is shaped like a circle. Red diamond at the center—*

My hiss grows until it's a low cry. It's no longer the aether scalding me; it's my refusal to let it go.

"Bree, release it—"

"No! I just need—"

"Release it!"

The magic bites into my skin, the burns going deeper. I scream—and finally release it.

The explosion blasts out and down, blowing dirt and dead leaves up into my face before the aether shimmers and disappears.

"Damnit!" I slam a balled fist into the ground—and punch a hole into the earth.

William coughs, waving a hand through the dust in his face. "Now there's dirt in your wounds."

I groan. He's right. *And* it's in my hair. I'll have to wash it again if I want it to look nice for tomorrow. *"Damnit!"* I repeat.

William kneels at my side, one silver-liquid-coated hand resting over my forearm. He'd called his own aether for a healing swyn so quickly I hadn't seen it. The bright, citrus scent of his aether signature floods my nose. "It's okay."

"No, it's not! I tried for Arthur's sword this time. Before, I'd tried for his shield. God, even just a plain gauntlet, William. I can't forge *any* of Arthur's armor, much less make something solid enough to do damage."

William takes my right arm in his gentle fingers and tuts. The burns sting like hell, even more so now with little bits of soil clinging to the raw and shiny red streaks. "Forging aether into solid matter was overwhelming to me, too, even after all that I'd studied—"

"I don't have a decade to study!" I shout.

Used to Sel's outbursts—far angrier and louder than mine—William doesn't flinch or even look up, just continues. "Even after all that I'd studied, it took long hours to visualize and forge Gawain's daggers. I visited the replicas in storage often to memorize their weights, feel their hilts in my hand. You must know the weapon to forge it. You need more time with Excalibur, I think. It is unique in our world, remember. An aether weapon made stronger by each Scion of Arthur who wields it, changing with each hand that holds it."

William's swyns are a literal balm. Calming, soothing.

"Your castings don't burn at all. You cool aether down from that"—I gesture in the air with my left hand—"to this." I point to my wrist, wrapped in shining silver-blue fluid.

"The aether I call is nowhere near as hot as yours to begin with. And I certainly don't call it in the amounts you do."

I frown. "What does that mean?"

"It means what we already know. That you are unusual. A new type of power—or rather, a new combination of powers. The invisible energy we call aether is a mutable ambient element manipulated by will, but that manipulation is somewhat defined by the user. Scions and Squires are limited by their knights' inheritances. I can cast Gawain's swyns and I can forge armor—not the exact sixth-century variety, no plates back then—but it must be a variation that works for Gawain's gifts. The only weapon we can cast is our knight's chosen weapon. With their demon heritage, Merlins can cast anything they wish: a staff, a hound, a protective barrier. You yourself have wielded aether in its mage flame state to burn demons in battle—something the Legendborn cannot do." He pauses. "What about your Bloodcraft abilities? Can you call the aeth—root—you create from within, then forge *it* into solid matter?"

I shake my head. "My Bloodcrafted root doesn't work like that. It's defensive, not offensive."

What the Legendborn have named "aether," Rootcrafters refer to as "root." Instead of forging weapons, typical Rootcrafters commune with ancestors to request access to ambient root—and there doesn't seem to be a limit with how they use it after that, from healing to memory walking.

But Vera's Bloodcraft spell takes it one step further. In the cave, red root flames ignited *within* me and flowed *from* my body, down my arms and hands. I breathed crimson fire that scorched isels and burned through their demon flesh—but only after they'd attacked me first.

William hums thoughtfully and switches his aether-drenched fingers to my left arm. The stinging burns on my right have already faded to a horrible itch. "What you did in the ogof . . . that was far more powerful than any Legendborn weapon casting could ever be. You didn't need a weapon; you *were* the weapon."

William's words remind me of Vera's. *You are my lineage, at its sharpest and strongest.* I breathe through the memory of her voice, every syllable its own type of cut. "All that power—Arthur's aether armor, Vera's Bloodcraft root—was out of my control. Just like now." I face him again, voice firmer. "And I need to *get* control before the Regents find out I don't have it."

"Why? You are the Awakened Crown Scion of Arthur. Control over his aether abilities, or lack thereof, doesn't change that. You can claim the title with the Rite, even be coronated, without forging a single plate of aether armor. *You pulled the sword.*" He flashes a grin. "You are his heir, burned forearms or not."

"But if I'm going to lead the search for Nick, I need to earn the Regents' and other Scions' *respect*. I need to be as good at this as Nick would have been."

"Well," William says, sympathetic. "My diagnosis? It's only a matter of time with Arthur's abilities. And until then, at least you know how your Bloodcraft works."

I scoff and kick at the ground. "Not as well as I'd like. I ran from my Bloodcraft at first, even if I didn't fully realize that's what it was, because I didn't want to deal with my mother's death. If I had just faced things head-on, I would have had access to root *months* ago."

William watches me. "Is that what you're doing now? Facing your challenges head-on?"

I think about it for a moment, and Vera's last words return once more. Hot and sharp and direct. *We ran so you would not have to.* Then my mother's, from the hidden memory she'd left behind. *When the time comes, if it comes, don't be scared. Fight.* My mother hadn't known half as much about our Bloodcraft powers as I do, and she used them to do what was right anyway. To save people.

"Yes," I tell him. "No more running."

"What the *hell* are you two doing?"

Selwyn's voice cracks across the arena—a whip of sound that lashes us both. I groan and look up. William sighs and shakes his head.

Sel is a tall, dark shape at the top of the cliff. Too far to make out his facial expression, but I don't need sight to sense his anger. Even from fifty feet away, his gaze scorches my cheek.

He steps over the edge. His coat lifts in the air behind him, a dark shadow fluttering against stone. As soon as he lands, he's moving—and at my side in a furious blur.

This close, his eyes are a harsh bright gold. He looks like he's just come back from hunting: flushed cheeks, wind-whipped raven-black hair, smudges of dirt on his dark duster, and his aether signature billowing in a cloud around him, fresh and burning. Whiskey, set ablaze.

"Explain yourselves!" Sel bellows, staring down at William.

William releases another, heavier sigh and continues his work. "Hello, Selwyn. Back from the hunt already?"

"The campus is clear," Sel snaps. "Imagine my alarm when I arrived home and you were *both* missing. I will give you two minutes—no, *one* minute to explain yourselves before I drag Br—" Sel's glare lands on my arm in William's hands.

He must be beyond furious for his situational awareness to be so delayed. In the span of a breath, the Merlin takes in the healing aether wrapping my arm from elbow to wrist. His nostrils flare, scenting the lingering ozone in the air. "You have burned yourself." He looks up, and his gaze hardens on mine. "Again."

It's the first time he's looked me in the eye since he arrived. The first time we've seen each other in a week. The first words he's said to me after *days* of silence.

And here we are having the same fight that drove us apart.

I bite my lip so I don't scream at him. "I told you I can't just sit in my room while you're all out hunting and fighting. I should be—"

"You *should* be back in the Lodge!" he snarls. "Behind *three layers* of wards, Briana!" He points at my wounds. "Is this not evidence enough of that?"

Shame and embarrassment flood my cheeks. And on top of those, I feel the sting of Selwyn using my full name to chastise me. "Once I can control Arthur's aether, I won't *need* the wards. And you can't give me orders forever, Kings-mage!"

He levels a stony glare at me. "I will give you orders right up until you take the Rite of Kings, and stop not a moment before."

This time I do scream—a wordless, frustrated sound behind clenched teeth. "What about everyone else?"

Sel lifts a dark brow. "Be specific."

"You—" I push to my feet, but William tugs me right back down. It's not yet midnight; I could break his grip with Arthur's strength, but it's *William*. He may not get in the middle of our fight, but he is a healer through and through—he'll never let me walk away with fresh wounds. "You ordered the others to follow me on campus!"

Sel's mouth thins. "I did."

"I don't need them to guard me—"

"Clearly you do." He shakes his head. "Do you have *any* idea—"

A short, screaming howl cuts him off from beyond the arena trench. The sound shutters our argument. My heart rockets against my ribs so fast it hurts. I know that cry. . . . I *remember* it.

"Sel—"

His expression flips from surprise to deadly focus in an instant. "Flank her," Sel orders, and speeds to my right with aether streaming toward both palms.

William is already on his feet, at my left in a blink. His aether armor builds itself in a rapid flow of clinking plates and chain mail. I stifle my envy.

The high-pitched screech comes again. It hits the cliff wall and bounces back against the trees, playing tricks on our ears. "How many?" I ask.

"Too many. Could be a pack." Sel glances behind us and above the cliff, where the forest continues back toward the Lodge in the pitch black of night. I know what he wants to do, what he's thinking. He wants to send me running back the way we came, to cross into safety behind his wards. "Go."

"No." I set my jaw. "I have Arthur's strength!"

His eyes flash. "But not his wisdom." Whatever calculus he's doing, whatever scenarios he's running in his mind, they don't include me. "William, we need Gawain's power. How much longer?"

William glances at the moon overhead. A quick check of the sky for the power in his blood. "Still a few minutes—"

Sel curses. "Too long."

"Get Bree back to the Lodge," William says. "I can handle this on my own."

Sel's eyes narrow into the darkness, seeing more than we can—and his face pales. "No, William, you can't."

"Selwyn!" Insult flashes across William's face. "I said I can *handle* it! Stop being—"

"Oh no . . ." I finally see what has found us in the woods.

William follows my pointing finger and blanches. "Dear God."

A dozen enormous, armored, fully corporeal hellfoxes emerge from the trees. These monsters may be lesser demon isels, but they are as tall as trucks. The line of them stretches thirty feet across in either direction. Green, smoky aether rises from their bodies, pluming upward into a dozen clouds with every swish of their scaled tails.

William rotates his wrists once—a sharp snap up—and two shining gauntlets appear on his forearms. "That's not a pack. . . ."

"No." Sel grits his teeth. "It's a legion." By now he's gathered enough aether to create a swirling cloud around our ankles—cool to the touch and perfectly in his control—but I don't know if it's enough. Sel and I were barely able to fight three together, and they were half the size of these and partially corporeal.

I've never seen this many fully corporeal Shadowborn at one time. How much aether have they been able to consume to become dense enough that Onceborns could see them?

The foxes snap at Sel's ward. Butt their heads against it. Testing it. Ripples of aether appear on impact, fanning out in abrupt, bright circles in the air.

"The ward will hold them, won't it?" I ask.

As if in answer, the fox directly across from us steps back and crouches low. It opens its jaw wide in an ear-splitting call—and the aether of Sel's ward begins to flow into its mouth in a stream of silver smoke.

"Oh, sh—" Sel is cut off by another scream and another, until all twelve foxes begin calling a section of his casting into their bodies . . . and his ward thins before our eyes.

SEL HAS FROZEN in place. Only his eyes dart up and down his diminishing ward, taking in the twelve whirlpools emptying into the foxes' mouths. I can't tell if he's thinking or freaking out. God, I hope it's not the latter. I don't want to see Sel freaking out.

This is the double-edged sword of using aether to fight powerful Shadowborn. It can be wielded as a weapon . . . or our enemies can consume it to grow stronger. Sometimes in the same battle.

William tenses beside me. A Gawain dagger now rests in each of his fists. "We could alert the others."

Sel blinks back into action, shaking his head. "No time."

I step forward, and the motion catches the attention of the largest fox. Its mouth snaps shut, and it lowers its head to level a dark green gaze directly at me. The foxes on either side of it turn too, fixing me with stares.

"They know who Bree is," Sel snarls. "They're here for her." He barks orders without taking his eyes off the legion. "Get her back up the cliff to the Lodge. If they get past me, head to the basement and open the Wall of Ages. Seal the wall behind you, escape through the tunnels." He sheds his duster to reveal the T-shirt below, freeing his arms and upper body for battle. "I'll hold them."

"How?" I shout. "They're eating the ward! They'll eat your weapon, too!"

His gaze darkens. "They'll have to catch it first."

Sel strides toward the foxes, growing his hurricane. The wind whistles and picks up speed then settles into the shape he wants: a single long, silver aether chain that keeps growing, link by link, on the ground. On one end, a heavy, round weight the size of a softball materializes; on the other, a handle attached to a wicked-looking arced blade.

I immediately recognize the weapon from training sessions in the arena, staged with Sel's own aether beasts: It's a chain scythe. A weapon to ensnare, pull close, and slice an enemy clean through.

Sel grasps the sickle in his left hand and, with a grunt, yanks the heavy-ball weight on the other end of the chain up into the air. The muscles in his back and arms flex as he pulls the airborne weight into a wide overhead spin. By the second rotation, the ball is moving so fast it's a silver, whistling blur against the darkness. The foxes' screeching grows louder.

Two warm palms pull my face away from the sight. I twist, gasping, to face William. His eyes bore into mine, now glowing the deep, pulsing green of Gawain. He yells over the noise. "If he has to protect you, he won't protect himself!"

"But—"

"We need to run, Bree!"

I gulp and nod. Okay.

We run.

But it's too late. We only make it a few strides toward the stone stairs on the cliffside before William shouts in alarm.

A large shadow streaks down the cliff, a black bullet in the shape of a man— and aims right toward me.

Without stopping or slowing, the shadow bends at the last second and upends me over their shoulder in a single, gut-swooping motion. The world twists upside down. Breath leaves me in a painful wheeze. They pivot in a blink, locking me in place with an arm across my thighs, and run back the way they came before William can react.

I'm already dizzy, but panic sends my mind spinning. My head bounces against my captor's back with each step, breaking my thoughts into jagged pieces.

A Shadowborn legion. Fully corporeal—powerful enough to take out the underpowered Legendborn. Sel on his own at the border, outmatched.

Captured. Someone took me from *inside* the ward—can't be a demon. Not a goruchel shapeshifter. A *human* figure attacked me, just as Sel turned away . . . timed perfectly with the demon attack, too perfectly—

Suddenly, the answer flashes through my mind.

"My mistress, Morgaine . . ." Rhaz had *warned* us, warned *me*—

Shadowborn and Morgaines working together. Allied against the Order.

My survival brain kicks in. Rage pumps clarity through my veins.

I won't be taken.

The Morgaine has us halfway up the stone staircase, with William giving chase in full armor. I pound at the figure's spine with a closed fist. Once. *Twice.*

"Oomph." The Morgaine grunts under Arthur's strength—*good*—and trips, nearly dropping me.

Before I can strike again, the Morgaine tightens their left arm against my legs—and springs up the rest of the cliff, landing us at the top in a single jump.

A heartbeat later, and they've leapt again. This time we land in the large lower limbs of the giant white oak tree that stands in the woods between the Lodge and the arena.

Still draped on their shoulders, my chest rises with theirs when they take a deep inhale—and jump again, and again, until we are six stories up in one of the tree's middle branches.

Abruptly, they bend, sliding me down to my feet until my back rests against the wide trunk. The branch below me is just broad enough that both of my feet can fit. The hard bark at my spine is somewhat reassuring, but we're terrifyingly far off the ground.

In a matter of seconds, the Morgaine has trapped me too high up to escape, even with Arthur's strength in my legs.

The fox legion echoes in the distance—shrieks and clicks, then angry howls. As my attacker darts along the tree limb, they are illuminated by quick flashes of green and blue aether. The person is my height, drenched in a belted black leather tunic and tactical pants. Fingerless gloves reveal pale fingers. The

Morgaine's face and hair are hidden by the heavy drape of a black leather cowl as they survey the ground below.

Doesn't matter. I don't need to see my enemy to fight them.

As soon as they are within striking distance, I step into a jab, throw my weight into it—only for my right fist to be caught tight in their own, shot up at the last second without a glance in my direction.

Their hand engulfs mine in a confident grip with plenty of strength behind it, strength that could turn crushing—

I twist. Find balance. Kick at their knee—force them to release me.

They shift back—I surge forward.

A right hook to their ribs. They pivot away before it lands—too fast—grasp my forearm, use my momentum, pull me off balance. I stumble into them, nearly slipping off the branch. They hold my wrist tight.

Then, the Morgaine chuckles.

Chuckles.

They're . . . *laughing*? At me?

An angry growl roars up from my gut to my chest—and my red root flares to life. Blooms bright at my elbow and rushes down my wrist until *both* our fists are engulfed in flames.

But only one of us gets burned.

My attacker yelps in pain, leaping back on the branch. They land deftly in a crouch, balanced on their heels, cradling one gloved hand against their chest and hissing lowly from the forest's shadows.

The light of my root pools around me. At my fists, it pulses in time with my heartbeat, words made rhythm. *I-won't-run. I-won't-run. I won't-run.* I know without seeing my reflection that my eyes have taken on the glowing crimson of my Bloodcraft.

Even my attacker's eyes shine with the flames of my ancestors.

I raise my chin. "Who's laughing now?"

Silence for one beat, two. Then, the low chuckle returns, followed by an amused, accented, *young* male voice. "Still me . . . my liege."

The root around my hands flickers. *My liege.* My eyes narrow. "Excuse me?"

"So it's true." The stranger's *r* rolls lightly. Scottish, maybe? "What they say about yer aether."

"What do you know about my aether?" I snap. Abruptly, he raises his head to look at me. Warmth hits my cheeks in a wave. My root flares again. "Who are you?"

He holds up a defensive hand. "I'm——"

Thwip! A bright blue aether whip cracks in the air, snaking around my attacker's ankle from below. He tenses. "Ach, shite."

The glowing whip tightens——and yanks him clean off the branch.

But my attacker is *fast*. While falling, he produces an aether blade in one hand and slices the whip through.

Selwyn is fast, too. He's on the other boy before he even hits the ground. In a millisecond, the newcomer is flat on his back with Selwyn towering over him, whip now lengthened into a jagged blade pointed at his throat. Sel's chest heaves; he's winded, or furious, or both. Yellow-green dust and globs of ichor run in streaks down his face and cheek, onto his shoulders. Bits of dead demon drape around his shoulders like a mantle. There was a dozen in that legion . . . did he kill them all?

Selwyn may not like me right now, but he is here to protect me. Even if my mind doesn't quite process that fact, my magic does. My root flames dampen, then fade. I sway a bit but hold steady. Small bursts of root don't drain me like they used to, thank goodness.

"I should kill you for touching her." I know Sel means me, but after our fight, the angry, possessive tone that reaches me up in the trees seems out of place. Like he's talking about someone else. The Crown Scion, not Bree. "I should . . . ," he murmurs, "and I think I might."

"Kane!" The newcomer tears his hood off, revealing tousled, dark auburn hair, long on the top and shorn on the sides——and a pair of glowing golden eyes. A young white man, not more than twenty.

Sel blinks. "Douglas?"

My captor is a *Merlin*. Not a Morgaine at all. A wave of confusion and embarrassment passes through me. Why would a Merlin try to . . . kidnap me?

"Long time no see." Douglas's soft Scottish brogue wraps its way around his speech.

"A very long time." Sel's stony expression sends a trickle of apprehension down my spine. I'm not the only one who notices that he doesn't lower his blade.

"Drop your weapon, Kingsmage," Douglas commands.

Sel's lip curls upward. "When I feel like it."

"Selwyn!" I hear William's voice and running footsteps. He pushes through the bramble and appears beneath my tree. "Where's Bree?"

"I'm here!" I call out. William's head tilts back to find me overhead, and his glowing green eyes widen.

Sel glances up at me for the first time. "She's safe."

"Thanks to me." Douglas takes the opportunity of Sel's distraction to elbow Sel's blade aside and jump to his feet.

"Why should I thank you for your services"—Sel smirks and points at Douglas's right hand with his blade—"when it looks like Briana herself already did the honors?"

"Heh," Douglas huffs, flipping his palm over. Even this high up, I can see the burned hole in the center of the leather glove. His head tips back until he meets my eyes. His grin is a flash of white teeth and long canines in the night. "That she did."

Sel is no longer amused. "Douglas, you—"

"Noswaith dda, Selwyn."

A new voice enters the clearing. Low and smooth like warm honey, it slips down my spine, leaving goosebumps in its wake. The new Merlin that emerges from the trees has warm olive skin and thick black hair slicked back into an undercut. As he steps out, he adjusts his long black overcoat. A silver Legendborn symbol is stitched on each wide lapel. Silver grommets at his shoulders wink in the shadows.

The man stares at Sel, expectant. In response, Sel widens his fingers to release the forged weapon. It dissipates into a sparkling cloud before it can hit the ground. To my surprise, Sel swallows audibly and straightens his shoulders before addressing the newcomer.

"Noswaith dda, Mage Seneschal."

My stomach drops. If the man below me is a Mage Seneschal, then he is one of the highest-ranking Merlins in the Order. An advisor on the High Council of Regents.

As if on cue, four figures melt from the woods, two on either side of the Seneschal. Mage flame swirls around their palms and wrists, alive and ready to be cast. Their eyes—golden, shining, bright—pierce through the dissipating mist and show me exactly who they are. But it's their attire that tells the full story. Tactical gear makes them deadly shadows at every turn: sleek boots; black pants; and heavy, hooded tunics, cowls raised high, casting their faces in darkness. Leather fingerless gloves striped with silver—aether-conducting thread. All of them, tall and broad-shouldered, radiate power and control. They have paused in unison behind the Seneschal like kinetic energy restrained.

Another realization strikes like a physical blow.

These Merlins are Mageguard, the elite military unit of the Order's forces.

Which means this is not just any Seneschal of the Council. This is Erebus Varelian, the Seneschal of Shadows. The most powerful Merlin in the world.

I gasp. Abruptly, heat like I've never felt before scalds my skin and cheeks. Burns from multiple Merlin eyes raised to find me, so harsh I wince.

Erebus, however, slowly, deliberately turns not to me, but to inspect the remnants of the destroyed demons on Sel's person. "It appears there are not wolves at your door, Kingsmage, but foxes."

"I am certain the wolves are not far behind," Selwyn says evenly.

Erebus eyes Sel for a long moment, as if deciding whether Sel is being impertinent. Whether Sel's comment was literal, about hellhounds, or metaphorical, about our new guests. Finally, he says, "They always are."

"I destroyed the legion." Sel looks beyond Erebus to the woods. "But we should search the area for an uchel."

"We *have* searched the area," one of the hooded Mageguard replies. "There is none."

Sel shakes his head. "It is known that isels do not work together without an uchel leading them—"

"And for many years it was 'known' that goruchel shapeshifters were extinct," Erebus counters. "Yet one infiltrated this chapter not six months ago."

Sel and I both stiffen at the mention of Rhaz. Sel never thought goruchels were extinct. In fact, he alone suspected that a goruchel could be among us, studying us and waiting. His one mistake was thinking it was me.

Protest sparks on my lips, and Sel clears his throat unnecessarily loudly. A clear message to smother that spark before it becomes words. I grit my teeth. *Fine.*

Erebus continues. "If we limit our hunt to only what is known, the *unknown* will soon hunt *us*." He tsks. "And as for your earlier declaration, are you quite sure you eliminated the full legion?"

Sel raises his chin. "I am."

"I see." The Seneschal's glittering eyes slide to William. "Scion Sitterson of the Line of Gawain, I presume?"

"Yes." William walks forward. "Good evening, Seneschal Varelian. Guards." He nods to the silent Merlins, faces still hidden in shadow. "We were not expecting to meet a member of the Council tonight."

"For security reasons, we do not broadcast our movements," Erebus says. "I'm sure you understand." He tilts his head, watching the bright emerald flicker of Gawain in William's eyes. "I have long been fascinated by the dueling inheritances of the Line of Gawain. The power to crush an opponent's bones in one hand and the power to heal in another. Poetic."

William's face is unreadable. "That is a word one could use."

"Diplomacy and tact." A smile spreads across Erebus's full mouth. His canines are long—a sign of his age and power as a Merlin. Just like Isaac's. "I have found that these are also inheritances of your Line."

William dips his chin. "My father would agree with you."

"If the area is secure and the niceties are concluded," Sel says impatiently, "I will retrieve the Crown Scion from her . . . tree."

When the Seneschal finally tilts his head upward to find me overhead, the full force of his gaze alone nearly knocks me off the branch. Erebus had already noticed me, of course. He *chose* to save my greeting for last.

A pause. The air crackles with anticipation. Silent to human ears, but at this point I'm certain every Merlin in this damn field can hear my heart racing. "No, you will not," Erebus says mildly.

Sel's head jerks up. "Excuse me?"

Erebus nods to Douglas. "Guard Douglas, could you please?"

Before Sel can protest further, Douglas takes two quick steps and leaps swiftly to a branch below me, then the next, until suddenly he's right back where he started. I step back—and my foot slips on crumbling bark. Douglas catches me at the elbow. "Steady there, m'liege."

Now that his hood is back, I can see that Guard Douglas has deep-set sun-gold eyes, brighter than Sel's. This close, they cast a warm glow on my face. Like Sel, this Merlin has tattoos, but his crawl like vines up the side of his neck, sprout wild from his collar, and trail down the pale knuckles exposed from his gloves.

Cognizant of the eyes below us—and indignant on Sel's behalf—I carefully extract myself from his grip. "Just get me down already."

His eyes twinkle. "Yes, m'liege." He steps forward slowly, forecasting his movements this time so that I can see his approach. When I nod, he dips down, slipping one arm behind my knees and the other behind my shoulders to lift me easily. Without losing balance, he turns, steps off of the branch with me in his arms, and lands so softly that I barely feel the impact when we meet the ground.

I do, however, hear the faint murmur of voices rise up from the earth the moment I get my own feet beneath me. Quiet protests from ancestors I don't recognize. That display of root was minimal, compared to what I did in the cave . . . but it was enough. Enough that the dead are complaining.

I swallow. I'll need to reach out to Mariah as soon as I can. Check to see if any living felt my root, too.

Douglas notices my discomfort. "Are you all right?"

I meet Sel's eyes, see the tension in his jaw. He's fuming for every other reason in the world right now, but there's recognition there too. He knows exactly what I'm worried about with the Rootcraft community, and he knows exactly why I can't say a word about it in front of the Mageguard.

"I'm fine." I slip out of Douglas's grip and come face to face with the waiting crowd of Merlins—and a Seneschal of the High Council of Regents.

Erebus's eyes are the darkest red I've ever seen. They are the color of thick heart-blood, on the razor's edge of black. His face is emotionless, but his attention—the very *act* of his consideration—scorches the tender skin of my cheeks. Before this moment, I'd have claimed Isaac Sorenson to be the most overwhelming Merlin I'd ever met, but Erebus Varelian's scrutiny would turn Isaac's regard into a hollow threat. My heart thunders in my ears. Fear splinters through my nerves—*When the time comes, if it comes, don't be scared.*

I am my mother's daughter.

I am also . . . covered in dirt.

I can only imagine what I look like to Erebus. The still-healing welts of my own making run in red stripes down my forearms. My once shiny curls have escaped their twists, the ends loose and fraying.

Suddenly, Erebus's gaze does not matter. His strength *does not* matter. What matters is how *I* respond right now, in this moment. I cannot cower before the first Council member I meet. I *will* not.

I lift my chin and stride forward to meet the fire of Erebus's attention head-on.

"Seneschal Varelian."

His crimson eyes widen. At this distance, his gaze is a silent, cutting thing . . . but interest and anticipation both flicker across his features at my approach. He is impressed.

"Crown Scion Matthews." His voice is loud and resonant for all to hear. "It is an honor to be in your presence."

Then, without warning, Erebus Varelian, the most powerful Merlin in the world, drops to one knee to bow before me.

3

THE MAGEGUARD FOLLOW suit, one at a time, until they have all kneeled to me. The ends of their robes lay over the dirt, covering the earth in black and shimmering silver.

To my left, William glances at the kneeling sorcerers, then back to me. Right. Now is the time to use the protocol I've studied. I clear my throat. "Rise, Mage Seneschal Varelian of the High Council and noble members of the Round Table Mageguard."

Erebus and the Merlins rise gracefully to their feet to stand at parade rest.

Erebus holds my gaze without blinking, and I realize he's waiting for me to direct the remainder of the conversation.

"I . . ." *Protocol, protocol,* come on, *Bree.* Start with formalities. "Welcome to the Southern Chapter, Seneschal of Shadows. Has your Regent accompanied you? I should like to meet her."

Erebus smiles, expression nearing something fond. "Regent Cestra, as commander of the military, is with the other members of the Guard. She will be in attendance at tomorrow's ceremony. As will the other two Regents and their Seneschals."

Panic hits the back of my throat. All three Regents and their Seneschals at the memorial. The full Council of six, nearly upon us. I am more grateful than ever that I warned the Rootcrafters on campus.

Sel is displeased, and does not hide it. "We expected additional Merlins to join prior to the ceremony. We did not expect the Council, or the Mageguard."

Erebus raises his chin. "The Mageguard clear every location in advance of the Council's arrival. Advance notice gives our enemies time to plan against us."

Sudden irritation flares within me. "Are we your enemies, then? Is that why we were not given notice that you would be attending tomorrow's memorial?" Sel's eyes cut to mine, brows lifted.

Erebus blinks. "N-no, my liege. Of course not." His mouth opens, but closes again, like he wishes to reconsider his next sentence before releasing it.

We have caught him off guard. *Good. Now he knows what it feels like.*

Finally, Erebus speaks—carefully, I notice. "A public appearance of Order leadership in one place has not occurred in several years, and, of course, Arthur has not Called a Scion in two and a half centuries."

"Does this mean all of the Mageguard has been assigned to this weekend's event?" Sel asks, eyes traveling over the silent figures behind Erebus.

"Yes, all twenty-four will be on-site," Erebus replies. "With a secondary support unit to follow."

"Quite a lot of firepower for a funeral," I murmur.

"In these times of uncertainty, with Shadowborn who could be hidden in plain sight, it is impossible to be overly cautious, my liege. Any large gathering brings with it added risk, and you are, after all"—Erebus shakes his head with a frown—"without a bonded Kingsmage."

It is a well-aimed barb. Lines of strain pull at the outer edges of Sel's eyes, but he remains silent.

I try to change the topic. "If you like, we can take you to the ceremony site tomorrow morning, early."

The small look of triumph on Erebus's face tells me that my attempt to steer clear of tension has failed. Instead, my words provided him with some opening I cannot see. "No need, Crown Scion. The other team is there now. We will remain here, because it is a Merlin's job to ensure that the level of security you receive is unassailable, day or night, wherever you may be. Within the chapter's Lodge, on its surrounding grounds—even at its borders."

A Merlin's job. He means Sel. Oh no.

"It is fortuitous that we arrived when we did"—anger simmers behind Erebus's eyes—"if what I have witnessed here tonight is the best that the Kingsmage of the Southern Chapter can do."

Sel stiffens. "I assure you, Seneschal Varelian—"

"You assure me not at all, Kingsmage Kane!" Erebus explodes. "Not when I arrive to see *a dozen* cedny uffern breaking down your ward." He gestures to me, my face and still-healing arms. "Not when I arrive to witness the Crown Scion of Arthur, covered in soil and dust, *wounded*, and running for her *life*."

When Sel doesn't refute Erebus's comment, I open my mouth to protest it myself, to say that my appearance and my wounds are not Sel's fault. But just as I do, William's hand is at my elbow. I don't know if he wants me to keep quiet for my sake or Sel's, but his grip is tight enough that I understand the warning. *Don't*. They've each stopped me once now. Do I trust them to know what's best, or do I challenge Erebus? There is some . . . procedure here, a flow of things in a certain order, a confrontation long expected, that I'm just on the outside of. So I hesitate.

Erebus's voice goes low and dangerous. "Bring forward the demon that Kingsmage Kane neglected to destroy."

Sel's head whips up, eyes wide, just as a sixth guard comes forward from the direction of the arena, dragging something glowing and green through the brush behind her.

The massive demon is alive—just barely. A spear I recognize as Sel's typical design bobs at the creature's throat as the fox growls at its captor. Thrown with Sel's usual force, but it seems to have missed its mark by a matter of inches. Sel scowls. "I believed it to be a killing blow, just like the others."

"Belief is not fact, Kingsmage Kane," Erebus murmurs.

A ruddy flush swims up Sel's throat to his cheeks. "Yes, Seneschal."

With a signal from Erebus, the Mageguard holding the dying fox releases the creature into the middle of the group of Merlins. Every Merlin—Sel included—steps inward as one to close the circle and prevent its escape. The demon collapses, eyeing its enemies.

"What's your point?" I turn to Erebus, fuming. "He missed one, but clearly your team found it!"

"My point . . . ," Erebus murmurs. As he trails off, the wind shifts, and the demon's snout snaps up and around to single-mindedly follow a scent until it finds its sole prey—me. Without warning, it launches itself toward the opening between Sel and Erebus, trying to get to me. Erebus pivots and, in one smooth motion, grasps the demon mid-leap with one hand. His fingers dig into its armor so deeply that gaseous aether leaks from where they are embedded down to the knuckle. "My point is that all it takes is a single, well-aimed death blow from a Shadowborn demon to kill an Awakened Scion of Arthur and undo fifteen centuries of Order and Legendborn sacrifices and victories, making those same sacrifices worthless."

The demon snarls. Then, Erebus's fist blazes with blue flames so hot and bright that they incinerate the fox almost instantly. His aether signature surrounds me with scents I associate with ancient trees and holy places: myrrh and saps, incense burning.

Erebus wipes his hands, rubs the dust from his lapels, and turns to Selwyn. "I gave you this post with the expectation that you would protect the Scion of Arthur's life with your own."

Sel is so furious he can barely speak. "And I accepted the post under that condition," he spits. "As a *child*."

"As a *prodigy*," Erebus corrects. "And yet you stand before me now, as a failure."

Sel's eyes spark with defiance. "Nicholas Davis was *not* the Scion of Arthur, so in *that* regard, I suppose we have *both* failed!"

In a blink, Erebus is a blur across the ground—then his hand is around Sel's throat. He lifts Sel easily, like he's nothing. Sel's boots swipe at the grass, then at the air. He gurgles, his hands scrabbling at Erebus's wrists—

"*Stop!*" I shout.

Erebus releases Sel at once, dropping him onto the ground in a heap—but he does not step away. "My apologies, Crown Scion." Instead, he watches Sel cough and wheeze, bent low on all fours.

I step forward. "Sel—"

Sel shakes his head once, halting me. After another moment of gasping, he pushes upright to his knees with glistening, bloodshot eyes and flushed cheeks—and anger barely contained in closed fists, behind tight lips. Erebus's hand had been around his neck for just a moment, but there are already deep purple bruises forming beneath his jaw. They'll heal and be gone by morning, but I know they hurt in the meantime.

"Kingsmage Kane, do you have an explanation for what occurred here tonight? If you do, by all means, speak"—Erebus's eyes narrow—"but do so with care."

A pause. Sel swallows once, twice, before he speaks in a strained voice. "I have no explanation for failing to protect the Crown Scion."

"I see." Erebus nods. "What *do* you have?"

Sel looks at me for a long moment before he turns back at Erebus. "Only my own actions upon which to reflect."

"In *this* regard," Erebus echoes Sel's earlier quip icily, "we are in agreement."

The Mageguard surround us on the walk back to the Lodge. I don't hear or see them, but if I so much as stumble on a branch, their eyes sting against my skin.

Erebus speaks in a low voice with William on my left. Sel is a silent shadow to my right. I try again to catch his gaze. To communicate my remorse, to let him know that I realize I messed up.

He won't look at me. The tension in his neck and shoulders speaks loud enough. As we approach the lights in the Lodge backyard, I see the injuries I'd missed deeper in the forest: A cut along his collarbone caked with ichor and dried blood. Blood at his temple, half-smeared from sweat. Even the silver plugs in his gauged ears are half-covered in dirt. A pair of claws must have sliced down his left shoulder blade, ripping right through the black shirt. Guilt sours in my stomach.

Sel's middle ward washes over my face. Two of the Mageguard materialize from the woods and turn to face the ward from the inside, raising their palms to the barrier.

Sel scowls at the Merlins tinkering with his work. "I just cast that ward."

Erebus answers. "And it will be reinforced."

Sel rolls his eyes, and we leave the two guards behind. When we reach the back lawn, more lights are on inside the Lodge than when I left. The rest of the Legendborn, returned from patrol. Eating late meals, rustling through the fridge and pantry, no doubt. William walks toward the side entry door. "Please excuse me. I always check in with the others when they return in case there are injuries."

"Scion Sitterson." Erebus's voice stops William in his tracks.

"Yes?" William turns. When he glances at me briefly, his eyes are a pale green in the bright floodlights of the Lodge exterior. Gawain's strength, still lit within him.

"Please"—Erebus gestures toward one of the Mageguard—"take Guard Olsen with you. I'll join you both in a moment to introduce myself to the other Legendborn."

The guard throws their hood back to reveal a tall woman with a short blond ponytail. Her hair is shaved above either ear. William nods, turning with her.

I frown as I watch them walk away. "William doesn't need an escort in his own home."

At the sound of my voice, the Mageguard turns on her heel, arms at rest behind her back. Her eyes flicker to me, then back to Erebus. I did not intend my comment to be an order, but this Merlin took it as one, and now she is wait-ing for clarity, from either me or Erebus.

"I apologize, my liege." Erebus blinks once, twice, appearing genuinely torn. "I sent Guard Olsen to *accompany* Scion Sitterson, not to escort him. She can offer a more casual introduction to the presence of the Mageguard than the formal exchange of titles and greetings. I thought that this would be easier on a Legendborn unit just returned from the hunt and no doubt eager for bed."

Erebus pauses, waiting for my response now, too.

Over Guard Olsen's shoulder, William shrugs.

"Fine," I say. "Thanks for explaining."

Erebus dips his head. "Of course." With a silent look, Olsen pivots back, and she and William walk together to the house.

"Kingsmage Kane," Erebus says, gesturing to the rear face of the Lodge and the rows of windows marking the residential floors, "which of these is the Crown Scion's room?"

Sel's eyes flick up to my window—and darken. "Second floor, third over."

Erebus's eyes narrow. "The one with the open window?"

Sel stares at me while directing his answer to Erebus. "Yes."

I flinch. "That's my . . ."

Erebus turns curious eyes my way.

I hesitate. If I say that the open window is my fault and not Sel's, then I'll have to admit that I successfully escaped Sel's efforts to keep me safe. And Erebus will add this shortcoming to Sel's growing list of apparent failures to do his duty.

"There is a third layer of warding," I finally stammer, avoiding an explanation entirely, "against the glass and brick, all the way around."

Erebus makes a thoughtful sound while studying the building. "A ward against impact and intrusion?" he asks Sel.

"Yes," replies Sel.

Another hum. A decision made. "Guards Zhao and Branson," Erebus calls.

Two of the three remaining Mageguard appear at Erebus's side in a silent whoosh and remove their hoods in unison. A tall East Asian man with a full mouth and bright golden eyes. A white man whose eyes are green-gold. Both wearing the signature undercut hairstyle of the Mageguard.

"Yes, Seneschal?" they ask.

"One of you at the driveway entrance, please," Erebus orders. "The other remains here in the yard." The Merlins nod, then split in two blurs going in opposite directions.

That leaves me, Sel, Erebus, and Douglas. Sel's expression is one of carefully crafted boredom. I wonder if anyone here is even buying it, honestly. I wonder if his usual insolence will only further annoy Erebus. "Are we done here?" he drawls.

"No." Erebus gestures to Guard Douglas, who steps forward on cue. "Formal introductions are in order, I think." Erebus looks between me and the Merlin. "Crown Scion Briana Matthews, please meet Guard Larkin Douglas."

I blink. "Larkin?"

"Call me Lark." He dips his chin. "My liege."

Erebus smiles. "Guard Douglas is the youngest member of the Mageguard, but trained by one of the best."

"You?" Sel asks drolly.

"No," Erebus replies simply. "His father, Calum Douglas."

"How *is* your father, Douglas?" Sel asks, eyes dancing. "Still angry his son lost out to a Kane?"

Lark doesn't rise to Sel's bait. "He got over my not being selected for Kingsmage when I was tapped for the Guard," he replies evenly. He turns to me, eyes twinkling. "Selwyn here might have the flashy title, but we get all the best field missions."

"Yes," Sel says with a sigh. "When not securing the safety of the Regents, the Mageguard operate in the darkest of shadows taking on the most dangerous Shadowborn legions, blah blah."

"Until a sovereign is crowned, anyway." Lark raises a shoulder.

"Yes, until a sovereign is crowned, then——" Sel stops himself short, eyes narrowing. His gaze darts between Lark and Erebus. "Then the Guard's sole duty is to protect the king."

The air thickens with some unnamed tension.

I clear my throat. "I'm missing something."

"I believe I am too, Briana," Sel murmurs.

Quiet regret pulls at Lark's mouth. "Look, Kane . . ."

Erebus turns to me. "My liege, you are aware of the Order's organizational framework? The body politic?"

"I am." The very first night I joined the chapter, Lord Davis explained the Order as anatomy, working together. "The Legendborn are the Order's beating heart."

Erebus smiles. "Yes. And you will be the head and the crown. But in the absence of a king, and even when one is Called, the Regents are the spine. As the Regent of Shadows, Cestra oversees the Merlin military, the Mageguard, the Order's intelligence network, and all of its security forces."

"Security forces that include the Kingsmage." Sel's voice has gone curt. His earlier arrogance has been wiped from his features. "Except that my Oath supersedes any order you or Regent Cestra might give."

"It did . . . ," Erebus replies slowly, "before your Oath was proven to be misplaced."

A muscle in Sel's jaw tightens. Abruptly, he steps closer and, to my utter shock, touches me for the first time in weeks. His long fingers wrap around my wrist—but his grip is not gentle, and his palm is sweaty. "If that medieval politics lesson is over, then I think the Crown Scion is due for rest—"

"Selwyn, I think you realize that I did not introduce Larkin here without purpose. . . ." Erebus's voice is not unkind, but it is firm. "Your services this past month have been appreciated, but—"

"Just say it," Sel grits out.

"Guard Douglas will protect the Crown Scion now, and he will remain her escort until they are bound together by the Kingsmage Oath."

EREBUS'S WORDS FALL like a lead blanket around us. My stomach plummets while Sel becomes perfectly, eerily, dangerously still.

Erebus looks puzzled. "Will this be a problem?"

"I don't . . . I don't need a—a Kingsmage," I stammer. "We need to find Scion Davis and bring him home safe."

Erebus ignores my protest about a Kingsmage entirely. "I have heard that you and Scion Davis are quite close? Is this true?" His eyes are curious, mouth lifted in a pleasant curl, but this question is not innocent.

The Regents do not permit Scions to be romantically involved if there is any chance a child could be produced from their union. Children who possess multiple bloodlines could challenge—or even break—the Order's ability to track and predict which descendant will become a Scion and which ancestral knight will Call them. Tracking the bloodlines with precision is the only way that the Table has remained organized this long. Of course, Nick and I are both living proof that there are gaps in the Order's oversight. No one in the Order knew our true lineages before Lancelot Called him and Arthur Called me.

So much for the superiority of their good intentions.

"We are close," I reply, voice neutral.

Sel drops my wrist and looks away. Clears his throat. "Prior to the revelations about their respective bloodlines, Scion Davis had named Crown Scion

Matthews his Page and chosen her as Squire at the selection gala. These intentions were publicly made."

Erebus fixes Sel with a stare. "An intention for an Oath that would not have taken, yes. Given that they are both Scions and cannot be bound to each other in such a manner. An unfortunate side effect of this truth, I'm afraid, is that some relationships must fall to the wayside in favor of others." The quiet note of warning in Erebus's voice slips between us on the heels of a restrained smile. "Like the relationship between you and the Council, Crown Scion. Or one between you and your new Kingsmage. You must understand that *your* safety is our first priority."

"And *my* first priority is saving those who may be in more immediate danger than I am," I counter. "Not bonding myself to someone I do not know."

Erebus sighs. "Please understand our position. Not only is it unprecedented for a Scion of Arthur of your age to be unbonded to a Kingsmage, but never before in our history has a Scion of Arthur been Awakened *and* become the Crown Scion without a Kingsmage at their side. Guard Douglas is the best candidate, but . . ." Erebus pulls out a tablet from his inside coat pocket. "If you do not wish to take Larkin as your bondmate, I have gathered six Merlin candidates for your consideration. Each within one year of your age, with a variety of genders, casting specialties, and personalities. Whomever you choose can be here within a day's notice. Regent Cestra and I can discuss each potential Kingsmage with you directly after tomorrow's Rite in the cave chamber."

My eyes flutter, shocked at the sharp turn. "The Rite? Tomorrow?"

Erebus lifts a brow. "Are you not . . . prepared for the Rite of Kings to claim your title?"

"No. I mean, yes." My heart knocks against my sternum. Everything is moving too fast. "I am prepared. I just didn't realize it would happen so soon."

"Should we delay?"

"No! But"——I add steel to my voice, feet on firmer ground now——"if there is time after the Rite, I'd like to hear about the search plan for Scion Davis. Again, he is my focus."

"Very well. But as you saw tonight, your life is already in danger, which means our Order is in danger. I have read the ogof y ddraig battle debrief, my liege. I am aware—and certainly, impressed—that you destroyed your would-be assassin, the goruchel Rhaz, on your own. But ideally, you would have a bonded Squire at your side to fight *with* you." His eyes slide to Selwyn, assessing. "And a bonded Kingsmage to fight *for* you. You have neither."

"That's not fair," I insist. I have been avoiding the thought of selecting either a Squire or a Kingsmage. What is the point when I am not allowed near danger? And I don't need one or the other to find Nick. "We all fought in that battle together. As a chapter. Sel, tell him."

Sel holds Erebus's gaze in defiance for a beat, then looks away. "You need a Kingsmage, Briana. We have discussed this."

We *have* discussed it. Once. When we stood on the balcony after Nick was taken, and when I was hovering between my old self and my new. A Brave Bree, shaken. A Before- and After-Bree, merged. A Medium and Scion, hollowed into a vessel for ancient powers I never predicted. I shake my head away from that day, that memory. "Isn't that what the Mageguard are for?"

"The Mageguard do protect the King, yes, but their other assignments sometimes take them away from direct security. The Kingsmage, on the other hand, is a life-long personal guard. Eventually, when your, ah . . ." Erebus's cheeks flush, but he clears his throat and continues, "When your heirs are born, the Mageguard will be reassigned to protect the children until they come of age, but the Kingsmage will remain at your side."

Jesus H. . . . Heat rushes up my neck, and suddenly the entire backyard feels far too small. I want to melt into the grass and down into the planet's core, clean through to the other side. Let me fall off this planet, *please.* I feel Sel's eyes on my face, Lark's and Erebus's too. "Can we not discuss heirs right now?"

Erebus flushes a deeper red. "Yes, of course. Too early in your young life, and much too late in the evening for that topic, I think." He smiles apologetically. "I need to make a call to Cestra, and you need to rest. Guard Douglas?"

Lark holds a hand toward the Lodge. "Shall we?" To my surprise, Lark leans across me to look at Sel, too. "Would ye join us, Kingsmage Kane?"

Sel blinks, surprised, but recovers quickly. "Yes, of course."

We circle the building in silence, a line of three weaving in and out of the shadows at the far end of the rectangular-shaped Lodge. Sel walks behind me, I'm in the middle, and Lark leads the way with his left hand extended to idly skim along the outside of Sel's innermost ward. The fingertips exposed by his leather gloves leave trails of silver through the shimmering barrier.

We slip into the front door braced for attention, but no one is here. Small favors.

Lark tilts his head toward the floor, listening. "Scion Sitterson and Olsen are downstairs, with . . . five? Other voices. The Legendborn, I assume." His eyes scan the foyer, the salon on the left, the grand staircases leading to the residential floor, the doors to the great room beneath the balcony. "Anyone else expected inside?"

"No." Sel is listening too. Both of them taking in far more information about the Lodge than my human ears can register. "I dismissed the Pages from their daily duties at the Lodge weeks ago and revoked their keycard entry. No one but Legendborn can enter the building. And Merlins, obviously."

Lark nods. "Good idea, Kane."

"I do know how to do my job, *Douglas*," Sel says.

Lark glances at us over his shoulder, pale eyes mischievous. "Call me Lark," he repeats.

"Fine," Sel snaps. "I do know how to do my job, *Lark*."

I groan silently. He honestly can't *not*, can he?

"Kane." Lark sighs and turns to face Sel directly. "Look, I don't think you, me, or the Crown Scion ever imagined we'd be standing here right now, under these circumstances."

I snort. "Got that right."

The corner of Lark's mouth turns down as he keeps talking. "But we *are* here, and these *are* the circumstances. For God's sake, I'm here to help. Ye should be thanking me!"

Sel gives Lark a leveling gaze. "Why exactly should I thank you?"

Lark's brows rise. "We were not friends at the academy, but we were not enemies. Our parents trained us in the old ways, to go beyond the title, beyond the Oaths, in order to do what must be done."

Something silent and resonant passes between the two Merlins and takes me aback. I hadn't considered this—that Sel has been isolated for months, maybe years, from people like him. He has always been alone at the chapter, in title and duty as well as origin. But in the blink of an eye, there are *seven* Merlins around him, in his space, connecting with him in ways that no one else can. People who truly understand what it is like to be a Merlin among humans, serving out Oaths that keep their demon nature under control.

Slowly, Sel nods. "This is true. Your point?"

"That we've known each other for a long time. I, more than any other Merlin, know how much is at stake for ye, personally." Lark steps closer to Sel, voice low. "Because I know this has been killing ye, Kane. You're torn between protecting your Oathbound charge and your Crown Scion, all the while worrying that your blood may come for ye in the night, just as it did your mother."

Sel flinches, and my heart lurches against my chest. The boy whose sharp tongue seems perpetually aimed at other people's tender spots . . . actually *flinching* when Lark hits one of his. I'm sure it doesn't help that Lark seems to know what Sel himself had only discovered a month ago: that his mother was not killed by a demon while on a mission, but arrested and locked away.

Anyone who knows about the former Kingsmage Natasia Kane likely thinks of her as a cautionary tale for "succumbing to the blood," what the Merlins call it when they lose themselves to the demon nature always hiding just under the surface of all part-human, part-demon cambions. The original Merlin, Arthur's sorcerer, had bespelled his descendants with a safeguard so that as long as they fulfill their Oaths of service and protection to the Order, they can keep that demon part of their blood from taking control. Twenty-five years ago, Nick's father framed Sel's mother—his original Kingsmage—for opening demon Gates in order to murder Onceborn humans so that suspicion would not fall on him for his act of betrayal. Lord Davis told the Regents that Natasia had become too powerful for even the Oaths to stop her from succumbing to her blood, and they believed him. When the Regents quietly took her title and had her imprisoned, it was assumed that the inability to fulfill her Oaths would erase anything that remained of her humanity.

But a restored memory of the night my mother died showed me that Natasia Kane had been there in the hospital, grieving my mother. Sel and I are the only people who know that not only had his mother escaped her false imprisonment but, somehow, she'd avoided succumbing to her blood while captured. We don't know how she did it, and we don't know where she is to ask. Whenever I have raised that memory of his mother with him, Sel dodges the topic.

Sel is not his mother. And with Nick gone, his Kingsmage Oath is unfulfilled. Right now I can see the pressing wound of *fear* in him—and so can Lark. A haunted, hollow look crosses Sel's face—and guilt pricks at my throat. Little daggers of *Why didn't I ask about this earlier?* and *What else have I missed?*

Another Merlin saw what I hadn't.

"Sel," I murmur, stepping closer, "are you . . . ?"

"I am fine," Sel mutters. Lark drops a hand on Sel's shoulder as he steps around him, continuing his casual stride toward the stairs. Sel moves to follow, leaving me to scramble behind him.

"But Nick . . . your blood—"

"He speaks the truth, Crown Scion. He *is* fine." Lark calls down to us from halfway up the stairs. "His Oath of Service to the chapter is helping him maintain. If it wasn't, and Kane here was anything other than in full control of himself, Erebus would have taken him down on sight. And *I* wouldn't be willing to leave ye alone with him."

Sel scoffs behind him. "You *haven't* left me alone with her."

"Getting there." Lark reaches the top before we do and turns on his heel, jerking his head down the hall. "Allow me to go ahead. I'll sweep the Crown Scion's room myself."

"You really do not need to do that," Sel says with a groan.

"Sure, I do. Besides"—Lark looks deliberately between us, smirking—"that will give you two a private moment."

Sel stiffens. "A private moment for what?"

Lark waves a hand at us. "To talk about whatever this quarrel is between youse."

My jaw drops slightly. Lark winks, then streaks to the left, out of sight.

"He's . . ."

"Annoying." Sel recovers before I do, taking the stairs in quick, quiet strides.

"Sel." I hurry up the stairs to stand in his path. "Wait."

He meets my eyes. "Yes?"

"I'm sorry," I blurt.

"For what?" he asks blithely.

"For . . ." I flounder, hands waving. "For all of this."

"Be specific when you apologize, Briana. It makes the act far more effective." He steps around me to the landing, turning left after Lark, hands stuffed deep in his pockets.

It is a near-physical effort to push past the continued sting of Sel wielding my full name like a weapon. To force us back to who we were when we first met—enemies, not friends.

"Okay . . ." I catch up to him again. "I'm sorry for sneaking out. For going to the arena with William."

He keeps walking. "That is a strange way to say you apologize for endangering not only yourself but one of your knights as well."

"Sel, come on. I didn't know there'd be cedny uffern at the arena ward!"

He scoffs. "Do demons usually announce themselves to you?"

"Well, no . . . but—"

Sel twists around. "Even if there were no cedny uffern at the ward, your actions endangered yourself and others. Again."

Our fight rises up behind my eyes, a script I could recite word for word even though it was weeks ago. "I told you what I wanted. I want to get better, stronger—"

"You could have done that in the Lodge training rooms. Inside. Behind my wards. Instead, you were reckless, repeating your same mistakes."

"I said I was sorry about that!"

"'Sorry' didn't cut it then, and it doesn't cut it now." He leans forward, snarling. "You convinced Greer and Pete to bring you on an unauthorized hunt and nearly got yourself killed in the process. And here you are tonight, doing the same with William."

"I didn't convince William of anything! He *asked* to join me."

His voice turns deadly quiet. "You put your Scion in an impossible position. William had to decide whether to go with you for protection or let his *very* vulnerable Crown Scion go off on her own, undoubtedly putting both her life and the spell that has fueled the Legendborn cycle for *centuries* in danger. You forced his hand. You just don't see it."

Shame wells up inside me, doubling, tripling what I felt earlier.

Sel, however, is not done. "Even if Erebus and the Mageguard had not arrived tonight, your actions put my title at risk. Does that concern you at all?"

"I stayed within the final ward. I was being careful!"

"No." Tension and anger lift the tips of his hair into smoky black strands. "You were being selfish."

"How am I supposed to be king if I can't—"

Abruptly, Lark exits my room, closing the door behind him.

"Room is clear," he says slowly. He looks at Sel, then me. "Everything all right out here?"

"Yes," I mutter.

"Peachy," Sel grumbles.

Lark appears unconvinced. "Right. Well, as far as I'm concerned, my job here is done. I'm heading to the infirmary next." He tips his head to me in a silent salute. "Crown Scion, see ye in the morning." Lark turns down the hall, tapping his fingertips on the railing as he goes.

"Douglas." Sel crosses his arms over his chest.

Lark looks back over his shoulder. "What now?"

Sel's brow furrows. "That legion didn't come from nowhere. They knew Bria—the Crown Scion was here. I've seen isel work together before. I know what I'm talking about. Either an uchel or goruchel ordered them to attack tonight, or someone else did."

Lark's face goes blank. "Someone . . . else?"

"No time for games, you know what I mean. I know our report about the Morgaine-Shadowborn alliance got to the Council within twenty-four hours of the ogof battle, which means the Mageguard got the intel within a day. It could be the Morgaines. The old man is in a mood. He won't listen to me, but . . ."

Lark holds his gaze for a moment, then nods. "I'll ask Seneschal Erebus to have the guards search again." His eyes flick to mine. "Night."

When Lark reaches the stairway and descends to the foyer, I step closer to Sel and whisper, "Erebus trained you himself and he won't listen to you? I'm a stranger to him. What if he decides not to listen to me? How can I be king if I can't—"

He holds up a finger. "Wait."

My mouth snaps shut. We wait. We hear the ding of the first-floor elevator. Hear the door open. Close. Even I can hear the wires and gears whine as it drops. In the distance, two floors below, another ding sounds in the silence. Far enough away now that we can speak in private.

Sel exhales and lowers his hand. "You need to be more careful, in every way. In what you reveal of your abilities or lack thereof, and to whom." He runs a hand through his hair. "And to answer your question, I do not know how you will lead. Just as I do not know what the Regents will say when they discover that the Crown Scion of Arthur cannot call aether on her own without varying degrees of self-destruction."

"They'll keep me benched," I say. "Keep me here, locked away, while you all search for Nick."

"'Benched'?" He steps closer, anger sparking on my cheeks from his gaze. "Is that what you think this is? A *team sport*? And you are the star player being held back from glory?"

"No!" I shout.

He shakes his head. "So you wish to rescue Nicholas yourself, is that it?"

I gape. "*No.*"

"You are *just* as stubborn as he is," he bites out. He glances at the door behind me and scowls at the sight of it, teeth flashing. "Just as foolish."

"This isn't about glory," I snap. "And I am not a fool!"

He gives a low whistle, followed by a hollow, mocking laugh. "Douglas really has no idea what he has gotten himself into with you."

"He hasn't 'gotten himself' into anything," I snort. "I'm not taking that Oath."

Sel eyes me. "Why not?"

"Because I don't even know him!"

He lifts a shoulder. "I didn't know Nicholas. Nicholas didn't know me. Not well, anyway."

"And I think that was cruel," I say. "You were children."

His eyes widen slightly. "Irrelevant. You should take the Oath. You can manage without a Squire for now, but you need a Kingsmage."

"Well, I don't need Lark," I protest. "I have you, don't I? Tonight was my mistake, not yours. You've kept me safe."

Some mixture of pain and frustration blurs across his face, leaving a heavy sigh behind. "I cannot keep you as safe as a Kingsmage can."

"You *are* a Kingsmage."

"Not yours," Sel counters lowly. "And that makes all the difference in the world."

"But—"

"*Not. Yours.*" He glares at me. "If I were your Kingsmage, I would have felt when Larkin took you tonight."

I scoff. "You were fighting a dozen armored foxes, by *yourself*—"

"I would have felt your mortal fear like it were my own, the *second* it arose—"

"You got to me within minutes—"

"Only because I sensed your root, and I know it flares when you're endangered." He shakes his head. "Yes, I came running, but you could have been killed half a dozen times before I arrived, don't you see?"

"Wait . . ." I ignore him. "Is that why you missed the last fox? Because you left the battle to find me?" Guilt rises again. *I* made this mess. Humiliated Sel in front of his superior, his peers.

"It does not matter." His jaw tenses. "The Kingsmage Oath is person to person, not title to title, and my Oath is to Nicholas. A fact you made sure to underscore with me the first time I broached this topic, Briana." With narrowed eyes, he watches the memory of that balcony conversation wash over me again. Sel hadn't offered to be my Kingsmage explicitly, but he had offered . . . something. Something we still haven't addressed.

Sel claimed me as his king.

More than that, he'd called me "cariad." A Welsh word, and one I didn't know.

It was an awfully Sel thing to do, using a phrase I don't know in a language I don't speak.

Calling me "cariad" was an open door without a direct invitation. He knew that I'd need to make the active choice to understand him. But that day on the balcony, I didn't make a choice. Or I guess, in a way, I did—by taking no action at all. Not asking him to translate, not pushing him to explain what sounded like an endearment. After the Regents' emissaries arrived and it became clear the dust would never settle, I became angry. If Sel truly wanted me to know what he meant that day, he should have said it in English instead of implicitly expecting me to look it up and do the work for him.

I can't help but wonder if that friction created the distance between us, before the guarding and the wards and ordering our friends to protect me behind my back.

"Nothing to say about our previous discussion?" he asks. "Or had you forgotten that detail in your current, immature display of defiance?"

My head snaps back. I resist the urge to stomp my foot . . . and further prove his point. "You are being *such* a jerk right now."

A callous smile twists Sel's mouth. "After your antics tonight? I think I'm allowed. You told Erebus you're ready for the Rite, but are you really?" The question stops me short.

The Rite will change everything. Make it all real. Finally get us—*all* of us—out of the holding pattern and into the fight we've been training for.

"Yes. I've been rehearsing with William." I raise my chin, steel my spine, because if Sel believes nothing else from me tonight, I need him to believe *this*. "I am more than ready."

He nods, satisfied. "Good."

There's one more thing I need him to know. "Sel, I *am* sorry about the position I put you in tonight with Erebus and the Mageguard."

He searches my features for a long moment. "If you are truly sorry for your actions, you will stay in your room for the rest of the evening." He chuckles darkly, backing away. "Or should I say *his* room?"

I flush. When the Regents ordered me out of the dorms, it was still sinking in that my life would never be the same again. I could have chosen an unassigned, unoccupied room; there are plenty in the Lodge. But I didn't. I chose Nick's. "It was just . . . where I felt . . ."

"Safe?" he asks.

I wrap my arms around myself. "I never said that."

His smile is tight and humorless. "You never had to."

After the events of tonight, what must my choice to stay in Nick's room feel like to Sel? Now that his title and ability to keep me safe have been so publicly questioned? When another Merlin has been assigned to protect me?

"Erebus is right, you know," he says. "About taking into account what the Council and the Order will need from you if you are to lead. And I am right about how you treat William and the Legendborn. Your priorities, your relationships . . . all of them have to change." He looks over my head to Nick's door once more, then back to me. "All of them."

My eyes sting. I know that things will change between me and Nick when we get him back. I know things between us can't be the same as they were. But still . . . I hate that Sel might be right.

An unreadable expression crosses Sel's face. An emotion that could become words if given the chance, but he presses his lips into a line, burying it. "I should go."

I don't want to end things like this, with remorse and pain beating between us like drums. "Sel—"

"Good night, Briana."

And with that, he's gone in a blur. Down the stairs, out the front door, and into the night.

5

THE NEXT MORNING, I am awakened by the muffled sounds of doors opening and closing downstairs and footsteps rushing up the stairs.

"Open up, Crown Scioonnn!" A voice sings on the other side of my door. "Your stylist is heeeeere!"

I check the clock: seven thirty—and the first day in weeks that the rest of the house is up and moving before I am.

I shuffle out of bed with a croaked laugh and am halfway there when another voice chimes in. "And she's got biiiiiscuiiitsss!"

Greer and Alice are grinning like fools when I open the door. Greer's wearing slacks and a black dress shirt with the sleeves rolled up. The exposed fabric under each cuff is tawny yellow in color, a subtle nod to their Scion's bloodline. The formal cloak of the Line of Owain is draped over their shoulder, still in the plastic dry-cleaning bag. Alice is in a buttoned-up blue-and-white-striped blouse over jeans, sporting an emerald-green leather wrist cuff on her left hand and holding a bag of Bojangles in her right.

"Crown Scion," Greer says with an exaggerated bow. "May I present Vassal Alice Chen?"

Alice does a mock curtsy. "To be in your presence, Crown Scion, is the most—"

"Oh my God, shut *up*!" I say, and yank her inside. She bursts into laughter.

"That's a weird way to say, 'Thank you, Alice, for coming to help with my hair at the last minute,'" Alice mutters. "Strange way to pronounce, 'Thank you, Alice, for bringing me breakfast.'" She waltzes past me, filling the room with the intoxicating scents of grease, fried things, and bacon. She sets the bag down on the desk and starts poking at the tools I'd set out for us last night: a thin styling comb with a pointed end for making parts, a short glass jar of freshly mixed hair oil from Patricia's home kitchen, a bit of gel, and a small pile of bands. She pulls her jet-black hair into a ponytail. "This'll do."

I roll my eyes. "Thanks for bringing her past the inner ward," I say to Greer. They're leaning against the doorjamb, chuckling. It's not just Pages who can't enter the Lodge without an escort.

"Yeah, no problem." They wrinkle their nose. "Actually, I come bearing some news you're not really gonna like. . . ."

I freeze. "Is it Nick? Did they—"

Greer stands up, waving their hands. "No, no. Sorry, nothing like that." Greer follows my gaze to the small collection of weapons braced against the wall on the other side of the door, but they're kind enough not to make a joke about it. It's not like I'm the only one who has collected a few extra weapons in their rooms these days, just in case. Hell, the basement armory door that used to be locked all the time is left wide open twenty-four seven now—also just in case. "No, it's about the, uh . . . lodging situation."

I frown. "What do you mean?"

"Well." Greer runs a hand over their dark blond hair, styled in a low bun for the ceremony. "You're gonna wanna go ahead and pack up a couple of suitcases. Regent Cestra ordered all of us to vacate the Lodge and move into the compound at Pembray."

"What?" I exclaim. "Why?"

They shrug. "Sorry, Bree. After what happened last night with the foxes, they want us in a more secure location. The Mageguard have barracks there, it's out in the country, and . . ."

I groan. "Fine. I'll pack."

"I'm gonna catch a ride over with Pete. That new Merlin, Douglas? Said he'll meet you downstairs when you're ready."

"Of course he did."

Greer smirks, stepping back into the hallway and waving to Alice. "See you later, Chen."

"That's *Vassal* Chen to you!" Alice exclaims. She raises her arm and shakes her bracelet. "To the Line of Gawain!"

"All of *that* going on behind me," I say to Greer, and gesture over my shoulder, "is William's fault."

"Mm-hm, but wasn't it *your* cover story?" Greer winks, then salutes before they turn to walk away.

I close the door and rest against it. They're right. I brought Alice to the Lodge the night of Nick's father's betrayal. Calling her a Vassal, a non-initiated supporter of the Order, was the first lie I could think of to explain why she was my guest. "I only recommended that we make you an *official* Vassal so that we'd have a paper trail to back it up, Alice. Not so you could go flashing around the Gawain greens."

"And it was good you did," she mutters, and digs into the Bojangles bag. "Otherwise, people would wonder why I was hanging around the Lodge all the time in the archives with William trying to get up to speed with your new Crown Scion lifestyle. Archives which are, by the way, *fascinating,* and I can't believe you aren't in there every day yourself."

I could be spending that time studying the ancient spirit whose abilities I've now inherited, and those Scions of Arthur who came before me. But I don't. It feels too much like reaching for the man himself.

My phone dings on the bed, saving me from having to explain that to Alice. I swipe it while she eats. A message from Mariah.

Saw your text. Okay to video with me and the doc?

Yep, I tap back. "Hey," I say to Alice. "Mariah texted. Gonna check in with her and Dr. Hartwood about last night."

Alice's head pops up, dark brown eyes eager and curious. "Oooh. Rootcrafter secret meeting. Need me to step out?"

"Nah, you're fine." Alice, William, and Sel are the only people I've told about the Rootcrafter community on campus.

I lean the phone up against Patricia's jar of oil and swipe the call open when the notification appears.

Mariah's warm, red-brown face appears on the left side of the screen. "Hey, Bree-Bree." She waves, grinning behind her glasses. Her hair is in long box braids, pulled up into a bun by a wide scarf.

"Hey, girl," I reply.

"That Alice back there?"

"Hi, Mariah!" Alice waves. "Don't mind me." She settles on my bed with her phone, happy to leave the conversation to us.

I peer around Mariah in the video. From what I can tell, she's in her dorm room. "What's going on?"

She shrugs. "Lotta nothing. Currently doing an excellent job of ignoring a take-home test. You said something went down last night. What happened?"

I blink. "You didn't feel it?"

She raises a brow. "Feel what?"

"A . . . root shockwave?"

"No! Holl*up* . . ." She leans closer, eyes searching my features. "Did you get attacked bad enough for your root to flare?"

"Yes. No. Not really?" Alice makes a frustrated sound and I turn to face her.

"Bad enough they're making her move outta the house," she adds, adjusting her glasses without looking up.

"Whoa!" Mariah gawks.

"I'm fine!"

"Aren't you the heir to the throne of white dude magic?" Mariah waves a hand around. "You should be surrounded by bodyguards."

Behind me, Alice snorts. "Oh, she is."

I glare at her. "It's complicated."

"Hello?" Dr. Patricia Hartwood, my former therapist, appears on the screen beside Mariah. We hear her voice, but the image faces the ceiling.

Mariah covers a laugh. "Can't see you, Doc Hartwood."

Patricia adjusts her camera until the image is mostly her wide smile, bright eyes behind yellow horn-rimmed glasses, and smooth, deep brown cheekbones. Her graying locs are wrapped on the top of her head today. "Better?"

"Yes," I say. I note Patricia's surroundings too. She's in a comfortable-looking cabin. Sunlight makes flickering patterns on the ceiling above her head. "That your rental?"

"It is!" Her eyes flick over the phone and around the room. "It's quite cozy. I need to thank your father for recommending it."

I grin. "Dad always knows the best places to stay in the mountains." It's true. He grew up in rural western North Carolina and he and my mom used to take me out there every year to see the fall leaves. Bright reds, vibrant golds, splotches of pink, peach, and grapefruit orange. Thinking about the family vacations we'll never have again makes my chest ache.

My eyes find the altar set up by the closet door. It's just a small wooden milk crate, nothing special, but the items on top of it remind me of the reason I came to Carolina in the first place.

In the center, a shallow ceramic bowl filled with dried medicinal wildflowers. Three crystals in a pile from my mother's jewelry box back home, sent by my father upon request: an oval-shaped bloodstone, a three-pointed rose quartz, and a carnelian that fits perfectly inside my fist. A tall jar of dried figs; sweetness grown from the ground. My mother's charm bracelet, laid open on top of a black cloth.

"The views are incredible," Patricia says, drawing my attention. "I could see myself staying in Asheville for longer than a week." She tilts her head. "And you still haven't spoken to him about what's really going on?"

"No." I'd called my father yesterday morning to check in, short and sweet. He told me he'd been having trouble finding good work at the auto shop. Been happy that my "fancy new digs" at the Lodge also came free of charge. Meant he could stop paying Carolina's dorm fees. "I told him that I think I understand Mom better now, and why she kept things about Carolina to herself. He said he wouldn't push."

My mother's gone and those family vacations are gone, and I couldn't prevent her death, but I'll do what it takes to keep my dad out of this.

Mariah shrugs. "Don't feel bad. A lot of Rootcrafter women keep the practice private."

"I hate lying, but he'd only worry. Plus, knowing the truth is dangerous." I gesture to Patricia. "You had to leave your home to be safe. I feel awful."

Patricia tuts. "It's just a short absence, Bree. I'm not losing that much time away from work."

"I know, but——"

"Bree," Patricia interrupts. "We are grateful for your warning last week. It was *my* idea to use the opportunity for a getaway while your Order Merlins are in town for the memorial service."

Mariah nods. "I'm glad you gave me the heads-up too."

"Least I could do," I murmur. "Did you get a chance to pass my message along to folks?"

"Yup. Told the Root network that it'd be a good weekend to lay low around campus. A lot of student practitioners don't work the real flashy branches of root, but better safe than sorry."

I gnaw on my lip. "I hope they're not mad at me about all this."

"Huh?" Mariah shakes her head. "You made sure the locals were safe. Gave advance notice the Merlins were coming. What's to be mad about?"

"After that first shockwave . . ." I tilt my head back and forth. "I understand why they'd be upset." The consequences from that night in the cave didn't solely land on the Legendborn side of things. A typical Rootcrafter opens a single pathway to one ancestor to borrow power, then returns that power when they're done. But when Vera possessed me, the red root furnace inside my chest had opened up like a wide, burning highway to every ancestor she'd called on to fuel the original Bloodcraft spell. There's a reason Rootcrafters believe that Bloodcraft—binding ancestral power to bloodlines permanently the way that both Vera and Merlin did—is cursed magic; it brings too much power from the realm of the dead to the realm of the living, disrupts the balance on both sides.

And I'm a Bloodcrafter twice over.

"'Wary' is the word I'd use." Patricia smiles. "When lightning strikes, the current travels along the ground and through the soil, but it doesn't destroy the earth. It was a jolt, and we recovered."

"That *was* one hell of a way to announce yourself to the community, not gonna lie," Mariah says with a wink. "I felt your root all the way on South campus."

"You're in a position to lead this organization that hunts magic users like us, Bree," Patricia says. "And you're already using that power wisely."

"Bloodcrafter and all?"

She smirks. "Bloodcrafter and all. Now, tell us what happened last night."

I recount the evening, stopping at the chorus of voices I heard last night when Lark got me down from the tree. Mariah hums. "I think you're good. That sounds like typical Medium 'noise' that comes and goes. You didn't tap into enough power to disrupt the dead beyond your immediate location."

"That's a relief," I say.

"The real question is, are you all locked up tight now?"

I don't answer right away. To Mariah, being "all locked up" means that I don't hear directly from the dead unless I ask for someone by ritual. But the truth is, some mornings, I wake up with the thirst for war in my mouth. Metallic and hot and hungry. I can't tell whom it belongs to, but I know it doesn't feel like me.

"Yeah, that answer is taking too long, girl," Mariah chastises. "You locked up or not?"

I grimace. "I think so? I haven't made an offering or done the ritual to invite anyone back in. No possessions. But sometimes, I feel . . . not quite myself."

Alice pipes up. "The Legendborn can gain personality traits from their knights, so maybe that's it?"

"Mmnnnnnn . . ." Mariah makes a low warning sound. "But you're not *just* Legendborn, you're a Medium. Imagine smoke escaping beneath a door, trying to reach you. There could be a fire on the other side. Bleed-throughs. Be careful."

"I'll keep an eye on it." I release a heavy breath, even though I'm not sure how to do that more than I already have. " I won't keep y'all. Alice is here to braid my hair."

"All *that* hair?!" Mariah rears back in the small video screen, eyes aghast. "Girrrrl, good luck."

"Thank you!" Alice calls.

"Talk soon, Bree," Patricia says.

Once we hang up, I swipe to a music app and press play. Alice pops up and stands behind me, pulling off my bonnet. She tugs at the loose twists, damp from my late night wash and detangle.

"Come on, Vassal Chen. Let's get this done."

6

MY FIRST PUBLIC act as Crown Scion is to say farewell to our dead.

However, since most of the people at this funeral don't realize that I *am* the Crown Scion, it's not really public at all.

Twenty miles southwest of the University of North Carolina, there is a large residential development called Pembray Village. To the public, Pembray is a quiet, private community situated on the rolling, picturesque acres of two-hundred-and-fifty-year-old farmland. The historic Pembray compound buildings include a three-story bed-and-breakfast, a five-star spa on-site, and a Michelin-star restaurant that only serves vegetables grown on the property from heirloom seeds. In the spring, the gazebo overlooking the postcard-perfect lake is one of the most sought-after wedding venues in the state. What the leisure magazines and locals don't know is that Pembray, like many such luxury compounds across the country, was constructed by the Order of the Round Table as a gathering site whenever needs required it. When Onceborn vacationers asked about making reservations at the award-winning inn this week, they were told it's been closed for "renovations."

I watch cars unload from a quiet spot under the awning of the inn. I barely remember my mother's service. But I know it didn't look this: a hundred rich white people in fancy funeral clothes spilling out of a steady stream of limos and luxury cars. Local celebrities, a few famous alums, the mayor, I think?

I'm not at all *surprised* that the only people of color here are a few Merlins and me, but it's still messed up. Even if my identity *were* out in the open, I'm not sure I could handle being surrounded at a funeral by this many emotional white people gawking at the Black-girl Scion of Arthur. On the one hand, it's true whether they want it to be or not. On the other . . . ugh. When Nick publicly claimed me as his Squire, the response at the gala was its own battle. I don't have the energy to fight against white folks' disbelief today.

A string quartet plays Bach on the perfectly manicured emerald lawn under a cloudy morning sky. In the distance, the glass surface of Llywelyn Lake ripples in silvers and grays from the occasional breeze. The air smells like rain and expensive cologne. I'm certain there had been flower displays at my mother's gravesite, but nothing like the ten-foot-tall living wall of fresh dahlias, carnations, and ranunculus that serve as a backdrop to the nine high-backed chairs spread across the dais. The guests walking toward the seating area wear black suits, long coats, dresses. They move with heads bent, whispering to one another while eyeing the urns that sit on a black cloth–covered table in front of the congregation.

There are four urns. One of them is empty because Evan's body was never found.

The unsaid thing about funerals is that directly after the communal mourning for someone you love, after everyone is gone and the connected grief dispersed, comes a solitude beyond imagining. A great, gaping *nothing* where a whole person and life and future used to be. The other side of a funeral is abyss.

On the other side of *this* funeral, however, my new life will officially begin.

I just have to get through the funeral to get to the Rite. Get through the Rite to claim my title. Claim my title to join the search for Nick. And when I leave for the search, the Council will leave Carolina too—putting needed distance between the Mageguard and the Rootcrafter network on campus. I can have all of that if I just *get through today.*

"Page Matthews?"

It's Theresa Hamilton, one of the Regent emissaries who'd arrived to take our statements the day after Nick was taken. She waves me over from the ceremony site's perimeter. She has to call me "Page" because to most everyone here, that's what I am.

I do not like Theresa. At all.

But before I join her I force my features into an expression that hopefully won't be read as hostile. The woman wears a high bun and narrow frameless glasses, and, even though I've only met her a couple of times, I'm pretty sure her patronizing chin tilt is a permanent fixture.

I come to a stop beside her. "Nice to see you again, Theresa."

"Please call me Emissary Theresa here, if you don't mind." Theresa does a double take at my appearance. "Oh." Her eyes travel my pant legs and hips up to my broad shoulders and the black robe clasped at my neck. By the time she reaches my hair, her plastic smile has melted.

"Something wrong?" I ask through clenched teeth.

She answers while staring at my hair. A set of Alice Chen—exact braided cornrows to keep my hair out of my face, flowing into loose curls—soft, shiny, and full—and styled with gel to fall over my shoulders.

"It is too late to change first appearances, but perhaps in the future, for decorum's sake, you might consider the care you take with your . . ." She gestures around her head to indicate my hair. "Perhaps smooth things down for a cleaner look?"

Heat flushes up and around my collar.

"Clean?" I bite out.

"Well," she says. "Yes."

Because she was curious, Alice learned to braid hair from my mother. My mother had laughed and sat her down for a lesson when we were thirteen. I could scream obscenities at this woman without messing up a strand. Instead I say, "Just because my hair takes up space doesn't mean it's *dirty, Theresa.*"

Her eyes widen, and she drops her gaze back to her clipboard. "The—the final guests have entered the ceremony site, so the Mageguard are ready for you now." Theresa taps her seating chart and then looks into the crowd. "Pages are seated in the second section, and you are to sit in the middle. If you don't mind?"

I do mind. After her comments about my hair, I'm not only impatient. I'm *angry*. I huff, eyes closing.

"Now, if you will, Page Matthews," Theresa presses, her voice low, "a funeral for our fallen is about to commence."

I open my eyes, smile returned to position as I face Theresa. "After the Rite tonight," I say, "you *will* stop calling me that."

Theresa raises a brow and taps the dark golden Order-symbol pin on her lapel. "I am the voice of the High Council of Regents, acting on their express commands. I will refer to you in the manner in which the Regents have advised me to, *Page Matthews*, until they tell me it is safe to do otherwise."

It takes everything in me to bite my tongue, but there's no real point in being angry with Theresa. She's a mouthpiece. She tilts her head toward the near-full seating area. "They need you in place before—"

I'm already moving, following her direction, weaving through the other guests finding their seats.

There are only a couple open seats left in the Page section, right in the center. Great. I get to be tucked between Pages who not only competed against me in the selection tournament, but who have no idea who I truly am now. As I shift down the aisle, Spencer waves hello from a seat next to the empty pair. Ainsley, who failed the first trial, narrows her eyes at me from the back row.

The Mageguard must have been waiting until I was in place, because the second I sit, my ears pop painfully. A gust of aether signature hits me from all sides in a wave.

This is *definitely* not like my mother's homegoing.

Whatever happened at my mother's funeral at Whatley Baptist Church in Bentonville, North Carolina, there wasn't magic crackling in the air.

I tip my head back to gaze at the largest aether construct I've ever seen. Most wards are close to invisible to those with the Sight unless disturbed or attacked, but a dome construct is an actual, physical barrier. The dome above the services for Russ, Whitty, Fitz, and Evan stretches a hundred feet in every direction, and shimmers silver against the Carolina blue sky.

Eight of the twenty-four Mageguard on site are spaced evenly along the circle perimeter, in black suits with hands outstretched. I watch them pull aether into their palms only to send it up through their fingers, where it flows into the shared casting. The density of this much aether—sharp and strong signatures, all blending together—burns my nose.

Someone at my side clears his throat, and I jump.

"It takes deep mastery over aether constructs to build an annistryw—indestructible—barrier. Extraordinary discipline and focus."

I blink at Lark. I hadn't seen him at all when I'd squeezed into my seat.

"Where did you—" I stop, taking him in. I'm not sure I would have even recognized that it was *him* without hearing his voice. "What are you *wearing*?"

When Lark dropped me off an hour ago, he'd been wearing what seemed to be the daytime version of the Mageguard uniform: dark grays instead of blacks, loose slacks, and a charcoal corded sweater, no tunic or cowl. Now he's wearing a black suit that looks like it's worth more than my entire wardrobe. His hair has been combed down to cover most of the shaved undercut. And the tattoos I'd seen last night are covered by a crisp white high-necked collar and long black suit sleeves. His amber eyes haven't lost their sparkle, even hidden behind a pair of high-end, near-perfect brown contacts that, I assume, are custom designed to hide his cambion heritage. Despite the designer suit, he looks like an extremely average college student. Nearly forgettable. Even his smile is set tight enough that his lips hide his Merlin canines.

"A three-thousand-dollar Armani suit." Lark tugs at the collar with a grimace. "Not what I'm used to, honestly, but it's what Theresa sent to my room here at the compound."

"Emissary Theresa *sent* you a suit?" Spencer twists in his seat, obviously eavesdropping. "Which chapter are you from?"

Lark has a lie at the ready. "I'm here to represent the Northern Chapter's current membership and to offer condolences on behalf of our Scions and Squires." Even his accent is less pronounced here. Another part of the disguise.

The university chapters of the Legendborn don't mingle much, not even for funerals. The Legendborn cycle means that when a Scion dies, there is always a family member trained and ready to take their place. If a Squire falls, there's another Page ready to be selected and Oathed. The only reason today's service was expected to be well-attended is because four Legendborn died at once.

Spencer sneers. "Are Armani suits typical gifts up at Northern? When it's not even *your* chapter members that died?"

And there seems to be a healthy amount of competition, even though we're all supposed to be on the same side.

Lark is scanning the crowd. In response to Spencer's question, he lifts a non-committal shoulder that can be read as a "yes" or an "I don't know" or nothing at all. Lark clearly couldn't care less about the treatment that other chapters' Pages get, but Spencer takes his silence for insult. He scowls. "You Northern kids. Spoiled, just like everyone says."

Without sparing Spencer a glance, Lark flashes a grin. "Southern Chapter hospitality at its finest, I see."

"Say that again . . . ," Spencer growls, moving to stand.

"Ugh! Stop!" I jump up before Spencer can say another word and shove at Lark's shoulder until he's forced to stand and exit the aisle. We push past the others until we reach a quiet spot under a tree. The nearest Mageguard, a short woman with dark hair and shining eyes, is about six feet behind us. She glances at me, then Lark, then goes back to her casting.

I huff, lowering my voice to Merlin levels of quiet just in case—more air than sound. "What are you doing here?"

Lark's mouth twitches in delight. "I'm here for the service, same as you, Page Matthews."

I roll my eyes. "You know what I mean."

He gives me a pointed look. "As it stands now, I am to be your Kingsmage. Where else would I be?"

I gesture at the Mageguard around us, the dome above. "This has gotta be the most magically secure patch of grass in the whole damn world. Aren't you—no offense—overkill?"

He chuckles. "No such thing when it comes to you."

"Debatable."

At that, Lark's true smile breaks through. "Not debatable to the Mageguard."

I *hmph*. "You sound like Selwyn."

He hesitates at first. "Your safety should not be debatable to anyone. Especially to a Kingsmage."

I blink at the turn in conversation. "What's that supposed to mean?"

"You and Kane . . ."

My eyes narrow. "What about us?"

He shakes his head. "Nevermind. None of my business."

"Probably not."

When we first arrived for the service, I searched the perimeter in hopes of seeing one Merlin in particular. I do it again now and still don't find who I'm looking for. I just assumed we'd see each other at the service and we'd get to talk again. Smooth things over somehow.

The Bloodcraft that gives me the ability to sense when a Merlin looks my way won't be tricked by contacts, apparently, so I feel the smattering of sparks on my cheek when Lark turns to survey me.

"What?" I snap.

"You looking for Kane?"

"I thought he'd be here." I sigh. "These were his friends too."

Lark tilts his head. "Kingsmages don't tend to run late."

I frown again at the second odd comment about Kingsmages. Does he mean Sel is here? Or that he won't be? Or is he trying to sell himself as my Kingsmage?

"He'll be here," I say. Together, our eyes roam the ceremony grounds, but there's no sign of Selwyn.

From where we stand, it's easy to see that attendees are in four groups:

Up on the dais and behind the table of urns, the Legendborn sit in high-backed chairs, dressed in Line-colored cloaks and formal tunics. The Scions are seated in rank order: Tor as third-ranked, Felicity as fourth, Pete as seventh, and William as twelfth. Next are the Squires: Sarah and Greer.

Directly in front of the raised dais are the families of the fallen.

Then the Pages.

In the back row in dark formal wear sit half a dozen Lieges—retired Scions and Squires, some of whom were never Called by their knight and some of whom were. They are adorned with sashes in the colors of their Lines, and bear both scars and hardened faces. A few have turned my way with curious, cautious gazes.

"Do you know many Lieges?" Lark murmurs. He's seen them watching me, too.

"Only the two that trained me," I reply. "Owen and Gillian."

He hums. "Lieges are a strange lot."

"What makes you say that?"

"Ah . . . I apologize." Chagrin overtakes his expression. "It's . . . not polite t'discuss."

"I already think you're rude," I comment. "So say it."

Lark's eyes widen. "I appreciate the honesty." He sighs. "Look, we Merlins have our aether abilities from birth, but you Legendborn only have yours for six years maximum, right? Sixteen to twenty-two." He shakes his head. "The ones of you lucky enough to survive that long face death from powers you don't even possess anymore."

"Abatement," I murmur. Lieges tend to die by thirty-five. If a knight calls his Scion to power, the Spell of Eternity gives them incredible abilities—but it burns through their lifespan, cutting it short. A form of Abatement seems to affect Vera's Line too. Mothers, gone too soon from their daughters.

"Aye. Lieges never lose the bloodlust. They don't leave the battlefield, even when their inheritances leave *them*. If you ask me, there are de-powered Lieges fighting Shadowborn out there who are far more dangerous than most Merlins. When you've got a ticking clock over your head, there's no reason to hold back."

I'll be a Liege someday, if I'm lucky enough to survive that long.

A woman with dark red hair in the very first row weeps loudly. Every time she dips her head to dab at her eyes with a handkerchief, the man beside her rubs her shoulders. The man looks familiar, like I've seen him on the news somewhere.

"Who are they?" I ask Lark, nodding toward the couple.

"The Coopers," he murmurs.

Immediately, nausea churns my stomach. Evan Cooper's parents. The *real* Evan Cooper. Not the Evan who was not Evan, but Rhaz . . . My hands curl into fists on my black slacks, nails audibly scratching at the material along the way. It's not the images of the fight in the cave—the ogof—that haunt me. It's the sense memories that come flooding back into my body.

In my palm, I *feel* the heavy, awkward weight of the demon Rhaz's body pierced on my blade, still writhing in his death throes. Smell melting, rotting flesh. Hear the garbled sound of the demon's screams. The ichor on my skin, root burning it away. Then, in a silent rush, I feel the heady bloodlust in my veins that might have been Arthur's, but might have been mine, too—

"Easy there," Lark murmurs. I turn to him with a question in my eyes, and he nods toward my still-clenching left fist. I scoff but open my fingers and press them wide into my thigh all the same.

"I'm fine."

"Good," Lark responds, wrapping my elbow in a light grip, "because we need you back in your seat."

"Why?"

He tilts his head toward the long drive at the top of the hill, and I see the answer to my question.

The Regents are here.

7

A WAVE OF murmurs flows toward us from the back of the crowd. Legend-born funerals are not uncommon, not in the business of an underground holy war. But this service, for four warriors at once and with the Regents presiding, will likely go down in Order history.

"Come." Lark tugs me along by the elbow. The low-pitched sound of gravel crunching under heavy vehicles pierces the barrier. The Regents' motorcade approaches, and the energy of the crowd sharpens with anticipation. Around me, everyone moves to their feet, adjusting their formal layers and robes, sashes, and sigils, so that the Regents will be able to recognize their Line and title on sight.

"Please rise," Tor commands imperiously from the front of the ceremony. I roll my eyes at her tone as we shuffle back in place. She's enjoying her role as the public Chapter leader pro tempore far too much for my liking.

Lark leans toward me. "Ready?"

"Yes." If Lark hears the slight tremor in my voice, he's polite enough not to mention it. "*They're* the ones who're twenty minutes late."

"The High Council of Regents has not convened in full in a decade. I reckon they can take their time."

The murmurs around us fade to anticipatory silence as three black stretch SUVs pull in at the drive at the top of the hill. They slow. A door slams. The sound sets my heart pounding.

"Head and chin up, shoulders back," Lark offers, his voice calm and close at my ear so that only another Merlin might hear. "Don't fidget. They won't acknowledge you here, but they *will* see you."

I glare at him, but stop tugging at my sleeves.

Silence falls as a tall white man wearing shades and a black suit folds himself out of the first car. A Vassal of some sort. He extends a deep bow to the seated Legendborn, who nod in return, then walks down the long vehicle to the door farthest back, opening it smoothly.

A tall white woman steps out of the car, adjusting her sleek auburn ponytail, and immediately I know who she is.

"Cestra," I breathe.

"*Regent* Cestra," Lark corrects, the amusement in his eyes at odds with the harsh, commanding tone of his voice. "A Page must never address a Regent without their title."

I press my lips into a thin line of acknowledgment, and Lark winks. He's clearly delighted by our temporary ruse.

Each Regent is selected by their predecessor, but must be of a Legendborn bloodline. I know that Cestra was once a daughter of the Line of Tristan, a distant relative of Tor's who was never Called, but when she took her title, she shed allegiance to her bloodline, forever abandoned its colors and sigil, and became the Regent of Shadows.

When Cestra steps away from the car, she is adorned in Merlin colors: a silver-edged black sash that trails down to the thighs of her wide-legged dark pin-stripe suit. Her sharp brows and eyes dart quickly over the crowd and the circle of Mageguard surrounding it. It occurs to me that her Seneschal isn't present.

"Where is—" I whisper.

"Erebus remains in the field while his Regent attends the ceremony," Lark supplies.

As Cestra approaches the edge of the shield, the closest Mageguard twists their wrist in a quick gesture, creating a doorlike opening in the magic barrier for her and the others to pass through. Cestra strides forward without stopping or turning to either aisle of standing guests.

Cestra's intelligence team has been running the investigation into Nick's kidnapping, mining the chapter members' debriefs for information. Within days of Nick being taken, they gained access to every document about me that has been recorded in any digital system ever. Medical records, school transcripts, Social Security number, addresses, you name it. Which means that Cestra knows exactly who I am and what I look like, but in this moment, she passes by me without a glance.

Why would a Regent spare a glance for a Page?

When Cestra reaches the dais, she takes the stairs to the center seats and nods to the standing Legendborn before sitting. As she settles, another door in a car up the hill opens, sending our attention back the way she came.

The next driver is already standing at the door. When his passenger exits, I recognize the white man in the dark navy suit as the Regent Gabriel, who, as the Regent of Light, oversees all of the society's operations in the Onceborn world, including those that have helped the Order move from medieval society to a modern power conglomerate. Gabriel leads the recruitment and management of thousands of Vassals across the globe. The Merlins that report to him are specifically tasked with maintaining the Code of Secrecy—and mesmering anyone who has seen too much.

Gabriel is pale, with an upturned nose and gray streaks at the temple of his light brown hair. Unlike Cestra, when he walks down the center aisle, he pauses every few feet to shake hands with someone he recognizes. *Glad-handing,* I think. *Like a politician.* As he offers condolences to the parents of the fallen, the final car's doors open.

The next man is the leader of the High Council of Regents himself, Lord Regent Aldrich, the keeper of Legendborn records, Order history—and commander of the Table when it is not gathered.

When Aldrich exits his car, he seems to rise and rise until he reaches his full height. A tall, tanned man, built like a warrior.

As Aldrich moves in front of the altar, his long, heavy cape swishes along the wooden planks of the raised platform at the head of the congregation. Tor signals for us to sit.

"Welcome, all." Aldrich's low, rich voice carries across the lawn and brings the whispering crowd to silence. The white-and-gold cape and sash radiate light beneath the low clouds. "To open our ceremony, a lament as ancient and precious as our great mission."

Aldrich takes a long, silent breath before he recites an elegy for the fallen, a poem for another warrior lost in another war long ago.

"As for the soul of Owain, son of ancient King Urien," Aldrich murmurs solemnly, "may we, as his fellow warriors, with today's families, sit at the knee of his creator to consider its journey . . ."

William taught me well. I recognize this portion of the ceremony. But I don't expect Aldrich's opening words to send a heated flush down my spine, followed immediately by an odd, cold sensation. Another wave of heat, then chill. The tall shape of the Lord Regent at the altar seems to smear at the edges and fade. My eyes have filled with sudden tears.

Aldrich recites the next lines in Welsh, echoing the ancient poem. "Rheged udd a gudd tromlas . . ."

I feel a tear slip down my cheek. Blink again.

Eyes close.

Eyes open.

"Nid oedd fas i gywyddaid . . ."

From one stanza to the next, Lord Regent Aldrich is replaced by a tall, robed figure. From a lament in English to one in Welsh, from a blue morning sky over a picturesque, professionally maintained lawn to endless gray clouds and a hidden afternoon sun . . . the scene before me has bled into another similar ceremony from long, long ago.

"Gan ni cheffir cystedlydd . . ."

The robed figure's voice is resonant, slow, overlapping with Aldrich's, but slightly off. Echoing like a minister's prayer in an enormous cathedral, but we are not inside a building; we are in a valley. And this speaker is not a holy man, but a cambion.

I know this because I recognize his long, narrow face framed by sharp cheek-bones. The dark brows and glowing red-orange eyes.

He is not *a* Merlin.

He is *the* Merlin.

I have never seen a depiction of the original Merlin, but in this moment, in this old world engulfing my own, I know his features like I know Alice's. They are familiar, reassuring, trusted. They are the features of a friend. *My* friend. No, *Arthur's* friend—

"Medel galon, gafaelad . . . ,"

Beside him lie bodies covered in shrouds and shields.

The ceremony for the Legendborn reminded me of my mother's funeral, but the losses are so far from one another, there is no comparison. And yet, in *this* world, for fallen knights I don't know, I feel a devouring echo of the pain I know, eating through my defenses.

It is Arthur's pain. *He* has just lost four more knights.

His grief *pulls* at the scar tissue of my mother's absence, tearing the wound open at the edges. It *drags* over the gaping hole of Nick's disappearance. The possibility of death coming to him, too, rises inside of me like a ghost to come, a haunting of what could be . . .

—*what if it happens again, it could happen again, loving them just to lose them, I'd lose them, I'd lose them, lose* him, *not again*—

Arthur's grief pulls words from my throat in a harsh whisper. "Eisyllud ei dad a'i daid . . ." The words don't belong to me, but I recite them with the sorcerer and with Aldrich both, our voices layers of past and present.

Eyes close.

Eyes open.

Now I am myself, speaking alongside Aldrich. "Pan laddodd Owain Fflamddwyn . . ." Aldrich and I say, "Nid oedd fwy nag ei gysgaid."

Jagged half images flash across my vision, horrors splashed over the shining world: Nick's body, broken and twisted at the feet of a laughing goruchel. Blood pooling beneath his skull because I was too late to save him. Sel, torn apart by a Shadowborn legion, his body carved open to the world—too much for any Merlin to heal. Alice, chased through campus, cornered by a fox that she can't see. My father, defenseless as a Morgaine hunts him down to find his daughter.

My mother, alone and dying from a hit-and-run—

"Oi." Lark nudges my shoulder, and I jump. "I didn't know you spoke Old Welsh."

"I—" I blink rapidly, try to free my eyes of the nightmares. They won't go. I can barely speak. "What?"

"Old Welsh? You speak it?"

"I—don't."

Lark tilts his head. "You just did." He pulls the silver pocket square from his breast pocket and offers it to me. It's only then that I realize I've been crying.

My hands tremble in my lap. I clutch the cloth in my fists and will them to stop shaking.

It takes another five stanzas before I hear a word Aldrich says.

"Will the families of the fallen step forward?"

One by one the families rise from their chairs to stand in front of the urn that holds their son. All except Evan's parents, who must stand before an empty vessel.

"Death walks beside our Legendborn Scions and Squires. We know this. We are not strangers to memorials, and yet these ceremonies never get easier and are never to be taken lightly. The loss of Fitzsimmons Baldwin, Russell Copeland, Evan Cooper, and James Whitlock is a blow to our chapter forces, multiplied four-fold. The sacrifices of your children will never be forgotten, nor were they in vain," Regent Aldrich says, his sonorous voice flowing easily over the hundred people in attendance. "I honor them as my brethren and as sacred members of this Table. I honor them for their clear hearts and dedication, and for their commitment to the vanguard against the evil we all must face. Scions serve a sacred role in our Order, and those who support and surround them serve sacred roles as well. As parents, you brought a child into the world knowing that they might be Awakened to power—and to risk. I am certain, too, that our fallen Squires felt responsibility for their Scions, and gave their lives so that their Scions could live. In this way, their will was done."

Behind him, the Legendborn manage to keep their blank faces, but Felicity flinches. Russ adored Felicity and loved being Oathed to her. If Rhaz had gone for her instead of him, Russ would have torn himself to pieces out of guilt, but that doesn't mean it was his will to die. The very idea makes my head swim for them both. So much death, so much blood . . . and more to come if I can't control these powers and lead as I should.

Aldrich gestures to Gabriel while gazing down at the families. "As with prior services, Regent Gabriel's Merlins are here to offer support to the families of the deceased. Our mesmer specialists will provide the relief of forgetting to any who desire it, without judgment or censure."

The relief of forgetting . . . I shudder.

Not long after Nick was taken, Vaughn Schaefer, a Page who'd aimed to become Nick's Squire during the tournament, announced he'd be meeting with a mesmer specialist. He didn't want to remember what he'd witnessed in the ogof. He'd seen a lot that night; we all did. Murders. A small army of demons. Rhaz, a walking nightmare. My Awakening and possession. I don't know exactly which part of that night was too much for him to remember. Don't know and never asked. And no one's seen Vaughn since.

Good riddance; there's a war on the horizon.

But now . . . I wonder if that specialist was one of Gabriel's Merlins.

When I see a few of the family members murmur among one another, discussing Aldrich's offer, any sympathy I feel is washed away with disgust.

My grief may tear at my insides still, but the wounds and memories are mine. *Mine.*

'*They are weak.*'

My head jerks back, and Lark's head turns. "You all right?"

That *voice.* "Yeah . . . ," I whisper, but my stomach flips.

I send a silent prayer that my mind is only echoing what I think Arthur might say—not that he can come to me like this without asking. *Speak* to me without an invitation. That would be far more than the vague emotional resonances that the Legendborn say they feel from their knights. Speech, connection to what I'm seeing and thinking in real time . . . that is interaction on the cusp of possession. Leaks. Bleed-throughs. Mariah warned me. Smoke under a door, reaching for its host . . .

My knee begins to bounce.

"And now, a few words from the ancient texts to offer solace in this time of bereavement—" While I was distracted, Aldrich had produced a heavy tome, and began to read from it.

"How *dare* you!" A voice crackling with anger and grief interrupts his reading.

Beside me, Lark shifts, his body strung with tension.

But it's not a demon at the service, staring down the Lord Regent. It's a middle-aged woman.

Evan Cooper's mother rises to her feet, shoulders trembling. Her seated husband grasps for her forearm, but she steps out of his reach and raises her head defiantly.

"How dare you suggest that we forget our children! Is that what you'd prefer?"

The crowd gasps, and even the aether barrier above ripples slightly, as if one of the Mageguard lost their focus.

Evan's father is on his feet now, wrapping an arm around his wife's shoulders. "Regent Aldrich, I apologize for my wife. We mean no disrespect. Bonnie—"

"No!" Bonnie Cooper wrenches away from her husband, thrusting her hand at the dais and the four urns wrapped in black satin ribbon. "We don't even have a body to bury, John!"

"Bonnie—" Evan's father protests, but even at this distance I can see his shoulders sag. John Cooper may not agree with his wife's methods, but each word she says rocks his body like another blow. Pain, linked and compounded.

Aldrich holds his hand out. "No, Congressman Cooper. The only one who would be acting with disrespect is me if I did not answer the call of a grieving Legendborn parent."

Evan's parents' faces are wracked with a mixture of brimming, sharp grief; confusion; and not a small amount of rage.

The Regent beckons Bonnie forward. "Please, speak."

Evan's mother pushes ahead. "Regent Aldrich, our Evan was taken from us by a . . . a monster." Her voice cracks, tears at the edge of every breath. "We called Evan on his birthday last year, and he spoke to us on video chats from his room. At least, we think it was him—"

"Regent Aldrich." John steps forward, wrapping his wife in his arms. "We knew it would be dangerous for our son to Squire. But this demon didn't just take our son from us, it pretended to *be* him—" The Congressman stops. Starts again, this time with the steel and passion of a man in politics, used to swaying an audience to his goals. "We want to know how and when our son was killed. When was the last time we spoke to the real Evan and not this Rhaz creature? How long did we welcome this demon into our home?" The Congressman opens his arm wide, gesturing to the other families seated around them. "We are not the only Legendborn parents grieving today. I know I speak for others when I ask, 'Where is this chapter's leader?' We deserve answers from the Scion of Arthur about what has happened under his watch! Where is Nicholas Davis?"

Lark's hand hovers over my knee. To guard against someone who might know my identity and attack me here in the crowd or to preemptively stop me from standing and revealing myself, I'm not sure which. No need to worry about the latter; I am frozen to my seat, deathly scared of what the Lord Regent Aldrich will say next.

At the Selection Gala, Lord Davis publicly predicted that Camlann was nigh in front of hundreds of Order members. Less of a prediction than a warning, since he was the one orchestrating and accelerating it behind the scenes. But it was too late, and word spread.

"A worthy question, and I can provide an answer." Aldrich looks out over the crowd.

What is said here today will not remain within this aether barrier. It will spread like wildfire to Vassals, to other chapters, to Legendborn families across the world—and potentially to our enemies.

The glint of readiness, of anticipation, in the High Regent's expression sends a chill slipping down my spine. This man is Lord Regent for a reason. He came prepared for this moment.

"The four young men we honor today fell in the recent wave of increased Shadowborn activity surrounding the four cardinal chapters of our Order. We have shared that Nicholas Davis and his father are preparing for the coming of Camlann, but I feel I should . . ." Aldrich tucks his chin, takes what appears to be a considering breath. "No. I feel I *must* share with you that this is not the complete truth of our situation. Nicholas Davis and his father are not on a leave of absence to prepare for his ascension to the throne."

A ripple of shock and uncertainty breaks across the lawn. I suck in a breath, exchanging glances with Lark. He shakes his head, eyes sharp on the stage and jaw tight with focus. He doesn't know what the Lord Regent is doing either. *Shit.*

"In light of the recent incidents that have resulted in incalculable losses, we, the High Council of Regents, decided to sequester Nicholas Davis for his own safety as the Scion of Arthur, and for the safety of the Round Table. He; his father, Lord Martin Davis; and Lord Davis's Kingsmage, Isaac Sorenson, will remain in a safe and undisclosed location—"

"*Someone* must answer for these deaths!" Bonnie Cooper remains undeterred.

A voice calls out from the crowd, "Is it not the Kingsmage's responsibility to guard this chapter from demon attacks?"

Another parent—Whitty's, I think—shouts, "How can we trust Kane to protect the king during Camlann if he could not protect our boys?"

Russ's father nods, visibly enraged. All of that pain, with anger just under the surface, bubbling up and out, seeking blame. The first tendrils of something like violence rise in the air around us.

"Steady." Lark's voice is calm, but he must feel it too, because he pulls both hands to his side, palms upturned. The ready position for calling aether.

Aldrich's mouth turns down at the edges. "These questions, too, have an answer. A truth that we owe you as parents of the fallen." Aldrich steps aside, waving Cestra to the podium. "I will let Regent Cestra, commander of our military and security forces, speak to your concerns."

Cestra steps smoothly toward the podium, displacing Aldrich without a second glance. Her pale blue eyes roam the audience, and when she speaks, her voice is lower even than Aldrich's rich tone.

"Someone the chapter trusted was opening local Gates purposefully in advance of the campus attack, and even during the events of the ogof y ddraig. Someone who has betrayed our Order."

My eyes widen. The Regents exposing Lord Davis's betrayal is something I'd never expect to happen here and now. Not during a funeral, not before the Rite. Not when they've just announced that he's been sequestered with Nick—a lie in and of itself. My chest goes tight with shock—but what Cestra says next takes me right out of my body.

"We believe that traitor is Selwyn Kane."

I'M ON MY feet before Lark can stop me.

At the podium, Cestra's gaze narrows to two blue daggers aimed right at me, daring me to say a word.

"Under my command," she continues icily, "Mage Seneschal Erebus and a select group of Mageguard attempted to bring Selwyn Kane in for interrogation early this morning. Regretfully, he chose not to go peacefully."

More gasps from the crowd. Behind Cestra, shock ripples through the Legendborn. Onstage, Sar rises to her feet—before Tor yanks her back down. Greer looks like they might fall out of their chair. William's eyes are round as saucers.

"Selwyn Kane injured two of our Mageguard and escaped custody." Cestra lifts her chin. "Given his evasion to even answer simple questions about the events in the ogof y ddraig, I hereby strip Selwyn Kane of his title as Kingsmage and declare him an enemy of the Order and fugitive from justice."

"No!" I shout.

A hundred eyes turn to me. Beside the Regents, William shakes his head urgently.

"Is there a concern from a Page about the military's actions in this manner?" Cestra asks, brow raised and voice dripping with threat.

Lark stands, wrapping a hot hand around my elbow. "I apologize, Regent Cestra—"

Aldrich steps forward, waving a hand. "No, no, Page Douglas. Let Page . . . ?" Aldrich trails off, tilting his head as if he's uncertain as to my identity. The affected gesture lights my insides up, lifts the hair on the back of my neck. The second where a regular Page might fill in her name for him drags out because I am not a regular Page. The world narrows and narrows to this . . . this *pretense* that he doesn't know *exactly* who I am—

'Enough of this ruse!'

That voice again. Not mine.

I'd felt Arthur's grief. Recognized it. That grief is gone now, with fury in its wake. I recognize that, too. Before-Bree, After-Bree, all over again.

I clench my teeth, stopping the next words from leaving my mouth with not a small amount of effort. I have kept Aldrich waiting, but if I speak now, I don't know whose voice the crowd will hear.

William leaps up just in time. "Regent Aldrich, this is Page Briana Matthews."

"*Matthews*, yes, of course! The Selected Squire-to-be of Nicholas Davis. My apologies!" Aldrich's voice carries an added false note of surprise and recognition that only makes my teeth grind harder. "I understand that this may be difficult for you to hear, Page Matthews"—he turns to the rest of the Legendborn, then to the crowd—"difficult for you *all* to hear." A low snarl begins at the back of my throat.

Lark pulls at my arm again, but I don't budge.

With Arthur's strength coursing through my veins, it will take more than a single Merlin to move me if I do not want to move. And right now, I do *not* want to move. I anchor my feet to the earth.

"Sel didn't turn against anyone!" I shout.

"Thank you, Regent Aldrich, for this update!" Tor springs to her feet. She pitches her voice loud enough to hit the microphone and carry across the lawn, drowning me out. "It *is* difficult for us to hear, but we appreciate your being forthright with those of us who remain."

Aldrich replies, but I don't follow any of it. I can't hear it. Blood rushes in my ears, the ground tilts beneath my feet, then steadies. When I look up again, only some of the crowd is paying attention to me, because Tor has successfully taken their attention away from the strange Page who no one really knows.

My heart pounds in anger, and a second heartbeat pounds behind it.

A battlefield soaked in red. My tunic and leathers, shining with it. Sweat running into my eyes. The stench of ozone and flash of aether in the distance. I am shouting with my first knight. We are arguing. We are always arguing, even here with our comrades screaming on the ground around us, bleeding—

"Please, lass. Leave it for now. . . ." Lark's voice, close in my ear.

Has he been speaking to me? I don't know how long I've been standing, immobile—moments, at least? The scene fades before my eyes, lifting like a layer of film until the world is sharp and clear and I am at a funeral where no one is bleeding. But now everyone is on their feet, chanting the Order's mantra with the Regents in a unified voice to close the ceremony.

"When the shadows rise . . ."

"He—Sel—didn't kill our friends. He'd never do that. They're lying—"

Lark's hand claps over my mouth. I lose balance. His arm loops around my waist and suddenly he's pulling me away from the shocked Pages around me and down the aisle.

"By the King's Table . . ."

At first, I let Lark drag me away, because I *should* let him do this. I can't fight a hundred people and the Regents with my bare fists. *I shouldn't be here anyway.*

But as soon as we clear the seating area, I tear his hand from my mouth.

"Let me go. Now."

He watches me carefully, hesitating against the order in my voice, then drops his arms.

I narrow my eyes, remembering what he'd said about Kingsmages earlier. How he'd spoken *about* Sel in ways I didn't understand. "Did you know?"

Lark flushes. All the answer I need.

I push past him. "Wait—" His hand shoots out to grasp my elbow.

This time I *do* use Arthur's strength to break his grip. Pull my hardest. I hear a pop. A bone, broken. Lark draws back with a sharp, pained sound, eyes wide.

"I—I'm sor—" I stammer.

'Do not apologize for doing what needed to be done.' I know it's his voice now. Recognize the deep baritone.

"No," I hiss. "I'm not listening to you."

Lark blinks. "What?"

I turn on my heel before Arthur's thoughts, his *disregard*, somehow shows on my face, leaving Lark blinking in surprise behind me.

I aim for the barrier and one of the Mageguard casters I recognize. One of the new arrivals from last night. Zhao, I think? His lips move quietly, murmuring the chant that helps join his aether barrier to the others'.

"Let me through," I demand.

The Merlin's amber gaze drops to mine as his brow lifts. "I don't take orders from a Page."

I inhale sharply. He *knows* I'm not a Page. Everything that just happened, and he expects me to play along with . . . today's publicity stunt?

"Let us through, Max." Lark is at my side before I finish, his injured hand tucked behind his back. "Matthews here needs to get back up to the compound and her room."

Max sizes Lark up and sniffs. "I don't take orders from you either, Douglas." Max shakes his head. "You think you outrank us just because you're Erebus's special pet?"

"How about taking an order from me?" William has found us, with iron in his voice and heat in his eyes.

"Scion Sitterson." Max dips his head and twists his wrist at once, pulling the shield open like a curtain. "My apologies."

William steps closer to the guard, eyes narrowing dangerously. "While you are in the territory of the Southern Chapter, you will *never* stop someone from seeking their own refuge, do you understand me?"

Zhao sputters. "But the safety——"

"Does *Page Matthews* appear to be in immediate danger to you?" William presses.

"No." Max shakes his head. "Apologies, Scion."

I push through without a second look and march up the hill away from the dispersing crowd. Max goes back to casting the barrier and Lark jogs behind me, matching my stride easily until we are shoulder to shoulder.

"I don't want to talk to you, Lark," I huff.

"I realize that." Lark's voice is sullen.

William catches up to us both, all long legs and black suit and emerald sash and two very furrowed brows. "I don't think we formally met last night, Guard . . . ?"

"Douglas," Lark replies, eyes widening. "Larkin Douglas."

William smiles. "Nice to meet you, Larkin."

"Likewise, Scion Sitterson." If I weren't so damn irritated, I might find the pink flush on Lark's cheeks curious and sort of precious. As it is, I groan and roll my eyes because Lark is a member of the group of Merlins that is hunting Sel down as we speak *and* he's a goddamn *liar*, so who cares if he thinks William's cute?

William is either oblivious to Lark's response to him, or he's ignoring it like I am. "Bree, I know you're upset. We all are."

"This is ridiculous!" I spit, and keep marching.

"I know—"

"Stripped of his title?"

"I know—"

"Hey, Matthews!" An angry voice reaches us, and my shoulders tense. Tor. She leads the group of Legendborn up the hill behind her: Sarah, close on her heels in matching Tristan blue; Greer and Pete in Owain soft yellow cloaks; and Felicity in deep Lamorak red trailing behind.

William glances at Lark, voice mild. "How about you go get that hand looked at, Douglas?"

Lark blinks in surprise. "How did you—"

William smiles. "Trade secret." He jerks his chin over his shoulder. "I apologize for the dismissal, but if you don't mind . . ."

Lark sees Tor approaching and takes the hint, hanging back. "Sure thing. I'll be around when it's time to leave, Crown Scion."

I grumble something unintelligible to all of humankind. William sighs as the group reaches us.

"What the *hell*, Matthews?"

I absolutely notice that Tor doesn't use any title at all with my name, and I pivot on a heel to return the favor. "Not now, Morgan."

Tor takes a beat to glance around her for listening ears before she continues. "Thanks for almost blowing your own cover," she says between clenched teeth.

"I wasn't going to blow my cover," I grit out. Even though I really almost did.

Tor crosses her arms. "You do realize that exposing yourself puts more than just you at risk, don't you?" She waves a hand at our fellow Legendborn beside her. "Shadowborn are still out there. Some of us would like to keep our abilities so we can actually do our job, thanks. Not sit in our room and pout."

"If I could be out there fighting with you, I would!" I hiss.

"Yes, but you can't, can you?" Tor says. She steps closer, voice low and sharp as a dagger. "Because you can't even call on Arthur's aether armor or forge your own weapon. Not without burning yourself to a pathetic crisp."

"Victoria . . . ," William warns.

Embarrassment floods my face in a hot wave. I hate that Tor knows what I can't do, has seen me fail. "And what about you, Tor? Were you just going to stand there while the Regents spread lies about Sel?"

"What lie did they tell?" Tor spreads her hands wide. "Sel's job was to keep us safe. And apparently he's run off somewhere. He needs to show his face if he wants to defend his actions."

"*Defend* his *actions?*" I move toward Tor, and she takes a step back, eyeing the clenched fist at my side.

Greer moves into Tor's space, where they tower over her by at least a few inches. "Take a walk, Tor. You're causing a scene at a funeral." They shoot me an apologetic grimace. "Well . . . a second scene."

Tor glances at the others. She was willing to chastise me, but she's smart enough to know she's outnumbered. "Sar?" She turns to her girlfriend, hand open to lead her away, but Sarah wraps herself in a hug and shakes her head.

"I'll see you back at the room, babe."

Tor looks stunned for a moment before stubborn fury returns to her features, bringing with it a flash of red to her pale cheeks. "Fine." She stalks off to the driveway, her ponytail bouncing with every step.

"All right there, Sar?" William asks, and Sarah nods.

"She's just . . ." Sar inhales, watching Tor's receding figure. "We've all been on patrol the last few nights. Out late." She looks at me, sighing. "No excuse to be rude to you, though, Bree. I'm sorry about her."

I hold her gaze for a moment. "Her behavior is not your fault."

Sar lifts a shoulder in a half shrug, looks away. "But I haven't stepped in to stop her either, have I? So, this is on me, too."

There's an awkward, uncomfortable silence.

Pete speaks up. "If you hadn't said something, Bree, I would have, I think. They sprung this on us. All of us." He sniffs, looking back over his shoulder and lowering his voice. "Never expected that the first time the Regents showed up, they'd take Sel's title and call him a traitor."

"Well," William intervenes. "Stripping Sel of his title doesn't mean much given the current circumstances." He looks at me meaningfully.

"Why would they interrogate him like he's a criminal?" I ask. "When we know it was Rhaz and Lord Davis opening those Gates—"

"Kingsmages *are* guardians of the chapter," says William. "Which means he's responsible for knowing how and why they died. I'm sure the investigation is just protocol."

"That has to be it," Greer says. They step closer, wrapping an arm around my shoulder. "Just part of the process, right?"

"Then why'd he run?" Pete asks, voicing the unspoken.

William shakes his head, his gaze on the ground. "I don't know."

"Bad time to skip town," Greer mumbles.

"I'm sure he has his reasons," William replies, but his voice doesn't sound very sure at all.

I groan as guilt swirls around in my chest. The way Sel and I left things last night . . . it wasn't good.

And now he's who-knows-where, running from custody. The Mageguard are formidable. What if they catch him? Lock him up, even . . . there are Merlin prisons. . . . I want nothing more than to get out there and find Nick, but I've never once imagined doing it without Sel. Is this what kings do? Make other peoples' lives harder with their own bad decisions?

I close my eyes and take a deep breath. When I open them, my friends are speaking to one another in low voices, but occasionally I see a glance in my direction that holds a faint shade of disappointment. Those glances turn my guilt to shame. Felicity is the only Legendborn who isn't looking at me at all. She stands awkwardly off to the side of our group with red-rimmed eyes trained on Russ's family. Her hands keep clenching and unclenching at her sides.

I know that look, that stance. As I watch Felicity standing there alone, struggling, the guilt and shame drain from my body. I remember what Alice did for me when my whole world had shattered overnight, when grief had obliterated me and I had no words to describe it. I remember needing someone, *anyone*, to acknowledge my broken pieces without trying to put me back together. Maybe I don't know what kings do, but I can still be a friend.

I step away from Greer and approach Felicity quietly. "Hey."

She jumps when I reach her elbow. "Hey, Bree."

I stare at her for a moment, making space for her grief, and mine. Let it seep into that opening, settle, then surface in words. After a few seconds, I say, "There's nothing anyone can say that will make things better."

"No, there isn't," she says. She smiles, but it doesn't reach her eyes, because they're already full of the other emotions I recognize. Anger. Resentment. And a wall, drawing itself up between us.

Once you get tired of folks offering sympathy that doesn't fit your pain, it's easier to draw the bridge up than it is to keep it open. Easier to stop the attempts to connect than it is to keep watching them fail.

"You . . . ," I begin. She looks up at me, her attention sharpened into something to cut. Something to maim. I recognize that urge, too. "You must be very, very angry."

Her eyes widen in surprise. Then she lets a bit of that sharpness slide back into her gaze, and into her voice. "You have no idea."

I could respond that I do, I do have an idea. But grief isn't a competition. It's not an identical pain that we all meet one day when death finds us. It's a monster, personalized by our love and memories to devour us *just so*. Grief is suffering, tailored.

I resist the impulse to run from her, but it is strong. I see the black hole, the dark place I've been. The event horizon I need to avoid, because it might pull me right back in without warning.

So I offer her the most I can. "I hope the pain lets up a little soon. Gives you a . . . a break."

She huffs a little. A hollow sound, edged with humor. "Yeah," she whispers, and turns away. "Me too."

Lord Davis and Rhaz may not have been working together, but they both tore this chapter apart in more ways than one.

"I better go get ready to patrol," Sarah says, stepping backward.

Pete looks at Greer and a silent dialogue passes between them. Bonded Scions and their Squires, and their secret looks. Some understanding met, Greer looks up and says, "We're off as well." They pull me into a quick, strong hug, and whisper into my ear, "If we see him, we'll bring him to you, not them."

Warm appreciation fills my chest. If Sel is on the run from the Mageguard, I doubt he'd show his face on the regular Legendborn routes, but if he needs help, they'll be there. "Thanks."

They stand back and squeeze my hand. "Finish the Rite and come find us?"

"Absolutely," I say firmly. I glance at the Regents still in the crowd, more eager than ever for the Rite of Kings to transfer power to me, to wear the crown for real. "Time to do this our way."

"Damn straight," Pete whispers. "Time for King Bree."

As the others walk away, Felicity looks back over her shoulder at me and gives a quick nod before joining them. "You got this, Bree."

"Thanks, y'all."

"We need to talk." William's voice is just over my shoulder, his footsteps soft in the grass behind me.

"William, I don't—"

"That wasn't a question."

William is rarely this demanding. He raises a brow.

"Fine," I mutter. "Let's talk."

9

WHEN I REACH my assigned room at the compound, William slips in behind me and shuts the door. Without a word, he heads right to the electric kettle on the sitting room table and moves to the en suite bathroom to fill it up.

My Page robes are stifling in more ways than one. I yank them over my head and throw them in the corner. It's cooler in my T-shirt, but blood still pounds in my veins. I don't want to sit. I want to race out of here and demand an audience with the Regents.

"Do you think Lark will take me to meet Erebus?" I ask, heading toward the closet to change clothes. "I'll do the Rite early if I have to, whatever it takes. I can't let them do this to Sel—"

"No, what you *cannot* do is what you *just* did," William counters evenly.

That stings. "But—"

"You *cannot* explode in front of your future subjects, Bree." He walks back into the room with the full kettle. "You've just shown an entire crowd of Order members—Pages, Legendborn, Vassals, Lieges, Merlins, Seneschals, *and* Regents—that you're hotheaded, impulsive, and lack protocol and decorum. An outburst that nearly rivaled one of Selwyn's."

I swallow around the truth of it. And the truth that not all of that outburst was mine. Or at least, I don't think it was. I don't feel Arthur anymore, don't hear him in my head. Does that mean he's gone? Or that a bleed-through could happen again? I wish I knew the answer.

I also wish I thought William was wrong to tell me what to do, how to be, but part of me thinks he could be right.

"So," I ask William slowly, "you came here to berate me?"

He shakes his head, smiles gently. "I'm not berating you. I'm telling you that you can't explode in public—and in front of the other Legendborn, who are looking to you to lead—but you *can* explode in private. Here."

I blink, caught off guard by the invitation. "What . . ."

"Go on." He gestures wide with one hand. "Let it out."

I try to find the words for everything that just happened. What's there left to say, even?

"You have a long day ahead of you still. . . . So now is the time."

Finally, I shout. "This is *bullshit*!"

"Good." William nods. "Agreed. What else?"

I start to pace, and I let myself just be *Bree*—and angry. "We agreed not to advertise Nick's absence, we agreed to say that the Davises went on leave, but then the Regents created *a whole lie* about Nick and his father being 'sequestered' for their safety! And now they're out there spreading lies about Sel. When they said they believed us that Lord Davis opened those Gates. It feels like a damn cover-up!"

"I agree."

That stops me in my tracks. "You do? You didn't say that with the others."

Instead of answering, William makes a questioning sound—so mild and curious that it confuses me at first. Then my eyes drop to his hands, where he's holding open a box of tea, extended in my direction.

I reject his silent offer with a wave and start pacing again.

William clears his throat. "I insist, Crown Scion."

I pause and glare at him. "I know what you're doing. You're letting me rant, then calming me down."

"And is it working?"

"No."

"Chamomile it is." He pulls two mugs out from the shelf beneath the end table with a sigh. "I didn't say anything outside because I didn't want to flame panic. Yours, mine, or our friends'. *You* are our best chance out of this mess. You were raised outside of the Order. You see things about our world that we can't. You can't go into the Rite of Kings without a clear head. We need to prepare, think it through."

I groan. The ritual. "I'll have to face the Regents at the Rite, but I can't act like everything is normal when they've just dragged Sel's name through the mud. When they're chasing him down like a criminal. Why would they show up and lie to everyone?"

William lifts a shoulder. "My guess? Control. But over what exactly? The war?"

I frown. "They can't control Camlann or stop it without us. Without me."

"No, they can't, but they can control the war's narrative." He plugs in the electric kettle on the coffee table and sits in one of the two nearby chairs while it heats. "Whispers that we are approaching Camlann have been circling for months. We may appear as one hierarchy, but the Order is made up of two factions—and the Regents must walk a fine line between them, as will you. Most are Round Table traditionalists. The thirteen Legendborn bloodline families that produce Scions—and the families of chosen Squires and the pledged Vassals that have served the Lines for generations. They expect their warrior children be treated with honor. They are waiting for a king. But the world is changed. The Order membership had to expand to maintain all of its access and resources. Now, there are a growing number of modernists pledging to the Order. Vassals who don't have decades of loyalty to a Legendborn family. They don't care about the Order's origins, only its money and reach." He taps his mug as he thinks. "But where does that leave the Regents *now*, I wonder?"

I stiffen, remembering Nick's father's indignation and ire over this very issue. What Lord Davis had said to me, sneering, while he'd held me captive and threatened me if I didn't leave the Order. "That's the reason Lord Davis wanted to start Camlann. To remind those modern members of Legendborn power and the mission. To them, the Legendborn are probably more symbolic than anything, just like Arthur was to me, before. A bunch of stories. Especially with the last Camlann so long ago and so many demon attacks stifled before they truly begin. They don't see the carnage because the chapters and Merlins do too good a job keeping it at bay."

William sucks in a breath. "And I imagine that the modern faction of quasi-believers would not be pleased if they found out a traditionalist like Lord Davis started a *war* under the Regents' noses. With enough momentum, they could challenge the Regents' grip on the organization. The Regents can't afford to lose one side's support or the other side's loyalty. The Order needs both to maintain its global status."

I remember the certainty of Aldrich's pivot, the way he'd been ready to deploy the new lie about Nick and his father. "Aldrich came here on a publicity mission," I murmur. "He'd want to use the public funeral and the grief and anger of its attendees to quell *both* factions with the same misinformation. Honor the Legendborn but cover up why they died."

William nods, eyes darting back and forth as he processes. "Which means Sel is their distraction. Directing the attention to this *investigation* story helps wrap the cave 'tragedy' up in a tidy bow by linking the entire situation to the actions of a single, volatile Merlin, who collaborated with a single, murderous goruchel. A contained incident rather than the first salvo of war."

I am stunned at the brutal logic of it all. And the high costs of their lies.

"They don't want to control the war," I whisper, "they want to bury it."

"Indeed. At least for now," William replies. It is well past noon, and yet I almost see the flicker of green in his irises. "It's not just about the factions. We should have at the very least expected that they would delay the announcement that Camlann has come as long as they can, in any way that they can, until the Table is ready."

I plop into the chair across from him, thinking the same exact thing. All of that *waiting* while they were *planning*. If nothing else, I feel an even stronger urge to control my powers now, and to gather the Table. Doing so means the Regents can end their smoke and mirrors.

The kettle whistles. William begins to pour our tea.

He eyes me carefully. "We still don't know if there are goruchel mimics in our midst. If an investigation into Sel's actions also takes attention away from you, I'm sure even *he* would say that it is a misdirection that is worthwhile."

I drop my head in my hands. "Aren't you worried for him?"

"I don't need to be. Selwyn is smart, strong, and more than capable of taking care of himself. If he doesn't want to be found, the Mageguard will not find him. And before you ask about the absence from his Oaths, he's been checking in with me regularly. Carrying out his Oath of Service to the Legendborn has kept him stable and so has, I believe, acting as surrogate Kingsmage to you."

"That's good," I breathe.

"Your life is in danger every minute, even when you're surrounded by a dozen Mageguard. Right now, we all need to keep level heads and play the game."

I shake my head. "Chess, not checkers."

"Chess, not checkers." William clucks. "Head up now, drink your tea."

I do as I'm told. We sit for a moment, and as the chamomile works its magic, a hot flush of humiliation washes over me. Anyone who saw me shout at the Regents could be thinking anything about me right now, and some of them won't care to hear about Arthur and uncontrollable ancestral bleed-throughs. I probably confirmed the worst assumptions of any racists in the crowd, too, like Theresa who already treats me like I'm unkempt and out of place. I can't care about them, not really, and don't. But I don't want this job to become harder either.

How much damage will I have to manage from things that aren't my fault?

I chance a question to William. "I made a fool of myself out there, didn't I?"

"Little bit." William takes a tiny sip of his tea, eyes twinkling. "Don't worry, when you ascend the throne, you can order everyone to forget it happened."

I snort. "Isn't that what Merlins and mesmers are for?"

William rolls his eyes. "Knew you'd be a despot." He studies me for a moment, humor fading, then sets his tea down. "Speaking of, there's one other thing."

I raise a brow. "Yes?"

"You broke Lark's hand, Bree."

I grimace. "I didn't *mean* to—"

"I saw what happened. You didn't mean to harm him," William says evenly, "but you also didn't care if you did."

I flush under his scrutiny and don't bother denying it. Of course William would notice Lark's injury and take me to task for my carelessness. "I hadn't even felt like *me*" is what I want to say. But I don't think it would make the situation any better or excuse things. I may be a Medium, and Arthur and his strength may be a part of me, may be leaking into my life, but it's *my* body doing the damage.

"It appeared to be a small break, and Merlins heal fast." He stands to take his empty mug to the sink. "But Lark was only doing his job. You'll need to apologize to him."

"I will."

"As his *Crown Scion*."

"I know."

William fixes me with a stern gaze. "You of all people cannot afford to use your inheritances recklessly, especially to injure those in your service. That is not what kings do."

"I *know*." I hang my head and sigh. "God, is *this* the berating part?"

"Yep, but I'm done now." He squeezes my shoulder on the way to the door. "Room service stocked the fridges for us; get something to eat. You've got to get dressed for the Rite, and I need to get back to the Lodge. If I see Alice in the archives, I'll give her a hug for you."

"A big one," I call after him, sitting up. "Like, the biggest hug."

"Extra-large hug. Enormous." William winks and slips out the door.

As soon as William leaves, I breathe a sigh of relief. It's not that William is stressful to be around. The exact opposite, actually. He remains as calming to me now as he ever was. But the constant company is . . . draining.

I open the fridge to see what my options are, and savor these last hours of solitude.

It doesn't last. Thirty minutes later, my phone buzzes while I pick at the platter of fancy cheeses and dried fruit that I keep wishing was a burger. It's Alice. How was the funeral?

I type back quickly. Layers of awful

Oh, so a normal Legendborn event then

I huff a laugh. She's not wrong. She types back before I can answer. Ready for the Rite?

Ready as I can be? Still not sure which clothes to wear under my robes. I'm a girl, but today is the first step to becoming king. There a fit for that?

Wear what you want. You're the ONLY person on the planet who can pull Excalibur. Wearing a skirt while you do it not gonna change that

You right

Always

I roll my eyes. K, gotta go get dressed for this thing

This "thing"?! The fifteen-hundred-year-old magical ritual thing where you Oath yourself in service to the entirety of the Order, and the Regents take the Oath of Service back to you?

I suck my teeth. Yup, that thing

Been reading up on these Oaths in the Lodge archives. Oath aether soaks INTO your body. Like, the commitment becomes a part of you, physically. In your cells. FOREVER

Thank you for that super helpful reminder, Alice

You're welcome! Have a great ancient blood ceremony!

In the end, I opt for a pair of thick but stretchy leggings under riding boots. A long tunic rolled up at the sleeves and belted loose at my waist. A green hooded cape. In the mirror, I pull at my curls and am reminded of Theresa's comment.

There really is no blending in, even though that's exactly what I'm supposed to do right now.

The last items I add are my mother's charm bracelet and Nick's Pendragon coin necklace.

What I truly want is for everyone to be safe and whole. For Nick to return. For Sel to be free to come home. I want Patricia and Mariah to live without fear. I want the same for William and Alice. For Felicity, whose grief has hollowed her out. I need to make sure Lord Davis doesn't destroy any more lives, like he did to my mother's, and Sel's, and Nick's.

That's *what kings do*, I think. *They protect their people.*

I may not be able to control my powers, but I have them for a reason. I am claiming this title *for a reason*. The only way to honor my mother and her sacrifices, and the sacrifices of the women before us, is to face every challenge head-on. They ran so I would not have to—not from the Order, this responsibility, this title, or these powers.

"Don't be scared," I whisper to the girl in the mirror. "Don't be scared. Fight."

10

BY THE TIME I step outside, the sun is near setting. Most of the ceremony guests have left, and the lot is empty. Except for one single armored car waiting at the curb with the back passenger door already open. I'd first laid eyes on this vehicular monstrosity this morning outside the Lodge when Lark picked me up to take me to Pembray. He'd called it the "Beast."

I'd asked him why the hell the car had a name and why I couldn't just ride with the other Legendborn. He said Beasts I through IV are named after the armored cars the president rides in to protect him during transport from place to place. Except *these* cars are designed specifically to transport valuable Order members like me and the Regents: each Beast weighs seven tons, is equipped with silver weapons strapped to the inside of the doors and beneath the seats, has silver seams embedded in the panels to help Merlins call on aether if necessary, and boasts seven-inch-thick doors with quadruple-layered windows. Frankly, it looks like it could withstand a small missile blast.

When I reach the passenger side door, Lark is in the driver's seat, facing straight ahead. His jacket is gone and his dress shirt sleeves are rolled up, displaying more of his tattoos. Right away I note that his right hand is bandaged.

I slip inside the back passenger side, close the heavy-ass door, and release a slow breath as I settle into the seat. I catch Lark's gaze in the rearview mirror. "I'm sorry I broke your hand. I didn't mean to, but I still did it and that's not okay."

He cracks a small grin in return. "I know ye didn't mean to, lass. I've had worse breaks, believe me. It's half-healed now, but I appreciate and accept the apology." His face sobers a bit. "I owe ye an apology, as well."

My mouth twists. "Because you knew about Sel and didn't tell me."

He nods slowly. "Aye."

Frustration boils within me. "Why?"

Lark sighs. "Because Kane asked me not to."

"What?" I sit up straight, thoughts churning.

Lark shrugs. "I'll hand it to him. Kane is . . . astute. He guessed something was up. Caught me before I left the Lodge last night. I think he was worried about what ye would do before the Regents arrived if ye kent Erebus and Cestra were coming for him."

I slump back in the seat. "And then he ran."

Lark nods. "Then he ran."

"And Erebus is hunting him?"

"Aye." He smiles slightly and turns the ignition. "But Kane's too good and too smart to leave a trail."

He pulls the car around and begins the drive back to the Lodge. When he turns the wheel, I notice that his left forearm bears the familiar mark of the Legendborn, but with the additional detail of black and gray mage flames pouring from the center of the four-pointed star. I've seen the same tattoo on Selwyn's left forearm, but thought nothing of it. It never occurred to me that there might be a tattoo shared by all Merlins. A sigil of their own.

We ride in silence until Lark speaks again. "Ye nervous about tonight?"

"No," I lie. "I just want it to be over."

"I have a question." Lark glances at me.

"Okay."

"Do ye truly think Lord Davis abducted his own son? Risked Onceborns by opening Gates *on purpose?*"

"I don't think, I *know.*" I tap my fingers impatiently on the seat's black leather. "He gloated about it to my face."

"Davis is a well-respected man," he begins. "A lifetime of service to the Order. Lots of allies, inside and out . . ."

I groan, irritated. "You don't believe people can lie? Hide their true nature?"

"Oh, I believe that." Lark chuckles. "Trust, but verify, princess."

I gnaw on my thumb. "Not your princess."

"King then."

"Not that either."

A crooked smile flashes across his face. "If that's the case, gonna be awkward being yer Kingsmage."

I lift a shoulder. "Maybe I don't need a Kingsmage."

Lark raises a brow in the mirror, but instead of pushing the topic, he changes it. "Got something for ye." My eyebrows raise. "Look in the center armrest."

I frown. I didn't think we were at the "gift" stage of friendship. Especially not after all the bone-breaking and lies. I dig into the center armrest and pull out a large leather pouch with drawstrings on the end. I feel something stiff but pliant in the middle. "What's this?"

He laughs. "That's the thing about gifts. Ye find out what they are when ye open them."

I bite back a retort and pull on the strings, tipping the bag over and into my lap. A pair of fingerless gauntlets spills out. The smell of fresh leather fills the cabin. There are straps up and down to adjust the circumference, and thick braces around the wrists. "Gauntlets?"

Lark glances up in the mirror. "A long line of Merlins in my family. Ma da makes leather armor and things, pieces we can wear under our clothes if we need to go hunting in public."

I gape at the gauntlets, taken aback at the craftmanship, the thoughtfulness. . . . "I didn't even know Merlins wore armor."

Lark flushes. "Some of us do, just so we don't have to cast it midbattle. I heard that you'd only started with the sword a bit ago. . . ."

Something in his voice gives me pause. No one knows I can't call aether armor except the other Legendborn and Sel and Alice. "Um . . ."

Lark's voice is suspiciously mild and neutral. "Ye haven't exactly had time to train. These are just temporary, until ye get the hang of casting and forging aether on yer own. Thought it might be a nice sort of . . . er, Rite gift." He knows, somehow. But he's not rubbing it in my face.

Lark might be decent after all. Doesn't mean I want him bonded to me for life.

I stroke my fingers across the leather, smooth without a single mark or dent. I wonder if they'll be strong enough to protect my arms the next time I call aether. If a Merlin made them, maybe they are. "I didn't know the Rite was something to celebrate with gifts."

"The old ways get forgotten, I guess. Anyway, if ye don't like 'em——"

"I do!" I clutch them to my chest. "I like them."

He chuckles. "I'll tell ma da."

I slip the gauntlets on one at a time and feel the waiting quality of the leather. Like they belong to me. I pull the gauntlet straps tight, and that feeling is confirmed. They're ready to be mine, and no one else's.

We ride a few minutes more into the darkness, turning farther away from residential lights onto a dim country road. Some classic rock song is on the radio, too quiet for me to identify it. Leaves kick up as we pass, swirling in the chill air outside. I use the time to mentally rehearse the Rite and my speeches.

Abruptly, Lark reaches toward the knob on the dash to turn the radio even lower, and the rhythmic electric guitar is replaced . . . by an otherworldly, low-pitched yowl.

"What the——"

A deep *thwunk* as the car hits something. Lark curses.

Like an animal shrugging, the front wheels of the vehicle lift with a grinding metal sound.

I scream, bracing as everything in the center cupholders falls down to the back seats. Cold coffee splatters across my face, a plastic cup hits my chest. I'm jabbed in the shoulder by a stray pen. Spare change rains down from overhead; my phone is lost behind me. I end up pressed against the seat looking at the sky through the front windshield.

"Fuck!" Above me, Lark's moving faster than I can see—Merlin-fast. Unbuckling himself, turning to me from the front seat. Pulling on my seatbelt, ripping it open. His hand grabs for my waist.

A crack streaks across the thick, bulletproof front windshield above us. It shatters—a shower of glass—and Lark is yanked skyward, away from me.

Something has him by the legs.

He roars, teeth bared. Punches his fingers deep into the leather cushions on either side of my hips, down to the metal bars that bolt the seats to the floor. Holds tight, stopping himself. He growls with the effort, eyes pinned to mine, body nearly vertical, feet to the sky. "Stay—in the—"

"What?!" I screech, heart pounding.

Lark nods once, firm—and lets go.

As he flies upward, he smacks a button beside the steering wheel. The opaque privacy shield between the front seat and the back snaps shut with a whoosh. The back windshield and left and right windows follow. The hissing sound of suction. I'm sealed in. Trapped in the murky dark of an armored cabin that is barely illuminated by dim emergency lights along the floor and ceiling.

Then, whatever is holding the car lets go—and the car tips forward faster than it tilted back.

Thousands of pounds of metal and steel hit the road with a bone-shattering boom. We're back on four wheels.

I shove my shoulder against the rear driver's side door. "Lark!" I slap at the door controls, trying to get *something* to open. The privacy shield, the windows—anything. They don't budge.

"Lark!" I kick at the front seats, but they're immovable. Outside there's a muffled shout, a growl—*BAM!*

The car tilts again. I go tumbling. Sideways and to the right this time. Like someone kicked the left side so hard that the Beast floats *up* on its right.

The car hovers on two wheels. Metal creaks.

For half a second, the passenger side door is nearly beneath my feet.

Then, gravity. We fall back.

The car lands on all fours again with another deep *whomp*. I hit the floor shoulder-first. Pain shoots across my chest.

BAM! Another kick to the rear driver's side door dents the metal a few inches from my head.

This time the Beast flips up and all the way over.

I'm tossed like a doll. The hood meets the ground, my back hits the ceiling.

The car lies still, but my breath is gone—knocked from my lungs.

Can't breathe.

Can't *breathe.*

Can't—

I writhe in pain, ears ringing, tears burning my eyes, *willing* my lungs to *work*—

Abruptly, air punches back into my chest, leaving me gasping, staring at the car seats overhead.

From outside, a muffled roar rips through the air.

I can't tell if it's from Lark or the demons he's fighting. Because it must be demons. Nothing else could lift this car like that, nothing—

A battle cry—Lark.

I twist myself around until my feet rest against the door closest to Lark's screams. Pull my legs back as far as I can. Kick the door.

White-hot pain rockets up my shins to my knees. I scream, grit my teeth—and kick again. This time the metal bends beneath Arthur's strength.

Again.

Again!

Finally, the center of the door bows outward, pulling away on one side. The outside world comes rushing in through that two-inch-wide opening—sounds of metal on stone. An unholy scream. Lark's aether signature, bright and burning in my nose. And another smell . . . sour and rotting.

I kick again, the opening grows. Twice, the door hangs off on one side. One more kick pops it free. I swivel around in the tight space, scrabbling for the sword strapped beneath the seat as I go. Wrench it loose. Crawl out onto the road with the sword held up, gulping fresh air.

Then I see what Lark has been up against.

An enormous demon made of boulders and green flame brings its joined fists down onto an aether dome. A mini version of the one at the funeral, but this one is just big enough for him.

Lark is there in the center, one hand held up, casting the shining blue-white shield around him. The demon brings its fist down again and again. Lark winces, but the shield holds.

His bandaged right hand—the one I broke—is tucked tight against his chest. His teeth are bared in fury and pain. He's been fighting one-handed.

Oh God.

Two foxes flank him. They suck the shield away, forcing Lark to make it smaller and smaller while the demon's anvil-like fists rain down, relentless.

"No!" I rush forward—but it's too late.

The shield cracks, breaks, dissipates.

Lark rolls away—but not fast enough.

The demon's fist sweeps down and up, backhanding the Merlin into the air. He lands on the asphalt forty feet away, body crumpling before it goes still.

Then the demon turns toward me.

Its eyes are two deep pits leaking smoke and emerald fire. It is shaped like a human, so a greater demon, an uchel, but one I've never seen before. This is a monster made of obsidian, the angriest and hardest parts of the earth, with glowing green joints. Its legs are four-feet wide and its jointed arms end in blunt fingers.

A wide slash of a smile tilts up in recognition.

"Awakened Pendragon," it says, a note of satisfaction in its deep rumble.

I'm strong now. As strong as a Merlin at least, thanks to Arthur's blood in my veins. But I need armor. I frantically pull at the air with my free palm, calling the aether around me. Drawing it in like I was taught. It bursts into bright flames, merges into a layer over my gauntlets, then flickers out. I pull again, focus through fear, but this time the aether simply flares into nothing. Not even a spark.

No, no, no . . . !

"Contain her," the demon orders, and the foxes chitter eagerly in response.

They stalk toward me on tall, scaly legs. Steam rises from their backs in the cool night air. The demon paces toward me, too, each step shaking the road, each step one last chance to decide what I'm going to do—run, or fight.

My eyes flick to Lark, body prone on the pavement. My fault.

Fight.

My fists clench, and the red flames of root erupt over my knuckles, roaring up the silver sword in my hand from hilt to tip.

A black blur flashes across my vision, launching itself up onto the uchel's stony chest. A crystalline blade, called and forged near instantaneously, thrusts through its eye. The uchel rears back, smacking at its attacker, but they're already gone. They're around the back of its head now—a shining aether blade plunges into its other eye. Both of the monster's hands reach up, but its fists find only air—their opponent is gone.

Selwyn Kane lands on the road in between me and the demon, his back to me, both hands spread wide.

The demon falls to the road, knees first. The asphalt vibrates beneath our feet.

Sel's already forging another weapon. Between his palms, an enormous shining spear forms, hard as a diamond. The foxes gallop toward us, screeching in the night.

His head turns slightly over his shoulder, his face in profile, eyes still on the roaring monster stumbling on the road.

"Run."

11

I DON'T RUN.

Instead I move to his side, and let the flames flare up to my elbows. We'll fight them back-to-back. Together.

Sel groans. "Can you listen to directions? For *once* in your life?"

Before I can snap at him, the foxes split, moving to box us in. Sel pivots. His spine presses tight to mine, and, despite his insult, reassurance and relief rocket through my veins. He's here, and he's safe.

He starts to reinforce his spear. The fox in front of me tenses, dips low, braces for a jump—and freezes. Its head whips down the street. It growls and begins a slow, backward retreat.

When I twist around, Sel's head is facing the same direction, looking back the way I came. His eyes widen. "Hide your flames," he hisses low in a voice I don't recognize.

"Why?"

"There will be too many questions before the Rite."

I hesitate.

He glares at me, incredulous. "Once! Just *once*—"

The sound of engines approaching, wheels over asphalt.

I turn, hand shielding my eyes against the white shining beams of half a dozen town cars. The doors of the first vehicle open before it has even come to a full stop. Dark figures blur out and into action, breaking around us toward the demons in the street.

Oh. I clench my fists to douse the root between my fingers. The red flames dissolve into mist around the sword until it's a plain silver blade in my hand once again.

The Mageguard are coordinated and deadly. The foxes are gone between one blink and the next. They make quick work of the demon as well, slicing it into pieces. Just as the uchel's head drops to the road with an earth-shaking thud, three cars pull up slowly behind me.

Even more Merlins. A shadow materializes at my shoulder, and inserts itself between me and Sel.

"Here to try again, Kane?" It's Max Zhao, the Merlin who wouldn't let me through the funeral barrier. His hand already grips Sel's upper arm.

Sel snarls but does not struggle. "Took you long enough."

"What was the plan?" Max scoffs. "Come out from hiding to attack the Crown Scion?"

"No!" I shout, confused but protective of Sel nonetheless. "He saved me. Saved both of us. Lark would have been dead if he hadn't shown up!"

Max follows my pointed finger to the far side of the road, where a barely conscious Lark is being helped to his feet by a member of the Guard. Still holding Sel, Max shifts his gaze to the right to examine the Beast upside down, its heavy metal door dented and tossed aside. "Or he arrived just in time to kill you while you were unprotected."

"Unprotected?" Sel rolls his eyes. "Come on, Maxwell. We both know Larkin, even unconscious, is far more protection than you could ever be."

Max growls, and it's too vicious, a precursor to violence. I move without thinking.

"Stop!" I lunge toward Max, palm open—and notice too late that my fingertips are still lit with root. As soon as my hand touches his arm, it singes through his coat.

The Merlin releases Sel with a roar and jumps back, teeth bared and eyes wide. He stares at my hand. "Holy *shit.*"

Sel squeezes his eyes shut, groans.

Max's eyes narrow. "What the hell—"

"So it is true. The reports about your red aether, generated from within." Erebus's voice flows over my shoulders, a rich blanket of deadly promise. He reaches my side with a long, silvery aether staff in his left hand, his right hand tucked in his pocket. His dark eyes are all for the root flickering at my fingers. "I have read the Legendborn's debrief reports of course, but it is . . . remarkable to see it in person."

I glance to Sel, who shrugs. *Too late to hide it now.* And like Erebus said, he knows about my root already. "Yes," I say slowly.

Erebus tilts his head, watching as I close my fist until the flames wink out. "Fascinating."

I swallow hard. The last powerful Merlin to say that I was "fascinating" was Isaac, and that didn't end well. But unlike Isaac's predatory scrutiny, Erebus's interest seems scientific. He turns back to study Max, who is still scowling at the pink skin exposed beneath the burned fabric of his jacket.

Under Erebus's gaze, Max straightens, glances at me warily, and speeds away toward the demon corpse in the street. The guards help Lark into the back seat of one of the town cars. It pulls away as soon as the door closes, hopefully taking him to get examined. If not by William, someone else. The sound of his body hitting the pavement echoes in my ears. Erebus's eyes slide to Sel.

"We've been looking for you, Selwyn. I assumed you'd be in the wind by now, but then you appear at the exact moment the Crown Scion is attacked. Did you orchestrate this?"

Sel groans. "You know I didn't. But someone did. Someone knew she would be in transit on this road. A goruchel—"

"Goruchels are not so easy to detect, as I'm sure you know. We have been methodically combing the other chapters for goruchel mimics since the appearance of Rhaz. A task that must be done without alerting a potential demon assassin within our ranks," Erebus replies.

Sel steps closer to the Seneschal, lowering his voice to a bare whisper. "Who else knew Lark was driving her tonight, Erebus?"

Erebus frowns. "I do not owe you intel—"

"Do you trust every Merlin in the Guard?" Sel asks. "Did you handpick each member yourself?"

Erebus's gaze flickers. Doubt, there and gone. It was fast, but I saw it. Sel saw it.

When the Seneschal answers, his voice holds a thread of uncertainty. "Cestra chose several. But all are Oathed. And a goruchel cannot mimic a Merlin—"

"Can't they?" Sel challenges. "A goruchel can mimic an Oath."

My eyes immediately find the Mageguard. Find Max, who has been cruel from the start, then Olsen. The others that have never spoken to me, but whose eyes always sear my skin.

"It knew who I was," I murmur, remembering the uchel's stone-and-thunder voice. "It called me 'Awakened Pendragon.'"

"Someone who knows Bree's identity was behind this." Sel's voice is a dangerous combination of urgency and defiance. "*And* the foxes. If not the Guard, what of the Council? Do you trust the Regents? The other Seneschals?"

Erebus's lip curls. "Be very, *very* cautious, Selwyn . . . these accusations will only make matters worse. Even I won't be able to protect you from the consequences—"

"The Morgaines, then!" Sel hisses.

"Enough!" Erebus drops a heavy hand on my shoulder. "Olsen! Ramirez!"

Two Mageguard appear at Sel's sides, one taking his elbow in a tight fist, the other holding a large black box.

"Let him go!" I lunge forward, but Erebus holds me still.

Sel stares straight ahead, jaw tight in what I can only interpret as resignation. He's not fighting this, and that sends fear rippling through me. Sel doesn't just give up. Sel doesn't just . . . *stop*. For the first time, I get a good look at him. Deep shadows have settled in under his eyes, the skin there thin.

The Merlin who had the box, Ramirez, approaches Erebus with two black iron handcuffs, heavy and wide. Erebus takes them from him. "What are those for?" I ask. "What are you doing—"

Sel lets the Seneschal lift his left hand, snapping the first iron cuff around his wrist. The loud click finishes with a silent pop in my ears, the pressure changed. Sel winces, like he'd just been dealt some invisible blow.

"Selwyn Emrys Kane," Erebus says, "you are now under arrest for six counts of negligence to the Southern chapter, one count each of gross negligence to your charge and to the crown, and one count of attempted murder of the Scion of Arthur. You will be detained until the date of your trial is determined."

"No!" I step in front of Erebus. "Aldrich said you and Cestra wanted to interrogate him about the Gates. What are these other charges?"

"The *Gates?*" Amusement and disdain color Sel's voice equally. He doesn't even address the other accusations. "Is *that* the story you're telling the Order? That I opened the Gates instead of Lord Davis?" He releases a humorless laugh, shaking his head. "Of course it is. Now you can use me as a scapegoat, and you'll not only bury the war, but you'll bury the betrayal of the Order's most visible and loyal servant. Lies and—"

"And misdirection, yes." Erebus dips his chin in acknowledgment.

Bury the war. I'd seen that one. *Misdirection.* William's words. But we were only half-right. Sel saw the rest right away; the Regents don't just intend to bury the war, they want to bury the betrayal, too. And arresting Sel for these other unannounced crimes? Not just a distraction.

They mean to put him away for real.

My still bruised, aching chest tightens painfully, like the air has been knocked out of me all over again. This can't be happening.

"What will the Council say to the Legendborn families and Scions and Squires about *why* I opened those Gates, I wonder?" Sel sneers. "Let me guess: 'The too powerful Kingsmage sadly succumbed to his blood. Just like his mother.'"

Erebus lifts a brow. "And how would you know about what happened to your mother?"

Sel laughs. "Secrets don't stay buried forever, old man."

"Some do. And some should."

"I don't accept this!" I spit.

Erebus turns to me, sighing low. "I apologize, Crown Scion, but if the High Council reveals that Lord Davis betrayed the Order *and* that Morgaines and demons may have aligned to send a goruchel assassin to kill both Legendborn children and the Scion of Arthur, there will be panic and unrest. We cannot afford widespread destabilization during a time of war and during your transition to king. The public, even that of the Order, wants their bread and circuses, and this fabricated reason for Selwyn's arrest gives them that while we take care of the reality of things like your Rite, like the search for Nicholas . . . discreetly."

"Fine, play your games. But why are you still arresting Sel?"

"Because we *must* arrest him. On the very real charges for a case we have been building for weeks, based on all that Selwyn and you and the other members of the chapter have told us about his actions leading up to the events of the cave. He must be held accountable."

I gape. "Negligence? Attempted murder? Are you kidding me? None of that is true. . . ."

Erebus's brows furrow as he produces his tablet from his breast pocket. After a few moments of swiping, he reads, "'At first, Sel thought I was a goruchel. He attacked me in the graveyard with his hounds, nearly killed me. . . .'"

Those are my words. What I reported to Theresa in the days following Nick's disappearance. "No, that's—that's not how it was."

Erebus puts his tablet away. "Your words tell a story, Crown Scion. Are you saying you lied to the investigators?"

"No, I'm—" I grit my teeth. "He attacked me because he thought there was a mimic among us, which ended up being true—Rhaz. And even if Sel wanted to murder me, I wasn't the Scion of Arthur then!"

As soon as the words leave my mouth, shock travels through each of the Merlins around me. Sel's gaze snaps up, brows furrowed. Ramirez and Olsen blink rapidly, amber eyes wide. Several emotions race across Erebus's face, one after the other: confusion, displeasure, annoyance, then pity.

It's the pity that creeps into my throat, makes it tight.

"Crown Scion Matthews"—Erebus's voice turns oddly gentle—"you have *always* been the Scion of Arthur. It was always you."

For a moment, I feel bare beneath their attention. Silly. Foolish in front of them, once again. I clear my throat. Try to regain my footing. "And as the Crown Scion, I order you to release Selwyn."

Erebus draws his head back, appraising. "I'm sorry, but Order law only recognizes those who have formally claimed their title before a governing body." He frowns. "You cannot stop due process."

His words echo Nick's from the day I demanded he help me infiltrate the Order. He'd spoken of process and titles and recognition then, too. When everyone thought he was the Scion of Arthur, he still had to claim his title publicly before he could sponsor me as his Page. This was one of the first lessons Nick taught me about his world: The Line is Law, but blood is not enough to conquer procedure. Even if that blood belongs to Arthur Pendragon himself.

"Crown Scion." Sel interrupts my thoughts. "My crimes—the real ones—are not for you to decide. Jury of my peers and all that."

The tightness in my throat drops to my stomach. Becomes dread, churning and dizzying. Sel . . . *believes* them. Believes that this is right.

Erebus moves to place the other cuff on Sel. "Let him go." I lunge to stop him on instinct, clasping the Seneschal's clothed arm in both hands.

The Seneschal freezes, as does every Merlin in our vicinity.

"Briana, please release me." Erebus could dislodge me easily if he wanted. Or try to, anyway. But he's hesitating, stuck between my title and his duty—and the inability to harm me dictated by his Oaths.

"*Bree!* Stay out of it," Sel says through clenched teeth. It's his low, strained voice that stops me from pulling further on Erebus.

"But—"

"Let him *go*, Briana!" Sel's command feels like a slap to my face. His eyes, a darker gold than I've ever seen, scorch my cheeks. The ends of his raven hair rise in a silent aether wind—a sign of his anger—the tips bright with magic that he's not using. Even his fingers are pulsing dimly, the way they do when he calls on aether unconsciously.

I step back, my hand dropping. Quickly, before I have time to recover, Erebus snaps the second iron cuff around Sel's right wrist. My ears pop again, painfully, at the same time that a sharp breath escapes from Sel's lungs. When the Seneschal passes a palm over both restraints, a curved symbol I don't recognize glows aether-blue on the back of each cuff, then disappears.

Sel groans through gritted teeth, and as soon as the magic is gone, his hair falls flat. The little color in his cheeks drains away. His hands are tight fists beneath the heavy iron, knuckles gone pale under pressure—and where there had been mage flames between his fingers, there is no aether in sight. Like the magic he'd called had just . . . disappeared.

"We know you can owl 'shift, Kane, so don't even try it," Ramirez growls. "These cuffs were custom designed specifically for you."

Sel's eyes remain blank. If he'd considered shapeshifting to evade the cuffs, his expression doesn't show it. I've only ever seen him transform once, and didn't realize it was possible at the time, or how rare the ability is among Merlins. They begin to lead him away.

As Sel passes, the Seneschal offers parting words. "You honor yourself by going peacefully this time, Kane. This, too, is service to the Order. It will help you, and keep everyone around you safe."

Sel nearly answers, but decides against it.

They pull Sel forward toward the cars. He passes without looking back, leaving me standing in the street.

Erebus is a looming shadow at my side. While the rest of the Mageguard are focused on the demon's destruction, his eyes are only for me. The Mageguard's aether constructs are silver-blue lightning bolts reflected in his irises.

Abruptly, the Seneschal speeds past me toward the Beast, and his focus on the broken metal door lying in the street chills me to stillness. He sweeps his coat back and kneels on the ground, long fingers trailing over the dents from my heels. Lifts the metal up, flips it over easily, like it's made of paper and not thick layers of heavy steel. Still kneeling, his eyes flick up to me, considering, then back down. He twists, finds the sword in the street, and makes a thoughtful sound. Stands. Is back at my side in an instant.

"You truly possess Arthur's strength." A statement, not a question. "You wouldn't be able to put a scratch on that door otherwise." My fingers flex at my side, and Erebus eyes them with interest. "To be appointed as Seneschal, I was first a Master Mage for decades, teaching young Merlins how to serve the Order. I've always been curious as to whether the fabled strength of the Awakened king would be a match to mine." His own hand moves, rubbing fingertip to thumb.

"Is that a threat, Seneschal?" I ask, letting every ounce of my fury wind through my words, bleed into my eyes. This man is not my ally. Probably never was.

Erebus's eyes grow wide. "No, Crown Scion. An observation."

I don't believe him. Even if I thought I could be a match for Erebus, the entire squadron of Mageguard is here now. I'd be surrounded by the most powerful Merlins in the world faster than I could blink.

"Let us continue this conversation in your alternate transportation," Erebus says, gesturing to the limo he'd arrived in. "I will escort you to the Rite of Kings myself."

I slip in the back seat with the nauseating feeling that something horrible has been happening, and I'm the last to know. Anger simmers in my chest, but I have nowhere to put it; the Seneschals only answer to the Regents and, for now, the Regents are still in charge.

The war is being covered up, at least for now. Lord Davis's betrayal is being covered up, maybe forever. Selwyn is getting publicly blamed for both, and privately treated like a criminal for mistakes and misunderstandings. And I'm just supposed to go through the Rite like everything's *normal*?

Erebus does a three-point turn to swing us back on the road toward the Lodge. I twist around to peer out the rear windshield just in time to watch four Merlins flip the Beast up and over, setting the enormous car gently down on the asphalt. Then my view is blocked by another dark limo pulling by to drive in the opposite direction. Sel's in there, held captive and restrained by God knows what magic.

Suddenly, desperately, I wish Alice was here. She's strategic and detail-oriented, just like the Regents. She'd know what questions to ask to trip up Erebus and the others, beating them in their own schemes. Or she might say that all I can do is keep pressing forward, use the power I have now while I fight for more.

"I won't let you keep him captive for things he didn't truly do," I say to Erebus. "After the Rite—"

"The Rite is our mutual commitment to each other, as Regents and the king-to-come. It is the first step toward honoring who you are and Oathing yourself to the good of the Order." Erebus's fingers tap on the steering wheel. "You would do well not to make your first act as king the release of an accused criminal. It would be better to command your forces toward more noble ends. The search for Nicholas Davis, perhaps?"

I swallow, tempted to scream at him that if I am king, I should be able to do both. I shouldn't have to choose between rescuing Nick and letting Sel be punished for crimes he didn't commit. But then there's the Mageguard, who report to Erebus and Cestra. I need their resources and their allegiance to find Nick. Would they follow me if I claimed my title only to immediately defy their Merlin laws? Would Lark stand with me after my carelessness earlier today broke his hand, especially when that injury nearly got him killed?

Fury rises in my throat. The Rite has just become twice as critical. Tonight has made it crystal clear that I can't do anything if I am not king. And if I don't have more information. *All* of the information. "Where are you taking him?"

"A Shadowhold. A place suitable for Merlins who succumb to their blood. He'll be treated with respect. His own quarters and food service until his sentencing."

"You act like he's already been found guilty."

"We have the evidence needed to convict in recorded statements. Only a Merlin on the path of succumbing to his blood would behave as Selwyn has. It is safest to keep him in the hold."

I scoff, and he looks at me sharply. "Selwyn isn't succumbing to his blood, or even on the path to it. He was clearheaded enough—and *good* enough—to rescue me tonight before the Mageguard even arrived. Someone more demon than human wouldn't help me; he'd enjoy watching my pain. This is about something else. A scapegoat, like he said."

"With respect, Crown Scion." Erebus's brow furrows. "What would you know about what it means for a Merlin to succumb to his blood when you were raised as an Unanedig? Whatever the erstwhile Kingsmage has told you has barely scratched the surface of our kind, our abilities, and our role in the Order."

"I know it means his demon blood could change him." I raise my chin. "He says he could go feral. Turn . . . evil."

"A simpler, less comprehensive explanation couldn't be expressed." Erebus laughs softly. "You think in terms of 'good' or 'evil,' but Merlin envisioned that his descendants could be both, with the Oaths as safeguards. Demons are selfish, solitary creatures. If our latent demonic natures overcome us, we lose empathy, sympathy, kindness. Humanity. Eventually, all that remains are the core hungers of demonia: the inescapable desires to create and consume human misery. Pain, chaos, anguish. Demons have no choice but to be drawn to these things, and *that* is why we are haunted by the prospect of such a descent. And why we must contain Selwyn for his own good." A pause. "It is what his mother would want."

I suck in a breath. "You knew Sel's mother?"

Erebus turns to the window and the passing darkness. "Natasia and I trained together before she was sent to live with the young Martin Davis. Like Selwyn, she was a prodigy. A wonder of a warrior."

I can't help my curiosity at the sound in his voice. The trace of pain beneath his stern brows. "You knew each other as children?" He dips his head and I make a guess. "You were close."

His eyes flick to mine, assessing before speaking further. Finally, he nods. "Natasia was my counterpart at the academy. She was on the path to become Kingsmage, and I was destined to become Seneschal of the Mageguard." His mouth twitches, the barest hint of affection. "It was Natasia who gave me the moniker 'Erebus,' from the Greek myths, as I would eventually command the Merlins who fight creatures from the darkest shadows. In turn I called her 'Nyx,' Greek goddess of the night. She moved like shadows fall, silent and swift. When she . . ." He trails off, losing the words to memory, or withdrawing from giving away too much.

I press him anyway. "You knew that she had been imprisoned in the

Shadowhold. You knew they lied to Sel when they told him she died fighting an uchel."

And you still know nothing *about what really happened to his mother,* I think, but I bite my tongue. Now is not the time to reveal that Natasia Kane has not only escaped the Shadowhold, but the danger of her blood as well. And now is *especially* not the time to share that I know these things because I broke her mesmer and saw the truth.

His face closes up tight. "Every Merlin who ascends to Seneschal is told which of our ranks has succumbed to demonia. Who, how, and why. So that we know what to watch for in our peers and we can keep the Order and its king safe."

"So that you can punish Selwyn for someone else's mistakes and make him out to be my villain, you mean."

"We are Merlins, Crown Scion. Cambions bound by Oaths that we hope will maintain our humanity for as long as possible, but in the end . . . we are, all of us, marking the days until we become your villain." He eyes me. "Do not think you know enough to judge our fates."

I don't want to hear the certainty in his voice, or the suggestion that Sel might hold that same certainty within himself. That he is on borrowed time. I swallow hard and look away. "I know that Sel is a good person, and a worthy Kingsmage."

"*Was* a worthy Kingsmage," Erebus says. "And yes, he was excellent. I should know; I hand-selected him for the title when he was a small boy and performed the Kingsmage Oath myself. But he is not serving that Oath at the moment, is he?" He nods in concession. "I will give him credit for coming to his Crown Scion's aid. Intention to serve counts for something and should slow his descent."

The care in his voice hurts, because it rings true. Erebus cared for Sel's mother, and he seems to care for Sel, too, in an almost fatherly way. Maybe even more than Sel's own absentee father. But that "care" is laced with horrifying disregard.

I take a deep breath and recite my way through the panic. Keep my friends safe, keep them from harm. No more deaths, no more damage. Get through the Rite, then get through the rest.

I wish Nick were here so I could tell him that now I understand how many emotions he had held in check every day. The loneliness, the doubt, and above all . . . the slow-building anger born from carrying the burdens of a power you don't fully possess.

We arrive at the Lodge just as the stars emerge from the dark blanket of sky overhead.

Erebus escorts me to the door alone, then walks down the steps so that he can confer with the Mageguard stationed around the perimeter. As I hover in the doorway, I feel the ripple of freshly layered protective wards, thicker and stronger than I've ever felt them before.

The Regents' motorcade arrives, three cars rolling to a crunching stop on the gravel driveway. As if choreographed, the front passenger side door of each car opens at once. Cestra emerges from the rear vehicle, still in her funeral wear, but with lower heels. Smart choice for the walk to the ogof.

Then comes Regent Gabriel and his Mage Seneschal, a tall, handsome white Merlin with dark hair, rust-colored eyes, and long fingers in a dark gray robe. Erebus is at my elbow, voice a low murmur. "Seneschal Tacitus, Master of Mesmer, born in Italy."

The one who can offer forgetting as if it were bliss. Oblivion as if it were mercy. I resist the urge to shudder, and fail. Tacitus grins—and I immediately despise him. He is cunning and charm personified. Sel's voice still rings in my ears, and I wonder if Tacitus could be the true traitor in our midst. When I glance up at Erebus, his furrowed brow tells me he is wondering the same thing.

If everyone is playing shadow games, then who can anyone trust?

Finally, Aldrich steps from his car. His Seneschal is a short, wide-framed, bronze-skinned Merlin whose fingertips glow a pure diamond-white, edged with a faint line of deep blue flames. The signature from his hands is a heavy, unsettling smell and his eyes are of the deepest orange.

"Seneschal Serren, Master of Constructs," Erebus supplies. "A powerful aethersmith from the Pacific Northwest, here in the States. The flames at his fingertips never go dark. He can change the form of his aether constructs without recasting them, and they are always unbreakable."

Erebus steps down and the six members of the Council look up to me with curious and expectant gazes. I wonder what they see. Arthur's Onceborn-raised Scion or the sixteen-year-old Black girl whom they never expected to pull the sword from its stone. Whatever they see, I need them to understand one thing: after tonight, I am their king.

"Honored Regents and Seneschals," I say, my voice clear as I recite the formal greeting. "I declare myself eligible for the Rite of Kings by way of bloodline, and invite you to bear witness to the return of our king, Arthur Pendragon, once again Awakened to lead our Table and Order to victory in the Shadowborn Holy War."

TWO OF THE Mageguard go into the tunnels to do a final sweep of the closed Gates before allowing all of the Order's leadership—current and future—to enter the underground cave. While we wait, the Council turns to me expectantly.

"Crown Scion Matthews." Aldrich appears at my shoulder with his Seneschal Tacitus close beside him. "I must apologize for the shock my pronouncement delivered at today's services. I assure you, my words were merely—"

"A strategy," I interrupt, smiling tightly. "To take public attention away from the investigation into Lord Davis, the individual who really opened the Gates. I am aware."

Aldrich's eyes widen slightly. "I'm impressed with your quick insight. With your emotional response, I assumed that you were taken aback, even pained by the ruse."

My lie is ready. "Not at all. I think, as Scion Davis's Squire-select, I needed to have a very public response of disbelief that my Scion's own Kingsmage could betray the Order."

"She is clever," Tacitus says, nodding approvingly. "There are many ways to feed a lie, but they are most sustained by elements of truth. Brava, Crown Scion." It is the first time I have heard him speak. His Italian accent is there, but so light I might not hear it if I hadn't known his background from Erebus. I wonder how long he has lived in the States.

I keep my face as even as possible. "I see the benefit of skilled subterfuge, especially as we plan our rescue of Nick."

"And when we bring Martin Davis to justice," Cestra adds. Her voice has lost the formality of the morning ceremony, her mask lowered. "He must pay for his crimes, privately of course, along with Isaac Sorenson."

Gabriel shakes his head. "It is still hard to believe that Martin would do such things."

Cestra's gaze darkens. "The Mageguard found a secured fridge in Davis's home full of cambion blood and vials belonging to both Selwyn and Natasia Kane that were presumably used to open the Gates. We have the evidence we need." The tone in her voice almost gives me hope, that at least in this way the Regents are pursuing truth and justice. Even if it's not out in the open yet.

"But his Oaths?" Gabriel says, spreading his arms wide. "That degree of betrayal for one so bound is unheard of."

"Not true," Cestra says with an elegant shrug. "We have heard of betrayal before. But the traitors' Oaths took their lives before we could get to them."

Aldrich clears his throat, cutting some tension in the air. He turns to me. "I hope you aren't insulted by our wish to perform the Rite before we discuss other matters and begin the transition."

I shrug. "I get it. The Rite is about mutual trust. And the first time the Scion of Arthur takes up the blade, it's usually a much more public affair. The Scion is Called, and then everyone gathers to watch him pull Excalibur to be fully Awakened."

I say it without emotion, like this fact isn't burned into my brain, said first in the voice of a demon. *"It'd be easy if all I needed was for Arthur to Call Nick like the others do, but that arrogant prick of a king won't fully Awaken his Scion until they take the blade."* I remember Rhaz chasing me in the dark not a few hundred feet from where I stand, and shudder.

"That is what the archives say," Aldrich agrees. "But we are the first Regents in two hundred years to even perform this ritual. Something you hope to never do, but must be prepared for. Not unlike war itself."

Olsen returns and waves us into the tunnel. It's time.

In the center of the cave, as before, is a small lake with a rock island in the middle and a raised stone extending upward. Excalibur, shining and sharp, seems to wink at me as I enter. My fingertips buzz with a desire to touch it.

Five Mageguard stand posted around the cave perimeter. The six members of the Council take their position in a line at the edge of the moat, alternating Regent and Seneschal. Aldrich gestures to the island with his hand. "We are ready when you are, Crown Scion."

I lift my chin and step forward, dropping the green cape from my shoulders until it pools behind me on the sandy bank. Underneath, the Pendragon coin shines bright over my sternum. I bend down, slipping the shoes from my feet, and step into the cold, clear water, letting it seep into my skin and bones, chilling me to the knee. I wade over to the island and circle it until I find the first foothold, taking one step at a time until I reach the platform beside the stone.

I haven't seen Excalibur since that night, only imagined it when I attempt to cast its likeness. But I think it remembers me; the crimson diamond in the center of the pommel absorbs light rather than reflects it, a reminder of what my touch—my Bloodcraft—did to the ancient blade to make it my own. As I stare into it, the diamond pulses like a heart.

"Crown Scion?" Erebus calls from below. My eyes flit to him and the others, standing with arms clasped beneath their robes, a mixture of curiosity and solemnity on their faces.

"I'm ready."

The Seneschals produce a copy each of the passages of the Rite—papers I've poured over in preparation for this moment so that I know what they're going to say before they say it.

Erebus kneels, hands wide on the bank, until a flash of aether encircles us, lighting the darkened walls in flickering blues and silvers and snuffing the lanterns out in a silent wind. His signature is harsh and fragrant. The smell of incense lit too close to one's face.

Soon, we are in the middle of a swirling hurricane of magic. Each time his mage flame rotates, it picks up other colors, some deep blue and near navy—the ghosts of Merlins' flames past still embedded in the soil. The Regents brace themselves on the bank, planting their feet against the rush of old power.

Aldrich calls to me. "Take the hilt, please."

My fingers hover over Excalibur. Its aether ripples against my palm, pulling my hand toward it like a magnet. With a deep, fast inhale, I grasp the hilt and grit my teeth against the energy that shoots from the aether-forged sword up my arm and into my elbow. In response, the blade hums a low and rhythmic pulse like drums in my skull, rising steadily to a hungry roar.

"Rhyfelgri," Cestra breathes. "The war cry."

"The shadows have risen," Aldrich's voice reaches me over the wind. "Will you swear, as king, to rise in return?"

I can stop any Oath from binding me, just as I can resist mesmer. But I have been preparing to take this one all month. To claim my title in full, the magic needs to be a part of me.

"I swear"—as I speak, the Oath wraps around my ankles—"that as king I will rise ready to dispel the shadows."

"Do you swear," Cestra begins, "as king, to take as your own the weight of the blood of the world?"

"I swear"—the Oath loops bands around my waist, pulling tight—"to take as my own the weight . . ." I gasp as the aether squeezes around my chest. "To take as my own the weight of the world."

The Oath is eating its way into my body, my cells, running down my veins. I remind myself that this is the price I've been preparing to pay, but it takes all of my strength not to put an end to it right now.

"And do you," Gabriel intones, watching me carefully, "as king, swear to serve the Order's mission above all others, unto your death?"

The cold fingers of the ancient Oath weave around my throat, stretching up my jaw and into my hairline, joining together over my skull to complete the network of promises.

"I swear," I swallow, "to serve the Order's mission above all others, unto my death."

"By your blood, on your heart, seal your Oaths with the Round Table," Erebus commands. "Unite the Table first in spirit, so that you may soon unite their Scions in flesh."

Only after these commitments have been made can I meet Arthur's knights in spirit, and pledge to lead and serve their Scions in life.

Oaths taken, received, and given. Oaths to spirits, to flesh, to bind.

I raise Excalibur in a salute, holding the blade upright before my face so that I see my dark eyes reflected back, and carefully set my palm against it.

"By my blood . . ."

I grit my teeth and draw my palm down in a quick jerk. The cut is so quick, there is no pain, no wound, and then blood swells.

"On my heart . . ."

Blood flows in a bright red line down my wrist, across the shining gold of my mother's charm bracelet. I lift my bloodied palm to my chest to wrap around the Pendragon coin.

"To unite the Table in spirit and in flesh."

For the second time in this cave, time slows, twists . . . and a vision swallows me whole.

No Scion of Arthur has ever written down or shared with anyone what they saw during their Rite. Not to the members of the Table, not to their bonded Squires, not to their Kingsmages. Not even to their own children. This part of the ritual is for kings and kings only.

I am in a great hall with a ceiling so tall that all I can make out are a swirl of shadows in grays and blacks. The floor is so dark that it devours light. And in the middle of this massive room there is a table.

I do not need to follow its curved edges to know its shape.

A dim light grows at the table's center. By the time I reach the sole empty wooden chair and stand at its back, the blue-white wash has spread just enough to illuminate a dozen pairs of gloved hands and gauntlet-wrapped forearms that rest atop its surface.

To my left, bathed in deep shadow, a man sits still as stone save for slow breaths that lift his chest in a steady rhythm. Wisps of light glint from the metal of his chain mail. When he inhales, his tunic rises just enough that I can glimpse the sigil in its center: the tawny yellow lion couchant of Sir Owain. The man to *his* left breathes in, out. His tunic bears the deep orange three-banded circle of Sir Bors. There is another man beside him, and another, and beyond that the light does not reach and there are men I cannot see, but I feel them still.

Listening. Waiting.

This is the Round Table. An echo of the final twelve knights of Arthur's army who were bespelled by Merlin so that their spirits could live forever-more. Their spirits have been waiting for me here. Something tells me that they will not move, will not speak, until I do.

I blow out a slow, calming breath. *Unite the Table in spirit, then in flesh.*

I grasp the back of the chair to pull it from the table's edge—and freeze.

The hands wrapped around the wooden chair back are not mine alone.

Flickering between my own fingers are the faint silver outlines of fingers broader and longer than mine. A wide, shimmering palm engulfs my own.

No. No.

Me. Arthur. My body. His.

Not again.

Heart thudding in my chest, I stumble back a step with a low, whispered moan. Shake my hands, try to throw him off, get him *away,* but it's no use. The silver outline of his body hovers over mine, long forearms covered in chain mail. A thick cloth tunic, longer than my torso and wider than my chest, hovers over the shirt I chose hours ago in my room at the Pembray compound. I cannot tell if I am layered over him or if he is layered over me. I don't know if this is what the other Scions experienced. No other Scion of Arthur has been a Medium. No other Scion of Arthur has been *me.*

I don't feel Arthur, don't hear him in my head, but this is almost worse. I can't plead with him to leave me alone or demand that he let me go because he isn't a sep-arate person here. He isn't even a *dead* person—he's a *living* spirit tethered to me.

My breath is loud in the waiting space, but the knights have not turned my way or moved from their position.

I came here to complete the Rite. I *have* to complete the Rite. *When the time comes, don't be scared.*

Just as the mantra rises in my mind, a gold light shines from my chest. I look down to see the dragon rampant stitched into the tunic of Arthur's body— pulsing in time with my heartbeat.

My heart. Not his.

I entered the Rite of my own volition, and the Table waits for *me*, not Arthur.

My—our—hands tremble, but I slowly, slowly clench them into fists, and his hands follow.

I step forward, dragging the silvery echo of Arthur Pendragon behind me. Reach the chair, pull it back, and sit.

"Hello," I say in my voice, not his.

A low, gruff voice rumbles from the shadows at the far end of the table. "Fy nglew." The ancient Welsh slides against my ears, shaping English in its wake. *My lord.*

So *they* see Arthur, hear Arthur.

Okayyy.

The knight who spoke to me—us—moves. Metal clinks on the table as he slides his arms forward across the stone, revealing the silver chain mail above his gauntlets, but not his face. "A yw'n amser?" The translation comes faster now, near immediate. *Is it time?*

There is shuffling as the others turn to watch and listen.

The greeting I rehearsed rises to memory. "It is time. Camlann has come." The words echo in Arthur's baritone a half beat after mine, in Old Welsh. I wait for them to land.

My words sharpen the energy around the table. Shifting of metal and cloth, sharp intakes of breath, low grunts.

"The Shadowborn have risen in number and in strength. I slew a greater demon who wore the face of a Squire of the Line of Sir Bors. I pledge myself to you for this war and the war beyond, and ask that you do so in kind so that the Table may fight as one, and so I may call on your Scions in life."

"May the Table always fight as one." The deep, rumbling voice comes from my right and belongs to a face whose features are not shrouded. The pulse of the dragon on my chest stutters when my heart does.

Lancelot.

The most famous knight of Arthur's Round Table sits beside me. He is a broad-shouldered man in a pale blue tunic bearing a great golden stag with a crown of antlers that gazes outward in challenge. He has Nick's coloring, and they favor each other. As I look at Lancelot, the connection I feel to Nick strikes me, familiar and true. I have never seen Nick wear a beard, but I study his ancestor's to imagine what Nick's might look like. I wonder if this is a vision of his future, Nick beyond the boy I know. There are half a dozen reasons that I can't look away from Lancelot, and I don't fight a single one.

Instead, I lean closer, searching the features within the helmet, looking for Nick, even here. Blue eyes so dark they could be navy peer back at me from either side of a silver noseguard. Lancelot does not retreat, but his head tilts in question. "My liege?"

I shiver. Even his voice affects me like Nick's does.

"Arthur?" he asks.

And I reply, "Lancelot."

Call and response. That's how it is between me and Nick. How it has *always* been. A bell rung in my chest that answers his. If this vision of the Table is waiting, then this moment with Lancelot is return.

I can't help it. I reach out to the gloved hand on the table between us. The moment our fingers brush, an electric pulse runs from my chest, down my arm, and sparks to his. Lancelot hisses, draws back—and his face begins to flicker. I gasp, watching the metal helmet glow, go transparent and thin, then go solid again. Back and forth, until it starts to fade.

Then, slowly, the metal bleeds away, taking Lancelot with it, until all that remains is tousled blond hair, a strong brow, and storm-blue eyes.

A face I'd recognize anywhere.

The face I have imagined every day since he's been gone.

A choked sob escapes me. Here in the waiting place of my forever Oath, my wish has taken shape. And even though I know it is not real, I call for him.

"Nick?" I ask.

And he replies, "Bree."

PART TWO

POWER

I SENSE THE warm hand wrapped around my wrist, but still do not believe.

"Bree?" Nick says my name again, but this time it's a question.

My hand flips to hold his wrist, squeezing. It feels like him. My voice cracks. "Nick. Is this real?"

"Where are we?" he asks, eyes darting over the table. The knights around us have gone so quiet that it takes me a moment to realize that they are bathed in complete darkness now, still.

"We're . . . this is the Rite of—"

"Kings. That must be why I . . . I felt something." He taps his chest. "Right here. A pull to *you* . . . then. . ." Nick takes in the outline of Arthur first, then he finds me beneath the king. "How . . ."

"I don't know. But I'm coming for you, okay?"

"No!" He shouts. "Don't come after me!"

The words are a slap against my face. "What?"

He shakes his head. "It's too dangerous. My father—"

"I don't care—"

"*Do not* look for me, Bree. Promise me you won't." He grasps my arm, tight enough to hurt. "Swear it."

A slicing sound, shrill in my ears. Nick's hair lifting in invisible wind—

"Are you ready to complete the Oath, Crown Scion?"

Without warning, Nick is gone. In his place, Sir Lancelot is a heavy presence. "Bring him back!"

"Are you ready?" Fierce expectation rolls off Nick's ancestor, in the way he peers at me under his brows, in the hungry way he scans my face.

I jerk back, attempt to pull my hand out of his grip, but his fingers tighten and hold me still. "Where is Nick? "

The low voice that reaches me from beneath the worn metal is now urgent. "You must pledge service to us if we are to pledge to you. . . ."

"Let me go!" I shout.

He releases me and I stumble out of the chair, breathing hard. When the other knights' helmets turn to follow me, I feel the full weight of the twelve men. No longer waiting, but demanding.

Lancelot's eyes harden. "Will you make this Oath, or not?"

My heart races in my chest. Blood rushes in my ears.

"Will you?"

"I . . ."

The room squeezes me like a fist. Will I make this Oath to the Table?

An answer falls from my mouth. "No."

At my refusal, the light from my—no, Arthur's—body floods into a bright red, dousing the room into deep black and crimson. Lancelot raises a hand to shield his eyes, just as Nick did when he first saw me with Excalibur. With a loud snap, the knights fade from their seats until the Table is empty.

And yet I am not alone. A beat of silence. Then—

"Estron wyt." *You are a foreigner.*

Arthur's voice reaches me from every corner, blasting all thought with its deep rumble.

He can see me even though I can't see him.

I shudder at his closeness, at the sound of his voice in my mind. He is here now, *truly* here. A presence separate from my own, but inhabiting my skin simultaneously. Messy and full, like I'd felt when my grandmother Charles had possessed me.

Sixth-century king. Of course he'd take one look at me and call me a foreigner.

Irritation hits me hard. It's sharp enough to cut through my fear, my trembling hands. "You mean I don't look like you? Well, you don't look like me either."

A long pause. When Arthur speaks again, I don't need to translate. "And you are a woman." I hear the surprise in his voice at this, as though my being a woman is the more shocking revelation.

I scowl at the shadows. "You just now figuring that out?"

"When we last fought together, I could not see you so clearly, daughter of sons."

That phrasing reminds me of Vera's *"daughter of daughters."* I don't like it. Don't like how familiar that is, how familiar he's being. "I have a name. Bree."

"Bri?" A low laugh. "Of course *that* is your name. You are bri itself. Your own, and mine."

"What does—" I shake my head, but again Arthur's Old Welsh supplies the answer. "Bri," to him, is a noun. Honor. Dignity. Authority. Power. I scoff. "I am not your *bri*. Call me Bree or Briana."

He presses forward as if I never spoke. "You are my Scion. Your fight comes from mine, and the battles that I have won—and lost—are yours to know and use. My power, yours to wield. We are kin and kindred."

"By force," I spit. "Not by choice. One of your 'kin' was a *monster*."

A pause. "It is only when I Call one of my Scions that I can bear witness to their lives, and Samuel Davis was never Called. It was when I Called *you* that I learned of his sin." Another pause. "I wish it had not been committed."

My confusion turns to anger. "You couldn't have stopped him?"

"Even if I had been Awakened with him, he would not have known me, *heard* me as you do. *You* are the first Scion with whom I can commune, Briana. The first in fifteen centuries. Never in my dreams or Merlin's could we have imagined that I could live and breathe alongside a descendant, the way that I lived and breathed and fought alongside you the night you allowed me to Call you."

Arthur's words feel infuriatingly true. I am a Medium. Of course the way he inhabits me is like no other Scion before. Of course the Spell of Eternity—and its caster, Merlin—had not accounted for me.

"You are *unique*, daughter."

My jaw clenches. "At what cost?"

A third pause in the darkness. "An immense one."

My thirst for vengeance simmers, boils, but Arthur's words keep it from spilling over the way I want it to. The fury I feel on behalf of Vera has nowhere new to go, but still it *grows*. Just as a flower turns toward the sun, my anger seeks a source to feed it.

"Yes." Arthur hums. "There. I recognize your desire to fight. Bloodlust, with purpose. Our battles are more alike than you know. We both fight monsters, be they demons or humans."

"Our battles are not the same."

"But they come from the same wish. The desire to conquer death. I saw my friends fall by the dozens to the Shadowborn. 'No more,' I once said to myself. 'No more deaths.'"

No more deaths. I said those words too.

"We are not alike," I whisper.

"Then whose grief is this?"

Abruptly, I am drowning. What I'd felt at the funeral hits me over and over again, filling my eyes and mouth with the screaming agony of *absence*. The gaping hole of love without a beloved. The memory of waking in the night, wishing it was all a dream. Like my body in the Round Table vision, I cannot tell Arthur's pain from mine. Where his leads, mine follows, and when I remember, so does he. Then, it's gone and I am gasping for breath, for light, chasing the remains of my own heart.

"That was . . ."

"Ours . . ." His voice breaks, as ragged and hoarse as my own. Like grief had just devoured him, and left him hollow too. "What truly ties us together is not blood, but pain. When we love someone and lose them, that loss imprints itself on everyone else we love too. I see it in your eyes, Briana. Have you not envisioned the faces of those you love, slack with death? Not because you wish to see such a scene, but because your mind and heart give you no choice?"

I remember the vision of Nick, Sel, Alice. My mother. Deaths that I could not prevent.

"I think . . .you do as I did. You invoke grief now so that death will never surprise you again. You imagine how it *could* happen, so that you can imagine how it cannot. You wish to destroy it before it destroys you. Is this the right of it?"

I'd just felt Nick, I'm sure of it. Held his hand, seen his face. The idea of never seeing him again in real life skips sadness and sends me to numbing rage.

Yes, my carved heart says. *Yes.*

"The power of the Table, Briana, is to stop the Shadowborn from destroying human life. But the power of a king? *We* lead from our pain. We make the choice to defeat death before it finds us, steals from us again. Half a heart is not enough to live a whole life, is it?"

That clawing grief reaches for me all over again even though I thought I'd escaped it. The fear of death hunting me, searching for the remainder of the heart it's already broken, and who it will take from me to get it.

Alice. Nick. Sel. Mariah. Patricia.

My father.

Kings can defeat death. Save their own hearts.

I whisper, "How?"

"I can teach you."

"I *have* teachers. William. Even Sel, when he's not being a jerk—"

"What you have are diluted lessons many centuries removed from their origins. The Scion of Gawain. The descendant of Merlin. The slower path is what they must tread, but you do not have to. Why borrow knowledge when you possess its source?"

There is no temperature in this almost-space, but a line of ice slips down my spine. "The bleed-throughs. The voice. That *was* you. The memory at the funeral . . ."

"Yes."

I shudder. "You *have* been trying to reach me."

"Yes."

"Why?"

"Because you left the door open, and because we are nearly at war. And because I can help you know strength, power, and control."

Despite my urge to push him away, to yell at him to leave, a deep expansive yearning opens up in my chest. A craving that bends toward his everywhere-voice.

Strength. Power. Control. Enough to fight back and defend myself. To face my enemies. To bring Nick home, save Sel, keep the Rootcrafters safe. No more running away, ever. *The point of our arrow. The tip of our spear.* Strength. Power. Control. Those three words ring deep inside me, make my mouth water. My voice is hoarse with want. "Tell me."

A long pause in the darkness.

"Summon me, and I will *show* you."

That open yearning closes tight. Immediately. Arthur is fifteen-hundred years dead in the ground, but that night, when the Legendborn and I faced a demon horde, he commanded my limbs in the here and now like they were his own. Like I was his puppet. It turns my stomach, makes my vision swim to even *think* about letting him control me again. "My body is my own. I won't let you use me again."

"I don't need to possess you to teach you. Power is one thing; control is another. There is so, so much more to learn. Our connection is a miracle. An opportunity across eons." Another low laugh. "And yet here you stand, obstinate."

I shake my head. "I won't obey a ghost just because he's ancient. Maybe I didn't close the door before, but now that I know I left it open, I'm going to close it." I imagine the house of my mind, just like Mariah taught me before. Imagine the windows shutting, curtains closed. Doors closed, keys turned and thrown away, cracks sealed—

"Do you fear your own greatness? Your own *bri*? Summon me, Briana, and I will show you what it means to be the Pendragon. . . ."

An image flashes in my mind. Iridescent scales. Smoke curled around a snout. Fangs as long as my own body. Heat and brimstone, then gone. A creation of his or my own mind, I don't know.

"I will leave because you wish me to, but I am only here because you sought me out. By your blood, on your heart."

"Stop *talking!*" Suddenly, my irritation at Arthur flares into anger, red root pulsing out from me in waves.

"We fought as one because you summoned me. You will summon me again, because we are each other's bri." His voice thunders in my ears. "Only a dragon may meet a dragon, Briana. Only a king can teach a king. . . ."

I won't let him force me into anything, no matter how alike we are.

"Leave me alone," I grit out. "*Now.*" As my root rises, Arthur's presence dissipates around me. Flames roar into the room to burn him out, burn him away, but they don't stop there. The walls catch fire. Then the floor beneath my feet. The entire *vision* is burning.

Startled, I stumble backward, falling. Brace myself to strike the ground— but instead of hitting the hard stone floor of the great room, I land with a . . . *splash.*

The stone floor of the medieval room is gone. In its place is a wide expanse of packed dirt and the shallow stream of water I'm sitting in. In the middle of a forest. At twilight.

Glowing water sluices over my ankles and around my hips, ripples over stones beneath my hands. The stream flows toward and then behind me, and I cannot see its end. Its banks are obscured by low clouds of glowing mist. Its shape is jagged, like a bolt of lightning over the surface of the soil.

'Daughter of sons . . . my bri . . .'

Arthur's voice is muted, far away, but it jolts me to my feet. As I stand in the stream, the light emanating from its water begins to dim.

'My bri . . .'

His voice is quieter this time. Fading with the light. I take two steps upstream and by the third, the water has gone dark, and somehow I know he is gone.

Up ahead, I spot a raised stone resting in a grassy clearing and decide that it is my target.

As I walk, other voices rise up on either side of me in bursts. Disembodied whispers in the darkness.

"The point of our arrow."

"The tip of our spear."

"Wound turned weapon."

As I arrive at the mossy stone and step up, the stream behind me—Arthur's stream—shrinks and dries into the barest trickle of water over the earth.

I marvel at how this place—wherever it is—is the near opposite of the ogof y ddraig: Instead of standing on an ancient boulder in the center of a pond in the middle of a stone cave, I am standing on a moss-covered mound in the center of a growing forest. Where the ogof feels sacred and preserved, this place feels both ancient and alive. Where Excalibur slept, I stand. In this place, *I* am the blade.

I turn back to face Arthur's stream. All that remains is a stretch of damp soil.

A voice behind me—crystal clear, proud—splits the silence open. "Daughter of daughters."

Relief floods my chest. "Vera." It doesn't take long to find her. She stands in a stream on the other side of the mossy stone. She is as I last saw her in my room in the Lodge. Bathed in blood and flame, hair a crown of its own.

"Where am I?"

"Where you have been before." She extends a hand for aid, and I lean forward to help her up onto the stone beside me. Her skin is warm, her palm and fingers firm. My lower body is chilled from the water, but she looks perfectly dry. Behind her, the small waterway she'd stood in babbles quietly. "The plane between life and death."

"It doesn't look the same." I wrap my arms around myself.

"The plane can appear as many things," Vera says with a smirk. "Before you visited me in *my* vision. Now, I am visiting you in yours."

"But it's not mine, not really. It was the Rite's."

She presses her lips into a line in the barest hint of displeasure. "Tell me about this Rite."

"It's a ritual for the Legendborn. It brought me to a room and a table and Arthur's knights."

"The king's men may claim the ritual, but they cannot claim the plane as their own." Her Southern accent wraps around the words like a blanket, pulling them close together in a soft drawl. "No one owns the space between blood-lines, between ancestors and descendants. Not even the dead." She huffs and trails a hand through the billowing mist at our knees. "The spellcraft the king's men use to create the plane in their image is but a poor sorcerer's fabrication of what a natural-born Medium can achieve in this place. What *you* can do as your power grows."

I shake my head. "I don't understand."

She hums and glances over my shoulder to the empty soil behind me then gestures to the stream from which she emerged, still running. "The streams are passageways. Your bloodlines made manifest."

I look out at the forest around us and imagine how many streams are there, waiting for me. My maternal line starting with my mother's life, my grand-mother's, all the way to Vera's. My father's parents', too, I imagine. Vera beckons me closer and points to the now dry streambed. "That is Arthur's lin-eage. You used intention and the king's blood in order to access their vision on the plane here, but then you broke away"—Vera points to where I splashed down—"and brought yourself back to the center." She opens her arm wide, gesturing to the ground all around us. "If you walk with intention and purpose on this plane, you can open the pathway to any of your ancestors. Or"—she looks at Arthur's stream again—"you can close it."

"I burned him away with root." I nod, the idea growing sharper and clearer in my mind. "Never done that before. Never been able to call on your power at will. It only shows up in defense, when I'm already in danger—" A flutter of excitement interrupts me. Possibility. "But *here* I used it because I *wanted* to. Not in defense . . ." I step toward her. "How can I attack like that in the real world?"

"I do not know." Her eyes drift over my shoulder, widening. "But I do know that before you learn to fight, you must first protect yourself."

My eyes spring open.

The real world surrounds me, bright. The ogof. Where the Rite started.

Time is back and moving quickly.

There's a sharp pinch in my right shoulder and *clang*! Excalibur falls from my hand to the stone below.

"Wha—" I'm stopped by the sight of a syringe sticking out of my upper arm and Emissary Theresa holding the plunger down.

Whoosh! Bright red flames erupt from my chest. Theresa screams and slips backward on the great stone, falling into the water below with a splash.

Movement below. The Regents, rushing away from the moat before my wave of root reaches them.

My crimson flames are met by a blue-and-white aether shield—the Mageguard, casting a barrier against my power. Protecting the Regents. Protecting themselves. From me.

The syringe is *still there*. I claw at it, pulling the needle out. Max appears at my left, teeth bared—I swing. He catches my fist easily. I crumple to the ground.

The last thing I see is his jeering face hovering above mine.

"Nighty night, Crown Scion."

14

A FAMILIAR POP of pressure in my ears jolts me awake.

An aether barrier opening—or closing.

The thought of being trapped sends me surging upward—against leather straps. The one around my right wrist snaps.

There's shouting. My eyes open.

"Hey!"

"Grab her!"

I'm in the back of a van on a metal stretcher, with a Mageguard on either side. Max and Ramirez. Max lunges for me—too late. My freed fist strikes him across the nose so hard blood splatters against his cheeks.

"Stop the van!" Max's voice is nasally and wet. Whoever's driving us slams on the brakes, sending both Merlins sliding, while my stretcher, bolted to one metal wall, stays put. I yank hard with my left hand, tearing the other strap.

Ramirez darts forward, dodges my second punch and throws his weight behind his palm, slamming down heavy on my chest, sending me back against the stretcher. Hard. My head cracks against the metal. I see stars. The van's gray ceiling spins, expands, threatens to turn liquid.

Ramirez screams, gripping his throat as a bright flare of silver-blue aether swarms his neck and face.

My thoughts run together. Logic feels loose, like threads unraveling and too hard to follow. Dimly, I think that if Ramirez is burning, he didn't just mean to restrain me. He wanted to *hurt* me. His Oath of Service to protect the Legendborn, to me, is *punishing* him? I blink, confused.

The back doors slam open—there's a scuffle. Ramirez is tossed to the floor.

"You fool!" Erebus, his aether signature rolling through the cabin like a heat wave.

"She attacked us!" Max cries. "She broke my nose!"

My head lolls to the side to see him cowering before his general. Beside him, Ramirez is moaning beneath the dimming flames.

Erebus advances on both Mageguard. "You are not to touch her again. Not that I care if your Oath takes you for it, but she is the *only* known heir to Arthur. If you kill her, the king's inheritance will go to the next eligible heir in the Line—a Line for which we have no leads and no other Scion to replace her."

"So what?" Max snarls, face bloody. "I'm supposed to let this little girl beat me?"

"She's worth more to the Order than you are, Zhao. You do the math."

No leads . . . no other heir . . . I can't follow him, my brain can't keep up, but something—

Max grunts. He pulls a third strap from the stretcher, binding my left arm against my hip. I couldn't lift it if I tried. Not with the metal ceiling spinning and my stomach turning. I moan, and Erebus's eyes snap to me, then to the open doors.

Someone shouts, "Dr. Reed is on the way with a stronger dose!"

"No . . . ," I moan, staring up at Erebus. "The Oath . . ."

His words reach me from very far away, whispered through a tunnel. "Our intention for the serum is to keep you safe, Briana, not to hurt you. Not a punishment, and not permanent. Else we could not administer it. Guard Ramirez, however, is paying the price because he knowingly took action with the intent to injure you. He *meant* to cause you harm. A critical distinction." Erebus crouches beside me, dips his hand behind my skull, then curses. Blood coats his fingers, shining and dark. He growls, "Bring Sitterson as well!"

William?

The van swims again.

Time passes. How much, I'm not sure. The ceiling blurs.

Another pinch to my arm. A needle slipping into my vein. I don't flinch; this pain seems beyond minimal compared to the searing hot ache at the back of my skull. A woozy, sickening sensation starts at my arm and floods up my shoulders to my spine—and then I'm drained. *Something* leaves me. Not energy, not quite. Something of my life that was in my limbs and flowed from my heart. Something that I had gotten used to feeling, even in that short time since Arthur Awakened. Gone now. I shiver.

A bright, citrus aether signature in my nose accompanies the achy, itchy feeling of my skull knitting back together.

"Bree?" William's shaking voice, and a warm palm on my cheek. "You had a small fracture . . . a concussion . . . should be healed soon."

"You're not here to chitchat, Sitterson." Ramirez, voice shaking with anger. "If they botched the formula and she overdoses, you bring her back. That's it."

My eyes open to find William hovering over me. He shines a flashlight into my left eye—it *hurts*. I squint, moaning. Light shines in my right, William holding my head still so I don't turn away. Then the flashlight's gone. He shoots a glare over his shoulder. "I have no idea what to expect or what to heal even if she *does* react poorly. I repair injuries, not . . . whatever your scientists have done here. This is *beyond* irresponsible! You didn't need to drug her—"

"Not my call, and not yours either," Max cuts him off.

"I swear to you, Maxwell . . ." William's voice turns to iron. "You will pay for this."

"Doubt it." Max sniffs. "Is she stable or not?"

"She is stable." William's eyes close, and he takes a deep breath before opening them. "For now."

"Then get out, Scion."

William's voice at my ear, his breath against my cheek. "I'm so sorry, Bree."

Then darkness once more.

15

"GOOD MORNING, BRIANA."

I blink the small room into existence.

I am wearing a pair of sweatpants and a T-shirt I don't recognize.

The back of my skull feels like one big bruise.

I am sitting in a chair at a table.

On the other side sits Regent Gabriel in a gray suit, with his jacket slung around the back of a chair that matches mine. He wears a practiced, pleasant expression. It is the smile of someone who wants the people around him to feel at ease. Right now, it does the exact opposite.

"What is this?" I croak.

"A secure facility," another voice says. Behind Gabriel, in the corner, stands his Seneschal, Tacitus. The Master of Mesmer is dressed in a gray ensemble. Slacks, a button-down jacket. When he notices me studying him, his attention marches like fire ants across my skin.

A red light winks at me from over Tacitus's head. A camera is mounted in the wall, its black iris pointed at me.

"We were at the Lodge. . . . The Rite—"

Gabriel temples his fingers. "That's correct. Last night we were at the Lodge."

Memories flood in, knitting my brow. The ogof. The needle. The van. "You shot me with something!" I surge to my feet—and nearly fall out of the chair in the process. Tacitus is at my side in an instant, lifting me carefully back into the chair before reappearing at his Regent's side. Bile rises in my throat, threatening to spill out, then subsides.

"Please be careful, Briana," Gabriel says in a low, soothing voice.

"Why did you—" Pain stops me short. For the first time, I feel the pricks in my right and left upper arms. I tug my sleeve up to reveal deep purple bruising around a constellation of small marks. Injection sites.

Gabriel answers before I form the question. "We have suppressed your ancestral inheritances. Arthur's physical strength and your ability to manipulate aether."

Alarms ring inside my skull as his words land, become concrete. My hand flies to my chest, clutching the shirt. That empty feeling I'd felt in the van is still there. A hole where my root furnace should be, where Arthur's heart sometimes beats. I feel hollow.

"This is for your safety and ours." His mouth twists as he watches me rub my sternum. "I apologize for your discomfort; it has taken us several attempts to get the dosage right. The serum is still experimental, you see? It works directly on your DNA, so the physical side effects are . . . not insignificant." He sits back, crossing one knee over the other.

"*Why?*"

"You are undeniably the Scion of Arthur, but you are also something new. Your aether abilities have been temporarily neutralized because we would like to speak to you without . . . surprises or unpleasantries."

I huff a laugh. "You could have just asked."

Gabriel's mouth quirks. "The High Council of Regents is responsible for making decisions that protect—or put at risk—millions of lives around the globe. I'm sure you'll forgive us our precautions. As the Regent who oversees the boundaries between our secret order and the Onceborn world, and who adjudicates potential violations of the Code of Secrecy, I have specific inquiries for you on these topics." He opens a tablet in front of him and spreads open a folder of hard-copy documents. "Why don't you tell me about your father, Edwin Matthews, and what you've told him of our Order?"

My heart thumps hard in my chest. "What have you done to him?"

Gabriel blinks. "Done to him? We have not 'done' anything to your father. He is under Liege supervision, unbeknownst to him." Gabriel spreads his hands wide. "We have no reason to harm your family, Crown Scion. We just need to understand how far information has spread. To that end, please tell me what you've told your father about the Order of the Round Table."

"My father knows nothing," I say quickly. Patricia's face flashes behind my eyes. Mariah's. Alice's. I shove their very existences down, down, so that nothing will show on my expression. No other names, no other people for the Regents to hunt.

"Consistent with what we've observed," Tacitus murmurs.

"Wonderful." Gabriel moves another folder across the table—with documents that I recognize immediately. "Your mother, Faye Ayeola Matthews, née Carter, witnessed fully corporeal Shadowborn murdering Unanedig twenty-five years ago. And she was mesmered to forget." He pauses, waiting.

My eyelids flutter. His words are simple statements, but they are also prompts. He doesn't know that I know the truth. No one except Alice and Sel knows about my mother's involvement with the Order or our shared history of resisting mesmer—an unheard-of ability too dangerous to expose. Even William doesn't know that my mother faked her mesmer for decades or that I can break them myself if I wish.

"What are you talking about?" I say slowly, fighting to keep my breath even. "No, she didn't."

"Her heart is racing." Tacitus narrows his eyes. "She could be lying."

"Or it's the serum's side effects." Gabriel's mouth thins briefly. "We will ask her again. Briana, are you saying you did not know about your mother's history with the Order prior to joining the chapter?"

I don't have to fake the effort to pull my focus together. "I'm sorry, I . . ."

Gabriel repeats his question. "Were you aware of your mother's history when you became a Page to the chapter?"

I shake my head. "No . . . no."

Something in Gabriel's politician smile ticks up. He is pleased. "Excellent."

I think I'm in the clear, until Tacitus speaks. "Then why and how would her daughter find her way to the chapter twenty-five years later?"

It doesn't escape me that Tacitus is speaking *about* me, not to me. Like I'm not a real person. When your mesmer is strong enough to wipe whole people from someone's memory, maybe no one is real. For the first time, I wonder if *he* was the Merlin who wiped Nick from his mother's mind. Tacitus catches me staring and smiles, long fangs wrapped in a devil's grin.

Gabriel hums. "Answer him, please."

"I—I saw a demon attack boys at a party, and Selwyn and Victoria killed it. The next night, I saw another demon on campus with Nick. No one else could see these demons. I wanted to know why I could. I figured the Order had the answers."

Gabriel regards me with narrowed eyes. "And had you seen demons before these instances?"

"No." The truth.

Gabriel sits back, eyes thoughtful. "Other questions, Tacitus?"

The Seneschal tilts his head, regarding me with hooded eyes. "Had you always planned to go to UNC?"

"Yes. My mother went here, and so I thought I would too." Not a lie.

"This is unlikely to be the sole result of family tradition." Tacitus shifts his weight, sighing. "If the archives are to believed, the Scion of Arthur is drawn to Excalibur's resting place. The girl and her mother share a bloodline, so the mother would also have been the Scion. It makes sense that they'd both be attracted to the university, even as they believed they were Unanedig. They could have written it off as a sense of alumni loyalty, connectedness to legacy, nostalgia, and so on."

"Agreed. Your assessment, Tacitus?"

The Seneschal shrugs. "Nothing in the witness observation files suggests anything to contradict her statements. Faye Ayeola Matthews, née Carter, was mesmered and never indicated any retained memories of what she witnessed the night that Natasia Kane opened the campus Gates. Her mesmer was administered by my predecessor, Seneschal to your own. A Merlin particularly adept at memory replacement."

"Jenna, yes, I recall." Gabriel pushes back from his seat with a thoughtful expression. "We'll stop for now. Let's repeat these questions at the next session to be sure."

Tacitus is at my side in a blink, hand hot and burning against my head, a blast against my consciousness. "Sleep. And forget."

"Stop . . ." His mesmer pulls me down a quickly swirling drain.

"Good afternoon, Briana."

I blink the small room into existence.

I am wearing a pair of sweatpants and a T-shirt I don't recognize.

The back of my skull feels tender.

I am sitting in a chair at a table.

On the other side sits Regent Cestra in a black-and-silver blouse, hair pulled back tightly against her skull.

"*Tch.* She can barely hold her head up. Will she even be able to answer any questions?"

A voice I recognize responds, "Her mind will sharpen, but her body will still experience side effects. If you'd like, we can try again later in the day?"

"I'd rather not." Cestra taps fingers on the table.

My head tips back against the chair, too heavy. My eyes follow Erebus, who has just walked into my field of vision. He settles against the back wall, face unreadable. The Mageguard general is in his typical black long coat. His black-and-silver aether staff leans against the wall beside him. The sight of him loosens a memory. Something happened with him . . . something bad.

Something that made me angry.

"Where am I?" I croak.

"A secure facility," Erebus answers. When he looks at me from this close, the bright sparks burn my cheeks. When I turn away to escape his gaze, I notice a camera mounted in the wall over his head, a winking red light beside the iris.

"Facility?" I shake my head. "No . . . we were at the Lodge——"

"Yes," Cestra says impatiently. "We were in the Lodge last night."

Last night? Memories return, breaking through cobwebs. The ogof. A needle. The van. My head, William healed me. "You shot me with something. . . ."

Cestra rolls her eyes at Erebus. "This repetition is tedious."

Repetition. The irritation on her face, laced with deep impatience. Like we've had this conversation before. But we haven't. I just woke up here— wherever here is.

She sighs. "Yes, you were in the Lodge last night. We drugged you with a suppressant that blocks your ability to use your inheritances. That is why you're"—she waves her hand in a circle near my face—"like this."

"Drugged?" I blink slowly and register the odd feeling in my chest. The empty feeling. Like there's a hole where my root furnace should be, where Arthur's heart beats sometimes. I feel hollowed out. "Why?"

"So that you'll behave."

Erebus clears his throat. "So that we can all keep level heads, Crown Scion."

"Listen, we're going to keep these conversations simple. I ask you questions; you answer. If I ask you for more information, you elaborate. Understood?"

I blink at her. "Was that one of the questions?"

She groans. "No."

She flips open a control panel in the center of the table, and a screen lowers on the wall behind her. As she works, my eyes find Erebus again. We stare at each other, and more memories return. My anger returns too.

"What's happening with Sel?"

Cestra doesn't look up, and speaks as images begin to appear on the screen. "Selwyn Kane's trial will begin after our debrief of you concludes." She says it so casually, like it is of no consequence to her either way.

"I'd like to . . . I'd like to speak on his behalf. As Crown Scion."

Cestra smirks. I don't like the glint in her eye. All of a sudden, I feel caught in a web that I cannot see. Every time I think I have footing with the Regents, it gets taken away.

"He is not your Kingsmage," she says. "You did not grow up with him. You are not bonded. From what I've learned from the other Legendborn, Selwyn

Kane was hostile to you from the first moment you arrived at the Lodge, threatening your life both publicly and privately on several occasions. Why would you speak on his behalf?"

I open my mouth, close it, and open again, like a fish. "He is my friend."

"He has been away from his charge and the service of his Oath for some time," Cestra murmurs, leaning forward on her elbows to survey my face. Erebus wordlessly takes over her search, flipping past images on the screen behind us. "Whatever friendship you may have felt will be buried beneath the symptoms of his . . . condition."

I shift in my chair, uncomfortable. Even if Sel changes, he'll still be Sel. Demonia is a part of him. "I don't believe he will succumb."

She sits back. "Then you are a fool. It is impossible to stop the process once it has begun. The stronger the Merlin, the greater their fall."

"If Sel was able to protect Nick again, his Oath would be fulfilled," I say. "Are you even looking for Nick and his father or is that a lie too?"

"That's *right.*" Cestra's expression turns conspiratorial. "You and Nick Davis are close. According to our intel, inappropriately so for two Scions."

Erebus only hinted at the nature of my relationship with Nick, but Cestra is much bolder. I say nothing.

"When your lineages were revealed, he, like the other Legendborn, must have realized that your relationship could not continue." She offers a sympathetic frown, but the cruel gleam in her eyes ruins the effect. "That must have been a difficult conversation."

I shift in my chair again.

"I *see.*" Her knowing smirk returns. "You two haven't had a chance to discuss it. Then let me do the honors: this relationship is forbidden. If it continues, the Council will take action to keep you and Nick from endangering the bloodlines."

My chest tightens and my ears go hot. "'Endangering the bloodlines'? You mean . . ."

"You know exactly what I mean. This may not be of concern to either of you yet, at sixteen and seventeen, but the Order has outlawed relationships between Scions who have the potential to conceive, and with good reason. We cannot risk a firstborn child born of two Lines, *confusing* two Lines, regardless of your intent or precautions."

When William first explained the rule about Scion-Scion relationships, it seemed far from my concerns. An awful sort of "modern fin'amor," he'd said. *Courtly love that can never be consummated.* I wasn't a Scion then, and Nick and I had barely explored who we could be to each other. But now, with Cestra's words striking at our future before we've even had a present, the law feels very real—and very much none of her damn business.

The Order's obsession with who has kids, with whom, and how, is stomach-churning.

"I see the defiance in you, Bree," she murmurs, "so consider this a warning, even though you'll forget it: We know everything about you. Who you love. Who you'd miss. . . ."

A fresh jolt of fear freezes me where I sit. I could never forget a threat like that.

"It's simple." She sits back, waving a manicured hand. "When this is over, find someone else to have fun with."

Erebus clears his throat, a relief. "If I may interrupt?"

He has finally landed on an image from the cave. Me, holding the sword high, palm against the blade, eyes gone red and blue. Then the image moves, and the blue-white mage flame swirls around my wrist and hands.

"You recorded the Rite?" I gasp at the video of myself, feeling exposed.

Cestra hums. "Keep watching."

In the video I stand, unseeing, lost in the ritual. In one hand, I clutch the Pendragon coin. In the other, I hold Excalibur high. Then, a roaring sound, a flash, and the flames shift from blue to crimson. The Mageguard and Seneschals work together, casting a near-instant shield to protect the Regents. Excalibur drops, and I blink back into the world around me, visibly shaken, eyes wide. Theresa appears and presses a syringe into my arm.

The entire segment had taken maybe thirty seconds. My vision of Arthur and Vera during the Rite felt like long, confusing minutes. Time had slowed and expanded.

"Pause," Cestra orders. Erebus stops the video, right as I fall to the ground at Max's feet. "Rewind to before the flash."

The video stops, and Cestra points to the screen. "Let's discuss what happened here, when the flames turned red. When you spoke to our emissaries about your abilities, you described yourself as a descendant of . . ." She taps on the screen of a tablet, scrolling through transcripts, then smiles. "'The Line of Vera.' Clever adoption of our nomenclature. These abilities, as reported by the other Legendborn, are impressive." She reads down a list. "Aether generation and manipulation into a wall, breathing red mage flame." She turns to me. "Is this correct?"

I nod. "That's what happened in the ogof the night I first pulled Excalibur."

"And you had not used those abilities before that night?"

"No." Not exactly.

"Why do you think it happened for the first time, then and there?"

"I don't know." Not exactly.

"Could it have been because of Arthur's Call?" Cestra prods.

The center of me, the very core of my being seizes up at the memory of Arthur's possession. Arthur, stretching at my skin. Moving my limbs the way he wanted, controlling me. I scowl.

Erebus raises a brow. "Something to share about the Call of Arthur, Crown Scion?"

My mouth turns sour. "It was not enjoyable."

Erebus nods. "It is written that the Call of Arthur in particular can appear quite violent."

"Sure," I mutter.

"Tell us about the other abilities of this Line," Cestra searches through her tablet for a note. "When you pulled the sword, were you a . . . Medium at this time?"

I'm so exhausted. "That night, both Vera and Arthur were within me."

"Within you?" Erebus questions. "As in, you could interact with them?"

"I . . . I could hear their voices, and they could control my body."

Cestra and Erebus go still and exchange glances. She clears her throat. "The other Legendborn reported that your voice changed during and after the battle.

Are you saying that the spirits of the dead can use your body without your will and speak through you if they wish? As in, possession?"

I nod weakly. "Yes."

Erebus inhales sharply. "I would like to explore this ability further, Regent. Perhaps without the suppressant?"

Cestra waves a hand. "Another time."

I look between the two of them, alarmed. This is what Sel said could happen. That the Seneschals would want to examine me. But I never imagined it in these circumstances. Not like this.

I should have.

Cestra has already moved on. "And Arthur's aether constructs and armor? Our intel says that you cannot forge them. That you draw on a large quantity of aether, and your attempts at castings result in burns."

My face flushes. "Yes."

Cestra crosses her arms and leans back in her chair. "Somehow, this interview has been both fascinating *and* disappointing." She gestures to Erebus. "We're done for now."

Erebus moves faster than thought, seizing my face in both hands. "Rest now, Briana. And forget." His mesmer tumbles me into dreamless sleep.

"Good evening, Briana."

Then.

"Good morning, Briana."

Then.

"Good afternoon, Briana."

Then.

16

"WHY ISN'T SHE responsive?"

The first voice, cold and distant, would have sent my heart racing—if it had been beating normally. Instead, it is a sluggish thump beneath my ribs.

"She *is* responsive. She just hasn't gone through a full sleep cycle." The second voice is stretched thin and taught, like piano wire. William is here.

"They want her alert today. Can you check to see if she's working or not?"

"She is *not* a toy." William's tone is hardened to a sharp edge. "She's a human being."

"Eh. Hurry up."

A hand against my brow. The room is bright before I open my eyes. Strong fingers wrap around my right wrist.

"She's stable, for now. But you can't keep drugging her with this . . . this *poison*. It's been three days, isn't that enough?"

"Not your decision, Sitterson."

Three days.

Three.

"Will—" I breathe, blinking between waves of nausea. Eyes open, fluorescent light, burning.

William's arm wraps around my shoulders, guiding me to sitting. The scent of his aether cocoons around me, a comforting thing in a jarring existence. Citrus, warmth, *William*.

Max sighs loudly from the doorway. "Can she walk?"

William looks me over. There are dark circles under his eyes, a strange tension down the line of his neck. "Can you walk?"

I squint, test my limbs. "Yes . . . ? Where are we?"

He helps me to the floor and kneels to slip shoes over my feet. "I hope this is the last time."

I grimace. Try to manage words around my dry, thick tongue. "The . . . last time . . . ?"

His eyes shine with unshed tears. "Yes."

"Get her moving. I need to check in with Erebus," Max calls from the hall. Silence follows.

William looks stunned by Max's departure. He holds a shaking finger up to his lips. He wants me quiet. Wants to be sure Max is gone.

Merlin feet don't make any sound.

While he waits to see if Max will return, I take in the room around me. There are no windows, no sunlight or moonlight to tell me the time, but the bright fluorescents flood the room in harsh white. I'm on the covers, fully clothed. Beside me on a tray is a plate with the crust of an eaten sandwich and an apple core. A half-empty glass of apple juice. A meal I don't remember eating, but the flavors seem familiar and my belly is full.

After another beat of silence without Max, William must decide he is gone. He leans in close to my ear, as if to rub my back, and whispers quickly. "Something's different today. This is the first time he's left me alone. The Council has been mesmering you. Wiping your memories of each day so that you can't build a lie between interrogations and so you forget what they're doing and planning."

Mesmers? I've been mesmered? He keeps talking, words coming so fast I can barely keep up.

"The Rite was an ambush. They drugged you with a *serum*—must have created it by studying Legendborn blood, to target our inheritances—"

Legendborn blood. Inheritances. Something is right there at the edge of my awareness. An unfocused thought . . . a detail . . .

"They dose me with it, too. Not as much as you. Enough to block Gawain's strength, make swyns harder. I don't know where we are, some sort of institute. There are labs, bedrooms. I don't see a way out—"

"Wait." I stop him. The thought grows sharper until it becomes *words*. "'M not just Legendborn. . . ."

"What?"

"I'm not just Legendborn. I can do more. . . . " I pull away and grasp William's forearms. "Need pain."

"You're hurt?" William scans my body. "Where?"

"No," I mumble. "Pain . . . it helps me . . . resist a mesmer."

His eyes widen. "You can resist mesmers?"

I huff a laugh. "Dunno about right now, but yeah."

William's gaze sharpens. His eyes dart to the hallway and back before he takes my arm in both hands. "Then I'm really sorry about this."

"Wha—" My mouth opens wide in a silent scream. A hot rush of aether floods my skull, spreading like fire through my senses. Bright, burning lemons and scorched oranges under a summer sun . . . William drives his power down through my skin, into my veins and muscles, burying it deep into my bones. Then, in a single lightning strike, my mind clears. My voice returns with a breathy, shocked "Owww!"

William releases me. "Will that work?"

I gasp. "What the *hell*, William?"

He winces. "I'm sorry! Aether burns when there's too much of it, too fast, remember?"

"Ugh." I nod. "Yes."

Max reappears right as William guides us to the door. "Let's go, Crown Scion."

Outside in the white hallway I follow Max, who, blessedly, walks at normal human speed. I take the time to put my thoughts and memories in order. The Regents captured me. Drugged me. They have interrogated me over and over for three days. *Three.* Does anyone else even know we're here?

This is not how any of this was supposed to go.

Another memory surfaces, this time about the serum. *Someone* told me about it earlier, I'm sure of it—*Gabriel*! His voice echoes in my ears. *We have suppressed your ancestral inheritances. Arthur's physical strength and your ability to manipulate aether.* That means no aether and no red root, but the other inheritances from Vera's Line, like . . . my senses, the mesmer resistance . . . the Regents' scientists wouldn't find those traits in Legendborn blood. Wouldn't even know to look for them. God, I hope those abilities aren't affected too. I need every defense I can get.

We make a left turn, go down a short hall, and end at a large wooden door.

Max cracks the door, peeks in. Nods to someone on the other side, then gestures that I proceed.

I enter a large conference room with windows that let daylight stream in.

The door clicks shut, leaving me standing alone in front of the High Council of Regents. In the middle of the room is a dark rectangular table. Lord Regent Aldrich, Regent Gabriel, and Regent Cestra sit on one side, while their Seneschals sit across from them on the other. But . . . they aren't even *looking* at me. Instead, Aldrich and Gabriel speak to each other in low tones. Cestra sits bent over a tablet. Tacitus flips through a yellow legal pad as he speaks to Serren.

I clear my throat to get their attention.

Aldrich waves me forward. "Good afternoon, Briana."

Words echo in my ears. *Good afternoon, Briana. Good evening, Briana. Good morning.* Memories of the other days, slipping back in place in dribs and drabs. The mesmers, breaking down. I give silent thanks to William.

Aldrich gestures to the single empty seat on the side of the table closest to the door. "Will you sit?"

I sit—and immediately feel déjà vu. We've done this dance before. *They want her alert today,* Max had said. Alert for what?

Aldrich smiles. "Briana, how are you feeling?"

I try to think past the sound of Cestra drumming her fingers on the table. *Tadum-tadum-tadum,* like a clock ticking down as they wait for my response. They still think I'm mesmered. That I don't know that they've had me imprisoned, drugged, and interrogated. I know exactly what to say. "Where am I?"

"Ugh," Cestra groans.

"Regent Cestra." Aldrich's lips press into a thin line until Cestra stops tapping. "Are we wasting your time?"

Cestra sighs heavily. "I simply tire of the ceremony, the repetition. Why support the ruse at this point? She's just going to be mesmered again."

The repetition.

The Regents wanted to reset me between interrogations, William said. They *pretended* that each meeting was the day after the Rite to keep me disoriented, unable to plan.

Tacitus rolls his eyes. "I know you enjoy making my job more difficult, Regent Cestra, but perhaps not today?"

"What are we if not the challenges we overcome?" Cestra purrs as she leans across the table. "And I thought you were the Master of Mesmer, Tacitus. You of all people can erase what's necessary without breaking her *entirely*."

Tacitus growls. "With *respect*, Regent, you have no idea how delicate mesmerwork can be. The more memories she accumulates, the more I will need to remove," Tacitus intones. "A quick discussion would be preferred."

Aldrich nods. "As you wish."

He clicks a button on a remote and a screen drops from the ceiling behind him. On it is a collection of images. My school ID from my first day at Early College. A blurry security camera shot of me walking through Polk Place with Greer—I squint—maybe a week or two ago. Me and Alice on the quad. Me and Selwyn pausing to talk outside the Comm Studies building. A zoomed-in shot of me, bent over a book in the undergrad library, a look of concentration on my face.

"This whole time . . ." My eyes sting, grow hot with humiliation.

"We've been watching you, yes," Aldrich says. "Since the moment Victoria Morgan informed our emissary that you pulled Excalibur from its stone."

I knew Tor called the Regents on her own, without alerting anyone in advance. Tor never kneeled to me. Tor never thought I should be here, sword or not. I don't even know if betrayal is what I feel.

But Tor isn't my immediate concern.

"You planned all of this?"

Aldrich regards me with measuring eyes, as if gauging my mood more than my question. "The Order would not have lasted fifteen centuries without adequate strategy, Briana." He turns to the rest of the table. "Regent Gabriel, your report from the Order's public domain."

Gabriel reads off a sheet of paper. "Over the course of three sessions, Mage Seneschal Tacitus and I have concluded that Briana's father is not a Code violation, although he should remain under Liege supervision for the time being."

"Good to hear," Aldrich says.

"We have also concluded that the Code of Secrecy has not been broken by Briana Matthews, nor was it broken by her mother. However—"

I hold my breath, waiting.

"Briana's responses did suggest that Scion Sitterson falsified records to add Alice Marie Chen to the Vassal network. These records claim she was sworn into the Code, but as it's an unauthorized invitation, we can't be sure."

The breath leaves my chest in a rush. *Alice. What did I tell them about her?*

Aldrich nods. "The fate of Ms. Chen?"

Tacitus meets my eyes and grins. "Mesmered. I allowed her to keep her memories of her coursework but erased everything related to the Order and her best friend's connection to it."

"No . . ." I press my hand to the desk to stand but crumple immediately. The injury William *shoved* into my bones and muscles sends a cold, searing pain up my shoulder and into my neck. "You can't do this."

"We can and we did," Tacitus murmurs.

Across the table, Aldrich's own Seneschal, Serren, releases a low whistle. "That is precision work, my friend. Not just any Merlin could distinguish between the girl's experiences as you have."

Serren is right. I'd seen Lord Davis's Kingsmage, Isaac, tear through Alice's mind without care, wiping away whole days like a tornado, leaving nothing behind. I'd brought her memories back with my ancestor's healing while possessed, but . . . I don't know if I can undo what Tacitus has done. I don't know where Alice is, I don't know when I'll see her again, *if* I'll see her again—

"Breathe slowly, Briana." Erebus sits closest to me, and he dips his head to meet my eyes. "You're hyperventilating."

Cestra rolls her eyes. "You are the most vicious warrior I've ever met, Erebus, and yet you are *soft* toward this girl."

Erebus cuts his eyes to his Regent. "She is the Scion of Arthur, whatever conclusions we come to today. Her health and well-being are of concern to us all."

Aldrich clears his throat. "Let's keep moving. Cestra?"

"My report is two-fold," Cestra says. "We spoke with Briana about her abilities and I have two proposals."

"Proceed."

Cestra rattles off her proposals without looking at any notes. "Briana's status as the Crown Scion has, up until this point, been deemed need-to-know information. I propose that we maintain it as such. With the Davises still at large, Camlann will appear to be two Scions away to ninety-eight percent of our constituents."

Aldrich nods. "And *how* do you plan to maintain Briana's status a secret?"

"My first proposal is that we divide and distract the Legendborn of her chapter. Let's send a bonded Scion and Squire pair from the Southern Chapter to join the hunt for Nicholas. Perhaps the Scion and Squire of Tristan, Morgan and Griffiths. We'll tell the other three, Taylor, Caldwell, and Hood, that the best way they can support the search party is to remain on campus continuing to fight Shadowborn crossings. It will take all three of them working around the clock to keep these Gates closed, even if we leave them with a guard or two."

"And what about Scion Sitterson?" Serren asks. "How will he be managed?"

"William Sitterson won't be a problem," Erebus replies. "As long as Briana is held here at the Institute, he will remain on-site and compliant, even without the serum to control his abilities. It goes against his nature—and that of any Scion of Gawain's—to leave her behind and uncared for."

"Exactly." Cestra agrees. "The most effective way to control someone is to understand their motivations. Which is why my second proposal is that we use this chapter's dedication to the mission and loyalty to one another to our advantage. We will inform all of the Legendborn who witnessed Arthur's Call to Briana that she has *chosen* to go into hiding to protect the Spell for the good of the Order. And in doing so, she has agreed to leave the Regency in place as the Order finds its new way forward. If there are questions, we can reiterate the importance of her safety and emphasize her own concern about the well-being of her friends."

"I'd never give up like that." I shake my head. "The others won't believe you."

"Won't they?" Cestra says. "Do you truly think they feel *safe* with you as their leader? On the worst night of their lives, when their friends were murdered right in front of them, you revealed yourself as a liar who infiltrated their chapter. You are at the center of their trauma."

Disgust and shame mingle in my chest. "My friends saw me kill the goruchel and the other demons. I fought *for* them, *with* them. . . ."

"You killed a goruchel when you were out of your own mind. Possessed, as you say. You are dangerous, Briana . . . and we have proof of that."

She reaches forward and presses a button, switching the screen to an image of me in the ogof during the Rite. This time, I see it through new eyes. What it would look like to someone who wasn't there, who didn't know what I was doing and had never witnessed the private Rite. I stand at the stone, with Excalibur raised and blood dripping down my palm. Root dances around the blade and my arms, flaring outward. I see the Mageguard shielding the Regents from *me*, not my flame. I see the translucent dome as the only thing standing between them and my power, while my eyes are distant, unfocused . . . and I am out of control.

Tears sting at the corners of my eyes.

"Proposals accepted," Aldrich says. "They are elegant, Cestra. Well done. Our final measure is, of course, how to proceed with Briana herself."

My head snaps up. "You can't keep me here forever."

"If I may," Erebus begins, and Aldrich cedes the floor to him. "My proposal is that we do keep Briana here at the Institute. My team and I will further study her abilities—safely, of course."

Cestra crosses her arms and leans back. "I agree. She can't control her power. Her aether draws hot and cannot be forged. This red mage flame appears only when she is in mortal danger, not unlike Merlin children before they are trained."

"Or Morgaines," Gabriel says, his voice cutting. "We have heard they are on the move. We have heard they have sent a Shadowborn to this very chapter."

"She is not a Morgaine," Erebus says dryly.

"How would you know?" Gabriel asks, drumming his fingers on the table. "A Morgaine has not been witnessed by this Council in hundreds of years."

Erebus hisses, baring long canines. "Because I can detect the sorceress's children. I can taste their magic. And because I say so."

Their voices drift to the background as I stare at the screen, trying to see myself through other peoples' eyes. Remembering Arthur's demand that my friends kneel before me. Wondering if he knew something that I didn't about what true power really looked like.

"Could she be trained to control her power on her own?" Aldrich asks.

"By whom?" Cestra counters with a snort. "We could train her like a Merlin, but to what end? As the Scion of Arthur, she is the anchor to the Spell of Eternity." She snaps. "One mistake, and Legendborn power is gone forever."

"And would we want to train her anyway?" Erebus murmurs. "To wield *either* of her aether abilities? We have already decided not to allow her near the blade. This is why, at this juncture, it is best to secure her for further study and testing under *my* supervision—"

Aldrich calls the room to order. He furrows his brow, turning to me. "Briana, we are not monsters. We will let you have a say in your own fate. I can't imagine you ever wanted to be king of all this, did you? I can see in your eyes that you yourself are frightened of these abilities. Surely you agree that being held secure, here, is the best outcome for you?"

The footage runs over and over in my mind on a loop. That girl, standing there *so* confident that all she needed to do was complete a ritual to claim her title. She'd studied all of the right words, all of the right protocol, but in the end, it wasn't her title to claim—I suck in a breath.

It wasn't my title to claim. . . .

Understanding, true understanding, finds me slowly, then lands heavy in my gut. I laugh, dry and bitter.

"Briana?" Aldrich prods.

I raise my head, leveling a gaze at the Lord Regent. "You're *still lying*."

The room goes still and Aldrich blinks. "This accusation, Briana—"

"You've *been* lying, from the beginning." I let a sharp edge creep into my voice. "You were never going to let me complete the Rite. It was a perfect opportunity to isolate me and take me out, because the Scion of Arthur must undergo it alone, without any Legendborn nearby. You didn't just *happen* to bring a syringe full of an experimental drug designed to suppress ancestral abilities to the ogof y ddraig. I didn't attack you . . . but you *hoped* something flashy would happen . . . something that looked dangerous. That's why you brought the cameras."

Their faces are answer enough. Gabriel frowns. "You must understand, tradition—"

"I pulled Excalibur from its stone! That *is* the tradition!" I shout, incredulous. "You saw it for yourselves. I pulled the blade, I am Arthur's heir, but that was never going to be enough for you." I tip my head back with a hollow laugh, delirious with the feeling of being *right*, with exposing the Regents, even here in private. "Bury the war. Bury the betrayal. Now . . . you'll bury the Scion."

Serren, who has remained quiet, shakes his head and spreads his glowing hands wide on the table. "You cannot blame us prioritizing the stability of the kingdom in the face of imminent war."

I jab a finger at him. "You should be prioritizing *winning* the war that is already here! Not scheming to stay in power!"

"What would you know about our war?" Aldrich scolds. "You were raised Unanedig."

"I was." I nod. "I *was* raised Unanedig, which means I know what you all look like from the outside. This isn't about the war. This isn't even about your refusal to hand the crown over to someone you don't know, because you didn't know Nick, either. Not really. If Nick were the Crown Scion, even with his father's betrayal," I ask, "would he have already been crowned?"

"Yes!" Serren asserts, as if it's obvious. "Because Nicholas would be able to control his abilities! Forge the weapons needed!"

"He'd have needed time to *adapt* to Arthur's inheritances," I retort, "just like any other Awakened Scion. And you would have given him that time. If control was the issue for Nick, you would have sent aid right away—a Master Merlin to teach him, or a Liege—but for me you didn't. You didn't even *try* to help me! This isn't because you fear my root either; Cestra just said that it only appears when I am in mortal danger—which should be a *good* thing for a Scion of Arthur." I shake my head. "This isn't about me being a danger to others. It's about you all preventing power from going to someone you don't think should have it."

"What does—"

"The Line is Law!" I sneer, teeth bared. "Y llinach yw'r ddeddf."

Gabriel seethes. "It is not that simple—"

"It *is* that simple. It has *been* that simple for *centuries*," I say, fist tight on the table. "I wasn't raised in your world, but I know that following the bloodlines is the most sacred rule you have. There are fifteen hundred years of one non-negotiable, unbreakable truth: the one who pulls the sword becomes king. That is the law." I glare at them all, one at a time. "Unless she looks like me."

"This is outrageous," Aldrich says, face paling. "As you said yourself, you were not raised in our world. You were raised without our—our customs," Aldrich insists, placing his hands on the table. "This is not about—about *race*."

I laugh icily. "When white people say something's 'not about race,' it's usually because it is and they don't wanna talk about it."

"Excuse me?" Cestra sneers.

"Excuse yourself," I sneer back. "It was about race to Lord Davis, but at least *he* had the decency to admit it to my face instead of"—I jerk my chin at the room, the screen, the camera—"all of this!"

Aldrich's face has gone slack. "You do not know what you're talking about, child."

Anger and shame burn me up inside. I should have known. I should have *known* better. I *did* know better . . . . I just . . . they wanted me to forget what else was at stake here. What's always at stake. I inhale a shaky breath. Try to keep my voice from breaking.

Maybe I let myself forget, but I won't let them see me cry.

"You know *how* I know it's about race?" I whisper. "Because in this entire conversation, not one of you have mentioned *why* I am the Scion of Arthur in the first place. *Why* I have his blood in my veins."

Aldrich looks as if he's choking on air. "Briana—"

"Crown Scion," I correct.

His face flushes red. The next words seem to be ripped from his chest, like he'd never say them if I hadn't forced him to. "We have heard the reports. This *claim* about how your bloodline came to be that of Arthur's. It is an accusation without *proof.*"

Everything inside of me lights up in rage. Roars out of me in an anger so rich I can taste it. Fury so cold, I grow completely still with it—or else I might explode.

"There it is . . ." My voice, low and merciless, tears at the silence in the room. I see Vera's hair, her voice. The suffering she carried, the suffering that followed, and led to me—her wound made weapon. "You don't believe history is true. You won't even admit it's possible. That I am Arthur's heir not by choice or honor, but by *violence.*"

The room freezes. Their arguments gone brittle. The air itself is desperate to hold me back, because I can break it, because I am the tip of the spear. The pain-sharpened blade.

"You won't say it out loud, but I will," I say. "I am the Scion of Arthur by rape. I *am* your proof."

For a long, long moment my heart beats wildly as all six members of the High Council of Regents sit, silenced. A muscle twitches at the corner of Aldrich's eye, but for the moment, even the Lord Regent holds his tongue.

Abruptly, Gabriel slams his hand on the table. "Is this Council to believe that Samuel Davis, the last *true* Scion of Arthur, would be so *irresponsible?*"

"'True'? 'Irresponsible'?" My lip curls back until my teeth are bared. "My *mother* was a Scion of Arthur. And my grandmother. Back *eight* generations!"

Cestra recovers in the only way she knows how, it seems: with a swipe at a fellow Council member. "Is it so hard to believe a man would be so . . . *irresponsible*, Regent Gabriel?" Something dangerous glints in her eye. "Samuel Davis's disregard for a woman he considered his property is, perhaps, the most believable element of any of the stories this Council has heard thus far."

"You will speak with *respect*, Cestra!" Gabriel narrows his eyes. "That man was a Scion—"

"Since when has a man's title *prevented* his brutality instead of further emboldening it?" Cestra hisses.

Aldrich stands, smoothing his hands over his suit. "We need to make a decision about the problem before us, not a problem from two hundred years ago."

Erebus sighs. "As Briana has just pointed out, these two 'problems' are one and the same." Aldrich glares at Erebus, but Erebus merely shrugs. "I am not wrong."

"The decision remains," Aldrich replies.

"There is no decision," Gabriel says. "Tacitus, take her memories, then let Erebus have her."

I say a silent prayer that my natural resistance holds against a fresh mesmer from a Master Merlin like Tacitus. With the serum in my veins . . . there's no telling.

Tacitus grins. "I do like it when they stumble on the truth."

"Really?" Serren asks without taking his eyes from me. "Why is that?"

Tacitus stands and is at my side in a blink. "Much more satisfying when I take it away."

His tight grip on my arm dampens some of the righteous fire inside my chest. I *have* to resist him. If I can't, then I'm lost.

"She leaves us no choice." Gabriel stands with a long sigh, buttoning his jacket. "It will be quite a lot of mesmerwork, Tacitus, but this girl has taken too much of our time. I, too, grow tired of the ceremony, and we have a dinner reservation."

"Agreed," Aldrich says, rapping his knuckles on the table. "Tacitus will clean things up here, and then Briana will be held at the Institute under Cestra's and Erebus's watch. We are adjourned."

My jaw drops. "That's all you're going to say to me?"

"What more is there to say, Briana?" Aldrich asks with a heavy sigh. "We must act in the Order's best interest, and as it is, if you are not in agreement with our decisions, you'll only create unnecessary strife."

Insult and indignation strike through me like lightning, and my anger roars back to life. "Is this how you treat the Scion of Arthur, Lord Regent?"

"You may have the king's blood"—Aldrich finds my gaze and holds it—"but you are not a Scion. You are . . . a camgymeriad. A mistake."

My lips part. Tears press at the back of my eyes, but I will not let them fall. I will not. I grasp for words, but they will not come. For vengeance, but I don't know how to take it. I almost wish for Arthur, burning for war. But they have stripped me of everything I could use to fight them.

My eyes follow the others. One by one, they prepare to file out of the room. As if everything had already been decided and my outburst was nothing to consider.

Of course it wasn't.

They have *a dinner reservation.*

The words leave my mouth before I can think better of them. "Regent Aldrich!" I call. He pauses at the door to look at me. I let the grin spread slow across my face. "Not here. Not today. But somewhere. Someday."

Uncertainty flickers across the Lord Regent's face. Quick, but I see it—and he knows that I did. Aldrich calls to the Seneschal of Mesmer. "Tacitus, if you would?"

As soon as the room empties, Tacitus wraps his hands around my face, squeezing tight. "Look at me." I flex my fingers, send pain shooting up the arm William burned until it clears my mind. Still, I stare into his golden eyes and feel the deep pull into his well. Today, his mesmer feels . . . warm. Invitational.

"You will remember the decisions made here as if they were your own, and release your dissents."

His words wash over me in a rhythmic wave, all care and generosity, and my thoughts start to follow them. . . . Releasing my dissents sounds lovely. It *is* lovely—

No. Tacitus's voice lifts the heavy anchor awareness from my mind, but I pull it back.

"If anyone in the Order asks you what happened here, you will say you were in conference with us for the past three days and agreed to remove yourself from the public eye for the safety of the Order and the Legendborn spell."

"Yes," I whisper. "I will remember what was said here today."

Tacitus's brow dips momentarily, pausing at my wording. "Your assistance is an act of kindness to help us save your friends and the lives of thousands. You want to help others. And staying here is the best thing you can do with the gifts you've been given."

"My . . . gifts?" I can barely keep the surprise out of my voice.

He nods. "Your inherited powers of Arthur."

"Yes, of course," I reply. "Arthur's blood is a gift."

My stomach twists into something rigid and painful. A knot burrowing into my gut. What happened to Vera was not a gift. It was assault. Theft. I want nothing else in the world in this moment but to burn this Merlin. Tear him *apart*.

Recognition flashes in Tacitus's eyes. I shutter my rage, but it's too late. He glimpsed what I've been hiding. He leans closer. "Briana, your heart is racing—and it shouldn't be."

I freeze. "Is that bad?"

"Only if it means this mesmer has not taken." He tilts his head, voice mild. "We will hold you captive here. But if, by some chance, you escape, I will hunt you down to the ends of the earth and rip your power from its source. Do you understand?"

I hold his gaze, keeping my own steady and blank. "I am here for my own safety. Why would I choose to escape?"

17

EREBUS ESCORTS ME to my new lodgings. We take an elevator near the conference room and walk down a long, enclosed suspended bridge with a glass ceiling and glass sides. For the first time, I see where they've been keeping me.

The Institute is not one building, but two. The building we've left looks like a conference center from the outside. The six-story building we're walking to now looks residential. Room windows punched in regular, near-identical shapes along the outer wall, no balconies.

The bridge is a few stories up, but it's high enough that I can see the grounds below. A garden maze, a fountain, a courtyard lit by electric lampposts. A kidney-shaped pool sits right beneath us; I hear a waterfall.

The Institute is undeniably, incredibly modern. More this century than any other building the Order has shown me.

The archaic language, the restored antiques in the Lodge, the robes, the rituals—I see them all for what they are now. Tools to immerse the young Scions and Squires and Pages in their own legends. The Regents keep the stories so alive that the Legendborn don't see the reality of what the Order has become.

When I see an aether dome overhead, it takes everything in me not to cry with relief. I have my magical Sight, even if the aether's color seems muted. I catch a whiff of signatures, several of them. The serum had been designed for Legendborn Scions, so maybe Vera's inheritances aren't fully suppressed, just dampened.

The dome starts at the edge of the sidewalk that circles the building below, arches up over the glass bridge, and curves all the way down to the other side, engulfing everything. I wonder if such a ward around the Institute is standard procedure, or if the Merlins are casting it just for me.

Erebus notices my gaze. "The Mageguard have been posted here since you awoke, and they'll work in shifts to maintain the barrier and keep you safe until I release them."

When we exit the bridge, it's like walking into a five-star hotel. Erebus takes me to another elevator, and we ride to the top floor. There is only one room at this level at the very end of a long hall. A faint silver layer of aether hovers over its wooden door.

At the door, Erebus produces a card from his coat pocket and swipes it over a keycard lock. The light on the side of the box flashes from red to green, but instead of opening the door like a normal hotel, he raises his other hand to the center of the wood. His palm presses into the sheen of aether, and an unwarded circle grows from his fingertips outward until it covers the entire entrance. Only then does he grasp the knob. The door opens with a quiet hiss.

Double locks: technological and magical.

At first glance, the room is a modern studio apartment. A kitchen on the right, with two cabinets over a sink. A living room furnished in gray and gold. A bed on the far wall and a door that leads to a bathroom.

"I think you'll enjoy your stay here. I need to rejoin the other members of the Council for our reservation." Erebus clasps his hands at his waist, giving me time to respond.

I swallow around a dry tongue. "What are you going to do to me now?"

His sigh is one of disappointment. "Nothing tonight." He looks down at me, red eyes like a heat lamp on my skin. "I will return for you in several days' time once the others are gone so that you and I may begin our work together, uninterrupted by unscientific minds."

Our work. Scientific. Whatever he has planned, with those words I know it will be invasive. Not work, torture. My throat closes. All I can manage is a nod.

"You are very brave, Briana." Erebus studies me like a Merlin, watching the effort it takes to hold my tears back, listening to the sounds of me barely hold-ing myself together. Even if I convinced the others that I chose to stay here, they can't expect me to not be frightened at being alone. "That will serve you well in the time to come." He closes the door behind me without another word. I hear the mechanism lock and assume the aether barrier went up as well.

I am used to Merlins' silent departures by now. I listen for the ding of the elevator to know that he's really gone.

Then, all at once, the strain of the past hour spills from my mouth in a low, long whine. My hands shake from adrenaline and tension and fear.

After a moment, I turn to inspect the door itself. There is no knob on the inside, and the solid wood surface sits flush against the doorjamb, surrounded by a crack so narrow I doubt I could slip a sheet of paper through.

Set in the wall to the right of the door is a small opening with a metal frame and plastic flap. I lift the flap up to see a covered tray of food, identical to the one by my bed this morning. When I yank the tray out to examine the opening, the cover snaps off, spilling the sandwich and salad in the process. It's no hope: the passage is just tall enough to fit a tray and nothing more, and I cannot reach through to the other side.

I dash to the single window near the bed—and see bars. No escape here, either.

A gilded cage.

They plan to keep me here for a long, long time. Maybe forever. Or as long as the experiments entertain them.

I squeeze my hands into a fist, but the strength of Arthur feels very far away, lost in that hollow space. With it, I could have pulled the bars back, but then there are the Mageguard outside. Even if I could break out, they'd hear me, and then I would be in worse shape.

I am *buried.*

I can wield Excalibur when no one else on the planet can, and "the Line is Law." That should have been enough.

But the Regents had been five, ten steps ahead. *Power is one thing; control is another.* They could have taken me prisoner right away, but instead they laid the trap so carefully and so slowly that no one could say they betrayed the Order's mission and laws. How could I have failed before I'd even gotten started? How could I not see it coming? All of that fighting, and it ends here. I step back from the window and clasp both hands to my mouth. If I don't, the scream I've been holding inside my chest will rip itself from my body.

All of my ancestors, and my mother, running so I would not have to . . . and I failed them.

18

TWO DAYS PASS.

Someone I can't see slips food into the small passage in the wall three times a day without a word. I call for them, but they never respond. They are human, though, because I can hear their footsteps approach and retreat.

I worry about William and Sel, and where they are being imprisoned. The other Legendborn are likely busy with Cestra's mission. I hope, for their sake if not my own, that they believed what the Regents told them about my departure; if they didn't, they'd likely end up drugged and imprisoned just like me and William.

I worry about Alice, too, but eventually find gratitude that she and my father are safe in their ignorance, even if hers is newly formed. I don't usually go more than a day or two without texting my father. I wonder what the Lieges are telling him. My stomach sinks when I think that maybe they used a mesmered and brainwashed Alice to tell him their lies about my whereabouts and why I haven't called. He'd believe her, because she's Alice.

I should worry more about myself, but it's easier to think of the others' fates than my own. Or to sleep and forget it all.

I wait for my powers to return, but the emptiness remains.

It doesn't occur to me until the end of the second day of confinement without the return of my abilities that the serum is probably in the food.

On the third day, I am leaning against the wall, waiting, when dinner arrives. The footsteps are critical. Footsteps tell me that the person approaching isn't Erebus, or at least isn't him alone. He has not come for me yet, but I know he will soon.

The steps pause outside the door and the flap clicks open. The metal tray slides in.

Now that I've figured out how they are still drugging me, it's hard to imagine eating or taking any of the so-called kindness offered here. I skipped breakfast and lunch. I pull the tray from its window and take it to the table.

When I uncover the entrée, steam rises. There's a steak covered in a deep brown gravy, mushrooms, and soft, caramelized onions. My traitorous stomach growls at the sight of it. Before now there had been sandwiches and fruit, oatmeal in Styrofoam bowls, cheese wrapped in plastic—all plain and tasteless.

This looks delicious.

I could skip this meal too, I think. *But when Erebus comes for me, there could be an opportunity to escape, and I'll be too weak to run.*

In the end, I decide I would rather be trapped, powerless, and full than trapped, powerless, and starving.

I unwrap the utensils from their white cloth and carve into the steak, sawing the knife back and forth until it stops abruptly.

Like it has hit something.

I nudge the blade through the entrée until I see what I'd struck: a tiny black case about the size of my thumb, underneath the gravy and beef. I dig with my fingers until I can pull the case out. There's a thin seal around the edge. My heart starts to race.

I lift the case and stumble on my way to the kitchenette, carefully rinsing and drying it off with shaking fingers. Once the case is clear of sauce, I snap it open, and inside, nestled in dry velvet interior, is a shiny black plastic device. It's . . . an earpiece. Like something you'd see in a spy movie.

No magic here. All tech.

I carefully slip the device into my ear, pressing until it's snug, then push the button on the side.

There's silence on the line, but I can hear that it's live. That someone *could* be on the other side, listening.

"Hello?" I whisper.

A release of breath through the earpiece. "Crown Scion Matthews." A voice I don't recognize.

I grasp the counter's edge, swallowing. "Y-yes."

The voice turns muffled, like they're facing away from the receiver. "It's her."

"Who are you?"

When they speak again, the voice is clear. Confident. "Someone who can create a five-minute window of escape for you. Tonight is the only option; there will be no second chance. Keep the device in your ear and do exactly as I say."

My mouth opens and closes around a dozen potential words, all fractured beneath the weight of shock. Finally, I manage. "Wait. Who *are* you?"

"Someone you can trust."

I snort. "I don't trust anyone right now."

"Fair. Listen, timing is everything. I can give you about . . . *three* minutes to decide if you want to stay there for months, if not years, of your life, or if you're ready to run."

I gape, stunned, trying to catch up.

"Now that's two minutes and fifty seconds to decide. Forty-five."

My heart slams against my chest. "What do I do?"

"Under the tray there's a keycard. Get it now."

I'm moving fast as they talk, reaching up underneath the tray, fumbling until I feel the edge of tape and something flat and hard underneath it. I pull, and the card drops into my hand.

"Two minutes. Are your shoes on?"

"Yes."

"Stand by the door until you hear the signal."

"I—I don't have my powers," I stammer. "They've drugged me with some suppressant; I can't do anything."

"You can follow instructions."

I shouldn't bristle at their tone, but I do. With all that I've been through, who the hell is this person to tell me what I can and cannot do? I'm the one who's being drugged and locked away and—

"No time for a temper tantrum." They clearly read my mind. "One minute. Are you in or out?"

"One minute until what? What am I looking for?!"

"One minute until the real clock starts. And you're not looking. You're listening. Stand back from the door."

"Stand back?!" I whisper-shout. "What are you going to do, blow it open?"

"Not quite. Forty seconds."

I grip the keycard in my hand. Not sure what I could possibly be looking—no, listening for. I count the seconds down in my head, my heart pounding and blood rushing in my ears.

One chance. One chance to get out of here.

Suddenly, there's a hiss like a vacuum being released. The ground shudders beneath my feet, and something in the ceiling groans overhead.

A heavy whoosh.

A loud pop that leaves my ears ringing.

An external alarm blares all around me, echoing outside of the window—like the fortress itself is screaming.

"What was—"

"The wards and dome are down. That five-minute window of escape I promised? Just started. Swipe the card." I run forward and slip the card down the reader. The door cracks an inch. Enough that I can push it open and slip into the silent, wardless hall.

"I'm out. What now?"

"Elevator."

I sprint to the elevator, heart pounding, adrenaline burning away my confusion. I grasp the edge of one elevator door to catch myself and swing around to face the panel of numbered buttons. "What now?" I screech over the high-pitched alarm, mashing the DOOR CLOSE button even though no one is coming behind me, no one is there, no one else is even on this floor.

"Hit B2."

I smash the button with my thumb and the doors close blithely, dinging. My fist clenches the keycard so tightly that the plastic starts to bend. *Loosen up,* I think. *Don't break it. Just watch the floors go down. Don't think about getting caught.* "What's on B2?"

Ding. Floor five. "Sub-basement parking garage."

"I'm on the sixth floor."

"I know."

Ding. Four.

"That's *seven* floors down. They'll catch me."

"You've got a head start, the building is empty, don't panic."

Ding. Three.

"A head start? Against *Merlins*? Are you kidding me?" They could be scaling the walls, tearing away the bars on my room's windows.

Tacitus could be on the lobby floor, waiting for me just like he said. Or outside the building, ready to hunt me down and take me apart to get to my power.

Another ding, and the elevator starts to slow. One more floor, then it's the lobby. "They called the elevator!"

"Shit. Time to adapt."

"What?"

Ding. Two. "Lie flat on the floor!"

I drop.

"There's an emergency overspeed governor that will—"

BOOM!

An explosion overhead, the elevator shakes, something heavy snaps—

The elevator drops into a free fall.

My body lifts a sliver off the ground, inertia holding me in its grasp—then gravity takes over.

I scream. A deep, ear-splitting whine from somewhere screams with me. The floor jerks. Decelerates. Another jerk. Stillness.

"Okay, get outta there."

I jump to my feet, mashing the DOOR OPEN button as I gulp oxygen into my lungs. The doors edge open about the width of my fist.

"Not opening all the way!"

"Pull. The safety will engage."

I work my right fingers into the wedge and swing to one side of the elevator, bracing my wrist with my left, and pull. The doors move another inch, then release on the track, opening enough that I can slip my body through and into the brightly lit garage.

"I'm out!"

"Run straight to the far corner; there's a door."

I sprint among cars as fast as I can. "The Mageguard—"

"Distracted. Use the keycard again."

I pull the card as I run, swiping as soon as I come to a stop, glancing over my shoulder. The door buzzes, then unclicks, cracks a few inches. A damp, earthy smell hits my nose, then the scents of dust and metal. I glimpse a dark hallway. When I get the door fully open, one light buzzes to life overhead.

"Okay, this is the hard part."

"Arguable!" I pant. I can only see about six feet ahead of me.

"Focus. These are service tunnels. You're gonna have to sprint through it, Bree. All the way to the end, but the lights are motion activated, so they won't come on all at once. Keep running."

I hesitate. Beyond the halo of light on the concrete floor, the tunnel extends into black nothingness. An abyss that I'm supposed to run through.

"They're coming around the building. They don't know which basement level you're on, but they'll find out quick. They'll have the ward back up in ninety seconds. You've got to get on the other side of it before they do, or you'll be trapped. *Run!*"

I sprint. In four strides, my lungs are burning. I'm running faster than the fluorescents can keep up, tearing down the hallway into darkness, leaving sputtering lights in a trail behind me. I can't see *anything*.

"The ward's coming up! Faster!"

"I'm—"

"You can go faster. You're running into pitch-black and you can't see, so your brain is fighting you. Fight back. It's a straight line. I *promise* you won't hit a wall. Run faster. Trust me!"

I grit my teeth and trust. My legs pump faster, arms swinging for momentum. The Merlins behind me can see in the dark. If they enter the tunnel before I get out, they'll be on me in seconds.

The thought of actually hitting a brick wall—exactly what the ward will feel like if I barrel headfirst into it at this speed—pushes me even faster, so fast I could trip.

"The wards—" I pant.

I can feel it in the air, aether crackling above me. The dome reshaping, spreading.

"Go!"

The pressure builds, the magic bearing down on me, like the ceiling is getting lower.

"Almost, almost, keep going, every step matters—"

They're right.

One heel strike, and the ward ripples down my spine.

The next, it snaps down to the floor only a step behind.

I can't help but glance back. The shining blue barrier illuminates the rest of the hall, clashing with the red emergency lights. I push forward again—and see an exit door.

I hit the crash bar. The exterior alarm rips into my ears, blaring overhead as I stumble out onto a concrete pad facing a service road.

"Come on!"

A familiar voice.

My heart stops.

I twist toward the voice, a small dark-haired figure hanging halfway out the door of a black Jeep idling to my right. A face I'd never expect to see here, never *want* to see here.

My heart starts again—and leaps toward her.

Alice.

19

I DON'T REMEMBER getting to the Jeep.

One minute, I'm staring slack-jawed at my best friend dressed in head-to-toe black tactical gear. The next, I'm being strapped into a seat as the vehicle peels out of the backlot with an ear-splitting screech. Inside my chest, my heart still thunders from that sprint and my lungs are burning. Outside the windows, security lights and trees blur by in a dizzying streak.

"Bree, oh my God, oh my God." Alice kneels in front of me, double-checks my seatbelt, then engulfs me in a hug as our getaway vehicle tears down the dark service road.

"Alice?!" My voice is muffled into her shoulder, lost beneath the engine. I cling to her arms, grounding myself. Willing my breathing to slow down. "How—how are you—"

"Strap in, Chen. Gonna be a bumpy ride." The driver who barks a command at Alice is a white woman in her late twenties. Dark-haired, with a thick silver streak over each ear. Alice shifts beside me and buckles herself into the next seat, fingers trembling slightly as she clicks the belts secure.

"How the hell did you get here?" I gasp. "Tacitus said he wiped your memory."

"Well . . . ," she begins with a sly smile. "He tried to."

Before I can ask what *that* means, we're interrupted. "Crown Scion," says a wry, familiar voice behind me. My head twists around immediately.

"Gillian?"

My old combat trainer smirks at me from the bench at the back of the vehicle. She's in tactical gear all over: a black sweater, black pants with one leg rolled over a sleek black prosthesis, and both feet in worn combat boots. Gillian's a Liege with years of field time under her belt, mostly outdoors. With this ensemble, she could melt in and out of shadows, easy. She leans over to pass me a bottle of water, and even her hands are wrapped in black gloves. "Here, you've gotta be thirsty after what Samira just put you through."

Someone scoffs. Sitting at Gillian's left, directly behind me, is a Black woman with short salt-and-pepper hair. "I knew she could do it."

The woman's ensemble is similar to Gillian's, except her cargo pants are rolled at the ankles and her black tank shows off broad shoulders and impressively curved biceps. Her brown face has barely-there smile lines and soaring cheekbones. She might be in her early thirties, only a few years older than the driver—but her hair color would indicate otherwise. She gives a two-fingered salute. "I knew you could do it, Crown Scion," she repeats.

I recognize her voice immediately. "*You* guided me out."

"Yep. And you did well," she says with a nod. "I'm Samira Miller. Our driver up there is Lyssa Burke."

Lyssa salutes me in the mirror. At her jacket shoulder is an embroidered patch displaying the gray wolf sigil of the Line of Geraint. On Samira's jacket, I see the amethyst one-winged falcon of Bedivere.

Understanding washes over me. "You're all Lieges."

"Did the early grays give it away?" Samira smirks. "Took you a minute."

I scowl. "I just ran for my life through total darkness with the strongest Merlins in the world on my heels. I think I get a minute."

Samira raises a brow. "Gill said you had spark."

"She's got more than spark," Alice butts in, eyes stern.

"That's what the rumors say too," Samira says, dipping her head in acknowledgment. She turns her head, calling out to the front. "How we doin', Lyssa?"

Lyssa taps her fingers on the wheel and glances to a display nestled in the center of the dashboard. "Nothing on our tail—yet. The extraction point seems to be out of their hearing range."

"Like I said it'd be."

"Like you said it'd be," Lyssa agrees in a dry tone. "Helps that we incapacitated them."

Samira grins. "They're Merlins. They'll recover."

Lyssa shakes her head, eyes scanning the dark road we've pulled out onto. "Anyone ever tell you you're absolutely terrifying, Sam?"

"Lots of people, yes," Samira says.

"Wait!" I shout. The Jeep doesn't stop moving but Lyssa's eyes flash up to the rearview. "William is still back there!" Guilt surges in my chest. I should have asked about him already. "They're drugging him, too, we have to—"

"We're taking care of it." Gill grasps my shoulder in a firm grip. "Deep breaths, Matthews. Panic is not helpful."

"But—"

"Ophelia's up and running." Samira leans over to hand Gillian a small device.

"Everyone secure?" Gill asks.

Samira gives an unreadable sigh. "Did what we could."

Is "everyone" William? Or . . . ? "They have Sel, too." I look between them.

"We know," Gill responds, frowning. "At a Shadowhold. Harder for us to get in and out of a 'hold. Lot harder."

"What does that mean?" I demand. "We have to save him!"

Gill shoots me a warning glance. "We'll do what we can, kiddo. Calm down."

"But—"

She tosses me an energy bar. "You need fuel. Use the time to get up to speed, Matthews." She climbs to the front and kneels down to speak to Lyssa, dismissing me. My fist clenches around the bar. Alice rolls her eyes, snatches it from me, and starts peeling the wrapper back.

"Alice," I begin, head spinning.

She gives me the bar. "Eat."

I snap a piece off and talk while I chew. It's some sort of thick, dry, chocolate-flavored thing, but I feel better after the first swallow. "Tell me what happened."

She takes a deep breath. "The day of the Rite, William and I were in the Lodge infirmary waiting for you and the Regents to come back upstairs. But then there was a loud boom, like an explosion, and the whole damn floor rattled."

"The Rite," I mutter, "was a trap. They ambushed me while I was in a vision, and everything went to hell."

She nods. "Felt like a bomb had gone off. It shook all of Will's tools off their trays, glass pipettes shattering on the floor. . . ."

I nod. "That was . . . that was me."

The Lieges exchange glances. Alice whistles low. "Wonder if the Root—" She stops abruptly, presses her lips together. "It's good that you were under-ground."

I drop my eyes to the floor to avoid Gillian's inquiring gaze, finishing off the bar. "Yeah."

I know what Alice was about to say, and I'm wondering about the Root-crafters now too. If my ancestral door was cracked before, the Rite opened it up again. In the stream, I'd connected to the Line of Arthur and the Line of Vera both, just like when I pulled Excalibur. This time I released just a pulse of aether—enough that the Mageguard had to shield against me—but it wasn't a sustained battle; maybe the wave didn't reach the Rootcrafters on campus.

Alice continues her update. "William knew right away something was wrong. There was no time. He scribbled a number on a piece of paper, shoved it into my hand, and pushed me out the back door. Told me to run. I didn't make it far."

"The Mageguard?"

"Yeah." Alice's voice goes quiet, and behind her glasses, her eyes go distant. "They were . . . I've never seen anyone move like that, look like that."

My chest tightens. Alice doesn't have the Sight, can't see aether, has never been in a battle. And she's never seen a Merlin in action, not even Sel. Before this, the only other Merlin she'd even met besides Sel was Isaac Sorenson, who mesmered and tortured her to get to me. I squeeze her hand. "That must have been terrifying."

"It was." Her brows furrow. "But so was finding out that they'd taken you."

"What happened with Tacitus?"

She shrugs, but something about it looks off. Affected. "They took me back to the Lodge. He mesmered me to think I'd been at the library all night, but as soon as it was over, my memories started flooding back, like filling a gap. I could tell that wasn't supposed to happen, so I pretended until he released me with an order to go home."

"How?" I exclaim. "Tacitus is the most powerful mesmerist in the world."

"That's what I keep asking," Gill says.

"I don't know." No one but a best friend could hear the lie in Alice's voice. See the small flicker in her gaze when she, fleetingly, catches my eye.

She *does* know, but she won't say here.

"What about the paper William gave you?"

Gill raises her hand. "That's where I come in. Got a phone call from a frantic girl—"

"I wasn't *frantic*!" Alice interjects, nose wrinkling in insult.

Gill shoots her a quelling look, but there's fondness at the edges. "Stand down, Chen. Considering how new you are to everything Legendborn, you were downright tranquil." Gill turns to me. "Your best friend here handled herself well. When we heard from Alice and couldn't get in touch with you or William, we tried to find Sel. No dice. The last time you were seen by anyone was six days ago, when Lark drove you to the Rite. The word has been that you and William were prepping to join the search party after Nick, but if that were true, the Lieges would know about it. So we did some digging. Heard through our network that the full Council had been gathering at the Institute, and we put two and two together, crewed up, and made a plan."

"Five minutes," Lyssa calls from the front.

"But you're *Lieges*," I say, confused. "You're part of the Order. Why did you . . . ?"

"We may be of the Order," Samira says in a low voice, "but we are *not* the Order. We are Legendborn. Our allegiance is to one another."

"The lies will keep the Regents in power for now," Gill adds. "If no one else knows that Camlann has come, that the Shadowborn have risen, there will be no calls for the king or for the Table to gather. The other chapters have been kept in the dark. We're on our own here."

A buzzing sound interrupts us from the front seat. Lyssa curses and pulls out a cell phone, barking, "Yeah?"

Samira and Gill exchange glances.

"Got it," Lyssa says, shaking her head. "Yep. We'll be ready. Out." She ends the call with a tap of her thumb and looks at us in the rearview. "The Guard found the extraction point back at the Institute, are on the road now. They know there's only a few places we could go."

"How much time do we have?"

"Ophelia said thirteen minutes, tops."

Samira nods sharply. "Let's act like it's ten. This is the Mageguard we're talking about. Their ears are probably good and healed now, so they will be *extraordinarily* angry."

I blink. "Their ears?"

Alice grins. "Supersonic bombs. Samira set one off near all six of the Mageguard keeping the barrier up. They were already distracted, and then they *became* the distraction."

"Six very wounded, blood-streaming-out-of-their-ears distractions," Gill says, shifting in her seat to pull a box from her back pocket. "That's the number of Mageguard required to keep that particular barrier up. Those six had to heal and recover to raise it again. Takes full focus to merge a construct that big."

I cringe. "You . . . blew out their eardrums?"

"They'll heal." Gill winks. "We don't have our knights' inheritances anymore, remember? And some folks, like me, never got them." I'd nearly forgotten that Gill is a Liege of Kay, a Scion from a Line that, prior to this year, hadn't been Called in decades. "Sans those powers, there's no fighting a supernatural being without a few tricks up your sleeve. Hand-to-hand isn't an option, so—"

"The only weapon against Merlins is incapacitation," Samira adds. "Overwhelm their senses. They heal, but it takes a little bit of time."

"And a little bit of time is all we needed," Gill says. "Here we go."

The van swings into a paved service road, skidding on the turn. Lyssa drives straight out onto a tarmac where, in the bright lights from a hangar, I see a private jet.

"We're flying?"

"Fastest way to get some distance between us and the Merlins. Ophelia's the best pilot we've got." Gill pulls out her own phone and shoots off what looks like a few texts. A second later, the engines on the plane rise in a deep rumble that I can hear and feel from the other side of the tarmac.

"But the others," I insist. "I can't leave them. William—"

"Already ahead of you, Crown Scion," Gill says.

We come to a stop before I can say much more. "It'll be okay," Alice says with a smile. She squeezes my hand before unbuckling her seatbelt.

"Wheels up in three." Lyssa cuts the engine and grabs a bag from the front seat. "Make haste, y'all. When it comes to Merlins, every second makes a difference."

Alice picks up a duffel hidden beneath her seat, and the doors slide open. The sound of the airplane engine blasts us. I'm pretty sure we're supposed to be wearing ear protection this close to a plane, but the game plan seems to be run as fast as you can. Board. Make haste.

Fair enough.

We sprint to the plane, hands over our ears. Or at least, the others do. My legs are still weak and that bar wasn't enough. Alice hangs back, arm looped tight in mine while we jog, bringing up the rear. As we reach the bottom of the stairs, a tall white woman with short black hair appears in the doorway, wearing a pilot's headset. Ophelia. She assesses us all in a single glance. "You two in the back. Gill, Sam, Lyssa, need you up front." Ophelia disappears into the body of the plane as we race up the stairs.

Once inside, Gill, Lyssa, and Samira turn left toward the cockpit, leaving Alice and me hovering in the carpeted entryway. I feel something like relief when Alice and I exchange both a stunned glance and nervous laughter.

"How are we here right now?" she asks.

"I don't know," I answer quietly, adrenaline still rushing through me, making my breath come in shaky gasps. "I don't know."

The curtain beside us yanks back—to reveal another familiar face.

"William," I breathe. He surges forward into my arms.

"Bree," he murmurs, his face tucked into my neck. "They took you away and you didn't come back. They kept me in a room on the residence side for days. Stopped drugging me but told me they'd hurt you if I fought back. Then . . . the wards dropped. Max went speeding off. Here." He draws back, reaching into his pocket. "These are yours." Jewelry spills into my palm. My heart stutters.

My mother's golden charm bracelet and the Pendragon necklace.

The coin is still smudged with dried, rust-colored blood. Mine, from the night of the Rite of Kings. I trace the thin, healed scar Excalibur left on my palm. My mother's bracelet is a little gnarled and smudged, but otherwise okay.

"Max leaving was our opening to grab Will." Gill reappears and leans a hand against the bulkhead. "We've got one more car coming."

"There they are!" Ophelia shouts from the cockpit. A squeal in the distance as a red sports car speeds into the lot. "Last one, let's go."

Gill pushes past us and jogs down the stairs. The rest of us exchange worried looks. I gnaw on my lip, hoping against hope. "Is it—?"

The sports car screeches to a stop near the stairs. The driver door opens, and a blurred figure speeds to the back—too fast to be human.

"Mageguard," I gasp.

"Oh God." Alice backs into the cockpit, eyes wide. "They found us."

20

"STAND DOWN." SAMIRA appears in the doorway, hand held out. "This is one of ours."

We turn back to the windows as the Merlin emerges from the back of the car, hoisting a still form over his shoulder.

I squint, but they're too fast to follow. Abruptly, the Merlin whooshes up the stairs to deposit—

"Sel!" William pushes past me.

"Man, that is one stubborn kid." Lark stands after dropping Sel's slumped figure into one of the bench seats along the back wall of the cabin. There's an angry, purpling bruise on the Kingsmage's left cheekbone. "Had to knock him out cold just to get him in the car. He's gonna be *pissed* when he wakes up." Lark turns to the cabin, a wry smile on his face. Finds me, winks. "Hey, not-princess-not-king. Sorry to report they tossed your gauntlets. I'll get you new ones."

I blink. "But you're—"

"The Mageguard were originally created to serve the king," he says, running a hand through his windblown hair. "Some of us still hold to that." He looks down at Sel, whose vitals are being checked by William. "Plus, I owe Kane for the other night."

"Thank you." William glances up at Lark as he holds Sel's wrist. "For saving him."

"No thanks needed, Scion Sitterson."

William stands with a tired smile. "Call me William. Please."

Lark holds William's gaze for a beat, then ducks his head. "William." If I wasn't looking for it this time, I'd have missed the pink on his cheeks entirely.

Gill calls from the door. "Better get out of here, Larkin. They'll get suspicious if you're gone too long."

Lark salutes me, then he's out of sight. The car he arrived in speeds away just as Gill pulls the door, and instructs us all to buckle in.

The engine changes pitch, then we're rolling down the tarmac.

My head is forced back into the cushion as we climb. Motion below catches my eye.

A convoy of Mageguard Jeeps careens around a corner and skids to a halt on the tarmac below. Half a dozen figures clad in black whoosh out of their cars onto the cement to stare up at us with glowing eyes.

"They're too far away to create a construct to slow the plane," Gill says reassuringly. Somehow, it still doesn't reassure me at all. "Promise."

Samira seems just as unbothered. In fact, she flashes me a grin. "We've got about a couple hours in the air, and you have questions."

"Where is everyone else?" William demands.

"They said they'd send Tor and Sar to the field to help the Lieges search for Nick," I say.

Gill nods. "They're at Northern now. We've kept an eye on them through the Liege network. And the others—Felicity, Pete, and Greer—they're grounded at the chapter, hunting the demons that have been crossing."

William shakes his head in disbelief. "They just . . . gave up on us?"

"They were told lies." Gill's face sours. "We thought about sending them a message about what really happened to you both, but decided against it. Greer and Pete would have begged to join the rescue, but too many people on a mission is how somebody gets dead."

I shift in my chair. "But they have no idea what they're facing."

"We need to tell them about the inheritance-blocking serum the Regents used to suppress our abilities. Bree's the Crown Scion, the king," William says. "If they'll do it to her, they'll do it to them."

"They won't need to," I say quietly. "Not if the Regents have convinced them I'm too dangerous for the Order." All eyes turn to me. "We already know Tor will never see me as king. She might even turn me back over to the Regents again if she ever finds me."

"Again?" William asks.

I nod. "I don't know what she told them, but her call that day . . . it started everything. They've been planning since the moment she reached out."

"I'm not surprised," Alice says, eyes narrowed. "I hate that bitch."

My jaw drops. Alice throws her hands up. "What? She was mad about you from the beginning. From the literal *actual* beginning, Bree."

William sighs. "Just because you're an outsider—"

"That's not it and you know it," I cut him off.

"Look, Tor's racist. Doesn't do us any good to deny it," Alice chimes in, crossing her arms. "Especially not now."

"I agree with Chen," Samira says. "We can't protect Bree if we ignore the forces working against her. How deep they go, how far, how wide."

"Tor'll come around," Gill says.

Alice snorts. "That's not generally how this works, but if y'all say so."

"And Felicity?" William whispers.

"She's struggling." Gill's voice is so low in the roar of the cabin that it almost goes unheard. "At least Owen's there now to help her through the agony."

"The agony?" Alice asks.

Gill inhales slowly, grimacing. "The agony is what we call the pain and grief from feeling an Oath bond break in battle. For the Scion or Squire left behind . . . it hurts like nothing you can imagine."

Silence in the cabin. Gill's and my eyes go to William, but he's already turned away from us. A stab of guilt in my heart. He felt Whitty die, too, and he'd never said anything. I hadn't even noticed, hadn't asked.

The thought of more deaths sends panic streaking through me. "Gill, the Regents said my dad is under Liege supervision. Is he safe?"

"The Lieges assigned to him are loyal to you, not the Regents. We made sure of it."

My shoulders soften in relief. "Oh, thank God."

Gill squeezes my shoulder. "We have burner phones that can mimic your cell number." She smiles softly. "Figured you'd want to check in. Tell him what you think he needs to know."

"I have no idea what that is, but yes." I release a slow breath. "And thank you." I consider using the opportunity to call Patricia or Mariah too, but decide against it. I need to keep the Rootcraft community as far away from the Order as possible. If their identities are exposed, if it gets out that I broke the Code of Secrecy with them, too . . . it's just too dangerous.

"The Lieges are watching my parents too," Alice says quietly. "Just in case. I told them we were busy with classes and it'd be a while before I could call." I know she hates lying to her parents. I wish she didn't have to.

"There's something else," Gill says in a low voice. She and Samira exchange a worried glance that makes my blood run cold. "The Regents will keep Camlann quiet for as long as they're able, but when it does get out that war has come, the traditionalists in the Order—including every Legendborn family—will demand a king. If the Regents are going to continue to claim the Scion of Arthur is 'sequestered,' they'll need a strong Plan B."

"What's Plan B?" Alice asks.

"Plan B," Sel's hoarse voice brings everyone's attention to the bench, where he's slowly pushing himself to sitting, "is when the Regents present a compliant high-ranked Scion to serve their interests. A perfect soldier." He glances at me. "Someone *they* think both looks and acts the part."

"So not Bree," Alice says.

"And not Nick," William adds.

Samira looks from William to me, brows knit tight. "The Regents have isolated the next eligible heir in the Line of Lancelot. No one knows where he is."

The cabin goes quiet. Alice looks among us all, eyes wide. "What does that mean?"

Gill shakes her head. "We're not sure—"

"Don't dance around the truth, Gill," Sel snaps. "The Regents need someone powerful enough to lead the Table, if not gather it in full. The Scion of Arthur is out of the question, which leaves the second most famous and respected knight: Lancelot."

My heart freezes. My mind flashes to a memory from the Lodge. Nick's own words come back to me from what feels like ages ago. *For a long time, men didn't care what the Spell wanted. They'd eliminate daughters to force it to the next heir. . . .*

"There is only *one* reason for the Regents to have the next heir in the Line of Lancelot fully under their control. One." His voice is sluggish but threaded with fury. "They aren't sending out a search party to rescue Nicholas. They're sending assassins to kill him."

I LOSE MY sense of self, my sense of time. The cabin shrinks, then expands. Becomes like liquid under my feet.

Voices surround me. Sel's and Alice's mouths are moving. William collapses into one of the seats, his head in his hands.

Samira claps, the sound echoing in the enclosed metal space. "No time for arguing, no time for tears. We're not exactly helpless here. The Liege network is already in motion, tapping everyone we know to get ears to the ground." She gestures to us. "We have two Awakened Legendborn, a capable Onceborn, and a Kingsmage—"

"Former Kingsmage," Sel interrupts.

Samira ignores him. "It's enough. All we need is an order."

"An order for what?" I ask, my voice a dry rasp.

Samira fixes me with a stare, walking closer. "You four can go after Nick yourselves with our resources. Supplies and the leads we've picked up. This rescue mission isn't going to be easy. The Regents have sent the Mageguard after him. The Shadowborn and Morgaine alliance may still think he's king, which means they want him dead, too." She pauses, looking around the cabin and to Gill, who nods. "Or . . ."

"'Or'? What exactly is the second option here?" Sel scoffs. "Rescuing Nicholas has been the plan for weeks, and that was *before* we thought the Order might kill him. We have to find him before the others do, end of story."

I nod. "Agreed."

"The second option . . . ," Gill says, taking a deep breath, "is that Bree goes into hiding. With all of you."

"Fuck no!" Sel exclaims.

"Are you serious?" I cry.

"You're all fugitives from the Order of the Round Table." Gill spreads her hands. "Bree, you're fugitive number one. The Regents need you more than they need Nick. Keeping Sel imprisoned means they'd know through his Kingsmage bond if Nick's in danger. Could be useful. William knows far too much. And Chen here"—she looks at Alice with a grin—"well, she's going to be on their radar after tonight if she wasn't before. You—all four of you—will have a better chance of avoiding recapture by the Regents and Mageguard and evading any Shadowborn legions who have somehow already found out who you are, Bree, if you get off the grid. If you go *truly* dark. Even from us, in case we get implicated in your escape."

"You want me to run away?" Indignation and disgust flood my chest. "I escaped the Institute. We're out now. We're together. The serum will leave my system soon, right, William?"

He nods. "Yes. Twenty-four, thirty-six hours max from your last dose."

"Great. So, give me a day or two, let's get our plans together . . . look at the—the intel," I stammer. "There's no way in hell I'm letting them win!"

Samira glances down at my balled fists and sighs. "Not every move is about winning. Not in a war like this one."

"Bullshit!" Sel's on his feet in a flash. "Bree and Nicholas *both* have Shadowborn after them. The demons who still think Nicholas is king and the ones who *know* Bree is. The difference is that the Regents will never kill her, but they *will* kill him."

"How could they even do that?" Alice asks. "Aren't they Oathed, too? Aren't the Merlins?"

"The Regents don't take that kind of Oath," Sel mutters, "and the Mageguard only swear to protect the Regents and the king."

My jaw clenches. "I'm not a coward. Nick needs our help."

"Nick needs you alive. We all need you alive." William says in a low voice, and my head whips up. William's gaze holds mine, his brows pinched. "We know there may be a goruchel in the Order's midst. You are right, Selwyn, that the Regents won't kill Bree, but that mimic might. We need to make the decision that puts her at least risk."

"Seconded." Alice sits back, arms crossed.

"This is not a vote," Sel spits, pointing at her. "And even if it were, you wouldn't get one."

"Hey!" I shout at him. "Lay off her."

Sel's lip curls, showing a hint of canines, but he looks away in silence.

"You're right about one thing, Kane," Gill says. "This isn't a vote."

A new type of stillness overtakes the cabin. I glance between her and Samira, expecting the more experienced Liege to lead us, but Samira's mouth curves into a rueful smile that drops lead into my belly. William's eyes are cast down. Alice drops her hand on my knee. I turn to Sel, but all he gives me is a dry, mirthless chuckle.

Samira's voice is low. "Either decision you make, the Lieges are behind you."

"I . . ." A chill drops down my spine. "Me? No, I don't . . ."

Sel laughs again. "She still doesn't get it."

"What's that supposed to mean?" I shoot back.

"It means you don't *get it,* mystery girl." He turns, eyes flashing. "This isn't a Liege decision. It's not a Legendborn decision. It's *yours.*"

Samira smiles sadly. "It's like we told you, Bree. We don't follow the Order. It's a false kingdom designed by the Regents. We follow the Legendborn, ruled by a king. Crowned or not, that's you."

I hold up my hands. "I'm not—"

"The Line is Law," Gill murmurs.

They are tired. Worn. Broken. Angry. And they're looking to me like I can lead them through it.

"What will it be, Crown Scion?" Sel says, eyes glittering. "Go into hiding to save your life, or go after Nicholas to save his?"

The cabin waits for my answer.

Sel's expression shifts to something dangerously blank. William stares holes into the floor. Gill and Samira are two soldiers, waiting for a command and ready to follow it. Alice's gaze is encouraging and soft.

During the Rite of Kings, I saw Nick's face. He'd called for me, and I answered. Call and response, a link held taut between us from the moment we met. I'd nearly forgotten the way our connection resonates inside my chest. How inevitable it feels. Like chimes ringing in response to the wind. The tide rising to meet the beach. I can't be king without him. I don't want to be.

I'm the reason Nick even came back to the Legendborn in the first place. Maybe it all would have happened anyway—no one can escape their blood just like no one can escape the truth. But the dominoes that brought us here today began with me when I ran from my mother's death instead of facing it. And now, if I choose to run again, someone else I love could die.

I can't let that happen.

"I won't run. We're going after Nick."

Sel smirks. William's eyes squeeze shut. Alice's fingers jerk on my knee, but she says nothing. Gill and Samira exchange a look.

The older woman stands, nodding. "The Crown Scion has spoken. We'll get you to a safehouse for the night. You all need a clear head, a meal, and a full eight." She jerks her chin toward a sliding door at the back of the seating area. "Two compartments in the back, each with bunks. Some sandwiches and bottled water in the mini fridge. Rest up. Gonna go update Lyssa and 'Phelia." She walks toward the cockpit and leaves us in silence.

William shoves to his feet and heads to the bunks without another word, pulling the door closed behind him. I hear his footsteps recede, then a second door slides open and closed. I stand up to follow, but Gill is there with a soft hand on my elbow.

"Let him go," she says. "It's not going to go away anytime soon, what it did to him when you were captive, what they made him do. First there was Whitty, now this. Just give him time."

I swallow and nod as she steps around me and follows Samira. I'll let William go, because I know she's right. He's not the only one haunted by what happened at the Institute. Even here, thousands of feet in the air and surrounded by allies, there's a part of me that feels like if I fall asleep, I might wake up disoriented. Confused. Certain that I was put to sleep like a toy left in a windowless room.

I jump when Sel abruptly moves to follow Gill.

"Sel—"

"Gonna go find out where they are taking us," he mutters without looking back at me.

"Matty."

Abruptly, I feel Alice wrap an arm around my shoulder and pull me to a corner as far away from the cockpit as possible.

"I come bearing gifts," Alice begins, opening up her duffel. She peeks into the bag, tilting it to the side. "Underwear, socks, a couple pairs of jeans, *Star Wars* T-shirts, tampons, pads, your favorite pajamas. Your shampoo and conditioner since I dunno where we're going, but wherever it is, I doubt they're gonna have anything but white-people hair products, so . . ." I choke out the most genuine laugh I've had in weeks. Her self-satisfied grin makes me laugh too, and then *she's* laughing and it's like when we were kids, setting each other off during sleepovers. Giggling and giggling in the dark.

But we're not kids. And everything is awful, and painful, and raw. And I'm so, so scared, and then I'm sobbing, and her arms are around me, and I'm shaking and crying until, eventually, I wear myself out.

I let the world go dark with Nick's Pendragon coin in my hand.

The clang of metal against metal in the distance. Grunts of effort, groans of pain. Sounds that I remember. Have remembered. Am remembering.

Am hearing, already and almost.

My eyes snap open. I am standing at the crest of a battle.

Down the hill, more than a dozen knights with spears. My men stand in a line on either side of me, in chain mail, leathers, and helmets, holding shields bearing their sigils. Here, some of their names, their original names, come to me in a rush of Old Welsh:

Boras, Cai, Bedwyr, Llameryg, Medrawd.

These names are who they were to Arthur, before hundreds of years of literature and songs were written across the globe. Before the world wrote his fictions and the Order began hiding the truth.

We circle a crackling black curtain, blinking in and out of existence. A Shadowborn Gate to the other side.

"A wyt barawd?" Are you ready? *The question is asked by my first knight, beside me—my chosen lieutenant. Llancelod, Sir Lancelot, eyes grim.*

"Dyfod yr amser." The time has come.

My words are whispered, but down the hill, a hundred feet away, a hooded, robed figure moves forward at my command. His footsteps leave smoking blue shapes on the earth behind him.

Myrddin. Merlin.

The sorcerer reaches a long-fingered hand high in the air and slices it down, rending the Gate open. A cut to cleave the veil between dimensions and finish our fight with the Shadowborn forever—bring the battle to their door instead of letting them pick us off at their leisure.

It is a mistake.

Immediately, my knights are swarmed by glowing, flying imps. Creatures on three and four legs stream out of the opening, leaping onto their backs. My knights fight back with wooden and metal spears that do nothing against demon hides. Merlin is a blue flash, conjuring an arsenal of weapons to obliterate the horde.

Lancelot curses beside me. "Cachu . . . !" We move as one, pulling blades as we go, driving into another battle that we hoped we would win, but did not.

Later, after the dead have come home and lie wrapped, Lancelot finds me at the north wall of the hold. "Arthur!" I sigh wearily.

When he reaches me, the angry stream of Welsh simply becomes meaning in my mind. "How many more have to die? How many, Arthur? Do you even know who we lost tonight, or are you already dreaming of the next strategy?"

His stag sigil is streaked with blood. None of it his. He swipes away the sweaty, flaxen hair plastered to his forehead. "Arthur, are you even listening—"

"Boras's son, Elyan." My voice is a low roll of thunder that stops him short. "Clawddyn. Brandylles. Morolld. Balan." Each name sinks deeper into my chest, alongside the others I have lost. We used to be fifty and one hundred. We are dwindling.

His eyes find mine, pleading and desperate. "Sixty-seven gone, now."

I advance on him, angry. "I know that number better than you ever will! See their faces more clearly. They pledged their lives, as well as their swords, to mine." I pound on my chest, where the dragon sits in shreds. "I feel it when that pledge is torn apart! I bear that pain every day."

"I . . ." Lancelot's eyes flutter. Look away. "I did not know, my liege. Forgive me." When he looks back, the image stutters, shifts—

And it is Nick's broad shoulders filling the tunic and mail. Nick's eyes, fierce and strained.

Then he is gone, and Lancelot is back.

I open my mouth, because this is when Arthur speaks. But this time, I pause, and he does not speak.

Lancelot waits, and I do not say a word, and this is not what happened.

Because this is not real.

I am not Arthur.

I am Bree.

And maybe I can control this.

In this frozen almost-past, my mind whirs toward the possibilities. I did not travel back in time. I am in Arthur's memory, but I am not walking it as an observer like Patricia in a memory walk. It isn't view-only.

When I channel Arthur, his spirit possesses my body in the real world, and he can do things that I can't control. But right now, his spirit has somehow channeled *me*. I'm possessing *his* body in a memory. Does that mean I can take control in Arthur's world, the way Arthur can take control in mine?

Twice I have seen Nick, who wasn't even born centuries ago. I wrap my mind around hope that this world is . . . mutable somehow. That I can influence it again. *Oh please. Please, please.*

I reach toward Lancelot—something Arthur did not do—and Lancelot does not react, because Arthur never reached toward him in the past. Because I am doing something *new*. Creating a branch in Arthur's memory dimension and bending it to my will. My heart races beneath Arthur's suddenly too-heavy mail, weighing my shoulders down.

My fingertips touch Lancelot's shoulder. The image flickers again, rapidly. My heart stutters, *hoping* . . .

Lancelot flashes bright—and becomes Nick once more.

He stares at me, eyes wide and searching. "Bree?"

22

"NICK!"

He stammers, "Wh-where are——" He looks out over the yard to the moorland and mountains.

"Wales?" I gasp.

He stumbles toward me, grasping my shoulders, eyes looking over my face, my clothing. When he pulls back, he drinks in my features, caressing my cheeks in gentle strokes, like he's relearning the curves and dips of my face. My face, not Arthur's. *He can see me, too.* "This is really you?"

I nod, smiling. "Really me."

Wonder runs like honey through his voice. "Was that really you . . . before? In the room? At the Table?" I nod. "Are you okay?" he asks, stepping closer.

I release a breathy laugh. "We're in a . . . memory dimension wearing our medieval ancestors' bloody chain mail and you're asking me if I'm okay?"

"Yes. Always." Nick rests his forehead against mine. "But I do want to come back to the memory dimension, medieval ancestor part."

I release a shuddering breath and smile a little. "I'm okay, considering . . . *this.*"

He leans back, looking beyond me to the castle, along the turrets, to the sky. "And this is . . . ?"

I lick my lips, flipping through a list of "where to start" responses like a stack of papers. "So much has happened. . . . I don't even . . ."

"I know." He swallows hard. "To me, too. But start with us, right now. You and me. How are we here together, B?"

You and me. I nod slowly. "Because I'm a Medium."

He blinks. A pause. "You can talk to . . . the dead?"

"Yes."

"Is that . . ." His eyes move rapidly, processing information quickly as ever. "Is that why Arthur was *with* you in the ogof?"

"Yes. It turns out the power I was born with, my Rootcraft, is that I can channel the dead, and they can channel me? But this"—I wave a hand around us—"is a whole 'nother level. Like a memory walk, which I can't do anyway . . . except this isn't a memory walk because instead of *watching* my blood ancestor's memory I'm *living* it, so this is like a . . . blood walk?"

He stares at me. "Makes sense."

"No, it doesn't," I say. "This is—"

"Completely bonkers?" he offers, half-smiling.

Somehow, that smile tips me over. A gurgled sort of whine escapes me as tears well up.

Nick's thumbs catch the tears before they fall. "Don't cry, B," he whispers. "This is wild, yes, but I'm here. You're here."

"But you're *not* here!" I gasp. "You're missing. Everyone wants me to tell them what to do, but I'm barely holding on. I don't know how to control Arthur's powers, and he wants me to summon him—"

He blinks, focusing. "Wait, wait, slow down. . . . Summon him?"

"Yes. His spirit. But that might mean him possessing me." I shake my head rapidly. "I don't want that."

Nick's eyes flash. "You don't have to do anything Arthur wants you to do."

"I'm not sure . . ." I shrug. "I'm not sure that's true." I wrap my hands around his wrists, pressing into the warm skin and bone. "Are *you* okay?"

He huffs. Hesitates. "Honestly? No. No, I'm not."

"Are they hurting you?"

His brows draw down. "Not me. Other people, though. Two Mageguard found us a few weeks ago. There was a fight."

My jaw drops. "They found you? But they said they were gathering intel."

He chuckles sourly. "Both can be true. I don't think those guards were meant to make themselves known to us. But Isaac is too good. He saw them watching us from an alley in a town near Brevard. Went after them. Came back bloody." He swallows hard. "I don't know if they survived."

The Regents never said they'd found Nick. I suppose, if the plan was to possibly murder him, they wouldn't have. "Nick, the Regents *are* looking for you, but not to rescue you. Gillian says they've secured the next in line to Lancelot."

I wait for shock, but it never comes. "I know. My father has contacts on the inside. They told him the Regents have already begun to prepare the next in the Line. If they track us down, they'll kill me to force the Spell to him, then place their puppet at the Table."

I study him, the acceptance written across his brow, settled into his shoulders. "You can't let them find you again."

"I don't think they will. Isaac takes more precautions now." Nick releases a low sigh. "He and my father keep us far away from their search teams. They seem to be able to stay one step ahead. I don't know what they're planning. If there even is a plan."

I press forward, uncertain of when our time together might end. "Where are you now?"

His brows draw tight, and I know he understands that I mean the real world, not here. "Isaac keeps us moving from place to place. Yesterday I woke up in a car headed east, toward the coast. Now we're in a hotel somewhere near a beach."

"You're on the coast?" I ask, desperate. "Okay, we're coming to find you."

His brows shoot up. "We?"

"I'm with the Lieges. And we have William, Alice, Sel."

"Sel?" Worry pinches his brow. "Is he . . . all right?"

I hesitate. "William says serving the Oath to the Legendborn has held off the effects of not serving his Kingsmage Oath to you. He says it might help that Sel's been protecting me too."

Nick draws closer. "But what does *Sel* say?"

"Sel says he's fine. But the Regents say he's going to succumb, or has already started. They publicly charged *him* with opening the Gates, said he was a traitor, then privately arrested him for completely different crimes."

"They are blaming him for my father's sins, just as they did his mother." Nick's gaze hardens to something venomous. Something that doesn't soften until he blinks. "Listen, I know more than anyone how much Sel cares about his duty. If he truly thought he was a danger to you, he would remove himself from the situation. You don't need the Regents to make that call, Sel will."

Warmth floods me at Nick's confidence in his Kingsmage, at how well they know each other even now. Sel's standards for his own behavior are terribly high, it's true—and they come at a terrible cost. I can't help but think of Sel's self-recrimination. His acceptance of Erebus's charges of negligence.

"But you can't come after me." Nick shakes his head. "It's too dangerous."

"I don't care!"

He grits his teeth. "I know you don't, B. But I mean it. My dad and Isaac together . . . they almost make each other worse. Don't come after me. Don't let Sel do it, either. Isaac will go straight for him and he's too strong. Isaac'll tear him apart."

"But it won't just be me or Sel. William has the power of Gawain, we have the Lieges, and I . . ." I pause, struggling to explain. "I'm getting better at my powers too."

He shakes his head. "It won't matter. It's just too risky, especially for you."

"For me?" A flicker of anger slips into my voice. "You don't think I can handle myself."

He runs a hand through his hair. "Jesus, Bree. You know I think you can do anything, take on anything and anyone in the world—and I thought that *before* I saw you freakin' breathe *fire* at a pack of flying imps!" He gasps in amazement. "I still believe in you, it's just . . ." His jaw clenches and unclenches.

"What?"

When he opens his eyes, the blue of them has turned thundercloud-dark. "My father is . . . completely gone. Erratic. Unstable. I can't reach him. He wants to control the Order, to go back to the old ways, but, in his eyes, he can't do either because of you."

"Me?" I gasp. I wrap my arms around my chest, clinking gauntlet to mail.

Nick inclines his head. "Yes. You. He *rages* about you. He's convinced you're at fault for it all. That you've ruined his life and my life and stolen our future from us."

My head snaps back. "But I didn't! I didn't *steal* anything."

"It doesn't matter. To him, you represent everything he can't have. Everything he was owed."

"Well"—I laugh nervously—"at least he can't kill me."

Nick's expression doesn't change.

My chest tightens. "But he *can't* want me dead. If he kills me instead of a demon, the Spell would be safe, sure, but the Line of Arthur would . . . disappear. I don't have any kids."

His mouth twists. "If you die, someone, somewhere will be Called to replace you. That's how it works for all of us. My dad is already looking for the next eligible descendant in your family. Trying to trace the direct bloodline from the last Awakened Scion of Arthur, find where it branched. They keep saying something about needing more than first names? They're having trouble, but they're not giving up."

My veins turn cold, tight. Then they widen, go hot. "They're having trouble because enslavers only cared to *write down* my ancestors' first names. Not because that's all they had."

"Christ," Nick says, wiping a hand over his mouth.

"I *hate* this," I hiss. "I hate that *your* father probably has the resources to go back that far and find . . . when *my* family—" I break off, chest tight with the layers of injustice, the sheer density of it. "I didn't ask for this. No one in my family *asked* for this!"

Some of the anger drains from Nick's face, replaced with a mixture of sorrow and worry. I realize he may not know the truth.

"You should know *why* it's me," I insist. "In the cave, I had a vision. You should know how . . ."

"How Arthur's blood came to be in your veins?" he asks quietly.

"Yes."

"I know," he murmurs. "My father and Isaac figured it out. They were obsessed those first few days, trying to understand 'what happened to the Davises.' They followed the power because they think that's the legacy. But that's the thing. The Legendborn legacy isn't power; it's violence."

We let that sit between us. That one word and all that it holds, all of the harm and the hurt and the theft. The brutality of men who design and destroy legends. The intersections of history that have brought us both here . . . There's a sour, metallic taste in my mouth.

I sigh, releasing what I can. "Maybe that's why I'm not very good at this Scion-of-Arthur thing."

"I wasn't very good at it, either." He steps closer, squeezing my hand to his chest. "Listen, Bree, I know 'I'm sorry' isn't enough—that there aren't any words big or deep enough for what happened to your ancestor." His eyes are soft, but his brow is set in a determined expression that I recognize. "But I *am* sorry about what that Scion did to her. Sorry that what he did to her then endangers you now, and takes your choices away. You've been forced into a world that not only puts your life at risk but shortens it. It's not right. Or fair. Or just."

I have an urge to shrug Nick's words away. He's right; they *aren't* enough. Could never be. *But*, I think, *no one ever apologized to Vera*. Maybe Nick's apology won't change things, but the very fact of it *is* a change. I look up and study his eyes, see the sincerity in them. I can't accept an apology on my ancestors' behalf, but I can accept it on my own.

"Thank you. For saying that." My voice breaks unexpectedly. "No one—no one else has apologized about that. Since . . . all of this." I release a shaky breath, feeling at least some of the weight lift. The pressure, eased. "Or said anything to me about my Abatement, for that matter. I guess, to them, it's just a given."

He takes a deep breath, brows drawn tight. "The Order steals something from all of us. Arthur multiplies the effect, concentrates it. Together, he and the Order have taken more from me than the others. But you . . ." He shakes his head, eyes hardening. "They've taken more from you than anyone else. More than anyone should bear."

My throat closes so tight it's hard to breathe. I'd forgotten the easy way Nick can just . . . find my heart and hold it between his hands. How effortlessly he sees me in the dark.

He lifts my palm to meet his mouth in a quiet kiss, and a memory surges back into place. Cestra smirking across the table. I suck in a breath.

Nick grips my hand. "What is it?"

"Something Regent Cestra said." I look up at him. "About our relationship being forbidden because we're both Scions."

His gaze darkens. "They truly only care about the Lines, not the people."

"What will it mean when you come back?"

"I don't know and I don't care," he whispers. He raises my palm to his mouth again, this time lingering. "I won't let the Order take this from us too."

Suddenly, the world around us shudders. Nick's head snaps up. "What was that?"

There's a deep tug behind my sternum. Instinctively, I *know* who it is, reaching for me. "It's Arthur. He's pulling me out. . . ."

Nick's face twists in a snarl. *"No!"*

"He's taking over again," I gasp. "I can feel it—"

Before I can say more, Nick's lips crash against mine, warm and fierce. I don't hesitate to respond, and then we are breath and rhythm. Hunger and satisfaction. Call and response, even here. Maybe *especially* here. What one of us wants, the other gives with lips, tongue, heat.

He leans back, panting, leaving us both dazed. "Please tell me I just kissed *you* and not a dead king." When I shake my head, his eyes widen in shock. "Oh God, you're Arth—?"

"No!" I grin, and his shoulders relax. "You kissed me. Not a dead king."

Warmth returns to his gaze, and he pulls us together again until our foreheads meet. Until his yearning and mine find each other in the middle. "Good. I prefer my kings alive."

I suck in a quiet breath. "Nick . . ." *Do you wish it was still you . . . and not me?*

A soft smile pulls at his mouth. "It was always you, Bree." His voice is low and somber, thick with emotion. "Always you."

With a snap, we part.

I am back in the plane between life and death, standing ankle-deep in the branch of the stream that belongs to Arthur. When I step up onto the bank, the mist floats up and around my knees.

Always me. First Erebus, now Nick. Reminders of the life I forget I'm living.

It is black as night and silent, save for the sound of water over rocks, but this time there is a cool wind rushing past my face. I hear a man whispering. Names, accompanied by sparking lights that flit around my head.

"Scion."

"Heir."

"The once and future."

I see a silver wisp growing in the distance. The wisp comes closer. It is taller than me, broader. Almost the shape of a man. I find some satisfaction that while Vera was fully formed here, Arthur is still ghostly. It makes me brave.

"Daughter of sons."

"Take me back to Nick," I order.

"Who is . . . Nick?"

"He is Lancelot's heir."

Silence that feels like confusion, curiosity. "And you saw him? In my memory at Caerleon?"

I suppose it's a *good* thing Arthur can't see what I do and say when I pull Nick into his ancestor's body. That what I say and do there branches off from his memory somehow. "Yes. I brought him into the memory."

"And yet his appearance is not a memory that I possess. Your powers are formidable, Briana." A pause. "In my time, there were women who claimed they could channel the dead. Walk the plane between life and death like a dirt path between one and the other. I did not believe them."

I growl under my breath, impatient. "Can you take me back or not?"

Another pause. "Let us make a bargain, my Scion."

I swallow. "I don't like the sound of that."

A low laugh. "You are smart to be cautious."

Silence then. The wisp hovers, waiting. It makes me wonder where he will go when I leave this plane again.

"Where were you before I was Awakened?"

"I rest in Camelot."

"Merlin sent you to Camelot?"

"Merlin sent me to my dreams."

I consider this. Sigh. *Damnit.* "What is the bargain?"

"Summon me, so that I may show you how to control my power. If you do this, I will bring you to memories of Lancelot so that you may visit his heir."

I shouldn't be surprised. Arthur made clear that he wants me to willingly come to him. And I made clear that I'd never risk letting him in again. Now that he has something that I want—access to Nick—he's going to wield it. What choice do I have? I need to see Nick again if I'm going to get him to tell me where he is.

But this offer is tempting for other reasons too; Arthur claims his power can help me stop death. Raw *need* pulses through me at the very thought. A desire so deep it feels shameful.

I raise my chin. "Fine. I will summon you, but on one condition: you will not possess me again unless I consent. Got that?"

"I understand. And I am glad of your decision."

"I'm not." I think back to the blood walk, to Arthur's supposed first lesson. "What was I supposed to learn from that memory anyway?"

He chuckles. "That dragons are fiercely loyal, and never forget what was taken from us. That eventually, we decide to protect what is ours . . . and burn the rest."

And then the old king is gone.

But even as I fly back to myself, I still feel Nick—across memory, across time and space, across life and death.

MY SKIN TINGLES. Like sunlight mid-burn. I jerk awake.

"It's me."

Sel's low voice reaches me from across the cabin, and the sensation disappears. He must have been looking at me.

"Oh." My voice is a rasp in the dark. Rough enough from sleep that, for a moment, it reminds me of Arthur's baritone. I shudder, and cough to clear my throat.

The safety lights are on, bathing the space in muted yellow along the center aisle. The engine hums beneath us, vibrating gently against the soles of my feet. My body feels drained and weak, like I haven't slept at all.

But one thought appears bright in my mind: I just saw Nick. I spoke to him. *Kissed* him. My fingertips graze my lips, remembering the feel and pressure of his. The small thrill is quickly smothered by the memory of the vision that followed.

If I want to see Nick again, I have to summon Arthur.

The way Arthur had spoken to me, it was like I'd come to him of my own volition. How did . . . . I look down when something falls from my grasp. In sleep, I'd held the Pendragon coin so tightly in my fist that the metal is warm and damp from sweat, and the old blood has stained my fingertips.

By my blood. Just like in the Rite.

In Rootcraft, we bring offerings to our ancestors. A collection of items, organic or edible, things that used to be alive, or things that are fresh. Mariah says we offer the favorite pieces of life to our dead, because they remind the ancestor of their time on our plane. But what kind of offering is blood?

My skin burns again. Sel's eyes are two golden beacons in the darkness. The silence between us is the awkward kind that fills space when there is too much to say and all the time in the world to say it.

"How long was I out?"

"I wouldn't know. I only returned a few minutes ago from a long talking-to in the galley from one Liege Gillian Hanover."

I frown. "So you came back, sat down, and decided to watch me sleep?"

He snorts. "Is that your immediate area of concern?"

"Not really."

He waits for me to continue.

"Something happened in my sleep. I saw Nick."

Sel's voice turns mocking. "Well, Briana, there are these remarkable things called *dreams*. . . ."

"It wasn't a dream," I insist. "It was a memory of Arthur's, but then it became something else."

"You have been drugged and mesmered, repeatedly, for days." Even his sigh is dismissive. "You cannot trust your own mind. Not until the serum leaves your system and you have gotten proper rest."

My eyelids flutter and my mouth goes dry. He's right. But still . . . "I told him we were coming for him. I think it was real, Sel."

He's listening now, not mocking. He narrows his eyes. "You *think* it was real, or you *know*?"

"I know. I'm sure." But I feel a tiny sliver of hesitation. Sitting here in an airplane cabin, with the engines rumbling beneath the sore thighs I earned from running away from a prison, the blood walk world feels like it's slipping away. Like a dream, it's already fading around the edges.

Sel leans forward, resting both hands over his knees. His face appears through the shadows to regard me with a scowl. "You are *not* sure. I don't want to talk about a maybe-vision, probably-dream. We will take action on facts and gathered intelligence."

The motion draws my eyes to his hands. The three-inch-wide black iron cuffs on each of his wrists are so dark they seem to absorb what little light there is in the cabin. "Those cuffs. What are they?"

"These lovely items are called cyffion gwacter. 'Void cuffs.' Cyffion are used for securing Merlins when your typical handcuffs just won't do," he says grimly. "When enchanted by a sorcerer, they block my ability to sense or call aether, or use it to shift forms."

That ear-popping sensation from when Erebus put them on. It had felt like a type of barrier snapping into place. "I don't understand."

"I said," he says, dragging each syllable out slowly, "they block my ability to sense or call——"

"I heard you," I spit. Why is he so irritating, even now? "I just mean, with those on you're . . ."

"'Neutered' is what Guard Ramirez said when he *absolutely* knew I was listening on the other side of the cell door. I am unable to cast aether constructs, forge weapons, or use it to fight and defend myself. The only one who can remove a pair of cyffion is the sorcerer who put them on in the first place."

Erebus.

An ache slices through me at this punishment. To not call aether, his element? To lose that additional sense that helps him do his job—the only thing I've ever known Sel to love unequivocally? "Sel, why didn't you tell me the Regents were coming after you?"

He stares at me. "What would you have done? Dive in to try and save me the night before the Rite of Kings, when you take the first step toward the throne?"

I scowl. "You ran when they came for you, but then you came back. Why?"

"I got bored," he drawls. "What does it matter? I saved you. Then I got caught. Now I'm here."

His response is bait, but I'm too tired and confused to take it. "That's not an answer."

"It *is* an answer; you just dislike it." He sighs. "Just like you disliked it when I forbade you from joining our hunts."

That fight feels so, so far away now. And silly. "What I dislike is that you're keeping things from me."

He laughs a short sharp sound and buries his head in both hands. His voice reaches me, muffled in his palms. "Breaking news: secret mystery girl suddenly tires of secrets."

"We trusted each other once, Sel. I know that I broke that trust, I know we've fought, but you didn't tell me you were in danger. You didn't tell me the Regents were targeting you." I don't bother hiding the hurt in my voice. "You told Lark, who you don't even like, but you didn't tell me."

Sel doesn't respond. The silence becomes painful.

"I just thought, after everything we've been through, after we . . ." I trail off, but the answers rise inside me, loud: *After you saved my life. After what we learned about our mothers. After the cave. After the balcony and 'cariad' and when you said I was your king.* Yours.

"After we what?" He looks up, fixing me with a bright, fierce stare. His frustration at close range hits me full blast. An involuntary shiver runs down my spine. Sel chases the slight movement, leaning closer to watch my physical response. Then his eyes meet mine again and for a breathless moment, it is like we are back on the balcony, or dancing together at the gala. Molten gold floods my vision, and the *something* between us ignites like electricity.

"After we what, Bree?" This time he wields the shortened version of my name like an axe, slicing our connection.

I squeeze my eyes shut. When I open them, he has leaned back. He's looking away from me and out the window, already moving on. "Erebus has already levelled the charges. Every Merlin in the world will know what I've done by now. If I am caught, they will bring me directly to trial."

"A trial that shouldn't even be happening, because you're innocent."

"No one has ever called me innocent before." He smirks. "You sure you want to be the first?"

I look away. He's mocking me now. "Well, you are. At least in this case . . ."

He lifts a shoulder. "I was going to plead guilty."

My head snaps around. "Why?"

"Because I *am* guilty." He balls his fist. "You never could just . . . let truth sit and consequences come." His voice is a low, damning growl. "I would plead guilty to every single charge, because I *am* guilty of every single charge."

"But, Sel—"

He holds out a hand, counting. "Negligence? Guilty. I took Oaths on my life to protect the chapter from any and all threats. I knew something was wrong *weeks* before Rhaz and Davis showed their true faces. I knew it and reported nothing." Another finger raised. "The isel I killed at the Quarry the first night we met? Entered through Rhaz's Gate. The uchel Lord Davis let in the night of the Oath? Davis's Gate. I should have captured and interrogated both demons about their origins. Instead, I—"

"Stop," I plead. "That's not fair."

"Why stop when I can keep going? Five more lapses in judgment to go." He bares his teeth. "How about letting you and Nicholas out of my sight at the gala? Leaving you two in that room alone"—he raises a brow, a knowing glint in his eye—"undefended and unaware of anything around you save each other . . ."

"Stop it." My cheeks flame at all that he leaves unsaid, at the heady whoosh of remembrance. Of the charged air in the anteroom after I'd accepted Nick's offer to become his Squire. How he'd held me. Kissed me.

"Is that kiss a bad memory for you? Oh my." Sel tilts his head, frowning for effect. "That is *unfortunate*."

"Shut up. You're trying to make me angry. It won't work."

"I am not trying to make you angry," he says, voice droll. "I am trying to make you understand."

"You weren't negligent! We were tricked!" I snap. "No one had seen a goruchel like Rhaz in years, and he fooled everyone. Even the Regents didn't see Davis's endgame because he'd put on a show for decades. If they missed their own Viceroy's betrayal, then aren't they guilty, too?"

"Nicholas is—I was his Kingsmage, and I failed to keep him safe within the Lodge." He rubs a hand over his face. "Because I was distracted."

"Distracted by what?"

"By *you*, if you must know." His eyes land on me again, heat now at a defeated simmer. "By all that I had seen you do. What you meant for my future and Nicholas's. By everything that changed in the span of one night, because of one sword and one girl."

"Oh," I whisper.

"But Kingsmages are not granted excuses," Sel says. He leans back, resting one ankle over his knee. "And let's not forget my pièce de résistance. Going after you in the graveyard with my hound . . ."

"You didn't know what I was," I hiss, my own fist clenching, "No one did. I was a Page then, not the Scion of Arthur."

"You have *always* been the Scion of Arthur, Briana." Sel repeats what Erebus and Nick have both said to me, but his tone couldn't be further from theirs. From Erebus, the reminder was a gentle correction. From Nick, reassurance and devotion. From Sel, all I hear is harsh recrimination, an indictment—and he's not done.

"You have been the Scion of Arthur from the moment we met, and long before. You have been the Scion of Arthur from the moment you were born. And neither of us can afford to forget it."

For some reason, my cheeks flood with heat. My eyes grow hot with unshed tears.

"The Regents will do whatever it takes to maintain the apparent sanctity of the Lines, even if they have revealed their disrespect for the Scions themselves." He keeps talking, ignoring my reaction. "As a member of the military, the incontestable penalty for the attempted murder of a Scion of Arthur is death."

The space tightens in on me, squeezing all thought from my mind. Then my fear and anger pivot to him. "And you turned yourself *in*? What were you thinking?"

Sel rises slowly, eyes earnest and ferocious, with one hand in his pocket. He closes in on me in two steps and captures my chin with his fingers so that I cannot turn away.

"Listen to me very carefully, Briana Matthews. I *wanted* to kill you. I imagined it. More than once. I never intended for you to leave that graveyard alive. For avoidance of doubt, let me be exceedingly clear: the hellfoxes that attacked us that night saved your life, because without their intervention, *I would have taken it.*"

I am bound to the seat, held in place. It has been a long time since Sel has looked at me this way. Like prey. He wants me scared, but his old tricks don't work anymore. "Fine. You wanted to kill me, but you didn't."

He releases me. "Not for lack of trying. The only reason they let me keep breathing is that I am still bonded to Nicholas. I can feel whether he is in mortal danger. If it were not for the handy alarm system in my brain, I would already be in a Shadowhold, rotting in a triple-layered iron cell awaiting a painful decline and death."

"You haven't . . . ," I begin, not sure how to ask. "Have you?"

"Have I felt Nicholas's life in danger?" His gaze goes blank as he focuses on something inside. Something deep and always there. "No. Not once."

The knot in my chest releases an inch. "Good."

He hums an affirmative. The engines seem to grow louder in our silence.

"You protected me that night on the road. And saved Lark. That counts for something."

He rolls his eyes. "I am a Merlin, Briana. Saving you is not a choice; it is an obligation." His head thunks back against the bulkhead. "And I am a Merlin who can't use aether. I'm infantry at best. Good for muscle and speed, which are not enough to kill a demon."

"Speak for yourself," a voice says. Gill walks in and takes a seat at the table. "Lieges go on missions too, you know. We don't stop fighting demons just because we age out of eligibility or lose our inheritances. I was never Called, so I've never had your 'muscle and speed,' and I do just fine."

"And of those Lieges who were Called by a knight, they keep fighting for how long again?" Sel drawls. "Thirteen years before the Abatement takes them?"

Gill shrugs. "We all gotta go sometime, Kane." She kicks his heel with her boot. "Don't be an asshole."

He laughs but says nothing as she hops up from the seat to open the fridge. I glance between the two of them, shocked a little at the interaction before I remember: Sel was bound to Nick at age ten, and Nick was trained by Lieges a year or two before. Gill has known Sel almost as long as she's known Nick—since the two boys were small children.

"Gill," I say, sitting up. "I saw Nick in a sort of vision. A Medium, ancestral . . . blood walk . . . thing."

"Uh." Gill's head appears above the fridge door, mouth full of sandwich. "Okay . . ."

"He said they were somewhere on the East Coast. That his father is behaving erratically. He said it was too dangerous to go after them. That he thinks Isaac may have"—I swallow—"killed two Mageguard trackers."

She stands up straight. "*That* is intel we did not receive."

"Erebus and the Council would have buried news like that immediately," Sel mutters. "Like everything else they want to hide."

"Can your team look into it?" I ask. "See if they can find them based on that?"

She nods slowly. "Of course. But tactically, they won't stay anywhere for long. And the Atlantic seaboard is a lotta ground to cover."

I sit back. She's right. Not enough info to do much of anything. The whine of the engines shifts, and the pressure in the cabin changes. Gill glances out the window. "Starting the landing cycle. May as well wake the others. Once we hit the ground, it's an hour drive."

"To this safehouse in the middle-of-nowhere Georgia?" Sel asks, his tone bored.

"Yep," she says winking at me. "Off the Order's grid."

"Off everyone's grid, it sounds like," Sel mutters.

"Keep up, Kane," Gill says with a wry smile. "That's kinda the point."

24

WE CIRCLE A secluded, remote airstrip at the top of a mountain. As soon as the landing gear touches the ground, an SUV's headlights flash awake from where it had been idling in the dark. Another Liege waiting for our arrival.

Alice, Sel, and William jog easily down the stairs to the tarmac. My pace, however, is slower through the cabin. Annoyingly so.

"You've been jailed and drugged, then you escaped a magical prison. You're probably really feeling it now that you've been sitting for a while. Your body's gonna need some time to recover, just like your powers," Samira says from the cabin doorway. I grimace in response.

I've just reached the door beside her when I pause. She's a tall woman who takes up space, wide shoulders and hips. Years of honed muscles at her biceps, wrapped around her thighs. She reminds me of Sel, somehow. The easy, confident movement and the coiled strength, ready to be used to protect or attack. Casually lethal. A pang of curiosity—mixed with envy—halts my steps, and I realize I have an opportunity that I can't pass up and might not get again.

Concern crosses her features. "What is it?"

"Nothing bad. Just wondering if I could talk to you . . . before we go?"

"Absolutely." She leans out the door to yell at the group down below over the sound of the engines. "Give us a couple minutes, yeah?"

From the tarmac, Gill sends a salute. She walks the others to the waiting

Jeep and opens up the trunk, pointing out supplies, but Alice hangs back. She catches my eye, makes a questioning thumbs-up. I smile. *I'm okay.* She nods once and jogs over to Gillian, who appears disturbingly willing to point out weapons to an overly eager Alice. Wonderful.

Samira squeezes my shoulder and walks away from the open door into the relative quiet of the cabin. I follow, stopping when she leans against one of the seats and crosses her arms and ankles. "How can I help?"

I glance over my shoulder, then turn back, debating how to begin. Easiest to start with the hard part, I guess. "Do you know why I'm the Scion of Arthur?"

Her features draw tight. "If you're referring to the 'how' of it, the rape of your ancestor, yes. Word spread pretty quickly through the Lieges." Then, slowly, starting from one corner of her mouth, a smile forms. "But why? 'Why' is a different question."

My brows shoot up. "Do you know the answer to that question?"

She laughs. "No. But I think there's a reason. Why did you ask?"

"Because," I begin, "it adds a layer to a situation that's already challenging, I guess. Because I'm the only Legendborn who's Black, and . . ."

She nods in recognition. "You wanted to ask how it was for me."

"Yeah," I say.

She smiles, eyes turning inward. "I was seventeen years old at the Northern Chapter. Parents were Vassals. I don't think anyone expected me to get as far as I did in the tournament. There were some difficult moments. I wasn't the first Black Page in the Order, so that barrier was present but not prohibitive. I wasn't even the first Black Squire, believe it or not. But I was the first Black Page to aim for, and win, the Squireship for a Scion of Bedivere." Her mouth kicks up in a smirk.

My eyes grow wide. "Bedivere's sixth-ranked. The highest—"

"The highest-ranked Calling the Order saw for decades, yes. Meaning it was almost certain that my Scion, John, would be Called. Which meant it was almost certain I would gain Bedivere's inheritance through our Oath. A Black girl, bonded to the highest-ranked Awakened Scion in the Order." She smiles in memory, shaking her head. "When I tell you the other Pages were pissed at meeeeee, whew."

I crack a grin. "I bet."

After a moment, she sobers. "At first, anyway."

"What changed?"

"John was Called, and we were Oathed, and then, when we were in the field during a rough patch"—she takes a slow breath—"we lost some Pages. A Squire. The jealous ones stopped being jealous when they saw us return to the Keep carrying the body of one of our own." She swallows, takes a deep breath. "The Vassal parents continued to be assholes, but the Pages never gave me crap again."

"That's horrible."

"It wasn't pretty," she says. "John and I fought together right up until we hit the cut-off age. And we're still at it, but we don't get to see each other as much as we'd like."

"You had good training, then," I say. "To last this long."

She gives me a meaningful look. "And you were the Page and chosen Squire of the Scion of Arthur. You had training too. It's just different now. Like starting a new job at entry level with zero experience, then getting promoted to CEO the next month."

I sigh. "Yeah, except I ended up as the CEO because it turns out one of the previous CEOs was a . . ." There are no other words for it. "A fucking monster."

She shakes her head. "It's not right, how you're the Crown Scion. The 'how' will never be right. But the 'why' is still open-ended."

I take a deep breath. "Yeah."

"Bree . . ." Samira's eyes go wide with something like admiration and pride. "You broke a *fifteen-hundred*-year-old glass ceiling. And even if the 'how' isn't right, I'm glad I'm here to see it."

A mixture of emotions swirls in me. Worry at the Abatement that I know is coming for her—and me. Shame that I'd never thought about what my role might mean to any other Black Pages and Squires, if there are any still living and if they ever find out about me. I *felt* so alone that I assumed I was.

She jerks a chin toward the side of the plane and the voices and people beyond. "They believe in you. Not just because of what you've done, but what you're gonna do. What you *could* do when you figure out how to control those powers of yours."

I flush, embarrassed. "I—"

"I'm not judging. I've heard that Arthur's casting isn't coming easy to you. Heard from Alice that your red flames don't show unless they wanna show. But I meant it when I said I serve the true king; I trust that you're the Crown Scion for a reason."

"I'm the Crown Scion because I pulled Excalibur," I reply, "the sword I'm supposed to wield that I don't even have with me. I dropped it during the Rite. The Regents probably have it now, locked up somewhere."

Samira's face breaks open in a grin. "But you pulled the blade when you did and how you did because you put yourself in the right place to do so. Not your mother, not your grandmother, but *you*. You brought honor to your Line, and I don't mean Arthur's. You don't need the sword, Bree. You *are* the sword. Their sword. *Our* sword."

My vision blurs. I wasn't expecting to hear all of this from Samira. It's a reminder that the only way to honor my Line, my people, and my mother is to face my fights head-on. I *am* the sword. I sniff a little, clear my throat. "Thanks, Samira. I think . . . I think I needed that."

"No problem, boss," she says with a wink. She holds up a finger. "One more thing. You need to know that the Liege networks are a bit more . . . worldly than the Regents realize. Always have been, with the work we do. We have our own contacts that are off the Regents' and Seneschals' radar."

I blink. "I thought everyone and everything were *on* their radar."

"That used to be true when the world was different. Now they just *want* it to be true," she says, an amused smile playing at her mouth. "Wanting something fiction to be fact and having the power to convince other folks of the same . . . that's how power stays put. The Order's surface networks tend to run down certain avenues, but Lieges? We deal with the world as is, so some of our channels are a little more *underground* than others." She pulls a pen and slip of paper from her vest pocket, and scribbles something down. "Based on what I've heard about your other abilities, I think you'll know what I mean when I say that in this part of the country, *roots run deep*."

I startle, searching her gaze. She winks. "Are you—"

Her brown eyes twinkle as she passes me the folded note. "Not me, but a couple aunts, some cousins. I'm sure you understand why I don't share that with anyone in the Order. Not even Gill."

"Yes, of course." I pull at the edge of the paper to open it, but she makes a negative sound and closes my hand around the paper until it's hidden in my fist.

"Wherever you go, things are gonna be dangerous. If you need resources or help outside of the Lines, I want you to use this info. Just be careful who you share it with, understand?"

I nod. "Completely." I clutch the paper. "Thank you."

Samira pulls me into a hug. "Black folks don't need Oaths to take care of each other. We never did."

Samira helps me down the ramp. Gillian watches us descend. The way her eyes roam over my careful movements is not unlike how she oversaw the training of Pages for the combat trial.

Jonas, the Liege who'd been waiting for us on the small airfield, is a tall man with warm, tawny skin and broad shoulders. I can't see his full build, but I *can* see that he has a full head of thick, bright silver hair. It gleams in the darkness. He looks me over, his dark eyes assessing and shrewd. "She gonna make it?" Samira shakes her head as if to say not to mention it, but the Liege ignores her. "Need to know if she can run on her own if we get attacked on the road."

"Bree'll be fine," Gill mutters, resentment sharp in her tired voice. "She needs food and rest. Time to get this serum out of her system."

Samira rolls her eyes. "Jonas is one of the senior Lieges, Bree. He manages the safehouses in this region, makes sure they have supplies and remain secure in case we need them."

"He's off active duty and put out to pasture, you mean." Jonas scoffs, but his eyes are fond when he looks at Samira.

Samira grins. "That too, old man."

Jonas isn't old at all, but by now I know that time works differently for Lieges. I'd thought earlier tonight that they'd gone prematurely gray, but it's not premature at all. Not with the Abatement on every Legendborn's horizon. On mine. I shove the thought away. I can't think about the next twenty years. The next twenty-four hours is uncertain enough.

"Jonas taught me how to use a dagger, believe it or not," Gill says with a smile. "And then I taught Nick."

"Can we reminisce another time?" Sel asks dryly, knocking the hood of the car.

Jonas nods, turning to climb into the car without looking back. "Agreed."

Samira watches us load in. Lyssa and Ophelia say their goodbyes and jog back to the plane. Their strides are so in sync, I wonder fleetingly if they are bonded Scion and Squire, aged out of their inheritances but still Oathed.

Gill looks us over—me, William, Sel, and Alice—and then returns her gaze to mine. "Rest overnight at the safehouse. We'll send Jonas the details."

With that, she and Samira stride back toward the plane, and we climb into the car and take off into the night.

The safehouse is a large home on a flat plot of land surrounded by a massive, dense forest. Sel was right. It's the middle-of-nowhere Georgia.

When we arrive, the moon is high overhead, a bright white crescent casting the world in silver and gray.

The house is a little dusty, but there's power and running water. The entry-way is chilly, and Jonas walks to a small gas fireplace in the corner of the main living room, calling over his shoulder, "Two rooms. One on the left, one on the right. Bunk where you want. I'll take the couch."

By some unspoken agreement, Sel takes the first room down a hall to the left. Or at least, it seems like Sel will settle there eventually. He opens the door, takes a look, then closes it before stalking out into the woods, mumbling something about the perimeter, leaving me in the hallway.

"Guess we're headed that way," Alice says, gazing down the dim hall on the right. "William can take the left room with Sel, and we can take the other one together, right, Bree?"

Our room is the owner's bedroom, if I've guessed correctly. In it is a full-sized bed and an en suite bathroom. Before we head inside, William jerks a thumb over his shoulder. "I'll be down the hall. Going to take a shower."

Alice chucks her boots off and immediately falls onto the bed. It takes me a minute to balance on still-weakened legs, but I slip my sneakers off and join her on top of the comforter. She tries and fails to mask a yawn against the back of her hand.

"I can't believe you," I murmur, shaking my head. "You helped stage a whole rescue operation."

She grins at the ceiling. "I did, didn't I?"

"How?"

"Pure adrenaline, mostly." She chuckles, turning on her side to face me. "If you ask me 'why' I did it next, I'm going to punch you. Like, in the throat."

I smile. "I won't ask why. I'm good on injuries for a while."

Her face grows solemn. "The suppressant . . . William said it's some sort of gene-blocking serum?"

I nod. "All of our powers are magically tied to our ancestors'. Somehow the Regents found a way to block that connection in our blood."

She blows out a breath. "With a big, global network and probably unlimited funding, they'd be able to put the resources into top-secret medical research like this. Gene therapy, I bet. It's disgusting, but honestly? I'm not surprised they came up with something to control a group of magical teenage warriors."

I huff. "Well, we were."

"It was indoctrination," she says gently. "Affecting the other Legendborn kids more than you, obviously, but even you learned the history of the Order from people who grew up with a paradigm. Misinformation baked into mythology. It's a classic strategy. Everyone is swept up thinking of themselves as the heroes, the romanticism of it all. . . ."

Everything she says makes sense, but it reminds me eerily of Cestra's precise logic and psychological machinations. Not that it will happen, but Alice would make a terrifying Regent.

We lay quietly for a moment, listening to someone rustle around in the kitchen.

"Lord Davis was manipulated, too," I say quietly. "His entire plan was based on the assumption that being the king actually mattered and that he and his son were the heirs to Arthur's kingdom."

Alice shakes her head against the pillow. "All that carnage to get Arthur to Call him. People were killed, your mother mesmered and tracked, Sel's mom labeled a traitor. And Arthur was never going to Call him anyway."

"Arthur was never going to Call Nick, either, but people believing he was the Scion cost him his mother. His childhood." I sigh. "No wonder he's so . . . frustrated right now."

"Right now?" Alice frowns. "You say that like you've spoken to him."

"Welllll." I pull a face, tilting my head back and forth. "I think I have?"

Alice sits up, eyes wide. "Tell me *everything*."

"I still haven't met the guy," Alice says, "but from what I've heard, Nick Davis doesn't give up on people, no matter what. And if Nick knows you at *all*, he knows you're the same way."

"*Hmnh*." I collapse into the musty smelling pillow. "Tell me something happy."

After a moment, she smiles. "I know how to throw a punch now."

My eyebrows shoot up. "You do?"

She shrugs. "We had downtime while plotting your epic rescue. I asked Gill to teach me, just in case."

"Just in case what?"

Alice rolls her eyes. "In case I end up fighting someone or something. She gave me these cool iron knuckles—"

I blink. "*What?*"

She digs into her front pocket, pulls out a wicked-looking set of metal knuckles, and loops her fingers into the holes so that they rest high over her hands. "Iron. It negates aether, just like Sel's cuff thing? And maybe a little like your Bloodcraft, based on what you told me about it burning through the foxes, except obviously these don't burn, so the effect is to a much different degree, but they should allow me to do some damage. I just need to get faster—"

"You have learned a *lot* more about the Legendborn world than I realize, haven't you?" I gape at her.

"And . . ." She smirks. "Samira said I could have one of *these* babies." She pulls a small, round black item out of her back pocket. It looks like a tiny hockey puck–shaped case with an unlit LED light.

She thumbs the case open to reveal a button. "An omnidirectional, ultrasonic acoustic device. A 'Super Mosquito.' What they used on the Mageguard. It's targeted specifically for certain types of demons with sensitive hearing and works on cambions too. This one is short-range and only lasts about ten seconds but could be useful in a pinch if we need to knock out some Merlins."

"Yeah, well, we're on the run with a Merlin, remember?" I caution. "I don't want to disable *Sel*, so let's be careful how we use that." I close the case, half-scared she could hit the button by accident. "You're legit scary right now, Alice."

"*Sel's* scary!" she exclaims. "And he's a jerk!"

"He's . . ." I trail off, not sure how to explain.

She rolls her eyes. "You have to admit he sucks. If not a lot, a little. Small amounts of suckage, scattered generously."

I groan. "I mean, yeah. Especially right now."

"Plus, he looks . . ." Alice shudders.

I bristle. "He looks like what?" I hate the idea of anyone mocking Sel's appearance. His Merlin eyes or his long canines—features that I forget stand out to outsiders. Cambion features that can compel or frighten.

She raises her hands in defense. "He can be kinda terrifying, Matty. Not to like, discriminate or whatever, but I don't trust him. He spent a lot of time trying to kill you for being a demon."

I slump back. "Not *recently* . . ."

Her side-eye could cut through steel. "Let's just say I don't feel a strong urge to go out of my way on his behalf. Ever."

"Again," I say, "you are vicious right now, you know that?"

She smirks. "I like excelling at new things."

She puts the device back in her pocket and glances toward the hallway, dropping her voice. "Do you know why Tacitus's mesmer didn't work on me?"

"Not at all."

"I have a working theory."

I throw up a hand. "Why did you ask me then?"

Alice rolls her eyes. "You know I like drama. I think it's because whatever you did to bring my memories back when you were possessed by that healing ancestor after . . ." She pauses, frowning. "After Isaac attacked me. Whatever you did that night, it stuck."

"Stuck as in . . . you can't be mesmered again? *Ever?*"

"I think so." She nods. "You were in *mega* Medium mode. Wide open to your ancestors, and you got possessed by . . . what was her name?"

"Jessie," I murmur. "Her name was Jessie."

"I mean, William told me no one can resist a mesmer, but *you can*. It's a passive component of your Bloodcraft, just part of your makeup. But you're also a Medium, so maybe if a healer ancestor used your already-mesmer-resistant body as fuel to break *my* mesmer, she made it permanent."

"I guess it's possible."

"At least you have Bloodcrafter ancestors to talk to about it," Alice says. "You could always ask them, see if they ever did something like that."

I sit up, mind whirling. "Alice, you're a genius."

She lifts a brow behind her glasses. "I know. But why at this exact moment am I a genius?"

"Because I need to learn to control my Bloodcraft in battle. Use it on purpose, use it to attack. And now I think I know how to do that."

"How?"

I grin. "I'll ask the dead."

IT TAKES A few minutes to catch Alice up on the ancestral stream conversation I had with Vera during the Rite and the way I'd defended myself against Arthur by burning him away from me.

"So, you think one of the ancestors between Vera and you knows how to activate your root as an offensive weapon, not just defensive?"

"Yes. It can't just be fight or flight." I shake my head. "I need to be able to fight my own demons—"

"Literally," she adds.

"Yes, literally." I pace the room. "I'll work with Arthur to control his aether and the Line of Vera to control my root."

I stop pacing. I think of what it feels like to call aether: the burns, the flare of power too big to control. "I need to *see* it, be there. *Feel* it. I need to . . . *reverse*-channel them. To blood walk, like I did with Arthur during the Rite and on the airplane." I check for the place inside myself where I can usually find my root, or Arthur's power, and it's still gone. "Serum is still active, so blood walking is definitely a Medium ability, not a Legendborn one."

Alice, ever logical, asks, "How did you initiate it with Arthur?"

I scowl. "'By my blood, on my heart.'"

She frowns. "That don't sound right at *all*."

"It's really not," I agree. I pull out the Pendragon necklace. "But blood is how this works. How it all works. You said it yourself, my body became an offering of sorts to Jessie. Maybe my blood can be an offering too. It's literally life."

Her entire face twists in disgust. "Okay, that's cool, but also gross."

"I summoned Arthur during the Rite with a fresh cut from Excalibur. I summoned him on the plane with dried blood on the Pendragon coin. Both items are deeply connected to him, and blood is the gateway for Bloodcraft, I bet." I shrug. "It's not a regular Medium thing, but I don't think I'm a regular Medium. I just don't have anything of Vera's Line. . . ."

"Oh yes, you do," Alice says, eyes wide. "Your mom's bracelet!"

My jaw drops. "Genius levels, maximum."

She darts toward me, holding my wrist up in the light. "You're gonna have to bleed on your mom's jewelry, which is a bit . . ."

"Witchy?" I offer hopefully.

"I was gonna say 'morbid,' but sure, let's say 'witchy.'" She wrinkles her nose. "I also think you should wait to try this until after you've gotten some rest and we find, like, a safety pin or something we can disinfect." Abruptly, with her hand raised, she sniffs under her arm. "Ugh, I reek like plane exhaust and sweat. I should shower. Unless you want first?"

"Nah."

"So," she says, voice suspiciously mild as she pockets her iron knuckles and moves toward the duffel, "you gonna go talk to him?"

"Wh—" I start to ask who she means, then realize who she means, and glare at her. "Oh. Sel."

"Yeah, Sel." She frowns. "I didn't hear every word of your argument on the plane, but I heard enough."

I sigh. "He's just . . . on the extreme self-loathing train, and I don't think he's going to get off anytime soon. He may need to be alone for a bit, and then we can talk. Or not? It's hard to tell."

"Oh, I'm certain he's prowling around, furrowing those dark brows at every woodland creature and shadow, but he should know he can't go it alone." With that reasonable admonishment, she waves and slips into the connected bathroom.

The metallic sound of pots and pans being shuffled around in the kitchen reaches me through the cracked door, and my stomach growls in response. Even the *idea* of food is making my mouth water; I haven't truly eaten in a day.

Outside the bedroom, the house is filled with small, homey sounds. Soft music plays on a stereo in the living room as I make my way through it, using one hand on the walls to keep balance. Somewhere in the house, another set of pipes protests before water flows through. William found his shower.

Jonas is riffling through one of the cabinets with his back to me when I walk into the small galley kitchen that runs along the back of the house. The window over the sink looks out onto the wooded backyard. Must be pretty during the day. Now, with no lights around the exterior of the cabin, the glass is a black pane staring back at me.

Jonas drops a large jar of pasta sauce on the counter without turning. Beside it are his other findings: a few cans of beans, two energy bars, a bag of rotini, and a jar of almond butter.

"Slim pickings," I say.

"Worse than slim," he mutters. He turns around, waving his hand at the counter of nonperishables. "Only thing that goes together here is the sauce and the pasta, so—" A cough cuts him short. "Sorry. So, I guess that's what we're having, unless I can find something else."

I shrug. "Could be worse. Can I help?"

He grunts in assent and runs a hand through his silver hair. "You get the noodles started. I'll keep looking for food that ain't expired." He coughs again, this time tapping a fist to his chest.

"You okay?"

He holds a hand up, nodding through another cough. "Just getting old, kid."

I swallow and turn away, hoping to hide the expression on my face. If I had to guess, Jonas is right around thirty-five. My heart sinks, but I don't think he wants my pity about Abatement. Besides, who would I be pitying here? Him or me?

We work in silence for a few minutes. He hunts for more food, and I stand at the sink, filling one of the pots he'd found with water, then taking it back to the stove to heat. I appreciate that he doesn't feel the need to cover the silence between us with casual chitchat. All the same, it feels strange not to at least acknowledge his support.

"Thanks, by the way," I mumble. "For helping us."

"Nothing to thank me for." He grunts again, this time from the small pantry near the back door. "I was a Squire before you were even born, Crown Scion. As far as I'm concerned, this is what I signed up for." He leans back to catch my eye, watching me for a moment. He hesitates before adding, "I know . . . I know you didn't sign up for any of it. I'm sorry this is how you were brought in."

"Yeah. Me too." I murmur. "It's been really, really hard."

"I—" He looks as though he might say more, brows furrowed in some thought I can't read, but instead offers a weak smile and shakes his head. "Anyway."

"Still," I say, trying to shift the mood, "you signed up to hunt Shadowborn. Protect humanity from evil. Not hide a group of kids from the Regents."

The pantry's accordion door makes a scraping sound on the floor when Jonas closes it, like the hinge isn't level. "Who says the Regents aren't the evil in this scenario?"

I turn. "Is that what the Lieges think?"

Jonas crosses his arms over his chest. He regards me fully for what feels like the first time all night. Taking in my face as if judging whether to proceed. Something in my expression must be convincing.

"There have been eight Camlanns in the fifteen hundred years since the Spell was cast, including this one. Every two, three hundred years or so. Some last a few months, others last years. They get hidden in bloody Onceborn wars— revolutions and coups and countries at one another's throats. But between Camlanns is what we Lieges call 'the quiet war,' and that's the war the Legend-born fight daily. It's the same Shadowborn war the original Table of one hundred and fifty knights fought in the sixth century, and it has never ended. There are only three people at one time who hold the title of Regent: currently Aldrich, Cestra, and Gabriel, and there's been hundreds of them elected by the Legend-born families over the years. The Legendborn cycle, on the other hand, has produced *thousands* of Scions. Thousands of young people fighting on the front lines of the same quiet war, year after year, either dying in battle or, if we're lucky, by Abatement. All of those deaths across all of those centuries, and not *once* have the Regents in power sought a way to end the war we fight every day." Jonas chuckles dryly. "They don't even allow formerly Awakened Lieges to become Regents and have a say in our own leadership."

The water bubbles behind me, ready for the pasta. "Why not?"

"Because we're war heroes," Jonas says with a dismissive flourish. "If we've made it long enough to lose eligibility, for our inheritances to leave us, we're more valuable as trainers for the new Scions and Squires. Or we're needed out in the field, still fighting. Or"—he reaches for the jar of sauce, rolls it in his palms—"we've lost our bondmate in battle and are too broken to do either."

"The agony," I whisper.

Jonas levels a gaze at me. Then his eyes lose focus, returning to a memory—or a person. His fingers pull at the label on the sauce jar, and the soft tearing sound echoes loud in my ears, over the bubbling pot, over the music, over the water running in the old pipes. Finally, he answers, his voice a low rasp. "Yeah."

"I'm—" I swallow hard. "I—"

He turns, moves to the stove behind me, picking up a small sauce pot along the way. The jar pops as he twists it open on the counter. He glances to my side of the stove, eyeing the bag of rotini. "Gonna need more pasta than that. Saw another bag in the pantry."

"I'll get it." I move past him, dazed with all he's revealed. I pull on the accordion door, and it catches on the floor. Pull harder—and a clawed hand reaches out from the darkness to wrap itself around my throat.

26

BEFORE I CAN make a sound, before I can struggle, the goruchel's grip tightens.

Pressure builds everywhere—behind my eyes, in my throat, the top of my skull.

The only oxygen in my lungs is what's already there.

I'm off the floor, airborne.

I blink to clear my vision, see my attacker. The demon has long brown hair, pale skin. White fangs that drip black saliva. Shiny red earrings that match her dress. Black-tipped claws. Dark-veined fingers and arms.

I scrabble at her hand with my nails, scratching at her skin, digging in.

I'm kicking, kicking—

One foot catches her in the kneecap. She snarls. Retaliates with a jab to the ribs—pain explodes in my side.

The demon spins me around. I gulp fresh air—before her hand covers my mouth again.

Then she's twisting my wrists behind my back, locking them tight in her grip. Pressing me forward. My shoulders burn, scream at the joints, while she pushes me through the back door to the lawn outside. She hisses in my ear, *"Come on, Scion."*

She knows who I am.

Every time I scream, her hand tightens around my jaw. Her nails dig in, sharp daggers of pain slicing my cheeks—and the furnace in my chest finally, finally wakes up.

Root flares upward from my fingertips, rushing hot and burning—she screams and releases me.

Through a curtain of tears, I see the lawn and the woods beyond. Selwyn is out there somewhere, hunting. *Sel!* I tumble forward, fall, then scramble toward the trees on all fours.

The goruchel dives after me, wrapping both hands around my ankles to yank me back and flip me over. She lands on my chest, straddling my waist, both clawed hands pressing my forearms up by my ears, down into the earth. I struggle, praying for Arthur's strength to have returned too, but her hips squeeze the sides of my chest until I can't scream or move again.

She could break my ribs without trying, crush me like a can.

Bathed in the porchlight, I see what my root has done to her face.

Her cheeks are streaked with still-smoking burns. Open, raw wounds that leak green wisps into the air and gape when she snarls.

"You didn't say she had aether!" she says, voice harsh and low.

Jonas is at her side, panting down at me. "She's not supposed to! What does it matter?"

Jonas. Jonas is helping her.

Oh God, no.

The goruchel eyes me hungrily. "Because with power like *that*, this girl is far more valuable alive than dead."

"No!" Jonas hisses. "Get her back inside. Finish it!"

The goruchel smiles, fangs white and sharp against a ragged face. "I don't think so."

"We had a deal, Kizia!"

Kizia grins down at me, drawing one hand up to my glowing palm. "Deal's off, Legendborn. This girl's got more where that came from, I can feel it. Enough aether to fuel an army."

"No . . . ," I croak. "Stop . . ."

Jonas pulls at my arm and Kizia shoves his body away so fast, he lands hard on his back ten feet away, moaning.

The goruchel leans close, hovering over me. "Show me that power, little girl. How did it go again . . ." Her hand wraps around my throat and she squeezes just like before, this time digging her claws into the skin of my neck—and the root in my fists flares bright, lighting her face in glowing red and orange. "Yessss." She grins triumphantly, pulls me up halfway, and brings my right hand directly to her mouth. But the second her lips touch my root she throws my arm away like it had burned her all over again.

"Fuck!" she yells, eyes wide. "No way . . . no, no . . ."

I collapse to the ground, air whistling through my throat, eyes watering. This time, *she's* the one scrambling, a red streak across the lawn, cursing and yowling. I've never seen a goruchel consume aether the way that the hellfoxes do, never seen one try and take it in deliberately. And never expected one to attack me, then react like I'd somehow attacked *her*.

"Goddamnit, *no*." Kizia wipes the back of her hand across her lips, like she's trying to clean my root from her mouth.

Nearby, Jonas pushes to his feet. The stunned look on his face says he doesn't know what's happening to Kizia either.

"SELWYN!"

William.

I see William at the door, backlit by the yellow kitchen light. Aether armor ripples into place across his body as he bears down on the startled Kizia.

Crashing sounds echo through the forest.

Close. Closer.

Here.

Kizia speeds away from William, toward the driveway—and Sel barrels into her, body a furious black blur overhead. They tumble end over end, all growls and fangs.

I twist on my side. Push up onto an elbow in the dirt. A searing arc of pain shoots across my shoulders from where Kizia had twisted them in her grip.

William's aether armor is fully formed now, illuminating the yard in glowing silver and blue.

Helmet. Shining pauldrons. Gauntlets. Leg armor. Chain mail flowing under and between.

He circles Jonas with an aether dagger in each hand.

Jonas has produced his own pair of metal blades, face bruised and bloody.

"Jonas," William says warningly. "Whatever you're doing—"

Jonas lunges, swipes. His weapon grazes William's chestplate with a high-pitched, metallic screech. William jumps back, surprise flashing across his features.

"Been doing this a lot longer than you have, kid." Jonas smirks. "How long can you hold that armor in place, do you think?"

William lowers his chin. "Long enough to stop you."

William dives toward Jonas, blades shimmering. Jonas is the larger, older opponent, but he doesn't seem to have lost any speed. He dodges William's attacks by striking, snakelike, before withdrawing just as quickly. A slash against a gauntlet. A swipe at the chain mail at his elbow.

William keeps up, but I can see the focus it requires. How careful his footwork becomes.

His opponent spent nearly two decades fighting demons, most of that time without inheritances. Without aether armor. William's armor and skills are formidable, but he's nowhere near as fast and strong as an uchel, and Jonas has been fighting them for years.

I know William; he doesn't want to hurt Jonas if he doesn't have to.

The demon's claws left stinging wounds around both sides my throat. Panting, I push up on both hands. Push again, get a knee underneath me. One more time, both knees. Then I'm on my feet, wincing through the pain in my shoulders, throat, and back, but standing.

A yowl splits the air, high enough to hurt our ears. Sel has bent the goruchel's arm back behind her. She swings wide with her free arm. He dodges her claws, doesn't let go.

A heartbeat later, William gasps loud enough to draw me back to his fight with Jonas. Jonas must have disarmed him, because one of William's daggers is blade down, upright in the ground.

Jonas's eyes flash in my direction, then back to William. To Sel and the goruchel he has trapped in his grip. Back to me.

He makes a decision.

Flips the dagger in his palm, adjusting its weight and his grip.

"No!" William shouts.

Jonas pulls back—and time slows down.

The blade hurtles toward me, aimed right for my chest—and a body crosses my vision, intercepting it.

Time speeds up.

Sel is on the ground ten feet to my left, with a handle sticking out of his shoulder.

"No!" I lunge toward him, falling after the first step. See up close how the blade has disappeared into his body down to the hilt. He rolls to his back with a groan.

A hand spins me around. The goruchel is standing behind me, black blood oozing from the side of her lip. "This is your fault!"

Her fist is already in motion when—*crack!*—her punch is stopped midair by a shining hand.

The demon's eyes go wide, stunned at the open palm that has stopped her attack.

My eyes follow the shimmering aether armor up the wrist holding her back, to the elbow, and finally to William's face. I expect to see a clenched jaw, gritted teeth, the full-bodied effort of holding back an opponent with preternatural strength. Instead, there is only the determined, steady power of Gawain.

William holds the strongest of the greater demons—a *full-blooded* goruchel—without strain.

Because for two hours each day, the Scion of Gawain's strength is unparalleled in either the demon or the Legendborn world.

And then, William uses that strength to close his fingers around her fist . . . and squeeze.

Kizia screams, loud and guttural. Struggles against his grip.

But he doesn't stop.

When bones crack beneath the skin, they make a deep, wet popping sound. That sickening crunch echoes around us in the yard until there are no more bones to break.

Between William's fingers, the goruchel's hand is now a ball of flesh and broken joints.

She's still screaming.

She tries to pull away again, but it's a mistake—her destroyed hand is still in William's fist. The pain must be excruciating. She'd have to break her own hand off at the wrist to escape him.

I've never seen William *use* his full power. I've been around him when it was present, but never seen it in battle. I imagined it would be flashier, somehow. Big swings of punches that send people flying. But this type of strength doesn't need flash.

All he has to do is . . . squeeze.

William is a healer, and he is a warrior. William is one of the kindest people I know—but the boy before me is an angry god, crushing a mouse.

Is that how I looked when I hurt Lark? It was William who warned me about using my strength to hurt someone, about being accountable for their pain. Now I wonder if this is why.

The demon snarls, black spittle flying from her mouth. "Let me go, Legend-born!" William doesn't budge.

The demon twists faster than the eye can track, this time sending an upper-cut into William's ribs with her free hand. The aether armor dents behind her fist, but William wraps his fingers around that wrist, pulling it up in the air too.

It's like her hands have been caught in cement. Nothing she does moves him or loosens his hold. There's only one way out.

The goruchel plants one foot and yanks hard with both arms—and howls in pain. The loud snap is her shoulders, popping out of their joints. I taste bile.

"Stop," William says, grimacing. "You're only hurting yourself."

"I'll kill you!" she shouts, red eyes blazing.

Without a word, William steps forward and, with one hand, smoothly pulls her into a chokehold. His forearm presses against her windpipe, not hard enough to crush it, but hard enough that she can't breathe. She kicks along the ground while both arms flail uselessly—one hand a bloody, gnarled mess.

Suddenly, Sel is on his feet beside me, fury marring his features. His right hand grasps the round hardwood handle in his left shoulder. A beat to inhale, then he pulls the eight-inch blade out with a roar behind gritted teeth.

A large, shiny red hole in his jacket reflects the light from the kitchen window. Blood flows in a stream down his chest, but he doesn't seem to notice. Instead, he scowls down at Jonas's thrown dagger in his hands as it drips red blood into the earth, like the weapon itself offends him. He shoves it into his belt, still wet. His head whips back and forth on the lawn. "Where'd the Liege go?"

"Ran," William mutters, jerking his chin into the woods opposite the back porch. "That way." He's still holding the goruchel with ease, watching her face carefully. It's now a blueish color. Her crimson eyes roll back in her head. "She's nearly out. Go get him."

Sel is off in a whoosh. Slower than I've seen him, but faster than I could run, especially now. William notices me swaying on my feet and his glowing eyes flick up to mine. "She got you pretty good. I'll heal you when we're done."

"Holy shit!"

There in the open doorway stands Alice, hair still wet and dripping onto her pink polka-dotted sleep tee and matching shorts.

She runs barefoot in the grass toward us just as William lowers the now unconscious goruchel onto the ground, but she stops a few feet away when she sees the demon. "Is that a . . ."

"Demon?" William nods as he releases the goruchel and eyes her for signs of movement. "Yes. Goruchel, the strongest and rarest. Although we've seen two in as many months now, so 'rare' may be an adjective we can no longer afford to use."

"She looks human."

William's jaw clenches. "She killed the human who looked like this. Goruchels don't leave their victims alive. They have to murder a human to replace them."

Alice's eyes widen in horror. Her head jerks from one part of the scene to the next as if she doesn't know where to look first. The very real demon bleeding black blood, half-broken and unconscious on the grassy lawn, William kneeling next to her, or me wavering on my feet.

In the end, she settles on me.

"Bree, your . . . you . . ." She steps closer, wide eyes traveling over my face, lingering on my throat. The careful way I'm standing. No, the way I'm tilting . . . She sweeps up under my arm to catch me. The motion pulls at my right shoulder and I cry out. "Sorry, sorry!"

"I'm okay, just—" It hurts to talk, so I don't.

"Set her down slow. Hold her head with one hand to keep it still," William orders, still kneeling beside the demon, his hand on her shoulder. In case she wakes, I guess.

Alice complies without hesitation, lowering me to the ground. It feels safer immediately. The forest was starting to spin a little. "I'm okay!" I insist.

William shifts the goruchel's body with one hand, hitching her upright so that he can wrap his other hand solidly around her waist. "Hold out your hand. I can't do it all, but I can start healing the worst of it. Close the lacerations at least."

I hold my hand out until our fingertips touch. His eyebrows fold into each other, his eyes close, and his teeth grit with the effort, but he manages to pull aether from the air around his left hand while maintaining his armor. It looks like a lot of effort to do both. Then I feel the familiar cool sensation of William's healing aether slip into my palm and travel up my arm and elbow, flow into my shoulder, and settle beneath my jaw, relieving my pain. The wounds from Kizia's claws begin to close.

My entire body grows warm with healing, and William's fingers withdraw. He pulls back to better hold the demon in place, panting slightly with fresh sweat beading at his brow.

"That was too much." My voice is still hoarse but it's nowhere near as excruciating to speak. "You'll overextend yourself—"

"I am *still a healer*." His voice is hard and sure, like he needs to remind himself, not just me.

I stare at my friend for a moment, fully processing what he's saying. William is a healer to his very core. It's who he *is*. The strength? The fighting? That's just what he does. What he must do. He doesn't enjoy battle the way Selwyn or Nick do. The way Greer does, or even Tor. How must it feel to hold death in one hand and restoration in the other?

There's crashing in the woods behind us, and irate shouting. "Shut up!" Sel barks in a voice made of steel and rage.

He clears the tree line, dragging a struggling Jonas on the ground behind him by his shirt collar. As he approaches, I see a glint of metal in his belt. The other dagger. Sel stops about ten feet away and swings Jonas loose onto the ground in front of us.

The older man falls forward on his hands and knees, wracked by a coughing fit. At first, I think it's because Sel had dragged him around by his shirt tight against his throat, but that's not it, because when Jonas sits back, the coughs keep coming. They turn wet in his chest. His eyes are bloodshot, his face flushed.

Sel crosses his arms. "Hoping Jonas here will stop hacking up a fucking lung long enough to tell us why he tried to kill Bree and why there was a goruchel-mimic *in his house*." His amber eyes flick to the demon on the ground and to William. "If she moves—"

"We need to question her, too," William says.

Sel makes a displeased sound in his throat, but doesn't protest. He growls at Jonas where he sits. "Come on, Liege. Speak up."

Jonas gasps for air. When he inhales, his whole body shakes and his hands curl into the dirt. He glares up at Sel. "I won't talk."

Sel rolls his eyes. "We can *make* you talk."

Jonas's laugh is hoarse. "*You* can't make me do anything, Kingsmage. Even if you weren't cuffed against using aether, you can't hurt me. Not with the assload of Oaths you're carrying around."

Sel's eyes narrow. "He's right. He's still Legendborn as far as my Oath of Service is concerned, even if he is a goddamn traitor."

"You can hold him in place, though, right?" Alice asks. She looks from the older man panting heavily on his knees, to Sel standing just behind. "Catch him if he tries to escape?"

Sel eyes her. "Obviously."

Alice ignores his sarcasm and stands. "I'll be right back." She jogs to the back porch and swings the door open to step into the kitchen.

Sel watches her go, confused impatience settling across his brow. "What's the Onceborn doing now?"

I make a negative sound, and he looks at me. His gaze lingers on my face, examining me for the first time since the fight ended. Sparks from his eyes travel down my throat to what I can only imagine are the marks left by the goruchel's hands. By the time he's done cataloguing my wounds, a silent, dangerous gleam has slipped into his eyes.

"How much time do you have, Will?" he asks, without looking away from my face.

William glances up at the sky, gauging when Gawain's powers will leave him. "Thirty minutes at most."

The door swings open and Alice jogs back out with a glass of water. She kneels down a safe distance from Jonas. "Here."

"What the hell?" Sel exclaims. "This isn't a tea party!"

Alice ignores him. Instead, she dips her head to catch Jonas's eye. "For your cough."

Jonas looks from her face to William's to mine, then back to hers, wary and calculating.

"It's just water. I'm, like, the newest of new kids here." Alice smiles and pushes her glasses up. "Learned about all of this a few weeks ago, so I'm all Onceborn city." She shrugs awkwardly. "I don't know what I'd even put in this, if you're worried about poison or something."

Jonas reaches out slowly to take the glass from her hand. Smells the liquid first, then watches her carefully as he sips it. The relief is visible on his face. "If you're that new, then you need to get out now while you can."

Alice sits down cross-legged. "Why? Bree's my best friend."

Over Jonas's head, Sel's eyes meet William's with a raised brow. William gives a stiff, tiny shake of his head. He wants him to wait. Let Alice work.

Jonas snorts. "Your best friend is the magical anchor to a centuries-old spell that's given sixty generations nothing but misery."

"She's the reason this war can be won," Alice counters calmly. "Bree will help stop Camlann."

Jonas coughs into his fist. His voice is mocking, sharp. "This one, maybe. But nothing truly ends Camlann, girl."

Alice sits for a moment, studying him. "You lost someone, didn't you?"

Jonas looks up, and I think about what he must see when he sees Alice. Her earnest brows and downturned mouth? The focused gaze that makes you feel like she's not thinking about anything else but you? A sixteen-year-old girl who can go completely still with attention, and who listens to people with her whole body?

The wind picks up behind us. William's armor flickers lightly but holds. Clouds shift overhead as we wait for Jonas to respond.

His first response is a silent one. Tears, filling his eyes. "My Scion."

Alice's face falls. "What was their name?"

Jonas's shoulders slump with something heavier than fatigue. Loneliness, the bone-deep kind, radiates from him. He's been out here for who knows how long, away from the other Lieges, away from the battlefield and a clear purpose. Living in the grief and only the grief. When he speaks again, his voice cracks on three syllables. "Lydia."

"I'm sorry," Alice murmurs, and I tense at the same time Jonas does. Wrong thing to say.

His scowl grows. "What would you know of the Warrior's Oath? You can't be sorry about pain you've never felt or seen."

Alice purses her lips, and I can see her brain recalibrating from her error. "I can be sorry about the pain I'm seeing right in front of me."

"That's why you can't understand. It was my fault!" he says, and this time when his voice cracks, the cough returns. He struggles for a moment, then downs the water with an audible gulp, wincing. "I could have saved her. Should have. Instead, I watched her die, felt her anger, her fear. She thought I'd be there to stop the demon, and I failed her."

Alice's own eyes shine in the night. "I'd want revenge if someone I loved was murdered right in front of me. But why would you try to kill Bree?"

Jonas's eyes sharpen on her, realizing what she's done. How she's maneuvered him. "I won't live long enough for a trial, so don't even try to get a confession."

"If you're not going to live long enough for a trial, why does it matter if you confess or not?" That stops him, and Alice keeps going, pressing her advantage. "Why go through all this trouble if you aren't going to make your mission crystal clear in the end? I'm new here. So is Bree. Tell us something we couldn't learn from anyone else."

Jonas's eyes flutter. "The Legendborn cycle saves human lives while destroying them in the same breath. I chose to become Legendborn, but Lydia didn't. And she was torn apart by a pack of hellhounds on her nineteenth birthday. The only way to stop that from happening to anyone else . . . the only way to stop the cycle is to kill the Scion of Arthur while she is Awakened and end the Spell."

"That only works if a Shadowborn kills Bree," Sel hisses. "That's why the goruchel is here."

"But after Sel disabled your assassin, you attempted to kill Bree yourself," William says. "Why? Your blade wouldn't have ended the Spell."

Jonas avoids my gaze, mumbling, "No. But her death would weaken the Table. Disorganize you. Keep you all from fighting, dying, if only for a little bit longer."

Sel rolls his eyes. "I don't know what Scions were like in your day, traitor, but weakening *this* Table wouldn't do a damn thing to stop them from fighting! It would only make them more vulnerable when they do."

"And you'd risk leaving humanity undefended," I say, pushing past the pain of speaking. I'm too inflamed at everything Jonas is saying, at what he's suggesting is the better path, to remain silent.

"If this goruchel had killed Bree . . . you'd let the Shadowborn rule?" William replies, confusion twisting his features. "So that even more Lydias can die, this time without the skills or abilities to defend themselves?"

"We can't be everywhere at once as it is!" Jonas shouts. "Humans are killed by demons in the middle of deserts, on islands, in the arctic . . . places we aren't stationed or don't patrol!"

"So, if you can't stop all evil, there's no point in stopping any evil, is that it?" Sel asks, his voice low and cold.

"You get to be as old as I am, Merlin, and the little and big evils start to blur together," Jonas says with a chuckle. "This was the best and only opportunity I'd ever get to end it on my terms."

I push to my knees, then to standing. "You waited until Sel was gone, and you knew he was cuffed," I say, piecing it all together. "You waited until William and Alice were both in the shower. You wanted me alone."

He'd even had music playing to muffle the sound.

"You find an opening, you take it. Aim for the head." His laugh turns into a violent, hacking fit. Worse than before. Longer. He pitches forward on one hand. When he coughs again, blood splatters onto the grass and down his chin.

"What's wrong with him?" Alice jerks back.

William starts toward Jonas, but Sel holds out a hand. "You know you can't stop this."

William's face contorts. Even if Jonas tried to kill us both, it goes against everything in him to watch someone suffer.

The Liege's face is turning a deep red color, like someone choking. He sits back, clawing at his own throat, breaking the skin. Alice screams and scrambles further away. Blood streams like tears down the inner and outer corners of Jonas's dark eyes.

"He intentionally broke his Oaths," Sel explains, a mixture of disdain and disgust on his features. "Oath of Fealty, Oath of Service—"

"Oath of Valor, too." Jonas wipes a shaking hand across his mouth. Sweat has gathered on his brow, and his pulse leaps against his neck. He repeats his Oath in a gurgling, halting voice. "'I swear to never knowingly allow my Awakened sovereign . . . to come to injurious harm.' That one hit . . . as soon as I told Kizia where to find you."

He coughs again, this time falling forward to vomit a pool of dark blood onto the grass.

My stomach turns at the sight and at the acceptance on Jonas's face. He knew what would happen here. He knew his death was coming.

Sel watches the scene unfold, eyes unreadable. "He swore to uphold those Oaths. And swore to accept the consequences for breaking them."

I'd seen what happened to Ramirez when he lunged for me in the Order's van. I know what an Oath does when its owner consciously takes action with the intent to harm me.

Which is why I am prepared for what happens next.

Silver-and-blue flames erupt around Jonas's throat. The Oath's power does not visibly burn him, but he screams as it spreads down his chest. Jonas turns onto his back, letting the flames cover his body. With one trembling hand, he scrabbles at something around his neck, barely manages to yank it out. Wraps his hand around it. The mage flame roars higher, blue at its core and silver reaching ten feet in the air. Alice can't see it, but William, Sel, and I watch the aether of Jonas's death light the yard.

Then, with a great sigh, they extinguish.

When we look down, a shining necklace with two coins lies atop a large, body-shaped pile of silver-and-gray ash.

ALICE SOBS INTO her hand. She hadn't seen the mage flames like we had, but she'd seen a man struggle against his own body, bleeding and vomiting life into the grass around him. That's bad enough.

Ash the color of Jonas's hair lies scattered on the ground, already dispersing in the wind.

"We didn't . . . do anything . . . we just stood here. . . ." Her voice is a ragged whisper.

William shakes his head, eyes somber. "Nothing stops the outcome of breaking an Oath. Oath magic becomes a part of a person's DNA. The stronger the Oath, the more severe the consequence."

"But . . . ," Alice falters.

"But *what?*" Sel jerks his chin at the ash. "This man did not deserve our *mercy.* He conspired with a Shadowborn to *murder your best friend in cold blood.* What part of that are you missing?"

"He . . . ," I whisper and turn to William. "He was coughing earlier."

William nods slowly. "That's what he meant about the Oath of Valor hitting him first. He'd planned to kill you before we arrived. The Oath was probably working on him when he picked us up at the airstrip." His eyes flick to the goruchel. "But Kizia here was doing the dirty work, so his symptoms were mild."

"His life ended the second he threw his dagger at Bree," Sel says. "The direct attempt on her life pushed the magic over."

"At his age, Jonas was close to Abatement," William says quietly. "I don't forgive him, or respect his decisions. I'm glad he can't hurt anyone else. The Legendborn have so few choices about how we might leave this life. I wish he'd chosen another path."

I watch the certainty on William's face and feel the opposite. Inside, my heart is in turmoil. I am relieved that Jonas failed. Angry that he deceived me, deceived us. Furious that he injured Sel. Terrified that he could let a goruchel into what should have been a safe place for us to rest and recover. But when I search for feelings of vengeance against Jonas, or happiness that he is dead, I come up short.

Suddenly, Kizia wakes.

She surges against William's hold, but he's been ready, and Gawain's strength is still flowing through him. He twists her around quickly and clasps both of her hands behind her back. She hisses in pain. "Let me go! Just let me go; I won't touch your Scion."

Sel pulls one of Jonas's daggers out and kneels over the goruchel, placing it against her neck. "Nice nap?"

"Blood traitor!" Kizia snarls, but the pain keeps her still. Her shoulders don't sit right in the sockets; the bones jut out alone at the ends of her shirt, and the arm muscles lie limp, an inch below where they should.

"You Shadowborn love calling me that, don't you? You always say it right before I kill you." Sel's mouth curves in a slow smile. "How did you meet Jonas?"

"Not telling you a damn thing, cambion." She spits into his face. Sel growls low in his throat and lifts his T-shirt to wipe it away. He presses the blade deeper, drawing black blood from her skin in a thin, inky line.

"Did you know the man behind you is studying to be a doctor?" Kizia's expression turns uncertain at Sel's measured, easy tone. His smile and bright eyes. "Currently, he's *terrifyingly* strong. Stronger than you and me combined. You've felt it, haven't you, Kizia? How he could, if he wanted to, take you apart"—he taps the flat of the blade against her neck—"bit . . . by . . . bit. Probably name each joint, ligament, and tendon as he goes."

She shoots Sel a haughty sneer.

"You Legendborn don't have the stomach for it." She looks at each of us, and a knowing smile blooms over her face. "Your precious *code* won't allow it. You're descended from the most self-righteous knights on the planet."

"Now, that last bit I won't argue with." Sel shrugs, glancing to William. "But the rest . . ."

Snap!

I jump as Kizia screams, mouth wide, eyes burning. Heart hammering in my chest, my eyes fall to where William's forefinger and thumb have just . . . twisted her elbow joint completely apart. Her limb is still held together by flesh. But now it's in two pieces. Not one.

She wails, but William holds her still. Behind the struggling demon, his eyes have gone flat.

Alice drops to her knees, vomiting on the grass. I'd do the same, except I know what it cost William to do this—the price he's paying to torture someone, even a demon. That thought scares me into action.

"I . . . uh . . . ," I begin, swallowing and wincing. Kizia's watering eyes dart to me, as do my friends'. "I've never seen him like this. Just answer. Before he has to do more."

She pants for a moment and eyes me shrewdly, then looks to Sel. Makes her decision. "Never met that old Legendborn before tonight. Said he needed a demon for a job and my employer brokered a one-day deal."

"Who's your employer?" Sel asks.

"Someone you don't wanna meet." She grins.

Sel narrows his eyes, as if deciding whether to believe her. He changes tactics. "Who else knows about your and Jonas's little murder plot tonight?"

Kizia shakes her head, eyes darting to me. "No one else knows where the pretty Scion is, if that's what you're asking. And no one else will, if you just let me go."

"And then what? You go back to your boss? Turn around and try and kill her again?" Sel asks. "I don't think so."

"I won't touch her!" Kizia cries. "I promise!"

"Sure, you won't," Sel drawls.

"I think she's telling the truth," I say.

Sel's eyes dart to mine. "Why would you say that?"

"She . . ." I swallow, putting together those rapid, desperate moments before Jonas tried to kill me himself. "She tried to consume my aether—"

"She *what*?" Sel snarls.

"Tried to," I continue speaking directly to Kizia. "And then you stopped. Like trying to take my root inside hurt you . . ." Kizia looks away. The fear from before is there in the taut line of her throat.

Sel taps his thigh with the dagger. "You demons like bargains. If you tell us what we want to know, we'll let you go. How about that?"

Kizia glances up at him, temptation written across her face.

"Tell us what stopped you from feeding on the Scion of Arthur, Kizia."

Kizia looks me over from head to toe, and finally relents. She swallows thickly. "He'll know it was me. That this was unauthorized. You're unregulated. Which is why you should let me go."

Cold fear slips through me. "Unregulated?" Sel asks. "What does that mean? And who will know it was you? Your boss?"

Her voice is hushed when she speaks again, eyes wide. "The Great Devourer. He who hunts humans for power."

Hunt. Power. Tacitus's final threat and red eyes rise to my mind. I shudder.

"Bullshit," Sel mutters. "Give us a real answer."

Kizia snarls. "This is full-demon business, *cambion*. I got nothing else to say to you."

"You sure?" Sel asks, a dark twinkle in his eye.

"Fuck you!"

"If that's the case," he says, "Thank you for your time, Kizia."

Sel glances up at William and nods. After a beat, William releases her. Kizia darts to her feet. She spares me a brief glance and turns, speeding into the woods in a dark blur.

Then, without a word, Sel hefts the dagger in his hand, dips his chin to follow her path—and throws the blade fast and hard.

A cloud of green dust explodes against the darkness, and I know that Sel's aim was true.

After a beat of silence, Alice shoves back onto her knees, looking between the woods and Sel, between Sel and William. "You—you . . . killed her?"

"Kizia was an undead demon. Never alive in the first place." Sel shrugs. "The woman Kizia murdered in order to mimic her body? *She's* dead."

Alice wobbles to her feet, dazed. "But she looked human, she spoke to us, she—"

Sel rolls his eyes. "Get your shit together, Onceborn."

"I have my shit together!" Alice waves her hands in front of her. "But you just killed a demon-person, and you're acting like that's . . . *normal*. Like killing is okay!"

"I killed a demon-person, too," I whisper. "Rhaz."

Alice's mouth opens and closes again, like she just can't find her words.

Sel crosses his arms, jaw set. "You did what was necessary. And just like Rhaz, Kizia had your scent. Neither one of them would have stopped hunting you if you'd let them go. It didn't matter what bargain we made. She'd have sought revenge."

I swallow. "She said she wouldn't come for me."

Sel scoffs. "Because of some Shadowborn boogeyman? Some assassination broker? No. You are the Scion of Arthur; your death at her hands would break the cycle and let demons reign free and feed forever. Whatever fear she had would fade soon enough, and she'd be back."

I swallow bile, but nod. "You're right."

"You *are* right, Selwyn. But it is different when they look human." I watch William rise. Finally, he releases his armor. The aether he'd cast it from crumbles, then dusts. He walks quickly over to me and assesses my face, gently lifting my chin. "Let's get you inside."

"I will carry Bree," Sel offers, stepping forward.

"*No*, Selwyn." Some silent conversation passes between him and Sel, until Sel's hand balls into a fist. Sel's eyes glow a deep, pulsing orange, and his lips pull back. His gaze darkens, fingers twitching at his sides. William says in a low voice, "Take a breather."

Sel relents, looking away. "Fine. I'll search the house. Make sure there are no more surprises. Find the keys to the SUV in case we need to leave quickly. I'll let you know when it's clear to go inside, then do another perimeter sweep." With that, he whooshes inside. Doors bang open and closed as he speeds through rooms and closets.

Suddenly, the world moves, and I'm in William's arms like I weigh nothing. He shifts me gently to better support my neck and spine.

"Is he okay?" I ask.

"He's being stubborn." William turns. "Alice, please find us a clear space while Sel finishes up? Couch is probably best."

Alice looks at me with tears staining her cheeks, then nods at William's request and jogs inside.

"This is a lot for her," I murmur against William's chest. I inhale the familiar scent of his signature until it calms my racing pulse.

"She will need our support." He smiles down at me. "When you first found us, you were attacked by a hellhound and its saliva had burned through both of your arms. And you came back for more the next day."

"But all the death," I whisper, shutting my eyes. "Seeing it right in front of you."

His hands tighten around me. "We prevent the ones we can."

"I want to stop them from happening," I reply.

He searches my face for a long moment. "I know you do."

I raise a hand to his chest. "William." My mouth crumples, tears springing to my eyes. "I never asked you about Whitty. I should have. I'm sorry."

He blinks, his eyes suddenly shiny as well. "We weren't bonded long enough to feel the agony the way Jonas did, or even Felicity . . ."

I press my hand against his heart. "But you felt it? Felt him die?"

William's expression goes distant. "Yes."

I clutch his shirt in my hand. "And you still feel it. And that matters."

"Thank you. He was a good man."

"He was." I give him a watery smile. "And funny."

William chuckles. "Very funny. Always wearing that damn camo jacket."

"Clear!" Sel calls from the driveway.

William moves toward the steps. As he reaches for the door, he says, "I'm sorry too, Bree."

"For what?"

"For not finding a way to stop the Regents from hurting you sooner."

"You saved me. You're why I could resist Tacitus's mesmer."

His chin dips as he continues into the mess of a kitchen, but I don't think he accepts my forgiveness. As he maneuvers us around the remnants of Jonas's meal and the pantry items strewn on the floor, something fractures inside my chest for William. William, who was forced to watch them torture me. Who prioritizes consent. And who, against his every instinct, tortured a demon tonight for answers.

There are many things that I will make the Regents pay for, but breaking William, making him question himself, will be chief among them.

I swear it.

28

THE COUCH IS musty, and newly freed dust motes circle the air above my head.

But the cushions are soft, and my body is warm. I'm laid out flat, feet on one end and head propped up on the other. Alice leans over the back of the couch on her elbows to watch William work. Or watch what she can, anyway.

Sel is perched on the armrest. He sniffs the air. "She's bleeding inside."

"Ew," Alice and I both mutter.

He raises a brow. "If I told you all the things I can smell and hear, you'd say a lot more than 'ew.'"

Alice grimaces. "Ew again. With *feeling*."

"Thank you for the announcement, Selwyn." William shakes his head with a smile. His aether-coated hands hover down to my ribcage and side.

"You should talk." Alice wrinkles her face at Sel. "You're sitting there still oozing blood out of your shoulder."

He glances down at his shirt, where the blood has dried and stuck to his skin around the still-open cut. "More upset about the jacket, to be honest."

"Are you healing him next?" I ask William.

To my surprise, he shakes his head. "Merlins can't be healed by my swyns."

"What?" Alice and I both exclaim.

Sel glances between us, looking like he's just tasted something sour. "Is this what the two of you are like all the time?"

"No," we say, and smirk.

He rolls his eyes in exasperation, but I can tell his ire is mild. Since we've all gathered in the same room—and he's collected every knife and weapon-like item from the kitchen into his lap—he's been less on edge. Leave it to Selwyn Kane to be comforted by a pile of sharp objects.

"Why is that, though?" I ask. William hits a particularly tender spot, and I do my best to stifle a quiet moan.

Sel's head and ear turn slightly in my direction, and a light flush hits his cheeks.

He definitely heard that moan.

"Merlin physiology is *just* different enough that my"—William tilts his head back and forth while searching for the words—"variety of aether isn't useful to their healing process."

"What does that mean?" Alice asks, eyes wide.

"It means mind your business, Onceborn," Sel interjects as he picks at his shirt. "I'll clean and bandage it myself once we figure out what to do next."

"I have a name," Alice says with a glare. "Three, actually. First, middle, and last. You're welcome to use any of them."

"Well." Sel tilts his head. "I'm honestly still deciding if I want to refer to you at all. I don't really know you that well, do I? Other than that you're Briana's Unanedig childhood friend."

"I don't speak Welsh," Alice says with a scowl.

"I am aware." Sel scans the room, looking it over for the third time in the past ten minutes. For more weapons, more hiding places, hidden threats, I'm sure.

"Is he always so damn rude?" Alice asks me.

"Yes," William and I respond.

"Call her Alice," I command. Sel's eyes flash to mine, then away. Closest thing I'll get to an agreement from him, I think, at least in front of the others. To Alice, I say, "'Unanedig' is Welsh for 'Onceborn.'"

"Your accent's getting better," William murmurs approvingly.

"Diolch," I reply, and he grins.

"Da iawn, Bree!"

"Da" means "good." That much I know. It didn't take long to pick up on a few phrases. I look up, proud of myself and pleased with William's praise—and find Sel's penetrating gaze already on me. Heat climbs up my neck, and my smile falters. He knows I've learned *some* Welsh now, but *"cariad"* still hangs between us, a word in limbo.

He looks away, pulling something out of his pocket. A cell phone.

"Found Jonas's phone in the car. Looked through it, but it's a burner. Nothing useful."

"Great." A rib shifts across a nerve and I stiffen. Pain shoots across my chest in a bright, sharp line.

"Sorry." William lifts his hands up, his face apologetic.

Sel stands, both hands on the end of the couch. "We need to proceed as if this 'broker' at least knows that they've arranged an assassination, and that they have an interest in ensuring that arrangement went as planned. If they find out that both parties ended up dead, we might have a serious problem. I'd say we have until the end of the twenty-four-hour window before they come looking for Jonas, Kizia, or both. That's tomorrow night. We should leave in the afternoon if not earlier."

"Terrific," I drawl.

Sel eyes me. "This information also means we have a new unknown entity to avoid. If this underground magic broker is aware of the Legendborn and the war, and they figure out who you are, Bree, they'll come after you, too." His face darkens. "That's the thing about kings. They're just as valuable dead as they are alive."

The room grows silent. "Well," I say with an exaggerated sigh, "I'm a Medium, so I'm a living king with a dead one in her head. Double points for assassinating me, I guess."

Alice thumps my shoulder. "Not funny, Matty."

Sel looks at me for a long time. "I agree with Alice."

Her jaw goes slack for a second before she recovers. "See? Even the grumpy wizard agrees with me."

"Sorcerer, if you must," Sel retorts. He taps the phone with a finger, pulling our attention back to business. "We need to tell Gill about Jonas and Kizia. If nothing else, so that she knows to watch her back."

A flutter of anxiety appears in my chest. "You think there's a chance Jonas was working with other Lieges?"

"I'd say we need to seriously consider the possibility. After all, he's not the only Liege who has lived the same story. We need to treat Jonas as a potential symptom of a greater problem. Any grieving, angry former Scion with nothing to lose could wake up tomorrow and come to Jonas's same conclusion."

If you ask me, there are Lieges in the field more dangerous than any Merlin.

Sel's lip curls back in anger. "Remember, Jonas knew you'd be vulnerable tonight. He'd had time to plan."

A sick feeling swims in my belly. "The serum," I whisper. "He thought I was still powerless."

"It wore off quicker than he'd anticipated," Alice says. "Thank *God*."

"No." I shake my head. "I figured out the Regents were dosing me in the food at the Institute. Stopped eating yesterday morning."

William sucks in a breath, eyes widening in understanding. "You missed three doses in a row. If you hadn't—"

"If you hadn't, your root wouldn't have stopped Kizia," Sel finishes, voice deadly. "And she would have killed you just like she was hired to do."

Alice gnaws on her thumb. "Jonas knew about the serum because Gill and Samira told him about it. Are we sure we can trust them?"

Sel taps his fingers on the hilt of a dagger. "I trust Gill."

I nod. "And I trust Samira."

"You're certain?" Sel asks.

I think of Samira giving me the slip of paper still in my back pocket. Her pride in me, her hope. "Yes." He nods once in acceptance.

"What about the Lieges watching our parents?" Alice asks apprehensively.

My heart tightens at the thought of my dad, the worry for him freshly renewed after Jonas's betrayal. "Can we ask Gill and Samira to watch our parents themselves? Or bring in Lyssa and Ophelia? People who have already put themselves at risk to help us."

Sel nods. "Good idea. We'll ask." He pulls the phone out again. "I think you both should contact your parents tomorrow. I'll make the call to Gill." He crosses one arm over his chest and holds the speaker end out with the other so we can all hear.

A voice comes across the line that I don't recognize. "Passcode?"

"It's Selwyn. I need to talk to Gill."

"Passcode."

Sel inhales through his nose. "Kane. Southpaw. Horizon."

"Thank you. Connecting."

Alice turns to me, whispering loudly, "Do we get passcodes? Why does he get a passcode?"

When I look up, her eyes are strained at the edges, and shiny with unshed tears and worry, but she's forcing a smile. She's doing her best with all of this. Trying to draw me back to the familiar: our banter, our inside jokes. The way we were before demons and assassination attempts. I lean in with my own exaggerated whisper. "I guess because Merlins get trained for field missions?"

She smiles to herself. "Chen. Mickey. Snorkel."

I grin weakly. "Not something literary?"

"You're right." She pauses. "Chen. Faustus. Nevermore."

"I like that." She presses her chin to my head and squeezes my shoulder. I hold her hand back in gratitude.

A buzzing sound from Jonas's phone, then: "Hanover."

"Gill, this is Sel." He clicks the speaker off and wanders down the hall.

"Done for now," William announces. He rotates his wrists, snuffing the aether out. Fatigue shows in the circles under his eyes, in the hunch of his shoulders. The only person here who looks remotely clean is Alice. "I apologize. If I had more energy, I could get you to one hundred percent, but . . ."

"It's fine, William." I put a hand over his. "I'm good."

Alice hovers over me, eyes traveling from my face to my stomach. "Wish I could see whatever it is that just happened."

Sel returns, tapping the phone against his palm. "That went about as well as one might expect, when one is informing someone that their mentor is a traitor who broke his Oaths and aligned himself with a demon."

"So . . . horribly?" I say.

"Yes." His jaw clenches. "She needs to update Samira. Will call us tomorrow. I say we all get some rest tonight. We're gonna need it." He looks at me. "Rest, and eat."

"I agree with the angry sorcerer. You need to rest." Alice stares at me hard, and moves toward the kitchen. "I'll go put something together." William follows.

I feel Sel's eyes on my back as I retreat to the bedroom.

The small, dust-covered lamp on the nightstand is too bright. Or it makes everything too real. I'm not sure. I swoop over and turn it off as soon as I return to the room, and that feels better. I fumble through the dark by the light shining through the cracked door of the bathroom.

When I go to the sink to wash my hands after using the restroom, I catch my reflection in the mirror—and suck in a shocked breath.

Whatever I looked like before William healed me must have been awful; the marks and scabbed-over wounds still ache and burn from Kizia's claws. There are five finger-length purple bruises and red scars pressed into my brown skin. Like Kizia had dipped her open palms in red paint and held my face, making deadly art. My lips are chapped and split. My hair is beyond wild. It's been days since I've been awake long enough to wash or style it. The curls feel dry. Parched. Like they could break at my touch. At the Institute, they didn't even give me a hair tie, and I've definitely been sleeping on a plain cotton pillow. I look like a wreck and feel like worse.

I lower myself on the closed seat of the toilet, then lean over to turn the light off in here, too. I can't face all of this in the light, not right now. Don't want to see myself, my injuries, the evidence of all that has been done to me.

By myself in the quiet and darkness of the small, old bathroom, the tears finally come, along with shivering that won't stop.

The Shadowborn attack on the Beast hadn't rattled me like this. Maybe because it felt like almost any other Shadowborn attack: demons appear, we fight them. Lark was there, then Sel. I wasn't alone, and the monsters hadn't even gotten close enough to touch me.

It should probably be unsettling that the almost-dying part of my life isn't new or jarring.

But this? Jonas had looked me in the eye and known my name. He knew that I'd been raised Onceborn, outside of this world and ignorant. He knew I'd only just become Crown Scion and that I was in over my head, playing catch-up to everyone else. And he'd invited a demon to murder me while he thought I was powerless and alone anyway.

Jonas wanted me dead so badly that he'd been willing to let his Oaths kill him in the process.

I remember that there's soap here, and some towels. Shampoo and condi-tioner Alice packed just for my hair. When I flip the lights on again, I see that behind a small door in the bathroom, there's a shelf with fresh underwear and a bra, clean jeans, a T-shirt, plus a zip-up sweatshirt in my size. Alice, again.

Bless her.

I have to lean against the tile walls to shower, and go slowly so as to not lose my balance. Arthur's strength is probably back now that the serum has worn off, but I am bone tired. Even as I lather up, take down my cornrows, and get clean for what feels like the first time in days, my skin buzzes with anxiety. I press my hands against the white subway tiles while my brain sprints from one worry to the next, unstoppable.

The Regents can't kill me, and they can't remove the power from my body. Just like Nick's father, they'll comb through my family tree looking for back-up Scions. My mother had no siblings, and neither did my grandmother.

Knowing what I know now, I understand why. One child, a daughter who would live only to see you die young, is more than enough. I don't know what happened before my grandmother, but if, for argument's sake, this one-daughter rule went all the way back to Vera . . . they'd have to find Vera's nearest blood relative's descendants. A sibling, a cousin. Some plantations kept records, I think . . . but how well? Was Vera born on Samuel Davis's plantation, or had she been sold to him from another?

Ironic that the Order, with the blood of chattel slavery on the hands of their founding fathers, with their Wall of Ages and thick tomes of family records, has to face the all-too-common challenge of researching Black American family ancestry. Maybe they actually have the resources to track down my ancestors, but then again . . . maybe not. Enslavers never expected the descendants of the enslaved to be free enough to look back in time.

I desperately want to know more about my own family, of course. Maybe even warn them. But any knowledge I gain could put my own distant relatives in danger if I'm forced to reveal it. Not knowing *enough* about my own past was dangerous before. Now, knowing *too* much could be worse.

I let the water sluice down my bruised back and decide I don't know which I prefer anymore: knowledge or ignorance.

29

EVENTUALLY, I EMERGE from the bathroom. As I pad over to the door, my damp curls drip water in cold rivulets down my back beneath the T-shirt, chilling my skin. I find a fresh hair tie in Alice's duffel and pull my curls up before I go find food.

When I open the bedroom door, I stop short—because Sel is leaning against the wall inches from my face, head tipped back, eyes closed.

"Jesus!" I exclaim. "Why are you out here?"

Without moving his head, his eyes open and settle on mine. Heart still hammering, I glare at him—and see that at some point during my mini breakdown, he's changed clothes. He's still in his black pants and boots, but instead of the bloodied and torn jacket and shirt, he's now in a simple black tank.

His voice is gravelly, tired. "Looking for a first aid kit. Thought it might be in the owner's bathroom."

Ah. I see the makeshift bandage over his chest and collarbone. A square of folded-up paper towels tucked in place by the strap of his tank top. I wince. "That *can't* be sanitary."

"I don't get infections," he says, turning slowly against the wall to face me. "But a clean wound will heal more quickly and a covered one will stop ruining my clothing." A pause. "Are you all right?"

I blink, processing the abrupt change in topic. "Yes. Just needed a shower."

His gaze holds steady. "And before that?"

"Before that——" I stiffen. "Were you listening to me cry in the bathroom?"

"Yes," he says simply.

"Ugh. '*mfine*." I start to rub my face with a palm, and he holds out a full-sized, clean paper towel. I take it, and he watches me wipe my face with the coarse paper.

"Thank you for saving me tonight." I move aside to let him into the room.

Sel unsticks himself from the wall and walks inside. "Why are you thanking me for that?"

"Right. It's not a choice. You're *obligated* to save my life." I don't mean to let the hint of bitterness leak into my voice, but there it is.

Sel hears it just fine, of course. He pauses mid-stride, turns his head over his shoulder to inspect me for a moment. Keeps walking and I follow. His nose lifts and wrinkles as he nears the bathroom, catching the synthetic floral body wash scent still lingering in the air.

I ball up the paper towel in a pocket and watch him kneel to open the cabinets under the sink. "Between me and Nick, you've done a lot of that, I guess."

He pushes aside bottles of bleach and glass cleaner. "Yes. That's my——was my job."

I lean against the doorjamb and watch him search for a kit. In the light of the bedroom, his eyes look sunken. "Your Kingsmage Oath," I say. "How are——"

"I'm fine," he says blithely. "Protecting you and William fulfills my Oath of Service, and that's enough to keep me from succumbing to my blood." He stands to set a small white first aid kit on the counter then opens the lid, lifting out supplies.

"Huh."

He shakes his head with a rueful smile that shows the tips of his canines. "'Huh,' she says. Completely unaware of what it feels like to have a living promise in her veins that will kill her if she severs it, or drain her humanity if she leaves it unfulfilled."

"Hey," I protest. "Just because I haven't taken an Oath doesn't mean I don't understand how they work."

He stops. "You still haven't taken an Oath? What about the Rite of Kings?"

Heat claws up my neck. "It got interrupted when the Regents attacked me." I don't know why I lie, but I know I don't want to tell the truth. I change the subject instead. "You told Lark that the Regents were coming for you. Then you ran. Where did you go?"

I watch the urge to shoot back a sarcastic retort pass over his features in the mirror, then vanish. "I was at my mother's cabin, near the Haw River."

I stand straight. "You found her?"

He sighs. "No, mystery girl. That first night after you were Called, after I set the ward layers for the first time, I took a car out there to check. It was locked up, dusty as ever. A few rodents had moved in."

The night I had been swept up in my ancestors' memories, tossed about like a loose stone in a river—or a stream. I'd wondered why he hadn't heard my desperate whimpering on the floor. Now I know he wasn't in the building at all. He was looking for his mother because I told him about my vision.

"She had to know that one day I would learn the truth and come looking for her." His laugh is quiet and dry. "But if the great Natasia Kane does not want to be found, she will not be found. Apparently"—his smile is all teeth and refined resentment—"she only makes special appearances for you and your mother."

That stings. "I'm sorry she . . ."

"Was happy to let her only son believe she was dead?" His eyes narrow. "She made her choice."

"What did you find at the cabin?"

"Her research, her books, same as they'd always been. I read them all over again, looking for clues about how she kept the demon from taking over—and found none. The night the Mageguard tried to arrest me, I went back to see if I'd missed anything, before they . . ." He lifts a shoulder, but does not finish. Pulls out a stack of disinfecting alcohol swabs and rips one open. "I've been told all my life that stripping a Kingsmage of their title and separating them from their charge is a punishment so severe it isn't done. I thought I could use what she learned to save myself, but whatever knowledge she found or ability she gained to preserve her humanity, she must have acquired it after she was taken away, or she never wrote it down, for fear of discovery. Or . . ." His mouth twists.

"Or?"

When he speaks, his voice is low, angry. "Or she left nothing for me to find, because she doesn't think I can handle what it will take to stop my own descent." He does not meet my eyes. "Going to the cabin was just staving off the inevitable, I suppose."

I nod, tracing an invisible pattern on the chipped wooden doorjamb. "And when you returned, you just *happened* to end up on the same route Lark used to drive me to the Rite?"

His eyes snap to mine. "Is this you being coy, Briana? I don't think I care for it."

A smirk pulls at the side of my mouth. "Just asking."

"Make your point, please."

"I *just think* that if you had the presence of mind to still do your job and protect me, then you're clearly not succumbing to your blood like the Regents said you are, or trying to hurt me, or even letting me *get* hurt." My smile grows triumphant. "Proves them wrong."

His eyes go flat, and he returns to the kit, pulling out a few bandages. "You don't know what it's like for demonia to bleed into your consciousness. All Merlins feel it roiling under the surface, there if we look for it."

Sel pulls his tank down on one shoulder, trying to stretch the collar with one hand to reach his wound. The fabric begins to tear. He curses and gives up, grasping the back of the shirt overhead and pulling it up and off.

My instinct is to look away, give him privacy. But he obviously doesn't care, because he took his damn shirt off while we were mid-conversation, so when he looks for my eyes in the mirror, I look back. He grins, then hisses when he presses the alcohol swab to the knife wound.

"We'll find Nick. For now, you have me and William and the Oath of Service."

He opens a package of gauze, chuckling.

Insult flares. "Why are you laughing?"

"Again, because you've never dedicated your whole being to someone or some cause greater than yourself. You don't understand what Oaths feel like, fulfilled or unfulfilled."

"Maybe I don't, but"—I step closer, even though I don't think William or Alice are listening to us—"I told you what I saw in my vision in the ogof. In the memories, your mother didn't succumb to her blood. So, you won't either. And even if you do, you'll still be you."

His eyes find mine in the mirror. "How do you know I haven't started to already?"

"Because I do. I have faith." I pause for a moment, then add, "And so does Nick."

His eyes widen. "What do you—"

"He said so," I murmur, "in the blood walk. He said you'd remove yourself from the situation before you hurt me."

Some emotion I can't catch crosses his face. "So you really did see him." He opens his mouth, closes it. Looks away. "How is he?"

"Okay, considering. He asked about you, too," I say. Sel's brows draw together, half-surprise and half-frown. "And yes it was really him. I could even touch him, somehow."

Sel turns back to study me, his brow softening. When he speaks again, his voice is quiet, almost hesitant. "Even if we do depose the Regents, what the two of you have . . ."

"The Order won't let us keep," I finish. "I know."

He holds my gaze for a moment, then turns back to his injury to examine the wound before covering it. From this close, I can see the shape of it, a deep incision about an inch wide, clean edges, but right below his collarbone and above the swell of muscle in his chest.

He presses the bandage in place, then pulls out the medical tape. Watching Selwyn Kane tear off a piece and struggle valiantly to apply it with one hand so that it stays taut is one of the most awkward things I've ever seen. So awkward I can't watch it without secondhand embarrassment. I step forward between him and the sink without thinking.

"Let me do it." I take the roll from his hand, and realize a second too late that we've both frozen in place.

This close, I can feel the heat radiating off his skin. Smell the hint of copper from his injury, like fresh pennies. The fading, muted smell of shampoo. Crisp fall air from the forest and pine sap on his skin from his patrol through the trees. I've never really known what Sel smells like underneath his magic. Or been close enough to see the detailing on the tattoo across his sternum. The Celtic knot is dark in the middle, with curled edges giving way to gray.

Oh God.

My gaze leaps to the top of his shoulder. I silently command my eyes to stay put. Like my life depends on it and I can't trust them not to wander.

"If you're just going to *steal* the tape and not use it . . . ," he murmurs, voice a low, rich echo in the small room, "then I think I'd like it back."

I shudder. Sel's voice always feels enveloping, like a physical thing I could touch. Right now, standing this close, it settles around us both like a blanket.

I feel his gaze on the crown of my head, on my forehead. Neither one of us is moving.

One deep inhale later and I drop my eyes to examine the tape. Lift a piece up, tear it off. Simple. Damnit, if it's so simple, then why do I have to focus on not letting my fingers shake?

I move to set the tape down behind me, but he takes it before I can shift away. *Keeping me close,* a small voice says.

Ignoring the heat from his skin, I stretch the material over the top of his bandage. One side down, three to go.

I reach for the tape in Sel's hand, but he grasps it tight in his fingertips. I pull, but he won't let go. I tug again, hear the smirk overhead. I sigh, and finally lift my eyes. The soft bow of his mouth is curved upward on one end, and his golden eyes—more burnt orange than I remember—twinkle with mischief and something that makes my heart stutter.

He tilts his head, eyes roaming across my features. "Briana Irene, forever leaping before she looks. Then she gets stuck and doesn't know what to do."

My voice sounds far away. "I don't know what you mean."

He idly examines the space between us, smirking at the inches that already feel like nothing. He leans forward with both hands on the counter, crowding me into the sink until I'm caged between his arms and his eyes are level with mine. "Liar. Your heart is *pounding* in your chest right now. Your breath just became shallow and fast."

My face burns, and it has nothing to do with his gaze. "I wish you couldn't hear all of that."

"Can I tell you a secret, Briana?" His voice slips into the sliver of air between us, silk and heat. "I *like* hearing the way people respond to me." A pause. "You, in particular."

I shiver. "It's involuntary."

"Oh, I know." His mouth quirks.

This close, I can see the pointy tips of his fangs. I feel an inexplicable urge to touch one. See if it's sharp or dull against my finger.

Sel's amusement skips across my cheeks. "See something you like?"

He'd seen my gaze wander to his mouth, and let it stay there. Let me inspect him. Hot embarrassment wraps around my entire throat nearly as tightly as Kizia's hands.

"J-just curious. Your canines are . . . are . . ." *Words, Bree. Find them. Use them.* "Not as big as—" His brows shoot up. "I mean, not as long as—" *Jesus Christ. Not* those *words.*

Finally, I expel a sentence. "Your teeth look different today."

His eyes are twin sunsets heating my face, and his voice flows between us in a honeyed growl. "Do they?"

"Yes," I murmur, my voice breathy. "I mean, they've always been different from Erebus's. Or the other Seneschals'. Or . . . or even Isaac's."

"Ah. For Merlins, aging brings us closer to our demon nature, and more power. That is why their fangs appear more prominent than mine."

"Does that mean if a Merlin has succumbed to their blood, to—to demonia, they look different too? And they're also more powerful?"

"Look different, yes. As for power?" He tilts his head back and forth. "Hard to tell because we are also more mercurial."

"Oh."

He huffs a laugh. "Current close quarters and *terrifically* entertaining circumstances aside, when I say you leap before looking, I'm referring to the fact that the minute you decided *we* were going to hunt for Nicholas, *you* deprioritized yourself. And you did so without acknowledging that those of us around you cannot afford to do the same. This is the same choice you made when you forced Greer to take you on a hunt. The same position you put William in when you set off on your own to the arena. When *you* take risks for a mission, we all do. But our risks are five-fold, because your life must be protected at all costs. Tonight, we were lucky, but there will come a moment when William or I will have to choose between your mission and your life."

I jerk back from his face, sputtering. "I thought you *wanted* us to find Nick. Wanted me to choose him. Don't you want to find him, too?"

His lips pull back in a silent snarl. "That very question is an insult. *Of course* I want to find Nicholas. I also need you to understand what you are asking of the people around you. You're not just Page Matthews hurtling into one dangerous, foolish situation after another anymore. You are the Scion of Arthur, and a king."

His chastisement stings, so the words leave my mouth before I can stop them, confrontational and biting. "*Your* king?"

Sel's eyes bore into mine, dizzying. That feeling from the plane returns. A sweeping sense of falling into him. Like I am losing all of myself, momentarily. Willingly. He goes so still, I wonder if he's stopped breathing. Then I wonder if *I* have. *You are my king now, cariad.* His words hang between us, rush loud through my ears. When he speaks, his voice drips with warning.

"Do not attempt to *bait* me into repeating myself." When he leans back, the air around me drops several degrees immediately, but his tawny yellow eyes are bright with anger. "And do not ask questions you do not truly wish me to answer."

His face shutters. I train my eyes on the floor.

"Alice is coming down the hall"—Sel tilts his head, inhaling deeply—"with food for you." He tosses the tape up in the air, then catches it. "I can take it from here."

I dash out of the bedroom, face on fire, and shut the door behind me. Flip around to press my forehead and hands into the door, the cool surface a relief to my hot palms. I squeeze my eyes shut, grimacing into the wood paneling. Guilt and irritation and embarrassment crash around my insides, bouncing off one another so fast I can't keep up.

What was that? All of that?

Your king? I tap my forehead against the door. *God, Bree, what the hell?* Sel had warned me about baiting him, and that's exactly what I did. I wanted to get a rise out of him. Why? Why did I have to push him?

I haven't been that *close* to Sel in a long time, but it also hasn't *felt* like this in a long time. Like we're on the same team instead of on opposite sides of a forever fight. The last time it felt like this was the balcony at the Lodge . . . his voice at my ear, low and insistent.

Cariad.

Earlier today, Nick had his arms around me, and his body pressed against mine. Sure, it was a memory-plane body pressed against my memory-plane body . . . but it was real. His lips were warm. He even *smelled* like him. Like laundry and cedar and *Nick*. Then later the same night, I'm—

"Are you okay?" Alice's loud, alarmed voice breaks me out of my daze. She has a bowl in her hand and is at my side in a second. "What's wrong? Why are you—"

"*Shh!*" I hiss.

"Why?" she calls. "Why are you plastered to the wall—"

"I'm fine!" I drag her to the window down the hall.

When I let her go, she puts one hand on her hip. "Explain?"

"Merlins have really, really good hearing," I say, waving my hands. "Just . . . I needed to not be right outside that room."

She sighs. "Sel's in there."

My head moves in a half nod, half shake. "Yep."

She rolls her eyes. "Only you would have boy drama the night you almost get murdered by a bloodthirsty demon. Part-demon boy drama, even." She groans and holds up the bowl. "Want to tell me about it over two a.m. pasta?"

My stomach growls so loudly I think the whole house must hear it, super senses or not.

She snorts. "So that's a yes."

I wake up in a warm bed, heart pounding in my chest. I shove myself upright and search the room for a threat, but it's empty. A shaft of late-morning light streams in through the old, moth-eaten curtains. The sound of clinking dishes reaches me from down the hall. Alice's voice. William's.

But my body doesn't believe that I'm safe. The same buzzing numbness builds in my hands. I shake them out, trying to relieve the sensation. My throat tightens. Panic is a heavy, invisible hand on my spine telling me to *run*. I drop my head on my knees. This is just residual fear, setting my system off. I close my eyes and breathe like Patricia taught me to. A single deep breath in, a slow one out. It takes long minutes before my racing heart slows to a trot, then a walk, until feeling returns to my hands.

The Scion of Arthur. A Medium. A Daughter of Vera. And I can't even handle waking up in the morning.

My left fist clenches over my mother's bracelet, seeking its comfort on my wrist. For grounding. For purpose.

When I reach for the glass of water on the nightstand I find more evidence of Alice at work: a shiny silver safety pin resting beside a lighter with a small pile of Band-Aids from the bathroom first-aid kit, and Jonas's cell phone for calling my father with a slip of instructions for faking a number on outgoing calls. Supplies for blood walking and a parental check-in.

I glance at the door and gauge how much time I have before someone comes in.

I prick my thumb. Watch the blood well up from a tiny red dot to a small droplet, then press my thumb into one of the charms on my mother's bracelet, and call out for an ancestor.

By my blood, on my heart.

I stand on the moss-covered stone in the ancestral plane, and pivot on my heel in a slow circle. Everywhere the earth is waiting for me. To call out with intention.

"Our sword."

"My bri."

"The sharpest and strongest."

I whisper, "Show me how to use our root to strike first."

A breaking, tearing sound. A stream splitting the earth and opening before me to my left. I step down into its waters and start walking. It widens with every breath. . . .

I am sitting cross-legged on the floor in the center of my living room, wearing a skirt and my short white socks, hair up in rollers. My roommate's out, and that's good, because I don't want her seeing any of this.

My name is Jessie. I am twenty years old. I live in Lafayette, Louisiana. And my mother told me that one day, I'd have her power.

I had no idea that power would look like this. My hand is flat on my chest, feeling the pulse of my own heartbeat. I close my eyes, smiling. I recently discovered that if I hold my hand here and concentrate on her memory, I can feel the heat increase against my palm.

Abruptly, red and orange flames erupt through my fingers.

I want to see how big they can grow.

The next day, I am at the diner.

I push through a pair of swinging doors into the kitchen to drop off an order. Laugh about a customer with an older cook at the grill. The smell of burgers and the sound of sizzling fat. Someone calls my name from the front, and the cook waves me away.

"Customer asked for you specifically," a coworker says. She smiles.

I laugh with her too. Probably my boyfriend, I think, and I tell her the same. The day's almost over and he's come to pick me up. I already know his order. This will be my last table.

But when I approach, it's not him. It's a student from the college up the street. The one that only just started letting Black kids in. His hair is slicked back and combed up. One of those motorcycle types, in jeans and a plaid shirt.

His eyes are black as night, with red pupils. They suck in the afternoon light.

His smile pins my feet to the floor. Fangs and satisfaction and knowing.

The customers from the table next to his stand up, pass between us, obscuring us from each other. I want to run, but I don't know why. When they clear, he is gone. My chest aches in relief.

I don't try the flames for a long while.

But I do try again, a few years later. I sit alone in my new-to-me but run-down basement efficiency apartment. I draw the flame from my chest, missing my mother, wishing for her wisdom and company. Her smile.

The next day, I walk down the street in my also-new-to-me city. Horns honking.

A man walking toward me. Long, brown hair. Black eyes with red pupils, looking at me.

I'm shaking. Shaking. Fingertips burning.

He comes toward me, eyes raking across my skin like knives clawing, searching. I feel stripped. Exposed.

He's closer now. My hands ball to fists. The crowd is too thick, nowhere to run. I grit my teeth, open up the flames inside my chest to get ready, wait until the last moment—the man passes me by.

Gone.

It takes everything inside of me not to freeze there on the sidewalk in New York. If I had, the people behind me would have drawn attention to me, shouting. Instead, I walk a few more paces and weave through bodies until I reach a storefront, flatten my spine against it, and look back. The man in black with red eyes and brown hair is at the crosswalk, pausing. Then crossing with his hands in his pockets. I don't know if he saw me, but I know the thought that he might have is terrifying. I know it would be bad if he did. Very, very bad.

"Pain-welded blade."

"You are *the sword."*

"Our sword."

I stand ankle-deep in the widest part of my ancestral stream, shaking my head.

"I don't understand. How did you call the flames on purpose?"

Jessie's low, husky voice comes to me from the forest. She sounds older than she did in the blood walk.

"I showed you what you need to know. To call our root with intention, think of the power you possess and the woman who gave it to you."

My mind flies to my mother at her writing desk. My mother in the kitchen. Her wide smile.

"But heed the rest of the memory, Bree: if you call too much, open the furnace too wide, the Hunter will find you."

I gasp awake, back in the bedroom. *The Hunter?* Who is *the Hunter?* The man I saw didn't look like any Merlin I've ever seen. Even Erebus's irises are a dark red, not *black.* Is that what a Merlin who succumbs to his blood looks like?

Kizia feared "the Great Devourer," some broker who punishes unauthorized demon feedings, who deals in "demon business." Jessie warned of "the Hunter," a roaming demon who came after her power when she used it. As much as I hate the Regents, at least I know who they are and what they want. Outside of the boundaries of the Legendborn world, all the rules are up in the air. Magic is currency, murder is business, and Rootcrafters are prey. How will we find Nick in all of this?

I don't have every answer, but at least I have one. A beginning. A how. I hold my hand against my chest and feel the furnace back where it used to be. Fire in my chest that feels like home and my mother, ignited by Jessie's memory.

I stare down at the bracelet in my lap, and the Pendragon necklace around my neck.

My legacy and birthright and decisions, all wrapped up in these gifts. My mother chose to fight even though she had no idea where her powers came from. She never knew about Vera. All she knew was that she had strength. That her mother had had that same strength, and her grandmother, and back even further . . . and that had been enough. She had been so, so brave.

I reach for Jonas's phone without thinking, punching in my dad's cell. He picks up on the first ring. "Hey, hey, there she is."

His face appears in my mind so fully formed it makes my heart ache. Graying bushy brows, salt-and-pepper stubble. Broad nose in a deep brown face, lines defining his smile.

"Hey, Dad." I hear muffled sounds of the auto shop in the background.

"Haven't heard from you in a week and all I get is a 'hey, Dad,'" he says, chuckling. As with every delayed call from me, there's admonishment and a bit of sadness, but something like pride too. Like living my own life and being busy and happy are worth the long breaks between calls.

If he only knew.

"Sorry." I force energy into my voice. "Been busy with school and parties and things."

"As long as you're all right, kid," he replies. "Long as you're safe."

"I am, don't worry." I swallow. "How you been?"

"Busy myself," he says. "Actually lost a couple of folks at the shop yesterday, then had two new folks show up asking for jobs this morning. Strangest thing."

I sit up taller. Did Gill already send replacements to watch my dad? "That *is* weird. Are they any good?"

"Seem excellent," he adds, and I can hear the smile in his voice. "Definitely know their way around engines. Two women. Lisa—no *Lyssa*, that's her name—and Ophelia."

My chest loosens. Lyssa, at the wheel of the Jeep. Ophelia, piloting the plane. Of course. "Lady gearheads. Love to see it."

"And when they teach the other guys a thing or two before noon? Even better." A voice in the background calls for his attention. "Hey, gotta run. You need anything?"

I hesitate. "Got one of your all-purpose pep talks handy?"

"Always." He hums for a minute, thoughtful. "Knockdowns happen. People say it's about getting back up again, but I think it's about *how* you head back into the ring. Make the *how* count and do it on your terms. That's what matters."

I whistle. "You had that one ready to *go*."

"That's the job, baby." He laughs. "I know you're busy, but call when you can."

"I uh . . . ," I clear my throat. "Might be extra busy over the next couple weeks. Exams."

"All good, I get it," he says. "Love you."

"Love you too."

I hold the phone in my hand for a long time, missing my father already but grateful for his words. They're always right on time.

It's not about getting back in the ring, it's about how you get back in. The strategy.

I need to find Nick and bring him home safe before the Morgaines, the Shadowborn, or the Order can find him. Sel was right about my choices risking putting others in danger. My choice brought us here, to Jonas and Kizia. But our enemies don't choose the safe path, and neither can we.

Dragons protect what is theirs and . . . burn the rest.

Suddenly, I have an idea.

When I enter the living room, I find William and Sel speaking in urgent tones in the kitchen doorway while Alice sits on the couch. The three look up when I walk in, as if sensing that something has changed. And it has.

"What if the Regents were right to lock me up?" I blurt. Sel's face is stricken, and I can tell he's about to argue, but I hold my hand up to stop him. "Hear me out. What if they locked me away because they were scared, and the demons are after me for good reason, and Jonas was right to try to get rid of me?"

"Bree, what are you saying?" William steps forward. "*None* of that was right."

"I know, but—" I shake my head, searching for the words. "You don't lock someone up or try to murder them because they *aren't* important. Jonas and Kizia looked at me and saw the anchor to the Spell of Eternity. A single life powerful enough to destroy the Lines, or completely change the course of the war. The Regents look at me and see a Black teenage girl. A *mistake* they can't undo and too much power in a body they can't control." I pace the room, the thought gaining speed. "I've been so focused on using the title of king, but everyone *else* is more worried about how powerful I am, magically speaking— and how powerful I could become. Not as king, but as *me*. Bree."

The room is silent for a moment. Alice taps her knee, eyes deep in thought. Sel's gaze pierces mine, but I avoid it for now. I have to get this out.

"I am Arthur's Scion." When I say it, it sounds like a declaration. Not just the result of a series of events out of my control, but a statement of fact and force. "And I am Vera's. They're scared of me because they know I can beat them. And that's what I have to do. I'm going to train harder than ever, use every possible moment, every fight, to get stronger. While we follow the leads to Nick, we should look for isel I can fight along the way—"

"No." Alice jumps up. "No, Bree."

Her stern tone shocks me into a confused laugh. "What?"

She swallows hard and raises her chin. "We've been talking and . . . we can't keep going. *You* can't keep going."

I frown. "Alice, what are you—"

William paces forward. "There is no overnight training that can keep you safe from hired demon assassins or allies who have turned against the Order. Your root is unpredictable and your Legendborn powers . . ."

My cheeks grow hot. "I need time to train . . ."

"You don't have that kind of time." William shakes his head. "I'm sorry."

"What are you saying?" I glance at William, then to Alice, and to Sel.

"What we're saying is . . ." Sel strides toward me, eyes boring into mine. "You need to run and you need to hide, and you can't do either if you're off searching for Nick."

The room feels as if it has tilted. The *world* feels as if it has tilted. I can't fully parse their words, because it's the exact opposite of what we came here to do.

"You have got to be kidding me!" I cry. "You can't just make that decision—"

Sel stops a few feet away. "You need to go into hiding for your own safety. Become a ghost."

I look among the three of them, waiting for this to be some sort of joke. Waiting for Sel to fight his own words. "You're asking me to run away?"

"We're not asking, Bree," he says slowly. "We're telling you. You have to run, or you'll die."

PART THREE

CONTROL

I CAN BARELY speak. My brain struggles to create even a single sentence in response to what they've just done.

There is only one word in my mouth: betrayal. And inexplicably, this betrayal feels worse than Jonas's. I didn't know him, but I know my friends. I thought we were on the same team, but suddenly here we are, one on three. Like facing a mirror in your own home with full faith in who you'll see, only to find it cracked and warped and *wrong*.

"*I* have to run?" I speak through gritted teeth. "Me?"

"Yes," Sel answers. "You."

"*Have to?* As in, I have no other choice?" My vision has gone blurry at the edges with tears and humiliation. "You expect me to just sit it out while you go after Nick?"

Sel's lip curls. "You're still talking about this like it's a game and we've told you not to play it."

I ball my fists at my sides, a scream just on the edge of eruption. "Isn't that what this is? Isn't that what you're doing?"

"No, Bree, no." William spreads his hands wide. "Listen to me. We've gone through every scenario. How do we search for Nick while keeping your identity hidden? How do we follow a trail that we know the Regents are already on? How do we prioritize his safety at the same time that we prioritize yours? It's impossible."

"It's not!" I shout. "You heard Gill and Samira, we just have to choose one or the other—"

"Gill and Samira sent us to a safehouse that was the opposite of safe!" Sel shouts back. "They had an Oath-traitor in their midst, willing to let his Oaths burn him alive in order to kill you. Their intel is out of date and their so-called allies can't be trusted. We need to get you out of here as soon as possible."

"There are four of us," I say, shrugging. "Let's vote on it."

"We already have," Alice mutters.

My mouth works open and closed. "But . . . on the plane . . ."

"A decision on a plane at thirty-five thousand feet means nothing," Sel says, "when we land and everything goes to hell on the ground."

I scoff. "Then I veto your vote!"

Sel barks a laugh and walks away, hands on his head. "Ridiculous."

Alice scowls. "You're not my king, Matty."

I thrust a hand out. "Apparently I'm not anyone's king if you all can go behind my back!"

"Bree . . ." William rubs a thumb across his forehead. "Sel and I have been in the field longer than you. We know when we're underinformed and out-gunned. We know when it's time to retreat."

I look between him and Sel and Alice, and no one is budging. No one is even looking like there's a discussion to be had, because they've already had it. Without me.

Eventually Sel will have to fulfill his Kingsmage Oath in order to preserve his humanity, and my logical brain knows it makes sense that he should leave to rescue Nick and save himself in the process. That maybe it never made sense for him to stay with me. But my logical mind is gone, gone, gone.

I'd walked into this room ready to keep fighting and suddenly, abruptly, I've hit a brick wall. Not just any brick wall, but *my friends*. I thought I was king, or close enough. I thought our decisions were "my call." They have *no idea* what I'd just learned in my blood walk, what I could keep learning, how much more powerful I could become—

A week ago, the roar of rage building in my throat might have felt like Arthur's, but right now? It's all mine.

"You know Nick is being hunted out there!" I shout at Sel. "He could die! Did you forget that part?"

He's in my face in a blur of motion, eyes like embers against my cheeks. "Say that again."

I swallow hard and lift my chin. "You want me to give up on him—"

His lips curl back in a snarl.

I face his wrath with my own. "I could save him. And you're telling me not to even try."

Displeasure twists at his mouth. "If you think that's what I'm doing, and why I'm doing it, if you think this is *easy* . . . then . . ."

"Then what?" I challenge.

He backs away, shaking his head. "Then you truly aren't ready to wear the crown."

"Selwyn!" William yells.

Sel rushes out so quickly, his coat snaps in the air behind him.

Hot tears streak down my cheeks; my chest heaves. This is all wrong. This isn't how it was supposed to go . . . this isn't what I *decided.*

William steps closer, rubbing my back in a circle. After a moment, he sighs. "I'll get some breakfast going, then go after him."

"Thanks, Will," Alice says. He nods and steps away, but as soon as his warmth leaves, Alice's arms wrap around me from the side. "I'm sorry. . . ."

My voice cracks when I speak. "I can't run away."

"You're not."

"I *can't,* Alice. . . ."

She tucks her head into my shoulder. "I know. But you can't do anything at all if you're dead. And you can't die, Matty. . . ."

I inhale sharply. Doubt slips in around my hard edges, even though I want to push it away. "I didn't—"

"You almost did, okay?" she whispers. "You almost did." I can't argue with her there, even though I want to. Not when I can feel her tears wetting the fabric on my shoulder.

"I'm not okay with this," I mutter.

"I'll be with you. We'll find another way for you to fight."

The mirror is still cracked, but Alice is here, trying to patch us back together. I whisper, "You promise?"

She nods. "Promise."

After lunch, Sel calls Gill. Once she hears our plan to go into hiding, she tells Sel to take us down to the basement before we leave. We didn't even know there was a basement.

Sel follows her instructions to kneel on the hardwood floor in the hallway, feeling along the baseboard for a hidden latch. Sure enough, once he pulls it, a four-by-three section of the floor raises an inch. Just far enough for Sel to lift it up and over, dropping it back onto itself and revealing a flight of wooden stairs leading down a stone-walled staircase.

"Holy moly," Alice whispers. "This is James Bond–levels of cool."

Already at the bottom of the stairs, Sel flips a switch and a row of overhead bulbs illuminates a concrete-floored room. We follow him down into a space the size of the house footprint.

Against one wall are lockers labeled with scribbled names on masking tape. Lining the back wall is a familiar rack of weapons similar to the one in the Lodge basement.

Sel walks along a row of clothing racks on the wall to our left. "Gill said to gear up with whatever you need." He points to the clothing, shelving units of boots and jackets, and a smaller rack of weapons that all look rather . . . collapsible and small. Meant for concealing on one's person.

Sel points to the desk and the massive gray-and-white machine in the corner. It looks like a printer, but I can't see where the paper would go. Instead, there's a stack of plastic cards nearby. "She's sending photos over for IDs. They've got a collection of fakes already. Said there's cash in the drawers." He pivots and heads back upstairs without another word.

William and Alice move toward the clothing, and I follow Sel's retreating form with my eyes until he's out of sight. He hasn't spoken to me since the fight before breakfast, and I assume that, with how we left things, he'll be taking off on his own to find Nick. I hope we can get a chance to talk before we part ways, but he's not making an opening for that very clear.

Alice waves me over, a smile on her face. "Come on, Bree, this is like shopping at the badassery store, except everything is free."

Ten minutes later, I'm back in our small bathroom, twisting around to see myself in the mirror while Alice makes her phone call to her parents. Everything the Lieges had in their communal closet was made for comfort and mobility. I'd found a long, flowing charcoal tunic split along the sides and a dark red embroidered V-neck top, matching leggings, and a hooded jacket. Alice found us both low-heeled, shin-high boots that are clearly used. The size isn't quite perfect, but the leather is supple and seems ready to fit and flex around my ankles and toes.

After contemplating my options, I decide to braid back the front of my curls so that my hair would be out of my face in the event we run into trouble. It's been twelve hours, but the back middle section of my hair is still damp to the touch. I'm debating braiding it, too, when there's a knock at the door.

"Come in," I call.

"It's me." William's voice is muffled through the door, and I swing it open to see him standing in the room wearing an uncertain expression and a pair of dark jeans, a black sweater, and a black jacket. A Sel outfit if I've ever seen one. "Do I look okay?"

I smile. "William, you look fantastic. I would not have guessed it, but black is definitely your color."

"Black is everyone's color." He lets one side of his mouth lift in an appreciative smile and ducks his head.

"I bet Dylan likes you in black," I say with a smirk. I finally got to meet William's boyfriend a few weeks ago. Dylan's a senior. Tall guy with deep brown skin and a wide smile. Adorable and kind and majoring in environmental justice.

William's face dims. "He does. Did."

"Did?"

"We broke up." He leans against the doorjamb. "Or rather, I broke up with him."

"What?" My jaw falls open. "When?"

William takes a slow, measured breath. "The day after Arthur Called."

"Why—"

"That night in the cave, I felt something," William says. "A sort of *pull*. In my chest. Did I tell you that?"

I shake my head. "No. Nick said something similar about the Rite of Kings."

"I felt it then, too." He nods. "I wonder if we all did. All of the Scions, our knights' spirits tugging at our souls like fish on a line. It reminded me that I am the Scion of Gawain no matter where I am or what I'm doing. We get so few choices. I keep saying it, but it's true," he says quietly. "And I chose to let Dylan go."

"Because Arthur Called? Or Camlann?" I ask, then swallow. "Or me?"

William pushes to standing. "All one reason at this point, don't you think?" Bitterness sweeps across his face, there and gone.

"Will . . ."

"Came to let you know that Alice figured out the ID printing." He slips me a driver's license that has my old Early College ID photo next to a new name and address.

I hesitate, but follow his lead rather than dig more about Dylan. "'Ramona Pierce'?" I ask.

"Yep." He jerks his chin over his shoulder. "We're ready when you are, Ramona."

I stare at myself in the mirror to evaluate whether Ramona Pierce is going to draw attention. The marks on my neck have faded to almost nothing, so I won't look like someone just tried to kill me. Again.

Before I leave the room, I add my chosen weapons. The safety pin and Band-Aids for my next blood offering get hidden behind the tunic in a small interior pocket. Next, I slide one of the retractable swords into my boot. I grabbed it because it reminded me of Nick's, and made him feel close even though I'm no longer running toward him, but away.

I wonder about the other Legendborn and whether Cestra's lies worked. Whether they'd believe I'd just give up on everything and go into hiding.

I suppose I can't blame them for believing it now that it's exactly what I'm doing.

I'm just lacing up my belt to pull the tunic tight when I walk into the living room. "Okay, Ramona is ready. Alice, who—"

"Alice and William are already outside, loading up Jonas's car."

Sel's voice stops me short. He's draped across the couch in all new attire. A black duster jacket with the collar flipped up and sleeves long enough to cover his cuffs. Black pants and what look like brand-new boots.

"Oh," I say warily. I expect another Liege would be on the way by now, ready to pick Sel up and fill him in on their most recent intel about Nick. "Is, ah, Gill sending another car for you?"

"No." He rises from the couch in that fluid, single-motion movement of his, and stalks toward me, hands in his pockets.

That's odd. "Why not?"

He gives me a strange look. "Because I never asked her to."

I blink. "I thought—"

"For as long as I can remember, my life has been pledged to keeping Nicholas safe." He holds my gaze as he steps closer, examining me like I'm a frustrating puzzle. He pauses just in front of me, and tiny sparks scatter across my cheeks. I can smell the soap radiating from his skin.

I nod, heart thumping. "I know. I understand."

"No, *you don't*." A quiet fire blooms across his features, turning them all burning. "You *don't* know what it feels like when the fabric of you, the very core of your being, has been modified to keep this person safe. So much so that when he's in danger, it feels like I can't breathe. That's how invasive the Kingsmage Oath is. It has to be, because keeping the king safe means keeping the Lines safe."

I don't know what to say, because he's right. I don't understand this feeling. I don't know that I want to.

"Nicholas is gone because I failed to protect my charge, among my other sins." He frowns, guilt and conviction at war on his face. Conviction wins out. "But I would be failing the Order's true mission, the spirit of the Oath, Nicholas, and you if I didn't stay by your side to protect you now."

I shut my eyes. Shake my head. That dizzying feeling swarms in my stomach at the passion in his voice.

"No," he chides, and lifts my chin with a finger. "Come back from wherever you go to hide. Look at me." I open my eyes to find him looking at me, uncertainty pulling at the corners of his mouth.

"I'm not hiding," I insist.

His thumb passes over my chin. "Do you want me to go?" I look away, but his voice draws me back. More insistent this time. "Bree. Do you want me to go?"

My voice is quiet, but sure. "I don't want you to suffer because you aren't fulfilling your Oath."

"I already told you," he says, his voice low, "protecting you and William is enough to hold me together. And you didn't answer the question."

I sigh, shrugging. "No, I don't want you to go."

He hums. "Was honesty so hard?"

"You were furious with me earlier. Why?" I ask, feeling brave.

"Because, silly thing"—his finger draws along my jaw before falling away—"you truly thought I would leave you."

My mouth falls open. "We fought . . ."

He smiles. "We'll always fight, I think."

"But . . . I can't—I won't force anyone to follow me just because I'm king. You have your own duty."

"I see you took my speech last night to heart."

"You said you protect me out of obligation."

"I did say that."

"You were willing to go to jail for nearly murdering me."

"And still am." He nods. "If we are being honest."

"So, are you protecting me now because you want to make up for trying to kill me then?"

Silence between us.

Finally, his face takes on a sad, wry expression. "Trick question."

"Why?"

"Because it's impossible." His mouth quirks into a self-deprecating smile. "I can seek absolution, but I will never be able to pay that penance. Not to you, not to myself, not to Nicholas."

I frown. "Why would you have to make it up to Nick?"

He squeezes my hand. "Rain check. I just professed my dedication to you. Rather dramatically, I would say. Can we focus on that instead?"

I am distracted by the pinch between his brows, the rhythmic clenching of his jaw. Then, I realize what they are—desperation. His question is not rhetorical. If I pushed him right now, he wouldn't evade the question with sarcasm or insult; he would explain. He wouldn't want to, but he'd do it if I asked, *because* I asked. I don't push. Instead, I say, "It was an *okay* speech. Did you practice that?"

He rolls his eyes, but relief ripples across his face. "I am a classics major, you know. I understand how to make a proclamation."

I grin. "Next time do it in Latin, and maybe I'll be impressed."

31

"'TALBOT AND LONGFELLOW'?" Alice exclaims. "That's not an address."

"No, it's not," Sel says, glaring at me in the rearview. He insisted on driving, and he and William are in the front of Jonas's Escalade, with me and Alice in the back. "Were you going to mention that part?"

"You're the ones who said I need to go underground." I'm starting to feel sheepish for claiming my lead to the Rootcrafters was, well, a lead and not a scribbled clue. "Samira gave it to me and said I should use it if I needed help. She must have thought I could figure it out."

Sel groans and props one elbow on the door panel. "Google while we drive. For now, I'm getting us away from the house and the airfield."

It all feels a bit too much like a family road trip to me. A deadly, demon-hunting, fugitive-from-the-magical-law road trip.

"Googling . . . ," Alice says, ducking her head to type on Jonas's phone. "Okay, Talbot and Longfellow are two roads near the town of, uhhhhh, *Clayton, Georgia*. Up in the mountains. The roads do intersect. But, uh, there's nothing there. It's literally a random crossroads in the middle of the woods."

Sel's eyes meet mine in the rearview. He looks back to the road, a fist to his mouth. "How far?"

"Three-hour drive."

"It'll be dark when we arrive, or close to." William takes the phone from Alice to help navigate. "I'm sure it's fine. Samira's a Liege. She wouldn't send Bree somewhere if it weren't safe."

Alice pushes her glasses up and frowns. "Is this the moment when I say Jonas was a Liege, too?"

"No," I reply. "This is not that moment, Alice."

"Got it."

An hour and a half later, Sel's thumbs tap on the wheel impatiently. "We need gas."

Alice leans forward to peer out the windshield. Ahead of us is a long, straight two-lane stretch of old highway with fields on either side. "I don't see a station."

"I do," Sel mutters. He squints. "A few miles ahead on the right."

Alice guffaws. "You can see that far?"

"Yes. The cyffion inhibit my use of aether, not my body's natural abilities." He glances to William. "We'll use the cash. Get in, get out."

"Agreed. I'll pay ahead." William raises his hand. "Except first I need to use the bathroom."

"Me too," Alice pipes up.

I grin. "Same."

Sel scowls at all three of us in turn, looking for all the world like a disgruntled parent. "Fine."

We pull into the gravel parking lot of a two-pump gas station that, if the lights weren't on inside the attached store, I'd absolutely think was abandoned. The pumps themselves look like they've seen better days, and there's a plywood sign propped up against one, facing the road. On it, someone has written the words SELF-SERVE ONLY in unsettlingly aggressive red spray paint.

Sel pulls up beside the pump farther from the storefront. "Let's make it quick."

William hops out of the SUV and strides around to the driver-side back door. As soon as he opens the door so we can join him, it dawns on me that William is probably the most innocuous-looking person in our group. Alice and

I exchange glances, and I immediately know she's thinking the same thing. We look dressed for some sort of . . . mildly hostile art gallery opening. Alice keeps her knuckles tucked into her back pocket, but slips off the military jacket.

The three of us make our way across the gravel parking lot and enter the store.

There are two white men inside, mid-conversation behind the counter when William opens the glass door. They look about mid-forties, and have similar features: dark hair, spotty noses, and wide builds. Brothers, I think.

Right away, the vibe feels sour.

They clearly saw us drive up and watched us walk across the otherwise empty lot, but take their time in turning our way. The taller brother nods. "How y'all doin'."

"Good, thanks," William replies. He pulls out his wallet. "I'd like thirty dollars on the pump out there."

"All right," the man says. He takes William's bills and rings it up while the other brother eyes me and Alice in a way that tells me whatever he's thinking is not a compliment. His mouth looks shiny, like he's just eaten something covered with oil.

William wears his mildest, most reasonable demeanor. "Do you have a restroom?"

"One. Back o' the store." The brother reaches up behind the shelf over the counter where all the large cigarette boxes are stored behind glass. Then he hands William a long, uncomfortably stained wooden rod with a string-tied key looped around the end.

"Thanks." William takes the rod without a beat. He turns to wave to Sel, signaling the pump is ready to go, but as he pivots back around, he checks in on Alice and me with his eyes and a raised eyebrow. *You okay?*

I nod. "We'll just look for some snacks," I say, loud enough for both men—and Sel—to hear.

Alice and I make our way to the stand of potato chips. I suddenly wish we didn't have to pee. This is awkward, and the hairs on the back of my neck are on end; we're being watched.

William exits the bathroom a blessed few minutes later and we move to the center of the store to join him. He holds the key stick thing out for one of us to take—and that's when the sour feeling in the store turns sharp.

"I'll take that back," the second brother says, coming around the counter. He's taller than William and wider, and he reaches for the stick before either of us can take it.

"Oh, we've got to go as well," Alice explains with a nervous smile.

The man tucks the key under one arm. "Sorry. Toilet's out of order."

Alice's jaw drops, and I stiffen. "What?" I ask, looking to William and back. "He just—"

"Out of order." The corner of the man's mouth lifts in a smirk full of sudden spite, eyes glued to mine as if to pin all that spite right on me. Paint it on my face, so I won't misunderstand.

I understand perfectly. And even without looking at her I know Alice does too. Her face flushes a bright, angry red, but she says nothing. We're in the middle-of-nowhere Georgia. There's the war, and there are battles. Neither of us chooses this battle.

William, however . . .

"Excuse me?" William asks, jerking a thumb over his shoulder. "Nothing's wrong with that bathroom."

"'Cept there is now." The man shrugs, but a low threat makes itself known in his voice, in the set of his mouth. "Simple as that."

Fear winds its way around my throat, jerks my heart into a quick rhythm. William could probably take these men in a fight, but there's no telling what could happen. They could have a gun on them or behind that counter; they could have a knife. If he wanted, this man could use that stained, nasty wooden rod like a weapon. I have the retractable sword, but we're in tight quarters, and what am I gonna do, slice these men open? Sel's outside—but anything *he* could do would expose him as someone not-quite-human. Too many unknowns. "Leave it, Will," I urge. I tug on his shirtsleeve. "We're fine."

But something inside William has snapped. His eyes flash as he steps closer to face the other man. "Are you going to explain to me why you're not letting my friends use your restroom?"

Alice's eyes grow wide, bracing herself. But the older man just shakes his head, that smile spreading across his wide, wet-looking mouth. "Nope."

The man behind the counter leans both hands on the sticky surface. "It's our store," he says with a shrug. "We don't have to explain shit to you."

The bell over the door dings. "Is there a problem?" Sel steps inside. He sizes the two men up, checks on us, all in the span of a heartbeat.

"What the hell are you supposed to be?" the man exclaims, looking Sel up and down. "Did Halloween come early? What's wrong with your eyes, kid?"

"Hey!" I say, stepping forward.

Sel holds a hand up to stop me. He forces a flat, emotionless smile on his face. "Is there a problem?" he repeats.

"Not unless y'all want there to be one." The brother comes around the cash register, and ever so casually leans on the counter, crossing his arms. He looks at Selwyn too, brows furrowed. "You one of them *goth* kids? What the hell is wrong with your—"

"Can I help you?" Sel asks, voice tight. "If not . . ."

The man pulls back, looks at us all. "I think y'all need to g'on and leave. Get to your rave or . . . whatever."

The only sign that Sel is agitated is the jump in the pulse in his neck. He grits his teeth, glances to William. "We should go, William."

"I agree," I spit, even though my heart is thundering beneath my ribs. "Let's go." Alice and I are already moving to the exit, but William hasn't budged. I don't even think he's noticed that his hands have dropped to his sides—a gesture that Sel, Alice, and I recognize immediately. The palm-open position for calling aether.

He wouldn't.

Sel is at William's side in two steps, hand wrapped around his elbow, fingers digging. "William." The pain gets William's attention. He looks between Sel and the other men.

"Better get moving, *William*," the man with the key sneers. He waves us away with the key we'd asked for, brandishing it out of our reach with a smile on his face.

William lets Sel drag him out of the store.

We make it back to the Escalade as a group and pile in silently. Sel starts the car and pulls out swiftly. As soon as we get on the highway, he shakes his head. "Will—"

"I know," William mutters. "I'm sorry."

"They had a gun behind the register," Sel says plainly.

I freeze. "You . . . did you see it?"

"Smelled it." Sel's jaw works back and forth. "If either of them had gone for it, I would have stopped them. I'm fast enough. But we can't afford to make a scene. Can't afford for the police to be called."

"These are the people the Legendborn are supposed to save from demons? The humans you're sacrificing yourselves for?" Alice scowls and drops her head against the window. "Those two aren't worth it."

After a long moment, William sighs. "Not our choice to make. We're born into that fight."

"Ha," I snort. "Yeah, well, what happened back there? Me and Alice got born into *that* fight."

Alice groans. "Just trying to freakin' *pee*. That's it. But then we end up with Racist Thing One and Thing Two. What the actual *fuck*."

"I shouldn't have let you go in by yourselves," Sel says. He looks up at me in the mirror. "I'm sorry that happened."

"Can't fight every demon," I say quietly. I watch the trees whish by, willing the adrenaline from my body. Squeezing my hands into fists to work it out of my system. "Just a reminder that it doesn't matter what my title is, whose magic I have . . ."

"I'm not Legendborn," Alice continues. "But if I were and a Shadowborn was coming for either of those assholes, I might have to look the other way."

The car falls silent. The fact that no one bothers to answer Alice, to counter her, should probably disturb all of us on some level. Her statement should probably shock someone into arguing for human life, even if those two men barely qualify. But no one says a word.

The first thing I notice about the Crossroads Lounge is the dragon-shaped skull mounted over the neon blue sign.

Immediately after that, I note that it sits on a hill at the intersection of two unpaved country roads in the woods. It truly has no address.

We park way down the road, half in some ditch. The gravel parking lot outside the bar is tiny, could fit maybe six cars at most. Parking everywhere else is first come, first serve, and the roads are piled with vehicles. Pick-up trucks, beat-up sedans, and the occasional luxury SUV. Eclectic crowd.

There are a few massive torches lining the pathway that are probably a major fire hazard even if they are useful. Beyond their light, it's nearing country-dark. No light pollution, so the early evening stars hang in the sky like diamonds strewn over navy velvet cloth.

"First things first, find a bathroom." Alice pauses beside me at the top of the hill and gazes up at the skull, jaw dropped. "Is that a real . . . ?"

"Dragon?" William supplies. "Seems so."

"What?" Alice says, looking at me. "Dragons are real?!"

"Dragons aren't real," I say, then hesitate. Turn to William. "Are dragons real?"

He shrugs, his hands in his pockets. "They were real in Wales, at some point."

"So, is this code for like . . . an Order-friendly bar or something?" Alice asks. "The Pendragon?"

Sel, who had sped up the path ahead of us and probably already searched every entry, appears in front of her in a silent whoosh. His eyes flash in the dark. "You are not to mention either of those words once we walk through those doors. Not the organization we're affiliated with, or the symbol of the crown. Do you understand?"

Alice flushes, but nods.

"Good. Now I suggest—" Sel's voice breaks off in a choking gasp. His eyes go wide and unseeing, and his hand flies to his sternum, clawing at the material.

"Sel?" William asks.

He inhales like a diver coming up for air—and doubles over, eyes pinched in pain.

"Sel!" I cry, stepping forward. His free hand shoots up to stop me and he stumbles back a step, two. "What's happening?"

"Is it . . . ?" The expression on William's face frightens me. It is the same one he wore when Jonas collapsed, when he watched a man dying in a way that his swyns can't heal.

Still bent to the ground, Sel nods. "Nicholas."

I suck in a breath. "Is he . . . ?" I don't even want to finish my own sentence.

"Alive, but . . ." Sel makes a low, frustrated noise, like he might fight his own pain if he could. His fingers pull at the shirt fabric, twisting it in his fist. "In danger."

I grab for the coin, rubbing my finger against the metal, but the blood has worn off. Scramble for the safety pin in my tunic. I flip it open and press the point against my thumb. "What are you doing?" William grabs at my arm, but it's too late.

"Blood offering," Alice explains, pulling him back.

"By my blood . . . ," I murmur—and the world instantly turns to black, like a curtain has closed all around me. *Come on. Come on.*

I stand atop the mossy stone.

"Arthur!" I call, and hope he responds.

A minute later, I hear Arthur's voice. Grating and irritated. *'You will not summon me like a pet on a leash to bring you to my knight's descendant.'*

My eyes snap open. The world returns around me. Alice is holding me upright, asking me what's wrong.

"Did you see him?" Sel pants, hand on one knee.

"Arthur wouldn't let me," I whisper. "He . . . he refused to channel me to his memories."

I've never felt so helpless. Thinking of Nick being in mortal danger is hard enough; watching Sel feel it and not be able to do anything is even worse.

"Well, we knew he was . . . an asshole." Sel takes deep breaths. "The sensation is passing, which means Nick has gotten to safety."

"We should . . . ," I begin. "Do something, we should—"

"No," Sel grunts. "He's alive. He's safe. Whatever it was has passed. We're not going anywhere. The decision's been made."

I wrap my arms around my middle. "No, I'm going to call Arthur again, give it a few minutes. Just to be sure."

"I am certain, Briana!" Sel barks. "These blood walks leave you unable to walk or run. We can't risk that right now."

His words feel like a slap and a defense at once. "Can we at least call Gill?"

"Can't." He shakes his head hard. "I crushed the phone and tossed it about ten miles back."

"What? Why?" I shout.

He looks up at me, jaw set. "You're either untraceable, or you're not." Finally, he stands. "I can feel when Nick's life is in danger, but I can *see* when yours is. *The decision has been made.* If I tell you to run, to leave. Do it."

I throw up my hands. "Fine."

He steps closer until he is all that I can see. "Swear it."

His eyes bore into mine, searching for my usual defiance. My mouth presses into a hard line, because I recognize the look on his face. Arguing won't work . . . and I know he's right.

They demanded I go underground and stop searching for Nick, and I accepted it against everything I am, but it was an acceptance nonetheless. Knowing when he's in danger—and knowing we can't go to him, or even try to, is part of that decision.

"I swear to run, if you say run."

Satisfied, he nods. Before he can speak again, his nose turns up, eyes cast over my head to scan the parking lot left and right. "I don't like the scent here."

Before I can ask what *that* means, someone approaches from the other side of the lot. A figure in a dark jacket moving so quickly to get inside that they don't see us. They knock on the door—three quick knocks, then a short one—and the door cracks. Distant voices. Sel tilts his head, listening. A hot pulse of magic hits me in a rolling wave, and William and I both gasp. As if compelled, I stumble forward, but the door shuts before I get far—and I feel a ward ripple in place across my cheek.

Sel watches the impact of magic on my face and William's. "What do you feel?"

"Power," I say. "Loads of it. Trapped behind a ward."

He makes an irritated, impatient sound. He can't sense the magic himself and it must be driving him beyond frustration. "Aether user? Or Rootcrafter?"

I shake my head. "Neither."

"Agreed," William says, tilting his head. "What I felt wasn't how the Legendborn wield power, but it's not Bree's, either."

Sel bares his teeth at the structure, as if the building itself was his opponent. "William." His voice is a scarcely controlled snarl. "Did we just bring the Scion of Arthur to a rogue's den?"

William tilts his head, unimpressed. "If we *behave* in this rogue's den, then we'll walk out with what Bree needs: information."

Sel fumes at no one and everyone. "If *half* of what is said about these places is true, then the second someone catches wind of who we are, we'll be surrounded by a bar full of furious rogue aether users. Aether users who have every reason to hide from—and hate—both the Order *and* Merlins."

"Why do they hate you?" Alice asks. "Also, you just said 'Order' even though—"

"Because the O-word used to hunt and imprison 'rogue' aether users for using magic they didn't understand and couldn't control," I answer dryly, crossing my arms. "Experiment on them. Lock them up in pretty buildings with wards on the doors and windows. Ask me how I know."

It's not just me, though. I think of Patricia, and how I'm still hiding her identity. Mariah, the only other root practitioner and Medium that I know. My mother, hiding her abilities. Then, the memory of the Salem Witch Trials manacles on display in the Lodge's library rises up behind my eyes.

Alice's nose wrinkles. "Gross."

"It will be fine." I nod to myself and walk forward. Alice joins me. "We stick to the plan even more. No Legendborn or Merlin or Order talk."

Sel flashes around me, blocking my path. "This is the *exact* type of place we're supposed to keep you away from. These are the people who would kidnap you, spread the word, and hand you over for the highest bounty."

I thumb the note in my pocket, remember the only other word on it aside from "Talbot and Longfellow"—a name. "I need to find Lucille."

"No, you *need* to remain alive. We are outnumbered and underpowered here." Sel steps forward and gestures between himself and William. "One of us will go inside to find the contact. You need to go back to the car."

I step around him. "No way!"

"ID?"

We all jump, even Sel. The tin roof–covered entrance had been empty. Now it's not. Instead, it's completely filled with a massive, red-brown-skinned Black man clad in dark red-and-black leather. The beard trailing down to his chest has shiny clasps nestled in its braids. The scent of deep forest rolls off him in thick waves. Pine. Loam. Damp bark.

Sel curses and pivots Merlin-fast, hands instinctively clawing the air at his sides. He seems to realize exactly when we do that there's no aether flowing into them. He straightens, his face flushed. "Who are you?" he snaps.

"Welcome to the Crossroads Lounge. I'm Louis, security. ID, please?" The man repeats.

Sel is eighteen and William is nineteen, and they could both pass for twenty-one if the bar requires it, but we can't. Alice and I exchange worried glances. Even though the fake IDs Gillian sent us to print say we're eighteen, it's a stretch. For her, especially.

Fortunately—or unfortunately?—that's not the type of ID the man is looking for. He calls over to us. "If you don't have a member ID, you'll need to be marked a guest. Wrists, please?"

William, Alice, and I exchange glances and take the final few steps to the front door. Before Sel can stop me, I hold out my arm. But instead of wrapping a paper band around my wrist, Louis swipes a palm over it. A symbol I don't recognize glows bright yellow and warm for a moment, pulses, then disappears. A circle made of four arrows, all following each other to make a closed loop. Beside me, even Sel's eyes grow wide. Next, Louis does the same to William, then to Alice.

The rest of us hold our breaths when he turns to Sel. "Wrist?"

"I think the fuck not," says Sel.

"Sel!" I hiss.

William drops his head into his palm. Alice goes stiff beside me. The man merely tilts his head.

"If that's your answer, all four of you need to be off the premises in the next ten seconds. Ten, nine, eight . . ."

"Sel!" I repeat. "Just do it."

Sel clenches his jaw so hard I think his teeth might break. Then he thrusts his left arm out. If the man notices the void cuff, he opts not to say anything. Instead, he puts the mark on Sel's hand too. "It'll fade in twelve hours."

"It better." He rotates his hand in the light, scowling at the mark.

The man's voice rumbles, bored, as if reciting a script. "With entry you agree to release the owners, staff, and other guests—be they human or nonhuman—of the Crossroads Lounge from any and all liability, including, but not limited to, liability arising from negligence, fault, agreements, or disagreements between entities that may occur as a result of your presence on the premises. You also agree not to instigate, continue, or intercede in any magical conflicts that are not explicitly permitted by the Crossroads Lounge owner or staff." Louis takes a breath. "Do you understand, agree, and swear to this verbal release and these behavior requirements?"

Surprisingly, Sel answers first. "Fine."

The man looks to the rest of us, and we mumble our agreements. It's hard not to follow up with questions. William's and Sel's brows are both furrowed, as I'm sure mine are. A sworn agreement is no light thing to the Legendborn.

"Any magic to declare?" From Louis.

"No." William's answer is fast and firm, like he'd prepared for it in advance.

The man grunts, and I pray he's not some sort of supernatural creature with demon-sharp hearing, because my heart leaps in my chest. I don't *feel* his eyes on me, so not a demon or part demon.

"You may enter." The bouncer gives us one last look and bends to open the door behind him. Then, with a sudden popping sound, Louis disappears.

Immediately, the sound of clinking glasses and classic rock stream out into the evening air, loud enough to make Sel slap his hands over his sensitive ears.

"Is he . . . that fast?" Alice wonders.

"No." Sel scowls. "That speed isn't his. I don't like this."

"Ugh, we *know*," Alice whines.

"Play nice, children." William holds up a hand. "Adaptability is the name of the game if we're to start coloring outside of the lines."

Alice chuckles nervously. "Lines. Get it?" She turns back to us, eyes bright with amusement. "Get it?"

"I get it." William winks.

"Everyone gets it," Sel says with a deep sigh of resignation.

Alice steps closer to me so that we walk almost shoulder to shoulder, her pinky finger twining with mine. I nod to the group with confidence I don't have. "Let's find Lucille and leave."

I tug Alice forward, bracing against the explosion of sensory input. The deep thump of heavy bass, the swirl of smoke, the ward dancing across my face and neck, and the smell of rich, thick aether pull me forward into the unknown.

32

THE CROSSROADS LOUNGE is a sprawling building of hodgepodge architecture.

The main room is a large, square, two-storied warehouse, but off to the left are three open-ended shipping containers attached to the warehouse wall, each labeled with a glowing sign overhead. To the right, the roof dips low, the floor flows from tile to wood and there's a long, shiny bar running from one end to the other. Straight across from the entrance, there's a stage set beneath a rickety-looking loft and a second level that stretches farther back into the building.

All of those structural oddities could be seen in a regular Onceborn bar, but a regular Onceborn bar wouldn't have shadowed corners that shift and waver, making it impossible to know exactly where the walls end. Even when I squint, I can't quite make out the warehouse's perimeter. What looked like a corner seems to melt before my eyes, as if distorted by the heat of an open flame.

I've seen Legendborn use magic to create constructs out of air, but I've never seen magic that could manipulate space. Some folks are huddled around tarnished silver tankards on low, sticky wooden tables with candles in the center. Other seating areas seem to be purposefully left dark; more conducive for shady business I suppose. The room smells like stale pipe smoke, desperation, and aether.

"Let's find a place to sit," Sel orders, his voice loud over the din.

William leans in close to shout in his ear. "I think we should blend in a little before asking around for Lucille. The sign says we seat ourselves. . . ."

Sel responds, but I don't hear him, because the magic of the space has saturated my senses. The *layers* here. Spicy. Sweet. Earthy. Sour. Bright. A heady mixture that sits on my tongue and fills my nose in a rush. A flavor so full that I gasp.

"Bree?" Alice looks at me sharply and I blink back into my group of friends.

"It's . . ." My eyelids flutter, and my words comes out in a slight slur. "It's a lot. I'm fine."

Sel holds my eye for a long moment. "There's a free table against a wall, with four chairs. Let's go." Sel points to what might be the back left corner of the building and gestures for us to follow.

A few patrons look at us as we pass, but at first glance, no one appears to be anything other than human. But the last time I saw this many Black and brown people I was on a ritual plane between life and death, and I was staring at my own family members. I breathe a sigh of something like relief. For once, I'm someplace where I'm more at home than the Legendborn are. A world of magic users who look like me, even if we aren't exactly the same.

I didn't even know this was possible.

A dive bar in the woods, for people who know aether, or root, or any of the other names for the magical resource that the Order has claimed for itself. If Nick hadn't been taken and I hadn't escaped the Regents, would I have ever known a place like this existed?

We make it to the table without issue and I get pressed into a chair against the wall before I can protest, with Alice to my left and Sel on my right, and William across.

The room was warm to begin with, but back deeper into the building it's sticky and hot. Alice worms out of her black jacket and I do the same with the outer hooded coat I'd worn in. Now that we're both down a layer, I can't help but compare our outfits: She's in a fringed, three-quarter-length black blouse that makes her look both badass and classy at once. I glance down at my own top, which looks expensive, but shows a bit more cleavage.

Damnit. I knew we should have coordinated fits.

I tug my shirt up, flushing. Alice notices and snorts. "Good luck hiding those," she says.

"You coulda said something before we left," I mutter back, hoping the music drowns out my voice.

"We didn't get dressed together, or I would have." She grins. "Besides, what am I supposed to say? 'Hide yer tits, Crown Scion'?"

I softly thump her in the arm. She smiles and thumps back.

Out of the side of my eye, Sel's head doesn't move, but the minute shift of his fingers on the table tells me he heard us.

"Oh, are we talking about Bree's outfit?" William leans forward, a wide smile on his face. "I didn't say it before, but I like it. Those colors look incredible on you."

"Right? Bree looks bangin' in any variation of red and black, honestly. Or gold," Alice says. A mischievous look crosses her face. "She looks great, doesn't she, Sel?"

An embarrassment bomb starts ticking in my chest. My entire face might explode. Gonna go boom. Just like that, face gone. *I can't believe her.*

Sel's eyes drift over me so slowly I have to clench the muscles in my legs to stop from squirming. "Briana looks nice." Then he looks away.

Alice's jaw drops.

Nice? Now I *do* squirm, because if I don't, I might hit something. "Nice" is how teachers describe your clothes on school picture day. "Nice" is how you describe a neighbor you don't know particularly well. The last time Sel and I were dressed up together at the Selection gala, he'd called me *stunning*. He'd stared at me like I was part-princess, part-goddess. Was that just because Nick was there? Or because I was just Page Matthews and not . . . all of the things I am now? I shake my head. Can't go down that road, don't even start. I'm not with Sel. It doesn't matter if he says I look good in the most boring way possible.

"'Nice'?" Alice, however, is already halfway down that road and gaining speed. *"'Nice'?!"* Alice scowls at Sel, and I extra-love her for being salty on my behalf. Thank God for best friends. "Does your vocabulary only include basic adjectives?"

Sel ignores her, looks around impatiently. "The service here is lacking. If I had my phone, I'd leave this establishment a horrible review for their horrible service."

"Sorry, sweetie," a voice says. "We aren't on any map, so 'fraid you can't leave the Crossroads Lounge a review."

A young woman with golden-brown skin and large eyes greets us. She's around William or Sel's age, wearing a bright red apron, black boots, and a red-and-black corset—an actual corset. It pushes her cleavage up in a way that's much more impressive than whatever this top I'm wearing does. If I'd known we were going to a place with this sort of dress code, I might have picked something different from the closet. Her outfit kinda makes me want a corset.

"Hello," Sel says in a low voice. His eyes catalog her ensemble in a heartbeat, then he meets her gaze with a slow grin. "I'd like to order a drink."

I shift in my seat, and tamp down the impulse to compare that grin of Sel's to the ones he's given me. Then I shake my head. That doesn't even make any sense. Why do I care about Sel's grin right now? It's an act anyway. I hope.

The girl laughs. "I figured." Then she drops a bowl of olives in the center of the weathered wood table, pulls a spiral-bound notebook from her apron, and tugs a pen out from behind her pinned-up curls. "I'm Emma, and I'll be taking care of y'all tonight. We've got a local brew on tap this week, 'Better Angels.' Sort of a spicy stout. A citrus-y wheat called 'Calamity.'"

"We'll take a couple of each, Emma," Alice says, smile much too big.

"Alice!" I hiss. No *way* they'll believe we're old enough to drink.

But Emma only smiles at me. "You want something different, honey?"

I blink. "Um, no. A couple of each is fine."

"You got it. Be back in a bit." Emma snaps her notebook shut. She glances at my shirt. "Cute top, by the way."

My cheeks heat. "Thanks."

When Emma leaves, Alice exclaims, "See? This is why I date girls. *Taste!*"

"I have taste," Sel mutters, wrinkling his nose.

Alice shoots him a dismayed grimace. "God, I am so embarrassed for you right now."

William snorts into his shirt sleeve, shoulders shaking with laughter. Sel scowls at the world.

I stifle my own laugh by clearing my throat and poking Alice in the leg. "'We'll take a couple of each, Emma'?"

Alice beams. "We wanna blend in, right?"

"By flirting with the waitstaff?" She shrugs.

"There are worse ideas," Sel says bemusedly. "But I'm afraid I agree with Bree. We aren't here to enjoy ourselves. We need to review the mission and keep our eyes out for anything sudden or suspicious or both."

"What exactly should we be looking for?" I ask.

"Unusual behavior. Conflict between patrons. Anyone staring too long at us, or who walks by the table more than twice."

Alice points at a man in an extremely deep V-necked black shirt. "Well, *that* guy has walked past three times. But mostly because he keeps going back for more shots." She jerks a thumb diagonally. "And those two in the enviable body-con dresses are arguing over their bill."

I look and, indeed, in the corner, a person and their partner keep jabbing their fingers at the tiny slip of paper on the table between them.

Sel's eyebrows wing upward. He's impressed. I'm proud. That's my Alice.

"Well done, Chen."

Emma returns with a small circular tray. "Here we go: two pints of Calamity and two Better Angels. Five each." She sets the drinks on the table and stands up with a hand on her hip. The glass in front of me is a light, frothy orange color and smells like citrus. "Pay up front when you're done." She looks down at Sel mischievously, then over her shoulder, before lifting a final, double shot glass I hadn't noticed out of her tray. I'd assumed it was for another table; at first glance, it looks like one of those flaming shots where the alcohol is lit on fire for added *drama*. "Look like you could use a lil' pick-me-up, cambion. On the house." And then she's on to the next table, a party of three at a high-top in the center of the room.

Sel, William, and I lean forward to examine the drink—and immediately go still. A small, silver vortex spins independently over the top, and trails slightly down the sides of the tall, narrow glass and onto the table. But it's not regular fire. It's *mage flame*.

Sel hisses, lips drawn back.

"What are you all looking at?" Alice leans across me to look at the glass, then glances up, shaking her head. "It's just a free shot."

I blink, then realize Alice can't see the aether. "Not quite." I look up at both boys. "Help me out here?"

"She, or someone else, called the invisible element of aether into visibility," Sel explains, eyes on the glass and voice low. "And with that called aether, cast a small, self-sustaining, spinning sphere over the liquor."

William's gaze has turned scientific. "Does she expect you to drink it?"

"It would seem so," Sel murmurs. The light of the aether is reflected in his own golden eyes, making them shine bright across the table.

"Can you?" I ask.

He looks at me over the glass. "Technically? Biologically? Yes. The cuffs block my body's ability to access ambient aether and use it. Ingesting it should be possible." He looks around the Lounge, a frustrated expression on his face. "I'm a bit more concerned that she could detect what I am so effortlessly."

I follow his gaze and immediately find at least three other people consuming beverages with wisps of silver aether spilling down the sides. I can't tell if they're human or demon.

"She said it would be a pick-me-up." William's attention sharpens. "Could this drink help fortify you? It's aether, but could it make up for the Oaths you can't fulfill?"

"Possibly." Sel stills and his fingers twitch at his sides, as if any display of aether can't help but trigger a reflex to call his own. "Probably."

"How?" I ask them.

William pauses, looking to Sel for permission. He rolls his eyes, tossing a hand as if to say, *Go ahead.*

"We know that all demons originate in the hell dimension, and that's where they thrive. But"—William leans forward, elbows on the table, eyes lighting with barely restrained enthusiasm—"when they cross over via Gates to the living, human plane, they become a form of undead, and require *two* metaphysical elements to survive." He holds up his pointer finger. "First, human energy. Demons are chaotic, spontaneous, animalistic creatures, so humanity in some form offers order through mental clarity. If a demon wishes to survive for any amount of time, they need to be able to think past their instincts." A second finger to join the first. "Aether, on the other hand, is like food. It affects the body and provides physical sustenance, and all pure-blooded demons need it in some capacity in order to maintain their forms on this plane."

"Back up a minute. When you say 'human energy,' do you mean eating people?" Alice asks, eyes wide. "Is that what Kizia wanted?"

"No. Kizia wanted Bree's aether. Her root. Human energy primarily means human *emotions*. Anger and fear, in particular."

I watch Sel, who looks for all the world as if he's not listening to a word we say. His eyes are on the rest of the room, the stage, and the world outside our table. "So, does Sel need human energy and aether too?"

"No again." William's eyes twinkle. "That's what's fascinating about Merlins. They are cambions. Well, this is *one* aspect of what's fascinating about them. There's a long list, frankly. . . ."

"I am *right* here." Sel groans loudly and fixes William with a stare. "Please hurry up so you can stop discussing me like I'm a science experiment, William."

William flushes. "Right. Sorry. Cambions are part human and born on this plane, so they don't need human energy *or* aether to survive. But demons are chaos creatures, and chaos favors imbalance. As cambions grow older, their demon blood grows stronger and, even though it's a very small part of their makeup, if they want to maintain control over their demon natures, they need to consume human energy to counterbalance it."

"The Oaths," Alice whispers. "They're the counterbalance for . . ." She pauses when Sel shoots her a look, and mouths the final word of her sentence in silence. "Merlins."

"Yes." William nods. "Oaths are belief and intention combined. Protecting others from harm is one of the most human things someone can do, the very antithesis to demonia."

I point to the still-flaming shot glass. "But in the absence of serving an Oath, could aether help?"

William drops his chin into his hand. "Because cambion physiology doesn't *require* aether, it acts more like a metaphysical drug. Dulls their physical pain, decreases stress, drops inhibitions. Bringing us back to this shot. My hypothesis is that a limited amount of aether would help temporarily soften the effects of humanity-demonia imbalance, maybe even tangentially restore vitality. A hypothesis Selwyn here seems to agree with."

Sel taps his fingers on the table. "A hypothesis is an informed guess, not a proven conclusion."

"Selwyn, this isn't shameful." William's sigh is exasperating, and long-suffering in a way I didn't expect. "Think of it like an experimental supplement. As your physician, I'd highly recommend a small trial—"

"For all we know, it could accelerate the change." Selwyn's fingers clench on the table.

"If that were the case at this dosage," William says, gesturing to the lounge, "they wouldn't risk serving it as *refreshment* in a packed bar."

"That's why you get aether-drunk!" I blurt.

"What?" Sel's ire is electric across my face.

I shrink back a bit. "When you administer the Oaths, you get drunk. Because you're a cambion."

"I don't 'get' aether-drunk. I become intoxicated as a byproduct of administering the Oaths, not something I do on purpose."

I nod to the shot. "But if it helps you now, then you should drink it. On purpose."

The immediate derision in his expression tells me I've said something wrong. "Unavoidable intoxication from the infusion of aether I receive when performing a duty I require is one thing. This"—he nods at the glass—"would be recreational. It wouldn't—" He pauses, inhales, and sits back from the table. "It's not a good idea."

I frown. "Why not? If it's temporary—"

"Because," he says sharply, "I *don't need it*."

"Oh, this was a mistake." Alice says abruptly, staring down at her halfway finished drink. She jumps out of her seat and pulls at my arm until I stumble out of my chair alongside her. "We still need to use the ladies' room. We've been holding it for two hours."

Sel stands. "You can't go alone."

"Why not?" I ask.

"I think it would be obvious. I'll escort you both."

Which is how Sel ends up leading us through a throng of people along the wall until we stand in front of three halls made of shipping containers.

"Respite. Desires. Delight." Alice blinks at the signs overhead. "Lot going on back here." Other guests weave around us, walking confidently down the hallways. "Do one of those mean 'bathroom'?" she asks.

Standing up on tiptoe, I can just make out shadowed doorways along one hall, lit by red bulbs. "Respite, I think?"

Sel leads us down the Respite hall. As the din of the main room becomes distant, we hear conversations coming from down the passageway. Farther in, we can see that each of the black-framed doors has frosted privacy glass in the middle. At the end of the container, there is a solid black door with WC printed on the exterior.

After knocking, Alice slips inside first. I lean against the exterior wall and close my eyes for a moment, taking a break from the cacophony of the main room. The music is so loud the bass shakes the metal walls of the shipping container, but at least I can think straight.

After a long moment, I feel Sel slide into place beside me, and the line of his body presses into mine. The contact startles me enough that my eyes snap open and I jerk away, losing balance—only to be stabilized by his palm on my lower back. "Thanks," I murmur. His palm is burning through my shirt, hotter than I remember it being the last time we touched.

"Of course." When I look up, his eyes are searching my features, roaming to my hairline, my shoulders. His fingers, still pressed against my lower back, twitch, then spread wide over my spine.

"What?"

"My vocabulary *does* include more adjectives than the word 'nice,'" he murmurs.

I flush. My voice comes out breathy and low. "Could have fooled me."

I'm halfway into sort of hating myself for sounding that way when I see the effect of my response on Sel's expression. The surprise and frustration and heat, all rolled into one. He holds my gaze like he owns it. I don't want to look away, but I couldn't if I tried. The floor beneath me dips, and the sounds around us grow muffled. My heart picks up, and even in a corridor rocked by thumping bass and distant voices, his ear tilts, listening to my pulse. Somehow, in this moment, I am filling Sel's senses the same way he fills mine.

"I suppose it doesn't really matter," I whisper. "Does it?"

His eyes dart down to my lips and my breath catches. His own mouth parts, the tips of his fangs just visible atop his lower lips. Without warning, he ducks his head and pulls me toward him simultaneously, and draws a breath near my throat. His voice is a hoarse rasp below my chin, a tease and warning both. "You are still asking questions that you do not truly want me to answer."

"What if I do want you to answer?" I reply, bold.

"Then I would say you look . . . devourable," he murmurs. "And that, for me, is something I don't wish to share in mixed company. For many, many reasons."

I swallow. "Many reasons?"

An intake of breath. "A great many."

Abruptly, his hand is gone, leaving my back cold in its absence. He stands upright and doesn't look at me again. My insides feel like those damn neon signs over the doorways. Flashing desire, delight half-lit, buzzing, bright. And a layer of guilt that tries to sour it all, and fails.

Alice emerges from the bathroom and breaks the spell, and I switch places with her eagerly.

Surprisingly, the space is clean. Much cleaner than whatever the gas station bathroom would have been, I'm sure. There are even scented soaps and a stack of fluffy hand towels to choose from. I splash my face with water and try to regain my sense of balance, but all I can think of are Sel's "many reasons" . . .

and the voice inside of me that wants nothing more than for him to list each reason out, one by one.

When I exit, Sel and Alice are speaking quickly in harsh tones, facing one of the doors with frosted glass a few feet away. He's at my side in a blink, his face dark with anger as he starts walking. "We need to get back to the table."

I have to jog to catch up. "Why do you both look like you've just swallowed an eel or something?"

"Worse than that," Alice replies, eyes looking over our shoulders.

Sel answers through gritted teeth. "Look at the signs next to the doors."

"What signs . . . ?" I trail off, then my eyes grow wide as I spot a plaque near a closed door on our right. My stomach drops. "Oh my *God*."

SEE THE BROKER/PROPRIETOR FOR A BARGAIN. NO UNREGULATED EXCHANGES ON THE PREMISES.

His eyes dart to mine and away again. "I told you this was a bad idea."

"Unregulated . . . ," I whisper. "That's what Kizia . . ."

"Yep." Alice gnaws at her lip.

Sel wraps a hand around my elbow. "We need to leave. Now."

"What about Lucille?" I hiss. "I need her help—"

"This establishment is run by the person who helped coordinate your assassination. We will find you help another way, Briana!"

Back at the booth, William clutches a pint glass full of water between his hands, waving when we approach. He clocks Sel's expression immediately.

"What's wrong?"

Sel leans close. "We found out what type of business goes on here. And who runs the place."

"Who?"

"The broker," I answer.

William stands. "Shit." He looks over his shoulder, sees the bouncer at the exit. "We have to pay for these drinks. . . ."

Sel scowls. "No, we don't."

"Wanna get put in magical-bar jail?" Alice hisses at his shoulder. She grabs both our coats. "Cuz stealing drinks is how you get put into magical-bar jail!"

"Comrades and gentlefolk, sorcerers and warlocks, witches and winos," a voice calls out in the darkness, using a sound system that cracks and garbles at the end of the words. "Let us put our hands together for the three sisters Morrígna!"

"We can't get distracted," Sel says. "I'm going to pay the tab if that's what it takes." He looks at me pointedly. "Stay here."

Our table isn't angled perfectly for the stage, so William has to scoot back when Alice whispers that she can't see. I can see it perfectly, though, which is why I see the aether fizzing in the air on its own at the same time William does. His brow furrows as I gasp. The deep yellow sparks twist in the air above the stage until they burst in a flash of embers so bright, most everyone in the room has to shield their eyes.

Then, just as with Louis, three women appear out of nowhere.

"What happened?" Alice moves to her knees on her chair to better see the stage.

"There were sparks," I explain in a low voice, underneath the slow drums of the intro to the performers' song. "Sort of like fireworks, but small. They flared up, and when they were gone—"

"Those three materialized as if from thin air," William murmurs without turning. "Just like the bouncer. How are they doing this if this power isn't theirs?"

A rise of angry voices at the bar draws my attention—and immediately sends dread down my spine.

"Who do you think you are, kid?!" A male voice spits, half-amused and half . . . not.

No. No, he *wouldn't*.

Yes. He would.

Sel stands at the end of the bar, both hands pressed into the sticky wood. "This is urgent. I need to pay my bill."

"Hey, is this kid jumping the line, Alonzo?" Another voice, this one belonging to a tall, brown-skinned woman with a high silver bun. I jump up.

"Bree!" Alice says. "He said stay here!"

I ignore her and push through the crowd to get to Sel.

"He's trying to," Alonzo, the bartender, shouts back to the woman. He's shorter than Sel, but much wider. He speaks around a toothpick. "Who are you here with again?"

I reach Sel's side and tug on his elbow. "What the hell are you doing?"

He spares me a glance, then leans forward. "I'm a customer. I'm asking for quality service. Something that seems to be beyond the staff here."

"What did you say?" The man's eyes seem to gleam brighter for a moment. The silver-haired woman pulls her companion back, and the rest of the bar patrons pull away, leaving us alone near the counter.

"Sel!" I urge, tugging on his arm again. It's no use.

Sel lifts his nose, sniffing the air. "I thought I smelled warlock." His lips curl back in a dangerous grin. "I'd hoped it was just an exaggeration, but the rumors appear to be true. Pact magic leaves an *awful* stench."

Alonzo inhales through his nose—and grows taller, wider, and the gleam in his eyes flares. I didn't know what Sel meant before, but I can smell it now—rotten fruit, sour and rancid. Like aether gone bad.

Alonzo hops the bar and lands with a deep, earth-shattering thunk on the wooden floor, earning gasps from the group around him. He towers over both of us, a boulder of a man.

"Say that again."

33

"STOP!"

I'm moving before I have time to think, stepping between the warlock and Sel, my hands pressed to Alonzo's chest.

WHOOSH!

All at once, my hands and arms erupt in flames. Activated by the threat of Alonzo, my root appears at a full, roaring burn. Taller than the warlock, wider than us both, surrounding us in a column of fire.

Alonzo grabs both of my arms, squeezing, and power bursts from my mouth and eyes, blazing bright against the warlock's face. He releases me, but my red flames stay with him, circling around his throat and his face, bringing him yelling to his knees.

Black smoke rises up from the warlock's skin, swirling and dancing in the air above him. The crowd gasps and points.

As soon as the smoke appears, it swirls into a tornado turning, turning— then dissipates into nothing. The entire building has gone silent, watching us.

The flames recede from my fingertips and arms, up my forearms and back into my chest. Sel stumbles to my side.

The only sounds remaining are my panting breaths and the warlock's, as we stare at each other in shock.

The man that had been massive before is now shrunken down to normal human size. Like his augmented shape had been stripped away and turned into smoke.

If I didn't already know, then the appalled faces near us would let me know I've done something terribly wrong. Alonzo looks down at his chest, anger warring with shock. His lips curl back, and his breath hits hot against my cheek, then abruptly, he curses and stands.

"And that"—a low, amused voice cuts through the tension—"is a demonstration of a new powerset I hope can be made available in the coming months, if supply chain issues work out." The crowd parts even further and a teenage Black boy wearing a long red jacket steps through. "Applause for our performers tonight!"

The boy is tall enough to partially block Alonzo when he steps between us and proceeds to clap in big, convincing slaps of his hands. The audience responds hesitantly, then with growing applause.

He speaks to us both through gritted teeth, gives an order in a sharp tone that brooks no argument whatsoever. *"Smile."*

Alonzo flashes his teeth unconvincingly but obeys. A shaky smile spreads across my face, and I tuck my trembling hands behind my back. Fury and fear cycle through Sel's features.

The boy turns back to us as if to applaud our "performance," but as soon as the crowd is behind him, his pleased grin disappears. "Get. Up."

As Alonzo stands, I get a closer look at the newcomer who commanded the entire Lounge.

If I'd seen him from far away, I'd have called him a Merlin on sight. A young one, maybe Sel's age. Gold-and-red light reflect off his warm brown face in the dim light of the Lounge. There's an unnaturally beautiful, inhuman grace in his stride and movements. Hair shorn close on the sides, but rising in thick, tight curls from his crown. Where others are in dark jeans and leather and denim, he wears dark-charcoal pinstripe suit pants, a gray button-down, and a tailored burgundy vest under his bloodred jacket. A gold watch is tucked in his vest pocket, with a delicate braided chain looped up from its hiding place over a vest button. As soon as the newcomer steps closer to Alonzo, I see his eyes sparkle like wine-red gems under dark brows.

Goruchel demon. Like Rhaz. Like Kizia.

Fear and rage spike in my body, turning my heartbeat thunderous. The newcomer's head whips in my direction—and his eyes are a deep brown. Not red.

I blink. Rhaz has haunted my dreams, just like every other horror from that night at the cave. Had I imagined it? I look to Sel for confirmation, but his face betrays nothing. I can't tell if he saw the boy's eyes change, or if the boy's eyes even changed at all.

The boy looks back at Sel, then tilts his head to Alonzo and gives him another order. "Wave and clap." The words are jovial, but the tone has a note of dark warning. Everything about this newcomer is balanced on a razor's edge between charm and threat. The warlock blows air out slowly from his mouth and waves like a performer who's just put on a scene.

"Let us return to our *regularly* scheduled show," the boy says, all charisma once again. "Applications for these abilities can be started at the bar, along with the usual deposit, of course." The newcomer raps his knuckle once on the counter and turns to the small crowd, a bubble of relative quiet while the show rages on at the stage. "Nothing to see here, friends, but if you insist on gawking, you may as well get a drink. Next round on me!"

A group rushes the bar, assaulting Alonzo with eager orders.

"You two." The newcomer has pivoted in the second that I glanced away. "Who are you?"

Sel narrows his eyes. "Who are *you*?"

The corner of the young man's mouth quirks. "My name is Valechaz. You may call me Valec. I am the proprietor of this bar."

"You're the broker?" I ask.

Valec smiles. "That I am."

Shock rockets through me, but Sel's face remains smooth.

"Every bit of magic that happens in this bar is authorized by me," Valec continues, "and I can have you tossed into my oubliette out back in a blink of an eye if I so wish. Faster than even you can move, Merlin."

"I don't know what you're talking about," says Sel.

Valec's face hardens a fraction.

"You announced the stage act, the Morrígna," I say. "I recognize your voice."

Valec's smile is pleased. "That is one of my favorite parts of the evening." He leans into me slightly, and I get a whiff of something dark, spicy, and burning. "I'm so glad you enjoyed it."

"Step back," Sel demands.

"For the final time. Who are you? Full names, please. First and last. Truth only—or the aforementioned oubliette."

"Selwyn Kane."

Valec's eyes brighten, then dim.

The handsome, strange boy turns to me. "And you, beautiful?"

"I'm . . . ," I begin, and pause with my mouth open like a fish. Do I say my real name? Or Ramona's? Should I bring out the ID to be convincing, or will that make it worse?

Valec senses my internal debate. "Truth only . . . ," he murmurs bemusedly.

Sel snorts. "Good luck with that."

I glare at him before turning back to Valec. "Briana Matthews."

Valec takes my name in with some consideration and hums. "Well, Briana Matthews and Selwyn Kane, you've violated the rules of this establishment, and so you must come with me. Both of you."

He snaps his fingers, and Louis appears between us, his large hands already wrapped around both of our wrists. I see Sel's other hand grasp at Louis's fingers, pulling—and then the bar goes black.

We pop back into the world in the same exact positions, but instead of being downstairs near the bar, we're upstairs in what looks like a large office with a desk, a filing cabinet, and two rickety chairs.

The bass of the music is muffled through the floor and a closed door. Sel's fingers are still curled around Louis's massive hand, but the snarl falls from his face as we both take in our surroundings. Then Louis blinks out of existence, leaving me alone with Sel.

With a deep sigh, I fall back down to my knees, still recovering from the burst of power that big. I don't think I've used flames like that since the Rite. I'm out of practice. Drained.

Sel rushes to the door and jerks on the handle, clearly assuming it would open beneath his strength—but drops his hand immediately, hissing. "Shit!"

"Are you okay?" I ask from the floor.

"Yes, of course I'm okay!" He snaps and raises his hand, palm out. There's a deep burn in the palm, red and round like the doorknob. "Totally fine, Briana. Obviously."

"You'll heal. Anyway," I mutter, "serves you right."

His eyes narrow. "Excuse me?"

"You started a fight when we were supposed to be leaving!" I stand.

"Well"—he inspects his burnt palm, prodding gently at the raw skin before hissing again—"from what I'd heard, warlocks are rather disgusting, and it turns out they are. I admit I lost focus—" He flinches, glares at me. "Or maybe I got distracted by the smell, is that better? I might have started a fight with him regardless. On principle."

"What *principle?*"

"Warlocks are humans who bargain for their powers." Sel walks to the window at a normal pace, pressing against the sill. "They've made a deal with the devil. Sell a few years off their lives, their firstborn, their soul, etcetera. And in exchange, they gain some of the demon's abilities." The sill singes his finger, but this time he pulls away before it does much damage, cursing under his breath. "It's tasteless. Abhorrent."

"Borrow, bargain, or steal," I murmur, Patricia's words coming back to me.

"Aether is a resource," he mutters. "The living cannot access and use it for free."

Valechaz enters the office without warning, nearly sending me tumbling backward to the floor. The air around the edges of his body blurs like a heat wave.

"You two!" He slams the door behind him. As he walks past he takes the heat wave with him. "You have *really* gone and fucked things up, haven't you? If it weren't for the wards, that pulse of power would have had every demon in a mile radius banging on the goddamn doors!"

When Valec takes a seat at the desk, he jabs a finger at the two cracked-leather chairs opposite. We are clearly meant to sit down.

"I extended a courtesy to the two guests that accompanied you tonight by letting them know you'd violated our mores. They agreed to wait peacefully while we determine your punishments."

I can't imagine William, and Alice especially, "waiting peacefully," but something about Valec and his control over the club makes me think they didn't really have a choice.

I try to imagine him authorizing my death. Did he sign off on it without knowing the details? Collect and disburse the money between Jonas and Kizia? The air around him is ready to spark into mage flame at any moment, hungry to burn the world where it begins at his shoulders, at his elbows, around his thick curls. Could this boy, barely a few years older than me, care so little for life that he helps people negotiate ways to end one?

As if he senses me watching him, his head snaps up, eyes flashing from brown to red and back again.

"*Sit. Down.*"

I move to take a seat, but Sel stops me. "Let her go down to the others. I'm the one who broke your rules. I'll take the punishment."

"No, you both committed sins tonight." Valec points a finger at Sel. "*You* initiated an act of aggression under my roof, in direct violation of the Lounge policies you agreed to upon entry." His finger travels to me. "But *you* have done much, much more than that. Do you have any idea the effect that little public display of power has already had on my business? Stripping a warlock's powers on demand? Whether it's temporary or permanent, it's a damn powerful parlor trick, and Alonzo is owed redress. I've got a pack of hungry, furious demons out there, half a dozen spooked warlocks asking for amendments, and a dozen human clients who think I've been holding out on them."

Valec pulls a drawer out from the side of his desk, producing a folder of paper and a pen. Without seeing his eyes flash demon, I'd assume he was just an annoyed businessman.

Sel tugs at his own collar. Even he feels the heat, and he always runs hot himself.

What *is* Valec?

Valec gestures vaguely over the documents, as if we are as familiar with them as he. "Altogether, you have violated Lounge policies, removed someone's rightfully owned and paid for abilities, *and* in the process undermined my authority as proprietor." He looks up, shrugging. "You are *both* in my debt until *I* call us even."

Beads of sweat begin to drip down my spine. Moisture at the roots of my hair making my scalp too warm, uncomfortable. "What do you want from us?"

"To begin, Briana, what deal have you struck, and which demon did you strike it with?"

Sel and I exchange glances. "She didn't strike a deal with a demon."

"Of course she did." Valec scoffs. "And I *am* impressed with that flame, I must admit. So impressed that I might let Briana go on all counts if she tells me everything she knows about that power." He looks between us, doing some calculus in his mind. "Yes. Her freedom in exchange for that extremely valuable information. This is balance." A smile spreads across his mouth. "So, who was your broker? If the contract has an aether-infused NDA, that's all right; I can break its bond to you."

Abruptly, the stifling air in the room thins. Sel and I look at each other, each thinking the same thing. He speaks before I can. "There's another broker?"

Valec blinks. "Yes, of course." He tilts his head. "Care to share which other broker concerns you, and why?"

Sel and I exchange another glance. The fact there is another broker in the area might change things. But if there is one thing I know about this new world I live in, it is that even if someone may not be who you fear the most, that doesn't mean they are safe.

"No, thank you," I mutter, just as Sel says, "We're good."

Valec raises a hand to his chest in a mock bow. "I *am* the only local broker that facilitates deals between humans and demons."

"What kind of humans?" Sel asks.

Valec raises a brow. "The regular, nonmagical human kind of humans. Why, what other humans do you know of?"

Sel goes still. Legendborn are technically human, but once they have their inheritances, they *become* magical. "Just a question."

Valec doesn't believe that for a minute. "As I said, I am the only broker of my kind. Which is how I know *someone* made a mint of a commission off a deal like yours. Permanent aether generation, demon-power destruction, tucked into such a pretty package." He whistles.

My jaw drops. "Are you . . . hitting on me right now?"

"A bit. What'd you give up in exchange? Something like that must have had an enormous fee, and yet you look, well . . ." He lets his gaze wander deliberately over my face and hair, shoulders and mouth. "Perfect to me. Soul still attached and everything."

Sel rolls his eyes. I step forward. "I'm telling you, I didn't make a deal."

He lifts a hand and sits back in his chair, feet on the desk. "Which of my competitors wrote the contract, and which demon shared their power with you?"

"No one did. I didn't sign a contract."

He goes perfectly still. "I hope for your sake you're lying."

I shake my head. "I'm not. I didn't sign anything!"

The temperature in the room kicks up another degree, the respite from before gone. His voice is a low, controlled purr. "An unregulated bargain, Briana? In this day and age?"

Dizziness threatens the edges of my vision. It's so hot in here. Sel's hand is steady at my elbow; he answers for me. "There was no bargain."

I swallow. "A demon didn't give me anything."

Valec crosses his arms. "Then where does your power come from, hm?" He sniffs the air. "You're human, but you smell . . . augmented. *Layered.*"

I press my lips into a line. Arguing with him doesn't seem to be helping.

Valec takes my silence for refusal, and his patience thins from barely there to nothing at all. Irritation and confusion evaporate at once. He's on his feet between one blink and another, leaning with both hands on his desk. I gasp and step back.

"I am being kind." His eyes flash ruby, then brown. "There *are* ways to find out more about your power without asking you directly. If you did not sign a contract for those powers, then I am not bound to treat you with, well, any respect whatsoever." His eyes glow a faint red, and this time they stay that way.

"We're here to talk to Lucille!" I blurt.

Valec goes still. His eyes dart between the two of us, suspicion bordering on pure aggression.

"Why would Lucille agree to see you when you cannot follow the sworn rules of entry? She is the Grand Dame of this territory, of which my establishment is a part, and any of the procedures I follow are approved by her. So, you see, Lucille has as good as endorsed whatever punishment I hand out." He glances to me. "But I've lived long enough to learn to live as the willow, not the oak. Perhaps you need more incentive to consider my offer. You're up, Selwyn Kane."

"No!" I challenge, but Sel's arm is already a steel bar against my belly, pressing me backward toward the exit.

"I'll be fine. Go," he says, and starts to pivot us around so that I'm facing the door.

"Aht, aht!" Valec stands, raises a finger. "Not the nature of this deal."

Sel's head swings back, outraged.

The boy smiles. "Even in our short time together, Kane, I can see that the best way to punish you"—he turns to me, his eyes glinting—"is to hurt her."

Sel's growl rips through the room. He lunges across the desk toward Valec, skidding on the surface—and into an empty chair. The broker's gone. Sel lands on his feet, flips around, eyes frantic.

"Too slow." A voice behind me.

Sel leaps on top of the desk—but Valec's hand is around my waist before I register that he has me in his grasp. I struggle, but it's like fighting iron. He's immovable, impossibly strong, even for me.

"Let her go." Sel's eyes drift down toward Valec's grip. "Now."

"Or what?" Valec purrs. He leans down to my ear. "What do you think he'll do, Briana? Jump down atop'a me with his angry eyes and flamin' fists? Not void cuffed like that he won't."

Sel's cuffs aren't visible underneath the long shirt, but somehow Valec spotted them, and Sel's not happy that he knows exactly what they are.

"Poor little cambion," Valec sings in my ear. That is enough to chill me, that he knows exactly what Sel is, just like the waitress did. But what he says next sends panic rocketing through my body and Sel's eyes both. "Little Kingsmage.

Leashed by the Order his whole pathetic existence and now manacled by them too?"

"How do you know who I am?" Sel's eyes dip to Valec's too-strong hand wrapped around my middle.

"I've been around a long time." Valec makes a thoughtful sound. "And I know what your Oath demands of you. Which is why I find it so curious that our Briana here"—he pauses, raises a hand to rub a thumb down the muscle of my neck—"so consumes your protective attentions. She's clearly a smart, brave, gorgeous girl, but to capture the singular focus of a Kingsmage? Who is sworn to protect the Scion of Arthur only?"

I stiffen in Valec's grasp. Valec doesn't know who I am—and can't, for my own good—but he's gotten too close to the truth for my comfort.

"She must be very special. I do like special things, Selwyn. I'm a special thing myself."

Sel's nostrils flare. "I will tear your limbs from your body."

"Mm," Valec considers. "Be a fun fight without the void cuffs, but as it is, I'd just get bored."

"Fight won't be fun if you're in pieces at the end," Sel snarls.

Valec laughs. "Better calm yourself, Kingsmage. Wherever he is, your Scion of Arthur can feel you right now, can't he? Your desire to kill me. From the whispers I've heard about Nicholas Davis, he wouldn't particularly like that—" Valec stops short, looking between us. He tilts his head in that listening gesture I know all too well. "Both o' your hearts flipped just now, and your breathing changed when I mentioned the Scion's name. Is there anything either of you would like to tell me about the once and future king?"

Sel jerks back, eyes wide with the desire not to panic Nick, at war with his desire to keep me safe. "Keep his name out of your mouth."

"Sensitive about your Scion, are you?" Valec snorts. "Kingsmages are so . . . single-minded. Play nice and I'll ensure everyone's limbs remain attached, and your precious Nick won't have to worry about what trouble you've found." He tilts his head toward me, voice low and conspiratorial. "I bet it's annoying, isn't it? So focused on protecting his king that he forgets about anyone else."

Heat swirls up my spine and burns my cheeks. Valec notices and chuckles. "Oh, I detect a *story* there."

"You have no idea," Sel growls—and lunges again.

Valec shoves me aside to meet him. In a flash, he grasps Sel around the throat and lifts him up in the air. Sel claws at Valec's fingers, his shoes scraping the carpet. "You are too young and too weak to beat me, so *stop trying*." He tosses Sel against the back wall—hard enough that his head cracks against the brick. Faded photos in old frames rattle from the impact.

"No!" I run past Valec, who doesn't bother stopping me. I reach Sel just as he moves into a sitting position with a grunt. My hand flies to his hair, past the thick waves to the back of his skull. My fingertips come away red. "Sel—"

He bats my hand away. Setting his back against the wall and using his legs more than anything, he slides to a half-standing position. "I'm fine!"

"No, you're not." Valec steps forward, casually lifting his desk to clear the way and pushing it aside like it weighs nothing. He stands beside me with his hands in his pockets, looking between Sel and then me. "Who you think you're fooling, pup? You're a *wreck*."

"Shut up." Sel's head snaps up. Fury and some other emotion I can't read mingle on his face.

"Why?" Valec tilts his head in confusion.

Sel glares at Valec, teeth bared. A silent warning.

That Valec ignores.

Instead, Valec looks between us, once, twice, then solely at me. "Wait—" He steps closer to me with narrow, searching eyes. So close that I almost see the iridescent red over the deep brown. After a moment, Valec draws back, devilish amusement dancing over his face. "Oh, I thought *I* might have to harm Briana to really stick it to you, Kane, but you've done that just fine all on your own. . . ."

"What are you talking about?" I demand.

Valec raises his right hand to my face and I flinch away—but can't escape. He already has a hand wrapped around my elbow like a vise. I hadn't even felt him move.

"Don't touch her!" Sel growls.

"First," Valec murmurs, almost gently, as he presses three fingers to my temple, "look at me."

If Merlins' eyes look both old and young, Valec's eyes look *ancient*. His eyes churn the space between us, creating a link like I've never felt before. Like mesmer, but . . . more like firm hands around my mind, *squeezing*—then letting go. By the time I think to resist, it's over.

"Now," Valec whispers, releasing me, "look at him."

Confused, I look back at Sel. "Why?" He has since dropped both hands onto his knees and his head is bowed, like he's trying to catch his breath—or control it.

Valec's voice is low at my ear. "Because he doesn't want you to."

Dread makes a heavy, dizzying cocktail in my belly. Heart thumping against my ribs, I step forward. Raise a hand to his shoulder. "Sel?"

"Don't—" He jerks away.

"Sel, are you—"

"Bree . . ." His voice is a low warning growl. Meant to scare and challenge. It stopped working on me ages ago.

Valec sighs. "If you don't turn around on your terms, Kane, you'll do so on mine."

Sel's spine goes rigid at Valec's threat. There's a long moment when I think he might let Valec force him, or that he might bolt. But he does neither.

Instead, Sel stands up slowly, twisting as he goes.

As his profile becomes visible, my mouth falls open in a choked gasp.

"Oh my God."

34

THE SELWYN I'D seen just five minutes ago isn't here anymore. This Selwyn is someone I don't recognize, even in profile.

Where Sel's skin is usually even and pale, this Sel's skin is flushed with bright red slashes across each cheekbone. His lips are a deeper color than I've ever seen. I catalog the damp black strands plastered on his temple and forehead. The rapid flutter pulse against the skin of his throat, strikingly *wrong* for a Merlin, whose hearts beat more slowly than people who are fully human. At his sides, dark veins line his fingers and hands, stretch past his wrists.

"Sel . . . ," I whisper.

Eyes closed, mouth pursed, he turns.

"Look at me. . . ." Breath catches in my throat. "Please."

And then he does, and what I see rips my heart open.

Sel's eyes have been a bright, tawny yellow in the sun. Glittering amber jewels at night. Even rich, liquid honey. But never have they been a burning sienna. This is gold, yearning for crimson. The sun, seeking blood.

And yet my hand reaches for his face before I can stop it, as if my fingers are compelled to touch the same features that have captured my eyes. Dangerous things draw you in like that, and he is a dangerous thing. Poisonous flora, gorgeous for a reason. Dancing flames, beckoning you forward. A lure in the dark by a creature who wants your death slow, not fast.

Then, realization crashes down around my heart, and my hand falls.

My voice is a bare whisper. "You said protecting me and William would be enough." Sel flinches, and his lips curl back. His canines, usually long enough to just touch his bottom lip, now extend to two sharp points. "Your . . ."

Your teeth look different today.

His voice, meant to soothe—and redirect. *Do they?*

The memories come back now, pouring in through cracks so small I didn't realize they were there. His eyes on the plane as we spoke. His flirting in the safehouse bathroom, how close he'd gotten and how *long* he'd held my gaze. The look we'd shared downstairs in the hallway. The hot press of his hand on my spine. . . . All of those moments. The guilt I'd felt being close to him, thinking I was somehow betraying Nick. Thinking that Sel *wanted* to be close to me, *wanted* to touch me. The parts of me that *screamed* that I wanted him to touch me, too . . . but no.

None of that was real.

What I thought felt like falling into him, maybe even *for* him, had been me, falling into Sel's illusion. A lie, wrapped around my senses, all by his design. Breath punches from my lungs. Pain burrows in, deep and wide, and nausea follows.

"You—you mesmered me." The well of tears, finally falling in a rush. "You've *been* mesmering me. Haven't you?"

His eyes fall shut. All the answer I need.

Valec rocks back on his heels. "A Merlin away from his Oaths is a damn ugly thing, Briana. Unbalanced cambions, all of 'em. Unlike myself."

Sel's eyes snap open. "You cannot be a cambion."

"Why not? Because I'm not on the Order's leash?" Valec sneers. "The original Merlin was balanced, born from a demon-human union. But that *lil'* bit of demon blood you Merlin descendants have is like a drop of rabid dye in a glass of calm water. The dye spreads everywhere, maybe tints the water a shade or two, but it will never fully turn that water the color it wants it to be. And that's the thing about demon blood: it *wants.*"

"Shut up," seethes Sel. His eyes find me. "Please, Bree, let me explain. . . ."

Valec talks over him, Sel snaps back; their words turn into a melted slurry of sound overhead. My hands tremble at my sides. My heart hits the same hurt over and over again, a steady drum of betrayal.

"That *imbalance* is what makes a Merlin so volatile," Valec continues. "Order favors balance, so when cambion blood is evenly split in a half-demon, half-human"—he gestures at himself—"it's much easier to control. Although, our Selwyn here is making a valiant effort not to succumb to his blood, I'll give him that. Touchless mesmer is *very* impressive work, Kane."

So dizzy I might vomit. So dizzy I *want* to vomit, get all this *wrong* out of me, all of it. I shut my eyes—and I'm back in the cave again.

Arthur, pulling my strings like a puppet.

Arthur, invading my mind at the funeral.

Arthur, making me wonder if I can even trust myself.

And now . . . Sel. Doing the exact same things.

Everything in my chest spills out in a low, trembling whisper. "You knew what the Regents did to me at the Institute. What *he* did to me." Guilt and horror splash across Sel's face, chased by recognition.

Valec raises a brow. "The Regents are in town? Who is 'he'?"

I ignore him. "You *knew* they drugged me. Manipulated my mind, my memories . . . so that I could be their toy to use or toss aside. You know what he feels like in my head, how I can't trust myself sometimes, don't know if it's him or me . . ."

"Who the hell is '*he*'?" Valec throws his hands up.

"Bree, please—" Sel holds out a hand.

I jerk back, shouting, "Don't *touch* me!"

His eyes darken to ruby, but he does not move.

"Is that what I am to you, too—a toy?"

Sel's fists clench and unclench. "No."

"I thought . . ." A sob wrenches its way from my throat. My heart feels as if it could collapse in on itself, taking breath and joy with it. I feel violated all over again. "You're *just* like *them* . . ."

The Regents. Arthur.

"No, I am *not* like them," Sel snarls, voice shifting into something wild, cracking.

Something hungry.

"I'm *nothing* like them. If you'd just *listen* to me—" He pushes off the wall, crimson flooding his eyes, blocking the white out. His veined fingertips reach the back of my hand—and Valec blurs between us. He shoves Sel away from me so hard, he hits the wall again. This time, Sel stays down, panting, shock across his face. "I . . ." Sel shakes his head, eyes unseeing. "I . . . I didn't . . ."

"Get it together, Kane," Valec snaps. "You're far too proud to thank me for that now, but I expect your gratitude later."

My jaw opens, closes. "What just happened—"

"Your anguish, his hunger." Valec's eyes simmer as he returns to my side, draping an arm over my shoulder. "Best if he takes a beat before he touches you, powerhouse. Right now, you're all anger and suffering, and so is he. Bad combination."

"I don't—"

"Your misery is *palpable*, Bree." He leans down to my ear, breath warm against my cheek. "I can taste it in the air, on the back of my tongue. Kane's demon isn't quite strong enough to take over, but if it were, he'd devour your pain like a fine wine, sweetheart."

William just said it downstairs. Full demons must consume aether and human emotions. Cambions don't need either to survive, but Sel away from his Oaths is more demon than ever right now. More demon than he'd let me realize. More like . . . Kizia.

Bile rises in my throat again; my stomach roils. The idea of Sel *feeding* from my misery. Erebus, Cestra . . . they warned me what Sel would become. Erebus told me what a Merlin who succumbs to his blood wants. They want what all demons want: fear and anger and strife. Creating pain in others just to ravage it for themselves. *"I would say you look . . . devourable."*

My voice is a broken whisper. "Did you do this to me . . . trick me, lie to me, to create pain you could . . . feed on?"

Sel jerks as if I'd hit him. "No!"

Valec's hands land on my shoulders and give them a squeeze before stepping aside to survey Sel with growing frustration.

"You're probably only a few weeks from your duties, but the minor Oaths wouldn't take a Merlin down like this. It's that goddamn Kingsmage Oath that packs a punch. Forever until death?" His face sours, like the words have turned rotten in his mouth. "The Order really does a number on Merlins with that Oath-and-service trick. And people complain about *my* contracts? My terms are child's play compared to theirs." His eyes flicker crimson as he sneers, "'The Line is Law.' An utter and complete scorching pile of rotting archaic garbage— and you can tell that pompous bastard Erebus Varelian I said that."

"*You* know Erebus?" I whisper.

His eyes narrow to red slits. "We've met."

Abruptly, Valec sighs, long and heavy. The red in his eyes swirls to brown, and he snaps his fingers. Louis appears beside Sel, a waiting expression on his face. Valec assesses Sel, then makes a decision. "His debt is paid. Take him away, give him a shot of the strong stuff, and tell the staff it's last call. We're headed to the roof."

Louis grasps Sel's arm. There's a beat before they go, when Sel could have looked at me. Could have said something, done something. But he doesn't look, doesn't speak, and then they're gone.

I stare at the spot where Sel had just been. The only evidence that he'd been there are the cracked bricks six feet up the wall, from where his head had struck it when Valec tossed him.

I scrub at my face with my hands, smearing tears across my cheeks. My voice comes out thick and far away. "Where did you send him?"

A pair of tumblers thunk onto the desk. My head whips to the cambion, who is kneeling, opening a cabinet out of sight. After a moment, Valec rises to standing, and it's like watching liquid flow upward. Preternaturally smooth. He has a small, glowing bottle in one hand and an ice bucket in the other. "Aether spirits on the rocks?"

I blink, taking the scene in. Thoughts in whiplash. "Where did you send him?"

Ice clinks into the tumblers. He pours one glass, then another. Sits on his desk and extends a beverage to me. "You look like you need a drink."

I stare at the tumbler, full of what looks like bourbon, and the silver mist swirling on top. "Can you please answer my question?"

He sips his glass, eyes dancing. "Why do you care? He lied to you. Cast an illusion without your consent, for who knows how long."

"Are you going to hurt him?"

He laughs. "He was hurting himself. I just helped seal the deal. He'll be unharmed by my staff, but tucked away for now with a dense shot of aether to help even him out for a bit. Speaking of—drink?"

Relief at this news floods me, but on its heels are fresh tears clouding my vision. "I'm underage." It's the only protest I can think to say.

He throws his head back, laughing loud. "Who's gonna arrest me for serving apple juice and magic to a teenager?"

I frown. "Apple juice?"

He shrugs. "Cuts the sharpness, I think."

"Why are you being nice to me?"

"This isn't kindness, little powerhouse." He smiles. "This is Southern hospitality."

I snatch the glass, and he watches me with silent approval. "What's aether do to humans?"

"To humans? If concentrated and concocted specially, they'll get what the Order folks call 'the Sight.' Temporarily." He nods at the glass in my hand. "With a little bit like that? Body buzz at most." He is at my side in a blink, silent and imposing. "But you aren't a typical human, are you?"

I stare up at him, bold. My emotions have been twisted into a knot and squeezed out into a liquid mess in the last hour. I don't even know if I have the capacity to be scared of Valec right now. If I do, I ignore it. "No. Which is why I'd worry about threatening me if I were you."

He grins. "Oh, I *really* like you."

I bare my teeth at him. Not a smile, but a warning. At least, I hope.

He looks down at my hand, then up at my mouth and features. "I've never met anyone or anything like yourself, so I can't say how you'd respond. For a cambion, drinking aether is like drinking a brief round of happy thoughts. Whole thoughts." He tosses his glass back. "Less of a concern for me than for Kane, but it feels nice nonetheless. And won't destroy your liver." He considers me for a moment, face soft—until it isn't. "Now that Selwyn's punishment has been met, you and I have unfinished business, Briana Matthews. I'll only ask once more. Your red aether. Who made your arrangement?"

I jerk away. The drink sloshes over my fingers and his carpet. "No one."

He takes my glass lightly and sets it behind him on his desk. "Well, never say I wasn't hospitable at first."

Valec walks us to an elevator down the hall, refusing to answer my questions any further. He doesn't bother taking my arm in hand or forcing me with him; I know he's much faster and stronger than I am. Valec's gait is unnaturally fluid and deliberate. Now that I've witnessed his power, I see violence in his every step and hear it beneath every long vowel in his Southern drawl. When we reach the old elevator, Valec pulls the rusted accordion-style gate open with a jarring clang. He gestures for me to enter first.

Once inside, the elevator shudders before moving impossibly slow to a higher level. Halfway up, Valec pulls the lever, stopping us with a shaking rattle. "I do have one question."

My fingers flex at my sides, a silent thrill at Arthur's strength in them once more. Imagining myself punching Valec in his smiling mouth. But what use would it be? Valec is faster than Sel—it doesn't matter how strong I am, he'd break two bones before I could even land a hit.

"What is it?"

He circles around to lean on the door opposite, eyes sparkling. "It's optional."

"Fine," I say.

He steps into my space, hands in his pockets. With a voice dripping in molasses, low and sweet, he says, "You and the Kingsmage. There's obviously chemistry, but I can't quite read the rest. Is it an exclusive thing, or . . . ?"

My eyes roam across the floor, as if his words—or the situation—could make sense if I could rearrange them and see them plain. I glare at him. "You know that's a rude question to ask someone, even in the Onceborn world?"

"'Onceborn'?" Valec barks a laugh, tossing his head back. "Oh, they have gotten you *good*, haven't they? The Legendborn with all of their honorifics and hierarchies, who gets power and who doesn't, who is worthy and who isn't. I've been around long enough to know that it's all several dozen layers of assholery. There's a reason a dragon's skull sits over our threshold." Valec's voice lowers. "The Pendragon and his ilk are *not* welcome here. The Kingsmage is *lucky* he's here suffering without his charge, because if the Scion of Arthur were here tonight, this crowd would tear him apart. In fact, I'd kill him right before Kane's eyes just to be able to watch them both suffer at once. With joy."

I swallow hard. "Is that so?"

Valec releases a long, frustrated breath. "If you of all people have fallen for their falsehoods and perversions of history, then you're perhaps more silly than I'd previously imagined."

"Me, of all people?"

He tilts his head. "A daughter of the enslaved. Your ancestors were once considered property by the colonizers and their descendants. Your body viewed as a means to an end. The Order is still upholding thousand-year-old traditions as if they had been written yesterday, so why would they release a four-hundred-year-old one?" His eyes flash. "Whatever knowledge or power these white folks have *deigned* to give you, whatever little Oaths they've let you make, it's all a gesture. You've seen the Regents' true faces. They may allow one of their precious Scions to share their knight's gifts with you, but instead of honoring your sacrifice, they'll demand your gratitude. When you die in service to the Order, instead of celebrating your life, they will brandish your death as evidence of their benevolent inclusivity."

Everything he says is true. I've seen it. I know it. Nothing about what he has said is off the mark. Perhaps the only thing I could clarify is that it doesn't even matter if I represent the very crux of those thousand-year-old traditions. They will still find a way to claim my power as their own. Ignore its origins, because

those origins discomfort them. And expect my humility for surviving the violence of a system they helped build, maintain, and benefit from.

"Thanks for the reminder," I whisper, nodding. "And the warning."

He hits the button, shaking the elevator to life. "A warning you best listen
to before it's too late."

I step onto the roof, and immediately shield my eyes from the bright glare of
stage lights. The rooftop of the Crossroads Lounge is high enough to look out
across miles of pine forest into an endless night sky.

The view would be beautiful, if there weren't an audience on one end and a
stage stained with old blood on the other.

Even outdoors, the air is thick with an aether smell that clogs my throat. A
bit sickly like the warlock's scent, but heavy and rich in my nose like Valec's. Are
these the aether signatures of those who live closer to the Shadowborn world
than the Order does?

"Bree!" Sel's voice reaches me from somewhere to the left. It takes a second
to find him, but when I do, my heart sinks. He's in a large rectangular cage to
the right of a stage. Metal bars a few inches apart on all sides, tall enough to fit
an adult standing up. He's shaking his palms at his sides, as if trying to cool a
burn—the bars must be enchanted the same as the doorknob in Valec's office.
I'm sure he tried to break them as soon as they threw him in there. Even from
here, though, I can see that his eyes have cooled to a burnt orange. Valec's
aether treatment must have worked some. I turn away, unable to look any longer without thinking of what he'd done to me. To us.

"Bree!" Alice's voice draws my attention to the audience. She and William
are seated in the center of the crowd, surrounded by people dressed in Valec's
dark red and gold colors. Waitstaff and bartenders, performers and bouncers.
Some of whom have made deals with demons, by the looks of the varying den-
sities of aether swirling around their bodies.

Alice's fists are balled on her lap, and at the moment, I'm grateful that she
doesn't have any powers of her own; whatever happens to me and Sel, Valec

doesn't seem the type to hold on to a regular human who hasn't offended him. When I look at William, he holds his wrist up at eye level and taps it with a forefinger, a reminder of the time. Is it close to midnight? And even if it were, would I want him to risk using Gawain's strength?

"Our offender is here. Say hello, everyone, to the lovely Briana." Valec sweeps forward, holding his left hand out to me.

The crowd releases a mixture of colorful insults and boos, which I can only interpret to mean they know that my "display" earlier with Alonzo was not a planned demonstration. That lie was for the patrons, not the Lounge staff.

The stage shakes when Alonzo steps up on the opposite side, already swollen to ten feet with biceps the size of watermelons. He doesn't hold a weapon; instead, he pounds a fist into one palm over and over. Each impact sends a ripple of stone over his skin, making him look like a hybrid between a human and a boulder. My mind flashes to the demon that attacked me and Lark. So, that was what Alonzo bargained for: the powers of an uchel.

The bartender with long silver hair appears at my elbow and pulls me up a set of stairs until I'm under the hot lights, across from Alonzo.

Valec steps between the stage and the crowd, turning with a flourish.

"Friends, we have here someone who refuses to hold up their end of the bargain!"

A rising "Boo!" ripples across the roof, echoing back from one side to the other in stereo.

"Yes, yes. And what do we say when terms are violated?"

"Death or deal!" someone screams from the back.

"Yes, indeed," Valec crows. He turns a sly eye to Sel, who is prowling from one end of the cage to the next. "Death or deal."

"What the hell does that mean?" I shout.

Valec regards me, hands on his hips. "Well, you can pay the price for your crimes against Alonzo and my business by offering a death—yours, his, one of your friends, I don't care—or by offering a deal." He grins wide, fangs glinting. "Demons do love a bargain."

"What's the deal?"

"That's up to you. Do you have information of value?" In a blink he is perched on a stool on the far end of the stage, a slow grin on his face. He looks up at Sel. "Last call."

"Stop!"

Approaching through the crowd is a tall white man in a disheveled suit and open collar, escorted by the waitress we'd seen downstairs, Emma. "Valec, I need to speak with you."

"He wouldn't wait downstairs," Emma says with a sniff. She pushes the man toward the stage.

Valec groans and stands, moving to the edge of the stage to look down at the newcomer. "Hello, Senator Anderson. Back again for another request for immortality? I told you, I don't do forevers—"

"No, no." The man runs a hand through his hair, eyes shifting to me, the stage, Alonzo, the crowd around him. "Can we please go to your office?"

"No, we cannot," Valec snaps. "State your business."

The man wrings his hands in front of him, nodding as if to encourage himself to speak up. "I'm in a bind, Valec."

Valec's attention sharpens. "Show me."

The man digs into his breast pocket and produces a wrinkled sheet of paper, folded longwise.

Valec takes the paper and skims it, his face darkening. "Can't help you."

The man looks like he's swallowed a frog. "But . . . but I need help renegotiating, he . . . abandoned his side of the bargain—you're a broker—"

Valec sighs. "This bargain was unregulated and it's been signed in blood. There is no renegotiating a done deal. If you wanted my guidance, you should have come to me first and paid my prices to broker the deal for you." He hands the paper back, disgust twisting his features. "What's done is done."

"No, no," Anderson pleads. "He said it would just require the last five years of my life, not . . . not this!"

The broker shakes his head. "There's nothing there about the final five years of life, Senator. All it says is 'five years of biological time on the plane of the living.' Let me guess, he's taking it from your sleep?"

Anderson's mouth works open and closed, and I see the prominent bags under his eyes clearly for the first time. "I can't sleep. Not for longer than an hour, maybe two. Every night I try . . . it's been *weeks*, Valechaz . . . my doctor says I'll die if I don't rest. . . ."

"You asked for lifelong riches and in exchange unknowingly signed away that which keeps you alive. Tale as old as time. Your suffering will feed the other party for years." Valec calls for Emma to come back, and another bouncer-looking person joins her. "When the language is not exact, creative license will be taken. What did you expect when you made a deal with a demon?"

Anderson falls to Valec's feet before he can be taken away. "I'm begging you! I have a family!"

A sneer lifts Valec's lips and his eyes flash crimson. "You were warned. Unregulated bargains never serve the weaker being, and yet now you come into *my* house and insult me?" Valec raises one booted foot, pushing the senator back up by the shoulder. "Leave. Before I kick you over this roof myself."

"Valec!" the man cries, but his screams grow faint when Emma and the other bouncer pull the Senator back by one arm each, dragging him to the exit and leaving a stunned silence in the crowd in their wake.

Valec crosses his arms and tuts. "The old white men lawyers always think they know best." He pivots on his heel, all anger and irritation gone as if it had never been, and spreads his hands wide. "Shall we continue?"

The crowd cheers in response.

"Wait! I offer a bargain!" Alice's voice rings across the crowd, sending my stomach plummeting.

Valec turns again, this time with interest. "Another interruption, this time by one of our guests in question?" He beckons her forward, stopping his security team from their approach. "Hello, small human. Come here and speak up."

"Alice, stop!" I shout, and she ignores me entirely.

"I have something to offer." She raises her chin as she walks, but I can hear the slight tremor in her voice. See the fear in her shallow breaths. What is she doing? "Y-you s-seem to value integrity and transparency in business, is that right?"

Valec gives her an appreciative look. "That's right. Anything worth doing in the dark is worth doing in the light."

Alice pushes her glasses up on her nose and turns on her lawyer voice. "If you let Bree and Sel and all of us go, and help us meet with Lucille, I'll tell you something happening in your business *right now* that violates much more than the terms of our agreement for entry. Something that's costing you customers. And money, probably in the thousands. Maybe more."

The crowd murmurs in low tones. Valec regards her for a long moment. "I swear to hear you out, and if I find your information as valuable as you say, I will release you and your friends." He shakes his head. "But you better make it good."

He urges her closer. Alice walks forward and cups her hand around Valec's ear. "Quiet as you can make it," he murmurs, and Alice nods. As she talks, his eyes grow wide in shock, then narrow in anger. "And you saw this yourself?" She nods again. When she's done, his eyes roam her features, looking for any sign of a trick. Then, without saying another word, he darts to the side of the stage and drags the silver-haired bartender out by her upper arm.

"Is it true, Miranda?"

Miranda's face is painted with a mixture of surprise and horror. "Is what true, V?"

"That you've been stealing vials of aether." The roof falls into a hushed, stunned silence. I can't imagine anyone being foolish enough to steal from Valechaz.

She shakes her head frantically and Valec tuts. "It'll be better for your health and safety if you hand them over now."

Miranda swallows audibly, then dips her fingers down the front of her corset, pulling out three shining vials.

Valec takes them from her hand without breaking their gaze.

He sighs heavily. "Well, this night has taken a turn."

35

ONCE THE ROOF is cleared and Miranda removed by Alonzo, Alice and William come running to me while Valec himself releases Sel.

Alice reaches me first. "Are you all right?"

I blink. "Sort of."

Valec snorts from across the roof. "You're fine."

William steps forward and tilts my face so he can get a better view. "You've been crying." He turns to Valec accusingly. "What did you do to her?"

Valec raises his hands. "You are a suspicious bunch, aren't you?" He points at Sel, who stumbles out of the cage. "I didn't make her cry, *he* did!"

"What's that mean?" William asks.

"It means Valec removed Sel's mesmer on me," I say.

"His mesmer?" William frowns. "On you?"

Alice glares. "What mesmer?"

"He's been tricking me. Hiding his descent in an illusion so I couldn't see him changing."

William's face pales. "You couldn't see it?

I shake my head. Of course it was just me. All of those times William and Sel had bickered over a simmering frustration I didn't understand.

"I said he looked rough . . . ," Alice says, face blanching. "I—I thought you saw it, too."

"I didn't," I mumble.

William whirls to Sel, eyes hot with anger. "How long, Selwyn?"

"Since the plane," I bite out, glaring at Sel. "He mesmered me on the plane when you all were asleep."

"Bree." Sel takes a slow step toward me, then halts at the look on my face. "I'm so sorry. . . ."

I turn away from him. "I don't want to hear it."

"Me neither." Alice's hands ball into fists. "You are a real piece of shit, you know that, Kingsmage? How *dare* you—" Sel flinches.

"Just . . . stop." I wave my hand. "I can't. Not right now."

Alice looks back at me, then to Sel, then to me once more. "This isn't over."

"We're not done talking about this, Selwyn," William says lowly. The disappointment and anger rolling off him are enough that even I would back away. Sel, for his part, nods once.

"Yes, yes, you'll all yell at Kane later. I don't need to be involved," Valec says, exasperated. "Here at the Crossroads Lounge, we like to expose dirty laundry, not clean it."

"The Crossroads," Alice repeats slowly. "I finally figured it out. The bar name. I get it now. My dad likes the blues."

Valec rolls his eyes. "Congratulations, you and your father have good taste."

"Can someone explain why we're talking about music?" asks William.

"Blues folklore says that a musician can go to the crossroads at midnight to meet the man in black," Sel explains in a hoarse voice. "The devil."

Valec's smile is disturbingly pleased. "Oh, do go on, I like a nice story. Especially told in that sullen, unhappy voice of yours, Kingsmage. Do you ever smile?" Valec turns to me. "Does he ever smile?"

"Rarely," Alice mutters.

"I like you," Valec says. "What's your name?"

"I'm Alice."

"I know this story, too," I add. "My dad used to tell it. If the bluesman sells his soul to the devil, he'll gain the ability to play the guitar like no one before or after. Like Robert Johnson did."

"The exact words were 'musical talent beyond human imagining,'" Valec says, tilting his head back. "One of my first deals."

"You're the devil?!" Alice screeches.

"No, sweetheart. But it makes for a nice story." Valec leans forward. "I just help with the deals. Greater demons don't need aether for physical form, but they do still need to feed. Raw, negative human emotions and energies are delicious, but it's like a whale eating plankton. Demons spend all their energy feeding, all day, just to get a full meal."

"So, you lure humans in for demon food," Sel says. "You truly are scum."

Valec grins. "I am scum, but there are worse, believe me. For example, I don't do murder contracts, while my competitors do. I find it difficult to assess the value of murdering a third party, especially when I don't know who the third party is." He frowns. "How do you begin to calculate that bargain? The math's impossible."

Alice laughs nervously. "Not at all terrifying. Not at all." She exchanges glances with me. "So, I'm gathering there are very unsavory brokers. What does that make you, Valec?"

Valec tugs on his vest. "Oh, I facilitate barters of musical genius, frozen youth, untold-of wealth, artistic brilliance. You name the skill, ability, or magical power, and humans want it. The right kind of demon can offer any one of those things, in exchange for fair payment. I draw up the contracts between the two parties, see to it that all are consenting and agreed on the terms, and help execute."

"For a fee, I'm assuming," I say.

"I ensure that everyone keeps their end of the deal," Valec says. "Speaking of—Lucille?"

"Yes, please," I say, back to business and ready to leave as soon as we can.

"Follow me." Valec walks to the elevator, whistling as he goes.

When we emerge in the lower level, the entire floor has transformed. Chairs and tables swept to one side, the floor open, and only a few faces tucked in dark corners of booths. A hot sensation of anxiety rides up my spine, making my skull tingle. When we'd arrived, I'd thought most of the people here were humans, but then there was the warlock who had become something . . . else. Now, I see an older blond woman smoking a silver pipe filled with swirling yellow aether. Each time she inhales, her eyes glow gold. Each time she exhales, they turn back to brown. She watches as Valec leads us to a hallway that loops around the main stage.

The five of us walk down the hall and Valec knocks on the door at the end.

A woman's voice calls out. "I'm not to be disturbed when I'm with clients."

"I'll make it up to the client. We've got a situation," Valec calls back.

The door swings open, and a Black woman with gray hair in braids wearing a long green dress exits. "I don't like being disturbed, Valechaz."

"Hi, niece." Valec smiles warmly. She scowls, then surveys the rest of us, pausing briefly on my face. "Everyone, the Grand Dame, Lucille."

"Niece?" I echo, looking between the two of them.

Lucille huffs. "He's my great-uncle seven times over."

I blink, head spinning.

"How old are you?" I ask Valec.

He gives a heavy sigh. "Two hundred and five."

We all gawk at him. Alice's eyes look like they might leave her skull in shock.

"You're . . . but you *look* . . ." I stop speaking when displeasure shifts across Valec's features. Sensitive subject, I guess.

"Balanced cambions are rare." Valec's lips press into a grim line, and he looks away.

"And arrogant," Selwyn grumbles.

Valec shoots him a hot glare. "I can afford to be arrogant. I've earned it. You and me, Kane?" He points between them. "We are *not* the same. Or did you not notice how easily I handed you your ass upstairs?"

Lucille groans. "Why did you bring these children to me, Valechaz?"

"Because," Valec says, taking Lucille's palm in his, "my many-times-great-niece demands that her uncle bring her any Rootcrafter that crosses his path."

I freeze. I never told Valec I practiced root.

Lucille's eyes find me again with new interest. "Was that *your* power I felt earlier? It knocked me right out of a reading."

"I'm sorry. But how did *you* know I know Rootcraft?" I ask Valec.

He lifts a shoulder. "I didn't, until just now."

"D-does this mean my session's done?" A white man sitting on a round, knitted ottoman in the room behind Lucille raises his hand tentatively. He's dressed in a Georgia-peach-colored button-up shirt and sports at least an eight-o'clock shadow.

"We'll make it up to you, sir!" Valec beckons the man forward and points him down the hall, leaving us in the doorway.

"Well? Comin' in or what?" Lucille huffs and sweeps back into the room.

With a shrug, we follow, and seated beyond the edge of the door on another ottoman, pouring tea, is someone I never thought I'd see here.

"Mariah?"

Mariah blinks at me, frozen with a tea kettle in her hand.

"Oh, this night keeps getting better and better," Valec says.

36

MARIAH RUSHES FORWARD to fold me into a hug. "Oh my God. I thought I felt your root earlier, but then I said, 'No, can't be Bree, she's back at Carolina.' What the hell are you doing *here?*"

"Same question." I laugh.

"I help out my Aunt Lu on the weekends."

Lucille turns to Mariah, and in that moment, I can see the slight resemblance. The slope of her nose, the shape and shade of her full upper lip. "Mariah, you know these folks?"

Mariah stutters. "N-no, Auntie. I know Bree. She goes to my school." Mariah pauses, eyeing the rest of the room as if carefully considering whether to add more.

"And yet you are accompanied by members of the Order." Lucille steps back, staring at Sel and William. "You are here with a Kingsmage and a Scion, I'd wager. Merlins mesmer first, imprison second. They've hunted root users for centuries, and at this point, I consider them my natural enemy. Why shouldn't I turn these two over to Valec and his crew for safekeeping?"

I explain, "It's not just me. We are all fugitives from the Order."

"Fugitives?" Valec grins. "Briana, you become more fun by the second." He looks to Lucille. "That's not even the best part, Lu. That power you felt earlier? She lit up like a volcano. Spontaneous root generation."

"Hmnh." Lucille moves to sit down. "Why would anyone ask the ancestors for

that? Too much power for Valec's lil' club, especially just to put on some show."

Mariah blinks twice at me, eyes wide. She knows exactly how it's too much power and why, but she won't tell Lucille about my Bloodcraft without my permission.

At the look shared between me and her niece, some bit of understanding flickers across Lucille's face. "You got something to say, Mariah?"

"No, ma'am. I'll get us some more tea." Mariah rushes to leave the room.

"I see." Lucille looks at me, then Valec. "How'd you get my name?"

"Samira," I say.

Her eyebrows raise. "Samira Miller?" She looks at William and Sel again, this time with suspicion. "Still cannot believe you'd bring a Merlin into my office, Valechaz."

"Well," Valec says, pointing at Sel. "This one's worth about two cents. They got him void cuffed, exiled, away from his Oaths, and he's generally and otherwise a miserable sonofagun." Sel rolls his eyes up to the ceiling.

"He a danger to others?" Lucille regards Sel's features.

Valec makes an iffy sound. "Looks worse than it is. He's not that far gone." He points to William. "This one seems like he has some power, but he's smart enough to not use it until he must. And that one over there, she's human. Clever and observant."

Mariah returns to the office with a tray of tea and sets it down on the low table off to the side. Valec moves swiftly around the table, bringing chairs to a circle and pausing to hold Lucille's chair out especially. She offers him a wry smile, and he winks back.

"Bree, is it?"

All eyes turn to me. "Yes, ma'am."

She holds a hand up. "Lucille is fine. I assume you and your friends are here for information, assistance, or both."

"Yes," I say, looking briefly at Mariah. "Mariah knows I'm still new to this. The root I make? It's my ancestors' power. I've only done it when I was possessed or scared for my life. I have to learn how to control it."

"You keep blowing up like that, you'll have every demon at your doorstep and every Rootcrafter nearby 'bout ready to pull out their hair when you knock them out of alignment with their own ancestors."

"I know," I admit.

"Is that why you're on the run from the Order?" she asks.

"Partly. We know how to lay low, we think. It's just the help with my abilities that I need the most."

Lucille takes a sip of her tea and considers this. After a moment, she looks up to Valec, not me. "Ideal thing for a crafter like her is to forward her on to a station, then to Volition."

Valec crosses his arms. "Best place to contain all that juice, I suppose. Especially with the attacks increasing."

"Attacks?" Sel asks.

"What's Volition?" William says. I notice he's already helped himself to the tea Mariah's offered.

"You'll see," Mariah answers. I give her a look, but she just smirks.

Valec responds to Sel. "Lesser demons have been crossing over more frequently lately. Hunting aether users, strong ones. Consuming them to gain power." Valec's eyes narrow. "Word has it that they're foot soldiers. Scouts, ahead of something big coming from the other side."

Sel's attention sharpens. "Camlann."

Valec's eyes snap to his. "One of the few ancient words our worlds share, but yes. There are rumors of Camlann. Well, the Camlann of Camlanns, really. Folks are talking like this could be the last one."

"Last like, final, and then there are no more Camlanns?" I ask. "Or last like . . . big boom and it might be the demons, might be the humans, but in the end, one group is in control of the world?"

Valec shrugs. "Either scenario is bad for business, as you might imagine."

"One of those scenarios ends with humans subjugated to demons though?" Mariah says, disgust plain on her face.

"Oh, sure. That's the worst one, definitely," Valec confirms. His grin does not at all instill confidence. "In that one, the Shadow Court comes to play."

"Excuse me?" I ask.

He smirks. "Ancient rumors about the endgame of Camlann and a demon court trapped on the other side that can match the Table in numbers and strength. Before they were allegedly put away, they were beholden to no law, no belief but their own pursuit of chaos and terror."

"Bedtime stories," Sel spits. "What they tell little Merlins who think they can single-handedly win the war."

Valec smiles. "I bet that was you, wasn't it?"

"Quiet!" Lucille waves a hand. "I have appointments and I don't have time to watch two cambions snipe at each other."

"Neither do I," I murmur.

Lucille nods curtly. "Listen to me. The stations are how we move Rootcrafters whose powers are big enough to draw attention from Merlins," Lucille says pointedly. Sel shifts in his seat as she sends him a hard look. "Hard-pressed to use our network to help hide you, your friend, and these two. I need a better reason than you've got powers you can't control and the Order's looking for you. And we got more than rumors about Camlann to worry about. There's word the Hunter's afoot again."

Valec curses. "Jesus."

I freeze. "The . . . Hunter?"

"Mm-hmm," Lucille says. "We have our own boogeymen that make the Regents and their Seneschals look like pests to trick and avoid. This one's a demon that wants nothing else but to devour as much power as he can."

Valec sighs. "An ancient sonofabitch that nobody's been able to see coming or stop. He wants aether, he gets it, and he wants Rootcrafters in particular."

"Why?" I ask.

"A Rootcrafter mid-casting offers a direct line to their ancestors—that's a lot of raw power to consume. Even goruchel are scared of the Hunter because he's been known to go after them, too." Valec wiggles his brows. "They call him 'the Great Devourer.'"

Sel hisses. I swallow hard and Lucille's eyes sharpen. "Y'all know him already." A statement.

"I've . . ." The room looks at me. How do we explain Kizia without explaining who I am? How do I explain the Hunter without telling everyone what I saw in my last blood walk with Jessie? Luckily Sel answers first.

"We came across a goruchel who was scared out of her mind about this demon. She was scared of Bree's power, too."

Valec's eyes light up. "Of course she was. I saw just a bit of that root and I have a feeling you weren't even firing on all cylinders, were you, power-house?"

"I . . . I don't know how powerful I am. I don't know how to call it on purpose." I swallow. "But I'd like to. That's why we need your help."

"Bree wasn't raised in root," Mariah intervenes. "But she's good people, Auntie. Just atypical."

I nod. "It's true. The women in my family didn't practice in a community."

"And why would that be?" Lucille asks, her head tilted to the side.

Mariah and I exchange glances, and she dips her head, encouraging me forward. If it weren't for her familiar face, I'd never say the words out loud. But I have to.

"My ancestor was a Bloodcrafter," I say, and add quickly, "out of necessity."

Lucille stills, and beside her, Valec makes a thoughtful sound.

"Bloodcraft is a sin," the older woman says.

"I know."

"There is no necessity worth its cost."

My anger flares. "You weren't there. You can't judge her."

"And you were?" Valec asks.

I nod. "I saw it happen. In a memory walk."

He and Lucille exchange glances. He shrugs, raising his hands. "I got nothin'. If she saw it in a walk, she saw it in a walk."

"Not my place to judge your ancestor, you're right." Lucille puts her tea down. "But I can judge *you* all I want. Do you think your power is worth its cost? Whatever that cost is, you must know it by now."

I blink, taken aback. Do I think my powers are worth the cost? The wound of grief from losing my mother sits open in my chest. It feels like it will never truly heal, no matter how much I acknowledge its presence. Then there are wounds my ancestors carried from one generation to the next. All the loss, multiplied and compounded and cumulative. All that running.

Don't be scared. Fight.

"I'm not scared of the risks, or of hard work. I'll fight what my ancestors wanted to fight but couldn't. I will *make* the power worth the cost by how I use it."

Her brows raise. "Bold claims. Tall order."

I glance at Sel, borrowing his economy of language. "I'm aware."

"Lu," Valec begins slowly. "If you can train Bree here to call up that root on command, she might be able to take the Hunter down herself. Hers is the only power I've seen that rivals his from all that he's consumed over the years." He shrugs. "Could be an advantage all around here."

Sel stands. "No, we're not asking for help just so you can use Bree for your own ends."

"It's not a bad idea," I interject. I hold a hand to stop him from going any further. "I can't just keep drawing attention to my community and leaving them helpless. If the Hunter is afoot again, I need to learn how to stop him. Not just for the Rootcrafters but for myself too. It's only a matter of time before he finds me," I say quietly, "just like he found my ancestors who had this same power."

"If your people had this root-generating ability, then I'm certain the Hunter was after them every chance he could get." Lu looks at me appraisingly. "I admire your ambition. And Valechaz has lived long enough to know when something or someone might be useful to the community. If we help you gain control over your powers, you will help us all in turn by facing the Hunter one day, when you're ready. Call it a bargain. An exchange."

I nod. "Agreed."

She smirks. "Excellent. You'll need to be at the station within the hour."

Mariah leads us out to a staff parking lot behind the Lounge, informing us that the next station is a house up the road. She asks me to ride with her to catch up, and I agree. Alice climbs into the back seat without asking, leaving William and Sel to ride together in Jonas's car.

Right now, I'm still not feeling great about sitting near Sel. Or at least, when we talk, I'm not ready to do it in front of other people.

But I don't expect Valec to hop in the back seat of Mariah's Jeep as well.

"I'd like to see y'all to the next stop," he says. Mariah looks at him in the rearview and rolls her eyes.

"You're no conductor; you're just nosy." She starts the engine and pulls out, pausing for Sel and William to drive up behind us.

She glances at me. "You look like you got a question."

I look at Valec, then back at her. "Are y'all related?"

"Not by blood. Not the way he and my auntie Lu are," Mariah says. "Thank God."

"Mariah," Valec chides. "You were so sweet as a baby; now you're just mean."

"But I thought Rootcrafters would," I say, shrugging, "avoid cambions."

Mariah sniffs. "We aren't a monolith. Some of us do. Some of us don't."

Valec sits back in the seat, draping his arm behind Alice. "Some of us cast our half-demon infants out to freeze to death at night."

Alice looks appalled. "That happened to you?"

"Yep."

"Why?"

Valec tilts his head back and forth. "My mother was seduced by an incubus, tale as old as time. Demons love chaos, love making trouble. I don't blame her. An enslaved crossroads child running amok on a plantation? Mighta been fine. Mighta made life a thousand times worse." His eyes flash red in the rearview. "When her life was already a thousand times worse than you've ever imagined."

I twist in my seat to stare at him.

"What?" he asks. For a moment, he looks like he could be a college-aged boy, out for a joyride with three girls. Mischievous and handsome and too aware of being both. But he's not. He's a two-hundred-and-five-year-old half-demon.

"It's a wild, random thought," I say.

He smiles. "I love those."

"Was . . ." I narrow my eyes, turning inward to my own memory. "Was your mother's name Pearl?"

Valec's eyes widen. "Yes, it was. And how exactly do you know that, Briana Matthews?"

I squeeze the seat between my hands. "A memory walk."

"With Doc Hartwood?" Mariah asks.

I nod. "Yeah. 1815. Her ancestor Louisa took me to see Pearl giving birth in a cabin. Cecilia, her other ancestor, was there too. A woman named Betty and another named Katherine. Pearl had a baby with glowing yellow eyes."

Valec grows very, very still.

"I . . ." In the silence, I realize I may have already overstepped. There is no clear path to reverse course, either. "I'm sorry that happened to you."

Valec rides in silence for a moment. Then he says, "Like I said, I don't blame her. Bondage is no way to live." He turns, gazing out the window. "Or die, for that matter."

He doesn't speak again.

37

"THIS CONDUCTOR, MISS Hazel, is so sweet," Mariah comments. She jumps out of the Jeep and walks around to the front to meet me. "Miss Hazel is Aunt Lu's partner of . . . God, thirty-five years? This house is a station we use sometimes. Hazel'll probably offer you a four-course meal so your bellies are full until the next stop."

"What's with the code?" Alice asks. "Stations, conductors, stops."

I answer before Mariah does. "Are we following the Underground Railroad?"

"Not quite," Valec clarifies. He comes to stand beside me, arms crossed, gazing at an old home up a ways from where we've parked. "There wasn't just one route, anyway, and no one really knew all of them, or even the full extent of any single route, for security reasons. But we're using the technology and knowledge left behind, yes. Keeping our people safe still looks a lot like hiding from those who would do us harm." He looks back at Sel pulling in behind us as we speak.

"Technology?" Alice asks.

Valec smirks at me, like we're sharing a secret. "Ingenuity is more than bytes and LEDs. Always has been and always will be."

Our conductor, Miss Hazel, is a short, round woman who is mostly apron and smiles. She greets Mariah at the door with a full-bodied hug, the kind where you sort of fold into the other person. When she does the same to me, my insides shine and vibrate at her touch. I inhale a heavenly cloud of lavender, mint, and sage. Cocoa butter and shea—from her tiny curls—swirl in my nose and mouth like magic.

"Come on inside, honey." Miss Hazel offers an easy, Southern welcome in a voice edged with age, but her glowing, deep brown skin is smooth and soft. She wraps a surprisingly strong arm around me, and guides me through her front door. Walking into her home is like entering another world.

The warm, rich scents of all-day cooking go straight to my stomach. I identify them right away: the sharp, mouth-watering smell of baked mac and cheese, fresh-baked cornbread sitting out to cool, and, underneath it all, hot oil hanging heavy in the air from something deep-fried. In every corner, green ferns and string of pearls plants hang from terra-cotta and sapphire baskets. Potted plants stand like guardians at each threshold, ushering us through a den and a living room with plastic-covered couches. In the back of the house there's a small, well-used kitchen with doilies on the table.

Hunger must show on my face, because an appreciative, proud smile spreads wide across Miss Hazel's face. "Looks like you need a plate."

Valec and Mariah join us and introduce William and Sel to Miss Hazel. Her eyes find his void cuffs immediately, and she raises a brow at Valec.

"A Merlin," Miss Hazel says, a negative hum in her throat.

He lifts his hands. "Approved by Lucille."

Sel dips his head, pink flooding his cheeks. "Thank you for having me, but I'll stay outside. To do a perimeter sweep and patrol. If you'll excuse me."

She makes a "hmph" sound that might be approval, and Sel leaves. I could intervene, I think, but this isn't my home, and Sel made his own decision. Pushing Miss Hazel to accept him would backfire, and the history here is too much for me to handle in the middle of the night as a guest in someone's home.

After we eat, Miss Hazel shoos William to the back of the house to settle in. William goes gladly, with a "Thank you, ma'am." Valec takes Mariah's car back to the Lounge and says he'll return tomorrow.

Mariah urges me and Alice to join her on Miss Hazel's screened-in porch.

Miss Hazel calls out, "Y'all girls sit. I'll fix us some tea."

I duck under bound herbs hanging at intervals from the porch ceiling. Mullein, sweet mint, and others I don't recognize in bunches of leaves and gathered roots wrapped tightly in wheat-colored twine.

The porch extends in a square out the back of the house, a peninsula in the green expanse of her backyard. Beyond the yard is a deep wooded area where daylight goes to rest. Woods like that pull you in because they feel like an adventure. But you just know those same adventurin' woods will send you back with all the souvenirs nobody wants: poison ivy oil, then a rash; ticks in your collar; chiggers in your socks.

"What do you think?" Mariah folds her legs underneath her on a wicker loveseat.

I drop into a dusty, creaking Adirondack chair and stretch my legs out. "I'm so stuffed that I'm not sure I can think right now. That was straight-up Thanksgiving food."

Miss Hazel calls to us through a window over her sink. "Used to be we'd eat like this every Sunday."

Mariah shakes her head with a smile. "Some of us still do. My mother lives in Fountain, North Carolina, and I think she makes fried chicken once a week. And hush puppies."

Miss Hazel whistles. "Yes, Lawd." The kettle clinks onto the gas burner. She pushes through the screen door to join us. "Pitt County Fountain?"

"That's the one," Mariah says.

"Coupla granny women out that way."

"Yep."

I drop my head back against the chair. "What's a granny woman?"

Mariah smiles. "Root doctor. Herbalist."

Miss Hazel taps her foot to get her rocking chair going. "Not many of us around nowadays, but I still see a few."

She sips her tea and fixes me with a long stare. "That Merlin boy. You trust him?"

Alice and Mariah both wait for my answer. "I trust him with my life. . . ." That's all I can manage, but it's true.

Miss Hazel hums, pushing up from her chair. "Then I'll go fix the Merlin a plate."

We all sleep in the next day.

By the time I make it to the kitchen, yawning every step of the way, Alice and William are at the counter chatting with Mariah over a book of pressed herbs.

Outside, the trees here have already released their leaves, save for a few that float down when a lazy breeze swirls through the forest.

I slide into a chair beside William. "Sel—"

"Out there already," William offers, sipping his coffee. "Came in to sleep a bit, but not for long. Wouldn't be surprised if he spent the day in the woods patrolling and licking his wounds."

"Ah."

"Mariah," Alice pipes up. "If we don't intervene right now, Bree is gonna head out to the woods and confront Selwyn instead of, I don't know, taking a beat to recover from the last day. Help."

"I have an idea." She smiles at Alice, then me. "Eat breakfast and meet me on the porch."

That's how I end up sitting on a cushion in front of the wicker loveseat with Mariah's knees at my back and her hands in my hair. "This *hair*!" she exclaims with a pin between her teeth. "Been waiting forever to get my hands in it."

"Not taking that as an insult." I say a silent thank-you that I'd just washed it a couple days ago, so whatever Mariah's doing back there will be done on relatively fresh curls. She sprays a moisturizing leave-in to coat the strands first.

"You shouldn't," she says with a laugh. She dips her hand into the jar at her hip. "It's gorgeous. But you're gonna need some sorta style to contain it while you're on the run."

"Getting attacked by demons definitely requires an updo," Alice adds. "Especially if the half-demon in your party who's supposed to protect you is an actual asshole."

Mariah makes a questioning sound. "I know we're not supposed to talk about the Merlin but, uh, there seem to be concerns."

Alice makes a face. "The list of concerns is *extremely high*. Not to mention she's dating his bonded charge."

Mariah leans over to stare at me. "*Girl!* Spill. It."

I flush and duck my head. "I am seeing his *former* charge; that's the boy he's still bonded to. Nick. He's missing in real life, but I see him sometimes when I channel Arthur. Because our ancestors, his and mine, knew each other . . . ? But Sel and I . . . my mother knew his mother. When she was hiding her Root-craft from Merlins, Sel's Merlin mother protected her. They were friends. Sel and I have a connection, but he tricked me and hid his true face. . . ." I look up to see Mariah's jaw dropped nearly to the porch floor. "What?"

"Run that back again," Mariah sputters.

"Which part?" I ask.

"All of it."

"Okay, so . . ."

By the time we finish talking and debating styles, most of my hair is pinned up in a bun with a dozen flat twists and a few curls loose at the front, and it's early afternoon.

Still no sign of Sel, but I'm not ready to talk to him just yet.

Valec returns for dinner with Mariah's car and reports in that we should be good to move on to Volition tomorrow. When I step out onto the unlit front porch after the meal, I find Valec sitting on a metal chair, long legs outstretched and booted feet crossed atop the wooden railing. "What it do, powerhouse?"

I glance down at him. Watch as he tips a silver flask back to his lips, throat working in the shadows. When he draws it away, he exhales, and bright silver vapor streams from his nose. He tips his head back and presses his lips together, then opens them to produce three shiny smoke rings that float into the air. "In need of some happy thoughts?"

"They never hurt," he says quietly. He starts to take another sip. Pauses. Offers me his flask instead.

I stare at it for a beat, then take it, tipping it back before I can hesitate. Hand it back as the liquid and aether slide down my throat. Cool, then warm. Hot, like a poker stirring the furnace behind my ribs. Not enough to throw sparks, but just enough to remind that it's there.

I find Valec watching me, brows raised. "What?" I croak. I have to cough to clear my throat.

He holds the flask out, fingers on each side so that its reflective surface faces up. A pair of bright dots stare back at me, then dim. My eyes, burning red and black, like two stoked coals.

"Interesting," he murmurs, and leans back in his chair. He puts the flask away in a breast pocket and rests his hands over his stomach, his crimson eyes peering out into the night. "Been following Kane out there. When that boy said perimeter sweep and patrol, he meant it." He jerks a chin to the driveway and field beyond it. "Started there, sweeping half a mile out. Real methodical. He's in the woods now, moving fast. Silent as death itself. If I didn't know to listen, even I would never know he was there."

I lean on the column, trying to find Sel in the darkness. I can't see him, of course. But even if no one told me he was there, I think I'd feel it.

"Sometimes," Valec says behind me, voice low. "Hunting and running blur together. You start out with a goal to chase down the bad thing, all good. But if you can't catch it, you dial your own hunger up, let your instincts take over . . . then alla sudden *you* become the most deadly thing in the woods."

I tip my head against the wall. Let the cicada song and the sky and the Southern accents soak into my bones. "You tryna tell me somethin'."

"Naw," he drawls. "Got a question though: You know why people hide things from people they care about?"

I startle at his shift in tone. "I—yes?"

"Example?"

I sigh into the darkness and turn around. "Before I knew Sel, I hid things from him. Other people too. I didn't feel safe, or I thought other people could get hurt."

"Ah." He raises a finger. "There are many reasons to hide the truth from those you do not know. But when there is care between two people, and trust built, there is only one reason that lies continue: not fear of safety, but fear of judgment. Shame and guilt are powerful motivators. Not easily overcome."

He's right. I know he is. Sel feared what I would think of him, but . . . he should have never—

Valec is at my side in a blur, tugging an onyx handkerchief out of his breast pocket. He offers it to me silently. "I may not approve of his methods—I'm very open in my business, as you know—but I admit to sympathizing. There have been times when I wanted nothing else but to be unnoticed for the thing clawing at me from within. Violations of consent and trust to the front, of course—but it's clear that he didn't wish for you to see him this way."

Valec's handkerchief is soft and smells like old leather mixed with star anise. I dab it against the corner of one eye. "He doesn't get to decide that."

"No. He doesn't."

The both of us let that sit for a minute. I'm grateful for the silence. And the perspective.

Valec opens the screen door but turns back before he goes, jerking his chin way to the left of the house. "Walk about fifty feet in, that way. He'll hear you comin'."

The door spring squeals as it closes. I take a deep breath, then walk into the darkness to hunt the deadliest thing in the woods.

The wind picks up a bit as I walk deeper into the trees.

I don't walk far. Don't need to.

"Can we talk?" I say to the swaying trees, then wait.

I feel his eyes on my skin a second before he drops down in front of me, light like a cat. I realize then that he's no longer hiding his true appearance. His eyes glitter, not ruby like Valec's, but some color in between what I knew and what he's become. The veins on his hands have disappeared.

I look around for a place to sit. A fallen log lies half-covered with moss behind me, and only a little damp. It'll do. I sit down, pulling my hoodie sleeves over my hands.

He stands before me, face resolute.

"I should never have mesmered you, and I apologize," he says. "I violated your trust. And our friendship."

I stare up at him for a long moment, try to see through the shield of formality to the person beneath. But all I can see are those times when he'd drawn me in only to lie. It makes me angry all over again. "Why?"

"May I . . . ?" He gestures to the log.

The knot in my stomach pulls tight. "Yeah."

"To explain, I think I need to start at the beginning." He settles beside me on the log, hands stuffed in his pockets.

He releases a long breath, head tipping up to the sky. "It would be easy to claim that my descent began when Nicholas was taken. But I don't think that is true. I think it started much earlier."

I put two and two together. "When you tried to kill me?"

He nods slowly. "Oaths are sealed through personal belief and intention. Belief is why Lord Davis could do all the evil he did and not be burned by his own Oaths; he believed what he did was right. I *believed* I was doing my job well when you first arrived on campus. That going after you was the right thing to do."

"I'm not excusing you," I say. "But back then, you were doing your duty. What you thought was right based on what you knew. I didn't know what I was either."

He laughs, but it's a hollow, cracking sound in his chest. "It is not my duty to be cruel."

He stares out into the woods as he speaks. "Oath bonds are extraordinarily powerful magic. Meant to elicit responses in the bonded parties almost before they can think. Under the bonded Oaths, decisions become instincts. Thoughts become impulses. Useful in battle, when life and death are decided in split seconds. The Kingsmage Oath links Nicholas and me very deeply. More deeply than I think he and I have ever spoken aloud. . . ." He shakes his head, redirecting himself from a lifetime of memories. "We've been Oathed to each other long enough to understand and anticipate the nuances of the bond. When I sense that he's in danger, I don't just detect his alarm or fear, I feel it myself as though *my* life is in danger. That immediacy of a threat, the desperation to live. It's mine as well as his, so that I am forced to act. And . . . when he senses my intent to destroy life, he has told me that that intent feels like his own. He hardly has to tell me, honestly; I can *see it* inside him, in his eyes. The bloodlust. For a few moments, what I want to destroy, he wants to destroy."

I stiffen, a sick feeling swirling in my stomach. "So, the night of the second trial . . ."

"By then, everyone could see how Nicholas felt about you. Me more than anyone else, I imagine. I was angry that he wasn't listening to my warnings, angry that I sensed something was wrong but didn't have proof." His eyes blaze when they meet mine. "You remember that I planned our partnership during the trial. Planned to trick you, corner you, and kill you. I knew Nicholas would feel a desire to kill someone that night, because it would come over from me to him through the bond. I planned for him to eventually discover that the person he'd wanted to . . . was someone he——" He shakes his head, eyes hard. "That it was you."

For a moment, breath feels impossible. All I can do is remember that night. The rage on Nick's face, threaded through with fear for me and . . . pain.

"Nicholas and I know precisely how to hurt each other. As children, we'd manipulate Lord Davis's regard. Pull rank and title to suit our whims. And that's *outside* of the sparring arena. Within it, as his Kingsmage, I could never strike with the intent to harm him, but I've given my share of bruises and black eyes and even broken bones. I always fought him in the name of making him a better warrior, better king, better opponent. All worthy intentions, as far as the Oath is concerned."

A small, dark smile tugs at the corner of his lips; their long rivalry flashes in his eyes. Fights won and lost.

"We both know how to exploit the bond, find the loopholes. It was a terrible thing for him to do, sucker punching me that night, because he did so knowing the only intent I *could* have used to strike him would be an unworthy one: retaliation. I won't defend what he did." He inhales, drawing himself up. "But I also can't defend that I was intentionally cruel. The morning after the first Oath, he came to me. Said he'd felt my desire to kill you and *begged* me to leave you alone, because of what it did to him"—he taps his chest—"here. He said it felt wrong, wanting to hurt you.

"So, I knew that what I sent through the bond would poison the part of him that was beginning to love you. Knew that if I failed, he'd have to live with the memory of wishing his girlfriend dead. Not just the memory, but the *feeling* of wanting to kill you himself, with his bare hands. Murderous intent like that is one of the worst feelings in the world. Haunting. Destructive. And for someone like Nick . . . it would tear him apart in a way he'd never forget and never heal from. And I did not care. I believed I was right, all in the name of *duty*."

There are no words to assuage Sel's guilt or accept his confession. I'm not the one to do either, even if there were. Cruelty and harm can be felt secondhand, but reconciliation cannot be offered by a third party. And I can tell by the desolate look on his face that he wouldn't want to hear any words of acceptance anyway.

"That's what you meant when you said that you could never make it up to Nick?"

"If I am honest with myself . . . I abused our Oath because it didn't seem fair that he was happy when I wasn't." A pause. "And because I could."

I remember thinking that night had changed the way Nick saw Sel; after we'd come back to the Lodge, the anger toward his Kingsmage had sharpened to an unforgiving point.

Now I realize that only Nick and Sel understood what truly happened between them. The abuse on both sides. Part of me wants to be upset with Nick for not sharing the full story with me . . . but how do you explain to someone else a cruelty specifically crafted to hurt you? There aren't enough words to capture customized malice, and the ache of trying to find those words sometimes does just as much damage.

"Is that night why you think you'd already begun to succumb to your blood?" I ask.

"Yes," he admits, "but only when I view it in retrospect. I'm loath to admit it, but at the time, I wasn't worried that I was losing my humanity." His voice is so quiet, I have to lean in to hear it. "That came later."

I frown. "When did you worry?"

He shifts on the log to face me, eyes darting across my face so quickly I almost don't feel the sparks.

"When I saw your bravery. Your fury. Your heart. When I started to see . . ." He swallows, brows knitting together. "When I started to see what I believe Nicholas sees when he looks at you. Only a monster could look at you and want to destroy you, Bree."

The knot loosens in my chest a fraction. "But you were still serving your Oath to Nick, then. So even though you were worried, you couldn't have succumbed that night, not technically . . . right?"

"Perhaps. But my behavior then affected how I behaved later, after Nicholas was taken." He inhales. "By the time the Regents arrived, I had been feeling the effects of not fulfilling my Oath for several days."

I look at him, alarmed. "That early? Sel . . ."

"I thought I had more time." He lifts a shoulder. "After I escaped, I did go to the cabin as I've told you. I tried to find my mother's cure. . . . When I didn't, all I could think about was finding a way to hide a little longer. From everyone. Once the physical changes began, I knew my nature would soon follow."

"But you *didn't* hide from everyone, did you?" I stand, fighting the tremor in my voice. "William wouldn't let you carry me inside after Jonas and Kizia. William told you to drink that aether shot to help balance you. Alice said she thought you looked rough, and I blew her off, because I couldn't see. And it wasn't just them. It was Erebus and Cestra and *Valec*. That—that random *waitress* you flirted with at the bar—" I grind my teeth. "They all knew, but I didn't. Because you didn't trust me."

Sel lowers his head, digs his fingers through his hair. "I was raised not to trust *myself*! But I do trust you—"

"Then why?" I cry. "*Why* would you lie to me about this, every time I asked you if you were okay? Did you think that I wasn't strong enough to deal with it?"

He laughs. "You are the strongest person I have ever met, Bree."

"What about Nick's trust in you?" I exclaim. "He said you'd leave before you'd ever hurt me!"

"And he would have been right, before! I *wanted* him to be right. Leaving you is what I should have done the moment I saw that I was changing." He looks away. "That alone was reason enough."

"Why didn't you?"

"Because . . ." His throat works. He swipes his tongue over his lower lip. Takes a deep breath. "Because my judgment is not what it should be around you, Bree. It never has been."

His confession sucks all of the air from my lungs, and in its place I am breathing confusion, gasping in pain, exhaling anger. Together, they close my throat tighter. When I manage to speak, my voice comes out in a thin whisper.

"Those times when we were close. The plane. The safehouse. Last night in the Lounge when you touched me, said those things . . ." I shake my head. "I don't know what was real, and what was an illusion created from your—your *fear.*"

Sel stands slowly, approaching me in careful steps. I look up at him, hoping to find something in his dark, piercing eyes to hold on to. "If you hear nothing else I have said tonight, hear this. My mesmers were only ever a visual illusion." His voice is low, determined. "Please know that I did not exert any other influence over you."

The knot breaks open in my chest. Tears prick at my eyes, in my nose. "So, I can't even blame your mesmer for . . . for how I felt."

Sel inhales a slow, shaky breath, releases it. "No."

I sniff, wrapping my arms around myself. "But you took *advantage* of those feelings, Sel. You abused our connection, just like you—" I stop myself short, the echoes rippling through me.

"Just like I abused my connection to Nicholas," Sel continues. "I know. But with you, I did not mean to. I did not want you to see the part of myself that feels inhuman. I did not realize—" He steps forward. I step back. There's a fierce, raw light in his eyes when he says, "Bree, those moments between us . . . they were *real.* I swear it."

"I deserve better than lies," I say through gritted teeth. "You were lying to me, lying to yourself. . . . How can I know what was real?"

His face twists in pain, eyes squeeze shut. "I suppose you can't," he whispers.

The warm thing opening up between us for weeks snaps closed. I don't know how to open it again. If I even want to.

I sigh and walk around him. "I'm going back to the house."

"Bree." His voice stops me. I can feel the fierce, fond expression on his face, even if I can't see it. I turn back to see him standing there, the fallen angel I know, more demon than ever. Not from how he appears, but by what he's done. "There's something else you should know."

As if my heart could break any further. I release a heavy breath. "What is it?"

"I feel better now, after the aether Valec gave me. I think I'll be okay for a while longer. He's given me a few vials to take with me. . . ." His voice fades away.

"That's good, Sel," I murmur, ready to turn away.

He's not done. "But before we keep traveling together, you should know that no one knows exactly what would happen if a Merlin killed an Awakened Scion of Arthur."

My breath catches. "What are you—"

"We are generations and generations removed from the original half-demon Merlin and our full-demon ancestor, all of us. But Shadowborn blood is *strong*. 'If a fully Awakened Arthur is struck down by Shadowborn blood, the Legend-born Lines will be broken forever.' I don't think it has ever occurred to any Kingsmage in history that that warning might apply to us. No one has ever considered it. I couldn't kill Nicholas even if the demon wanted me to. Not without killing myself. But *you* . . . we're not . . ." His eyes are pleading and helpless and wild in the night.

I watch him for a moment, too thrown off guard to respond. "Are you saying you're going to kill me?"

He shakes his head rapidly. "No. I'm saying that it kills me that I *could* have. And it scares me that I might still."

I lift my chin. "I could send you away. Tell you to find Nick."

He stuffs his hands in his pockets. "You could."

The possibility hangs between us, because I am the blade that he's waiting for. The one that could sever him from me and from us. I think of the place in my mind still healing from what the Regents did. From Tacitus, wiping my memories and sending me to sleep. The serum, robbing me of the magic in my veins. Arthur, holding his knowledge over my head, keeping me from not just Nick, but the knowledge and power I am owed.

He swallows hard. "I won't ask you for forgiveness."

A month ago, I would have already offered him exactly that. Maybe more.

Tonight, I offer him nothing.

Instead, I turn on my heel—and walk away.

When I get back to the house, it is silent. Not an empty home, but a resting one. There's no sign of Valec. Fine by me. I don't want to talk to anyone here.

In the room I've been assigned to with Alice, there are two twin beds with a large chest between them under a window. Alice is a rumpled shape in the bed farther from the door, her soft snore a steady rhythm in the room. I ease the door shut behind me so as not to wake her.

My thumb is punctured before I fully find my seat on the floor. By the time my legs are crossed, the coin is a smeared mess in my hand, and I am whispering.

"By my blood . . ."

38

'*YOU ARE ANGRY, my Scion. In pain.*'

"Yes."

'*Good. Then I will show you why dragons never die.*'

Clang!

The wind is an icy claw, tearing at my skin. It funnels down to us in the shadow of Cadair Idris, skips over Llyn Cau lake, and brings the winter chill to our small band in the ritual space below.

Clang!

We stand on the edge of the stone circle set low into the earth, surrounded by lit torches held aloft by Pages, and watch the sorcerer do his work.

Clang!

"We are all that is left." Lancelot at my right, speaking my thoughts aloud as he is wont to do. "They have brought our numbers down to nothing, Arthur."

"We are not nothing," I rumble in response, my eyes still on the movement of Merlin's arm, the heavy swing. The words of forging guiding every strike, pushing power into the boulder in the center of the ritual cerrig. "We are thirteen."

Clang!

A wave of silver aether pulses through the ground, stopping at the raised stones beneath our feet, most of it bouncing back and into the earth, back to the boulder. Over and over, Merlin drives power into the stone, but each wave that hits and returns also sends a reverberation outside of the circle. An echo that sends lightning up my spine.

"This plan that you and Merlin have devised." In the light of the torches, his hair gleams gold. "How will we know if it is successful?"

"We will know we have succeeded," I reply, "when we are dead, and return."

"In spirit, but not flesh."

"Not in flesh, not in our lifetimes. But when every Cysgodanedig is dust, the war will be won."

Clang! *White sparks arc high in the air, falling on Merlin's cloak.*

"How many generations?" Lancelot asks.

"As many as it takes."

I turn to his profile, watching. "The Spell will not hold if we do not all believe. Our Oaths bind us to it. Do you doubt, my knight?"

His brows furrow. Clang! *The aether sparks fly; this time they are reflected in his eyes. Embers of power glowing silver and blue, then fading, then rising again. He turns to me then, and his gaze is as I know from the battlefield: storm and steel, fury and focus. "I do not doubt. The Table, forever."*

I clasp his arm in mine, our fingers wrapped at the elbows. "The Table, forever."

At my touch, Lancelot *flickers, thins,* then reappears as the boy I know.

Nick squeezes my elbow, eyes looking me over in a concerned sweep. "What's wrong?"

I shrug helplessly, voice low. "A little bit of everything, but I think I should be asking you that. You were in danger the other night."

He releases me. "Mageguard. It's over, but my father was injured. We're in a safe place. I am, was, sleeping, actually—" He stops short. "Sel felt it, didn't he?"

"Yes," I whisper.

Something must show on my face—pain, anger, disgust—because his brows draw tight, and his voice lowers. "Something happened."

I stare at him, gauging how much to say, how much I want him to know. Emotional exhaustion and the shadow of guilt leave me at a loss.

I take a shaky breath. "Sel made a bad call. A messed-up, selfish decision that"—I squeeze my eyes shut—"really hurt me."

Nick's hand cups my face. When I open my eyes, his expression is sympathetic, but hard. "He does that."

"Advice?"

"About Sel? If I had any to offer, I'd have given it to myself a long time ago." He frowns. "His Oath, is he—"

"Not great," I say, and scowl. "But stable, for now. We found a sort of potion at a demon bar. . . ."

His eyes grow wide. "A demon . . . bar?"

I nod. "Long story. But Sel's okay. Back to being more asshole than demon."

I inhale slowly, looking out at the scene that is the beginning of the Legendborn. Our origin. Even mine. "This is where it all started. And eight Camlanns later, it's still going."

Nick follows my gaze to the knights surrounding us, held still by the diversion I've made in Arthur's memory. "Where are we?"

"Arthur is more show than tell."

Nick's face twists in a scowl the way it always does when I say Arthur's name. I find it oddly validating. "He brought you here to show you this place and time? Why?"

I look up at the mountain, the lake. The ritual circle, power held within. The knights with bare heads, in tunics, stripped down, and the answer surfaces.

"Because . . . this is the night the Spell was cast. This is the first time the original Table received their aether abilities. He said he would show me how to control his power, and this is the first time he would have used it."

"Then that's why he brought you to this memory. So you could feel for yourself how he gained control." He frowns. "Too bad they're frozen."

"When I break from his memory, it creates some sort of . . . split in the stream. That's why I can bring you here when you weren't there to begin with." I focus on the memory again, will it to go forward. At first, nothing happens. Then . . .

Clang! *Merlin's aether hammer strikes the stone.*

Nick kneels beside me, then he freezes. "Holy . . . I just saw—"

"Yeah," I whisper. "It's—" My breath catches, because something inside me has just expanded to fill my chest. When I look at Nick, I know he felt it, too. "I remember what happens next."

He nods. "So do I. I know where to go, what to say, what he did." He stands, blinking at the world with fresh eyes, finding the other eleven knights now moving, shifting, alive around us. "Do you think they see us, or Arthur and Lancelot?"

I rise to meet him. "They are figments of what has already happened. So, I think they see them, not us."

"Arthur!" A voice pulls my attention to the center of the circle. Merlin, chest heaving. "It is time."

I glance at Nick. He pushes at my shoulder. "Go."

It is strange, remembering something that didn't happen to you, but I let the impulse to call back take over. *"Very well." I step as Arthur stepped, past the stone, to the grass, to his sorcerer.*

Merlin throws back his hood to reveal a wild shock of black hair, long enough to touch his shoulders if it wasn't lifted up, swaying in mage flame. He is a handsome man—half incubus, so that makes sense. A strong jaw, a face both old and young. A full mouth and narrow nose. But his eyes are like nothing I've ever seen: red like Erebus's, but rimmed with yellow.

He bows slightly as I approach. "This last strike will crack the boulder. When it opens, take the blade."

Arthur nodded, so I nod. With a mighty, final blow, Merlin's hammer splits the massive stone in two—revealing Excalibur in its first form. Long, near transparent, and missing the center diamond. Smaller crossguard, rougher edge, but still the sword I know. My hands itch to hold it.

My fingers have to dig around the crumbling bits of stone caked against the hilt to get a grip on it, but when I lift it up, Excalibur sings in my hand, a primal scream I would recognize anywhere.

"Rhyfelgri," Merlin whispers.

I raise the blade high, and my knights roar in response. The aether streaks down my hand and into my chest.

Merlin beckons the others down from their perches. "Into the circle. Kneel. Pledge
yourself as knights once more, and your power will be multiplied, and woven into your
bloodline for all time."

Nick climbs down, watching me with something like pride, like awe, like fierce joy.
He is the first to kneel. The first to take the flat side of Excalibur to his shoulder, and,
gasping, receive the jolt of aether it sends through his body. The first to look up at me
with glowing silver eyes.

"The Table," he says. Because it is what Lancelot said.

"Forever," we say together.

The Spell of Eternity weaves through all thirteen bloodlines like living
lightning, leaving everyone near drunk with magic, covered in it, made of
it. Nick and I included. After it is done, Merlin bids us all farewell, walks
alone to the foot of the mountain, and disappears.

The party splits across the hill. Some tell stories around the circle,
some drink mead by the camp near our horses, others retire for the night.
It is easy to find the other eleven knights, because their eyes are still
glowing silver with aether. Laughter finds us across the grass, and I can't
help but laugh back. I wanted to escape, and this is more than I could have
asked for.

I feel like the blade tonight. Aether, forged into life.

Nick stands beside me smiling, his eyes twin orbs of silver blue. "This
is . . ." When he sighs, aether leaks from his lips in a cloud of smoke.

"Amazing," I whisper. And it is: every nerve in my body feels alive, electric.
I relax into it, giggling, spinning, enjoying the sensitivity of my skin as I twirl
through ambient aether everywhere. When I stop, still dizzy, and hold my arm
out, wisps of mage flame draw themselves to my skin like a magnet. "I'm not
even doing anything."

Nick grins, and holds his arm out too—and aether wraps his wrist and bare
hand in a smooth silver layer. Lancelot's power flows over Nick's skin and down
to his palms, stretching into a pair of twin swords. Lancelot's blades.

"It was easy for Arthur. It's not easy for me. I pull too much, too hot." I lower my arm.

"I dream about us, Bree. Fighting side by side. Together. But lately, I dream that one day, we won't have to fight at all." He releases the swords back to the air.

He closes the distance between us, palm hovering over mine. "Can I . . . ?"

Nick grips my fingers, and I feel the power flow between us like the boulder to the circle. It leaves me in a wave, hits him, returns. "Oh," I gasp.

His glowing eyes widen, find mine. "Your eyes are still . . ."

"Yours too."

He glances over his shoulder. The camp is nearby. "I don't remember this part."

"Me neither." I follow his gaze, and the memory has frozen again. "Which means—"

"It's just us now." His eyes sparkle with dark satisfaction, and my heart skips. He pulls me close, and sparks jump between my chest and his, zipping up my throat and wrapping his shoulders. His eyes fall shut. "God, B . . ."

"All this power," I murmur, voice slurring. "Why is it like this?"

His hands slide up and down my arms, dragging fire in their wake. "Dunno. The ranks, maybe . . . Arthur first, then Lancelot second. Because it's fresh, and what we feel in the real world is watered down, generations away from now?" He laughs, breathless joy in his voice. The first I've heard in a long, long time. "Or maybe it feels like this because it's *you and me*."

Here we can be Bree and Nick without the Order's demands. Without their rules and laws. Here we can forget that people want so very much from us and instead we can want from each other.

"Nick . . . ," I plead, tugging his face down.

His eyes snap open and lock with mine, pupils swallowed in silver. "Yeah." He nods, wraps a hot palm around the base of my neck, slides it up into my hair. "Yeah."

And then his mouth is on mine, and every call and response we've ever felt pales in comparison to this one. Power cycling from his body to mine in a slow loop between his skin and mine. Everywhere we touch speeds the rotation until I can't tell whose breath is whose, whose flame arcs higher, which spark starts the fire that surrounds us. He moans, tugging us to the ground. I open my eyes—and see that the stars over his shoulder shine in our rhythm, too.

"What if the Regents find us?" I whisper, breathless. "And we can't have this again?"

"They can't find us here," he replies, and presses his mouth against my throat. I shiver. He pulls back, grinning at his effect on me. "Bree, I—" He stops short, eyes dimming to blue irises, black pupils.

"Nick?"

He gasps, eyes seeing something that isn't there—or isn't here, in the memory. "Oh God. No." He clutches at my arm. "The cabin—we're at the cabin!"

And then he disappears.

"Nick!" I push up to sitting, but he's gone. The stars go out. Cadair Idris's shadow disappears. Even the ground fades, until I am falling back, back. . . .

"Bree!" My eyes snap open as Alice shakes my shoulder, shouting in my face. "Wake up!"

"I'm . . . I'm awake," I mumble, blinking hard. The room is blue-gray dim, the last bit of night before morning. "I was . . ." My chest tightens. "No, no, Nick is . . ."

She nods. "I know. Sel came running in; William has him now, but it's not good." Her eyes scan my face and stop at my hairline. "What happened to your hair?"

I dig a finger through the curls. "Nothing." I push to standing. "Listen, I know where Nick is."

"You do?" She jumps up. "Then we gotta go. Now!"

It's a fight, but I manage to convince both Alice and William to stay behind. Alice, because I can't risk her getting hurt, and William, in case anyone from the Mageguard—or a demon—follows our trail back to Miss Hazel's.

Sel almost leaves without me, too, but I shoot him a glare hot enough to melt metal and clench my fist around the keys. "Don't you dare."

Two minutes later, we're in the car.

Sel knows exactly where the cabin is, and lets loose a stream of curses as he reverses in the driveway, tiles squealing on gravel. "The goddamn cabin," he finishes. He whips out onto the main road, foot heavy on the gas.

"What is the cabin?" I ask. I'm in the back seat, looking through the collection of weapons we brought from the safehouse.

"Exactly what it sounds like, Briana," he snaps. "A house in the woods."

I swear I see red without any magic at all. "I *know* you are not being rude to me right now, Selwyn Kane. Because I have *plenty* of rude for you."

His jaw clenches, but he keeps his eye on the road.

I take a deep breath. "Let's put our issues aside for the moment. We're going to rescue Nick; that's the priority."

He nods. "Agreed."

I start over. "Where is the cabin? And why are they there?"

"Sapphire Valley, near Gorges State Park." He presses the pedal again. We must be going at least eighty. "And my guess is they're there because it's the only Davis property the Regents wouldn't know to search. The other seven were raided weeks ago."

"*Seven?*" I gasp.

"Focus."

I scowl at him in the rearview. "Why don't the Regents know about it?"

"Because technically, it won't *be* a Davis property until Nick's eighteenth birthday. Anna left it to him." His smile is grim. "The Regents would never suspect they'd take refuge in a Rheon-owned house. It's smart."

Cold slips down my spine at the hard look on Sel's face. "Anna is his mother."

"Yes."

"His mother was mesmered," I say. "Nick was totally wiped from her memory, why would—"

"Anna's family, the Rheons, kept in touch with Nick, occasionally." Sel rubs a hand over his face. "Called. Sent cards."

"How?"

"They disowned her, but still wanted to remain connected to Nick because he was a Davis."

"What?" I cry. "But she'd lost her memory. Her son and husband were gone. How could they—"

"Anna broke Order law." Sel sighs. "But the Rheons are an old Vassal family. One of the oldest." He changes lanes, gets us onto an on-ramp, following the GPS built into the car. "They sided with the Order because it meant remaining in the Regents' favor. No Rheon would ever harbor a fugitive from the Order, so it wouldn't seem like a good option, but it is. The house has sat empty since . . ."

"Since Anna was mesmered." My fingers curl into fists on my knees. I never thought I'd feel connected to Nick's mother. I felt for her, yes, but now . . . now I'm just *angry* for her. "Who did it?"

Sel's jaw works back and forth. "Tacitus."

"Of course," I mutter. I climb into the front seat with my pile of knives and snap my seatbelt in place.

"What happened to your hair?" Sel asks abruptly. Alice had asked the same thing, and I hadn't had time to look. While he changes lanes again, I flip down the visor in the front seat. There, above my right eye, is a streak of shiny silver curls.

"I don't know. . . ." I pull at the curls, twirl them around my fingers. "They weren't that color last night."

"No, they weren't." His eyes narrow on the road. "That looks like Liege hair. How much power are you using?"

Liege hair. I swallow. I don't know how one earns the hair that Gill and Samira and Lyssa and Ophelia have. Never asked. Assumed the gray hair was just from some form of accelerated aging, not from power use. "You think . . ."

"It's not just that. . . ." He lifts his nose, inhales. "Your scent is different."

"Excuse me?"

His nose wrinkles. "You smell like Nicholas."

I shift in my seat, skin suddenly hot against the leather.

Sel glances at me, at the bandage on my thumb. "You summoned Arthur. When?"

"After I left you."

A long pause. "I see. And Nicholas?"

"He was there as Lancelot in Arthur's memory."

"And . . . ?" He shakes his head, confused. "You were doing what, exactly?"

I gnaw on my thumb, shrinking in the seat. "I—I don't know how the magic works."

Sel's golden eyes flick to mine, brow raised, then back to the road. A pause, a consideration. Then his head whips toward me. *"Seriously?"*

I squirm, heat burning my cheeks. "I don't have to explain myself to you."

He grits his teeth. His thumbs tap the steering wheel. "No, you do not. And I didn't ask you to."

"How long?" I ask.

He groans. "Another hour at least." His nose scrunches up again—and he punches the button to roll down both our windows.

39

WE ARRIVE AT the cabin in forty-five minutes instead of sixty, because Sel speeds the whole way. By the time we pull off the exit, the sky is streaked in reds, peaches, and golds. Near sunrise.

"There's the sign." A billboard on the right displays a fifties-looking family in front of a lake house. "Sapphire Estates and Villas."

Sel freezes as soon as he pulls into the parking lot. "Merlins."

"What, where?" I twist in my seat.

Sel sniffs. "Not close by, but they were here recently. In the last hour."

My pulse quickens, imagining Nick in their hands. Or struggling. Gone already. "We're too late."

Sel's voice is stone. "Maybe. Look." He points to a row of three dark vehicles in an open-air garage off the main welcome building. "If they already had Nicholas, why would they still be here?"

"Would they have . . . ?" I trail off.

"I would have felt it already," he mutters, craning his neck slightly to look past the cars. "There are Merlins inside the cars still. Heat waves rolling off the engines."

"They just beat us. How did Nick know they were coming?"

"You said Lord Davis had spies on the inside, yes? Probably got just enough warning to hunker down. There are over fifty private cabins up and down this mountain, with outcrops and forest and private roads between. If their cars are still here, that means they only got a tip about the location. They don't know which cabin they're in. Yet."

"Do you?" I ask, stating the obvious.

"Sure, but even if we get there first, there's Isaac."

A door slams, and we duck down instinctively. A tall man in a pair of jeans and a dark denim jacket steps out of one of the three cars, long legs carrying him toward the front entrance. He's making an effort to walk like a normal person, but I know a Merlin gait when I see it. Smooth, long strides, silver-ringed fingers loose at his sides.

"What if they get there first?" I ask.

"Might be a good thing, actually. Unless they find a way to get void cuffs on him, they'll have their hands full with Isaac. Should be enough of a distraction for us to grab Nick, and if he's free and able to fight—"

"What if he's not?"

"Have not exactly thought that far ahead."

The Merlin walks back to one of the cars, and they pull out in front of us, accelerating left, and Sel follows.

He pulls the SUV into a tight left turn—then clutches his head with a roar of pain, letting the steering wheel spin in one palm. I lunge forward, holding it tight, just barely keeping the car from flipping. Instead of tumbling, we fishtail out, spinning one hundred and eighty degrees and coming to a jarring stop facing the way we've come. Both of Sel's hands clutch at his hair, pulling it as he yells.

"Sel!" I shout, reaching a hand out to his wrist.

"Don't touch me!" he yells, his voice hoarse. "Don't—"

I withdraw. "What's happening, what's—"

He releases his head and grabs the wheel again, panting as he grips it. His eyes flare a deep orange.

"Nick."

"What—"

Sel puts the car in reverse, swinging it back up onto the road, and slams his heel on the pedal.

"Is he—"

"In mortal danger?" Sel grits out, his voice strained. "Yes."

We take the final turn on the mountain road barely slow enough to remain on it, and come around at the base of a drive up to a cabin on a hill.

Battle mage flame flares bright in the windows, flashing like lightning inside the cabin's walls.

They're already here.

Sel's out of the car before I can even unbuckle myself. I'm shouting at him to stop, that he'll get himself killed, but it's useless—and hypocritical. I'm sprinting after him, no thoughts of my own safety. Sel and I share the same single thought, I know it: Nick.

Nick. Nick. Nick.

Sel stops in the middle of the road, listening. "Something's happening. We need to get off the road."

He moves around to my front, hand turned awkwardly to guide me to his spine.

I blink, confused as he crouches.

He turns around and rolls his eyes. Mouths, "Get on!"

I climb onto his back—just barely settled—and then he's racing us through the woods toward the fight, silent and swift.

He slows when the trees thin, listens for a moment, and takes the next few steps at a human pace. He doesn't set me down and it's obvious why—my footsteps will break every twig and pine needle. His don't make a single sound. I peer over his shoulder, following his gaze as he assesses the area.

A smooth driveway. Three black Mageguard Jeeps out front.

Shouting from the inside.

It happens so fast.

One second, the cabin is a rustic, two-story getaway with big picture windows under an A-frame roof.

Then . . . it explodes.

Every single one of those picture windows blows outward in a shower of glass and bright flames. The A-frame roof erupts into a fountain of splintered wood and broken shingles.

Sel grips my thighs tight enough to bruise.

"Oh my God. Sel—"

He shakes his head hard, hisses, "Wait."

Just then, the door is shoved off its hinges from the inside. Four Merlins come tumbling out with it, covered in bright white flames and screaming.

Sel pulls me tighter to him and drops to a crouch.

I gasp. He doesn't bother to shush me. The Merlins' faces and clothes are in shreds—blood streams down their chins and shirts. One Merlin's arms and hands are a mess of blood, like she'd thrown them over her face to protect herself. It hadn't worked. She trips over her own feet and falls. Doesn't get up.

The other three don't fare much better. They stumble through the lot toward the cars, barely able to see. Two fall to their knees—their pained moans echo against the trees overhead.

I don't realize how badly I'm shaking until I feel Sel's hand smooth down my leg and up again. It doesn't help. It takes everything in me not to make a sound, not to run, not to move.

The only Merlin left standing turns our way briefly; there's a pool of blood on a shirt, a deep wound through a sternum. And then I'm back in the tunnels.

Fitz on the stalagmite in the cave. Fitz's chest burst open, ribs broken and spread—I tuck my head into Sel's shoulder.

I feel Sel's silent intake of breath beneath me and open my eyes just in time to see Isaac Sorenson standing in the blasted-open doorway, completely unscathed. Isaac's eyes blaze a fiery red. The mage flame wrapping his arms is silver, feeding twin clouds of smoke around his fists. His mouth opens in a silent snarl as he surveys the broken Merlins outside.

He looks nothing like the refined Master Merlin I last saw in a tuxedo in a country club.

One of the less injured Merlins throws herself in Isaac's path, hands spread wide. I recognize her as Olsen, the guard that escorted William to the Lodge that first night. Silver aether gathers in Olsen's palms as she prepares to fight the Kingsmage.

It's nothing against Isaac's fury: the Kingsmage bares his teeth, and mage flame from his hands flows in a thick rush toward Olsen, looping around and around her chest until it solidifies into a construct—a glowing band. Isaac holds one hand out, pulling his fingers in slowly. The Merlin scrabbles at her ribs with bloody hands, dropping to her knees once more.

Isaac's fingers pull in tight. He is choking the life out of Olsen, and enjoying it.

I'm shaking again. Olsen gurgles, a rattling sound emerging from her mouth—and then it's Fitz all over again. The imp with its claws in his back, his last screams when he realized what was happening. Sel's hands smooth up and down my legs in a steady rhythm.

But there is no soothing this. We're watching a woman get murdered and doing nothing. We're witnesses.

A car door opens to our left. Slams shut. Then, another. The trees block our line of sight. Neither of us dares to move.

Isaac releases an unconscious Olsen—she tips forward. A dull thud as her face and head smack against the pavement. Isaac doesn't seem to notice or care. His eyes are only for the new arrivals. "Bore da, old friend."

From behind a wide trunk, a tall figure in a long coat emerges. Sel's fingers dig impossibly tighter, and I return the favor with fingers like claws in his shirt.

Oh no.

It's Erebus Varelian.

And beside him stands Max Zhao, his second-in-command and agent of my torture at the hands of the Regents. I fight to keep my breaths quiet, but my heart is a freight train in my chest.

Erebus pauses, surveying the carnage in the driveway. "I would not call the morning 'good,' Isaac, when you have used it to wound four of my guards."

Isaac offers a lazy shrug. "It could be worse. I killed two others. At least these four will heal."

Erebus sighs, hands clasped before him. "Where are the Davises? Did you shield them from your blast inside?"

As if on cue, Lord Davis walks out onto the step beside Isaac. He is more gaunt than I'd last seen him, running from the ogof, but his pride has only spread, wild and overgrown in his every movement. It fills his eyes, lives in his sneer. This is a man undaunted.

"The Council deigned to send the general o' the deep shadows after all these weeks? I was beginnin' to feel insulted."

"Where is the Scion?" Erebus asks.

Sel and I both hold our breath.

We see him at the same time. Against his instincts, Sel nearly rises to standing—before he forces us both back down.

It's Nick. Finally. Emerging from the destroyed cabin in slow steps.

He is as I have seen him in the memories. Thinner, perhaps. But still broad-shouldered and regal—and angry as he takes in the wounded Merlins on the ground. Before he can speak, a silver aether shield snaps around the group on the stairs.

A casting, brought up by Isaac in an instant around Nick, his father, and himself. Lord Davis grasps his son's arm tight.

Erebus tilts his head. "A barrier, Isaac?" He looks past him to Davis and Nick, then deliberately turns to the left and right. "You have nowhere to go."

Isaac smirks, drawing one palm out in front of himself while the other arm continues to hold the shield. Offense and defense both.

Erebus's gaze sharpens. "You cannot fight me and hold that barrier at once."

Isaac responds with a blast of silver flames, swiftly blocked by Erebus. Max looks between them both, eyes wide.

Erebus sighs. "Have it your way." He pivots, holding his own palm out toward Isaac's barrier. For a moment, I think that he might send his own blast back, but that's not what happens at all.

Instead, Isaac's dome shudders. Cracks. Isaac growls, using both hands to reinforce it, but it splits as fast as he repairs it, faster. Then it peels away in layers, rushing across the driveway—and right to Erebus's open palm.

Isaac roars, charging for the Seneschal in a blur of motion, blades forming in his hands as he moves. The two Master Merlins battle it out, aether
weapons meeting again and again, flames roaring and swirling across the
pavement.

Then, several things happen at once:

Up on the stairs Nick wrestles from his father's grip and makes a break for
it, darting down the stairs.

Lord Davis shouts after him, running.

Erebus barks an order to Max, who summons an aether spear in an instant,
throwing it in a blink at Nick's back. Sel jerks forward, but someone else gets
there first—

And the spear pierces Lord Davis's chest straight through with a wet, loud
thunk.

Nick's father falls in slow motion, hitting the ground on his side. The spear tip
glows, bloody from his back, and the shaft hovers above the pavement, shuddering with his final breath.

Isaac's guttural scream splits the air.

Nick dives to his father's side.

Sel releases me to the ground completely, jaw slack and open.

I just . . . stare.

Lord Davis's body is lit an eerie blue, illuminated by the aether spear dissipating into nothing.

It leaves behind a bloody hole in Davis's red plaid flannel, and a growing pool
soaking the pavement beneath him.

Isaac is at Lord Davis's body in a blink. "Martin . . . *Martin* . . ."

"Dad?" Nick's voice breaks me, and Sel, too. Beside me, his fists are balled
at his side.

Erebus steps forward. "I am sorry that it came to this, Nicholas."

Nick's head jerks up, eyes red and shiny with grief and fury both. "No, you
aren't."

In an instant, full armor flashes into place around his body, and twin blades appear in his hands.

Max lunges.

Faster than a Merlin, Nick's crossed blades meet his opponent's throat, then part—cleaving Max's head from his body.

THE BODY FALLS at Nick's feet. He stares down at it, panting, eyes wide, stricken. His face is covered with red spray.

I forget to breathe. Beside me, Sel's hand grips my wrist. Neither of us can move.

Erebus releases a long breath. "Nicholas, drop the swords."

Nick shakes his head, but I don't know if it's at Erebus, at the sight of Max's head on the dirt below him, or at what he's done.

Before Erebus can ask again, Isaac rises slowly from Lord Davis's body. Turns, chest heaving. For a split second, I recognize his face, because it's one I have worn myself. This agony, I know. I remember.

It is rage, expanding so fast and so hot that it fuels itself beneath your skin. Grief so deep you are only an open wound, only pain. Pain so fresh that the world itself feels like it should be burning.

In a flash, he and Erebus are locked together, rolling in a blur of aether, punches rattling my teeth.

Sel is already at the tree line, eyes darting between the two Merlins and his charge. The motion catches Nick's attention, and he finds us across the driveway. His eyes widen at the sight of Sel, then me. Flutter, as if he's not sure he can believe them.

I have imagined this moment so many times. What it would feel like to see him again. I never imagined that Nick would be standing before us splattered in blood from delivering a death blow.

Sel steps forward again, nodding. After a moment, Nick nods back. He sees us. Good. We can't go to him without exposing ourselves; right now, no one else knows we're here. We're his escape, his rescue.

Sel and Nick's heads turn in unison, both checking for the tactical opening. The Merlins are still fighting, Isaac too lost to hold back and Erebus calling on every skill he has to fight him off. The opening is here, now. Sel and Nick turn back to each other, eyes meeting again.

Then, some unspoken, silent understanding passes from charge to Kingsmage, and Sel sucks in a breath. "No . . ."

Nick takes one step back. Then another. And then I'm saying it, too. "No."

He shakes his head, and the meaning is clear.

He's leaving.

Without us.

He's leaving . . . *us*.

Two more steps, and then he's gone through the woods on the other side of the cabin, armor blinking out as he moves, until he's lost between the trees.

A loud crack reaches us from the end of the driveway. Isaac lies still on the ground, too far away for us to know if he's alive or dead. Erebus stands triumphant.

Sel curses. Then hoists me up on his back again and we're moving. Fast. The forest is a blur around me, wind in my face and open mouth. I tuck my head down, gritting my teeth against the sob in my chest that has grown into something primal.

Sel comes to a stop deep into the woods, where shadows are stripes against his cheek and sunlight is a band of light against the black of his hair.

"Nick . . . ," I gasp into his shoulder.

"I know."

"Sel, he left us. . . ."

"I . . . know. I—" He inhales. His whole body is trembling beneath me. Between my arms, against my chest. He sucks in a breath, willing his body still. Another. Then: "Nicholas made his choice, Bree."

"But, it isn't supposed to be this way. . . ." My voice is muffled through tears that soak his shirt, nasally and wet. "He was supposed . . . to come . . . *with us*," I choke out, fisting my hand to my mouth. "Nick killed Max. Oh God . . ."

"Zhao was going to kill him," Sel whispers, and I don't know if he's reassuring himself or me. "Zhao *did* kill his father."

"But that wasn't—" I grip his arms in clawed hands. "That wasn't self-defense—"

"No." Sel turns his head, catching my eye over his shoulder. "That was revenge."

His brows are furrowed with every emotion I feel colliding within me, too: Sadness. Confusion. Horror.

"That was murderous intent," he whispers in a hoarse voice. Nick's eyes burn in my memory, their blue turned hot and ruthless. "He was in bloodlust. I should know."

"He—he was in shock. I don't . . . I think . . . we can get him back—"

"He doesn't want to *be* back. You saw it in his face, I know you did. *He* left *us*, Bree, after all that we've done to—" He stops short, twisting his head back the way we've come. "Shit. Erebus found our car."

And then we're off again, rushing through the forest. Over streams, doubling back over logs, zigging across deep loam, the only sound his breath and my own, loud in our ears.

Sel runs us another mile to a clearing that looks to be a part of some sort of ropes course. There's a wooden sign nearby: CAMP ATKINSON. We must be on the grounds of one of those adventure retreats for tourists.

In the center of the clearing is an enormous oak, with metal foot- and hand-holds built into the trunk at intervals. At the top, nearly thirty feet in the air, is a wooden platform with rotting wood railings on all sides and a square opening just big enough for one person to fit through from below. The kind of structure built for team-building exercises.

Sel takes several steps back. "Hold on. I'm going to jump to the tree. Try and clear our trail."

It's got to be another fifty feet to the trunk. I'm certain he can make it on his own, but he's never jumped this far with me on his back before. I have just enough time to squeak and clench my legs and arms around him before he speeds forward, jumping us both up in a long arc. The wide trunk shudders when we land, Sel's fingers digging into the bark, but the tree holds. And then he's climbing. At the top he pauses, clambers up on one side, and swivels so that the handholds are in front of me instead of him.

"Go."

I climb the rest of the way up and onto the platform. It's maybe ten by ten. On all four sides broken, weathered ropes hang limp from old hooks.

Sel climbs up after me and presses me down until I'm flat against the platform surface. He moves to the edge and crouches, peering through the canopy with eyes that can see much more than mine can. Light-footed, he makes his way back to me, a finger to his lips.

The wind whistles through the trees. A branch creaks to our left. This far out, in the shadow of the mountain, the woods are twilight dim, even though it's day.

Nothing. I hear nothing.

No birds or insects, like they have fled from a predator in their homes.

Which means the woods are not empty.

"Briana." Erebus's baritone reaches us through the trees, and I thank every fiber of my being for not reacting to the sound. I know he's listening for me. It's what Sel would do. This is how Merlins hunt.

I release a slow, silent breath, and Sel stiffens.

Bright silver light flares up all around us in a wide circle. Erebus, trapping us.

Across from me on the other side of the platform, Sel's fingers are tensing and relaxing, reaching for his own aether by instinct, and not finding it.

My own root hasn't shown itself yet—maybe because Erebus isn't here to hurt me, exactly? Because my life isn't threatened?

This is when I need to control my own abilities, I think. *This moment.* I can't risk burning myself with Arthur's aether, but armor's not what I need right now anyway.

I need root.

I remember Jessie's vision and hold my hand to my chest. *The power I possess and the woman who gave it to me. The power I possess and the woman who gave it to me.*

I imagine my mother's face, her smile.

And nothing happens.

Her voice, her cool hands against my cheek.

Nothing.

Sel's eyes find mine across the flickering light of Erebus's aether closing in on us. The empathy on his face nearly breaks me. Neither of us can use our powers here.

Jessie showed me the way, and it's not working.

"Briana, it would be so much easier if you would simply give up. I don't want to drag you and Selwyn out by your ankles, but I will." Erebus's voice is flat, emotionless. Like he's confident this is the end.

I dig deeper, curl my fingers inward, clawing my own sternum—

The power I possess.

The woman who gave it to me.

The power I possess—

Suddenly, Erebus's voice fades. Time slows.

I take in a deep breath through my nose, and when I exhale, the flames of root blow to life in my hands, red and fierce. I extend my hands before I can talk myself out of it.

Sel's eyes rise to mine, drop to my lit fingertips, then back up to me. I will him to understand, because I don't know how to say what I want him to do. I don't know how to ask for this, don't even know if it will work.

But we have to try. It can't end like this.

Sel reaches out, fingers stopping just short of my own. For a moment, nothing happens.

Then, he closes his eyes, brows furrowed—and there is a tiny tugging sensation behind my sternum. Frustration darkens his face. He doesn't think anything is happening, but I do. I can feel it.

I push the root out, open up the furnace a little more, let it burn hotter—and the flames on my hands arc to his fingertips, wrapping around each of them and flowing up his wrists. I visualize my root circling the cuffs like a layer of red heat.

Sel holds his breath.

Burn hotter, I think. *Break them.*

The flames tighten around the void cuffs, settle into the metal. A small line appears, a fissure claimed by my root—and then another. Another . . . until the cracks spread like crimson spiderwebs over the iron.

The cuffs fracture, then fall to the wooden planks.

"Briana, don't fight me," Erebus calls, and his voice is directly underneath our feet. "Whatever you're planning in there—"

Sel gasps, head thrown back as my aether climbs up his forearms, spiraling around his elbows. For a moment, it feels like *I'm* wrapped around him. His eyes snap open, and then he's on his feet, bringing his hands together so the flames spread faster.

FWOOOM!

We explode, together.

SEL'S EYES GLOW the color of my root. Not demon-dark irises, red streaked with black, but the shade of fresh blood, pulsing and alive. We inhale together as one, and exhale as one. Inhale again, deeper. Exhale—and this time, he breathes out two streams of smoke. A dragon in the night.

We walk to the edge of the platform together, flames stretched between us in a fiery link.

Erebus is down below, eyes wide and hands outstretched, blue-white aether swirling in a cloud around him. When he sees our flame, he growls. "What have you two done?"

"Leave us alone!" I shout.

"I can't do that," Erebus says, eyes sliding back to me. "A power like yours . . . can't roam free. An anchor to the Spell of Eternity who can generate aether to this magnitude? The Shadowborn would love nothing more than to destroy you. The Morgaines would hold you hostage. We—"

"You held me prisoner!"

"Better with us than the others." Erebus throws out his palms, casting a crackling net of aether over us and drawing it down. His fingers claw at the air, bending his trap. It folds around us, a sphere closing us in.

In response, Sel shoots one palm out to create our own sphere. A red circle of protection on all sides, pressing back against Erebus's, burning through his construct as fast as he can cast it.

"You're safer with me than him, Bree." Erebus's voice is closer than before. My head twists toward it. He's just outside of the warring constructs, thirty feet in the air, on top of a shining blue column cast beneath his feet. "Selwyn is already succumbing to his blood; I see that now." Sel grits his teeth, focused on holding Erebus back, but hearing every word.

"What you're doing now, giving him your power . . . it will only push him over faster. All of that aether?" Erebus takes a step forward on crystal. "All of *your* aether?" Another step. "No cambion can take that in without craving it forevermore." Erebus stands outside of the warring spheres of blue and red, eyes boring into mine. "If you run with him, you won't be any safer than if you'd been on your own."

"Shut up!" I scream, and the flames on my arms flare higher.

I grab Sel's hand, but instead of letting him pull from my power, I push into his, feeding his construct until it grows bigger, stronger.

Erebus strains to keep his sphere together, eyes squinting against the light.

I lock gazes with Sel, and he nods, understanding my meaning without words.

Our construct expands outward with a massive cracking sound, shattering Erebus's. The force knocks Erebus back, sending him flying.

When it is done, and he is gone, I finally let myself collapse.

Sel catches me before I fall over the edge, and the last thing I see is the light of my power fading from his eyes.

When I come to, I'm draped over Sel's back again. The woods are still dim, but the dark soil of the forest floor at this altitude is turning speckled white with early snow. Silent flakes that won't stick, won't stay. We're moving at human speed, and his hands are clenched beneath my thighs. When I groan, he pauses.

"Bree." He's out of breath.

I've never even heard Sel out of breath before. It shocks me alert.

"Put me down."

I can't see his face, but I see him shake his head. The black strands of his hair are plastered against his head and neck. "Not yet. Not until you can walk. The air is . . . thinner up here." His voice cracks on the last word, and fear shoots through me.

"What's wrong? Is that why you're out of breath?"

He shakes his head. "No, that's not why." He starts walking, and that's when I notice his gait. Each step feels purposeful. Careful.

"Sel, stop." I slap at his chest. "Something's wrong."

"'M fine," he pants. "We have to keep going."

I wriggle against his grip. The fact that I can move against him, and that his fingers loosen, tells me he is not fine. I shift my weight around until he's forced to stop, and press back until he's forced to let go.

Immediately, his shoulders slump forward, and his hands go to his knees. He turns to the left, to the right, eyes narrowed in profile.

"Are we lost?"

His jaw clenches. "I just need a minute."

"Erebus—"

"Our construct," he says, standing up with a hand in his hair. "It burned him pretty badly. I could smell blood and muscle. Gonna take him a while to heal."

Memories flood back to me. How I'd saved us, but only barely. How Jessie's solution worked so easily for her, but not for me. "I used my root. A lot of it." I whisper. "The Hunter—"

"No one's found us. Yet. That's why we need to keep moving—"

"You need to rest."

He breathes out a hollow laugh. "I'm not tired."

"Then what—"

He turns to me, and the look on his face makes me gasp. The red in his eyes is gone, but what's left behind is the rich, bright color of liquid gold. Heavy lids. Mouth open in a quiet pant. "You're aether-drunk."

He shakes his head. "I know what aether-drunk feels like. This . . . this isn't that." He takes a step to the side to lean against a tree, his head tipped back against the bark. I follow him, half-worried he might fall even with the tree at his spine. "Aether-drunk is dull bliss. Temporary balance. Relief. This is . . . better and worse."

Suddenly, my heart is pounding, because whatever he's feeling, it's not from the aether in the air around us, or from an Oath. It's from me. He's drunk on *me*.

His head lolls in my direction. "You told me you could smell my magic. At the gala."

"I did. I can."

He turns against the trunk to face me. We are so close I smell whiskey and smoke. His aether signature, back again. "I wanted to know what that was like. Wanted you to describe it. Didn't know how to ask."

"Oh," I whisper.

"Do you want to know?" he asks in a low voice that makes me shiver. He reaches for my hand, and his fingers are hot against my palm. "What your magic smells like?"

I swallow. "I . . ."

"Honey wine. Amber. Green things growing. The tiniest hint of copper, like fresh blood. Something else . . ." A deep inhale, and I feel him shudder. *"Power."*

"Sel . . ." The day has turned chilly, but his skin is burning.

"Mmm?"

"You said you didn't want to drink aether. You didn't want to use it . . . recreationally."

He chuckles and leans back, pulling his hand from mine. The glowing light of his irises are thin bands around drowning black pupils. "That was a cheap casting by a warlock with parlor-trick power. Valec's juice is a temporary dampener at best. There's no comparison. This flavor . . . your aether, your root . . ." He shakes his head, voice low with wonder. Swipes a tongue over his lower lip. "I can still taste you."

"Oh my God." I emit a strangled sound, and clap my hands over my face in mortification. "You can't just *say* stuff like that, Sel."

"I'm sorry." I look up to see his face darkened, pinched with sudden shame. "I'm *so* sorry, Bree. I kept telling you not to hide from me, but then I . . ." His eyes squeeze shut. "Then I did everything in my power to hide from you. I will never . . . I should have *never*—"

"This looks like fun," a voice says in the darkness.

THE NEW VOICE makes us jump. "I hope I'm interrupting something."

Sel hisses into the trees at something I can't see. "You."

"Me." The figure melts into shape from the shadows, hands up for peace but eyes glinting for battle.

"Valec." I groan.

"Bree." He grins.

"What are you doing here?" Sel steps in front of me, and Valec and I both roll our eyes.

The afternoon light finds all of the shadows and planes of Valec's face, the outline of his fangs as he smiles, the deep red of his cravat and vest. "It's nice to see you, too, Selwyn."

"How did you find us?" Sel snaps.

"Mariah called me from Hazel's. Said you'd gone off in a rush." He stuffs both hands in his pockets. "Imagine my surprise when I'm in the middle of restocking the bar and a wave of *your* power"—he points at my chest—"hits the Lounge like the blast radius from a nuclear bomb. Whatever you did put two of my waitstaff on the floor, and they still haven't woken up."

"My—" I start, then close my mouth. Sel glances at me and curses, wiping his hand over his mouth.

Valec watches the two of us. "Something happen here?"

I nod. "Erebus attacked us."

Valec's brows shoot up. "That old goat. I hope he was extremely, intimately close to that blast you let off. Please tell me he's dead."

I shake my head. "Not dead. Burned, apparently."

"Yes," Sel says, sharpening. He grabs my hand. "We need to keep going. Get as much distance between us and the Mageguard as possible."

"Them and everyone else," Valec mutters.

Sel pauses. "What's that supposed to mean?"

Valec curses. "I knew it. I *knew* neither of you would realize what you've done. Hades, I hate being right."

"Speak plainly, trickster," Sel growls.

Valec points to me. "You, my dear, set off an aether bomb that reached my bar all the way in the hills. If I felt it, so did every Shadowborn or Shadowborn-adjacent creature in the Southeast. You're lucky I found you first. That much power? Any hungry demon worth their salt is going to be looking for its source. Forget Erebus, you need to clear out before you get cornered by a pack of isels hoping to go corporeal in a jiffy."

Sel goes still beside me. "That much power could help dozens of demons go corp."

"Hundreds," Valec adds. "And even a fully corporeal demon will want to know where that wave came from." He shivers. "It felt like . . . rage and pain and chaos. The good stuff."

"We gotta go." Sel pulls me onto his back.

Valec sighs. "That's what I've been saying. And not just right now." He points at me. "You need to get to Volition before you set off another one of those root bombs."

Sel starts to jog. "I hear a road that way. We can get a ride, maybe—"

Valec shakes his head. "I've got a Porsche parked a few miles west. Follow me." The cambion disappears through the trees with the crack of wind closing in the vacuum behind him. Sel follows, eyes seeing more than I can. I tuck my head into his back and pray he can keep up.

We run like that for long minutes before Sel drops out of his sprint, stopping abruptly.

"What happened?" I whisper.

He hushes me. His head turns back and forth, searching.

Valec comes careening back to the clearing we've paused in, skidding to a stop. "I smell them too."

My heart lurches against my rib cage. Shadowborn.

"How many?" Sel drops me gently to the snow-dusted ground, swiveling so that I'm between him and Valec.

Valec inhales. "Dunno. Four maybe? Five? Not just isels."

"Obviously."

"Well, I wasn't sure—"

"I can tell the difference," Sel sneers.

I push between them, and Sel shoulders me back. "Stay behind us."

"I can fight," I insist. "We can fight. Earlier—"

"You're why they're here now." Sel shakes his head. "Any more of your aether will be—"

"Blood in the water." Valec shucks off his jacket and tosses it.

In the forest around us, a pack of isels and uchels emerge. Hounds and foxes, jaws snapping. I see at least two uchels made of stone, one moss and rot.

Blue mage flame hisses to life around Sel's hands and arms, gathering in a rush and extending out to two huge scythe-tipped spears. To my surprise, Valec spreads his hands wide, a long line of golden root snapping into place between his palms. He claps both hands together, combining the light into a bright mass, and when his hands part, two wicked-looking crystalline flails fall from his fingers.

The isels roar and snap, paws clawing at the earth—and launch themselves at both cambions at once. Without speaking, Valec and Sel separate, circling behind the pack faster than the lesser demons can change course, slicing and striking as they move. It's a technique I've seen Nick do before: lash out from the side as you pass, use the creatures' own momentum to drag your weapon down their flesh.

Sel is a black-and-silver blur blocking my vision. "Run, Bree!"

I hesitate. I could call root to myself and burn the demons away, like I did with Alonzo's borrowed power. Like I did to Erebus . . . but if that brings more monsters to the fight, Sel and Valec could get overwhelmed.

For the first time, I reach within for Arthur without a blood offering. *I am your Scion! You cannot let me die!*

Before I can decide what to do, an uchel appears before me. A towering creature on two legs, with long spindly fingers and a wide smile of dripping teeth. It draws back, claws spreading wide, and—Arthur responds, if not with words, in action.

Just as I imagine it, silver mage flame erupts across my chest and snaps into a solid breastplate to block the uchel's attack.

Its eyes go wide. *"Legendborn!"* In a flash, it strikes again. And again, beating me back with each blow even as its claws scrape down the armor. With every strike, the armor begins to crack. It flickers beneath two particularly strong blows, then returns and holds. I trip on a root and hit the ground.

From twenty feet away, Sel's scythe comes swinging overhead, neatly decapitating the uchel in one blow.

Across the clearing, Valec looks down at one of the piles of dust with a considering expression. "You know," Valec pants, pulling out a handkerchief to wipe his palms, "I think one of those demons was a customer of mine."

I fall back against a tree, suddenly unable to stand. The world blurs. I don't know why. "Sel . . ."

Sel is at my side, eyes searching, his nostrils flaring. "No . . ."

I start to slide. He catches me, and I hiss at the contact. "Easy . . ." Valec's voice at my side. They're both lowering me onto the ground, Sel's palm cupped under my head.

Arthur's gleaming armor lights both of their faces in faint blue. Valec's eyes flash between us in confusion. "This armor . . . you're not casting it."

"No." Sel shifts closer, nose to my chest. Searching for the wound. "She is."

Valec shakes his head. "How?"

"The armor is covering your wounds. A demon must have gotten to you, sliced it open before you could recast. I can't see what's happened." Sel's eyes find mine. "Bree, relax. Release the armor."

I try to release Arthur's armor, but I don't know how.

Valec gapes. "She your king's Squire, is that it?"

"Not his Squire," Sel mutters. "My king."

"Your *king*?!" Valec cries. "If that's true, then——" His eyes grow wide. "Sel——"

"Take a deep breath," Sel says to me. The hand at my temple is gentle, but his voice and body are tight as a piano wire. "Imagine the armor fading."

I take a deep breath. Try again. I know when it goes, because he and Valec go stock-still.

"Jesus Christ." Valec rocks back on his heels to standing. Pulls out his phone with trembling hands.

"Is it . . . bad?" I croak.

Sel doesn't answer me. "Who are you calling?" he barks to Valec.

"An ambulance, who do you think?"

"No!" Sel shakes his head. "We can't take her to a hospital. They'll ask too many questions. She doesn't even have an ID."

Valec thrusts a hand toward me. "She's been clawed open, man!"

"Sel——"

"You are going to be all right. Be still," he says shakily. I shift, try to look down at my chest and he pushes my head back, hand gentle on my chin. "Valec, call Hazel's place, ask for William, he can help her."

Valec's already calling, phone to his ear. "Too far away, what can he do?"

Sel shakes his head, swallows. "Scion of Gawain."

"That's great, but it's still too far . . . ," Valec says impatiently. "She's not gonna last that long——"

"Shut *up*!"

Valec looks between the two of us, then out through the trees. "I'll pick him up myself. Run him through the woods." Valec's gone in a gust of wind.

Something about his departure, or the lack of distraction, brings sensation flooding back to me. A scream builds in my throat, but the pain catches my chest before I can release it. Lightning through my stomach, up my ribs. Pain so deep my brain can barely process it.

"How bad is it?" I manage.

"William's on his way," Sel whispers. His hands are pressed against my side.

I tip my head over and see . . . enough. My right ribs and side are opened in stripes. Muscle, glistening wet. A steady stream of red flowing down into the dirt.

"I'm not gonna . . ."

"Yes, you are!" The muscles work in his jaw. His eyes shine—he blinks it away. "You are. You just have to hold on a little longer, Bree. For me—"

I start to respond, but when my mouth opens, nothing comes out but a low groan and a few dribbles of salty, metallic-tasting blood. I want to grab his wrist. Get him to look at me. Say something. He feels very far away. My body feels far away. And heavy. I hear his voice calling my name, but it's garbled, like he's speaking underwater. Sounds but not letters, not a word.

I drift in that heavy space, and everything—memories, thoughts, sensations—gets soft around the edges.

Dull. Gone.

Sel's voice is still a slur of sounds, but they change. Grow fluid. And the cinnamon and spice scent of his aether signature brings me up from that dull place. I open my eyes. His eyes are fixed on my side, a strained grimace on his face. His hands hover an inch above my flesh. Aether shimmers in the space between my body and his palms in a thin layer.

"Don't move," he grits out.

"What are you . . ."

"I've got you. Stay with me."

The floating dullness claims me again, but Sel's magic is there on the edges, keeping the darkness at bay.

"Stay with me, Bree."

43

MY EYELIDS FLUTTER open—a lamp nearby, too bright—and I immediately squeeze them shut.

"If I didn't adore you, and if it wasn't against every healer code ever in existence, I'd shake you half to death for scaring me like that."

William.

I open my eyes again to see him standing over me. It's evening. I'm back at Miss Hazel's in one of the twin beds and—I shuffle around a bit on the mattress—in just my bra and underwear beneath the thin blanket covering my midsection.

"Welcome back."

Memories return in a jarring stream. Sel. The forest. The smell of copper, so much blood, mingling with his magic. "'M alive."

William's mouth quirks. "Yes."

"Valec," I murmur. "Went to find you."

"It took Valec and me three hours to get to you both. That was three days ago."

I blink. I don't know which number to tackle first.

"I've been lucky as a Scion of Gawain," William whispers. "I'd never had to triage between two dying friends, and I never want to do it again."

I frown, and remember the speed of the two cambions, flashing around their opponents. Sel was in his element, and still powered by my aether. I don't remember seeing a mark on him. "Two dying friends?"

William releases a short sigh, and steps aside.

Behind him, on Alice's bed across the room, is Sel. Paler than I've ever seen him, skin striking against the shadows. Still, like a reclining statue carved out of stone and clothed in a pair of jeans and a black tee.

"He's alive. Although neither of you should be."

"What happened?" My eyes are only for Sel. His eyelids are pinched tight, like even in sleep he can't relax. Unlike me, he's lying above the covers—*he runs so hot*, I think.

William points to the blanket, pulling my attention with a question in his eyes. "May I? Easier to show you."

"Sure, but—"

William lifts the blanket up, revealing my bare midsection and several dozen butterfly bandages closing four long, jagged red stripes stretching from underneath the cup of my right breast to my hipbone. Newly healed wounds, fresh scars.

He points to one of the darker lines. "They were all bad, with massive hemorrhaging, but this one was the worst. Deep tissue lacerations, through the fat layer and through muscle. Claws sliced clean through to the marrow of your ribs. Air got into your chest cavity, between your right lung and chest wall, resulting in a pneumothorax, collapsed lung."

I feel it then, the ache in my chest. Like even mentioning it was enough to remind my body of its healed wounds.

William watches me carefully, pausing before moving on. His finger hovers over the scar, following it down to the bottom of my rib cage. "Demon split your diaphragm and opened your liver up on the way down. Grazed your stomach and missed your colon, thankfully, else sepsis would have been an issue and . . ." He shakes his head.

Tears prick at my eyes. I don't know if I want him to keep going. I do know I want to understand what happened. But every word he says, every organ he mentions, wakes up in response. My insides are burning by the end.

William replaces the blanket. "In the nonmagical world, you'd have gone into shock and died within minutes."

It takes a few attempts to find the next words. "Sel healed me?"

He shakes his head once, his eyes soft. "No. Sel held you *together* with his constructs. Kept your organs intact, pulled the muscles in place, reconnected the veins and nerves, and kept the blood moving to avoid necrosis. Kept your oxygen flowing."

I know I faded in and out. I remember Sel's face above mine, twisted in a grimace. His voice, chanting.

"The average Merlin knows how to cast large weapons that are hard and sharp, and the harder and sharper, the better. But what Sel did was unprecedented. He cast thousands of flexible microscopic aether constructs, and manipulated them to keep you alive. More than bandages, they were"—William shakes his head, voice half in awe—"life support. For three hours. Even if another Merlin could have come up with this that quickly, could have pulled this off, the effort would have killed them." William frowns. "Sel collapsed as soon as he saw me. Held on as long as he could."

Air leaves my battered chest in a rush. "I . . . I don't know what to say."

William's smile is sympathetic. "Whatever you say, it should be to Sel. Not me. He almost died to keep you alive."

It's hard to focus on his words. I'm caught between the fractured memories then and my broken body now. I'm terrified of what could have happened, and what did. Dizziness overtakes me, and my eyelids begin to droop.

"Rest," William says, as I slip back into unconsciousness.

When I wake again, the light has changed. Sel's bed is empty. Impossibly, there is a sticky note on my chest.

> He woke up early. Refused to lie back down. You are both going to kill me with stress one day. I would ask you to rest, but I know you won't. At the least, please drink the water on the table. You've lost a lot of fluid.

"Water?" At the foot of my bed is Alice, quietly holding the glass of water William left behind. I hadn't noticed her.

I nod from my pillow.

She leans forward with tears in her eyes. "Matty . . ."

"I'm okay." I grimace and push to sitting and take the glass in both hands. My middle feels tight, but I can already tell I've healed some since the last time I was awake. "I'm okay." The water is delicious.

"Matty, you're incredible. The strongest person I know, even before all of this. But you have *got* to stop almost dying. It's not cool."

I drop my hand over hers. "It's a lot cooler when it's small stuff, that's for sure."

Her mouth quirks. "I don't like the small or large stuff, I don't think. I prefer the no-stuff."

I chuckle, then catch my breath. "Same."

She raises a hand to my hairline, lightly drawing her index finger over the silver curls that have not gone away. "Still here."

I pull on the locks of curls she's found, drawing them down over my eyes.

Alice studies them. "From using your power?"

"Dunno. Seems like." I release the curls and look toward where Sel had been sleeping. "He's up. Does that mean he's okay?"

William walks in the room, seesawing his head. "Physically, sure. Mentally . . . unclear. He told us what happened with Nick. And then, right after that you were attacked. The way Valec described your injuries, I was certain you'd be dead by the time we arrived. Selwyn was there with you the whole time, thinking you could go at any moment, right in front of him. I wouldn't wish that type of terror on anyone." He perches on the other side of my bed, tilting my chin gingerly back and forth to look in my eyes.

I nod, guilt flooding me at the strain still there on my friend's face. "I know . . . the Lines—"

"The Lines?!" William exclaims, startling me. His face is twisted in long-simmering frustration—and fear. He releases a hollow, sour laugh. "The Lines, Bree? You nearly died."

"Y-yes," I begin, hands worrying at the blanket. "I know what it means if I fall. I do. I'm sorry. I just . . . don't like feeling coddled and useless. I'm not some damsel—"

"Stop." William holds up a hand. "Just stop." I've only seen that line between his brows when he's treating the most critical patients. "You're more than the Lines, Bree. And the fact that you think that was the first thing we thought about? It makes me wonder if you know any of us at all."

I have trouble holding his gaze, and shame in the form of heat floods my neck and chest.

"I was thinking about saving my friends. Not the *damn Lines*." He rubs a hand over his mouth, and the brown stubble of his chin stands out against the pale skin of his fingers.

"I'm sorry for worrying you," I murmur. I wonder if I'm numb to it all, now.

He heaves a breath. "I know you mean well."

That doesn't sit right with me, but I'm not sure how to fix it.

He nods to a pile of clothes in a chair beside me. "You're discharged. You can get dressed when you're ready." He stands up and slips out of the door before I can say another word.

Alice watches him go, but says nothing. Instead, I'm left with my thoughts and an eerie silence from the wooded landscape around Hazel's house. Alice turns to me just as a tiny thread of panic starts to enter my consciousness.

"Sel's been walking the border most of the day. He knows you're awake."

I swallow, understanding her meaning.

Don't hide in here forever. You need to talk to him.

I get dressed and make my way through the main room of the house, turning down the hall that leads to the screened-in porch. I pause before opening the door, knowing that wherever Sel is, he'll be able to hear me step outside.

What do you say to someone who nearly gave their life to save yours? I remember the expression on Lark's face that night in the Beast and shudder: immediate and total willingness to face whatever attacked us, as long as it meant I was safe. Not just willingness, but a resigned acceptance. Like he'd anticipated this day, envisioned it even. Not a death wish, but closer to one than I want to admit. The eyes of someone who'd imagined what it was like to die in service many, many times.

I may not understand the why of it, truly, but I can express my gratitude. I don't want to die, and I didn't because of him. I push the door open—and immediately stop when the shadow on the bench beside me melts into a familiar shape.

"Valec?"

The half-demon is dressed to the nines, as always. A purple-and-red brocade vest over a black button-down with the sleeves rolled up to his elbows. Black slacks and shiny boots. "Hey, powerhouse. Nice to see you with your insides inside."

"That's gross, Valec."

He winks. "So was seeing you bleed out in the dirt, sweetheart."

I open my mouth to shoot back at him, but stop. He was there that night, and I owe him my gratitude too. "Thank you," I say quietly, "for going to get William. And fighting with us."

Valec studies me for a moment before nodding once. "Wouldn't want word to get out I helped the Legendborn. Happy to kill your enemies, but I need to keep my good name as dirty as ever."

I huff a laugh. "Right. Speaking of, why aren't you back at the Lounge?"

He drifts over to the screen and peers out into the woods beyond. "I returned after you were stabilized. Came back when the doc called to say you'd likely wake up today." He turns, leaning against a wooden post. "Wanted to see you again, in the flesh. Make sure you were real."

The way he looks at me is a mixture of wonder and envy, and not a small amount of hunger. I resist the instinct to retreat.

"You gonna stare at me all day to make sure I'm real, cuz that's really not necessary."

Valec grins. A flash of fangs. "I like how present-minded and witty you are."

"I don't feel that witty right now." I shake my head. "I feel . . . like I'm tired of almost dying."

He nods slowly. "The best thing you can do is get strong enough to defend yourself, and keep living. No kinda life running, looking over your shoulder all the time. I heard about what happened with Erebus and Davis. Remember what I said about becoming the deadly thing yourself?"

I pick at the wood railing. "Yeah. I remember." Nick has became the deadly thing. A killer. I don't know yet how that changes what's between us.

His eyes stray to the woods again, and he tilts his head in a direction the way I've seen Sel do. Listening.

"When you're a cambion, you're caught between two worlds. Always. Not just two cultures or two communities, but literally two states of being. Life. Death. This plane, and the one that calls us back home in the middle of the night." His eyes return to me. "Most of us go a very long time without feeling like we belong anywhere."

I look over his shoulder, knowing that he's not just talking about himself.

"Sel belongs to the Order. To his chapter."

Valec sighs, shaking his head. "You can't belong to an idea, Bree."

"What does that mean?"

"You're a smart girl." He claps a hand on my shoulder and opens the back door to go inside, calling behind him. "Figure it out."

It's still morning. Chilly, but warming up under a lazy sun behind clouds. Someone put a ward up around the house. I'm not sure if it was Valec or Sel until I pass through it and taste the cinnamon whiskey of Sel's power—but the burn is welcome; it means Sel's aether abilities are back.

They're back because the cyffion are gone, and the cyffion are gone because I burned them away.

I may be mostly healed, but my body knows I'm not at one hundred percent, and slows my steps into the woods before I've even gone ten feet. I listen to it, and stop.

"Sel?" I whisper. I stand waiting for thirty seconds, nearly a minute, and wonder if he's too far away.

I shouldn't have worried.

I'm surprised; even though, as William said, he'd nearly died to save me, he looks much better off than I do. Even his hair looks thick and shiny in the shafts of sunlight.

He stops a few feet away, hands at his sides, and lets me study him.

"You saved my life."

"I did."

I didn't think I'd cry, but my eyes start to burn anyway. "God, Sel. What if we'd *both* died?"

His gaze hardens. "Are you suggesting I should have let you perish?"

"No, I just—" I blow out a puff of air. "Of course not. I know the Lines—"

Hurt flickers across his face before anger blankets over it. "Be very, *very* careful what you say next, Briana," Sel says, his voice low.

I sigh. "I know what it means if the Scion of Arthur dies. I'm not going to just forget that, okay?" Shame from William's anger is still close to the surface, but I can't shake what I know. What I've seen be important to the Order and Legendborn. "I'm not going to act like the Lines aren't part of this."

He speaks through clenched teeth. "You think I did what I did . . . because of the Lines."

"That's not what I'm saying."

"And yet you're saying it anyway." He laughs humorlessly.

"No, I'm saying thank you for saving my life." I clench my fists. "But you're the one who said saving me was an obligation, not a choice. So, yes, I do think you saved me because of the Lines, because of your Oaths—"

He takes a step toward me, eyes flashing. "My Kingsmage Oath is to Nicholas! As you've helpfully pointed out in the past. Some days it is nearly *impossible* for me to fight that instinct, but with you—" His brows draw tight as he stares down at me. He shakes his head, some decision made. "No other Merlin can protect you like I can, because no other Merlin feels about you the way I do. I want you to live, because I want you to be happy. Not because of a spell, but because so very many things would break and go dark if you weren't in the world. Myself included."

His voice is a warm pressure against my chest. A pressure that gets bigger and brighter until it spills out in a shaky breath and a tear that he catches with a gentle finger. I don't even know why I'm crying.

In a hoarse voice, he says, "And because those moments between us were real, and you know it."

"Nick . . ."

Sel's eyes are unreadable, his voice even. "Do you truly think Nicholas would begrudge us this? After everything?"

Sel is never imprecise.

"This?" I whisper.

Sel watches me carefully. Long enough for the wind to catch his hair. Release it. Lift it again.

"This" could be the feeling between us, all warmth and sharp edges that we keep almost touching. "This" could mean how close we're standing, and the breath shared between us. "This" could mean my heartbeat, thundering in both of our ears. Sel could define our "this" in any number of ways, but right now he chooses one.

"Yes, this," he finally murmurs, eyes cautious. "A Kingsmage and a king who needs protecting."

My throat works, swallowing around every other answer he could have given. "Right."

"Right."

I back away toward the house. "I need . . . to go find Alice."

He shoves his hands into his pocket. "You do that."

"R-right," I stammer.

His mouth twitches in the beginnings of a smile. "You said that already."

I pivot on my heel before he can say anything further. Even though I leave with the air lighter between us, I know that things aren't the same.

I don't have to turn back to know that he watches me all the way to the house. His attention is hot and steady on my skin.

A Kingsmage's gaze is unwavering.

44

THE NEXT MORNING, Miss Hazel heads out to see about the next group of "passengers" coming through. More aether users who need protection moving around. She gives me a kiss on the cheek and the last bit of pecan pie before she goes.

While I gather our things, Valec knocks on the door to the room Alice and I shared.

He strides in wearing a change of clothes from somewhere. "I'll be leaving in a few." He eases the door closed, dark eyes taking in the room in a single sweep.

I make a guess. "Alice is outside on the porch talking to Mariah, if you're wondering if I'm alone."

"Less worried about Alice than Kane." He pauses. "Although, maybe I shouldn't be. Your friend's mind is wicked sharp."

"You have no idea."

Valec's voice is wily once more. "I wanted to send you off with something, if you don't mind."

I give him a skeptical look. "What kinda something? And if I take it, will I be in your debt?"

He laughs. "This gift is free. No deal, no contract."

I nod and hold out my hand, but he shakes his head, curling my fingers back into themselves. "I told you I had a direct way to find out more about your abilities."

"Yes."

He steps nearer, until that leather-and-star-anise smell swirls thick in the air, and my cheeks prickle. Valec's gaze had never felt like anything on my skin, I realize. I look up at him, and his eyes have shifted to their full crimson. I gasp, but don't step away. Instead, I feel a pull closer, to see exactly how his irises look in the light. How much his smooth brown skin needs to be touched. And I *could*, I could touch it—he chuckles, catching fingers I didn't know I'd raised. When he speaks, his canines are longer than I remember. I'm up on my toes, and his mouth is a whisper's width from mine. "And now you understand why it's unethical to let the demon out when working with clients."

I jerk back, shaking my head. Subtle, no more attractive than the most attractive human in the world . . . but powerful, nonetheless. "I'm . . . I'm sorry."

"I could have warned you," he drawls. "But I didn't."

Ugh. "Is that why you do the contracts? Because you're half human and half demon?"

His mouth quirks. "The only balanced cambion in the region that both parties can trust. If the deals are going to be made, and they will be, as they have since the beginning of time, then at least I can see to it that humans aren't taken advantage of."

My eyes widen. "You're . . . you're *good*!"

He rolls his eyes, but there's a tiny tug at the corner of his mouth. "None of that puritanical judgment. I'm not 'good,' I'm fair."

"Well, it makes me trust you a little more."

"I'll allow it," he says with a smirk. "At least that makes me feel a bit better about doing this."

"Doing what?"

"It takes a special skill to weigh the metaphysical. How does one determine the quality of a soul offered against a once-in-a-lifetime supernatural power? How much is eternal youth truly worth? What does beauty weigh? There's no single answer. It's case by case, and sensitive business." He presses his palm to my sternum, hot fingers on my collarbones, and holds my gaze. "Before I make a deal, I like to assess the goods, so to speak. I could take a look around, if you let me. As a favor." His mouth pulls on one side. "Thing is, this here is . . . not gonna feel great."

I grit my teeth, and nod. "Do it."

His hand grows hot on my skin, and his eyes glow until I am falling, soft and harsh, slow and fast. Until the world is tinted red, a darker and darker and darker shade until it is no longer red, but black. His eyes reach me from far away, and a warmth, low and encouraging, spreads through my chest. Like a powerful mesmer, but so, so much deeper.

If Sel's mesmer feels like the tide pulling me under, and Isaac's a wave, Valec's mind is the ocean rising up in a wall and crashing over me all at once.

A burning, searing heat pulls through my veins. The furnace in my chest that is my Bloodcraft birthright opens up to burn his power back—and voices rise from within me, my own joining them:

'Help me see the danger before it strikes. Help me resist their entrapments. Give us the strength to hide and to fight. Protect us. Protect me. Protect her. Please.'

Valec's power is too close, too much like theirs.

Burn. Him. Out.

An explosion inside me. I am flung back into my body—and a root fireball sends Valec flying across the room.

The cambion twists in midair, kicking off the wall with a loud thunk instead of hitting it. The root, without a target, dissipates into a cloud of smoke. Valec lands in a crouch, red eyes wide and glowing, teeth bared at the smoke as if it might come for him again.

The door slams open, and Sel stands between us, snarling, his back tensed for combat. My chest seizes at the sight of him. His face is all fury and fangs, the ends of his hair raised high and smoking. His fingertips have darkened. William, Alice, and Mariah come tumbling in after him, shouting. The floor tilts beneath me, and my chest itches. No, it *hurts*—

Sel advances, and Valec holds his hands up. "I'm done, I'm done!"

"Sel . . . ," I whisper, and he whirls back, eyes growing wide when he sees me.

Even though I can't see it through my clothes, I know the mark starts at my chest, where Valec's palm rested. As we watch, the mark spreads into deep red vines that climb up my throat and down my arms to my elbows, curling into small buds at my hands. I gasp, looking down at my body.

"What did you do to her?" Sel demands, his voice a low rumble. I look up to see his eyes flooding back to a deeper yellow. His hair drops down against his head, and his fingers flush to their normal pale color.

Alice lurches toward me, but William holds her back.

"I didn't do that," Valec says, walking around to get a better look with both palms still raised. "*That* was already there."

A slow realization creeps through my body. Valec didn't put that mark on me. He *revealed* it.

As we watch, the vines fade in color until they disappear entirely into my brown skin. Like they were never there. Or like they always were. I'm not sure. With trembling hands, I pull my sweater up over my shoulders, uncomfortable under both Valec's and Sel's gazes.

Valec tips his head back in sudden understanding. "The Bloodcraft. Of course!" He looks at me with new interest, and not a small amount of awe. "Your ancestor called for power. And if *you're* the end result, I'd say she called on a *lot* of power."

"Yes. She did it to escape. To protect her unborn daughter."

Valec curses. "Two hundred years ago, when a Black woman running meant a white man chasing after his property. In your ancestor's case, she was carrying his blood—what the Legendborn value most in the world."

I nod. "Yes."

Valec snaps. "Well, that's one part of the mystery solved. Your ancestor made a bargain. I knew it!"

"Valechaz," Mariah warns. "Not a game." William and Alice begin asking questions at once.

"Wait!" I shake my head. "No, Vera and the Legendborn are

Bloodcrafters. They bound power to their bloodlines. Vera didn't—"

Valec interrupts. "Bloodcraft and Rootcraft are practitioner ideologies. Belief systems about how to best *use* aether. Some folks get very"—he sniffs—"*stuffy* about how they were raised in magic." He gives Mariah a pointed look.

"So, Patricia was . . . wrong?" I ask Mariah.

She shakes her head. "Nah. Doc Hartwood's not wrong. She's just *particular* about her tradition. I know lots of practitioners like her, and lots who aren't, like Aunt Lu." She smiles, shaking her head. "We're all raised on slightly different beliefs."

Valec rolls his eyes. "There are a *thousand* different philosophies about the 'right way' to handle power once you possess it, metaphysical or not." He turns back to me, eyes glinting. "But in the case of magic, there are only three methods that the living can use to access it."

"Borrow, bargain, or steal . . . ," I murmur.

"Exactly. Your chosen belief system determines your acquisition method. Rootcrafters believe in balance, that magic is not theirs to own, so they preach borrowing. Fine, that's their way. Bloodcrafters believe there is value in binding magic to their bloodlines permanently—as a morally questionable philosophy in the first place, its practitioners are *usually* the type to access power through theft. See: the Legendborn and the corresponding Abatement that is the universe correcting for that theft. But Bloodcrafters aren't *required* to steal power. Nothing is stopping a Bloodcrafter from making a permanent bargain for her power instead." He grins. "So, let's review, shall we? Vera used magic for the practice of Bloodcraft, but how did she get that magic in the first place . . . ?"

I think back. The request. *Protect us, please.* Then thousands of voices answering. *A price.* "Oh God. A bargain."

He gestures to me with an open hand. "And who did Vera make the bargain with?"

"*Her* ancestors. Mine."

"How many?"

"All . . . of them?"

"Well, damn." Mariah looks at Valec, who whistles long and low.

"High reward like that requires a high price."

I bite my lip. "'One daughter at a time, for all time.' And the mothers, my mother . . . they all die early."

His eyes flicker with pain. "That'll do it. But it wasn't your ancestors who gave you that mark. Couldn't have been."

I blink. "Who did?"

"And what is it?" Sel demands.

Valec regards us all for a moment, and satisfaction turns to concern. "None of you know?"

Sel groans. "You're enjoying our ignorance."

"Yours, mostly."

"*Valec.*" Mariah chides. "Even I don't know. Just spit it out."

Valec draws a deep breath through his nose. For the first time since I've met him, something like sympathy crosses his face, and his brows turn up in the middle when he faces me.

"To most demons, humans are fickle, short-lived things who lie. A lot."

"Don't demons lie?" I protest.

"Well, of course," he says. "But not about promises. Demons can't resist a bargain and can't break their word once one is made. Humans, however . . . say a young human being promises something of *themselves* as their half of a bargain, something big—their soul, their future child, a powerful ability only they possess—there's a high likelihood that when the time comes to make the exchange, that human will get cold feet, turn tail, and run. The only thing that ties a human down to that demon or prevents them from giving their promised bounty away to another demon with a better offer is a binding magical contract. Hence, me."

"Get on with it, Valec. . . ," Mariah urges.

Valec makes a face at her. "But in the old days, before brokers and paperwork, there was another way for a demon to claim a human bounty for themselves. Especially if that bounty is something they have to wait for, and they don't want any other being trying to claim it in the meantime."

My chest clenches, burning where the glowing mark had spread across my skin. Valec's eyes soften.

"I'm sorry, powerhouse, but you've been bloodmarked."

I press a hand against my chest. "There's a demon out there who is waiting on *me* to fulfill a bargain?"

He nods. "Yep. And nothing and no one—in either dimension—can stop them from coming to collect."

45

THE ROOM LOOKS at Valec blankly, waiting for him to continue.

"Wish I could tell you more." He scratches the back of his neck. "Really do."

Sel shakes his head. "Don't listen to him, Briana. He's trying to convince you he has use here. He's made up some reason to give you information, hoping it'll turn into a debt you owe him."

Valec's had enough. "You getting close to the edge again, Kingsmage? Jumping to the worst-case scenario first. Assuming I want to tie Bree to me beyond the bounds of this conversation. Keep her for myself?"

"Don't you?"

"Well," Valec considers, smiling with not a small amount of fang. "Yes."

A minute tilt of Sel's chin. "Watch yourself."

Valec's smirk blooms wide. "The difference between you and me, Kane, is that *I* am a transparent sort, who's happy to say out loud all that I desire." Brown eyes flicker to red and back. "You want the same, you just can't come out and say it. Not really."

Sel's answer is a stunned silence. William flushes pink, and Alice looks downright disgusted. She pokes a finger at Sel's face. "You watch *yourself*, Kingsmage. That's my best friend and I don't like or trust you *nearly* enough to—"

"Stop. *Stop.*" I wave my hands while fighting the heat building around my collar. I blow out a breath and turn to Valec. "How could a demon be waiting for me to give them something I never agreed to give?"

"You didn't agree to it. Vera did. He marked her first and you've inherited it. And since the bargain was unregulated, this demon could have claimed anything they desired." Valec straightens his vest. "All I know is that particular mark is strong as hellfire, which means the demon who applied it is ancient. Never seen one carried out over generations."

"It's what burned Kizia," I whisper.

"Kizia?" Valec says. "That trash goruchel always on the lookout for a score? How do you know her?"

"Knew her," I murmur. "She's . . . dead."

Valec inhales sharply. "Don't say another word. I need plausible deniability. But tell me how your mark burned her?"

"A lot like it burned you," I say.

"She feared the Great Devourer," Sel says, eyes on me. "Said he would find her for unauthorized feeding."

Valec whistles. "The Great Devourer. You mean the Hunter? You're sure she said that?"

"Hundred percent sure," I whisper. My chest aches and burns, as if speaking his name is enough to call the demon's mark to the surface.

"Bloodmarked by the Hunter himself. . . . Damn." Valec rubs his chin. "I need to get back to the Lounge. Put my ear to the ground on this, find out what I can about the Hunter's last sighting." He points at me as he moves to the door. "And you need to get to the protection of Volition. ASAP, powerhouse."

"Wait!" I step to the door. "I saw Vera's bargain. There was no demon. And she would have said something by now, I'm certain."

"Some opportunistic demons can piggyback onto a verbal bargain, if you're not careful," he calls over his shoulder. "You're a Medium. Call somebody up and ask."

"It's not that simple!" I protest, but even as I say so, I think of Jessie's warning. Of *him*—the man following her in the days after she drew on her Bloodcraft with intention.

"Sure isn't. Not out in the open where any demon nearby might find you. Which is why you need to go to Volition." And with that, he saunters to the front door and out onto the porch, without looking back.

Mariah mumbles something about Valec being "a damn nuisance" and jogs after him.

After a moment of silence, Alice Chen decides now is the time to stir the damn pot. "I think Valec likes you, Bree."

"Agreed," William says, voice amused.

"Valec likes playing games." I scoff. "I'm a shiny new thing he got to play with."

Sel turns at that. "Play with *how*, exactly?"

I flush. "Figure of speech."

Sel sneers. "He's a demon. We can't trust anything he says."

"He's a cambion," I reply. "Just like you."

In a blink, Sel's in front of me, eyes blazing. "Valec is *nothing* like me."

"Is this a one-drop rule thing?" I ask, brow raised. "Because, ew."

"It is not the same." He runs both hands through his hair, pacing. "That is . . . white supremacist *bullshit*. I'm talking about the *actual*, *active* evil in someone's blood."

Alice taps her chin. "So, what percent actual, active evil are you, then?"

Sel glares at her. "Don't try to be clever."

She laughs. "I don't need to try, fang boy."

I throw my hands up in exasperation. Behind me William groans. "Now would be a wonderful moment for me to intervene and remind you all that evil deeds are not written in hemoglobin. You can't see them under a microscope."

"No, but you can see them in action," Sel spits. "Valec arranges for humans to become food."

"The humans come to him, actually," I reply reasonably. "He said it himself. Clients on both sides of the deal approach him. I'm not saying it's something I would do, or that it's objectively 'right,' just that if they're consenting adults, I'm not entirely sure what the problem is. It's better than letting the demons ravage the human population. And less work for the Legendborn to manage. He might even be making your jobs easier."

"Or creating more work for us, because goruchels and uchels have a steady source of food and all the time in the world to plot with one another, or join forces with the Morgaines!" Sel thrusts a hand out. "There is no reality in which making it easier for demons to survive is a good thing, Bree. The Order——"

"Are you really going to quote the Order to me right now?" I spit back. "You of all people? The Order has lied to you your entire life. Locked you up. Why are you clinging to made-up rules by an organization only in place to serve itself?"

"Because those made-up rules are what can keep me remotely human!" Sel roars. "And the Order, even Davis, even Isaac, even Erebus, took me in and kept me alive and trained me when my parents left me behind! Because no matter how awful the Regents are, our Oaths mean something. Which you wouldn't understand, because you've never sworn yourself to anything or anyone in your life." Sel curses, then he's gone in a whoosh of black.

Tears spring at my eyes, and I fight them away. My chest is heaving. When did I start breathing hard? When did this turn into a fight? Why does it always have to with him?

William releases a slow breath and wraps his arm around my shoulders. "Valec hit a sore spot, and Sel took it out on you. He'll get over it."

I exhale. "Does he . . . does he have to be such an ass about it?"

"Yes," William and Alice answer together.

Three hours later, with all five of us loaded up, Mariah pulls in past a gate to a long, long dirt drive and stops partway down the road when we reach a painted wooden sign that says VOLITION.

She beckons us out of the car. The chill in the air slices right through my hooded jacket and leggings. When she rounds the hood, the corner of her mouth lifts. "This used to be called Guthrie Plantation. It used to *be* Guthrie Plantation, 'til other crafters got together to buy it from the state in the twenties. Good thing, too, 'cause they kept it from turning into one of those 'plantation venues' white people book for weddings." She wrinkles her nose in derision. "Getting married, right where we were butchered and assaulted, raped, whipped, and starved, families torn apart. Taking family photos on top of centuries of blood and death. Shit is fucking *gross*."

I shudder, nodding in agreement. I look up the road, past the sign, but it seems to rise up toward the horizon.

Mariah follows my gaze. "It's a whole lotta land. The big, historic house is still there. Lots of smaller homes preserved for our private use, and a couple new residence structures they built that the state heritage folks woulda never allowed."

She beckons us forward, then holds out an arm. "Stop here."

Sel's brow furrows.

"What?" William asks.

He shakes his head. "May be my imagination, but I could have sworn I just felt . . . aether."

Mariah smiles. "Just you wait."

She steps forward and pauses, pulling out a pack of dried nuts and fruit and a small mason jar of water, unscrewing the top. Then she sets both down on the ground.

Gold mage flame sparks to life beneath her hands. Sel, William, and I each step back, startled. In a flash, it spreads like fire in a thin, hot line out from Mariah on either side, curving wide and rushing through the underbrush and trees out of sight.

"Mariah . . . ," I whisper. Alarm is a low sizzle in my belly. Mage flame doesn't catch things on fire the same way normal fire does, but seeing the smoke and light flickering over the dry ground is still unnerving.

Mariah throws a smirk over her shoulder, the light reflecting in her glasses as she follows its path. "Wait for it."

BOOM!

All at once, the midmorning sky turns a crackling, shimmering gold.

"A barrier," Sel says, sheer awe plain on his face.

Mariah lightly touches the surface. I watch the gold ripple against her fingers.

"That's it," Alice declares. "I'm getting *somebody* to Oath me."

I glare at her.

"I can't take this—you all can see things I can't see, and it's getting old." She feels me staring, and doesn't even look back at me when she argues. It's decided in her mind, I can tell.

"May as well," William murmurs in agreement, eyes back. "This is . . ."

Sel's shaking his head, taking in the enormity of the structure, the reach of the transparent shield arcing across the sky. "Who is casting this?" Like mine, his eyes are darting around the woods, looking for aether users, but there are none.

Mariah steps back with a satisfied smile. "First, this barrier is always up. I just let it know that we were here so it could show itself. Second, no one here is casting it."

"Well, then, who is?" William asks.

Mariah looks to me, and beckons me closer until we're side by side next to the shield. "Can you feel them, Bree?"

As soon as she says something, and I stretch outward with my senses, the hair on the back of my neck lifts.

"*Oh . . .*"

I drop to my knees, press my hands into the earth, and listen. Gold mage flame encircles my arms, flowing up in a rush to my shoulders like hands seeking me out, searching over me. The light spreads into my chest. Sel is at my side, reaching down.

"Stop!" Mariah says. "Don't touch her."

"Excuse—"

"Don't, Sel," I whisper. The light is flooding up my neck and over my throat, into my mouth, my ears, covering me. "They're reaching for me. It's not . . . it's not painful. They just want to know who I am. Why I'm here."

His eyes search the ground around me. "Who?"

"The dead. Ancestors who died here." I pitch forward, struck by the force of them. "Oh *God*, there are so many. The death, and the life. Dozens of them. Asking me . . ." I tilt my head. By instinct, I press my ear to the earth. I look up. "They want to know if they should let you in."

Sel startles. "Me?"

I shift to my knees. "All of you."

Mariah steps beside me, turning with a smug expression. "This site is reclaimed from our oppressors. Rootcrafters have cared for it for a hundred years, and spent the first half of that helping the ancestors who wanted to move on from their trauma go to rest. The spirits who remained control this place in death, because they never could in life. Which is why y'all need permission to come inside the barrier."

Sel nods, looking at the ground with new eyes. "With respect, they don't know Bree . . . do they?"

"Most were crafters in life, so they know enough." Mariah turns to me. "So, Bree, you've got to let *them* know."

I nod, because *yes*. Yes, of course. The land beneath my body is rich with voices, so close to the surface, blood in the soil, lives spent in whole here, from birth to death. I sag when the light spreads from me, inviting me to respond.

"Yes, please," I whisper, placing my hand against the barrier. I look over my shoulder at Alice, William, and Sel. "They're with me. They are here to help me."

The barrier shudders, and an opening spreads from my fingers outward, growing into a circle wide enough for them to walk through. I step through and wait beside Mariah.

Once the circle is wide enough, William and Sel walk through together. I can see on their faces that they are paying attention to the sensation, looking for differences. Finding what is similar.

"This is the biggest construct I've ever seen. I . . . I didn't know aether could be used like this. Cast by the dead." William's wonder is infectious.

"That's because it's not aether," Mariah says with a smile. "It's root."

Alice stumbles through after William and Sel, landing in my arms. "Bree . . . ," she whispers, eyes wide behind her glasses. "I can see it."

"You can?"

"Feel it too." She laughs dazedly. "It hurt, and then it didn't."

As the barrier closes behind us, Mariah turns. With hands spread wide and the rolling hill of the reclaimed plantation behind her, she smiles.

"Welcome to Volition. Where our will be done."

PART FOUR

VOLITION

46

"WILL THE BARRIER go down?" I ask. We walk the rest of the way on foot. Behind us, the barrier remains high, sparkling in the midday sky.

Mariah shakes her head. "No, never. Just gets more visible or less. The ancestors are awake now. You're a new Medium on the grounds. It'll probably stay lit up like that for a few hours."

Sel looks overhead, holding his hand up to the sky even though the barrier is at least half a mile up. His fingers play against the air. "It is . . . *strong*."

"Don't, Kingsmage," Mariah warns. "You can't use root without permission here."

I expect Sel to argue, especially after being so restricted by the cyffion, but to my surprise he doesn't. His hand drops. "Understood."

"The boundary is marked by bottle trees here and there." She points to a tree about six feet tall a little ways behind us, on the other side of the gold root barrier. Colorful glass bottles cover the end of each branch. The light of the barrier plays off the blues and greens, illuminates the yellows and reds. "When the barrier goes invisible and you're walking around, you gotta 'look left and right, keep two bottle trees in sight.' If you see two, you can draw a line between them and know where Volition's protection ends. Don't expect y'all will be venturing out, but just in case you do. And if you do, you can't get back without one of us."

"Similar to a ward," Sel murmurs. "Designed for certain entrants, and restricted for others."

Mariah points out the grounds of Volition as we walk. "Okay, so on the left and right side of the main drive there are some modern buildings. An office. An archives room. Three updated residential buildings for guests."

"Guests?" Sel asks.

"Yeah, *guests*. Like you, you're a guest." She points to a massive rust-red barn up ahead with a pair of large doors open on one end. "We don't keep livestock here anymore, so the barn's been finished inside and remodeled for community gatherings. Volition was a site of subjugation and is now a living cemetery, and we are that cemetery's caretakers. While the ancestors buried here were brought to Guthrie Plantation against their will, the descendants of the enslaved *choose* to call on Volition. Choose to learn, to rest, to arrive, to leave."

I fall behind on the walk, overwhelmed with the energy around us, my lids half-closed. With each step, I have to resist the urge to take my shoes off or run my bare hands over the ground. With each structure and stretch of lawn we pass, my Medium vision shows me what is and what was: ghostly outbuildings with mud sill cabin doorways that lead to interior dirt floors, gone now but there once. Black women in loose shirts and skirts flicker in and out of existence as they stride toward me with buckets of water from a river I hear in the distance, running high then but dry today. A small kitchen building up ahead that sits quietly now, but whose bleed-through shows me the smoke that used to curl from its chimney. The scent of cooking meat from over two hundred years ago makes my mouth water. By the time my friends notice I'm not with them and turn back, they find me kneeling in the grass, hands brushing over the pointy tips but lost in a vision of muddy hoofprints from the past.

Mariah laughs. "You really gotta get better at closing up shop, girl, or you'll never get past the driveway. You'll get bleed-throughs of this whole plantation if you're not careful."

"Too late." I push to my feet.

She smiles. "Every Rootcrafter communes with the ancestors, but Volition is more intense for Mediums than any other practitioner, just by the nature of our particular gifts. That's why it's the best place to go when you have questions to ask without being disturbed, when you have ancestor work to do. But for *you*, Bree-Bree?" She laughs at me. "You're probably half in the stream just by walking around the place."

Sel shakes his head. "But is it her power or theirs?"

Mariah laughs again. "Thinking like a colonizer, Kingsmage. The ancestors have access to the power. We're *borrowing* it, letting it flow through us, but ultimately, it's not ours to keep. 'Temporary' is the key word here for most Rootcrafters." Mariah looks back at me, linking arms with mine. "But because of Vera's Bloodcraft bargain, Bree here is a faucet that doesn't turn off."

"Fire hose, more like it," I mutter.

"Yeah, well, there's a reason Valechaz calls you 'powerhouse.'"

I pause. "Can Valec come on the grounds here, or would he be a guest?"

Mariah makes a strange face. "Valec was born on a plantation, to a mother who practiced. His mother's people cast him out, but he ended up enslaved elsewhere. He's welcome at Volition and always has been. Doesn't come by much, though." She looks around. "You and I may feel the dead, see them, but we don't carry the memories of what these places were really like. He does. He lived it. Survived it."

"Hard to remember that sometimes, with how young he looks," Alice says.

Rising up in front of us, imposing and grand and painted in fresh white and grays, is the main house.

"That's the original big house, for the most part. Some additions about fifty or sixty years ago, and of course the inside is different. Ritually cleansed to hell and back, for one thing."

"Mariah?" A voice calls out from a large, low-walled garden in the side yard.

"Aunt Lu!" Mariah says. "Hazel called you about us coming by?"

"Yep." The Grand Dame appears around the corner, smiling at me. "Hello, again."

I gape at Lu. "I didn't know you'd be here."

Lu folds Mariah into a hug, then looks over at the rest of the group with a wry smile. "You aren't our typical passengers. Figured I'd handle some things myself. My abilities are stronger here, too." She steps closer to me and offers her hand. "So, let's check in, Bloodcrafter."

I stick my hand out, preparing for a simple handshake. Instead, her fingers buzz against mine. Lu winces with a slight smile, other hand up as if to block light. "Who you been talking to, all that power?"

Mariah grimaces. "Well, that's just it, Lu. Bree isn't channeling anybody right now. This is just inside her."

Lu steps back, squaring me up. "Always on, huh?"

"Not always in control of it," I correct.

She hums and runs a hand over her braids, twisting the ends around her fingers with a thoughtful sound. "Well, the ancestors wouldn't let you in if you hadn't had protective intent. And your aura looks good to me, but the colors . . ." She looks at William, then back to me. "You're Legendborn, like he is. A Scion. Arthur's, I'd wager."

Selwyn curses.

"Were you gonna mention that?" Lu asks, not unkindly.

I swallow. "Not exactly safe to say at the Lounge. And Valec's not a big fan."

Lu crosses her arms. "I'm not a big fan myself, but I am curious how one of us got mixed up with one of them."

The others turn to me, because that's my story to tell. "I can fill you in. Later, if that's okay."

She nods, but her eyes narrow in thought. "Agreed." She moves toward Mariah and points up at the house. "Hazel's coming by later to help with the meal. Get the other three settled in to the guest house, Mariah. I'll take Bree to her room. Y'all have had a long couple of days. Everybody rest, take a nap, we'll see you at dinner."

"We've all been traveling together. I can stay in the guest house too," I say.

"You can't stay in the guest house." Lu shakes her head. "Not if you're here to do ancestor work." She beckons the others to follow Mariah as if there's no further discussion to be had. "The rest of y'all are gonna work, too. Help keep up the grounds, or help keep an eye out on the border—one or the other. Make yourselves useful. You'll still see plenty of each other, don't worry."

Sel shifts his weight, torn between protesting and biting his tongue. He looks beyond Lu to the house. "Can we visit Bree's rooms? See where she's staying?"

"Nah." Lu shakes her head as she guides me toward the house. "The ancestors say who comes in the house, and they decided a long time ago it's descendants of the enslaved." She lifts a shoulder. "Can't argue with the ghosts of the enslaved. Wouldn't want to, wouldn't recommend it." Lu nods out over the grounds of Volition. "This is their final resting place. The ones who died on it, bled on it, suffered. They make the rules, not us."

Sel follows her gaze, nodding once without comment. William's face is solemn, thoughtful. "In the Legendborn tradition, we call ourselves Awakened when our knights call us. But we don't really talk about them as if they're still alive. Beginning to wonder if we should."

"Well," Lu says. "Awake ain't the same thing as living."

It feels like more than a temporary parting. The four of us have been together for so long, and this is where I undergo something that they can't share.

Alice steps forward to give me a tight hug. "See you soon." I hug her back.

William squeezes me from the other side and kisses my cheek. "We'll still be close."

Mariah rolls her eyes. "Y'all. It's not like she's going away forever. Jeez."

They drift away behind Mariah while Sel lingers. I glance to Lu, who rolls her eyes and starts up the path, muttering something about "teenagers" and "drama."

Sel steps into my space, frowning. His eyes follow the silver curls at my forehead with a displeased expression before they drop to my gaze. Displeasure still present. "I do not have to tell you that I am not okay with you being out of my sight, no matter how protected you are on this property."

"No," I reply, mimicking his low tone. *"You do not."*

He rolls his eyes in mock annoyance. "But I do need to say one thing."

"Of course you do."

He reaches for my hand, tugs me close, and leans down to my ear. "I am . . . sorry about this morning."

Tension in my chest releases, but I'm still feeling prickly. "You were mean," I whisper.

He nods, dark hair a soft caress up and down my cheek. "That is because I am a mean person." A pause. "But everyone else deserves it. *You do not.*"

My heart fills with warm honey, and Sel smirks like he can see it. Like he knows he did that and doesn't care if I know, too. I haven't fully forgiven him for mesmering me. I don't know how we'll heal that rift, but maybe in a place of protection and peace, it could be possible. At the very least, I won't be worried about being choked, attacked, or disemboweled.

It should shock me that I've been living with all three of these threats for weeks now, but it doesn't. It shocks me more that I could be somewhere where those threats are guaranteed to be absent. I'm somewhere—we're somewhere—where we don't have to look over our shoulders. Don't have to lie about who we are. Don't have to worry Erebus could be around every corner, or a Kizia, or a Jonas. My face must show some odd emotion, because Sel tilts his head.

"Just thinking," I say. "About going to sleep tonight, not worried that I might be murdered. Or that you or Alice or William might be attacked because you're with me. Maybe a whole part of my brain will be able to relax, at least a little."

He chuckles, nodding. "I'm glad. We aren't meant to run from trauma to trauma."

I look around the grounds. "I think this place understands that."

"I'm glad someplace does," he adds. "No one can run forever." His eyes have gone distant. I can tell who he's thinking of by the pinch between his brows.

"I haven't tried to contact Arthur again, to find Nick," I say. "Maybe I—"

"No. If you reach out to Arthur, do it for you, not Nick." He hums, jerking a chin to Lu a few yards away and the house beyond. "Go on. We'll be here." He waits until I reach the stairs, then follows the others to one of the brick houses up the drive.

"You ever been in a spirit's home before?" Lu asks when I catch up to her at the front door. I see the family resemblance between her and Valec a little more clearly. The expression that sees more than you want to share.

"No." I reach my hand out instinctively, and a barrier around the house sends a zing of energy zips down my fingertips and up my neck.

"Another root barrier?" I look back at the one still overhead. "Why did they want a second one around the house?"

Lu crosses her arms. "I asked my grandaddy the same thing when I was your age. He said that the foundation of root is protection, and it's up to the ancestors to decide how much of that they want to offer and how much of that we need." She looks back over her shoulder to see the others enter the low guest house. "Didn't want to alarm anyone, but if any of your friends try to get in, the house won't let them."

"I can't ask, like at the driveway?" I ask.

"The house is nonnegotiable." She shakes her head. "Volition is both a gravesite and a refuge. A site of mourning and a site of hope. If there's any place in the country where the spirits of the dead can reclaim a place for themselves and their own people, it's a house like this, don't you think?"

I nod slowly, thinking of Vera's escape from her plantation, the origin of her Line of power. Even as I have prepared myself to confront the Regents and force them—and the Order—to face the truth, I have run. I have hid. I have had to escape, time and time again. I have survived, but I have scars to show for it—inside and out.

"A place of our own," I say. "To rest."

Lu links an arm with mine. "Where we get to decide what to preserve, and how."

47

THE ROOM SHE invites me to is a mix of modern elements—outlets and a charging cable for a phone I don't have—and nods to history. A washing basin in front of a heavy, gilded mirror. Wood paneling on three sides, and an accent wall of some sort of brocade in reds and yellows and greens. There's a bathroom down the hall, and four other rooms on the second floor. I don't have anything to unpack, but there are clothes laid out over a four-drawer, antique dresser that look like they might fit me, and accessories to keep me warm: leggings, a long dress with wide sleeves, a scarf, an oversized jacket with a hood. I change into all of the clothes, grateful for fresh laundry, and sit on the bed, eyes drifting shut within minutes.

I wake up on the bedcover in the late afternoon, face smushed into the floral comforter. I hadn't even really intended to nap, but my body had other plans.

Lu meets me outside the house, or rather, I meet her. She looks settled on the porch by the time I arrive. Changed into an old pair of wide-legged jeans and a loose black shirt, hunched over a basket, picking through items. Her gray braids have been pulled up into a pile on her head.

Without preamble she says, "Folks who come here for work have to state their intention to their ancestors directly."

"Makes sense." I nod. "I know my intention: I wanna get stronger."

Lu snorts, keeps hunting through the basket. Pulls out a couple of stones, a wrapped bit of herbs, a white cloth. "Maybe."

Something like insult rips through my chest, surprising both Lu and myself. "What do you mean 'maybe'? I've been through a *lot* to get here, even before I knew what Volition was, I knew I needed a place like it. I know what I want."

"Intention isn't want. Intention isn't even need." She looks up out at the yard, taps her pointer finger to her chest, then tips it outward. "Intention is the bare bones of desire, but it requires fuel. That fuel is your will." She looks around. "'Volition,' the word, is your choice to attach and align yourself with your desire. The strongest of our workings come from this place of alignment."

Sounds like something Patricia would say, except more nicely. "I already have a therapist," I mutter.

"Good for you," Lu says with a laugh. "I ain't your therapist. I just work here."

A lot more nicely.

Still, when I consider her words, I can't help but think of the Legendborn Oaths. There are some overlapping principles, at least to me. Different words for the same ideas, different executions for similar goals. "Huh."

"'Huh' what?"

I shrug. "The Legendborn, the Order, they work with intention magic, too. Their Oaths are based on that."

Lu wrinkles her nose. "Their Oaths bind to their bodies through intention, and live within them to punish deviations from a given promise. Volition isn't a place of punishment. It's a place for teaching."

Tension flows from my shoulders. "You have no idea how good that sounds right now. How much I've been running, we've been running. Even when I've been able to call on my ancestors, it drains me after. I'm . . ." I look out at the grounds, the gold sheen of the barrier marking the safety of this space. "I'm grateful to be here. Relieved."

"Good." Lu stands with her collection of items tucked into a satchel, and places the basket on the table. "We'll get started first thing tomorrow morning. You hungry? We've got dinner to prep. The others are already started."

Ten minutes later, I'm maneuvering around the dining room in the barn with a handful of plates, setting the table for seven.

Lu walks into the room with a pitcher of tea then sets it down and pivots back out the way she came in. The door to the kitchen area swings open and closed behind her, and I get a glimpse of Mariah and Alice laughing as they prep a salad. Hazel pushes through a side door holding another foil serving platter and a pair of tongs, heading to an outdoor kitchen.

When Lu walked us across the grounds, she pointed out where cabins used to stand. "Outdoor prep in plantation kitchens was pretty common. We centralized it at the barn, updated the spaces, added gas and electricity, but we still use some of the old ways of cooking. We don't have to live in our ancestors' footsteps to know them, but cooking the way the plantation cooks did . . . that's its own type of magic."

William and Sel asked to walk the Volition border from the inside to get to know the layout of the grounds. Alice stayed behind but she asked too many questions of the cooks, which meant she got put on food prep with Mariah.

The dining room of the barn feels more like a camp building than I'd expected. Lots of long picnic tables, a kitchen at one end, big windows open to the field beyond. The room's big enough that it could fit a hundred Rootcrafters, easy.

Hazel walks in and sets a large bowl down on the table, reaches in, and pulls out a smaller plastic one, setting it down too. Then she pulls a green bean out of the first, snapping the end.

The sight of her snapping beans reminds me of my dad. The sound reminds me of my childhood, and the only food prep task my parents would give me when I was six and eager to help. I slide down the table to join her and reach into the large bowl, pulling out my own long green bean.

We fall into a rhythm, grabbing beans and splitting the pointy ends off as we talk. It's meditative work. Something about feeling along each casing to find the breaking point, one at a time. Thirty minutes later, the beans are sizzling in Mariah's pan under Hazel's supervision, and Alice is walking around the table opposite me, putting down glasses while I pour the tea.

Sel and William walk in right when the smell of food starts hitting us in steady, mouth-watering waves, and offer to chip in. William grabs the napkins and Sel picks up the utensils, falling in behind me. His silence tells me he has something on his mind, but I don't push.

The meal is splendid. Warm, filling, and lively.

I shift in my seat as we sit and digest, anticipation fluttering up above the itis in my belly currently luring me to sleep. "What exactly happens tomorrow morning?"

Lu pauses, looks at me. "Depends. Mariah says you haven't been using material offerings for your communions . . . ?"

"Blood offerings seem to be the most direct approach. Dunno why, but that's what lets me blood walk. Live the memories they choose to show me."

Hazel stirs her tea. "Offerings honor the ancestors with gifts of life. That's why it's better to provide something that was once alive, fresh, or something close to its original form, or created by nature. But Blood-craft, for you, connects you to the dead in two ways: to the power of thousands of ancestors on one lineage, and to the power of one who lived over a thousand years ago on another. Reaching that far back, asking questions that cover that many lives and years . . . it makes sense you may need something richer than fruit and sweet cakes. Especially if they're inviting you to their memories."

"I use more than blood." I raise the Pendragon coin necklace with my left hand, shaking it so that the coin and the bracelet shine in the same light. "I use these, too."

Lu eyes both items. "Focal items, connected to each bloodline. I use focals for aura work sometimes. Have the client hold them so I can help read the dynamic between them and their objective, or relationship."

"But when you summon Arthur, you see Nicholas as well," Sel says, voice low. There is no rancor or spite or frustration on his face, only a quiet sort of contemplation. "Who isn't an ancestor."

"Yes." I explain to Lu. "His ancestor is Lancelot. When I'm in Arthur's body in Arthur's memory and touch Lancelot, if I focus on Nick, Nick takes his ancestor's place."

Lu blinks. "Medium possession—channeling a spirit forward to the living—is rare. Channeling in the opposite direction, even rarer. But bringing *another* living being into their ancestor's body in the stream? Never heard of it."

"Maybe because Nick gave me the necklace?" I offer.

Hazel and Lu exchange glances, talking to themselves more than us now. "That was a one-way gift, not an exchange." Lu questions her wife with wide, excited eyes. "Haze, is she tapping into his genetic memory?"

"That'd be epigenetics," Hazel muses. "And yes, could be. Mediums travel the ancestral stream, a type of spirit DNA. Bree is more powerful than a typical Medium, with a seemingly endless source of root powering her. . . ."

"Wait. *Epigenetics?*" William leans forward, eyes wide. "Miss Hazel, you think Bree can navigate DNA memory?"

"It's a hypothesis. But yes, I do." Miss Hazel smiles at William's slack jaw. "You all call me 'Miss,' but my students call me 'Doctor.'"

William grins. "Dr. Hazel, I like you very much."

She laughs. "We are biology and magic both, Scion." She pours herself another glass. "Communing with ancestors requires a connection that runs in both directions. Spiritual and physical. An open channel on both sides, tying each party to the other. Like blood."

"Or like an Oath," Sel murmurs. "Our Oaths bind to our DNA and bind people together, either as individuals one to one, or one to a group."

"It makes sense, actually," Alice says. "You're tapping into his lineage."

"Thanks, y'all," I murmur after a quiet moment. "For being here."

Alice rolls her eyes. "Are you kidding? Not running for our lives is the new vacation."

Sel's mouth twitches. "She's not wrong."

William groans. "We need *actual* vacations."

"What are those again?" I ask. The table laughs.

"I am glad you are here, too, Bree Matthews." Lu sits back at the table, eyes thoughtful. "I hope, for all our sakes, that you find the answers you seek."

THE FIRST THING I think of when I step inside the large, packed-dirt communion circle at the back of the property the next day is that it reminds me of the Legendborn training rooms. Circles for bouts and practicing combat skills. Circles to establish boundaries for the opponents, keeping the fight inside.

I hope my ancestor work doesn't turn into a fight.

"Do you know all of their names?" Hazel asks. She and Lu walk in opposite directions around the boundary to "set the circle" for the revival. Lu says that the communion circle has been on the property for ages, but they have to wake it up in some way. Bring it to the ancestors' attention that something big is about to happen, I guess.

Whenever the two women cross paths, one passes a small hand-rolled cigarette back to the other, who puffs on it on her rotation, then passes it back. It doesn't smell like nicotine to me—at all—but that's none of my business.

Alice watches the entire process with wide eyes. She, William, and Sel are behind me, perched on a collection of boulders that are worn smooth from observers past.

"Yes," I say. "Starting from the beginning, there's Vera, then—"

Hazel waves a hand. "Don't tell me. Wait until we start the revival, then recite 'em all in reverse order so that them in the ground can hear and know who you're trying to reach."

"Mm-hmm," Lu says, crossing paths with her wife and slipping the joint in her hand. "Almost done. Then you'll stay there, say their names with your whole chest, and we'll get started."

"Did you bring a blade?" Hazel asks.

I pull my trusty safety pin from my pocket and rest it on my knee, sharp, freshly disinfected tip closed in. "Yep."

She eyes the tiny silver pin and huffs a laugh. "Guess that works too."

"Blood is blood." I shrug.

She and Lu circle one more time, until there's a deep trough in the dirt in a near-perfect circle around me. They brush off the bottoms of their shoes and sit on opposite sides of the circle. Hazel gets settled, then explains the revival ritual once more. "Think of this place and ceremony like an amplifier for the ancestral stream. Volition and the communion circle will boost your call so you can talk to all of them at once, 'stead of one at a time, and ask for who you need directly, no guesswork."

I nod. We've gone over this before, but it's a good reminder. The last time I saw all of the women in the Line of Vera at once, I was sweating bullets on the hardwood floors of the Lodge, burning up inside a flaming circle. The last time I had this much ancestral juice at my fingertips, I was in the ogof y ddraig, blowing flames at imps. This circle will contain anything that happens to me, or anything I do—and the barrier over Volition is a second layer of protection. "Okay, I'm ready."

I press my finger into the tip of the pin, then smudge it on the links of my mother's bracelet. "By my blood . . ."

Immediately, a bonfire of golden root flames explodes into existence in the center of the circle.

"Holy . . . ," Alice whispers, somewhere behind me.

Amplifier indeed, if even Alice can see Rootcrafter magic.

I knew I would call my mother's name, but knowing is not the same thing as saying it, out loud, for the first time in a very long while.

"Faye."

For a moment, nothing happens. Then, the yellow and orange bonfire in the center grows, burning brighter, until it is tinged dark Bloodcraft red.

Then, out of the flame, my mother steps forward.

She is just as I remember her, but illuminated. Shimmering in gold and white and wearing a dress edged in crimson. Her smile is wide and warm as she walks toward me, barefoot over the sandy earth.

I am running toward her, hoping, praying that I can touch whatever matter she's made of now. *Please. Please, just* one *hug.*

When she wraps her arms around me, all I feel is heat. Not the cool, smooth texture of her brown skin, but a growing flame pressing outward, as if I could wrap my arms around root itself.

Hugging my mother in death feels like my magic in life. Hot-bright burning beneath the surface, a near eruption. Weapon turned wound, open and raw.

'*Hey, honeybunch,*' she murmurs, and pulls back. Her flame-tinged hand rests on my cheek.

"Mommy," I whisper.

She smiles, looking me over. '*I'll never say you're too big to call me that, but you are growing up. Seventeen soon.*'

I laugh through tears. I'd completely forgotten. "You keep up with my birthday on the other side?"

'*That's one moment in time I will never forget, wherever I am.*' She pulls me close, pressing my head underneath her chin. '*Our Brave Bree.*' She looks over my shoulder, beyond the flame circle. I follow her gaze—Alice has leapt to her feet, with tears streaming down her face.

My mother dips her chin. '*I knew you would be there for her, Alice.*' She surveys William, then Selwyn. A smile tugs at the corner of her mouth. '*It appears I need to thank you all for caring for Bree.*'

Movement and sound behind me. Alice crying so hard, I might start, too. "There's so much I want to ask you. Things I need to know. I need your help—"

She spots her bracelet in my palm. '*Did you find the hidden memory?*'

"I did," I whisper. "How long can you stay?"

She leans back, pressing a hand against the curls at my temple, with that line between her brow. She pulls at the white strands, frowning. *'Not long. Ask your questions.'*

I know the question I need to ask. Know it now, here, more clearly than ever. "Did you ever call on our root of your own volition?"

Her brows pinch in the middle. *'No.'*

I try to mask my disappointment, but mothers notice everything.

She smiles and hugs me tight. *'No ancestor can direct you how to live your life in the present. But they will show you their lives, and hope you glean what you need. Keep searching.'* A beat, then she whispers, *'I know you want to stop death, Bree, but be careful. Grief takes many forms. Be certain you aren't still in its throes, but callin' it somethin' else.'*

Her warning strikes at the part of me that is drawn to Arthur and his promises, but I set it aside when I sense that she's leaving. "Wait."

She pauses, but I see the light within her growing dim.

I glance over my shoulder, but Sel hasn't turned away, and I know he's listening. "The woman that helped you hide the memory. Was that Sel's mother?"

My mother smiles, fond and sad at once. *'Yes. Natasia.'*

I have to ask. "Do you know where she is?"

She glances to Sel, and I know her answer is for his ears and mine both. *'No. Even if I could speak to her now, she would not tell me.'*

My mother gives me a final squeeze, and a frown. *'I love you, Bree. Tell your father I love him.'*

I laugh through tears. "I will. I promise." She turns and walks away before I can beg her to stay. "I love you, too." I see her smile lift, and then she is flame and light, and I can barely make out her features.

"Keep going," Hazel whispers.

I drag my palm across my eyes, sniffling, nodding. I take a deep breath, focus on the voice I will never forget. The spirit I first channeled in my life as a Medium. "Grandmother Charles, Leanne."

Leanne pulls forward out of the fire, a wide, short woman wearing an apron over a full skirt. She smiles. *'We meet again.'*

"Yes, ma'am," I whisper.

She frowns. *'You gettin' enough to eat? Your face looks thin.'*

Someone snickers behind me. I ignore them, and her grandmotherly disappointment. "I need to ask you a question. Did you wield our power to attack, not just to defend?"

She shakes her head, face sad. *'My mother had so trained me to stay away from danger, that I lived most my life without the power ever manifesting. Didn't matter that I never used it. It was going to take her no matter what.'*

The grief in her voice digs my own down deeper, burrowing like a drill. "I understand . . . ," I whisper.

'Sorry, baby.' She waves, and steps back.

Jessie I've already spoken to, but she comes forth anyway, glancing to her left where her own daughter had just appeared, sorrow in her features. *'I showed you what I know. That the Hunter will come if you wield our power, grow it large enough to do harm.'*

I feel my friends' eyes on me, and Hazel's and Lu's too. "Who is he?"

She shakes her head. *'I never found out. I could only run.'* She steps forward, eyes hard. *'I am a healer, but know one thing: My mother wished to be a hero. And fighting took her life. But the power woulda taken her life anyway.'*

Next is Emmeline, the hero. More hope there. *'I fought the creatures I saw in the night.'*

She puts her hand to her chest like I'd seen in Jessie's memory. Pulls it forward to extract a whip of flame. I echo her, excited to learn how to do more—then abruptly, she drops her hand. *'Until one night, foxes cornered me. Later, the Hunter found me as I lay dying in the street. He watched life leave me, and said not a word.'*

My heart is a drum in my ears. The bonfire rises in a matching rhythm. At the edge of the circle, Lu and Hazel exchange a look. They are helping me, in part, because I could become powerful enough to face this demon. The presence that has haunted my bloodline and pursued Rootcrafters for generations. "Is the Hunter . . . the demon that bloodmarked us?"

Emmeline shudders. *'I do not know that word, but I do remember him,'* she whispers. *'Eyes black as night, dark as the space between stars, red glowing coals in the middle. Those eyes were the last thing I saw.'* She steps back. *'Be wary, Bree.'*

I do not have time to be wary. I've already run enough.

I have five to go, including Vera herself. I raise my chin and call again.

"Corinne."

Corinne shakes her head when I ask about using our root. *'I died bringing Emmeline into the world. I cannot help you with what you seek. I could not even help my daughter. I was gone before I could tell her where our power came from.'*

Regina is next. *'The power came to me when I needed it. And when I asked.'*

My heart leaps in my chest.

She stops my hope cold. *'But then I started seeing him. From out of nowhere, he'd find me.'*

"But how——"

She shakes her head. *'I won't show you, lest he find you too. We have all lost enough.'* She pauses to examine Volition before she goes, expression curious. With quick mental math, I realize that she'd lived through Emancipation. She looks to Hazel and Lu. *'This place is ours, isn't it?'*

Lu dips her chin. "Yes, ma'am."

Regina smiles, soft and hopeful, then fades. *'Good.'*

Then, Mary. *'Demons were everywhere back then. But then so were other monsters. I saw that Hunter one time and made sure he never had cause to find me again. I just knew he wanted to kill me and I couldn't let that happen. Not after I lost Mama. So I ran. I cannot help you, baby.'*

Selah, Vera's daughter, listens to my question and shakes her head. *'After Momma died, I ran and I survived. I suggest you do the same.'*

By the time Selah fades, I am on my feet, pacing. "No one knew how to use root as a weapon? No one? And if they did, the Hunter came to find them!"

I whirl around to call the last figure, my voice no longer a request, but a demand. "Vera!"

I stand, staring at the flame for a long time. Vera steps forward, eyes burning like the furnace we have all carried, cultivated, lost our mothers to.

She dips her chin. *'Daughter of daughters.'*

My voice comes out low and angry, and I don't try to hide it. "You know why I have called you. "

'I know.'

I wait for her to elaborate, until I am done waiting. "You say I am the spear, the pain-welded blade." I thrust my hand out. "You say I am the wound turned weapon, but you won't help me *become* that weapon! Either no one knows how or they do and they refuse to tell me. I've been running for my life, nearly *killed* because I have to almost die before I can defend myself! What kind of power is that?"

'None of us can help you become . . . anything. We can only show you what we know, enough for you to make your own choices.'

I scoff. "You have got to be kidding me. We don't get to *make* our own choices; you made sure of that!"

Vera's flames burn hotter. She glides toward me, and I can feel her displeasure from here.

Oh well. I'm displeased, too.

'I bargained for our survival.'

"You trapped us," I hiss. "And you don't even seem to care. And the Hunter? Do you know about him? Do you know about the bloodmark?"

'I do not know of this Hunter, I will admit.' Vera bristles, lifts her chin. *'But you know nothing of a trapped life. A bound life.'*

"No, I don't. Not like the one you lived," I admit. "I won't dismiss that, or diminish it."

'Good.' She nods, begins to turn away.

"But 'one daughter at a time, for all time.' That was the deal that you knowingly forced on us. That was *your* Bloodcraft spell," I call out. "And Bloodcraft *is* a trap for the descendants who bear it. It is a binding from birth. That's why other crafters call it a sin," I argue. I glance around the empty circle, where my foremothers once stood. "You bargained for our survival, but *you* never had to bear the consequences. I *see* the agony still in their faces. It's baked into their voices. I can hear it, because it's *mine too.*" I step toward her, teeth bared.

"Bree . . ." Hazel's voice is an urgent plea.

"You got your wish, but you never inherited it at the expense of losing *your* mother, you just bound us to lose ours, over and over and over again. . . ."

Vera's voice roars over me, a hot wave. *'You wish to wield my power, but you cannot manage your own tongue. I saved our bloodline.'*

"That may be true, but that's not the full story." I step into her flames, fury making me bold. "You said that our family ran so I wouldn't have to, and I thought you meant we ran from the Order. What you missed is that some of us ran from the Hunter and we *all* ran from *pain and grief*. You didn't just save our bloodline, *you cursed it*."

Her image flickers, then recovers. *'That is not true.'*

"It is true, you just haven't had to live with it." I shake my head. "The least you can do is tell me how to make my mother's death count. How to use the power to keep myself alive!"

'You are the one who decides now how to keep our Line alive, Briana Matthews.' Vera narrows her eyes. *'I have done my part.'*

She pivots on her heel, and disappears in a flash of light. The circle is cast in darkness. Its edges only lit by the small candles that sit in metal trays on the outer lawn.

I collapse onto my knees, rubbing my palms into the earth. "Come back," I demand. "Come back here!"

"Bree, stop this," Lu calls. She stands at the edge of the communion boundary. "I can't enter the circle right now. I need you to come out."

My chest heaves, taking in great, furious gulps of air. My lungs and chest rise and fall like bellows, feeding the fire still lit in my chest from this calling. "No." I dig my fingers in like claws. *"Come. Back!"*

Fwoom!

A column of flames explodes upward from the circle around me. I *scream* into it, roar alongside it. *"I'm not done with you, Vera!"*

The swirling pillar of my root and fury gets hotter, brighter, and blasts upward in a powerful rush—burning a round hole through the protective golden dome of Volition.

49

SHAME DRIVES ME to my feet.

Fear douses the great column of flames.

Terror sets me running.

Tears blur the way, but I know the direction. I feel the buzz of the barrier—and then I'm on the other side, crashing through the forest that surrounds Volition, red flames streaking from my fist and mouth.

"Stop!"

I keep running—until I trip on a log, and tumble to the other side, knees knocking painfully against hard earth.

"Bree, stop!"

I grunt, scrambling to press back against the wood and pull my knees tight. "I'm sorry," I whisper. I drop my head back against the log harder than I intend to, but the pain feels good. It zips, electric, across my skull. I deserve it, for what I've done. "I'm sorry, I'm sorry. . . ."

Sel leaps over the log, twisting to land in front of me in a crouch. "Are you all right?"

My root flickers around my palm, illuminating the woods, painting stripes of light against his dark clothes.

"The barrier . . . I'm so sorry, I didn't mean—"

"It's okay, Bree," Sel assures. "They're getting it back up. The ancestors are filling it in."

"But that much root." I drop my head into my burning palms. "Any demon looking could have seen that, they'll find Volition."

He inches forward. "They're calling Valechaz. Asking him to tap his network, see if anyone noticed. It was quick, Bree."

"The demon who bloodmarked me, what if he saw. . . . He could come," I say weakly.

"He has not come for you yet," Sel says. "And he may not today. If he does, we will meet him."

My hands ball into fists, pressing into my eye sockets. "I just got so, so angry."

"I know," he whispers. "Look at me." I peer up at him through the flames of my fingers. "No one is mad at you. No one. We all saw what happened, we know how disappointing this is to you."

I shake my head. "I fucked up. Ruined this barrier, this place."

I sob into my hands for long moments, wishing I had chosen a different response. Wishing I hadn't come to Volition at all. Wishing . . . God . . . wishing my hope had not been thrown back in my face.

Exhausted finally, I sniff, and rest my head against the bark. "I don't even know if Vera will ever come to me again."

Sel's voice is quiet. Patient. "You are harder on yourself than anyone else around you, Bree. You excel at so very many things, punishing yourself is a great example."

At that, I look up to find him watching my root with wary eyes, as if he wants to reach out, but worries it will burn him.

"I don't want to hurt you," I mutter, and I rub the heel of my hand over my nose, "so I don't think the flames will, either. Like last time."

"I had hoped that would be the case." Something sad in his voice brings my eyes to his. "As for 'last time,' that is what I am afraid of."

"Afraid?"

"Yes." He moves to a cross-legged position, our knees inches apart. "Touching you when you're like this . . ." He laughs quietly. "Dangerous in more ways than one. Burning is the least of my worries."

"Oh," I whisper.

"'Oh' is right." He sighs. "Maybe it is because I am mid-descent, not quite myself and not quite the demon, or maybe it is because your root is like no other form of aether I have ever encountered, but it took the entire time you were recovering at Hazel's for your scent to leave me. Those three days, and then some."

My eyes widen. "Oh."

He chuckles. "Again?"

"You didn't tell me," I whisper.

His golden eyes follow the flames as they dance across the backs of my hands. "I didn't know how to. Was ashamed, really."

"Why?" I shake my head. "Like William said, aether—or root—affects you differently, but it's nothing shameful."

He leans forward, holding his palms over mine, letting the tips of the flames just kiss the undersides of his hands. After a moment, he finds my gaze and keeps it. "Your power is intoxicating, as are you. I was ashamed because as soon as it was gone from my system, I wanted it back. Craved it—and you. It wasn't . . . right." He breaks our gaze, glancing down. "Can you . . . ?"

"Yes, sure." I sit up straight and curl my fingers in. "I can pull them back inside at least. . . ."

I visualize withdrawal, the flames returning to my chest. We watch as they grow dim, then slip back beneath my brown skin.

When they are gone, Sel looks over my face. "Eyes still glowing red."

I groan. "I bet. I can still feel the power-up from the circle. My veins feel *hot*."

He reaches a thumb to my cheek. "And you are still crying."

"Ugh." I scrub at my cheek. "I'm sorry, I just—"

"What do you feel right now?" he whispers.

I look up at him, at his golden eyes so concerned, intense as always. "What?"

"What are you feeling?"

I blink once, twice. "I feel horrible? Embarrassed. Ashamed, like I'm not ready to go back there and face everyone. I feel terrified, and I just want . . . I just want to feel—"

"Safe?" he asks.

I gulp, but don't deny it. "Yeah. I want to feel safe."

A sad smile lifts the corner of his mouth. "I thought you might." He reaches into his back pocket, and produces my pin.

I stare at it, closed in his palm, and realize what he's suggesting. What he's offering. I pull inward in shame. Sel's hand cups my kneecap, holding me in place. "It's all right, Bree. I've already told you. I want you to feel safe." He gently tugs my tear-stained hand forward and flips it over, pressing the closed pin into my palm. "If that means being with him right now"—his brows lower and tighten together, swallows audibly—"then so be it."

I am not sure what to say. The last we saw Nick, he'd killed someone. I don't know what I'll say to him when I see him again, but I know my heart wants him near. I pull the Pendragon coin out from under my shirt.

Then I catch my reflection in its silver surface. Glowing red irises, just like Sel said. Just like Valec had seen that night on Miss Hazel's porch. I swallow, wondering what could be possible right now that might not be possible ever again. Wondering about genetics and epigenetics, root power and streams.

"Do you feel safer with him too?" I ask quietly.

Sel studies me, surprised at the question. "I . . ." He releases a heavy sigh, and a confession. "Sometimes. Safer. More whole."

"Do you trust me?"

His head jerks up. "You know I do."

I press the tip of the pin into my palm and clutch the coin in my fist. "I don't know if this will work, but . . ."

"If what will—"

I grasp his wrist with my free hand, and whisper.

"By my blood . . ."

50

THE MEMORY ARTHUR chooses to show me is not like the others. There is no vio-lence, no blood, no magic ripping through my body.

The castle is filled with subjects, laughter, joy. Long wooden dining tables lit by tallow candles stretching away from the dais. Overhead, the iron chandelier holds the finer candles, made of beeswax to last late into the celebration, lighting our way to a new Camelot.

I sit with eleven of my knights at a long table. They are shouting with their families and neighbors, laughing with one another.

"The Shadow King is dead!" I roar, because Arthur did. But it takes me aback—the Shadow King? My subjects pound the tables beside their plates, raise their leather tankards.

"And the Court will fall in his wake!" The voice beside me carries across the room, rousing another round of applause from the crowd.

My first knight. My Lancelot.

At the end of the table, Bors knocks his helm against the wood, calling for attention. He rises, toasting our victory, giving Arthur—and me—a free moment.

I remember the rules. I hope Nick does, too. My fingers slide to my right, and press against his forearm. The scene shudders, Lancelot flickers . . .

And Nick is there beside me, eyes heavy with sorrow. He looks out at the memory, and I can see the images fill into his mind as he reacquaints himself with what his ancestor did in this moment, why we are here, what will come next. After he surveys the dining hall, he turns back to me.

"Why?"

"Because I miss you."

His mouth lifts, half-sad and half-fond. "I miss you, too."

Nick's fingers tap against the wood, anxious. "We should talk, as Nick and Bree, not as Arthur and Lancelot. Can we . . . ?"

"Wait," I urge.

He frowns, eyes darting back and forth to search Lancelot's memory of what happens next. "For what? There are more toasts and then . . ." His eyes narrow, catching a stronger moment from the ones we could relive. "Then the crown?"

I swallow. "Yes. Let's wait to see if it worked. Play it out." I lean toward the entrance to the hall, and pray that my experiment was not a waste. I will the memory forward.

"To see if what worked?" Nick asks. "What did you do?"

The doors bang open, and a hooded figure in a long cloak strides in, soaked to the bone with rain from the moors, steaming with magic and heat. The hall falls to nervous excitement. The knights are used to Merlin, but the subjects are both fascinated and wary.

The sorcerer moves with silent footsteps through the hall, though they leave wet marks on the stone behind him. In one hand, he holds a large black bundle. He ascends the dais, past the knights, nods to them in greeting and stops to stand before me.

"My liege." Merlin throws his hood back to reveal his thick, ink-black hair striped through with silver, long enough to hide the tips at his ears. Blazing, unmistakably super-natural golden eyes study me from above high cheekbones.

Nick and I nearly miss the next moment, because we can't stop staring at Sel's ancestor. The originator of all Merlins everywhere. The architect behind the Spell of Eternity. We see all of this, but we are also looking for something—someone. Looking for the part of Sel that is this cambion, even here. Merlin does not notice. Instead, he tosses the heavy bag onto the table with a metallic-sounding thunk.

"You have it?" Arthur had asked, and so I ask it too.

Merlin nods. "He could not survive without it. And no one will ever wear it again. His Court has been broken."

Arthur stood with trembling hands to pull the fabric away from the Shadow King's crown, and so I do too.

It is towering, menacing, and obsidian black. So dark it absorbs light even now, dimming the little illumination offered by the chandelier overhead. If solar crowns have a circle of radiant spires, the Shadow King's crown is the exact opposite. Its spires are blades of night, as long as a man's hand, nearly daggers themselves.

Worry curls in my stomach. When Valec described the Shadow Court, Sel behaved as though they were less than a folktale. A made-up story as unbelievable as the stories the Onceborn world tells of Arthur. Maybe Sel and the other Merlins are taught that the Shadow Court is a legend, but I know better than anyone that legends are only half a shade distant from truth. And this memory proves that not only was the Shadow Court real, but the Round Table fought it.

And that Court once had a king that Arthur defeated. A king that neither Valec nor Sel seemed to know about. I hold the crown between my palms, finally, and raise it high. "The Shadow King has fallen, and his Court has scattered, weakened without their leader. The Round Table will force them behind the Gate our sorcerer has crafted, to be barred from our world for all of eternity!"

The room erupts. The celebration will go long into the night.

"I will take it from you, brother." A pale young woman with dark tresses and deep green eyes appears at the table, her approach nearly as quiet as Merlin's. Arthur recognizes her immediately, and so do I.

"Thank you, Morgaine." I start to pass the crown to her waiting, open palms, when Merlin intercepts the handoff, lifting the heavy headpiece away before she can take it.

"I will keep it for now." Merlin's voice is low, laced with something between an admonishment and a worry. "Thank you."

Morgaine flushes red and dips her head, a small bow to her mentor. "Apologies. I did not mean to overstep." Morgaine catches my eye, then Lancelot's, and flushes a deeper red before mumbling a farewell and making her retreat—likely back to her and Merlin's shared laboratory.

"Your apprentice yearns for your approval, sorcerer." My eyes widen, but Nick smirks back. This is what Lancelot said. He is following the script. "Perhaps she yearns for more than that, as well."

Merlin watches Morgaine's figure disappear into the shadows beyond the candlelight. "I am aware."

Nick and I both freeze; the phrasing is so Sel's, said almost in the same tone, that I nearly miss Arthur's next line. "Please keep talk of 'yearning' to quiet tones when it comes to my sister, and far from me."

Lancelot answers before sipping his mead. "Half sister, so I will remain half-quiet."

Merlin wraps the crown back into its covered bag, ignoring Lancelot's jibes. "I will be the one to keep it safe, my king." *He glances at us, then out to the room, back again.* "If that is all . . . ?"

I swallow. Now or never. I am Bree, in Arthur's memory. This is not the past; it is not a dream. It is an experience, recreated. An experience that I can manipulate. Nick gasps beside me; he knows what I am doing. I reach toward Merlin's silver-ringed fingers where they rest atop the Shadow King's crown. When our skin touches, I hold my breath. The room shudders. The memory flickers.

The rest of the scene freezes . . . and this blood walked world is ours.

Sel stares down at my hand on his.

Sel's eyes follow my fingers to my wrist, my wrist to my elbow, my elbow to my shoulder and face. His field of vision expands. His eyes find Nick. He inhales sharply, then exhales two words.

"Holy fuck."

Nick stands, eyes wide and glistening. "Sel?"

"Nicholas?" Sel breathes.

Nick reaches out first, right hand grasping Sel's shoulder, pulling him closer over the table, sliding to cup the nape of Sel's neck. Sel's right hand mirrors his—and then they are forehead to forehead, eyes squeezed shut, breathing each other's air for the first time in months.

As I watch them connect, I realize that the feeling Sel offered me, the feeling he knew I wanted, is here. It's between both of them, and between us all. Safety grows warm in my chest, expanding to some other emotion, twisting into something painful and beautiful at the same time.

51

THERE IS A balcony of rough-hewn stone carved into the castle above the dining hall. While the rest of the celebration had frozen, by some unspoken agreement, the three of us decided that we couldn't stay there. Didn't want to see or feel the presence of a crowd. We walk up the curving stone staircase three across, each step one more thought or question building in the silence.

When we reach the top, we move as a group to the wide wall. The clouds overhead are thick and enormous in the sky, brightened by the full moon behind them. Across the moat and wall, a body of water reflects the light, mirroring the sky.

"Like a memory," I murmur.

Sel and Nick follow my gaze. Sel sees farther than Nick does, and combs the bank on the other side of the lake. "What is like a memory?"

"The reflection on the lake," I explain. "It looks like the sky above, but there are small differences. Movement in the water. One is preserved, while the other shifts."

"I see." Sel turns away from the water, leaning on the wall to face us. "We are in Arthur's memory, but we've stepped away from it, for now."

Nick leans over the balcony with both elbows on the stone. We both wait for what we expect to come next.

"I won't ask you to explain yourself," Sel begins.

"I'm not sure I could if you did," responds Nick.

"I *will* ask you where you are now. If you are safe."

Nick answers. "I am safe."

Sel waits for Nick to reply to the rest. Narrows his eyes, glares at the stone floor. Clenches his jaw. When it's clear the answer is not coming, he curses. "Goddamn you, Nicholas."

"I need time," Nick says evenly. "I've never had time to myself, Sel."

"How much time?" Sel demands. "To do what?"

Nick folds his hands together. "To figure out how to stop this."

"The war?" I ask.

He shakes his head. "To stop the cycle."

I suck in a breath. Sel's voice is low and dangerous. "There is only one way to stop the cycle, Nicholas, and you had better not be considering it."

Nick's head jerks around. "Jesus fucking *Christ,* Selwyn. Do you *really think* I could kill Bree?"

"I *really think* you should explain yourself!" Sel retorts.

I step between them before things escalate. "No, he doesn't think that!" I release a breath. "But there is a lot of that going around."

Nick flips to face us both. "Which is why I want to find another way."

"What way?" Sel asks.

Nick points back toward the dining hall. "This is the beginning of the Order. You do realize that, right? At first it was the one hundred and fifty knights, then it was the thirteen—enhanced by Merlin and binding power to their bloodlines—but that down there? That's the beginning of the society. The public praise. The bragging. The display of power, crown of our enemy. Hubris, organized."

Sel crosses his arms. "Your point?"

"This is the beginning of centuries of taking things from children and their families." Fury twists Nick's face, pulls his lips back. "The Order took all three of our mothers, in one way or another. My father did the deeds, he was its loyal foot soldier, but even he saw that there was corruption. Political games. Even a petty, evil broken clock is right twice a day."

"And yet you killed for him," Sel muses.

"I didn't kill Zhao for my father." Nick's eyes burn. "I killed him for me."

Sel's eyes widen incrementally. "We should . . . come back to that."

Nick rakes a hand through his hair. "The Order took our childhoods from us, Sel." He looks at me. "If I go back, the Regents will never let us be together, B, if they let me live at all."

Sel rolls his eyes. "They will never let you and Bree sleep together, you mean."

My jaw drops. I resist the urge to slap his arm.

Nick glares at him. "Don't be crass. It's more than that, and you know it. Even if we find our way back to each other, safe and whole, and even if the Regents are disposed of, the Order's logic will still stand. As long as the cycle continues, no one will ever risk the intertwining of the Line of Lancelot and the Line of Arthur."

"My question remains. How do you think you can stop the cycle without harming Bree?"

"I . . . I don't know." He turns away, leaning over the balcony again. "But I believe there is a way."

"You *believe*? You do realize you sound like that . . . that cartoon bug thing, don't you? Wishing on a star for your dreams to come true?" Sel mocks.

"I think there could be another way, too," I mutter. "And it was Jiminy Cricket."

Sel scowls. "Excuse me?"

Nick snorts into his palm. "From *Pinocchio*."

Sel looks between us both. "*I* cannot *believe* I am stuck with you two."

The tension lifts, and I smile. "You are, you know. Stuck with us."

Nick makes a sound of disagreement. "Nah. I think *you're* stuck with *us*, Bree."

"Agree to disagree." I drift to the edge of the balcony, eyes overhead. Looking for a star, maybe. Glad that we are together in this pocket of time that isn't time, in a place that was real and a space that is not.

I feel Sel's gaze on the back of my neck, on my cheek, before I hear his voice.

"Mae hi'n brydferth."

"What?" I ask. Nick turns when I do, just as confused. Arthur's memories don't recognize modern Welsh, and I only know a little. I do recognize the words for "she" and "beautiful" though.

Or maybe Nick *isn't* just as confused as me, because a slow, laughing smile spreads across his face, like he understands Sel's game already. He leans a hip against the wall to watch me beside his Kingsmage, eyes teasing. "Ydi, mae hi. Yn *dragwyddol*."

Maybe that last word was "forever." "Beautiful forever"? No, "always"? I flush, then pout.

"Because of Arthur, I'm only fluent in Old Welsh, not modern. You know this isn't fair."

"We know," they respond together, and laugh. It's hard to be mad, watching the rare humor shared between them. When was the last time I saw them joke with each other? When was the last time their smiles echoed each other's? Something unclenches in my heart to witness it: the familiarity of long cohabitation, the bonds forged outside of Oaths and despite of them, the wavelength of understanding tuned to the frequency of Sel and Nick.

Sel sighs, pauses. Clears his throat. "Mae hi'n gweld dy eisiau di." I don't get a word of that, but the look on his face tells me that his mood has shifted slightly. Nick looks from Sel to me, and his long, solemn gaze on my face confirms it.

"Mae hi'n gweld dy eisiau di hefyd," Nick replies softly.

Sel shakes his head. "Mae gen i ofn *amdani*, Nicholas. . . ."

Did he say "scared"? "Her"? Is Sel is scared . . . *for* me?

Nick faces Sel, eyes earnest. "Dwi'n hyderus y medri di gadw hi'n ddiogel."

I think I hear enough: Trust, you, keep her, safe.

Sel's laugh is a hollow, empty bark. "You shouldn't, not after all I've done. Not after the last few weeks. After——" He stops short. "My demon is at bay for now, but you shouldn't trust me with her."

Nick tilts his head, considering Sel's words and his expression.

They lock eyes and it takes everything in me not to interrogate them both further. Because even though they're speaking in English, I'm missing something.

Then, it clicks: Sel didn't caution Nick about trusting him to *protect* me. He cautioned Nick about trusting him *with* me. Because Sel doesn't trust himself with me, either.

Nick doesn't know about Sel's mesmer. The lies. But he responds as if he does. "Dwi yn," he murmurs, then translates. "I do trust you."

It gives me the push to answer Sel for myself, because he is many things, but he is also my friend. And right now, in this world that is just for us, our own sort of protective dome in time, away from danger, he needs to hear it from both of us. "I do, too."

Their heads turn to me. Nick's gaze goes soft and fond. Sel flushes, but doesn't say a word.

And that's okay.

The scene around us crackles, goes fuzzy, then crisp.

"What's that?" Sel asks. His eyes go alert, assessing. "What's happening?"

I inhale shakily, uncertainty creeping into my chest. "I don't know. . . ."

"You brought us both here," Nick replies. "That's a big disruption of Arthur's memory."

The bricks beneath our feet tremble and begin to go transparent. Overhead, the night sky grows unearthly dark. "This world is unstable . . ." Sel's lip curls. He looks between us. "Can we be hurt here? Die?"

"I don't know," I say. But I can't leave yet. I look to Nick. "Nick, please let us come to you—"

He gnaws at his lip. "There are other ways to live than what the Order has shown us." He shakes his head. "I've . . . I've seen it."

"Seen what?" Sel exclaims.

But before Nick can respond, the blood walk cracks like a mirror. Jagged lines through space and time appear among the three of us, dividing us back into our own bloodlines, back into the real world.

"Nick!" I lunge, stretching to reach Nick, but my hand hits an invisible wall.

"Be safe, B," Nick says. His eyes flit to Sel's. "Both of you, be safe."

Eyes close.

Eyes open.

And Sel and I are in the woods once more.

His eyes glow yellow in the darkness, jaw clenching and unclenching. The sounds of the night fill in the silence between us.

THE NEXT FEW days at Volition are quiet. Lu and Hazel hover, reassuring me that they aren't mad and that the ancestors are a little rattled, but okay. We all breathe more easily when Valec reports in that he hadn't heard rumors of a root surge.

One day in the garden with my friends nearby, I show Lu my mother's brace-let, and actually talk about her. She asks questions about my immediate family, my mother, my father. Somehow, here among the heavy presence of loss and death and grief, it's easier to speak about her. Maybe after I saw her, living but not here, it became easier too.

I have not touched root in over a week, but one morning, I ask Lu if I can practice using aether without calling Arthur. She agrees it's a good idea. If the ancestors of Volition don't like it, she says, they'll let us know right quick.

Sel and I split off from the group after lunch to head to a clear area, but I stop us before we get far and turn back the way we came.

"Can Sel call his power here with our permission?" I ask. Lu and Hazel are getting settled in the rocking chairs on the front porch. "Or is it only outside the barrier?"

Lu nods. "With permission, sure. Some might say we shouldn't let a Merlin practice here, but those folks might be just as worried about a Bloodcrafter practicing on the premises. In the end, neither one of y'all will be able to harm anyone else inside this barrier. If you tried, the ancestors would fight back. So." She shrugs and calls out loudly, "Go ahead, Merlin. Show me what all the fuss is about."

Sel looks between us, a bright light in his eyes that I don't expect. I've never seen him cast something just because. From the look on his face, I don't know if he ever has. "Thank you, Lu," Sel says. She gives him a hurry-up gesture.

Slowly, as if he's not certain, Sel twists his palms up to move his fingers in a gentle, pulling motion. Aether streams into his palms, and he releases a short, relieved chuckle.

I laugh. "Worried it wouldn't be there when you called?"

"A little."

He takes a deep breath, eyes fluttering closed. Silver-blue aether floods into his palms, wrapping his wrists and arms, swirling along his tattoos. Wind cycles up from his feet, bringing wisps of blue and silver with it until his limbs are all flame and power and light.

When Sel's eyes finally open, the reckless grin curving along his mouth is our only warning.

In a flash, his wrists flex up, then down, and aether flows out from him in a steady rhythm along the ground. When he rotates his wrists, light rises around us overhead, stretching wide like a cloud—and then bursts, raining down like blue embers. Tiny fireworks sparking and exploding into nothing before they hit the ground.

Lu claps. "Impressive light show. And I thought Merlins were only good at making weapons."

Sel's head is tilted back, a slow smile on his face as the aether falls around him. "So did I."

The next day, William sits across from me on a stool while I stand in the grass before him.

"Aether is cast and formed because we will it so, just as Oaths only work when you hold the full intention to comply with them." He holds both arms out, palms up. He forms a crystalline gauntlet from nothingness on his left, then, with narrowed eyes, releases it, only to recast it into a gauntlet on his right.

"How do you do it so quickly?" I ask.

"Because Scion constructs are always the same," Sel says. "Merlins can technically cast whatever constructs we wish." Sel grins and squeezes both of his hands into fists. Aether armor snaps into place, faster than William's more instructional display, and more complete than any Scion's. He even has a helmet.

William cheers. "Show-off," I mutter.

"And maybe Bree can cast what she wants, too," Alice says from where she sits on the ground. She can't see our practice, but likes hearing about the mechanics.

I shrug. "Maybe."

"Not maybe." Sel walks closer to me. "I've seen your flames raw and loose around your hands and arms. Seen you throw up a shield even. You and I made something more contained than mage flame that night in the woods with Erebus. It was focused, like a bomb."

"That was you, though," I point out. "I just gave you the—the raw materials."

He shakes his head. "Nope. We did that together. Try again."

I try calling Arthur's armor. The most I can manage, after an hour of work, are a pair of loosely fitted bracers over my wrists. Solid to the touch, but soft like leather—and they burn so hot that I have to release them almost immediately.

Nothing I've done would protect me from a Shadowborn attack.

"Casting is both faith and intention," William reiterates. He flexes his fingers to pull aether onto them in a slow-growing silver mist. "I *know* the aether is in the air around me, even though I can't see it in its inactive form. But my intention is set on using it before I can see it. I call it to me knowing it's there."

"Is that how it feels to you, Sel?" Alice asks.

Sel stares at me. "No."

"So helpful." Alice rolls her eyes.

⤙⤛

"You cast armor in the woods with Valec," Sel says one day, frustration evident on his face.

"I begged Arthur for that."

"You were still yourself when it was cast, though. That's why we're going to see if you need a little nudge."

"You mean a fight?"

"Exactly."

There's an unspoken agreement that some things don't happen on Volition grounds. So, for this session, the four of us walk through the barrier to a flat space near some trees.

Birds whistle overhead. The trees here will release their leaves soon. Not this week, but the next probably.

Sel calls together a quarterstaff, his weapon of choice, and points it at me. "Let's go, Crown Scion. No Merlin speed, and I'll hold back on strength for now." He casts another weapon, a smaller shining staff fit for my hands, and hands it over. "I'll even make your weapon for you."

A few whoops from William and Alice.

When I don't answer, William calls from the sideline. "You feeling up to it?"

"Yeah," I say. "Just—"

"Intention."

I walk out into the clearing we've chosen, feeling the weight of the aether staff in my hand. Rotating my wrist. Expecting it to feel strange after not having handled a weapon in weeks . . . but it doesn't. I swap to my left hand—Arthur's preferred grip—and it feels just as at home there. *Huh.*

The fight starts. I lunge forward with the heavy staff, and Sel strikes and twists out of the way. I disarm him, but he lets the staff fall and pulls a new one in the air. Too slow. I push forward and use my momentum to topple him over, and we go spinning over the leaves scattered on the grass.

Sel rolls me once, twice. I manage to twist enough to draw my left knee back—and kick his chest.

Arthur's strength sends him *flying*. He lands flat on his spine with a thud.

My pounding heart stutters in my chest. "Sel!"

His laughter reaches me first. In a flash, he pulls both legs in and executes a perfect no-handed kip-up—a flip forward and into a crouch. He grins, fangs at his bottom lip. "Oh, this is *very* fun."

When he raises his staff, the light hits the aether—and a pulse of searing red heat spikes through my mind, boring into the space behind my right eye. I drop my weapon onto the grass, and pitch forward to one side with a moan.

A scene splashes across my vision, painting over the trees in a fine layer of red.

Memories I've seen before, rising unbidden.

I'm walking through the French Quarter. A trumpet howls nearby and a piano dances beneath it. Jazz is in the air.

A Black man walking toward me. Bloodred pupils, searching.

I'm shaking. Fingertips burning.

His eyes rake across my skin like knives clawing, searching. *I feel stripped. Exposed.*

He's closer now. My hands ball to fists—the crowd is too thick, nowhere to run. I grit my teeth, open up the flames inside my chest to get ready, wait until the last moment—the man passes me by.

Gone.

"Bree!"

I gasp, inhaling the scene into my lungs and away from my line of sight. Like smoke, it's drawn back into my body.

Sel and William are kneeling in front of me. "What happened?"

By the time I rock back on my heels, Sel is already standing. He peers down at me with questions in his eyes. I stand up, brushing my sweaty palms down my jeans. "I don't know."

"What did you see?"

"A bleed-through from Emmeline, I think."

"Which daughter was that?" Alice asks.

"The one the Hunter found and watched as she died."

Jessie saw two white men in two different cities, Emmeline saw a Black man in New Orleans, and I am the only one who has seen them all. For the first time, I wonder if the Hunter is not one demon, but several. Or a roaming court of demons working together on a single mission. *The Shadow Court.*

After everything I've seen, anything feels possible.

I shudder. Adrenaline and fear are still under my skin from Emmeline's memory. But that was from another time, and the Hunter is not here. "Go again?" I ask Sel.

"No. Enough training for the day." Sel's eyes dart to the wood around us. "She could be warning you. Let's get back inside the barrier."

The next day, I stop short when I emerge from the steps of the main house and see two long picnic tables joined together on the lawn in front of the barn, with balloons floating on each end. "What in the—"

"Surprise!" My friends are cheering and clapping, and then Hazel is there bringing out a tray of cupcakes, and I'm dizzy from the attention.

"What—"

"Heard from a little birdie that it was your birthday," Mariah says, gliding over to where a lone balloon has been tied to a chair at the end of the table.

"She heard it from me," Alice corrects. "After your mom reminded us."

"Alice," I whisper, touched.

She wraps me in her arms. "It's what she'd want and it's what I want. So don't be stubborn about it, just smile and eat the cake."

I hug her back. "You give the best orders."

"And don't you ever forget it."

Tears sting at my eyes. "I honestly don't know what I'd do if you weren't here for all of this."

She squeezes me before letting go. "Be sad, not have cake, forget to drink water—"

"Okay, okay!" I laugh.

"Not much here in the way of decorations." Mariah offers a broad smile, looking up at the balloons. "But still, your born day is something to celebrate."

I let her herd me to the seat and press me down, and they sing "Happy Birthday" raucously off-key. Sel leans against a nearby tree. He doesn't sing, but he looks like he may have hummed along a little. Alice slides in beside me for a quick hug as William pushes a cupcake toward me with a single candle.

I look up to the group of friends crowded around me, and decide that if they can take a moment to celebrate me, then maybe I can too. I blow out the candle, and let the war go for one night.

It's not until well after midnight, when I sit down in the garden on my own, that I realize how long it's been since I've celebrated anything, much less myself.

"Hey, birthday girl."

I feel Sel's eyes on my face from somewhere to my left. Smile. Hop down from the garden wall, and move in the direction of his attention. "That's me."

Sel emerges from the shadows, hands in his pockets. "Didn't know your birthday was in November."

"Not like I know when your birthday is either."

He sniffs. "June."

"Ah," I say with a smile. Only a couple of months before we met.

He looks over my shoulder. "You headed inside soon?"

I look back to the barn, where the lights are on everywhere. Voices, still talking. "Nah. Just wanted the quiet."

He nods and makes a thinking sound in his throat. "I have a present for you," he says. "If you'd like."

My brows shoot up. "You got me a present?"

He walks closer. "It's not a . . ." He looks around, shrugging. "It's a present, not a gift."

"Okay." I breathe a laugh. "Now who's the mystery boy?"

He grins. "Oh, that's always been me." He extends his hand, gesturing back over his shoulder. "It's on the other side of the barrier. Not too far. And I scouted the area earlier."

I grasp his fingers, fully anticipating the zip of electricity on my skin. It does not disappoint.

We walk to the golden barrier together, and stop at its edges. He holds up a hand, fingertips hovering over the surface. "There's one around the main house, I noticed."

My eyes widen. "You felt that, did you?"

He lifts a shoulder. "I'd want to protect my own, too. Not everybody needs to be in every place."

I push through the barrier around Volition, and Sel follows. "You'd put a barrier around me if you could, wouldn't you?"

He smiles, and tugs me close. "Don't tempt me." He pulls my arm over his shoulder, and tilts his head. A silent request. I nod, and he pulls me up, then we're off.

He stops at a dense collection of trees. I peer around him but can't make out more than a few feet. "I can't see out here, you know."

I hear his laughter. "I know. I just stopped because we need to walk the rest of the way."

I tuck my head against his shoulder and close my eyes. No point in looking up if I can't see what's coming at my face—although as we move, Sel's arm reaches up every once in a while to pull a branch away from our path. I let myself breathe in the scent of his aether, feel the familiar cinnamon and smoke burn at my nose and warm my insides. "Your aether signature is back," I mumble into his neck. His response is a low, contented hum. Nearly a purr that I feel more than hear.

Eventually, I hear water.

"Is that—"

"Shh," he says. "You'll spoil the surprise."

"Mmn," I respond.

He releases me, and I drop to the forest floor. He tugs me through the last bit of trees into a starlit clearing with mist floating low over the damp ground. And there, at least two stories high, is a waterfall crashing down into a pool surrounded by wet boulders the size of small cars. "Whoa . . ." I pull away from him, and step carefully through the mist. It shifts and breaks around my knees, but coalesces behind me in a thick layer. I turn back to Sel to see his reaction, but he's not watching the water. He's watching me.

"Is this my present?"

He moves through the mist to meet me, feet silent across the ground. "No."

Something on his face stops my quick retort. A flicker of nerves. Rare, on Selwyn Kane. "What is it?"

He looks around the clearing, brows drawn tight. "I didn't think about this part. For it to work, you have to close your eyes." He smiles at me. "But I have to be honest, at this point, I have no trust in your ability to follow instructions."

I glare at him. "I can cover my eyes." I put both hands up, more than happy to prove him wrong.

Instead of responding verbally, I feel his hands slide over mine from behind.

I drop my hands. "You *really* don't trust me," I huff.

"Not for this." He takes a small step forward, until I can feel his breath at my ear. "You don't listen. You're the most stubborn creature I have ever met."

I shiver. "And?"

A pause. "And . . . you're also the most wondrous being I have ever encountered, will ever encounter. And I believe there is nothing in this world that you cannot do."

I swallow. "Oh." I take a beat, then speak a truth that I think he will understand more than anyone. "I just keep thinking about what Nick would have done, if he had truly been Arthur's Scion."

Sel scoffs. Nudges me forward with slow steps until I start walking again.

"What?"

"You weren't there when he was younger. You didn't see him stumble, then fight his way through acceptance. Just two years before he met you, Nick wouldn't have done . . . any of what you're doing. He went through a rebellious phase in high school."

"Really?" I laugh.

"It was dreadful." He snorts in disgust. "Drinking plastic-bottle vodka behind bleachers with Onceborns."

"Not studying?" I ask, somewhat shocked at this vision of Nick. When we met, he was a star student.

"Oh no, he studied," Sel replies. "Drunkenly, sometimes."

I snicker and he chuckles, breath warm at my ear. It seems time to say the quiet things, ask the quiet questions, so I do. "Do you miss him?"

Silence for two steps, three. "'Miss' is . . . not the word. It is deeper than that." A pause. "I suppose you don't miss him because you see him, or used to, on the blood walks."

I take a breath. "Are you jealous?"

A pause. "Of what, exactly?"

"Sel, I know you used to have feelings for him. Do you now?"

Sel lowers his hands, rounding to face me. He inhales deeply and shakes his head. "The Nicholas I fell for is gone, I think, if he ever existed at all. So, no. My feelings for him run deep, but not in that direction. Not anymore."

"Do you wish they still did?"

He laughs quietly. "What I felt for Nicholas before wasn't healthy, Bree. It was adoration poisoned with mutual spite. I understood how to be his body-guard but didn't understand how to be his friend. Or how to ask him to be mine. I don't want that."

"Do you wish for something else then?" I press, feeling brave. "Something . . . healthy?"

"I don't know if that's in the cards for me." He seems poised to protest, then stops, studying me. "If I allowed myself that wish, it would be truly something. But wishes are the dangerous mind games we play with ourselves. The only way to win is not to play."

He reaches for my eyes again, a request. I nod and he wraps his hands around my face gently until the forest is gone once more. We keep walking. After a moment, he says, "The point is, you are leagues ahead of Nick, ahead of all of us, I think. . . ." He swallows. "One of my deepest hopes is that one day you will finally believe this yourself, but alas . . ." He clucks his tongue, voice faux-wistful. "You are too stubborn."

I huff. "Maybe I'll start buying into my own hype just to prove you wrong."

He laughs. "Please do."

For a moment, I wonder at this entire exchange. Selwyn at my ear in the dark, telling me what he likes about me. I might have questioned his compliments a few weeks ago. Questioned his motives. I want to believe he means every single word, but a small sliver of my heart won't let me. I can't shake the thought that his voice is the same honey in truth that it is in lies. I clear my throat. "Are we there yet?"

"Almost."

I wait, listening. There are crickets here. A trill beneath the rushing water. The mist and spray mingle together in my nose in occasional gusts. And Sel's hands are hot against my forehead, gentle over my eyes.

"Okay," he whispers, and drops his hands to reveal my present.

The clearing is much, much brighter than before—because it is filled with blinking fireflies. They float around us, lights pulsing lazily on and off. There, then invisible again. So many that I can't follow any single insect, but instead feel surrounded by gentle, slow bursts of light. I rotate where we stand, feeling dizzy and delighted at once. "There are so many . . . !"

Sel nods. "It's late in the season for them. I didn't think they'd still be present, but they must like this clearing." He watches me curiously. "Do you like it?"

I grin. "I love it."

His smile grows until it's reckless. "I knew you would."

I wrap my arms around his neck and pull him down for a hug without asking. After a beat, his arms encircle my waist. This time he's the one who tucks his face into my neck and shoulder, mumbling, "Happy birthday, Bree."

I pull back slightly. He releases me, face turning suspicious.

"That's your question-face," he murmurs.

I nod. "Yeah."

"Go on."

I gnaw on my lip, fighting myself. It'd be easier to not say anything.

Sel's eyes are thoughtful. Patient.

I release the words in a quiet rush. "You called me cariad."

He raises a brow. "I did."

"I didn't know what it meant then."

His eyelids flutter before he steels himself. "I . . . was aware. So?"

"So, I want to talk about it," I insist. "What you meant."

I do not expect the sound of his dry laugh, edged with amusement. Or the mixed expression of frustration and sheer awe. "Really? Now is when you want a Welsh lesson on something I said months ago?"

"Be nice, it's my birthday," I shoot back.

He regards me for a moment. "All right." His voice is low and careful. "Well, that was a statement, not a question. And if we're going to discuss this, I'd rather feel as though you're not hiding from it. So, I'd like you to say that again, please."

The overtone in his voice is that of a challenge, but beneath it is something I rarely hear from Sel: vulnerability.

I lift my chin and repeat myself, holding his gaze on every word. "You called me cariad."

"I did." He takes a step closer, eyes searching mine before he speaks again. "Is that your question? You want me to tell you the English translation?"

I shake my head, and his brows lift. "No. I asked William the other day."

"Ah," he says, surprised. "I see."

I flush beneath his gaze. Roll my eyes to cover a rush of embarrassment. "Still mad, by the way, at you and Nick for talking about me in Welsh in that blood walk while I was right there."

He doesn't fall for it. "No, you're not."

I gaze up at him, heart thundering in my chest. "A little."

Something sharp flashes across his brow. "Is *that* why you're raising this now? Asking me what I meant by it? Because you're angry with Nicholas for leaving you?"

My jaw drops. "No! It's not like that. I'm not angry with him. I never was. More . . . hurt."

"Ah." His nostrils flare, and his voice goes flat. "So, you're asking me about why I said what I said because Nicholas hurt you?"

I nearly choke with shock. "No. God, Sel. No."

He narrows his eyes. "Then why bring this up now, Briana?"

But guilt leaks into the back of my throat in a cold, steady drip. My tongue feels frozen in my mouth. If Nick were here, would I have ever revisited this conversation with Sel in the first place? Ever *actually* voiced it out loud and con-fronted him about it as I'm doing now? A small voice inside of me answers both questions in an instant. *Yes,* I would have thought about "cariad" again, because I've *been* thinking about it, and *no,* I would not have confronted Sel about using that word if Nick were by my side.

A petulant part of me wants to shout at Sel that this moment right now is his fault. He started it.

Sel had been prepared to leave this attraction between us alone, but that was before he betrayed me, before his demon, before everything. And here I am reaching past *all* of that to bring a single moment on the balcony at the Lodge back to life, just to remind myself that some parts of us could be real. And if Sel's feelings were real then, then maybe I could trust him now. But it's a selfish wish. And silly logic. Because I can't erase everything that has occurred, and we can't go back to the way things were before he used my feelings for him against me. And if I let *this* moment go any further . . . I could be betraying what I have with Nick. Even though, in his own way, Nick betrayed us both by leaving us in the woods that day.

This is a mistake.

"I don't want to . . ." I step away from him. Sel's eyes follow me, but he does not move. "I shouldn't have said anything."

His eyes soften. "You don't want to what?"

I blow out a breath. "To make things confusing!"

"Are you? Confused?" Oh God. I can feel his eyes on my mouth.

"No." I shake my head. *"Yes."*

"Okay. All right." His voice is low and soothing. He takes a slow step closer with an outreached hand, as if waiting for me to bolt. "This isn't an interroga-tion. I am sorry. It is your birthday. And I had questions . . . but I don't want you to leave." His fingers wrap around mine, and he rubs a slow circle across my palm with his thumb.

I nod. "Okay."

"Let's keep this simple?" He smiles softly. "Tell me what you learned about cariad?"

I swallow, and keep my eyes focused on our hands joined together. "It's a term of endearment, but there's more than one meaning."

"And what meanings did you find?"

"I . . ."

My heart is rattling around in my chest. I bet he can hear it. In fact, I know he can, because he frowns, and after a moment of hesitation, raises my palm and nuzzles his face in it, eyes half-closed. It's grounding. He's here. He's not rushing me or accusing me or making fun of me. He's listening.

I wonder, not for the first time, how much he's been touched with affection. At the thought, my fingers flex against his temple—and he presses forward, forcing them farther into his hair, seeking contact. So that's a yes; starved for touch. When my fingers curl into the silken dark strands over his ear, his eyes open wide, bright gold against the fireflies' blue-yellow glow. "What meanings did you find?"

"'Cariad' can mean 'sweetheart,'" I whisper.

He nods, and leans down to graze his lips across my cheek. "Yes."

"'Darling.'"

His eyes on my face as he moves to my other cheek. Kisses it lightly. "Yes."

"'Beloved.'"

His lips are warm against my forehead. "Yes."

"Also . . . it means 'love.'"

He pulls away, eyes molten. This close, his gaze burns against my skin. Scalds, but I don't want him to look away. "Yes, it does."

I take a ragged, useless breath. "Which . . . did you mean?"

His smile is soft, wry. "Trick question."

"Why?"

"Because I meant all of them." I bite my bottom lip, and he smiles, drawing it out with his thumb. "But you already knew that. Didn't you?"

I nod, because there's no point in lying. "Yes."

He frowns. "So why . . . ?"

I half-shrug, flushing. "I . . . I just wanted to be sure . . ."

His eyes dart across my features, then widen in understanding. "You wanted to be certain of what I felt for you before I manipulated how you saw me—literally and figuratively." Sel studies me, eyes a swirl of pain and regret. "Because now, even though you trust me with your life, you don't trust me with your heart."

It pains me to meet his gaze, because I know he sees right through it.

"I see." His mouth lifts in a small, sad smile. Resignation. "I understand wanting to go back in time to help unpack the present. I mixed lies with truth when you needed me most. And when others did the same to hurt you." He sighs quietly, nods, as if steeling himself. "I understand why you might not believe me now, so I will need to be happy that you at least believe what I felt about you then. That can be enough for me, if that's what you need."

It's my turn to laugh. He tilts his head, confused. With all of my affection and frustration, I say, "Liar."

He blinks owlishly. "I am not lying—"

"Well," I say, biting my lip. "Maybe it's not enough for me."

Before he can respond, I pull his head down and press my mouth to his indignant scowl until it turns soft and warm. He shudders against me. Then, his palm wraps around the nape of my neck, turning the kiss fierce, his mouth open and hot. He pulls me in by the hip, closer, a pulse building between us, a shared demand. There's a whoosh, movement, and I am against a tree, bark digging into my back, Sel's mouth working against mine before he tears himself away entirely with a low groan. "We shouldn't," he pants. "Not like this . . ."

"I—" I gasp and shut my eyes, heat flooding my cheeks. Embarrassment and desire mingle so thickly I can't tell one from the other. Sensation swims, churning me from the inside out. My mouth *burns* from his while my mind tilts around the axis memory of his hand on my hip. Logic and words feel far away. My heart is beating fast somewhere in my fingertips, in my belly, in the entirety of my chest.

When I open my eyes again, Sel is watching me with unguarded hunger and amused awe, like he knows everything my body is feeling, the warmth and torture and shock . . . and hopes it never ends. "Oh my God . . . ," I exclaim. "Stop looking at me like that."

"Then stop looking like *that*. Like you're desperate to be back in my arms." His brow rises, his voice lowers. "I like that look on you."

I drop my head in my hands. "You're the one who stopped us."

"I know," he whispers. "And I like that, too."

My head snaps up, anger flaring. "You're enjoying this!"

"I'm part incubus, of course I'm enjoying this," he counters smoothly. "Start, stop, and everything in between, if it's with you."

I groan, unable to take anymore. "Sel, please . . . I . . ."

He sighs, relents. "It's not that I don't want . . ." He turns away with another groan, fists clenching at his sides. "I *want*"—he shakes his head, voice softer now—"but there are too many questions, Bree . . . between you and me, between you and . . ."

Between you and Nicholas.

He doesn't have to finish the sentence. We both hear it well enough without the words.

I nod. Of course he's right. Not like this. "I'm sorry. I didn't mean—"

"No." His eyes snap back to mine, scalding my skin.

I blink to find reason. Can't. "No?"

"Don't say you didn't mean to kiss me." He steps closer, voice desperate, hand warm against my cheek. "I couldn't stand it if that were true." When he kisses my cheek this time, his lips are a firm, hot promise. An admonishment. A wish. Against my skin he whispers, "Instead, tell me you meant it."

My mouth goes dry. He draws back, eyes serious and waiting. "I . . ." I take a shaky breath and listen to my own heart racing in my chest. Feel the buzz of magic from his skin rippling across mine. Stand in the blaze of his attention and request, and speak the truth. "I meant it."

It doesn't seem to stick. I repeat it again for good measure. "I meant to kiss you, Sel."

He takes in my face, assessing as always. Then, after a beat, he laughs low, shaking his head, his expression quietly pleased. "Reckless girl."

I lift my chin. "And?"

He grins. "And . . . never change, Briana Matthews."

When we make our way back to Volition, it is with slow steps and shy smiles and hips and legs that keep touching as we walk. Early morning is just beginning to tint the darkest blues of the world a pale peach, while the forest remains asleep. Sel stops abruptly, tugging me back into his arms. His hand cradles my jaw. "Say it once more . . . ," he murmurs.

I grin against him and push up to my toes to whisper in his ear. "I meant to kiss you." I expect him to respond with more sweetness, a joke, a gentle nudge into his arms—but he turns his head at the last second, his body a long line of tension as his ears pick up something mine can't. "What is it?"

"Trouble." He yanks me onto his back and runs us toward the border.

We stop just outside of it to see ten Mageguard in a semicircle on the far side, hands up against the barrier, trying to break through.

53

AS SOON AS I pass us through the Volition root barrier, we both breathe a little easier.

Only a little.

With this many dead maintaining it, the ancestral dome of Volition is far stronger than any Merlin-cast aether barrier could ever be, but the Mageguard don't know that. And their presence is alarming enough, even if they can't see or hear us, because somehow, they've found where we've been hiding. Where we've been safe.

Lu and Mariah stand in the middle of the main road, bodies rigid with anger. William and Alice turn to meet us. Hazel must be back home, thank God.

I slide from Sel's back. "Are you all okay?"

"We're fine," Alice gasps.

"How did they find you?" Lu's eyes don't leave the Merlins.

"I don't know." Her question wasn't accusatory, but it still stings.

William and Sel stand together, talking tactics. ". . . Nothing shameful about waiting it out," William says.

"They know she's here. They will wait as long as they need to," Sel replies, eyes dark.

"But the barrier . . ." Alice points.

"It'll never come down for their magic, but that doesn't mean we're safe,"

Mariah says with a scowl. "Means we just went from being protected to being trapped."

Sel flexes his fingers. "I could make a run for it, get them to follow. Put up a good fight. Long enough for you three to get to a car."

"No," I say. "We're not splitting up."

He hums instead of fighting me, which is how I know things have changed between us. We watch the Mageguard in black on the other side, faces hidden by their dark hoods. A few of them have shifted positions and now walk alongside it. Their hands curl against the barrier as they go, as if prodding the surface, searching for an opening. "I've studied that barrier, too. They're trying to call its aether to them. Manipulate it into an opening." He shakes his head. "It won't work."

"Then what are *they* doing?" Alice points to a group of three Merlins circling down where Sel and I have just passed through.

He growls. "Tracking us. We were just outside and they've found Bree's scent. If there had been any doubt that the Crown Scion is here, it's gone now."

We watch in silent horror as a caravan of SUVs drives down the road, stopping at the edge of Volition's barrier. Several more Mageguard file out in black gear, hoods back. I don't know whether I want to see Lark or not, whether him being there but on our side would help us or hurt him. But when he does not appear among the other guards, a lump of worry takes shape where Lark should be. Did they find him out? Did Cestra realize there were Merlins loyal to the Crown Scion in her midst?

I don't have time to fear for Lark, because the final car slows and Erebus Varelian emerges. Dressed in black slacks and a dark gray overcoat, silver grommets winking in the first rays of sunlight, made gold through the barrier. My fists flex at my sides.

Erebus Varelian has come to Volition, and I will drive him out.

Then, in a terrifying moment, Erebus calls out directly to me. "I am sorry for the delay, Briana," he says loudly. "The car you and Selwyn left behind at the Rheon cabin had unregistered plates, but a working GPS. Eventually, we discovered a very perturbed, vengeful waitress who let on that she knew where the illustrious Valechaz may have taken you. Miranda, I think her name was?"

"That thief?" Alice's face darkens with memory and fresh ire both. "Oh, Valec is going to *kill* her. . . ."

I don't disagree. Miranda isn't long for this world.

Erebus walks slowly along the barrier. "I've seen a barrier like this before. Rootcraft-made, ancestor-forged. Impressive." His eyes look past the magic. He can only see what he's meant to see—an empty historic property—but for just a moment, I swear I'm looking straight into his gaze. "I know that you're on the other side, Briana, watching and listening. Aren't you?"

I hate that he keeps saying my name. Keeps emphasizing that he knows where I am, how close I am. It's meant to get under my skin and it's working.

Alice wraps a hand around my elbow. "Don't answer."

"I won't. And he can't hear us, remember?" My voice doesn't sound very reassuring. Instead, it comes out breathy and high-pitched.

She swallows visibly. "Right. Right."

The wind picks up, and Erebus turns toward it with a raised nose. "And you are still with the former Kingsmage? Selwyn, you must be desperate by now, starved for humanity without your Oaths and weakened by your lack of access to aether. I imagine that, currently, your eyes are only good for seeking the pain you might consume from others. Briana, I'd be very, very careful with him. . . ."

A smirk grows on Sel's face, but he does not respond. Erebus doesn't realize he has Valec's aether vials. That's an advantage.

"I know enough about ancestral barriers to be aware that you could very well choose to never leave this place." Erebus makes a sign behind him to the second car in the caravan. "So, I brought reinforcements to encourage you to make a *different* choice."

The doors open behind him, and my stomach turns to ice.

Olsen, recovered from her injuries at the cabin, drags a familiar face out of the truck—Patricia.

"No!" I shout. Mariah screams with me. Lu wraps a strong hand around her elbow and Sel does the same with me—yanking us both back before we can run toward the barrier and our mentor.

Sel pulls me in tight to his side. "He's baiting you, Bree. She's fighting back."

It's true. Patricia isn't strong enough to fight Olsen, but she isn't coming quietly either. I can't make out what she's shouting from here, but I can see the scowl and hear the tone. She's telling that Merlin off something fierce. I feel a rush of gratitude that she doesn't appear to be mesmered into compliance or too injured to move. But then I wonder why they brought her and the gratitude dissolves into apprehension. Patricia is brought just out of Erebus's reach, and held still by Olsen, who has clapped a hand over her mouth.

Erebus walks closer to the barrier. "I have not lived this long without moving strategically in battle, Briana. Without studying my opponents' histories. I will tell you, Aldrich considered taking your father, but I advised him it was too dangerous a ploy. Too risky to endanger the sole parent of a child who has already lost one—particularly when that child is you."

I hate that I feel relief. Hate that, for a brief, terrifying moment a vision of my father flashed before my eyes held tight in a Merlin's arms instead of Patricia, and I was grateful it's not real.

"You are a girl who had been willing to go to hell and back, even endanger her own life as an outsider in our Order, to enact revenge for her mother's death. I told the Lord Regent that taking your mentor would be most effective."

"Are you supposed to *thank* him?" Alice hisses. She is pacing back and forth nearby, lips curled over her teeth. Her fingers rub over her already donned silver knuckles. "*This* asshole."

"Mm-hmm," Lu agrees.

"Dr. Hartwood is someone you know well, someone you care for, I said, and"—Erebus looks up and over the dome of Volition—"she's a Rootcrafter. Someone with connections to the very sanctuary in which you have hidden yourself. It would be a shame to harm Dr. Hartwood, but I think you know I would be willing." Patricia's eyes are wide above Olsen's hands. I can hear her muffled shouts.

"Goddamnit," says Sel.

I grit my teeth. Fury has taken my breath. Turned air into hot knives at my throat, in my chest.

Erebus flashes long fangs. "I propose an exchange. If you, and only you, exit the barrier, you have my word that we will send Dr. Hartwood through, where you know we cannot reach her or anyone else in your party."

"Don't even think about it, Bree." Sel is in front of me, blocking my view of Erebus.

"She's not replaceable," I hiss.

"Bree, you are——"

"*No one* I love is replaceable, Sel. The Order deals death so easily, accepts it so easily, but I refuse. I will *never* be a king who throws one life away for others."

But this is Rootcrafter business, on Rootcrafter property. I look between Patricia and Mariah, from Mariah to Lu. Lu nods once. "The ancestors trust you to make the right decision."

I know what I have to do.

I pull on Sel's arm. "Do you trust me?"

He replies in an instant. "With my life."

Alice reaches a hand out to catch mine. "I don't like the look on your face, Matty."

"I have a plan," I say, squeezing her fingers tight before releasing them.

"Does it involve crossing that barrier?" Sel's eyes narrow.

"That's the 'trust me' part."

Sel blinks. "I take it back. Don't trust you."

I roll my eyes. "Sel, please." I look between him and William. "You're the only one fast enough to grab Patricia yourself if they don't let her go. I need you with me. And William, I need you to care for the others if something goes sideways."

"On it," he says.

Sel eyes me for a long moment, the indecision and fight in his eyes making them glow brighter. Eventually, he nods, too. "I am with you."

I hold my hand out for his, and he takes it. Together, we walk close to the border, and stop with ten feet to go. "Okay," I say, looking around at the open space nearby. I inhale, exhale. "This should do it."

I don't tell him my plan, because I know he won't like it. *I* don't even like it.

I near the barrier, and rub at the pin, then the coin in my pocket, opening up a new wound.

By my blood . . .

'Daughter of sons.'

"Enough of that. I need your help," I say out loud. I feel Sel stiffen abruptly beside me, his hand squeezing mine. He wasn't ready to hear me speak to Arthur, and he won't be ready for what I invite Arthur to do next. "Don't take me away to a memory. See what I see, right here and now. Know what I know."

A beat. The uncomfortable sensation of Arthur shuffling through my recent memories. Images ripple quickly across my mind, then slow. The Mageguard in their dark cloaks. Silver rings flashing beneath fingerless gloves.

'The children of Merlin.' Arthur lingers on Olsen and Patricia. *'Coordinated against you under a strong leader.'* A consideration. *'You cannot fight this group alone.'*

I groan, impatient. "I know."

A pause. *'I can best them.'*

"Then let's do it, before I change my mind."

'On my own.'

"What?" I hiss. "Let you drive?" Sel's grip turns into a vice. "No way. Together, like last time."

'Inefficient. You have seen my power. This is life or death, in your palm. A king would do what needs must.'

I swallow. I have to let him in, fully. Without losing myself. Without losing total control.

"Fine."

I know him before I see him, because his presence flares in my chest at the same time that he appears before me. A ghostly figure brought to life, more real than a revival.

Arthur Pendragon, son of Uther Pendragon, wielder of Excalibur, stands before me, because I called him here.

Arthur is massive. Broad-shouldered, gleaming with aether-cast Legendborn-style plate armor. White-blond hair in thick waves around his scalp. Even in the light of aether, I can make out the silver streaks in his coarse beard.

It is the exact color of the lock of curls I've been sporting lately.

And suddenly I understand. My hair's premature gray isn't the sign of how much power I'm using. It's not Liege hair. It's the sign of Arthur . . . and I know in my gut that I earned it from walking in our shared blood for long stretches of time.

The world around us melts away. A silver-blue sphere barrier snaps into place to surround me and my ancestor, and then the world is just me and the king.

I hear Sel shouting my name, but the sound outside the small dome is muted. I don't know if I am casting it, or Arthur, or both of us together. Sel bangs on the barrier with both fists, but it doesn't break or dent.

Arthur takes two steps forward to examine me. I raise my chin.

"You are exactly as I thought you would be, on this plane." He lifts a translucent finger to my temple, tugging at the curl of white hair that matches his own. "My bri."

I jerk away. "Don't touch my hair." I grit my teeth. "Just do it."

One bushy brow lifts, and the left side of his mouth follows suit. Amusement coloring his face and his voice, he says, "You finally summon me in full when Camlann is upon the world and your own Court rises against you, and this is how you treat me?"

"Yes," I spit.

His eyes flash, molten silver turned to steel. He holds out his hand, palm up. "Say the words, Briana."

Sel is still shouting, and Alice has joined him. They bang on the barrier together, punching at it in silent blows. But instead of hearing the words they say, I look at them and hear their voices from earlier, and wonder what would happen if I let myself believe them. If I could be the person they see: the girl who was already powerful, even when she didn't think she was. The girl who was already their king.

You're also the most wondrous being I have ever encountered. . . . And I believe there is nothing in this world that you cannot do.

Matty, you're incredible. The strongest person I know, even before all of this.

And Nick, who saw me from the beginning. *You know I think you can do anything, take on anything and anyone in the world. . . .*

I can do this.

I grasp Arthur's hand in mine and squeeze. "By my blood, on my heart . . . to unite us in spirit, and in flesh."

Together.

Together.

Together we approach the barrier.

We step close, directly before Erebus.

His red eyes don't see us yet.

We don't have to coordinate, or talk to each other, because we are one. We step through to the other side, the barrier of Volition opening before us with a loud crack, then closing behind us with a low boom.

Our voices mingle, a deep thunder of sound. *"An exchange."*

Erebus's eyes widen, searching our features, the streak of white in our hair. "Briana, your appearance . . . your eye color . . ."

"Now!" we shout. *"An exchange."*

The conflict in Erebus's face disappears. He snaps his fingers, and Olsen releases Patricia. She rushes from the Merlin's grip and hesitates. When she looks at us, alarm twists her features. She knows who we are, *what* we are. She walks with the memories of the dead, and her power sees that we are flesh and memory both.

"Bree, no . . ."

"Go," we say. She jumps, but moves quickly to the barrier. The ancestors are ready, and an opening appears before her. With two steps, she melts through the golden shield, and disappears on the other side, where Sel is waiting for her.

Erebus steps forward, and takes our arm in his hand, gripping to hurt. He beckons to Olsen, who is at our side in a blink. "Let's go."

But when they pull us, we do not move. We have the strength of kings.

Olsen strains.

Our mouth smiles.

Olsen pulls again. The effort of a child trying to pull a boulder from its ancient rest.

It makes us both chuckle—our amusement puts fear on her face.

Erebus is smarter than his guard. He steps back, hands loose and palms up—ready for the fight he suspects is coming. "Briana, what . . . what are you doing?"

"We agreed to cross the barrier," we say, and hold our palms out and up to mirror him. *"We never agreed to go with you."*

Erebus snarls. The Mageguard whoosh into position. We snap our armor in place with a loud pop. A sword materializes in our hand between one breath and the next—not Excalibur, but it will do.

Then . . . the next few minutes are a blur.

We rip through the Mageguard like a fiery blue hurricane.

We are speed and light, laughter and destruction.

We move as one—but so can the Mageguard.

It takes two of them on each limb to take us to the ground, and even then, we are fighting. Their Oaths hinder their attacks: they seek to contain, not harm, or risk the Oaths turning on them mid-battle. We shove one off and into the air. A deep snapping sound, mixed with wet. A bone breaking as he lands. The other Merlin twists out of reach, is joined by another.

A warrior's roar to our right—Selwyn is a black streak rushing through the Volition barrier, spinning a chain overhead. Clipping Erebus in the shoulder with a sharp scythe. Taking another out at the legs. The Seneschal is on him in a second, power rushing to him as he attacks. The Kingsmage screams—

The two Merlins nearest us move as one, but we meet them mid-stride. Slice at the one on the left while twisting low, spinning, meeting the other with a backward thrown elbow to the face.

But they are replaced by two more—

Suddenly, the screams multiply. Merlins, clutching their heads. Merlins, falling to their knees. Selwyn, too, gasping with eyes wide, curling into a ball to cover his ears.

And Alice, standing just outside the barrier. Her face is stricken with fear, but she holds a small black device with a blinking red light high over her head in a fist that does not waver.

The ultrasonic weapon, taking the cambions out all at once. Every Merlin, on the ground in pain, incapacitated.

Except one.

Erebus stands with blood streaming from his ears down the front of his black overcoat and surveys his fallen Mageguard. His troops are writhing masses on the ground, disarmed by their own bodies. When he turns back to face us, his face twists in an inhuman growl.

The device has injured him, but not enough.

And then, its ten seconds are up.

Alice tosses the now-unblinking device down on the ground, and dashes toward one of the moaning bodies. Selwyn! Behind her, the barrier opens to reveal Mariah, shouting for her to hurry.

Alice lands at Selwyn's side, heaving until his arm is up over her shoulders, trying to drag him back to Volition.

Selwyn's body is heavy, and his legs drag in the dirt. Alice's progress is slow going, she gasps, straining—

Erebus looks from us to our friends with vengeance in his eyes, aether gathering around his fists, lifting his hair high.

He's not going to let them cross that barrier.

We're running to intercept just as he snarls and leaps to stop them.

We reach Alice and Selwyn before the Seneschal does—barely. Block his attack and return with one of our own—a punch that sends him flying spine-first into the barrier. He collides with the concrete-hard surface with a deep crunch and slides to the ground.

A hand grasps at our shoulder—

We pull the attacker up and over by their arm, throwing them into the broadside of the van with a heavy thunk. The person falls motionless to the ground.

Oh God.

Oh no.

Alice's black hair. Her glasses, shattered. Her limbs, too limp. She doesn't get up.

"ALICE!"

It wasn't a Merlin who grabbed us; it was Alice.

Because she thought we were . . . me.

Alice! I scream, but the sound hits the walls of my own mind and bounces back, useless. *Let me go. I need to go back. Let me go now, let me—*

But Arthur's consciousness expands, pressing me further and further away from the place of possibility, from control.

'*Though I may fall, I will not die.*'

Those words. Every Scion utters those words the moment they are Called, except when they speak, the voice that emerges is that of their knight's, announcing that their spirit has Awakened. Arthur twists them in my ear, and I realize much, much too late that he is not announcing his return—he's announcing my departure.

Arthur!

'*I will not die . . . ,*' his voice rumbles, a storm closing in, '*but call on blood to live.*'

Let me go!

'*No, my bri. Not now. Not ever.*'

He lied. And I believed him.

The cord between my spirit and my body *snaps* . . . and I fall away from myself.

ONLY A KING

54

THE WORLD IS brighter this way.

Warmer.

Louder.

Alive.

Around me, the destruction Briana and I had wrought together. The Mage-guard, broken and scattered. Some appear more dead than even I am, but I don't bother to check. Their general, the Seneschal, is felled where we left him.

Briana's friend—the girl with the Merlin-incapacitating noisemaker—lies still and pale, mouth slack. The golden barrier nearby is open, the Scion of Gawain running through it, too late to save her.

Briana would be devastated.

"Nnnghhhh . . ." A groan to my left. The Merlin boy, Selwyn, awaken-ing. He is groggy, disoriented. His cambion eyes are unfocused as he surveys the chaos that remains. His gaze fixes on Briana, and focuses at once. "What happened . . . ?" He rises to standing and reaches toward me. Toward Bri-ana. "Are you all right?"

Quaint.

I let him pull Briana's body close. He wants to hold her. He dips his nose into her neck—inhaling, then freezing. "Bree, you smell . . . different . . . ?" He inhales deep against her skin a second time.

I stop him with a hand around his jaw, I dig Briana's nails into his skin—and squeeze. He jerks back, yellow eyes gleaming. "What the hell—?"

My laugh in her chest is a slow, delicious thing. I like the sound of it. The Merlin boy does not. His face and eyes remind me of his ancestor. If only Merlin could see his children now.

"Bree?" asks the boy.

I pull her full lips back into a smile. "Dydi Briana ddim yma."

Briana is not here.

Blood drains from his cheeks. He takes Briana's appearance in just as Erebus did. The gray hair. The flash of silver-blue in her eyes. The smile. All the little places where bits of me are mingled with bits of her. Have been mingling, in fact. One memory at a time.

The Merlin hisses, fangs just bared, palms opening to the sky. "You're Arthur."

"Yes." I search for the words in modern English. They will hurt more that way, said in her voice and in her language. "I am Arthur Pendragon, and I own this body now."

A growl rolls up through his chest, out through clenched teeth. "No, you do not."

He launches himself at me and I laugh, dodging him easily. Briana is much faster than she thinks she is. He stumbles in the dirt, shock gripping his features.

He has never seen her move this way.

But the boy, Selwyn, is smart. When he rights himself, he does not do as some opponents would, and try the same attack—or similar—again. He gives up on his first strategy, and searches for another. His eyes dart across her positioning, the distribution of her weight, the sword in her hand, and all the while, he pulls a ball of aether into his palm to form a long, shining staff, hard and dense as any sword. "Let her go, Arthur."

We circle each other. I chuckle again. "I have only just arrived, boy. Don't be rude."

"I will fight you."

At that, I throw my head back in a laugh. "Do not lie to your elders. You would never—could never—harm this body. You know it. I know it."

His resolve flickers, as does his staff. "I won't let you manipulate her again."

"Again?" I say, brandishing my sword. "I have been manipulating her for months. Playing on her desire to wield my abilities—an impossible feat with an overdraw of ambient aether that no one could ever hope to control."

Selwyn's scowl deepens. "You were doing that to her. Letting her burn herself . . ." His eyes flash. "So she would be forced to summon you for aid, bleed for you? Live your memories?"

"Indeed."

"Why?"

He is stalling for time. Looking for a way to attack his beloved without permanently injuring her.

I grow tired.

"That would be telling, descendant of Merlin," I say, and lunge toward him. He follows the feint. I draw back and strike the temple behind his eye with a closed fist—and all of Briana's strength.

The crack against bone echoes in the early morning air.

He crumples into a heap. Goes still.

I never intend to allow Briana to regain control of herself, of course, but if she did, and she found her Merlin dead, she would be extremely distraught.

Extremely.

I step over his body and continue toward the still-running vehicle.

I kick the most alive-looking of the Mageguard—a young woman. Olsen, I believe. She stirs, and I kick again. "Get up. Take me to the Regents."

Olsen glares up at me. "Matthews," she snarls.

"Not anymore." I point to the sleek black beast. "Take me to the Regents." She blinks as though she cannot believe her eyes. *"Fy duw,"* I mutter. How useless.

A whistle of movement. A black aether spear slams down in the earth an inch from Briana's foot, still vibrating from its journey and the strength of its thrower. It swallows light in on itself, a weapon meant to bring night and death with it.

The sunlight above and around me dims. The air grows cooler. The world, darker.

Ah.

I whip around to see the spear's caster. "I thought I killed you, old friend."

The voice cracks from long disuse.

"Only for a time."

55

I AWAKEN SUBMERGED in Arthur's bloodline. The stream is in my throat, in my ears, filling my mouth when I gasp for air. I shut my mouth tight and kick up *hard* toward the distorted red light of the forest above. My fingers claw through ice-cold water, grasping for *anything*—oxygen, the stream bank, the sky itself—and instead they collide with a smooth invisible barrier. A dull *thunk* sound greets my nails, as if they have struck thick glass.

I punch this time, with purpose, and pain rockets down my wrist. Again, harder—the pain zings into my shoulder. I scream. A mistake. My lungs fill with water. I flail weak, oxygen-starved arms, muscles protesting. Sel asked if we could die in a blood walk, in our ancestor's memories. I didn't know. But can I die? In my own mind?

Black spots enter my vision. The answer never comes. I sink down and down, waiting for the bed of the stream to meet my back. . . .

But it also never comes.

Instead, I land spine-first onto a cold, hard surface. Overhead, arches rise in a bright chamber so tall that, without the sunlight streaming in from long glass windows, I would not be able to see the ceiling. A *room*, not the stream. Daytime, not night. I *recognize* this place from the Rite of Kings.

I gasp for air with lungs free of water. The sound is lost beneath a sharp chorus of masculine laughter that bounces off the walls. The joyous uproar after someone at a party delivers the punchline to a joke.

I jerk my gaze to the right. Recognition takes away the breath I just fought for.

Six knights are seated along the curved stone on my right: Geraint, Gawain, Bors, Mordred, Caradoc, Erec. And six are seated on my left: Owain. Bedivere. Kay. Lamorak. Tristan. Lancelot. The Table gathered, whole and hale, smiling at one another, but without a glance in my direction.

I roll, scrambling to my hands and knees—and see that my hands are my own. Solid, brown, covered in callouses from training. Each one half the size of the hands I usually see when I blood walk Arthur. My clothes are mine, too. Thin cotton and denim instead of worn leather and heavy cloth. I lift a hand to my face, my hair—all me. Confusion and fear lift the fine hairs on the back of my neck.

The conversation flows around me uninterrupted. I wave a hand in front of Sir Bors's face. "Hello?" He absentmindedly strokes his short beard, nodding at Mordred beside him as the other knight regales him with a story. His eyes never turn my way.

None of them see or hear me.

Another time, I might be relieved not to be seen by all of the original knights at once. Relieved to not have to explain why I am here, who I am, when I'm from. But right now, it just feels wrong. Because . . .

I shouldn't be *me* here.

I should be Arthur.

Immediately, my eyes find the single unoccupied chair across from me. With a sinking feeling in my gut, I inch toward Arthur's place at the table.

Just as I reach the edge, tall, wooden double doors open in the far corner of the room. A young Arthur himself strides through in full regalia: a long fur coat, bronze circlet over his thick, blonde-brown hair, eyes dancing like they hold a secret.

The Table cheers at the approaching king. "There he is!" a voice calls.

"You're late, my liege!"

"We started without you, Pendragon!"

I clamber off the table to meet Arthur halfway. "You asshole!" I attempt to call on the aether in the room—but nothing comes.

Even on my worst days with Arthur's power, I could at least bring *some* aether to my fingertips. Here, it's like it doesn't exist.

Arthur's stride doesn't falter, his attention never wavers—and he walks right through me.

A dizzying, awful sensation shoots from my stomach to my throat.

"Let me guess," the young king calls with a laugh, "Caradoc drank all of the mead?"

While the table roars in delight and Arthur reaches for a tankard, I shudder. Even air gets displaced, but he moved through me as though I was less than air. Like I was nothing.

Truth settles in my throat.

This is *not* a blood walk.

The last time I was in the Table's chamber in Camelot, I had arrived via the Rite and the world felt like a fiction. Every man there was an otherworldly spirit, dormant and waiting. But here the knights are so solid I could reach out and touch one of them.

This is not a vision.

Light catches my eye—Caradoc reaching across the table through a sunbeam. Candle stands spread about the room offer a warm glow, but the sharp, pungent odor of tallow-candle smoke from Arthur's memories is completely absent. The tapestries hanging on golden rods around the room look as if they've just been woven. Colors saturated and threads perfect . . . all is pristine.

This not a memory.

My stomach tightens. What had Arthur said when I'd asked where he'd been before he'd Awakened?

I rest in Camelot.

Merlin sent you to Camelot?

Merlin sent me to my dreams.

I suck in a breath. Arthur's dreams. I'm *in* his dreams, inside the waiting realm of an imagined Camelot. I stumble backward, away from the fabricated men and mirth.

Arthur spent *centuries* in this place, only ever seeing the real world when he

Awakened, when Camlann came, when the Table of Scions needed him to lead.

But like so many things in the Legendborn world, the Spell of Eternity wasn't designed with me in mind. The magic didn't plan for me or what I can do. Or what Arthur can do, has done.

I am a Medium *and* Arthur's Scion, and my connection to him works both ways. His spirit has been in my mind, and I've been in his. Over and over again, for months. He tricked me into trusting him, and eventually, I caved. Which was all he needed to force us to switch places.

Panic slips between my ribs. My eyes squeeze shut, tears hot at the corners. A low, fearful whine escapes me before I can stop it, but the knights can't hear it, can't help me, keep laughing. My pulse picks up. I breathe deep, force it to slow.

"This . . . this isn't real," I whisper. "It's just a dream."

Abruptly, the world around me shudders and blurs, then grows dark. Thunder growls outside the windows, as if rumbling in response to my words. Like the dream itself *heard* me.

"What—"

A great ripping sound, like thick fabric torn apart. A sizzle and deep pop, like a log in a fireplace. Then, lightning slices through the room from above.

I leap back just as the bolt hits the center of the room, and with a teeth-rattling *boom* . . . it cracks the Round Table in half.

The two heavy semicircle slabs collapse inward, slamming onto the ground with enough force to shake the floor.

I am so stunned it takes a second to realize two things: one, that the knights are still in their chairs, as if nothing had happened, and two . . . the lightning is not done.

Smaller strikes hit the floor in rapid-fire succession, so loud I have to cover my ears as I scramble away. They surround the Table, inching closer with every bolt.

I watch, helpless, as twelve bolts strike at once—directly hitting each and every knight in a single blink—and leave cobweb-covered skeletons behind.

This isn't Arthur's dream anymore.

No, this . . . this just became his nightmare.

Crackling above is my only warning before a bolt strikes closer to me, splitting the stone six feet away.

Real or not, instinct takes over.

I sprint to the farthest wall, to the doors Arthur used to enter the room, heart thundering. *Please have an exit. Please—*

I reach for my root, but nothing responds. My root doesn't exist here, either—

Clang! Clang! The metal candle stands fall as the floor breaks open.

I'm running too fast to stop, and skid shoulder-first into a door. Only when I grasp the door handle with both hands do I risk a glance over my shoulder.

The tapestries have caught fire. Steady hits of lightning inch closer to me, following the path I'd taken to the exit. One strikes ten feet away, another, nine—

I pull hard on the heavy door. It cracks open, just enough. I squeeze through the opening. I don't care what's on the other side.

All I see are the crumbling bones of twice-dead men.

I stumble into another room—bright, warm—and push as hard as I can to shut the door tight behind me. I back away, chest heaving for air, watching the cracks of the door, waiting to see the deadly lightning flash beneath it.

It doesn't.

And yet there's no doubt in my mind that if I open it again, a bolt will meet me.

"Arthur!"

A woman's muffled voice reaches me, accompanied with muffled footsteps that draw near.

I finally take in my surroundings.

The whole room is cast in the orange-gold light of the sunset outside of a wide, stone-edged window. On one end are two wide wooden chairs, a hide rug, and a low table between them. And there's a *massive* fireplace on one wall. So tall I could stand fully upright inside it.

It only takes one glance to see that the flames flicker in a repetitive rhythm. There are no sparks, no smell to the fireplace. It is perfect.

I swivel back around, expecting to see the door through which I entered, but it's no longer there. A blank, gray stone wall stands in its place.

Another dream.

The single door in the room swings open and Arthur walks in, harried and distracted. His hair is loose and unadorned, his face drawn, and instead of the fancier attire in the throne room, he wears a dark blue tunic and loose brown pants with matching boots.

"Arthur!" Close on his heels comes a dark-haired young woman I recognize from my blood walk with Nick and Sel: Arthur's half sister Morgaine. She pursues her brother to the hearth with both hands clutched at her sides. "You know I wouldn't ask if it weren't important!"

Arthur's low rumble is fond. "I do *not* know that, dear sister."

When Arthur walks past me to the window and grips the stone sill, I edge closer. Wave a hand between his face and the view of the hills behind us; he doesn't blink. The lines at the edges of his eyes may have been earned with joy, but those at his mouth follow the path of solemnity and worry.

"As I'm sure you're aware, you are known to ask for a great many things . . . and, quite frequently, you receive that which you ask for." Arthur's smile makes an appearance as he glances over his shoulder.

Morgaine takes this comment as encouragement and bounds forward. "Stop resisting my demands and accompany me!" She can't be more than twenty-five, but here she behaves like an impish teenager. She waggles her dark brows. "I have something to show you, brother. And don't ask what, because it's a surprise."

Arthur peers down at her and releases a long-suffering sigh. "I am tired, Morgaine."

She tugs at her brother's hand, and he smiles down at her. "Then you should come with me before your old bones get lost forever in this chair."

Arthur surprises me by murmuring words that do not quite feel like they are for her ears, but for his own. "Were you always this mischievous, sister?"

"Yes." She laughs. "Come with me," she begs, and pulls again. "Quick, before Merlin returns."

"Are you hiding something from Merlin?" His eyes widen, with a glint of their own mischief. "Nothing good can come of this."

She giggles. "Like that has ever stopped you."

Arthur watches Morgaine like I might watch him, wondering if she is a fig-ment of his imagination. It gives me an idea.

I step forward so that I stand between them. "Arthur, I don't know if you can hear me. But this is a dream, she isn't real—"

Behind them, the flames of the fireplace roar higher, hotter. A second later, and all is as it was, except I am left reeling. This world reacted to my words, just like it had in the throne room.

Morgaine frowns at her brother. "Must you be so stubborn?"

Arthur's eyes sharpen on her face. "No. Let's go, then. Show me your surprise."

"Stop!" I hold out a hand, but his body passes through mine just like before. Dizzying, nauseating. "None of this is real—" The light shifts in the room as if night has abruptly descended. Thunder rolls nearby, foreboding. The precursor to lightning.

Then, as I hold my tongue, the fire quiets down and the thunderclouds clear. The light shifts outside and the sky turns calm. The dream, warning me again that if I continue, it will break down around me. That the only way to keep things peaceful here is to behave as though this place is real, *believe* that it's real. Ignore that there is any other world than this one made of magic and con-sciousness. If I acknowledge the dream is a dream, then it becomes a nightmare.

Are these Merlin's rules? Or did Arthur turn on himself after centuries of waiting, and make his own dreams a prison?

No wonder he was so eager to meet me and see the world through my eyes in the beginning.

I was his escape.

As the last bit of thunder quiets, Morgaine and Arthur chatter happily, like the volume turned up again. They walk to the door and exit the room to turn right down the hall.

Something tells me I can't remain in a room without them, so I trail behind.

I have no choice but to follow the dreams that don't belong to me and never will.

If I want to stay alive here, then I must become a ghost.

56

THE SHADOW KING looks as he always did.

Black smoke in the shape of a man, filling the air with the scent of brimstone. The air nearest his form is leeched of light. Wings made of ink flare out from his spine, lifting up in claw-tipped curves overhead.

His eyes are the same obsidian, with pulsing red coals in the centers.

His gaze burns Briana's skin. *Ah yes.* Her ability to detect the attentions of demons. I grit my teeth against the near-unbearable sensation. How does she *stand* this?

I search inside for her so-called root, the red aether connected to her keen senses, and while I feel the dormant furnace, like her, I cannot activate it at will. Our spirits have switched places, but even I do not have access to her greatest gift. I look down at the glowing silver-blue sword still in her hand. The only aether I can access on this plane is my own.

"Is something wrong, Pendragon?" The King's voice is a low, amused crackle. His voice is the sound of wind rushing through the mountains at Cadair Idris. The voice that villagers once feared could beckon forth the Cŵn Annwn, the hounds of the otherworld. The voice that once commanded all Cysgodanedig, all Shadowborn.

It is a voice that once haunted me, too . . . before I silenced it.

I do not acknowledge his question. "What shadow did you use to gain access to this place, demon?" I quickly search the lawn of strewn bodies, seeking the darkest, deepest shadows on the grounds; his passage for jumping from one space to the next, as the eye blinks. There are a few possibilities by the trees, back up the gravel path, near the waiting vehicles. He could have used any of these shadows to arrive . . . but that is not the question I need answered. "And how did you know I had returned?"

His ink-like wings flap, pushing burning smoke against Briana's face. Her body coughs. Another annoyance of physicality. "You are as arrogant as ever, Pendragon."

"You are mistaken, king of Cysgodol," I say, sniffing. "Arrogance is what severed you from your Court, not what separates me from mine."

"Your Court is in as much disarray as it ever was." As he speaks, his form grows dense, becoming more corporeal. The red coals grow, become two flames in black. A split red tongue flashes, then disappears in the smoke. In a blink, he becomes shadow once more. "I have been watching them. Hundreds of years later, and they are factions within factions. No longer riding under the dragon-rampant banner of Arthur, son of Uther."

He has watched my Legendborn? I dislike this. I pace toward my former opponent—and am surprised to see him glide backward. As if to avoid me.

Something is . . . amiss.

I glance down at his black aether spear still in the ground. Fifteen centuries ago, his aim had been sharp enough to find a man's eye through his helm across a darkened battlefield. The Shadow King does not miss his mark.

Not unless he wishes to.

A theory forms.

I dart toward him, using Briana's speed. Swing the aether sword—a weapon that can harm him—in a wide arc. It meets a shield, hastily shaped from smoke. I attack again—another block. A pivot, strike—and he dissipates and re-forms a few paces away.

He is defending himself only.

"Is there something you wish to share with me?" I ask. "In regard to your unwillingness to attack this body?"

The King swoops back ten paces on long, curved legs tipped with black claws. "Let us say that this girl is an investment that I would like to maintain."

He does not move, but sends a whip of thin smoke my way. A tendril manages to graze Briana's chestplate before I can escape it.

A flash of pain, burning, spreading.

I stumble back, clutching at Briana's sternum. Tear the aether chestplate away, let it dissolve on the ground, and watch in horror as a branching, glowing tree grows over her skin beneath her top garment, down the brown skin of her biceps, to her wrists. It pulses red—in time with the King's grinning, eager eyes.

An invisible mark, activated by the magic of the Shadow King, lord of demonkind.

Rage fills me. "You have *bloodmarked* this girl," I snarl.

"Yes . . . and no." The Shadow King makes a shrugging motion, wings rising, then settling. "I bloodmarked her ancestor. She has merely inherited it."

Briana is not tall enough to tower over the King, but I advance on him like she is. "For what reason would you do this? Tell me!"

"You mistake me for one of your subjects, Pendragon!" The King's wings flare wide, twice the height of a man on each side. "Demanding answers as though I have pledged you as my liege lord. As if I kneel to you. 'For what *reason*'?" The King laughs, a crackling, scraping, fading sound. His voice reaches me on the wind. "My own, of course . . ."

With that, his black aether form swirls and dissipates, bringing light to the grass and battlefield once more.

But that does not mean he is gone. I know better than to make this mistake ever again.

I twist in a circle, both hands wrapped around the hilt of Briana's cast blade, searching the dark corners of the open field for my oldest opponent.

"Hiding in your shadows again, old friend?"

The King's laughter rolls past in a wave from one direction, then returns in another. It could be real, or it could be my memory, tricking my ears and Briana's both.

He could be anywhere. Any shape.

And now, he is gone.

But we have visitors. Vehicles approach, their sounds grow louder—the reason why the King departed, perhaps? I turn to meet the three metal beasts rolling closer on the gravel—and without warning, I feel Briana's arms wrenched behind her in a powerful grip. A flood of magic fills her nose: resin-soaked heartwoods set aflame, myrrh and oud.

"Arthur, isn't it?" A harsh voice whispers in Briana's ear, filled with venom. *"My liege."*

I recognize the wheeze of a man whose breaths are hindered by broken ribs. The aether signature and injuries alone identify our captor. "I do not think we have formally met. Is this how you treat your king, Seneschal Varelian?"

Erebus yanks Briana to his side with one hand clamped around an elbow. I allow it, curious to mark his injuries: his chest, held tight on one side with his left hand; his gait, slow with an injured leg. "Your arrival complicates things," he grits out, wincing as he speaks.

"Because your Oaths keep you from truly harming Briana?" I ask, smiling. "That's unfortunate. For you." I pull against his hold and am pleased when it takes both of his hands to keep me in place.

We reach the vehicles, and their doors slide open. Four Mageguard emerge from each car, blurring into place around us.

"Bree?" one of them calls. Ah, the young Merlin who helped Briana escape.

"Hello, Larkin Douglas," I say.

His eyes widen in surprise, then dart between me and his Seneschal commander, concern warring with duty. "Seneschal Varelian . . . what is going on?"

"Take heed, all of you," Erebus announces. "This individual is no longer Crown Scion Briana Matthews. She has been possessed by the spirit of Arthur Pendragon, and it is he who attacked the squadron behind me."

"Bree!" Erebus turns us both around. Behind us, the root barrier has come down just long enough to permit its occupants to leave.

The three figures still remain on the ground: the Scion of Gawain, bent over Selwyn and the Onceborn girl, Alice. But now, standing guard between the healer and us are the Rootcrafters that accompanied Briana. Their names come back to me from her memories: Mariah, the young one. Lucille and Patricia, the elders.

This ought to be interesting.

It is Mariah who stares at the Merlin entourage, eyes blazing. "Let Bree go."

"This isn't Briana, Rootcrafter," Erebus replies. "I think you know that."

"It is Bree's body. *Bree's*. She is still inside," one of the elders responds. Patricia, recovered from her abduction. "*We* will exorcise the spirit. You don't know how."

"The girl may not be herself," a new voice says. "But she is still a valuable chip to play."

The Regent, Cestra, steps beside Erebus. She must have just emerged from one of the Order vehicles. "We will control her our way."

"Control?" I spit. "This is *treason.*"

Cestra smirks. "Against whom? The Regents are the current leaders of this Order." She shakes her head. "Attack me just as you attacked my Mageguard if you like, my liege, but something tells me you did not come here to fight your own kingdom."

"I did not," I concede to the woman. "I came to rule. To reign. To win this war."

She produces a pair of cyffion. Erebus's grip grows tight. "Then you will wear these while we negotiate."

I study the cyffion. Have not seen them in ages. Never seen them applied to any of my Court, much less myself.

Before I can protest, Patricia interjects, voice shaking with anger. "You wouldn't *dare* put those on her."

Cestra raises a brow. "And why not?"

Lucille, the smallest of the women, steps forward, her voice low and hard. "The ancestors of Volition will not stand for chains of any kind on our people, ever again."

Cestra's eyes narrow infinitesimally. "I do not fear ghosts."

"You should fear ours." The younger woman, Mariah, lowers her chin, fist balled at her hips.

"I would listen to these descendants if I were you, woman," I say with a low, throaty laugh.

"If you only knew how silly you sound in that body." Cestra steps forward, clicking open the first cuff. "The Order will never allow a mistake like you to lead. And I have worked too hard to be toppled by a mere girl whose ancestor was in the wrong place, at the wrong time." Her head whips toward the Mage-guard, Larkin. "Douglas! Tell Sitterson to gather up the wounded. I want Kane and the Chen girl with us."

Larkin looks between Cestra and Erebus, hesitant.

"Douglas, move!" Cestra barks. The Merlin moves closer to the Rootcrafters with both hands raised for peace. Lucille turns to the Scion of Gawain, who gives a short nod. The line of Rootcrafter women allow Larkin through and the two boys begin speaking in quick, hurried tones over the wounded.

"Apply the cuffs, Seneschal," Cestra orders, and hands them to her subordinate.

Erebus's voice remains even. "For what reason, if I may ask?"

"So that we can deal with her and the rest of the Table all at once."

The mention of the Table gets my attention. Are they all together at this moment? Waiting? Ten Scions and the Scion of Gawain . . . a near fully gathered Table already prepared for my arrival. And Cestra knows where they are. Hope flares, even as it wars with irritation at this obnoxious woman. To be with my knights again is impossible, but to see their descendants, to feel their spirits . . .

Cestra glares up at her mage. "That is an *order*."

Erebus hesitates a moment longer. He glances at the Rootcrafters, the barrier, then back at Cestra with a sigh. "As you command, Regent."

Erebus slowly takes Briana's—my—arm, and steps around so that we are face to face. I could run, fight, as Cestra says, but I wish to see my Table. I would give up my advantage if it means that we could be gathered again, in spirit and in flesh.

I begrudgingly hold out both of Briana's arms.

When Erebus snaps the first cuff around Briana's left wrist, the internal effect is immediate—a searing, cold pain freezes the power within her. Her root furnace, my sense of the aether in the air, the armor we both cast around her body, gone. All flattened into nothing.

A heartbeat. The hair on the back of Briana's neck lifts. Erebus himself grows still.

Silence.

Then, the Volition barrier explodes, blooming wide until the dome spreads far enough to encompass the vehicles. As it moves outward, a deep cracking sound follows, shaking the earth between our feet.

"What is that?" Larkin asks. The other Merlins step back, staring at the dirt with eyes wide, like they are hearing more than we can with our human ears.

The rumbling is enough to shake even Merlin balance.

"That is Volition!" Mariah yells. "Our ancestors are warning you, Legendborn. Leave now, and quickly, or be trapped here and die."

Cestra shakes her head, mouth set in a stubborn line. "Other arm, Erebus." When he hesitates again, she grasps Briana's right wrist with her own impatient fingers. When she snaps the other cuff on her wrist, the earth around us opens with a mighty *crack*. A dozen lightning-shaped fissures split the ground around the Merlins, isolating the group on a patch of crumbling soil.

Shouting erupts around us as the ground opens wider with another crack, and another—and the back wheels of one of the Order's empty vehicles drop into the earth. A loud, blaring alarm sounds from inside the car, and its lights begin flashing.

Cestra stumbles at the next wave of the Volition ancestors' power. I nearly laugh at her fall, but the loud splitting of the ground beside me steals the humor from my voice.

"Arrogant woman," I sneer.

"Indeed she is." Erebus holds Briana's elbow in one hand and, with a single swoop, lifts Cestra up by the other, carrying her toward a remaining vehicle. "We need to go, my Regent!"

"Take us to the Northern Chapter!" Cestra demands furiously.

Erebus's jaw clenches. "Yes, Regent."

The earth rocks beneath us all, nearly swallowing the other Order vehicles whole. There is only one left, and it could fall into the ground at any moment, blocking our escape. "Larkin!" Erebus calls over his shoulder, but the other Merlin is struggling to keep his footing carrying the Kane boy in his arms in the direction of the house and away from the Order cars. Beside him, the healer has lifted the Onceborn girl and is hurrying her to safety as well.

"Leave them!" Cestra calls. "Get us out of here!"

Erebus curses and speeds the three of us to the vehicle, tossing an angry Cestra in the front seat. Immediately, she produces a thin black brick and brings it to her ear. "Aldrich, we're on our way—"

I cannot hear the rest because Erebus rushes Briana around to the back, buckling her into a seat. Before I can protest, his palm presses hot against Briana's forehead, sending sleep rushing into her body. In one slow blink he is in the front seat, bringing the vehicle to life with the touch of a finger. Then, her eyes close, and we are speeding away.

57

THE MOMENT BRIANA'S body recovers from the Seneschal's mesmer, I awake—and am assaulted on all sides by the sensations of living.

My—her—stomach swims with nausea. Her head is filled with down. Her mouth and lips, both dry as summer straw. All is made worse by the uneven travel over a rough road. These cars' heavy metal bodies move swiftly over the land, but cannot they carry us with more ease?

I did not enjoy vomiting in my own body. I will not enjoy it in Briana's, of that I am sure. I swallow the bile in her throat and gather my thoughts.

The Seneschal moved too quickly for me to use Briana's ability to resist his power. I won't let that happen again.

The sky outside of the car shows a late-afternoon sun. We have been on the road for most of the day.

"Are you taking me to the Table?" I ask in Briana's raspy voice. I should demand water.

In the front seat, the woman Regent twists back to smirk. "Our intel says they are gathered at the Northern Chapter's Keep, holding a vote about how to proceed against us, the Regents, now that some . . . whispers have spread about our treatment of the Crown Scion and her allies. We shall see if your presence is enough to gather the Legendborn to sense."

"I have seen these children through Briana's eyes," I say. "Unlike you, they are loyal to the mission."

Cestra's eyes, stony and unfeeling, find mine in the mirror. "We shall see."

Unlike the secluded Southern Chapter's Lodge, the Northern Chapter's Keep is a gray-bricked castle set high on a hill.

Cestra and Erebus flank me as we weave through the stone pathway that winds around the front lawn. The Seneschal's gait loosens with every step as his cambion body heals from its recent injuries. There are no guards, no Merlins awaiting our arrival. "Where are the sentinels?" I ask.

"They are not expecting company." Erebus gestures toward a stone archway to the side of the building.

"They think they have called a private meeting of Legendborn—the remaining Scions and Squires, some just recently Oathed—to discuss the growing rumors about the truth behind the disappearances of William Sitterson, Briana Matthews, and her best friend, the so-called Vassal Chen."

"Ah," I say. "Your machinations have gone awry, have they?"

Cestra's scowl tells me the answer before her words do. "We successfully convinced the Legendborn that Sitterson and Matthews were together, in hiding for her own safety, at first, but requests for contact can only go denied so long. This wild goose chase your descendant has taken us on has lasted far longer than we'd planned. Too long. Chen's parents are asking questions, and so is Matthews's father. Nicholas Davis has gone completely underground, and his father's body has been found by the Onceborn authorities. The Legendborn still believe, for now, that Selwyn Kane is in a Shadowhold, but even that story may have begun to form cracks with whispers from certain Lieges." Cestra tucks her hands into her long coat. "We have allowed the children to host several of these, with our eyes and ears on the inside to gather information, of course. This is the first time all of the chapters have gathered together, and so we as the Council have decided now is a good time to . . . how do they say it?" She chuckles. "Enter the chat."

I do not quite follow this reference, too abstract in Bree's memories. "Why allow them to meet at all?"

"Because it is far easier to understand and guide sentiment than it is to squash it outright." Cestra smiles. "Warfare is not all blades and bows. Perhaps if you and the original Table had understood that, we would not still be in this war." She trails a hand along a wooden railing.

I do not rise to her bait. "You have never seen the full bloodshed and chaos of Camlann, child. That is the only reason that you toy with it now." I consider sharing that I have seen the Shadow King, that this Camlann will be as no other, but after I am crowned, the Regents will be advisors to me. The only people who need to hear the truth are my Legendborn.

Behind the building lies a strange sort of arena surrounded by four sections of carved stone steps that create entry from every direction, with a field in the middle. On the far end lies a gauntlet course made of suspended rings and thin beams on which to balance. "Is this place for training purposes?"

Erebus nods. "One such location for the Legendborn, of many."

Erebus directs my attention to the other side, where a growing crowd of young people has gathered in a loose circle. We move toward the nearest set of steps, approaching from the east.

Even at this distance, the clamor of an argument is audible. As we walk down the stone steps toward the crowd, some voices and faces become clearer. I recognize many of Briana's friends from the Southern Chapter: Peter, the Scion of my knight Owain, and his Squire, Greer. Victoria, the Scion of Tristan, and her Squire, Sarah. Felicity, the Scion of Lamorak, still without a new Squire. The new Scion of Bors, a young, untested boy of sixteen, Squire-less as well.

Children who possess mere echoes of my men.

There are others gathered here whom Briana has not met, Scions and Squires from other chapters. I assume that I am also seeing the Scions of Kay, Bedivere, Erec, Caradoc, Mordred, and Geraint.

I wish that their faces were familiar to me. Wish that I could feel their bloodlines and spirits, but I do not.

All of the current Table members are present, save her friend the Scion of Gawain and her beloved Nicholas. I require a fully gathered Table to finish what I started, to live truly on this plane and turn back Camlann myself. This incomplete group of ten Scions and assorted Squires will have to do, for now.

Cestra shouts as she walks. "Honored Legendborn of the Round, may we have a moment?"

The group turns as one—many producing aether weapons on instinct.

"A Regent . . . ?" "Regent Cestra!" "That's a Seneschal."

"Bree!" Greer and Peter move to the fore of the group.

"Not quite," Cestra says with a smile. The two children stop short, glance at each other, then back at Cestra.

I glare at her. "I can speak for myself."

"Where is William?" Greer asks. With a flick of their wrist, they call forth the aether lion of Owain.

"And Selwyn?" Felicity strides forward, the armor of Lamorak flowing into place along her shoulders.

Cestra holds her hands up for peace. "William tends to the injured. One of whom is your dear Kingsmage, near succumbing to his blood."

The crowd gasps. "Enough of this," I say. "Let me speak to my Table."

"*Your* Table?" A haughty voice joins the group from behind. The Regent who plays politician descends the stone stairs from the west, with his Seneschal in tow.

"There you are, Gabriel," I say. "And Tacitus."

The crowd parts to let them through. Regent Gabriel's eyes narrow as he comes closer. "You do not even speak like the girl, and yet here she stands." He glances at his Seneschal. "What do you think, Tacitus?"

Tacitus stops several paces from me and leers, ringed fingers twitching at his sides. "I'd like to take a tour of that mind." His fangs show his age, and his eyes burn nearly as dark as the Shadow King's.

"Bree, what are they talking about?" Greer says, faltering. "Why are you cuffed?"

"That's not Bree," says Victoria. She uses Tristan's speed to dart forward, reaching me before the other Legendborn do to peer closer. "Can't you tell?"

Her Squire reaches her side in a blur. "Is that . . . ?"

"I am King Arthur Pendragon of Britain."

A mocking voice calls out from the east. I pivot on my heel to see Lord Regent Aldrich stride down the stairs from the south toward our group, eyes bright. "Son of Uther Pendragon. The first wielder of Caledfwlch, the blade Excalibur, and first-ranked of the Round Table in the Shadowborn holy war."

"You recognize your king, Aldrich," I reply. "All the better to cede leadership to me, and with haste."

"Bree——" Greer calls.

"She's *not* in there!" Victoria shakes her head, shouting back at the Legendborn. "That is not our Scion of Arthur! She's closer to a demon than Legendborn. Look at her! She's possessed by a ghost. The Regents should have kept her drugged and locked up!"

"Victoria, my dear," Aldrich says with a furrowed brow. "Give us some credit. We did try, but there were traitors in our midst."

"Tor . . . ?" Sarah steps back from her girlfriend. "The Regents told us that Bree had gone into hiding with William for her own safety. All those weeks trying to figure out if they were lying and you . . . you knew what really happened to them?" Similar gasps from the group.

Victoria raises her chin. "Camlann has come, and Bree has no idea what she's doing. She shouldn't even be here, Sar!"

Sarah's face is a tumble of emotions—shock, fear, then a haunted type of disgust. "You spied for them? This whole time?"

As the girls argue, I notice the cloth-wrapped blade Aldrich has kept hidden behind him. Even without seeing it bare, my hands and my fingers itch to claim it. Briana's body knows the blade because our shared blood calls for it, even when cuffed. "You have Caledfwlch."

"This?" Aldrich raises the sword by the wrapped flat of the blade, pulling at the strings as he talks. As he unravels it, the weapon becomes exposed for what it is when it is not held by the blood of the Pendragon: a narrow, thin, old metal longsword of no remarkable feature and no greater strength than any other metal-forged blade.

Except that it has been broken in two.

"What have you done, boy? That blade was forged by Merlin himself." My blood runs cold, tendrils of panic seeping through my veins in drips. "It cannot be forged again by anyone else."

Aldrich barks a laugh. "Boy?" He shakes his head. "Truly you are Arthur before me. As for Excalibur? I had my Seneschal break it for safekeeping after Briana failed to return it to its resting place in the stone."

"Safekeeping?" I roar. I extend my hand for the pieces. "Give it to me! It is mine by birthright!"

Aldrich eyes me, then turns to the crowd of Legendborn. "If you are the true king, I think you should fight for your broken sword before your Table. Three Seneschals should suffice, don't you think?"

The tension thickens the air around us, but sets my blood singing.

"I am prepared to do what it takes," I murmur and extend a palm to cast a shield and blade from aether—only to remember the cyffion circling my arms.

Aldrich turns toward the listening Legendborn. "Will you be ruled by a king who allows herself to be manacled like the rogue magic user she is? If we take those off, will she show us Briana's unnatural root? Or her inability to control even the most basic of Legendborn powers?"

This is the Regents' goal, is it? Force the Table to witness their king out of control, possessed by a spirit, and weak in battle? Discredit Briana before she has even begun? The Legendborn look between me and the Regents, to the three Seneschals, and back to me again. Uncertainty ripples among those who don't know Briana, and confusion spreads on the faces of those that do.

But it is the gleeful look on Victoria's face that makes "discredit" seem the lesser evil. "She doesn't belong here," Victoria says. "She never did. And now she is compromised. Just like she wishes to compromise *us*, can't you all see?"

Victoria is not a born leader, but she knows how to command a crowd. At her words, confusion turns to suspicion for some, then fear.

I sneer at them all. "Why don't you have Erebus remove these cuffs, Aldrich, and we will see who triumphs."

"Enough!"

With a loud crack, aether descends around the six members of the Council, encasing them in a near-translucent, blue crosshatch-patterned prison.

The Council members shout in protest, but the Legendborn barely react. Instead of responding with alarm, the gathered Scions and Squires part, allowing four of the Squires unfamiliar to Briana to stride through the opening. While the Seneschals within the constructed prison do everything in their power to break it, the four unknown Squires surround them with arms outstretched and teeth gritted with effort, reinforcing the structure with whispered spellwork and words that sound foreign to Briana's ears.

But their castings, their chants, their hand movements . . . they are a form of magic that I have not seen in a very, very long time.

I see now that these "Squires" that Briana did not recognize were not Squires at all, and that this clandestine meeting the Council interrupted was not solely a gathering of members of the Round Table. These four aether-users were invited too, and in their squabble with the Legendborn children the Council had not realized that the outsiders had been watching, waiting.

"Who the *hell* are y'all?" Victoria demands. It seems that the Council's mole, Victoria, was not privy to all.

"Victoria?" Cestra shouts. "What is this?"

"Not what," a new voice says. "Who."

Three of the newcomers break away to absorb the work of the prison casting, leaving their final member free to move. She is a young woman with short brown hair wearing brown leathers and boots.

I suck in a breath when our eyes meet.

It cannot be. It should not be.

In this moment, the war, the Shadow King, the foolish Regents all fade to lesser matters. Even Caledfwlch is forgotten beneath the roar of blood in my ears, the heartbeat hammering against Briana's chest.

The young woman's gaze slides away from mine and to the Regents as she continues talking. "We have watched, we have listened, and we have simply, *finally* had enough."

The mischief in her eyes has dimmed, but it is still there. Her face is shaped differently, her hair, but unlike when gazing upon my knights, I can *see* her spirit hovering around her. I do not know why it is different with her than the others, but I know I recognize her and feel her before me.

I know my sister.

"Morgaine?"

The young woman's gaze snaps back to mine, as fiery as ever. "Do not speak to me."

I swallow past the shock and pain, stumble forward on Briana's shaking legs. "Is it truly you, sister?" I whisper. "My Morgaine?"

The woman's eyes flash. "I am not your sister," she says with unnerving still-ness. "But we are her descendants. And it is time for the Regents and the Order to come to an end."

"To . . . an end?" I stammer. "Morgaine . . ."

"My name is Ava," the girl corrects. Her eyes are twin daggers, aiming right toward me.

This girl says she is not Morgaine and her features are different, but I cannot shake the feeling that I am standing before my very own sister, my flesh and blood.

"Your reign, your *Order*, is what eventually drove your sister to exile," Ava shouts, "or did that history get lost beneath your many wars?"

I dig through what Briana knows of my sister's descendants. There is frus-tratingly little. "The Order . . . accused her descendants of treachery. . . ." Anger floods me. "No, that was a mistake," I say. "I will make this right. I swear it."

"It's too late for that, old man," Ava replies sourly. She raises a hand, aether crackling around her fingers in that same crosshatch style. The way that my sister's magic came to her.

Boom! The Seneschals strike at their prison as one, forming hairline cracks that spread like a web. It is only a matter of moments before they break through.

From within her crosshatched prison, Cestra shouts at the Scion of Tristan. "You hid this, Victoria. You hid that the Table has aligned with Mor-gaines!"

Tristan's Scion raises her hands. "I didn't know, I swear!"

"The Morgaines approached us with their intel about what the Regents were really doing behind the scenes," Greer says. "The Morgaines are the reason we know that you'd drugged and kidnapped William and Bree. They told us that you'd locked Sel away in a Shadowhold without a trial. They're the reason we know that the three of them escaped, and that you wanted to murder Nick. The enemy of your enemy is your friend, and the Regents have proven themselves to be the enemy of all Legendborn."

Rage fills Victoria's features. "And you kept this from me?" She casts an angry glare at her fellow Legendborn. "All of you?"

"Yes." At Victoria's side, her lover's face is shrouded in disappointment. "Because we didn't trust you."

Victoria stares at her girlfriend, eyes wide. "Sarah?"

Sarah shakes her head. "You kept trying to get us to trust the Council, even when we all knew that they were lying to us. . . . You've gone after Bree from the beginning, Tor, for all the wrong reasons." Her eyes shine with unshed tears. "So I told the others they couldn't trust you with this."

In the moment of distraction, Serren, the Seneschal of Constructs, finally breaks open the prison, releasing all six occupants at once. Without stopping, he creates two scythes and whirls against the Morgaine closest to him. Erebus and Tacitus follow close behind, casting weapons as they blur against their opponents. At first, it appears as though the Morgaines might hold their own, but the three Seneschals are older, stronger, and cambions built for war. And yet the Morgaines do not fight alone; it takes but a moment for the Scions and Squires to join them and face off against the three Master Merlins.

The traitorous Regents begin a hasty retreat, leaving their Seneschals and their magic to face the crowd of nearly twenty trained warriors.

But they won't escape me.

As the battle grows in volume and violence around me, I stride toward the escaping Regents, but on my third step, I feel a tug from the ground and look down to find the broken pieces of Caledfwlch. From where Aldrich has let it fall to the earth, the blade calls to me once more.

I kneel to the ground to reclaim it. As soon as Briana's fingers grasp the hilt, the short section of blade still attached blazes blue fire, shining bright and wide and sharp once again. One swipe at my wrist with the jagged edge and the first cuff falls. Flip the blade to sinister, slice again, and the right cuff follows. My armor roars to life up my arms and across my shoulders, down my chest and over my hips, knees, feet.

By the time I am wrapped in aether and breathing easy, the Seneschals are retreating, outnumbered by the nearly full Round Table and Morgaines.

My triumph is short-lived, however, because abruptly, my sister's descendant Ava stands before me, regarding my armor and Excalibur both with solemn eyes. "I wish you had not called on your aether."

I toss the broken end of Caledfwlch to my left hand, the hint of battle crackling between us. I pull aether toward the edge of the half blade, hastily rebuilding its shining length from memory until the sword is complete. "And why is that?"

Ava casts her own sword in a blink, drawing it close and dropping into a well-honed battle stance. "Because while we came here to fight the Regents, you are the heart of the Order, Arthur. And for it to truly die, so must you."

"I do not wish to harm my own sister's descendant, but I will if I must." I raise my half-aether blade into position.

Before either of us can strike, there is a screeching sound from a dark tunnel set between two stone staircases. A large vehicle exits, careening across the lawn and over the grass straight toward us.

58

AS WE MOVE through the hallways of the castle, I follow Arthur and Morgaine close behind, but try to get a sense of how big it is, how many rooms. I get lost, or the rooms shift as we move. Arthur's dream of Camelot seems part real, part fiction, part wish. I have no idea how much time has passed in the outside world, whether the dream moves quickly or slowly. I have no idea what Arthur is doing while in possession of my body. I am terrified to find out.

Wishes are the dangerous mind games we play with ourselves. The only way to win is not to play.

Sel's words ring truer here than ever.

The Shadow King's crown rests in a dungeon deep in Camelot, on a metal stand behind a near-translucent, hatch-patterned aether construct. Although I can tell that we are somewhere underground, the crown sits in a patch of sunlight, delivered down several stories from a small, round, open skylight overhead.

"I cast this barrier myself," Morgaine is saying. "Merlin taught me how."

"Truly?" Arthur asks, and she beams with pride at her brother.

It is hard to listen to their conversation, because my eyes are drawn to the crown.

If inanimate objects in Arthur's dream world look shiny and unreal, the Shadow King's crown feels like a beacon of reality—dented and dinged, streaked with dirt. Its claw shape, the color, the way that light seems to be absorbed into the metal rather than reflected.

"And what did you wish to show me?" the dream Arthur asks.

I consider not for the first time what makes this interaction between Arthur and his half sister a dream and not a memory. Sometimes, our dreams are memories revisited, sure, but other times, dreams depart from what was, and become something else.

I wonder if the easygoing, open nature of Morgaine is the quality of this vision that makes it a fiction. How much she shares with her brother, and how proud she is of her apprenticeship. The girl I saw in Arthur's banquet memory was far more nervous and withdrawn. An object for him to protect and care for, not an advisor or a confidante to share secrets with.

Morgaine circles the crown. "Do you see the way it seems to have grown dim since you took it from the Shadow King?"

Arthur steps closer, and I join him. "Yes," he says. "Is it dust?"

She shakes her head. "I have a theory."

"Do share."

She preens at his attention. "I think that this crown is not unlike your Caledfwlch." Morgaine draws closer, inspecting the crown as she speaks. "Caledfwlch absorbs your power, but it's also tied to you. Connected. That's why no one else can wield it in battle *but* you. When it is away from you, it grows dim, too."

A line appears between Arthur's brows. "An aether weapon?"

Morgaine nods eagerly. "Yes. And since it is the Shadow King's aether weapon, then he was not just bereft of his crown, but he has lost his ability to lead and fight. That is why he became weak and why he perished. Isn't that wonderful?"

Arthur rubs at his beard. "Will this stop the war, forever?"

Morgaine sighs and leans down so that the crown is at her eye level. "I don't know. The Court will be trapped on the other side, but as for the other Shadowborn? The chaos may make them stronger. That is why Merlin is working on the Spell of Eternity for you and the Table. . . ." Her fingers hover over the barrier. "But what if there were a way to *harness* even the dying power of this crown, brother? Use it to our advantage?"

Arthur pulls his sister back gently by the shoulder. "Nothing good can come from playing with Shadowborn magic, Morgaine."

She resists him for a moment before relenting. "You don't know that."

"What does Merlin say?"

She stands. "That he does not trust demonkind, and that he would know better than most why their magic cannot be trusted."

I step closer to the barrier, my hand outstretched before I can stop it. I don't know why this ugly, gnarled, evil crown calls to me, but it is the only thing of this world that is unabashedly real.

Maybe that's why I can't help but reach for it.

Just like the dream Arthur walking through me as if I am nothing, my fingers pass through the dream barrier like it never existed at all.

But the crown is solid mass. The instant my fingertips touch the tallest point of the Shadow King's crown, a black wave of power pulses from its center, right up my arm, and across my chest.

I feel the bloodmark come alive before I see the light shine through my shirt.

And my root comes roaring back to life with it, crimson flames covering me like a blanket and casting the dungeon the color of sweet, furious Bloodcraft. I could cry with relief.

Morgaine's bloodcurdling scream cuts that short. "Merlin!" she shouts.

I whirl around, bringing the Rootcraft flames with me. Morgaine and Arthur already have blades drawn, both of them.

"Who are you, monster?"

"I-I . . . ," I stammer, shock that they can see me temporarily overtaking the relief at having my power—*any* power—back in this realm. "You can see me?"

Morgaine pulls a ball of spinning aether into her palm and draws back as if to throw it. "Whom do you serve?"

"No one!" I say, but make the mistake of holding both hands up in defense. The red flames only climb higher and brighter between us.

A familiar screeching sound splits the air, slicing across the sound of root flames. An eagle owl in flight overhead, then diving down the skylight. A second later, Merlin himself descends between me and Arthur, his eyes reflecting the deep red of root. The murder in the sorcerer's eyes takes me aback and I nearly fall scrambling away from him. "Diminish your power, or I will do so for you."

I pull as hard as I can on my root, but it does not disappear, only withdraws enough so that Merlin can see my face—and the glowing bloodmark on my chest.

"You bear the Shadow King's mark," Merlin hisses.

"No, it's the Hunter's—" The protest dies on my lips.

The Hunter . . . the Great Devourer . . . *is* the Shadow King.

Which means the Shadow King survived Arthur's attack and lived long enough to bloodmark the Line of Vera.

Every demon that haunted us, no matter how he appeared, was one. A single, ancient demon who marked our power—and who is waiting for his prize.

Before I can process any further, Merlin lunges.

I throw up a wall of flame at the last second, and he roars in pain, jumping back as it burns his palms and arms.

I don't wait to make my escape. I dash toward the open wooden door that brought us to the dungeon, running as fast as I can to the hallway—and run right into an aether-plated chest of armor.

This armor is more than tunic and mail; bright, shining, and silver-blue, it could only be cast by a knight after Merlin enhanced the Table's blood with magic. Strong arms grip me at the shoulders, lift me up, until I am eye to eye with Sir Lancelot.

"Who are you, girl?"

I do the only thing I can think of. "None of this is real!" I shout in his face. Startled, he opens his mouth to reply, only to be interrupted by thunder shaking the walls around us. He drops me, and I run down the hall searching for a door, any door that will let me out of this dream.

Lancelot is close on my heels, shouting. And Merlin's aether signature claws at the insides of my nose. I hear his mage flames as he sends his power rushing along the walls of the narrow hallway.

I spot my exit up ahead and throw my shoulder into it, pushing the door outward—and land in the middle of a bright summer day in an empty, sawdust-covered courtyard bordered on all sides by racks of wooden practice swords and, beyond them, towering trees.

I twist back, expecting to see the door disappear as the other one did, but Lancelot and Merlin burst through behind me, weapons in each hand.

"This isn't real!" I scream. "You're not real!"

Thunder claps overhead, breaking the sunlight into night. Lightning strikes all around me, and torches bordering the courtyard bloom to life with smokeless fire. Lightning flashes again, blinding me temporarily—all is white, bright spots across my eyes, and sawdust thrown in the air—and I scamper backward, crabwalking and coughing, waiting for my vision to return.

I immediately sense that I have pushed the dream's boundaries too far. If I keep going, the world will fall apart around me, if the lightning doesn't find me first.

"Come out, demon!" Lancelot calls to me. He too is coughing in the smoke; somehow he evaded the lightning. He can't possibly see me. "We know you are of the Shadow Court."

I dash for a rack of weapons and hide behind them, clasping both hands over my mouth, pushing my root down and down until it fades. Merlin is half demon—does he move like Valec did? If he hears me, will he be at my side in a blink, ready to kill me without mercy?

The wooden weapon rack behind me is wrenched up and away. I dart toward the trees—but a hand grabs my collar and holds me fast, lifting me up and around until I am facing Merlin's fierce gaze beneath bushy brows. "There you are, little Cysgod."

"I am not Shadowborn!" I shriek.

Merlin releases me to the ground, freeing both hands to gather aether around him, whipping up a storm of it that churns so quickly it clears the smoke away. "Your mark says otherwise."

There is no time to explain further before Merlin cuts me down. There is no escape.

My bloodmark pulses in time with my racing heartbeat. Instead of dimming, as it has in the past, here it is *alive* and bright, shining through my clothes, winding up my throat and down my arms and elbows.

Merlin is right. The Shadow King *did* mark me . . . .and waking his mark up brought my root back. Not just back but . . . more. I realize suddenly that for the first time since my root first rose, it doesn't feel like Vera's power.

Here in this world, somehow, the red flames are mine to wield.

They belong to *me*.

I won't fall to the mercy of these figments, these ghosts, of people long dead. This may be Arthur's dream, but I will burn it down myself before I die in it. I will make it a nightmare on my own terms if I must.

"I won't go without a fight," I say, scuttling backward.

Lancelot reaches Merlin's side, brandishing two glowing swords. "I was hoping she'd say that."

I press both palms into the earth, calling my root to the surface just long enough to send it roaring over the ground toward their feet. Merlin leaps backward before my flames reach him, and Lancelot speeds away until we are facing each other, two on one.

The surprise in Merlin's eyes delights me. He has fought demons, but he's never fought me. He and Lancelot exchange glances, shifting their weapons as they assess me.

I don't wait for them to form a strategy. Instead, I draw my root up and out of my chest to my arms and ask it to do what I never could with Arthur's power—become solid.

And here, it responds.

Root flows over my chest and down my legs, hardening as it goes until I am covered with flat, iridescent rubies layered on top of one another that look like—

"Scales," Lancelot hisses.

Merlin shakes his head. "It cannot be. They are extinct—"

"Dragons never die," I whisper, and rush them both, moving like a blade through liquid—and pivot at the last second to lash out at Lancelot with a clawed gauntlet, cleaving the mail in two. My claws bite into his shoulder down to the muscle, then I dart back.

With eyes wide he recasts the chain mail, melding the split pieces together.

A spear whistles—I duck, twist, and push off from the ground toward Merlin.

The sorcerer calls up a wall of aether just as he did before, this time circling me tighter, closing me in. His voice is chanting overhead, casting a harder and harder construct.

A prison meant to hold me.

It won't work.

I punch through the closing circle—it stutters.

A blade strikes my wrist from the other side. A blow from Lancelot, meant to break bones—

It barely pierces my scales.

I withdraw. Pull root from my chest to counter Merlin's spinning prison, moving my flames in a rush in the opposite direction until the two dissipate against each other.

Merlin stands across from me, panting, hands outstretched and eyes wide with horror. "Demon!"

Lancelot adjusts his grip on his injured shoulder. "Monster."

"No," I say in return. "My name is Bree."

"Bree." Lancelot blinks, shakes his head. "Bree?"

"Yes!" I shout. "Bree!"

Before they ready another attack, I remember Sel's chain scythe. With a thought, my mage flame spreads to the ground, forming chains one link at a time. The heavy ball weight in one hand, the curved blade in the other.

I pull it up and overhead as Sel did, and laugh at the sensation of my own root power in my hands, deadly at my command, because I made it so.

"Surround her!" Lancelot shouts. Merlin yells something to me that I cannot hear. More accusations, more lies, more condemnations.

I ignore him, and spin my chain faster.

After what looks like a frustrated growl, Merlin drops down to punch the ground with a flaming blue fist. His aether ripples out around me, but instead of a cyclone to close me in, the aether solidifies itself into six animal constructs.

The silver hounds form a circle, snapping and yowling behind me, beside me, in front of me.

Behind them, Merlin and Lancelot back away. Merlin sends his constructs in to fight in his place.

"Coward," I whisper. "Sending creatures as fodder."

Merlin and Lancelot exchange heated words that I cannot hear above the whirl of my weapon and the cries of the hounds. They seem to be fighting with one another now, likely over how to best defeat me.

No matter. I won't give them time to plan a counterattack.

The sorcerer's hounds are gone—sliced into shining bits and pieces—in fewer than three rotations.

This takes Lancelot and Merlin by surprise. I grin. Good. I lengthen my chain so the blade whizzes just by them, and take a step closer.

"Stop!" they shout. "Bree!"

Another step.

As one, they begin to retreat when a thunderclap overhead shakes the earth, and the sky flashes bright with lightning.

The dreamworld, fighting back again.

Lightning strikes at their feet, sending them flying in opposite directions.

Before either of them can lift a blade or raise a hound or use any of their aether against me, I let the chain scythe melt back to flames on either side of me. Then I feed the flames with root, pushing even more fuel toward them, *imagining* them into the shape I want.

Into the *wings* I want.

Massive. Claw-tipped. *Powerful.*

With one mighty flap, I am in the air.

The glittering, red, leatherlike wings spread ten feet wide on either side of my ruby-scaled body. Thunder rumbles, giving me just enough warning to swoop to the side and away from a flash of lightning. I am faster in the air, stronger.

I don't ever want to come down.

Lightning splits the sky in three places at once. The patch of trees closest to the castle goes up in flames. The fire jumps and spreads. Soon the whole forest will be ablaze.

Below me, Lancelot and Merlin wave their arms, calling me back.

"Come down!"

"What do you care?" I shout. "You just want to kill me."

"Not true, mystery girl!" Merlin shouts, and my eyelids flutter.

The wind whips around my ears, probably distorting the sound this high up. I steady myself, adjust my wings to remain airborne.

"Bree, please!" Lancelot yells, and just barely dodges another lightning strike at his feet.

The dream, Arthur's dream . . . is changing. It's turned on me now, like it knows my own hopes and wants me to believe them. Like a drug, it wants me to absorb the lie. It is building a new story that it thinks I will accept, I'm sure of it.

A lie in which they are here with me.

But that can't be.

Not when their faces are still Lancelot's and Merlin's, men many years older than me and long dead. Men that have never met me, never will, and couldn't possibly understand who or why I am.

"No," I shake my head. "This is the dream. This is what trapped Arthur . . . rewarding him if he believed, punishing him if he questioned. . . ."

"Do you remember what I said to you?" Merlin calls to me. "That you are the most stubborn creature I have ever met."

"You didn't say that to me . . . ," I whisper, but my subconscious has already turned toward the memory, toward hope, and I have drifted steadily closer to the earth without realizing it.

A silver cord wraps itself around my ankle—and yanks. "No!" I shout, but my wings are dematerializing without my focus. They flap against the aether rope pulling me downward, but lose strength with every wingbeat, the construct losing structure until it is flame and fire with no substance.

A final, hard pull brings me crashing to the ground, but before I can recover, aether-reinforced arms wrap themselves around my chest and pull me tight against solid armor. "It's me—"

I scream—and my root flares outward and up. Lancelot ducks his head—helm and all—against my shoulder and waits it out.

But there is no limit to my root. I send more flames out in waves, and more still, but every time they burn his armor away, he recasts it and pulls me tighter.

I lie panting in his grip, red flames surrounding us. He does not let go, and I do not stop.

Until I feel a pull on the very center of my furnace. My head snaps up—to find Merlin kneeling before us, one open hand hovering a foot away, collecting a swirling ball of my red root into his palm. It's just enough that my flames weaken, briefly. I send them roaring back to life—and aim them straight at him.

Merlin absorbs the rush of power but winces at the effort, fangs bared. "Nicholas," he grits out. "It's not enough. She's . . . too strong; she doesn't believe we're real. She'll kill us in here if she gets free."

At my ear, Lancelot looks up. "And they'll kill her out there if we can't bring her back! Try again!"

Merlin raises both palms, taking in double the amount of my aether, sucking it nearly as quickly as I create it, just like a hellfox would.

"Still not enough." He grinds his teeth together, shaking his head.

"Keep trying!"

A pause. A growl. "You know what I have to do."

"No!" Lancelot's helmet is gone now. I can see the scruff on his chin now, the dark blond hair matted in sweat against his forehead. "I can't lose you; I *won't* lose her. . . ."

"You'll lose us both if you don't let me try," Merlin says.

The two meet eyes over me. Something about that shared glance, the worry there, the care . . . makes the dream feel too good to leave. Makes me want to stay there between them, even if it's all a lie in the end.

Lancelot's voice is tight when he finally answers. "Do it."

Merlin crawls closer on hands and knees. "Just know, Briana Matthews," he says, "that you are worth this and more."

Without a second's hesitation, he pulls me close enough that we nearly kiss—and inhales my power into his body. Devours it whole. My wings shrink and turn to smoke. My armor melts, then sparks, then turns to dust. My gauntlets shatter into shimmering pieces. And all of it—all of it—flows up and into the sorcerer's mouth, draining my root until the furnace grows dim. With every breath, Merlin draws more deeply on my root. And with each breath, his eyes turn a deeper and darker red, until they are the color of heartblood. His fingers hold mine and I gasp at the sight of them—nails turning dark, veins crawling up his wrist in black lines.

Lancelot grasps my face in both palms and holds it tight. "Come back, Bree. Come back to us."

My root has left me. The only thing of my own here, the only thing that kept me safe in this hellscape. "No . . ." I shake my head.

"Please." Merlin's voice is nearly unrecognizable. "Come back to us."

"This isn't real," I whisper. "It can't be. If this is real . . ."

Then Sel is almost gone, more demon than human because he consumed my root.

Then Nick is back, but broken and bloody at my hand.

If this is real, then Alice . . .

If this is real, then the nightmare won't end when I wake up.

"Oh God," I gasp. "It's . . . it's real."

The world cracks open, breath forced from my lungs.

Thunder shakes the earth beneath us. Smoke from the trees fills the air, clogs my nose, clouds my vision.

The world goes dark. In the distance, trees on fire pop and break, falling into themselves.

Finally, my vision clears, and I see what I'd been too scared to hope for. Both boys, real and here.

But Sel is not the Sel I recognize, not anymore. In a brief flash, I see what he's sacrificed to save me—his eyes have turned bloodred, his fangs sharper, his features more angled and beautiful and terrifying. The hands at my shoulders withdraw, and there are black-tipped claws instead of fingers. He shoves away from me and Nick, scrambling back into the smoke before I can see any more of his transformation.

I shift forward and Nick releases me, holds a warm hand against my back. I turn to him, see his familiar face, the dimples, and the worn blue eyes. The soot smeared onto his cheek from my root, the singed tips of his hair. "Hey, B."

"You . . ." My lower lip trembles. "He . . ."

Nick follows my gaze. "I know. We need to get him out of here."

This is the worst thing I can imagine: that all we fought for and everything Sel had done to keep his demonia from overtaking him would happen right before my eyes. Not just through me, but because of me.

Nick squeezes my shoulder, pulling my attention. "Don't suppose you know how to get home?" In the distance a burning tree falls, sending a rush of flames to the sky. "And quickly?"

"I don't even know how you got here in the first place," I reply.

"A long story." He grasps my hand. "But we need you now. How do we leave?"

"I . . ." I squint, pulling my thoughts together. "Merlin didn't build this place for someone to leave voluntarily. It's a place for Arthur to wait until he's Called."

"But how did he switch places with you?"

"He didn't," I whisper. "I—I let him. I accepted his offer to live through me."

The edges of his mouth turn down. Another tree cracks to the ground.

"You accepted Arthur to get here," he says slowly, "so what is the opposite of acceptance?"

The lightning of the dreamworld threatens the edge of my consciousness, waiting for me to challenge it, but I won't. Because if Sel and Nick found their way in, I can find our way out.

I push to standing on trembling feet and Nick helps me rise. Somewhere nearby, Sel moans, and I hear him push to his feet as well, see a flash of black hair in the flame-lit dust.

All at once, I know what I have to do.

"I . . . ," I whisper to the dream, "I reject my title as Scion of Arthur."

Around me, the world quiets. Beside me, Nick sucks in a breath.

"I will not rise to dispel the shadows," I murmur.

The dream fire dims, grows still. The world darkens.

Then, the figure of Arthur appears.

He is in my body in the real world, but here I see him as he appeared at Volition. Shining armor near translucent. But this time, the look in his eyes is of pure rage—multiplied when he sees Nick. "You."

I don't know what Nick did to him on the other side, but Nick raises his chin defiantly, eyes like flint. "Yes. *Me.*"

I step in front of Nick to face my ancestor eye to eye.

"I will no longer take as my own the weight of the blood of the world—"

Arthur's image grows solid, dimming while my, Nick, and Sel's bodies begin to brighten. "Stop—"

I look up at Nick, who takes my hand. Nods. From the shadows, Sel's now-glowing fingers grasp my arm.

"Briana—"

"I reject everything your blood has ever given me. I will not serve the Order's mission above all others," I murmur. With every word, we lose density, become as light. "I reject these Oaths, by my blood . . . and on my heart."

I wake up in my own body, gasping, my heart racing so loud that I can't hear the soothing words Nick murmurs against my cheek. All I can see are the bright stars overhead, harsh reality flowing back in around me . . . or the other way around. Me, coming back to life. He shifts so that his hand supports the base of my skull, a warm palm holding me steady.

"Nick . . . ," I rasp.

"I'm here." When he presses his mouth to my forehead, the stubble at his chin scratches the bridge of my nose. "You're okay. We're back."

"Sel . . ."

He goes quiet, mouth working open and closed. He draws back so that I can see Sel behind us, where he lies flat on his back, unconscious. Sel's fingers are tipped with black claws, and the dark veins I'd seen in Arthur's memory have followed him here. "He's alive."

Nick's words are careful. "Alive" is not the same as "okay."

A fresh gash runs across Sel's open, upturned palm. Beside him lies Excalibur, broken in two. My eyes fall to Nick's hand next, where a matching cut travels the same path.

The sticky smear of blood on my cheek. The wide strip of red on my forearm.

They'd blood walked to find me. Blood walked to bring me back. "We did what you showed us." Nick says. "Didn't know if it would work . . . had to try."

"You and Sel . . . came after me? Even though you didn't know how we'd get back out?"

"We had faith," he says quietly. "That you'd know how to get us all out safely."

"And if I didn't?"

We look at each other for a long moment, then to Sel, and back to each other. When he finally speaks, Nick's voice is warm enough to wrap the three of us together, a bond of its own. "Then the world would be broken in more ways than one."

My eyes water. "Sel needs help. I don't know how—"

Someone clears their throat, and our reunion on the plane of the living is broken.

I realize that we are in the middle of a field at night.

Standing around us in a loose circle are faces I recognize, and many I don't. Greer and Pete, Felicity and Sarah. Other Scions and Squires in crystalline aether armor. Mixed between them are Gill and Samira, even.

There are four other people that I don't recognize, each holding a crystalline sword that points my way. One of them, a young woman, stares down at me with an expression I might call hate, except that she doesn't know me and I don't know her. She scowls at me, then Nick, then pivots on a heel to stalk off into the distance, spine stiff with rage. "Let's go." The others lower their weapons and follow, but I have a feeling I'll be seeing them all again.

"Where . . ." I croak, cough, try again. "Where is Alice?"

I'VE NEVER SEEN someone in a coma. Never seen Alice this still.

I've been watching her for over two hours now, after William healed my own injuries, and nothing has changed. Each inhale is a quiet draw of breath, more movement than sound, and each exhale is just as silent—but accompanied by a wisp of blue aether drifting slowly from her lips.

While Gill and Samira brought me to Alice and William, Lark and Nick moved a still-unconscious Sel to one of the Keep guesthouses separate from the main building.

"I don't know if I did the right thing," William whispers. "I don't know."

"You saved her." I blink away tears. "You saved her, William . . . after I . . ."

William continues as if he didn't hear me. "When it happened to you, it was different. The healing aether I applied to your injuries the first night we met? It was a risk, but nothing that would affect you long-term. And it turned out, you weren't Onceborn, so there had been nothing to worry about. But Alice . . ." His voice cracks. "I had to use so, so much, Bree, and the aether in her isn't fading like it should—"

Another slow exhale, and a puff of aether—bright and citrus, William's signature—rises from her lungs. The air over her bed is a low, silver-blue cloud now.

"I don't know what it's doing to her. I don't know what will happen when she wakes up."

"You're worried this is permanent." My voice sounds far away.

He nods. "Yes."

I want to scream that it doesn't matter, that she's *alive* and *that's* what matters, but I don't. She wouldn't have even come close to dying if I—we—hadn't hurt her.

I can't even blame it on Arthur, because it wasn't just his choice that led us here. It was mine, too.

"There is, truly, nothing else I can do." William shakes his head, like even he can't believe it. Like there should be more healing at his fingertips for everyone who needs it, regardless of their injury.

A soft knock at the door interrupts us. When it opens, Lark peeks his head through. "Looks like Kane is waking up, Will," he says quietly. "Still pretty out of it, though. If ye want to come check on him."

William squeezes my shoulder and gets up. "I should go see Sel."

Lark notices me hesitate, caught between going with William and staying with Alice. His expression turns rueful. "I'm sorry, Bree. I don't know . . ."

"You don't have to explain." Lark isn't sure it's a good idea that I be there when Sel wakes up. I'm not sure it's a good idea either, after what happened. I offer Lark a watery smile that threatens to break my own heart even further. "He gave up his humanity to save me. Maybe I shouldn't be the first person he sees."

"I was going to say," Lark says gently, "that I don't know what Kane will be like when he fully comes to. I've put a barrier around him, just in case, and Nick is guarding the door."

I blink, swallow. "Right." Because Sel might be dangerous now. Demons want fear and rage and pain, however they can get it.

William begins to speak, then stops. "Let me know if anything changes. And get some rest tonight. We'll all know more in the morning."

When he shuts the door behind him, I move closer to Alice's bedside, slipping her cool fingers into my hand. It takes a moment to find my words. I struggle twice before they come.

"I'm so sorry, Alice," I whisper, voice cracking. "This is my fault, my . . . my arrogance, that did this to you."

Silence. Another wisp of silver-blue rises from her open mouth.

"William says that coma patients can hear you," I whisper. "I don't know if anyone has told you what happened after"—I swallow around the lump in my throat—"after Volition, but I can. I know you'd want to know."

I take a deep breath and nod, putting the pieces together for myself, then I tell her everything that happened, both in Arthur's dream and ours.

Voices pass us by in the hallway outside. I wait for them to move on before continuing with what I'd learned in the last several hours.

"As soon as Erebus arrived at Volition, Nick felt Sel's murderous intent through the bond. It was so strong that Nick called Gill from one of Isaac's throwaway phones, freaking out, and demanded that she come get him. They picked him up near Sapphire Valley but didn't know where to go. Fortunately, when Erebus and Cestra left you and William and Sel at Volition, they left Lark, too. When he called the Lieges to say that we'd been found, they told him Nick was already with them." I gnaw on my lip. "Things got worse when Arthur shoved me away and attacked Sel. All of the murderous intent Nick was feeling through the bond just disappeared. Nick thought Sel died."

I try to imagine what it would be like to feel Sel's rage for almost your whole life, recognize it like your own, then suddenly feel . . . nothing.

"Sel woke up not long after everyone figured out where the Regents had taken me. The Lieges and Nick got here first, but Lark, Sel, you, and William arrived not long after. Nick attacked in full armor just as the lead Morgaine, Ava, was going to kill Arthur. Forced them all to stand down until they could get Arthur out of my body. The Regents and Seneschals had already escaped."

I shudder. "And well, the rest is . . . the rest was its own kind of bad, I think." A pause. "But also . . . its own kind of incredible. Because Nick and Sel saved me, and then I saved us." Another pause as I frown. "That doesn't sound right; it wasn't a good thing."

I wait another beat, and realize too late that I had been waiting for her to jump in. Make fun of me. Ask questions.

My eyes burn with tears. I don't know if Alice will ever wake up again.

I squeeze her hand and drop my own back to my lap, where the metal pieces of Excalibur sit wrapped in cloth.

I wipe at my eyes with the back of my hand and take a long, slow breath before releasing it. I kiss her forehead. "I want you to know that I love you and if you see my dad before I do, tell him I love him, too?"

She doesn't respond. It's the best I can do.

When I step outside the room, everything feels numb and I'm not even sure I want that to change. Maybe "numb" is okay, if this is the price of loving people just to find new ways to lose them.

EARLY THE NEXT morning, the main hall of the Keep is packed with Legendborn Scions and Squires, and Lieges led by Gill and Samira.

I avoid it entirely.

I step out onto the back patio of the Keep and walk up a hill I'd found last night that will work nicely. It is a good hiding spot.

There's a small bit of grass before a large copse of bushes and towering old trees, with shadows growing deeper among them as the sun shifts overhead.

I am ready for the first step.

I take a seat on the soil, set the wrapped, broken pieces of Excalibur down beside me, and close my eyes.

When I open them, I am standing in the center stone of the ancestral stream.

"Wound turned weapon."

"Our sword."

"Crown Scion."

The voices crowd me. Maybe they have *always* crowded me.

I think of all the women before me, all eight, and then Vera herself, and the streams that open up before me widen. I imagine Arthur's and, even now, his stream appears in the soil.

So many different voices and paths to follow, ready for my steps.

Vera is at my shoulder. "What are you doing?"

"Giving myself room," I mutter, "to be someone other than who you all keep telling me to be."

"What do you mean by this?"

I turn to face her. "I realize now why Jessie's mantra to call root didn't work for me. She said, 'Think of the power you possess and the woman who gave it to you.'" I smile, sadly. "I used to think that woman was my mother, and, through her, you. Tried it her way, and it didn't work."

She tilts her head. "And why is that?"

"Because you all didn't give me my power." I kneel to face the streams, thrust my hands into the earth from which they came. "I did."

At once, the furnace of root is in my chest, and I let it grow from my hands. Let it burn hot, hotter, hottest—until it is a swirl of fire at my feet. I use it to burn through Arthur's inlet, until the bed beneath is dry, but I don't stop there, because the whispers and expectations and pressure don't stop with him.

"Pain-welded blade."

"Our resistance."

"The tip of our spear."

I kneel in the next stream and let my root burn through the water until it boils around me. Hot. Hotter. Hottest again.

No longer the point of the spear, the tip of an arrow.

Not the strongest girl anyone knows.

Not the most incredible girl, or the impossible one.

No longer the pain-welded blade. No longer a blade at all. No one's weapon but my own.

I burn the ancestral plane until it dries up, until the bed turns to dust, and the voices die down to silence.

Vera gasps beside me. "What have you done?"

I turn to her, and everything feels so clear.

"You said they ran so I wouldn't have to," I say. "But I think they ran so I could choose one day. And today, I choose me."

"You are a child. Too young to understand what you've done." Vera shakes her head slowly, turns transparent. "I can no longer help you."

I stand. "Don't you see? I don't want your help. Not when it ends this way, feels this way."

She is near-fading, a red wisp of light. "Then take my warning instead."

"And that is?" I whisper.

"You don't want the weight of us, but consider where that leaves you. Consider that chaos favors imbalance."

When I open my eyes again at the hill above the Keep, the furnace inside me is still lit. Part of me worried that it would not be, after scorching the streams to my ancestors. Part of me worried that might be the price I would pay to live without their voices and their influence.

But I shouldn't have worried at all. My instincts were right.

Arthur's dream world showed me a way of using my power outside of the stream and away from my own body, away from my own *blood* even. The king's dream made clear that I don't need to follow my ancestors' instructions or heed their warnings to survive. All I have to do to control my power is decide that it is *mine*.

By burning away their roots, I am finally free to grow my own.

And my power is ready to grow with me. I feel it. Ready for my call. Burning at my volition.

Hot enough to forge whatever I want.

Excalibur is a pile of scrap metal beneath my hands in the dirt, but I won't let it stay that way.

I take a deep breath, hold my hands out over the blade, and command aether and root both to layer themselves over and over again, up and down the blade. It is a weapon, cast and forged for my bloodline—and I will cast and forge it again.

Within moments, the heavy longsword shines in the dirt, its stone now a deep purple, its blade silver and sharp, its hilt ready for my hand. It will need a scabbard for traveling.

There is one final step to take. One last decision. One last choice.

I sit on the patch of grass facing the darkening forest, release a quiet, bright pulse of root, and wait.

It doesn't take long.

Red pupils glow in the darkness, and a great shadow moves through the trees toward me, wings in silhouette.

"I knew it was you," I whisper. "I know who you are. And who you've been."

"Oh, I doubt that."

"You are the Hunter. The bloodmarker. The Great Devourer. The Shadow King."

The shadow pulls inward into the shape of a man. The man from Jessie's memory in the diner. From Emmeline, standing over her as she died in the street. Then, to the shape I recognize most. Dark hair, olive skin, a long black jacket, and an aether signature older than the ancients themselves.

How many people has he killed, just to walk among us? I look up at him without moving, and he stares down at me with a calm, curious expression, waiting for me to call him by the name I know best.

"And you are the Seneschal." I smile. "Hello, Erebus."

"Hello, Briana. Scion of the Pendragon, Scion of Vera, Daughter of Faye." He drops his hands into his pockets. "How did you know it was me?"

"My many mothers told me, in their own way," I say. "They kept saying that the Hunter always shows when our root grows powerful enough. And the Root-crafters said that the Hunter is afoot."

He smirks. "And?"

I glare at him. "When my root flared bright during the battle of the ogof, that should have been enough to bring the Hunter to me, but he never showed. *You* never showed, or so I thought." I climb to my feet. "Then I wondered, what if the Hunter *was* someone I came to know after the cave? Someone in disguise?"

"That could be any number of people," Erebus says with a shrug. "Anyone you met at the funeral. A member of the Mageguard. Larkin, even, or Valechaz."

I shake my head. "No. It was Valec who told me what a bloodmark was. Explained why Kizia was terrified to feed from me. A very old demon was very interested in keeping my bloodline—and me—alive."

Erebus hums. "Go on."

"My bloodmark responded to your crown in Arthur's dream realm. It made me realize what a defeated Shadow King who survived Arthur's attack might want most of all: revenge." I spread my hands wide. "What better position to seek revenge than that of a Council member, who are the first to know when Arthur's Scion is Awakened."

He claps slowly. "Bravo."

"Figuring that out was the easy part," I say. "I know what Vera pleaded for the night she bargained with our ancestors, but your bargain with Vera was unregulated. How did you find her? And what did you exchange, exactly?"

"I knew an opportunity might present itself with a Scion of Arthur one day, and waited for one to arise. I had no idea it would arise with Vera's spell. I was simply at the right time and place. She pleaded for protection of her bloodline, and I joined the bargain," he says. "When one of your Line is in mortal danger, I feel it and can locate you."

I shake my head. "That is why you appear when we use a great deal of our root. You're not trying to kill us, you're coming to protect us. That's why you tried to protect me from the other Regents."

"I protect the Line of Vera if I can, when I can." His eyes go distant. "Sometimes I have been too late, and others, I am merely checking on my investment." He grins. "Now ask me what I am waiting for in return. Ask me why I bound my mark to your bloodline."

"I don't follow your orders," I point out.

Erebus hums. "It is true that I seek revenge, but I also want my crown and my Court. I need the power in your blood and your connection to Arthur to regain both. The day Vera called for help, I answered, so that I could mark as mine what I hoped would come to pass: The Bloodcrafted child of a Rootcrafter and a Scion of Arthur, Awakened. A child who could draw an endless supply of ancestral power, who will expel that power when she dies."

"'One daughter at a time, for all time.'"

"Open to interpretation in an unregulated bargain." Erebus's grin widens. "I demanded one daughter, out of all time, of my choosing."

"But your bargain with Vera; you can't harm me."

"I cannot. But I am a very old, very patient demon, who needs a very powerful resource to retake the Shadow Court. *When* you die, and eventually you will, I will consume your aether myself." After a moment, he tilts his head. "You are not surprised by this."

I'm not, but it was good to hear it all confirmed. "I have heard that no demon can resist a bargain."

His eyes narrow. "I am listening."

"I will go with you, and stay by your side so that you can claim my power as your prize without trouble, if you do me a favor in return."

He tilts his head. "Why would you go with me anywhere?"

"Your bloodmark brought my power back to me in Arthur's dream. You are the only being on the planet who is strong enough to keep me safe, and you're bargain-bound to do so." I look out into the woods, considering. "You are the only being old enough, who has seen enough, to teach me."

"And what do you wish to know?"

"Strength, power, control. Over my own destiny." I look up at him. "Only a king may teach a king."

"You do realize that the second you reach your magical peak, I will ensure that you die, and devour all of that strength and power you currently seek to gain."

"All the more reason for you to teach me," I say, shrugging. "The more powerful I am, the more powerful you will be when you consume me."

He smiles. "I am impressed. You are your mother's—all of your mothers'—

daughter. But I need to hear your requirement of me. What do you wish for in exchange, Briana Irene?"

I take a slow, deep breath. This is what I had planned for, and yet asking for it means that it might not come true. I am gambling on an educated guess.

"With your long life," I begin, "and your long time infiltrating the Order, you must know where Natasia Kane is."

Erebus goes still, studies me. Finally, he says, "I do."

I swallow around the knot in my throat. "You travel through shadows. Go directly to Sel's room at the guesthouse. If you take him to her, I will go with you."

Erebus shakes his head slowly. "The boy is far gone. There's no guarantee Natasia can save him."

"I know." I clench my fist. "But it's his only chance."

Erebus's lip curls. "The minute he is well, you could escape me. Return to your friends."

"I am asking you this for me!" I say. "And I will not escape you to return here." My laugh is sour, sad, both. "Because nothing I do will ever be enough for them. The Regents made sure of that when they put me on display in Arthur's possession, dangerously out of control and powerless at once. I used to think I shouldn't be here, but now I know I can't. And maybe I don't have to be. This world wants my suffering, and I cannot keep giving it to them."

Erebus considers this for a long moment, then nods. "I accept your terms."

I stand. "Bring Sel to me first. Please."

"As you wish." He inclines his head, then melts into shadow and disappears.

He reappears a moment later with Sel struggling in his grip. Abruptly, Sel's nose lifts to the sky, following a scent, searching. . . .

When he finds me, I am caught frozen by eyes turned molten red. Then his gaze loses focus, burrows past my features, slices through my hope . . . and a slow, dangerous predator's grin overtakes his mouth, displaying long black-tipped fangs.

"Your anguish . . . ," Sel purrs, voice low and hungry, "is wrapped around your very heart."

Before I can react, he darts forward, claws outstretched, reaching for me and my pain—just as he did in Valec's office. Erebus snatches him back in an iron grip, holds him still.

"Selwyn senses your misery," Erebus mutters impatiently. "That is all you are to him now."

Tears blur my vision. Mystery Girl. Scion. Cariad. King. All that I am, all that I was . . . I wish Erebus, the Shadow King, was lying. But I don't think that he is.

We are all marking the days until we become your villain.

"Make haste," Erebus insists, ear tilted toward the Keep. "Nicholas has noticed he is gone."

"Heartache." Sel's eyes drink me in, his attention a low simmer. "And so, so much guilt. . . ."

I risk a step closer. "Sel, you've saved me over and over again. Now let me try to help you."

His head tilts, and I hope he's listening, but his expression turns rageful. "What have you *done?*" he snarls.

Erebus's hands wrap around his shoulders.

And then they are both gone.

The wait is longer this time. I keep Excalibur in my left hand, blade-down at my hip while I pace.

Then, Erebus appears, alone, brushing his hands down his suit. "It is done."

"She can help him?"

He lifts a brow. "His mother made no such promise."

I knew she wouldn't.

"Bree!" Nick's voice at the bottom of the hill. William beside him. They see Erebus behind me and start running. Nick speeds through the grass, armor snapping into place as he shouts. He calls for me and it takes everything I have left not to respond, not to reach for him too. He's halfway up the hill, a few steps away.

I extend my right hand before I change my mind, and Erebus snatches it.

"I'm sorry," I whisper to Nick. "Please know that I—"

The last thing I see before I disappear with Erebus is Nick's hand, reaching out—and closing around smoke and empty air.

RANK	BLOODLINE	SIGIL
1	King Arthur Pendragon	Dragon rampant
2	Sir Lancelot	Stag at gaze
3	Sir Tristan	Three arrows sinister
4	Sir Lamorak	Griffon courant
5	Sir Kay	
6	Sir Bedivere	One-winged falcon expanded
7	Sir Owain	Lion couchant
8	Sir Erec	
9	Sir Caradoc	
10	Sir Mordred	
11	Sir Bors	Three-banded circle
12	Sir Gawain	Two-headed eagle
13	Sir Geraint	Wolf courant

COLOR	INHERITANCE	WEAPON(S)
Gold	The King's Wisdom and Strength	Longsword
Storm Cloud Blue	Speed and Enhanced Vision	Dual Longsword
Azure Blue	Marksmanship and Speed	Bow and Arrow
Carmine Red	Preternatural strength (enduring)	Axe
~~	~~~	~~~
Amethyst Purple	~~~	~~~
Tawny Yellow	Aether lion familiar	Quarterstaff
~~	~~~	~~~
~~	~~~	~~~
~~	~~~	~~~
Burnt Orange	Agility and Dexterity	Longsword
Emerald Green	Enhanced healer abilities; preternatural strength at midday and midnight	Dual Daggers
Stone Gray	~~~	~~~

AUTHOR'S NOTE

Just as *Bloodmarked* is a sequel to its predecessor, this author's note is a sequel to the one at the end of *Legendborn*. I encourage you to read that note if you have not already, then continue here.

GRIEF AND TRAUMA

While *Legendborn* drew inspiration from my personal, acute grief journey, *Bloodmarked* pushes that journey forward to look at how expansive grief can be. How it can transform into new desires and missions, how it travels between generations, and how it can become the type of burden that masks itself as "duty." When Bree hears Vera's declaration that the generations of women between them "ran so that you would not have to," and that she is "the tip of our spear," she internalizes those words as an all-consuming responsibility, and applies it broadly to her own life because she *cares* and their lives mattered. This process is familiar to many Black women that I know, and yet it can be the source of damage. While I believe Black women are magic, we are also human. Though we cannot be our ancestors' every wish, we often feel compelled to try. This, too, is a manifestation of intergenerational trauma and grief. In the Legendborn Cycle, I explore how these processes can play out in families, between Black women, and within Black girls.

ON BLACK EXCELLENCE AND BEING THE "FIRST"

This book is dedicated to "every Black girl who was 'the first'" because there are burdens that come with breaking barriers. We are in a landscape where micro and macro "firsts" are still being achieved by BIPOC. We live, work, and learn in institutions that find ways to shift their structures and rules in order to stop certain populations from becoming powerful, that move goalposts and redefine excellence just as equity can be reached. I was raised by a Black woman who was "the first" in areas of her educational and professional life. I myself have been a "first." Bree is "the first" in many ways—and often "the only." She must grapple with external expectations from a judgmental world as well as the confusion of her own internal desires, all while doing right by her family. I sometimes see this struggle portrayed as if forced resilience is "strength" and harrowing solitude is "empowerment," but these images come with high costs. I don't want Bree to be seen as "strong" to the point of not being cherished. She is allowed to be a teenaged girl. She is worthy of being protected—regardless of what she can do for others.

As I wrote *Bloodmarked*, a friend observed that Bree's arc echoed elements of Simone Biles's journey before and during the 2020 Olympics in Tokyo. To Simone, thank you for your choice. It means a lot to me.

KING ARTHUR

The greatest delight and challenge of working within Arthuriana is balancing my own personal wish for accurate historical representation with the creative fictions of the canon. The Legendborn Cycle navigates this balance in many ways: For one, Camelot as a "castle" with balconies of stone did not exist in sixth century Wales, nor did the "Round Table," but I could not resist the imagery. Arthurian writers often generate the roster of their own Table, incorporating knights that were created centuries apart from one another. (Lancelot du Lac, for example, first appeared from Chrétien de Troyes in the twelfth century, and in France, but he is frequently presented as an "original" member of Arthur's Table.) In my case, I wanted Bree to meet the same knights in Arthur's blood walks that make up her court today. I decided to work with my Welsh medievalist, bardic tradition consultant, and translator, Dr. Gwilym Morus-Baird, to create sixth-century Wales "origins" for the names of knights whom we may now know by other names, echoing the globalization of Arthurian traditions in the real world. So, Sir Lancelot in the Legendborn Cycle began as "Llancelod" and Sir Lamorak began as "Llameryg," et cetera.

All credit goes to the incredible Dr. Morus-Baird for modernizing the orthography of *Marwnad Owain ap Urien*, the very real ancient elegy originally written in Old Welsh by the sixth-century poet and bard Taliesin and recited by Aldrich and Bree during the *Bloodmarked* funeral scene.

ROOTCRAFT AND VOLITION

It bears repeating that I drew on my own life experiences and African American history and spiritual traditions to create the fictional magic system of rootcraft. Rootcraft is not represented as an institution, because that doesn't make sense or feel true to the inspirations. I *do* see Rootcrafters as a sort of flowing coalition, with communities that may overlap around core tenets. In this spirit, I created the fictional plantation site Volition as a place that could be reclaimed in the name of common values by a group of Rootcrafters.

Volition is imagined to be in the southeastern United States. As Mariah says, Volition was a site of subjugation. As a living cemetery, it centers the ancestors who died enslaved on its grounds and what they might wish for as spirits, rather than centering the enslavers, the historic plantation, the land itself, or modern-day visitors.

Volition is also the site where I chose to crystallize the specific tensions Bree is navigating, of seeking to understand our ancestors' choices and contexts while giving ourselves permission to build on those choices, and perhaps seek different ones. She, like many of us, lives the challenge of honoring the path her ancestors walked while doing her best to forge a new one.

ACKNOWLEDGMENTS

THIS STORY AND book have taught me so much about myself as a writer, as an artist, and as a person. I am proud of the final product, but I am just as proud of pursuing that final product in incredibly difficult times. Thank you to everyone who supported this second-book journey and the evolution of this series now known as the Legendborn Cycle.

Thank you, eternally, to my parents. I hear you more clearly every day. I miss you both and I know you're watching and cheering.

Gratitude always to the ancestors who laid the path for me to travel.

To the readers: whether you are on your second (third, or fourth!?) reread or you are just joining the Legendborn world, thank you for your support and love for these characters. They love you right back.

I will run out of pages if I try to capture all of the gratitude and appreciation I have for my agent, Joanna Volpe. Jo, your massive support and advocacy for my books is incredible, affirming, unwavering. But throughout this process, you never let me forget that I am a creative human being worthy of support and advocacy, as well . . . and that impact is impossible to measure. Thank you times everything, raised to infinity.

Endless thanks to my editor, Kendra Levin, who always dives into the Legend-born world ready to tackle it in every direction. Our calls are story structure and magic, emotional arcs and romance, and everything in between. Thank you so much for all you have done for me as an author, for the series, by always asking the absolute *best* questions.

Huge thanks to Laura Eckes and Hillary Wilson for returning to make a wonderful cover and tackling our boy Selwyn for the first time. His hair is *perfection*.

Enduring thanks to everyone at Simon & Schuster, and especially the teams at Simon & Schuster Books for Young Readers and Margaret K. McElderry Books. In particular, I am thankful for these folks for working so hard to get this book and series into the hands of readers: Justin Chanda, Anne Zafian, Jenica Nasworthy, Kaitlyn San Miguel, Kathleen Smith, Olivia Ritchie, Chel Morgan, Emma Saska, Hilary Zarycky, Elizabeth Blake-Linn, Caitlin Sweeny, Alissa Nigro, Ashley Mitchell, Emily Ritter, Michelle Leo, Nicole Benevento, Amy Beaudoin, and the education and library team. Special thanks to Tara Shanahan, Morgan Maple, Nicole Russo, and the publicity team. Thanks also to Lauren Carr.

Thank you also to the team at New Leaf Literary & Media who have supported my work, including but not limited to: Jenniea Carter, Abigail Donoghue, Jordan Hill, Veronica Grijalva, Victoria Hendersen, Pouya Shahbazian, Katherine Curtis, Hilary Pecheone, and Eileen Lalley.

Special thanks to additional folks in the industry and in the "Team Legendborn" community: Andrea Barzvi, Cassie Malmo, and Liesa Abrams.

Enormous gratitude to my research consultants, subject matter experts, and authenticity readers: Dr. Hilary N. Green once more for your work, support, and insight; Dr. Gwilym Morus-Baird for medieval Welsh knowledge and modern Welsh translations and creations; Dr. Chanda Prescod-Weinstein for helping me to dream in the space between physics, genetics, and fantasy; and Bezi Yohannes for helping me to envision what it would be like when Arthur and Bree finally "meet" and, further, what Bree means for the culture (both pop and community) and for medieval studies as a discipline. Thank you to Papa V. for your medical advice.

To Karen Strong: Bree's forever champion! I am so grateful for your early reads, your honest feedback, and steady, brilliant eye for craft and structure. When we look at the work together, I always know you have my creative best interest at heart. Thank you.

To Lillie Lainoff: Every conversation with you is a gift and I am so fortunate to have your support and incredibly sharp (haha!) eye on my fight scenes, my emotional beats, and more. You are truly a dream craft collaborator and fierce friend. I am grateful to have your sword, and you will always have mine.

There are so many authors in my life to thank for their support, advice, and love during the writing of this book: Daniel José Older, Bethany C. Morrow, Susan Dennard, Kiersten White, Sabaa Tahir, Roseanne A. Brown, Namina Forna, Jordan Ifueko, Antwan Eady, Elise Bryant, Adam Silvera, Julian Winters, Brittany N. Williams, Tiffany D. Jackson, Mark Oshiro, Maya Gittelman, L.L. McKinney, Dhonielle Clayton, Kwame Mbalia, Leigh Bardugo, Eden Royce, Lora Beth Johnson, Charlie Jane Anders, Monica Byrne, Chloe Gong, Olivie Blake, Victoria Lee, Ashley Poston, and Ebony LaDelle.

To Annalise and Alyssa: Thank you for being the best part of my internet and the best part of fandom. Our friendship has been such an anchor, our coven so empowering.

To Adele: You are Team Legendborn, Team Tracy, and Team Bree, and I truly could not fight for it all without you at my side being your rockstar-collaborator-warrior self. Thank you for wearing all the hats while somehow making new ones. Let's gooo!

Immense gratitude to all of my family members across all of my families, for being enthusiastic about my future and this series. Thank you.

To Walter: Quite simply, there would be no *Bloodmarked* without you. Even if there was, the Tracy who wrote it wouldn't be as proud, brave, and hopeful as I am now. (Or as hydrated.) You made it all possible. Thank you for believing in me and being my partner on this grand adventure. I love you.

ABOUT THE AUTHOR

Tracy Deonn is the *New York Times* bestselling author of *Legendborn* and a second-generation fangirl. She grew up in central North Carolina, where she devoured fantasy books and Southern food in equal measure. After earning her bachelor's and master's degrees in communication and performance studies from the University of North Carolina at Chapel Hill, Tracy worked in live theater, video game production, and K–12 education. When she's not writing, Tracy speaks on panels at science fiction and fantasy conventions, reads fanfic, arranges puppy playdates, and keeps an eye out for ginger-flavored everything. She can be found on Twitter @tracydeonn and at tracydeonn.com.